Ellen stood numbly before him, not fully understanding what he was doing. She saw him expertly push the blouse from her shoulders, then drop it. His hands moved very fast and she watched them in a sort of stupor. He stripped the flannel skirt from her waist, her legs, and then her three petticoats. He bent to pull off her shoes, stockings and garters, and then he laughed softly and kissed her. She started, drew back, trembled, and a flood of fiery heat and delicious weakness fell upon her. She put one arm across her breast and one hand over her revealed sex, in the ancient gesture of a virginal woman, who was at once appallingly afraid and surrendering.

Jeremy took her by the shoulders and pushed her before the mirror. She stared at her reflection, her bare flesh shrinking, her loosened hair flowing over her shoulders. She caught a strand of it and pulled it quickly over her breasts.

He stood off from her a little, and surveyed that white perfection of her tall young body. Ellen was far more delightful and lovely than he had suspected, and now he was filled with tenderness.

"Sweet love," he said. "Look at yourself. Haven't you ever looked at yourself before? Are you blind? Wouldn't any man want that?"

Fawcett Crest and Gold Medal Books
by Taylor Caldwell:

THE ARM AND THE DARKNESS
THE FINAL HOUR
MAGGIE—HER MARRIAGE
GRANDMOTHER AND THE PRIESTS
THE LATE CLARA BEAME
A PILLAR OF IRON
WICKED ANGEL
NO ONE HEARS BUT HIM
DIALOGUES WITH THE DEVIL
TESTIMONY OF TWO MEN
GREAT LION OF GOD
ON GROWING UP TOUGH
CAPTAINS AND THE KINGS
TO LOOK AND PASS
GLORY AND THE LIGHTNING
THE ROMANCE OF ATLANTIS (*with Jess Stearn*)
CEREMONY OF THE INNOCENT

TAYLOR CALDWELL

Ceremony of the Innocent

A FAWCETT CREST BOOK

Fawcett Books, Greenwich, Connecticut

For ROBERT J. GIBBONS—one of the very few real friends I had in my life—with gratitude and affection. He is also a great gentleman who has cheered me and is responsible for this book, for without his constant encouragement I could not have started or continued.

FOREWORD

This is a story of a tragic woman and a tragic country. It is two stories, but they parallel each other and often touch and briefly merge, and at the end they are one.

The historical details in this book were given in an earlier book of mine, *Captains and the Kings,* which carries a complete bibliography, and need not be repeated here. The conspiracy does indeed exist, but under other names.

While this book is not my autobiography, and Ellen Porter's background is not mine, nor her appearance—and I was born many years later than she was born—her thoughts have been my thoughts and her experiences mine also. I have encountered many of the people in this book and have endured from them what Ellen Porter had endured, though they are a composite picture here and so cannot be identified. Many of them, too, are now dead.

So in many ways though this is a bitter book it is a true one.

There is an old saying, "Only a man can hurt himself. But only a man can hurt a woman."

TAYLOR CALDWELL

Part One

Love—or perish? No! Love—and perish.

—ANON

1

The pastor pointed out his toes to the limit of extension, spread his arms like wings, and lifted his head in an utmost pose of rapture, his old face exalted, his eyes staring as if with ecstasy at the mildewed white ceiling of his church. It was as if he were embracing a vision of angels suffused with dawn, and his congregation stared at him in fascination. His emaciated features appeared to be rayed with another light and his smile was transported.

He spoke softly and with tremolos: "Love or perish, love or perish. That is the Law and there is nothing else. If we do not love our neighbor with all our hearts, after God, we are as poor as the dust and lower than the beasts. What if we possess the riches of Midas and do not love? We are nothing. Trust, trust. He who does not trust his fellow man is evil. He is wicked. There is black sin in his heart. Love! Trust!"

The organ groaned in sympathy, then rose to an accusing note. The meager little church vibrated all through its sifting plaster. The hot noon sun glared through the plain glass windows. As if with grief the pastor slowly dropped his thin arms, his gaunt head; a dry sob sounded from his channeled throat. He was an old man and he was very stupid, only a little less stupid than his congregation. He whispered in awe, "Trust, trust. Love, love."

He had never been so moving. Women wiped their eyes furtively under their cheap straw hats and peeped at their neighbors to see if their "feelings" had been noted—and approved. Men coughed hoarsely and shifted their heavy boots. The organ almost wept. A child whined in the midsummer heat; the yellow dust blew through the open door. The light was intense, burning, harsh. The pastor began to hope that the collection plates would hold more today than usual, for he had not tasted meat for nearly two weeks except for a lean fowl last Sunday. He studied his people from under his pale lashes and was gratified to see that he had quickened them as never before.

He knew them all well, and intimately. He had married many of them, had baptized even more, and had buried their dead. He knew their guilts, and had no compassion for their weaknesses, their spiritual and bodily sufferings. It was all sin, all wickedness. The children reeked of it, even those in their mothers' arms. All women were inherently dissolute, all men fornicators and adulterers and faithless and liars. Trust! Love! What did they know of these? He sobbed drily again and let his half-hidden pallid eyes rove over every subdued face, every weary face, every sad face, and every young face. Sinners, all, ripe for the plucking and the burning.

He saw his young granddaughter in the middle distance, prim and clean in her dotted-swiss Sunday dress and her straw hat with the red cotton roses. Amelia, ah! She was a saint, the only saint in this church. Like most of the girls present, she had a small pink tight mouth, demurely fixed, a pale complexion, long dropped eyelashes, and polished tubes of hair hanging on her maidenly shoulders. Near her, but not too close, sat that hideous girl, Ellen Watson, in her coarse dress which had been washed so often that its original blue was almost white, and the hem, let down several times, was lined and resisted ironing. She wore no hat, and this was an insult both to the church and to the pastor. She was the only female present who had no head covering, and he was affronted. Moreover, her eyes were not cast down in girlish shyness and meekness. They were fixed on him intently; he could see the brilliant blue shine of them, the great blue stare. She was nodding as if he was still speaking, and she in entire agreement. She was thirteen years old, the same age as his dearest Amelia. Her offering, as usual, would be only one copper penny, and this again was an outrage.

He was pleased at her hideousness. There she sat, poised on the edge of the hard bench, waiting for him to speak again, and her hair was an immense mass of flowing red, all tendrils and waves and glitter in the sunlight, and it was not confined by a proper ribbon as was the hair of all the other girls. It had a turbulent, even uncontrollable, appearance, and was so vital that it seemed

to crackle, to rise of its own volition at her slightest
movement. It resembled the leaping of fire. She was
larger in every way than the other girls. Thirteen, it was
said. She looked all of sixteen, at least, and her breasts,
nubile and pointed, pushed against the faded cotton, as if
trying to burst through it. The pastor felt an ancient
stirring in his loins, and hated the cause of it. No one
with hair like that, and with that slender but ripe young
figure, could be anything but evil, anything but a snare
for the virtuous. Her face! He had never before seen a
face like this on any girl-child or woman. It was almost
square, and lustrous as china and very white, except for
the apricot blaze on cheekbone and on wide full lip. Her
chin was dimpled, her ears carved of marble as was her
bare throat. Her nose was clearly molded, and impeccable.
Her large hands, long and slender and very clean, were
scoured with hard work, the nails chipped.

She possessed grandeur, and a kind of classic grace. The
pastor did not know she was extraordinarily beautiful and
striking to the point of perfection. He noted her arms,
bare to the elbow, round and gleaming and without a
single freckle or mole, and again his loins stirred. A snare
for the unrighteous. A wicked girl who would soon be a
bad woman. A hideous girl.

Ellen gazed at him patiently with those enormous blue
eyes which were fringed with thick bright lashes, as vivid
as gold. Her soft breast lifted the worn fabric over it. Her
hands were clasped in her lap. Her feet, in their broken
buttoned boots, were crossed lightly. Her old dress was
too short and her smooth calves were encased in darned
black stockings. The other girls her age had hems that
touched the tops of their boots, as was proper. Had Mrs.
Watson, her aunt, no decent shame that she could send
her niece to church, to listen to holy words and admonitions, in such clothing, in such revealment? The girl was
like a flaming bird in the midst of brown hens, and there
was an uneasy if derisive space about her as if she were a
pariah. She had no friends, no relatives but her aunt, who
was both a dressmaker and a household drudge. True,
Mrs. Watson was poor, poorer than most of the others in
the church, but could she not find a length of cotton to
make a dress for the girl so she would not be a scandal
in this company?

The organ rose to a higher wail and the congregation

stood up with hymnbooks in their hands. The pastor said, "Hymn fifty-nine." Voices lifted, feeble and uncertain:

> *"Brightly beams our Father's mercy*
> *From His lighthouse evermore,*
> *But to us He leaves the keeping*
> *Of the lights along the shore!"*

The singing was stronger and more sure now, and louder, but above it rose an amazingly lovely voice, full and passionate and fervid, and it was the voice of Ellen Watson.

> *"Let the lower lights keep burning,*
> *Cast a beam across the wave!*
> *Some poor sinking, drowning seaman*
> *You may rescue, you may save!"*

"Amen, amen," moaned the pastor, only too aware of that powerful and exultant voice rising over the other voices like a shining and melodious wing. Why did the strumpet have to bellow like that? He frowned at Ellen, but her eyes were lifted and a beatific smile widened her lips and her white teeth caught the sunlight. She was making a mockery of the hymn! Her neighbors were glaring at her, eyes narrowed, some vindictive, and all disapproving. She was unconscious of them, as always she was unconscious. She did not recognize viciousness even when it intruded upon her, sneered at her, rejected her, and hated her. She did not know she was despised. She only knew that she was always alone, except for her aunt. This did not disturb her. She believed, with sometimes a little childlike sadness, that no one wished to be with her because she and her aunt were very poor, even poorer than any of these poverty-stricken village people. She accepted life with simplicity and hope and sometimes joy, for she was innocent by nature and trustful.

The pastor knew all the gossip of the little village of Preston. He had often heard, snickeringly, that Mrs. Watson was no "Mrs." but a stranger from another place and that Ellen was not her niece but her illegitimate daughter. She had arrived in Preston from "upstate" when Ellen was but an infant, and said she was a widow and a dressmaker, and that she would "help out" in any household which needed emergency aid. She never came to church, though she sent Ellen. The pastor did not question the slanders, the innuendos, the slurs. Ellen was enough to arouse instant hatred in the drab, and instant rejection from the dull and sly. It was rumored, whisperingly, that she was often seen in the fields "with some boy," at night. Her beauty did not move anyone but an occasional youth or lustful field hand. She was considered "showy" and repulsive, and ignorant, above all. For she never seemed to be aware of the animosity which was constantly about her.

Because she was so unusual—a bonfire on the cobbled streets—she was detested and avoided by the other girls, who were of a piece and as undifferentiated as the kernels on a cob of corn. She was singular, uncommon, spectacular, both in face and body and in movement, and so she awakened enmity among the uniform, who could endure no variance, no distinguishing characteristics. Ellen's very innocence, obscurely recognized, was an affront to those who were not innocent however they were meek and conforming in speech and manner and opinion. She was suspected of every vileness, of every corruption. She was accused, among the girls, of acts and behavior and words that were unspeakable and not to be openly mentioned and designated. Of this, too, Ellen was unaware. She accepted jibes and sly smiles and insults with a still serenity and patience which confirmed the slanderous whispers and made heads nod. If a classmate lost a cherished ribbon, a five-cent piece, a book, a pencil, a pen, Ellen was the thief.

She never understood that the wicked and the mean accused others of wickedness and meanness, especially if those others were at all unusual. Occasionally she would become aware that her peers held her guilty of something mysterious and unspoken, and as a result she felt a confused guilt in her heart, a self-deprecation that made her uneasy and sad, for a little while. But she was too innocent and innately too joyful, too trusting, too eager to please and conciliate, for prolonged melancholy. She excused her defamers on the grounds of misunderstanding. She was often sorry for them, for she knew their poverty and their laborious lives. Love. Trust. She alone knew what these meant in their fullest revelation, and this was unconsciously suspected and so aroused malice. When the male-

volent behavior of others was forcibly thrust upon her
attention she was only bewildered. "You are a fool,
Ellen," her aunt would say with shrillness and impatience,
and Ellen would not answer. She suspected that her aunt
was quite correct, and would suffer a thrill of shame. But
why she was a "fool" she did not know.

She thought she was ugly, for she was so much taller
than her small and ungenerous schoolmates. Sometimes
she envied them their ordinary prettiness, their mincing
ways, their sweet little simpers, their tiny little voices, and
she would gaze at them wistfully. They laughed at her
hair, her height, her great blue eyes, and she did not
know it was envy, though subconscious. She felt herself
gawky and graceless and odd. When she looked at herself in the little smeared mirror above the kitchen sink in
her aunt's house she did not see miraculous beauty, or
color, or perfect contour. She saw distortion and did not
know it was the distortion of others.

Her aunt would say with a sigh, "You are no beauty
like your mother, Ellen. She was small and dainty, with
black curls and bright gray eyes. You don't look like other
people, and I worry about you. Never mind. Well, you
must make yourself useful and that, in this world, is very
important." Even May Watson's opinion of her niece was
distorted by the memory of a strange laughing sister, who,
though not of Ellen's coloring or nature, had been enigmatic and sweetly mocking. Mary had been as "different"
in her tragic way as Ellen was "different" in her way. May
did not as yet know that she truly feared for Ellen, as she
had feared for her own sister.

When Ellen left the church this Sunday noon no one
spoke to her, though eyes trailed her malignantly and
mouths were twisted in ridicule. As always, she was unaware of it all. However, some other sense often made
her briefly alert to dislike. She had little of the instinct
of self-preservation and did not know, and would never
know, that this was extremely dangerous in a most dangerous world. If only I had a pretty new dress, she
thought, instead of this old thing I've had for ages. Then
people might love me, too. Well, anyway, the Bible says
God loves me and that's all that matters. She thought of
what the pastor had said: "Love or perish." She nodded
to herself. She felt a familiar bursting in her heart, a
peculiar longing, and a kind of exaltation that hinted of

a future full of love and joy and acceptance. She had only to work and be useful; that would answer all her yearnings.

Her long and exquisitely formed legs carried her smoothly over the rough stones of the one long street of the village. Her tumultuous hair tossed behind her in the hot and dusty wind. Her face was alight with eagerness and expectation. She thought of the coming Fourth of July celebrations and the band that would play patriotic songs in what passed for a park in Preston, just outside the village limits. Music, to her, even the roaring Sousa marches, was an ecstatic experience. When she heard a mechanical piano clamoring out a "piece" from some parlor, or heard the high grinding of the new phonographs emanating from a house, she would suddenly come to a halt on the street, incapable of moving, unaware of anything about her, her face transfigured, held in ecstasy. This would excite laughter and open jeers from passersby, particularly children, but she was always unconscious of this, transported to another dimension where all was harmony and a thousand voices sang, and everything was understood, everything revealed. She had, as yet, no discrimination; she only knew that she winced and even cringed when she heard modern and maudlin ballads sung in trembling pathos. She would say to herself, "Cheap," but did not know exactly what she meant.

She loved music even more than she loved books. She had a little library at home, culled from garbage pails or bought for a cent at Sunday school, and this consisted of a tattered copy of *Quo Vadis?*, a coverless collection of Shakespeare's sonnets, *David Copperfield, The Adventures of Tom Sawyer,* and a sifting ancient Bible with print so small that it strained even her young eyesight. She read these over and over, elated to find something new at each reading. But she had little time to read.

As she passed the various houses along the street she heard the occasional banging of a piano and stabbing voices raised in some disharmonious hymn. She cringed at these also, but did not know why. She had a dim feeling that God deserved more grandeur than this and she also felt a vague guilt—growing in her daily now—that she ought not to object to any sound raised to a somewhat cloudy heaven. But there was something in her mind which demanded majesty and stately glory.

This longest street in Preston boasted the "finest houses in town," houses standing arrogantly beyond careful lawns and with trees plated with dusty gold. There were water troughs for horses here, and carriage blocks, and narrow gardens behind the houses. Ellen would look at the houses with pleasure, and without envy, for she knew nothing of envy and was incapable of it. Somewhere, she insistently believed, there was a house like these waiting for her, with cool dim interiors, portieres, lace-covered windows, rich carpets and polished floors and carved doors.

She came on a lawn in which little white daisies crouched in the grass. She immediately knelt to examine them, and was filled with delight. She touched one or two flowers with the gentle finger of love and awe. The satin petals immediately conveyed to her the euphony of music, infinite dulcitude; the diapason of perfection. She gazed, marveling, at the minute golden hearts, powdered with an infinitude of almost microscopic points. It never occurred to her to pick one, to ravish one with death. They had their being, which no one should violate. She could not put these thoughts into actual words, but the emotion was there.

As she knelt there on the grass, her hair a tumbling effulgence in the sunlight, a handsome carriage rolled along the street, containing a middle-aged man and a youth of about twenty-two. The latter was holding the reins of two black horses with gleaming hides. He pulled the horses almost to a halt as he saw the girl. "What a beauty!" he exclaimed to his companion, who looked past him at the girl.

"Yes," said the older man with admiration. "I wonder who she is. Never saw her before in this misbegotten town. Perhaps a newcomer. But a little too gaudy, isn't she? Like a young actress."

The young man laughed. "Look at her clothes. Hardly an actress. I wonder how old she is."

The older man said with indulgence, "Now, now, Francis. Every pretty girl takes your eye; it's your age. She's probably a servant; maybe sixteen or fifteen years old. We can ask my dear brother, the Mayor, today. Look at her, indeed. What an elegant face; I wonder if that color on her mouth and cheeks is real. You can't tell with servant girls these days. Their mistresses are too lenient with them. There was a time when servants had a half day off a month; now they have two whole days, and that can lead to—paint."

"That face is of neither a servant nor a girl of a brothel —if there is any brothel in this town." The young man was inexplicably annoyed. The carriage rolled away. Ellen got to her feet, not knowing she had been thoroughly inspected and commented upon. Her face was alight; she felt that she had received a revelation from eternity and she no longer heard the hymns whining from the houses. She began to run again; the street was pervaded with the robust smells of roasting beef and pork, and the delicious effluvia of frying chicken. She experienced a pang of hunger, and only smiled. She had a secret: The world was infinitely beautiful, infinitely alive, infinitely moving. Winged with this knowledge, her running feet seemed to fly over the pavement, to dance on the cobbles of the road. She wanted to impart what she knew to someone, but there was no someone and she had no words. She had no real destination.

She came to the end of the long street and there was an open place before her, unmarred by houses or people. Now she could see the distant Pocono Mountains, all mauve and gold with an opalescent mist floating over them against a sky the color of delphiniums. This was her favorite spot, wide, uncluttered, uninhabited except for high wild grass and trees, butterflies and birds and rabbits. She gazed at the far mountains and again that sensation of exalted joy came to her, the hidden joy with a hidden promise. Here she could pretend that there were no human beings about her but only peace and intimations of rapture, of poetry and music. When, as she sighed with bliss and her eyes fell on a sign which read, "Lots for Sale," she felt a deep and nameless distress. Soon there would be imprisoning houses here, shutting off the mountains, walls and roofs and chimneys desecrating her little world.

As she stood at the edge of the street gutter, her newly restless foot scraped against a page or two of a book. She looked down at the pages and eagerly bent to seize them. But they were stained brown by some disgusting liquid, and only a line here and there was visible. She read: "Pope." There was but a fragment of a poem and she read it:

> *"Where every prospect pleases*
> *And only man is vile."*

A profound melancholy came to her, as usual wordless, and charged only with emotion. "But, it is true," she whispered to herself, and was startled at the new and disquieting thought. Again, she felt guilt, and shame, but why she did not know. She tucked the stained page down her neck, then ran on, though less exuberantly than before. She only vaguely understood that each day brought a new knowledge that made her briefly miserable. However, she was very young and soon she was skipping again. She remembered the daisies and their mysterious dream of hope, for herself alone.

She entered a street of little crowded houses, all bleakly illuminated by the sun and showing unkempt lawns and broken picket fences and falling porches. Here there were more people than on the long street, howling and jumping children, screaming and frowzy adults, cracked pavements, decaying paint, and scruffy steps. Above all, here, the phonographs ground away with the latest obnoxious songs. Men in dirty overalls sat on wooden stairs and drank beer. Ellen ran swiftly, and was followed, as customarily, by hoots and whistles. A sense of shyness and degradation almost overwhelmed her and she felt dirty and exposed. A dusty tree, dying for lack of water, spiraled down a dry yellow leaf on her head and she brushed it away. She had begun to sweat; her face was reddened both by mortification and by heat. Then she thought, as always: It is because I am so ugly and so big and don't look like other people, so I must forgive these men and children and women.

She ran on more quickly, anxious to outrun the derision and hostility. Love and trust, the Reverend Beale had admonished. I am very wicked, she thought. It is all my fault—someway. I should love and trust; that is all there is.

She came to the very smallest house on the street, which contained only four diminished rooms, with an outhouse in the rear. However, Aunt May kept it clean and neat, an anachronism among its neighbors. The windows were polished, though most of them had no curtains. The grass was scythed, the little yard bare of everything but yellowing turf. A careful sign hung in the one front window:

"Dressmaking and Alterations. Household Help." Ellen ran to the one door, on the side. Aunt May had painted it pink against the gray clapboard wall. Ellen opened the door and went into the dark little kitchen, which smelled of cabbage, boiling potatoes, and spareribs. Ellen was delighted again. Spareribs was her favorite dish, and one cooked only on Sundays or other holidays. Her foot caught on the seam of the torn linoleum, and an exasperated thin voice said, "Why don't you pick up your feet, Ellen? You are so clumsy. And you're late. You know I have to go to the Mayor's house at two o'clock because he has company, his brother and nephew from Scranton. Go wash. Your face is all red and wet. Dear me, what a provoking girl you are. Your hair is all messed up, too."

"I'm sorry," said Ellen in her resonant voice. She was always "so sorry," so always, recently, overcome with guilt. She went to the pump and threw cold water over her face and tried to smooth down her rioting hair. She looked into the crackled mirror over the tin sink and her face and hair filled it with color and vitality, and she sighed. Why could she not look like Amelia Beale, the prettiest girl in town?

"What did that fool of a Reverend talk about today?" asked the exasperated voice near the rusting wood stove.

"He isn't a fool, Aunt May," said Ellen. She hesitated. "He talked about loving and trusting."

"Loving and trusting who?" asked May Watson, rattling a plate against the pump.

"Why—everybody, I suppose, Auntie."

"More fool he. Never love or trust anybody, Ellen. I ought to know!" She fell into a short brooding. "Set out the plates, if it isn't too much trouble."

Ellen set out two crocked ironware white plates on the table, and sniffed the boiling meal with anticipation. Again her exaltation came to her. "I guess there's a lot to love and trust in the world," she said.

"What?" Her aunt's voice was now sullen and bitter. "Ellen, you are really not very bright, as I keep telling you."

The voice belonged to a little spare woman, flat as a shingle, with a tight thin face and hair the color of a gray squirrel. Her eyes were also that color, and disillusioned, her mouth a line in her colorless face, her nose beaked, and constantly wrinkling and twitching. Her calico dress, of gray and white, was fresh and ironed and she wore a white apron. She moved briskly; she was just forty and she was withered and wrinkled and dry as a dead weed. Her eyes sparkled only with anger and vexation, and they were sparkling now as she looked at her tall niece. Ellen could already sew carefully, and could keep house. Next year she would be put out to service, when she was fourteen, and no more nonsense about school. It was outrageous that "they" now kept young women in school until they were fourteen and would not permit them to work until they reached that age. Two or three dollars a month would come in very handy in that struggling household.

"You'll have to clean up the kitchen and wash the sheets and pillowcases, and sweep out the outhouse and scrub the floor in your bedroom, after I go," said May Watson. "Mind you do it well. You are so careless."

"Yes, Auntie," said Ellen. She looked through the minute window of the kitchen, and again the melancholy came to her.

"I am going to ask Mrs. Porter, the Mayor's wife, if she can hire you next spring," said May Watson. "She pays her cook eight dollars a month! A fortune. I heard she needs someone extra to wash. I hope to get the work, then you'll have to take care of this house—after school," she added with angry contempt.

Muttering, she put a steaming yellow bowl on the table. "Spareribs. Eights cents a pound. Outrageous. I got two pounds. Don't eat it all. We will have the rest for dinner tomorrow night. Ellen, why are you standing there like a gawk? You fill up the whole kitchen. You are too big—like your father." Then she caught her breath, for this was the first time she had spoken to Ellen of her paternal parent.

Ellen became alert. "My papa? What was he like, Auntie?"

"Brown-faced and black-eyed, and big as a house, and with a loud voice like yours," said May Watson, sitting down on one of the creaking kitchen chairs. "Never mind. He was no good. Never could see what your mother saw in him. Don't take too much of the spareribs. You're always so hungry, and that's funny. You don't work." Then she was saddened, for she loved her niece. Maybe, she thought, I can bring some scraps home for the girl; they eat well at the Mayor's, he with that rich farm and all. Perhaps a piece of meat or the heels of fresh bread, or a slice of cake or pie. Or a handful of strawberries. Mrs. Porter is very mean, though; watched every crumb of food, and her cook's worse. May Watson touched her wide pocket. She could slip something in there, when no one was looking. So, it was stealing and maybe it was sinful, but Ellen was still growing and was always hungry. The bitterness in May Watson's heart increased. She was to receive one dollar for an afternoon and evening's work; the housemaid was ill. It was said the Mayor's son had got her "into trouble." At any rate, she had been sent off. Lucky for me, thought May Watson. She thought of little Alice, fifteen years old, an orphan. She had worked two years for Mrs. Porter, and had never had an afternoon off in all that time. She had labored from sunrise to midnight, every day. Don't seem right to me, thought Mrs. Watson. But then, the girl had been brought up "wrong." No decency. May looked at Ellen with sharp intensity. No need to worry there; the girl was too ugly to attract any man. But maybe some elderly farmer might want to marry her; she was big and strong and healthy and could work well, when prodded. It was the only hope May Watson had, for herself and her niece. Before she herself died she wanted to see Ellen "settled," with enough to eat, a Sunday dress, and a sound roof over her head.

"Loving and trusting," said May Watson. "That's the story of your mother's life, Ellen. But she was always a fool. Nobody could tell her anything different. Dreaming. Everything wonderful for the future. She never learned that wasn't no future for people like us. Only work."

"I don't mind work," said Ellen. The meat was a luxury, a joy, in her mouth, and the cabbage and potatoes were delicious. She looked longingly at another of the spareribs, but refrained. They were for supper tomorrow.

"Well, that's an improvement—over your mother," said May Watson. She hesitated. "You can have another potato, if you want it."

"I'm filled up," said Ellen, and turned her eyes away from the enticing bowl. "It was so good, Auntie May."

A pang in the chest struck May Watson. She spooned the potato onto Ellen's plate. "I got two more I can boil up," she said. Somewhere in her arid and horizonless mind there was the somber conviction that somehow, someway, "things were not right" for her kind. Something was awry in the world she knew. She would swallow down this rebellion with warnings that she was not thinking sensibly, that things were the way they were and there was no sense in questioning. Questioning and arguing only brought about the sort of punishment that had overtaken Mary, her sister. When May Watson prayed, which was rarely, she prayed that Ellen would understand that in this life the poor kept their heads down, their voices meek, and worked diligently and asked for nothing but the right to live—which was not often granted them. Mary had died of the "consumption." She had reached beyond herself, and so probably her fate was "just."

"You can have another piece of cabbage, too," said May Watson, but Ellen, smiling, her blue eyes shining with what could only be tears, shook her head. "I'm filled up," she repeated. Her mouth was still watering. "Auntie, the clock says half past one. It's a long walk. You'd better go, and I'll clean up."

Were those really tears in Ellen's eyes? thought May Watson. Why should she cry? She had just eaten a good meal, first meat in three weeks, and the bread had been only three days old. Ellen was a fanciful girl, though, like her mother. She, May Watson, had never known why Mary had wept or laughed or had sung. "I'm going," said May Watson with abruptness. "While you are at it, Ellen, you can wash out the kitchen safe, too."

She stood up and folded her apron carefully, for she would wear it in the Mayor's house. She suddenly paused and looked at her niece with mingled pity and warning. "This here is a wicked world, Ellen," she said, and did not know why she said it. "You got to make your peace with it, and expect nothing."

"Yes, Auntie."

May Watson sighed. "You don't understand a thing I say," she said.

Perhaps it is because I don't believe it, thought Ellen, and once more the darkness of nameless guilt overflowed her. Her schoolteacher always told her class that one should be respectful of "superiors" and adults and those in authority, and she, Ellen, was always inwardly protesting. Hence her guilt. She stood up and kissed her aunt's cheek. "Don't work too hard," she said, with shyness, for affection between them was almost never expressed.

"What else is there?" May Watson said, and went to the bedroom for her battered hat and the gloves she kept for "respectability." It wasn't very clever to go to work looking like a drab with no self-respect. People paid you less then. The hat, black and bent and ten years old, was pinned to her thin hair. But the gloves were white and clean and she carried her purse haughtily. She would ask for an extra fifty cents today. The Mayor's wife was notoriously "stingy." Suddenly May Watson was uplifted and defiant. An extra fifty cents would buy almost a week's supply of turnips and potatoes and perhaps a little meat for next Sunday, not to mention a pint of milk and a loaf of bread, and a bar of Ivory soap and maybe a towel. The three towels in the house were falling apart, frayed and tattered. It ain't right, thought May Watson, but she did not know why she had come to this conclusion. It wasn't "respectable." She marched out of the little house, however, as at the call of a trumpet, her head high, her thin bleached face defiant. Fifty cents. She deserved it, for hours of work, besides the dollar she would be paid. She would also manage to conceal a tidbit for Ellen, too. The poor had to do something if they were not to starve, sin or no sin. God was awful hard on the poor. It looked like He hated them. I guess I'm no Christian, thought May Watson, moving rapidly along the street. Well, then, maybe that's good, too. We got to look out for ourselves; no one else would. "Gentle Jesus, meek and mild," said the parsons. They forgot His anger. Maybe they was scared of His anger. Nothing's right in this world, thought May Watson, and she was dismayed and confused. She thought of her sister, Mary, who had laughingly defied the world and had gone her way, to her death. My thinking's not right today, she thought. She remembered the tears in Ellen's eyes, those huge blue eyes so like— She sighed again. Better just to work, and accept. No use asking for things that weren't "proper" and deserved. The Lord had it all worked out—the rich were rich and the poor were poor, and it was ordained. "Where's your red-haired hussy?" a man shouted to her from the broken steps where he sprawled, and May Watson shuddered. Maybe God was right, hating the poor. Sometimes they deserved it. Guess most people get what they deserved, anyway, and she smiled wryly. I was born without much brains, she thought, and so's my life what it is, and Ellen was born homely and that's why she'll have to work hard all the life that's coming to her.

May Watson reached the Porter house, the handsomest one on the long street, and walked down a path of flag-stones bordered by shining laurel leaves. Shadows danced on the hot stones but it was cooler here and beyond the house she could see the many-colored gardens sloping down to a gazebo and green spruces. She passed windows heavy with intricate lace, the glass reflecting her weary features. She heard laughter on the veranda at the rear and the tinkle of lemonade and ice in crystal pitchers and she sighed. Maybe Mrs. Jardin, the cook, was in a good humor today and would save her, May, a glass to refresh herself. Not likely, though. Mrs. Jardin was very like her mistress and even surpassed her at times. May knocked on the kitchen door and then entered. The kitchen walls and floor were made of red brick, polished with wax so that they glimmered in the sunlight pouring through opened windows, and the sink was of "china" and had running water in it, both hot and cold, fit for a king's kitchen. The wood stove exuded odors of burning fruit-wood, and the fragrance from large iron pots was more than inciting. But the room sweltered with heat and for a moment May could not get her breath.

Mrs. Jardin was a plump short woman with a jovial face and small black eyes like bits of coal, and her black hair was wound tightly in a knot on the top of her head. Her cheeks were crimson and wet; she wore a flowered dress which May had made for her, and a starched white apron which came down to her arches. She was always smiling, usually gay, and so she had the reputation of being a jolly woman. But behind that comfortable façade, as May knew, lived a soul of ice and granite, obsequious to "betters" and malicious and cruel to inferiors, and totally without mercy. She was also a gossip and in-variably believed the worst of everybody and she was always dissatisfied with May Watson, who never had any luscious morsels to impart to her concerning the village. She looked at May now with her lively eye. "Suppose you couldn't have come before this," she said. She had a voice like a very young girl, piping and immature, which she considered beguiling, especially to the male sex. She had

had two husbands, who had thankfully died not long
after they had married Florrie Jardin, and whom she
called "them no-goods." A widow and childless, she was
not without prosperity. There were gold earrings in her
thick pink ears.

May said, taking off her hat and gloves and putting on
her apron, "Isn't two o'clock yet. I'm early." She sent a
furtive eye about the wooden counters which lined the
brick walls, seeking a slice of pie or cake she could
purloin for Ellen, or even the small end of a ham.

Mrs. Jardin perceived that eye. "If you wasn't so late
you could've had a cherry tart from yesterday. Kept it for
you. Then thought maybe you wasn't coming, so I ate it
myself."

May shrugged, rubbed her dry scoured hands together.
"Just ate," she said. "Not hungry. Well, what should I
do first?"

The hot wind rattled the twigs of a tree against the
window and the leaves were gilded with light. But it was
dusky in the large kitchen and the stove fumed. The red
bricks appeared to steam. "You can husk them strawberries in that bowl over there," said Mrs. Jardin. "Then
you can peel them potatoes and wash the lettuce and shell
the peas." The girlish voice became somewhat shrill.
"All this work to do, and nobody to help!"

May Watson had a thought. "Well," she said with an
air of uninterest, "there's my niece, Ellen. She could come
in to help out, during the summer. Maybe a dollar a
week, for six days."

Mrs. Jardin's eyes widened incredulously, and snapped.
"A dollar a week for maybe only a few hours a day!
Alice didn't get but that for a whole month's work, for
twelve hours a day, seven days a week! Think we are
millionaires in this house? I been here for fifteen years
and just got another dollar a month, first raise in all that
time. That makes nine dollars a month, a whole month,
and I'm down here in the kitchen at half past five in the
morning and never leave until eight at night! Besides,
ain't that girl of yours still in school?"

"I want her to be educated," said May. "Leastways, to
finish her last grade. Only right. She writes a fine hand,
too, and can keep house. She'd be a help to you, Mrs.
Jardin. Always friendly; no sulks. And very willing.
Nothing too hard for her to do."

Mrs. Jardin's little eyes narrowed so much that they almost disappeared behind her fat red cheeks. She smirked. "How old's she? Heard she was fifteen. Too old for school."

May hesitated. Then she said, though she winced inwardly, "Ellen's only fourteen. Not fifteen."

"Last I heard from you, May, was that she was just thirteen."

"She had a birthday last week, making her fourteen," said May, wincing inwardly again at the falsehood.

"And you letting her go to school again in September? Foolishness. All right. I'll speak to Mrs. Porter about Ellen helping out this summer. Seventy-five cents a week, and her supper, and that's pretty grand, too, May."

It could be worse, thought May. At least seventy-five cents a week would be of considerable assistance, and then Ellen would have a meal here, and that would be a saving. She shrugged. "Anyway, think about it and ask Mrs. Porter, though I'm saying it's slave wages." She drew a slow long breath. "And before I get to the work I can tell you now: I want an extra fifty cents for today, and that's for sure."

"You're crazy," Mrs. Jardin said, and giggled and shook her head. "Better hurry with them strawberries. They got to soak in sugar seeing they are the first of the season and still a mite sour."

May, in spite of her usual brusqueness, was secretly yielding. But all at once she felt a sharp thrust of despair. Her moving hands slowed, stopped. She seldom felt despair, but now it was like a grief in her, sickening, drying her mouth. She said, "I got to have that extra fifty cents. You do the marketing around here. You know how expensive things are these days, prices always going up and up. Four cents, now, for a three-cent loaf of bread, and even that's smaller."

"You want a dollar and a half for not even a full day's work?" shrieked Mrs. Jardin, aghast. "You really mean that? You ain't just crazy?"

"No. I'm not crazy. I won't get out of here until maybe eleven tonight, and that's nine hours' work, and on my feet every minute, and serving and cleaning and washing the dishes, while you go upstairs to bed at eight, nine. I'm human, too, Mrs. Jardin."

Mrs. Jardin's florid face became cunning and was no

longer jocular. That's what you think—being human, she thought. You and that girl of yours! You ain't got any decency, either of you. Human! She shook a ladle at May. "A dollar's a dollar, and that's what you agreed, and it's a lot of money. Men work twelve hours a day for that, in the sawmills down at the river, and on the barges. A dollar's a dollar."

May did not often feel courageous, but the despair in her had heightened as she thought of Ellen. She lifted her hands from the bowl of strawberries and deliberately wiped her hands on the apron. "All right, then. I'll go home now—unless you go out there to Mrs. Porter and tell her I want the extra fifty cents. Then what'll you do? They got company and all, and you can't do it all yourself. Or maybe Mrs. Porter'll come in and help you out. She's big and fat enough."

"Mind your tongue, May Watson! You got a bad tongue on you, impudent and such! Talking like that about a lady like Mrs. Porter. No respect for your betters!" But Mrs. Jardin was full of consternation at the thought of sending May away and being left to do all the work herself, and the folks from Scanton being so hoity-toity and wanting everything done right, and Mrs. Porter with her eyes that saw everything.

"Fifty cents extra," said May Watson, and she could smell the drunken scent of approaching victory. "Well, why you standing there?"

Mrs. Jardin was seized with a savage desire to beat May on the head with the ladle she held in her hand. "Outrage!" she cried. "Well, I'll ask Mrs. Porter, and you better think of putting on that hat of yours and those damned gloves you walk around in!"

May reached for her hat and held it in her hand and looked inflexibly at her old enemy. "I'm waiting," she said.

Mrs. Jardin threw the ladle into the sink and stamped furiously out of the kitchen. May had begun to tremble. Perhaps she had gone too far. A dollar for nine hours' work was generous. Her tired eyes wandered, helplessly. She saw that a pie had been cut and a large wedge taken from it. She moved as fast as a cockroach, cut a thin new piece and dropped it into the pocket of her apron. Her trembling increased, but so did her despair. Ellen had only one pair of shoes, and they broken and mended too many times, and getting smaller. May shut her eyes and squeezed the lids together tightly, and felt ill and undone. If Mrs. Porter refused, she would have to submit.

The door opened again and it was Mrs. Porter, tall and massive and flushed in her dark-blue silk dress and ruffles, who entered, followed by the newly smirking Mrs. Jardin. Mrs. Porter was not only jowly and fat; she resembled an aging milkmaid, for her skin was coarse and her mouth brutal. There were gold bangles on her thick wrists, and her fading fair hair was a pompadour of rolls and braids. Her light eyes, wide and red-rimmed with sparse lashes, were the color of skimmed milk. She looked shocked and disbelieving.

"What is this, May?" she demanded, her usually genteel voice roughened and harsh. "Fifty cents extra for just a few hours, when you agreed to that dollar, which was more than generous." The silk ruffles rattled about her throat and at the hem of her dress. "His honor, the Mayor, pays his head bookkeeper only six dollars a week, six days a week, and sometimes at night, and Mr. Hodgins is grateful, too! At the rate you're asking," and she did a rapid mental calculation, "you'd be getting nine dollars a week! You must be mad, May."

" 'Tisn't like it was for a week," May said, and visibly trembled now. "It's just one day, and the landlord's just raised the rent another fifty cents a month. And my niece, Ellen, has just got to have a pair of shoes. I can buy a pair at the secondhand store for seventy-five cents. She's just got to have them, Mrs. Porter. I can't let her get crippled."

"I'm not engaged in running an orphan asylum, May," Mrs. Porter said, and moved her hand impatiently as if waving away an impertinent fly. "Your—niece is old enough, Mrs. Jardin tells me now, to be working for her own living instead of lying about your house only sleeping and eating, a big girl like that! Fourteen." She glanced at Mrs. Jardin, who was enjoying herself. "Mrs. Jardin tells me Ellen is for hire. I'll pay her seventy-five cents a week, if you are just sensible, May, and realize the enormity of what you have been asking."

Ellen, Ellen, thought May Watson. But she sensed victory again. Mrs. Porter's voice had taken on a hint of wheedling. So May said, with a stubbornness which pleasantly surprised her, "I got to have the extra fifty cents, ma'am. I really have. Maybe this once, only."

Mrs. Porter smiled grimly. She threw out her hands. "Very well, May. But I'll remember this, I surely will. I never heard of such ingratitude. I've been your good kind friend, May, and have called on you often to help Mrs. Jardin in an emergency. But your sort is never grateful! Never. That's what's wrong with this world these days. Ingratitude, imposition. You have me at a disadvantage, May. Otherwise I'd dismiss you at once. You should feel deeply ashamed."

She looked down at her dress. "And you charged me a dollar for mere slight alterations! A dollar! Just to let out the skirt and add the ruffles."

"It was all handwork," said May. "Not machine work, like all the rest of it. Handwork. Took me three nights. Was more than just letting out the skirt and adding the ruffles. I had to take it all apart, every piece of it, and fit it together. Thought I'd never get it finished. Your waist," said May with uncommon bluntness, "has got real thick the last two years, Mrs. Porter."

The large coarse face above her darkened and appeared to become bloated with anger. "We're very saucy, aren't we? Very loose and heedless with our speech, too. The world's becoming a very ungodly place, May Watson."

"It always was," said May, amazed at her own courage. "Never was any good."

Mrs. Porter smiled again, with even more grimness, and said, with meaning, "You ought to know, should you not, Mrs.—Watson?"

"I certainly do," said May, and bitterness came to her and she was sick with it.

The flush on the woman's face became scarlet and the milky eyes glared. "What did you expect, your kind? Very well. I have guests; I am demeaning myself arguing with you, May Watson. You shall have your extra fifty cents today." She glanced at Mrs. Jardin, and hesitated. "You can send your girl, Ellen, here tomorrow morning at six sharp, in this emergency. Seventy-five cents a week. We will try her out, at any rate. From six in the morning until Mrs. Jardin dismisses her at about seven. Is that settled at least?"

"Yes," said May. "It is settled."

Mrs. Porter turned briskly about and did not glance again at the staring and very vexed Mrs. Jardin. She lumbered rapidly from the kitchen to rejoin her family and her guests, her every movement expressing exasperation and disgust.

"Well, you won," said Mrs. Jardin to May, who was again squeezing her eyelids together, but now to control tears. "Never thought to see it happen. When Christmas comes, I'm going to get another dollar a month or she can look for somebody else. Maybe I should be thankful to you, May."

This new alliance startled May, and she opened damp eyes. "Starving folks to death, that's what they're doing," she said in a quavering voice. "One of these days we're not going to stand for it any longer."

"Amen," said Mrs. Jardin, and she chuckled. "Get along with them strawberries, now. Dinner's at five, same as usual on Sundays." She playfully slapped May on her thin rump with the ladle, and burst into a shrill hymn, in a rollicking tempo again filled with apparent good humor:

> *"Yes, we march to Beulah Land, Beulah Land,*
> *Yes, we march to Beulah Land, in the morning!"*

Beulah Land, thought May, her hands swiftly hulling the berries. Now, where's that, I wonder? It's not for my kind, anyway. Hell, more likely, when we got it here, too.

During his wife's short absence the Mayor had quickly poured a good quantity of rum into the glasses of his brother and his nephew. He winked at them. "Now fill them up with that damned lemonade," he said. He was as stout as his wife, but shorter and of a better temper. But he was no less exploitative. His hair was thick and white and silky and he dressed with rich style on Sundays, though he wore decorous black suits during the week in his offices. Today his cravat was broad and held a diamond pin, and his coat was of a gray and white large check, which he considered "sporty," and his trousers were a gleaming white.

"Where's Jeremy?" asked the Mayor's nephew, Francis Porter.

Mrs. Porter emerged onto the veranda, frowning, but at the sound of her son's name she smiled deeply and with pride. "He is having dinner with the undertaker's niece, from Scranton," she said. "Her father owns the biggest ironworks there, and she is an only child, like our dear Jeremy. We have hopes," she added archly, seating her-

self in a huge wicker chair and sighing softly. "This is
the second summer, and I believe the young people write
to each other regularly. A very pretty girl, too, and well
brought up."

"Speaking of pretty girls, I saw a beauty today," said
Francis. He was a tall and very slender young man with
fine flaxen hair and open blue eyes, a very delicate complexion with a sharp flush on the high cheekbones, which
gave him an interesting appearance, and a wide and gentle
mouth. He was almost pretty himself, Mrs. Porter thought
without generosity, for she resented the young man's
obvious if somewhat frail handsomeness, unlike her dear
Jeremy's "manly" aspect.

"Oh?" said Mrs. Porter, arching her pale eyebrows, so
sparse that they seemed hardly to be there at all. "Who,
I wonder? There's only one nearly pretty girl in this
town." Her mouth writhed as if with amusement, for she
hated Preston, having come from Scranton herself. "Fairly
comely. That is the Reverend Mr. Beale's granddaughter,
Amelia. Very nicely brought up, too, and well mannered.
About fourteen?"

"About that," said Francis. His father, who resembled
the Mayor very closely, though he was slightly less
massive, laughed. "Francis was bewitched. We saw her on
the street this morning, obviously coming from that shabby
little church on Bedford. Francis drew up the horses to
look at the girl. I confess I thought her beautiful, too."

"A sweet little face with a pink mouth, and soft brown
hair?"

"No, Aunt Agnes. She wasn't sweet at all; she had a
strong and lovely face with remarkable coloring. And a
great mass of red hair, floating far down her back. A tall
girl, a graceful girl."

Mrs. Porter drew her brows together, considering. Then
she cried, with hilarious delight, "Oh no, Francis! That
could be only the very ugly girl called Ellen Watson,
whose presumed aunt is right now in my kitchen, helping
Mrs. Jardin!"

"Then it couldn't be the same girl, for the girl I saw
had a magnificent face, very arresting. And I have never
seen such gorgeous hair in all my life before. Like a
cataract of copper in the sun, and not tied back with any
ribbon."

"You will observe," said Walter Porter, "that my son

was bewitched. Yes, and I thought her beautiful, too. Very unusual young wench."

Francis' color deepened. "She is not a 'wench,' begging your pardon, Papa. She had a look of—well, grandeur. Prideful, even noble. Angelic in another meaning of the term. I have never seen any girl like that before. She was not in the least like anyone else. Especially not in Preston, where everybody looks alike in some peculiar fashion."

"I agree with you there," said Mrs. Porter, sighing. "Very dull people in this town." She looked at Francis with new animation. "If you hadn't said she was beautiful, this mysterious girl of yours, I'd think it was Ellen Watson, or that's the surname her aunt alleges it is. There are quite a few stories— No, it couldn't be Ellen Watson. Ellen is quite unattractive, a very big girl who looks older than she is. By the way, she will be working for me this summer, and you can see for yourself, Francis, that she is not the one of whom you have spoken." She laughed lightly. "Still, I wonder who the girl is whom you saw. Red hair. Ellen's the only one in town who has really red hair, though I see you prefer to call it copper."

She had another thought. "Was she prettily dressed, this girl?"

"No, very poorly, in fact. I noticed her boots were broken, though polished."

Mrs. Porter was startled, but she gave her husband's nephew a sly glance. "I wonder who she is. Well, we will see, tomorrow, Francis."

Walter Porter had been musing. Now he said, "It has just come to me. I saw a woman like that, or rather her portrait, when I was about Francis' age and visiting a friend of mine in Philadelphia. She was young, but was already dead. Let me see: An Amy Sheldon, of a great family, in Philadelphia. She was the mother of my best friend, John Widdimer, but had died shortly after he was born. I visited him during university holidays a few times, and he visited us in Scranton. Remember him, Edgar?"

The Mayor nodded. "What became of him? I thought he had a glorious future. One of the best families in Philadelphia, and very rich, too, and he was a clever young feller."

"Don't you remember, Edgar?" asked Mr. Porter. "They had a fine stable of horses and he was always riding. He was killed by a new stallion he had bought, a

racer of which they had expected much. Old Widdimer
had the stallion shot, which I thought was a dreadful
waste of good horseflesh. John was a reckless chap in
many ways and insisted on riding the stallion at once,
though he was hardly broken to the bit. Very sad affair
indeed. Very sad." He sighed. "I'll never forget the
portrait of his mother. Very like the girl we saw this
morning, hair and all, and with such a face! Pity."

"Was he married?" asked Mrs. Porter, intrigued.

"No, no," said her brother-in-law, shaking his head.
"But I believe he was engaged to marry one of the
Brigham girls, very rich, very pretty. Sad. I think her
name was Florence. John had quite an eye for the ladies."

But Mrs. Porter was gazing suspiciously at her husband. Was Edgar "drinking" again, after his many promises? He gave her a beatific smile, and she was infuriated.
She had never forgiven him for buying that farm and
moving to Preston, for all he had become the Mayor and
so the most important man in the village.

2

Ellen, guilty once more, sipped a spoonful of the cooling
liquid in the bowl of vegetables and pork. Then she put it
in the kitchen safe and covered it carefully. She then pro-
ceeded to clean the kitchen floor, the bare wooden table,
and the two old-fashioned chairs. She polished the warm
stove, washed the window, rinsed out the three dish towels
and other cottons, then went into the other rooms, her
own minute bedroom without a window: it contained but
her narrow bed, neatly covered with a white sheet, and a
small commode which held her few articles of clothing.
Here she dusted and straightened, glanced with regret into
the crocked mirror over the commode. After this she went
into her aunt's bedroom, where she repeated her duties.

Following this she opened a door and went into the "parlor," a room hardly larger than the bedrooms, but here, according to May Watson, there was a "richness." The furniture consisted of a real mahogany settee, all twisted wood and verdigris velvet, the wood scarred but brilliantly polished, the velvet worn down to the nap. A similar chair stood near the tiny little window, the only window in the house which possessed a curtain, and this of coarse machine lace starched to the stiffness of cardboard and almost of that texture. There was a square of imitation Brussels rug on the floor, the rose pattern nearly obliterated by time and constant cleaning. A little table close to the settee held an old lamp, unexpectedly elegant with crystal drops and a chased white shade shaped like a bell. Here, on this table, lay Ellen's beloved Bible, but only she read it. Unlike the other rooms, plastered and stained with damp, this room had wallpaper, painfully and inaccurately hung by May, and it was of a violently rose design, roses like carmine cabbages valorously leading vines of an intense and improbable green. Ellen hated this wallpaper, which May considered "grand." The vines seemed, to Ellen, to writhe and to choke and the enormous roses were like large blobs of blood among them. However, she always assured her aunt that the paper was indeed "grand," and worthy of the most expensive rooms in town, even while she inwardly cringed. At these times she felt an emotion which she did not know was an internal weeping, dark with sorrow.

It was very rare that she and May ever entered this sacred room except on holidays such as Christmas or Easter, or on the visit of the very infrequent lady, usually a client seeking May's expert alterations on a cloak or a dress or a robe. Behind the settee, discreetly hidden, was May's elderly treadle sewing machine, which she had bought for two dollars ten years ago. It had a "real" walnut case, and was polished as assiduously as the other furniture, and cared for with anxious zeal, for it stood between woman and niece and starvation. It was not beautiful, but it had utility, and henceforth worth, and so Ellen admired and cherished it. To her still unformed mind a thing should be either bright with beauty, for beauty was its reason for existence, or it should be useful, for labor itself had sanctity, and was muscular and strong. Ellen dusted every spotless surface, moved the chair an inch nearer the window, and avoided looking at the wall-paper.

She took the washed and wet towels and sheets out to the clothesline in the yellowing backyard. This yard had a low picket fence which May had zealously whitewashed; the outhouse was also whitewashed and stood proudly at the rear. Ellen hung the cloths on the line, and her only other summer dress, a gay pink cotton, worn only on the most elevated occasions, such as visiting the park on Sundays to hear the band concert. It was nearly three years old and had been made by May, and the telltale hem had been covered by a rickrack braid also made by May. It had a flounce about the neck and flounces on the sleeves, and a narrow blue ribbon sash. Ellen had just washed it carefully, for it was to be worn on the Fourth of July, at the church picnic. Ellen regarded it fondly; she believed it made her almost pretty and acceptable.

She heard a woman's bass voice chuckling, and turned her head. Old Mrs. Schwartz, gigantically fat and squat, and with a thin face like the blade of a knife, was leaning on May's picket fence. She had a raveling mass of dyed hair, frankly of an unlikely shade of auburn, and little glittering sherry-colored eyes, a long and very protruding nose, and a mouth always twisted sardonically. She made her living by "fortune-telling," and scrubbing and "helping out" at village parties, and was believed to be a witch. She was also an excellent cook and had often been kind enough to recommend May for household tasks and washing and ironing. But May was both afraid of her and hostile towards her, for all her frequent kindliness. "I don't like her heathenish and unchristian fortune-telling," she would say to Ellen. "Pagan, it is. Keep away from her, Ellen. She can bring you bad luck if she has a mind to."

Ellen thought her fascinating. There was, to the young girl, something gay and inspiriting about the old woman, something antic if very malicious. She had a ruffianly way of speaking and gesturing, which appealed to the innate honesty of the girl. Mrs. Schwartz was never "mealy-mouthed" or "nice." She never said polite things, and all her rude remarks were underlined by significant sneers. She held a book with a broken cover in her spotted hands now, and she poked it in Ellen's direction.

"Got you something, gal," she said. "To wear out those pretty eyes of yours."

Ellen ran to her eagerly and received the book and
held it in reverent hands. *"Walden and Other Writings,*
by Henry David Thoreau." She opened the stained and
darkened pages gently so as not to break them. Mrs.
Schwartz watched her cunningly; she saw the radiance on
the young face and pursed her satirical lips and nodded
to herself with a sort of fatality. She pointed to a page
Ellen was skimming. "Read that," she said.

Ellen read aloud:

> *"Mourning untimely consumes the sad;*
> *Few are their days in the land of the living,*
> *Beautiful daughter of Toscar."*

The girl could not fully comprehend what she had read,
but she experienced that old and familiar stab of sorrow.

" 'Beautiful daughter of Toscar,' " said Mrs. Schwartz,
gazing at Ellen and again nodding her head. "That's what
I always call you, Ellen my gal."

Bemused, yet puzzled, Ellen glanced at her briefly and
continued to turn the pages as an avid man examines
the meal put before him.

"That man, Thoreau, wasn't no coward," said Mrs.
Schwartz. "I don't believe in any unpardonable sin, but if
there's one, it's being a coward. Afraid of your own
shadow; smirking and cajoling just so folks'll like you,
and won't stick a knife in you—the way people do when
they get the chance. Afraid to offend the Devil, or them
that comes in his form, all smiles and teeth and talk of
'love.' That's really wicked, Ellen. Nothing so wicked as
them that calls themselves 'a brother of mankind.' You
got to watch out for them all the time, and run like a
rabbit when you sees one. Yes, sir."

Something distressful and faintly denying rose in Ellen,
and she was struck with a vague despondency though
she did not know why. But she said, "Thank you, Mrs.
Schwartz. I'll return the book after I've read it."

"No, it's for you, my dear. Found it among the rubbish
in my cellar this morning. Thought you'd like it. You'll
like it better as you grows. I did, long ago." She smiled
at Ellen with a wry fondness. " 'Daughter of Toscar,' "
she repeated.

"Why do you call me that?" asked Ellen.

"Because you are, seems to me." She looked at the pink
cotton dress on the line, and heaved a gusty sigh and for

a moment dropped her head. Then she stared at Ellen and
her formidable eyes, so compelling and insistent, so knowing, moistened. "Ach," she muttered. "Those damned
gnats." She rubbed her furrowed eyelids. "What an innocent you are. Probably nobody can help you, not even me.
Doomed—that's what you are. Innocent."

Ellen looked at her in baffled silence. Mrs. Schwartz
returned the lucent gaze piercingly. "I know your aunt
don't cotton to fortune-telling. She thinks it's heathen or
something even worse. She won't fight 'less she's pushed
to the wall. Not genteel, she thinks. Well, poor woman.
A good woman, too. Very sad. Ellen, don't you ever trust
nobody, and keep your love careful, like gold too valuable
to spend on the worthless. That means almost everybody.
Know what the Bible says? 'None save God is good,'
and sometimes I don't believe that either. Or the world
wouldn't be so stinking a place. Never mind. I'm a
heathen, a Romany they calls me, though I come of
German stock. But I got eyes to see and ears to hear.
Read something by a heathen poet:

> *"O Thou who man of basest earth did make,*
> *And e'en with Paradise devised the snake,*
> *For all the sins the face of man is black with,*
> *Man's forgiveness give, and take."*

She chuckled at Ellen's young face, so suddenly alarmed
and sober. "Gets down to your heart, don't it? It's something to remember, always. That's why I got my doubts
about God. But not about the Devil! He's real. What does
the Bible call him, 'Prince of this world.' Couldn't be
righter. I'm telling you this, Ellen, because I'm scared
about you. Give me your left hand," she added abruptly.

Ellen hesitated. Was Mrs. Schwartz "of the Devil," as
the neighbors said? Then she gave Mrs. Schwartz her
long and slender hand, so lovingly formed, and Mrs.
Schwartz looked at the calluses on it and she no longer
grinned.

"Yes, a borned innocent," she said, and her voice
roughened as if she were attempting to restrain some
anguish. "An innocent—cursed. But that was always true.
The innocent are cursed. They never learn what this
world is, and all the people in it. Kill 'em, and they'll only
look surprised—never learning. Stupid, I call it. And yet"

—she paused a moment—"maybe if there's a God He put the innocent here as a 'reproach,' as the Bible calls it. He don't have real sympathy for them, seems like. Just kind of victims to prove something we don't understand, and never will." Her lips contorted as if she had tasted something infinitely acrid. "Maybe the Devil, and God, understands. Nobody else will."

She began to scrutinize Ellen's work-scarred hand. Ellen said, "The minister today said we've got to love and trust."

Mrs. Schwartz glanced up and her eyes were fiery and her grin was malevolent.

"He did, eh? What does he know about it? 'Love and trust.' Formula, as I would say, for death. Cruel death— in this world. Yes, it's right here in your palm, my child. Written out clear, and terrible. Terrible. Hate and suspect —that's how you can prosper in this world, and it's the only way. Afraid you'll never find out, and that's what's terrible, for somebody like you."

Again she studied Ellen's palm. "Not all bad. You got some luck here, and very soon, too. But won't lead to what the silly world calls happiness. And, money! Lots of money, lots and lots. That's one consolation. Ain't no substitute for money, ever. Not love, not joy. Just money. Well, that kind of satisfies me. But money can be a curse, too—for the innocent. 'Daughter of Toscar.' "

But Ellen was naïvely pleased. She studied her palm also. "Well, I'd like to help Aunt May, with money. When will I get it?"

"Not for some years, gal, but you'll get it, that's for sure."

She stared for a long minute or two at the rosy palm. Then she uttered a short hard sound as if frightened, and dropped the hand. Her eyes leaped violently. "Don't mind what I said, even if it's true. I got just one thing more to say and that's don't ever trust and give your heart fully. Not that you'll remember. Innocents never remember anything that hurts them. Like a snail without its shell, that's what you are. Snatched up for eating. What else can I tell you, that's the truth? An innocent pays no mind to truth. It likes to dream, and believe."

She turned away, and despite her bulk she hurried as if she had seen a fearful sight and must flee. Ellen watched her go, more baffled than ever. At the door of her battered house, which was hardly larger than May Watson's, Mrs. Schwartz stopped and looked back at Ellen. "Know what the Bible says, gal? 'The wicked flourish like a green bay tree.' And something else: 'The children of the wicked dance in the streets with joy.' Keep that in mind. Might help you when you most need it." She shook her head, and disappeared into her house.

Ellen examined her palm. It told her nothing. But Mrs. Schwartz had spoken about money, and money would help Aunt May, and that was all that mattered. Money would take away the chronic misery from her aunt's face, the weariness, the tight despair. Yes, that was all that mattered. Elated, Ellen went singing into the house.

She looked in the kitchen safe but kept her eyes away from the tempting yellow bowl. Her aunt was always complaining that she was hungry, and she supposed she was. There was a morsel of cracked cheese, a spoonful of tea and a slice of bread and a bit of wizened cake for her supper. It was enough, she said valiantly to herself. Why did she want to eat all the time, anyway? Her heart was still uplifted by what Mrs. Schwartz had said. Soon—there would be money for both her aunt and herself. She leaned against the scrubbed kitchen table and devoured the cheese and the bread and the cake, while the kettle seethed with hot water for a cup of tea.

The sun was beginning to set. All at once Ellen decided to go into the parlor and sit near the window. She ran into the other room and threw herself into the chair. The window faced west, and now the falling sun lay on the side of the cracked clapboard of the corner of the house, showing every stain, every bulge, every blister. It was a lonely sight, lonely and still, and Ellen was struck into that profound melancholy which she did not understand, but which pervaded her whole spirit. The street was silent for once; only the bleak light was clear and lamentable and foreboding on the clapboards.

Then Ellen's gaze mysteriously shifted and she was looking through a tall, narrow leaded window which revealed rosy brick beyond its damask red draperies, and the lonely light stood there on the wall and not even the climbing rose bushes on their trellises could dim its ominousness. The girl stared, half holding her breath. The light deepened, even brightened, but its cheerlessness only increased on that motionless brick wall. Ellen felt a large room behind her, dim with evening, and utterly silent though tenanted by bulky masses of excellent furniture, and glimmering mirrors in tall gilt, and a vast unlit chandelier of crystal.

Ellen uttered a faint cry of fear, and the scene changed again and there was only the clapboard wall and the descending light and the echoing stillness. I was dreaming, she thought, and glanced about the little dolorous room in which she sat. I was dreaming, she thought again. The melancholy lay in her breast like a crushing disease which would kill her, like a direful memory which was not part of her experience, of a life she had never known, of something she had never seen. It fell upon her with devastation, and she jumped to her feet and ran into her bedroom and threw herself upon her hard little bed, and whimpered.

She was awakened by a sound and sat up on her bed in darkness, for she had slept. "Aunt May?" she called.

"Yes, and where are you, Ellen. It's half past ten."

Ellen ran into the kitchen. May Watson was lighting the kerosene lamp on the table. "I've had an awful dream," said Ellen.

"Haven't you anything else to do but dream?" asked May with vexation. "Oh, dear heaven. I'm awful tired." The lamp jumped pale jaundiced streaks about the desolate kitchen. "Here. I brought you a slice of pie, a piece of bread and a smidgen of ham, and a hand of strawberries." She emptied her apron pocket, and Ellen exclaimed with glee and May smiled reluctantly. "What an appetite you always have," she said, and she reached out her scored hand and fondly touched that mass of turbulent red hair. Ellen might be ugly but she was only a child after all, and loved eating like the greedy little pig she was. Ellen began to stuff the food into her mouth and May watched with faintly smiling compassion.

"I've got good news," she said. "You are going to work for Mrs. Porter as her housemaid all summer. Seventy-five cents a week, and a supper. Beginning tomorrow. Isn't that wonderful?"

"Oh, Auntie May! Mrs. Schwartz just told me this afternoon that I was going to have lots and lots of money! She was right!"

"Didn't I tell you to stay away from that awful witch?

She can bring you bad luck, but you never pay attention to what I say, Ellen."

Ellen tossed back her hair and smiled wildly, the strawberries staining her white teeth.

"But it's good luck! And she gave me a book, a marvelous book, to have as my own."

May Watson took off her gloves and her hat and stood, sagging, in the center of the kitchen. "Oh, Ellen, Ellen," she murmured. Then she straightened. "And I got fifty cents extra today and you can get those shoes from the secondhand. Be sure they are big and wide enough to fit you for a year or more. Ellen, Ellen."

Ellen stopped eating and stared deeply at her aunt, then ran to her and embraced her, almost crying, bending down to enfold her smaller relative.

"Don't worry," she murmured. "Please don't worry. Everything is good, so good for us."

"Nothing is ever good for our kind," said May Watson, and suddenly she was passionately exasperated at the girl, for she was exhausted, her feet swollen and throbbing, her shoulders aching, and her hands smarting from strong soap. She pushed Ellen from her and Ellen stepped back and regarded her aunt anxiously, and with the now familiar sinking of guilt in her heart. "You got to learn that, Ellen, before you're much older. Don't ever expect anything from this world, ever." May's squirrel-gray eyes darted little lights of anger, and yet she wanted to cry.

Ellen's voice trembled somewhat when she said, "I was sitting a minute in the parlor." Her eyes became enlarged, intense. "And I saw something—I don't know what, but it was awful rich, but it made me sad, too."

"What on earth?" said May, pushing back her thin and grizzled hair. She put the kettle on for hot water for a cup of tea, and reminded herself that she must get more of the tea; it was the only thing which revived her after a long day's work. "Well, aren't you going to tell me?" For Ellen was hesitating, her ruddy head bent, her teeth biting her lower lip.

"It was just a dream," she said in apology, "and I don't know why it made me—gloomy, and frightened me. I never saw that before, and yet I was me, though I seemed to be older, a grown-up lady about twenty, I think. But I looked like me; I know it. And I was looking out a window, it had little leads in it like the Mayor's stained-glass door, but this window wasn't stained glass. Just clear. And it had heavy red silk draperies with gold tassels and fringes and silk balls on the sashes." She stopped, again in apology, but May's face had turned quite white and her mouth had fallen open and she was staring almost stupidly at Ellen.

The girl spoke more hurriedly. "It was only a dream. And I was looking out at the brick wall of the house, and it had a trellis with roses and leaves on it, and behind me I could feel a big room, bigger than any room in Preston, and though I didn't see the room I knew it was full of grand furniture, and there was a big lamp of little bits of glass hanging from the ceiling, rows and rows of glass, prisms I think you would call it, and the room I was in had dark walls of wood all polished like furniture, and there were lots of books—Aunt May, what is it?" she cried, and went to her aunt again, for May Watson stood there, stupefied and almost glaring in the weak light of the table lamp.

May pushed her hair fiercely back from her face, then stared about her as if she did not know where she was. She fumbled for a chair. She sat down, and now she fixed her eyes on Ellen, distraught.

"I knew such a room, for years; I dusted and polished it for years. And I remember the wall of the house and how it looked—" Then she came to herself and clenched her hands on her bony knees and wet her lips and appeared to see Ellen fully for the first time. She was aghast. "How did you know about such a room? Who told you?" Her voice was high and acute, even terrified. She reached out and grasped Ellen's arm and shook her. "Tell me; who told you?"

Ellen was affrighted. She tried to draw away from that hurting grasp but could not. "Nobody—told me," she stammered. "It was just a dream, a dream. You are making my arm ache, Aunt May."

The woman released the girl's arm, and then she was suddenly weeping, hiding her face in her rough palms. "It can't be," she groaned. "It can't be. You never saw such a place. Only I and—only I did. I must have told you about it, sometime."

"When I was very little," Ellen urged, eager to comfort her. "That must have been it."

May rocked on the chair, weeping dolorously, her face

still hidden. But she nodded. "That was it," she moaned. "It could only be that. You were never there, never there." She dropped her hands and her deep premature wrinkles were filled with water which ran down to her chin and dripped. Ellen had never seen her aunt weep before, and now she was shattered with guilt and remorse. She put her head on her aunt's knees like a puppy deserving of the most drastic punishment.

For a long time May could only look down on that vital and disordered mass of hair on her knee. Then she put out her hand and touched it, smoothing it. Ellen sobbed. "There, there," said May. "It's all right. I'm just terribly tired. When I'm tired like this everything—everything—seems not right, or something." She wiped away her tears with the sleeve of her calico dress. "Now, you just stop crying, hear me?" She tried to make her voice severe, but it broke. "You got to get up at five to be at the Mayor's house at six, and it will be a long day for you. Ellen, Ellen? Listen to me. I told them you were just fourteen. Remember that."

Ellen raised her head; blue wet light swam in her eyes. She felt forgiven, and there was a rush of love in her for her aunt. "Fourteen," she repeated. "Well, it isn't quite a lie, is it? I'll be fourteen in January, and that's only six, seven months away. Fourteen."

"Yes. Now you go to bed. I'll wake you at five. You'll work hard and be polite and obedient, won't you, dear? Mrs. Jardin is a hard woman and Mrs. Porter is even worse. You've been in their kitchen a couple of times, and you've seen them, and they paid no more attention to you than if you'd been a fly. Never mind, though. Just work hard and earn seventy-five cents a week, and maybe they'll let you have a good meal at supper." Then she said savagely, "A good meal. Steal it if you must. They got plenty. They save the scraps for their dog, and you're better than a dog. My Ellen."

Ellen, all distress gone from her, and happy that her aunt had recovered from her mysterious collapse, kissed May warmly and went to bed. May sat for some minutes, thinking. "It can't be," she whispered aloud. "She can't remember—that. She was never even there. Just me and Miss Amy and Mary. Why, she wasn't even born yet! She wasn't born in Philadelphia. She was born in Erie!"

Now May was swept with an old grief and her eyes

flooded again and she bowed her head and whispered, "Mary, Mary." Then she was horribly frightened, and she stood up and blew out the lamp and scuttled to her own bed, where she lay sleepless for some time listening to the voices of the wind and the few trees on the street. There was a gas lamp outside and it poured its ocher light into the bedroom and flickered on the damp walls and May Watson thought she saw ghosts and covered her head with her sheet.

3

"I bin up an hour, since five," Mrs. Jardin grumbled to Ellen, "while you were still slugging in bed. Your auntie knows that the home folks eat their breakfast at six, even though their visitors don't eat till seven, a heathen lazy way of living, in the cities."

"I'll come at half past five tomorrow morning," said Ellen, again sheepish with guilt. "But Aunt May thought you said six, Mrs. Jardin." It was still barely light outside; the laurels had a ghostly reflection on them as seen through the kitchen window. By bending forward over the sink and peering to her left Ellen could see that the eastern sky was a vast sheet of gold into which, at the horizon, were being intruded long thin fingers of scarlet. Birds were already arrowing through the dimness of dawn and their cries and calls made an exciting music to the girl. She had walked through the dark streets in which only a few early workers had been moving, and they still half asleep. At least she had escaped the mocking cruelty of the children on her way to this house.

"What are you staring at through the window?" demanded Mrs. Jardin. Her jaunty face became sly. "You look peakish this morning. Didn't get to bed 'til late, I reckon."

"It was about half past eleven," said Ellen, rubbing the silver.

"Oh?" asked Mrs. Jardin, pausing by the fuming stove, which crackled cheerfully with the fresh wood. "Where was you?"

"Well, I fell asleep, waiting for Aunt May," said Ellen. She thought of the clean winds of dawn she had just encountered, the sweetness of the air even in this dusty village by the river, and she smiled happily to herself. Mrs. Jardin saw that smile, and she smirked.

"Anyone with you?" she asked in a voice deliberately uninterested.

Ellen was surprised. She turned her head to look at Mrs. Jardin. "No, there isn't anyone living in the house but us."

"I didn't mean that. I meant a kind of visitor maybe," Mrs. Jardin said, and winked at Ellen. The girl was puzzled. Yet a sense of degradation without a name attacked her, a shapeless embarrassment. "We don't have visitors, except the ladies who come for Aunt May to make them dresses and alterations."

Mrs. Jardin nodded significantly to herself and her smile was slyer. If ever a girl was a natural-born strumpet this one was, with all that wild red hair and bold face. You can't fool me, my girl, she thought. I know a bad one when I sees one and you're bad, clear through. End up on the street in Scranton most likely. Born for it. You didn't sleep alone last night, and nobody can tell me different. While your aunt—if she is your aunt and not your mother—was out working.

The kitchen was lighted by gas, new to Preston, and its light was harsh and depressing. It also smelled badly. It flickered on Ellen's hair and her suddenly mournful profile as she vigorously rubbed the cutlery. It was now half past six, and the Mayor and his lady had already had their breakfast. In half an hour the visitors from Scranton would have theirs. There were sounds of movements above. The Mayor's house and furniture were considered very "grand" in Preston, but to Ellen they were both ugly. She did not yet know the full meaning of the word "elegant"; she only knew that there was something grossly missing in these large rooms, in which huge dark furniture brooded and every corner was occupied by fringed chairs and tables, ornament cases, vases filled with

pussy-willow branches or violently colored plumes; draperies were everywhere, not only at the narrow slits of
windows. They curved over the fireplaces, fringed and
balled, and were mostly dark red or navy blue, and
dripped from the grand piano and hung at the doors.
They even swathed the backs of giant sofas and festooned
themselves over all the pier mirrors, which reproduced
only the furniture and the dim expensive rugs and windows in the wan light that pervaded the house even on
bright summer days. They glimmered like ghosts and had
never reflected sunlight. The ugly flowered walls were
almost covered by dingy if expensive paintings of somber
mountains and darkling seas or stags at bay or a glum-
faced child with a basket of flowers in her hands which
resembled the asphodels, the flowers of the dead.

"The Mayor's house is a palace," May Watson often
said. But Ellen, though she had never seen a truly beautiful house in all her life, vaguely understood that this
house was hideous, tasteless, oppressive. It never occurred
to her to wonder why she knew this; there were so many
things she knew without any experience of them. The
house smelled of lavender, wax and strong soap, and
mustiness; the lurking stairways were haunted in the
gloom of a house where little outside light was permitted
to enter. Hollow booms of no discernible source echoed
constantly through the house and enhanced its ponderous
dreariness. Suddenly Ellen believed she could not breathe
here, that her chest was being weighted down by something beyond her knowledge, and she was both despondent
and frightened and wanted to run out into the free air
where there were no threatening crepuscular walls and
stairways with polished brass balustrades and bowls of
dried flowers and Meissen china figurines under glass bells
on tables, and fringes and silk balls and crouching furniture of deep-stained mahogany, and thick creeping rugs
that harbored dust. How terrible to have to live here,
thought the girl. In contrast, the wretched little house
she occupied with her aunt was cheerful and open, for all
its poverty and destitution. Innately buoyant though she
was, Ellen felt crushed and hopeless in this "mansion,"
and could hardly hold herself back from cowardly flight.
The black hall clock chimed a quarter to seven in a loud
grave voice, and Ellen's feeling of dismalness increased.

The kitchen window was filling with sun, and Mrs. Jardin turned off the gaslight.

Ellen said, "Are there many houses in Preston like this, Mrs. Jardin?"

Mrs. Jardin lifted her head proudly. "No. This is the grandest. But then, Mrs. Porter comes from Scranton and brought her family's furniture with her. People love to come into this house and stare at everything. Never saw anything like it before, they didn't."

Ellen was not given to irony but now she said within herself: They're lucky. This made her feel both guilty and mirthful, and she carried a dish of stewed prunes and figs into the dining room, which resolutely rejected any daylight or starlight at all, and so existed in gaslight by night and duskiness by day. Aunt May had called this room "luxury," but Ellen flinched at it. Its four long slender windows were shrouded in blue velvet draperies and almost opaque lace; the enormous buffet, to Ellen, resembled a closed coffin for all the mass of silver trays and teapots and sugar bowls and pitchers on it, and candlesticks, and for all the painting of dead fish and fruits and flowers which overhung it. The table was a gigantic wheel of mahogany, now covered with a white damask cloth centered with a silver bowl of roses and two silver epergnes. A glass chandelier hung over it, motionless in the torpid and smothering atmosphere that filled up the house. There was a china closet here which appeared to threaten the whole room with its crowded masses of porcelain and silver; it leaned slightly towards the center, scowling at the table, which was surrounded by colossal chairs paved with crimson velvet. Ellen laid the dish she was carrying on the table and looked about her, and shivered. She did not know what was wrong with the room but to her it was far more appalling than any poverty she had encountered. One day, she said to herself, I will have a house full of beautiful slender furniture, painted and pale, with delicate rugs and smiling walls and big windows full of light. She could vividly see such a dining room, scented with flowers and ferns, open to gardens wide and tranquil, and her depression lifted as if an aromatic wind had blown over it. She went back into the kitchen with a bemused but joyous expression on her face.

"Lovely room, ain't it?" asked Mrs. Jardin with pride.

The vision of the dining room she would have some-day suffused Ellen's thoughts, and so she said without hypocrisy, "Lovely."

In honor of the occasion of her first working day in the Mayor's house May Watson had permitted her niece to wear the pink cotton frock usually hallowed for holi-days, and a long white apron. She had found a blue ribbon to hold back Ellen's hair and it had a flaunting look in that tumbling mass of triumphant red. Ellen brought gleaming plates from the china closet to the table and carefully laid out the silver. There were sounds on the front stairway and she fled back into the kitchen.

"They finally got up," said Mrs. Jardin with disfavor. "In the middle of the day!" The hall clock struck seven ponderous notes. "Most folks are at work now; the Mayor's in his office and the Missus has gone marketing. Wonder what the world's coming to these days!"

As Ellen's working day had been changed by Mrs. Porter from eight hours to the customary twelve and her wages to one dollar a week instead of seventy-five cents—a magnanimous gesture and one which elevated the self-approval of the lady—the girl was entitled to two meals rather than one. The first would be at dinner, at eleven, the next at supper, at about five. Ellen's breakfast had consisted of a piece of toast and a cup of tea, the latter enhanced by a luxurious lump of sugar purloined by May Watson from this kitchen. Ellen, therefore, was hungry. Mrs. Jardin was frying sausages and pancakes and there was a sweet smell of maple syrup in the room mingling with the other fragrance, and the pungent excitement of coffee. Ellen had never tasted coffee, and she wondered if the actual beverage was as intriguing as the odor. There were pitchers of cream ready to be carried into the dining room, and a plate of hot pork chops and browned potatoes and a platter of luscious fried eggs and a basketful of fresh steaming rolls, several assortments of jams in crystal pots as well as a small oval dish of crisp hot fish. "Are just two gentlemen going to eat all this?" asked poor Ellen, her mouth watering.

"Why not? They're healthy, ain't they? Though Mr. Francis got the malaria in the war." Ellen looked long-ingly at the sausages and the other edibles and Mrs. Jardin saw this. She said, "Be careful, and get no com-plaints, and you can eat the scraps from their plates, though there won't be many, I warn you. You really ain't entitled to anything but something at eleven and again at five—no breakfast. But do your work well and you can have the scraps and even a cup of coffee. Don't say a word to the Missus. She has me save the scraps for Fido, out back in his kennel."

Ellen was grateful in spite of a first shiver at the thought of eating from the plates of others. Though she and her aunt were beset by the most stringent poverty and were always hungry in consequence, they had never eaten a morsel the other had left, not even the last crumbs. However, the odors in the kitchen, the array of food she had never encountered before, incited the girl to a passionate craving which she could not control. "Fido's too fat anyways," said Mrs. Jardin, congratulating herself on her charitable nature.

She placed many of the dishes on a large silver tray and motioned to Ellen to take it into the dining room, and followed her to give her her first lesson in serving. The gentlemen were just entering the room through the velvet portieres and Walter Porter said genially, "Good morning, Mrs. Jardin. Fine day, isn't it?"

"Just lovely, Mr. Porter," said Mrs. Jardin, giving the older man her most impish and confidential smile. (He always gave her a substantial tip on his departure, but not Mr. Francis, a poor figure of a young man, so thin and so "washed out" in appearance. In anticipation, however, she often, in a maternal fashion, urged him to "eat hearty, it's good for you, Mr. Francis.")

Francis, waiting courteously for his father to seat himself, suddenly saw Ellen, who was stretching her long young arms to place everything neatly on the table, as Mrs. Jardin had taught her this morning. He stopped in the very motion of sitting and both he and his father stared with pleased astonishment at the girl. She did not see this, but Mrs. Jardin, who saw everything, observed the reaction from the gentlemen and her face was avid again, bright with curiosity.

"This here is Ellen Watson, the new housemaid, Mr. Walter," she said. "If she doesn't please, just tell me. She's new and raw and I'm trying to be patient in training her."

"Of course. Capital," murmured Walter Porter, shaking out the big square of white table napkin. "I'm sure she will be splendid, won't you, Ellen?"

The girl flushed a bright rose at being addressed so directly by so distinguished a gentleman, and could not answer at once. Mrs. Jardin gave her a sharp thrust in her side and she almost dropped a platter, and she said in a trembling voice, "Yes, sir. Thank you, sir."

What a beautiful voice, thought young Francis. What a beautiful girl. She is like a fire in this awful room which is always chilly and dank. He was suddenly breathless. When Ellen presented him with the pancakes and sausages he could only, for a moment or two, look up into that miraculous face and see only those large blue eyes, so brilliantly shining and so timid. Mrs. Jardin keenly watched not only the table but the young man, and she felt gleeful. Another scandal in this house, unless one watched out. But what could he see in this ugly girl, such a gawk, so clumsy and with such rough hands? A real hoyden as well as a wench of bad repute, as the minister called it. Not like Miss Amelia Beale, who was a real lady though poor, too.

It isn't possible for anyone to be so beautiful, Francis was thinking, finally looking away from Ellen. She had a noble face, the face of an aristocrat, as well as being too exquisite to be believed. And what eyes! Like a newborn infant's, clear and glowing. His character was somewhat listless, due partly to nature and partly to the malaria he had contracted a year ago during the war with Spain. But now the listlessness was gone and he felt totally alive and moved and even joyful. He wanted to touch Ellen as a shivering man wants to move from dimness into the warm sun.

Mrs. Jardin was muttering commands to Ellen and the girl was following orders in a hurried confusion and with a desperate desire to escape admonitions. If she did well she would be permitted to eat the scraps from this banquet, and she was forced to repeated swallowings so that her mouth would not openly run. Francis saw the spasms in the white throat and he thought, with astonishment: Why, the poor child is hungry. Now he was filled with compassion, a compassion so strong that self-congratulating tears came into his eyes. She can't be more than fourteen; that face is too immature. What a beauty she will be in a few years, if such beauty can be increased by maturity.

Walter Porter was giving Ellen swift close glances, and

when she offered him a dish he smiled at her kindly. "Did you come from Philadelphia, Ellen?" he asked, extraordinarily stirred by Ellen, who so resembled the portrait in the Widdimer house. Was it possible there was some connection somewhere, though it seemed improbable? Perhaps from the wrong side of the blanket, he added to himself, and smiled again.

"No, sir," the girl almost whispered, filling his coffee cup with extreme care, for her hands were shaking. "I was born in Erie. I've never been in Philadelphia."

"You have no relatives there, child?"

"No, sir. None. Aunt May—my aunt—she was born in Erie, too, and was never in Philadelphia."

Now Francis spoke to her for the first time, and his breathlessness had returned. "Are your parents alive, Ellen?"

Her hands empty now, Ellen stood stiff and tall, hiding those hands under the white apron. She glanced down into Francis' candid eyes and saw there only a soft tenderness, which she could not interpret. She only knew that he was not hostile and she wanted to cry in gratitude. He was so good; he was the best person she had ever known. Who else cared about her parents, or wished to know about them? She swallowed nervously and forgot her hunger.

"No, sir, my mama and papa are dead. Papa was from New York and Mama was from Erie. They both died when I was two years old. That's what Auntie May tells me. She was Mama's sister." She had never spoken so freely to anyone before, and certainly not to a stranger. Her aunt was always warning her mysteriously not to speak to strangers and never to answer them, but there was no harm in it, was there? She was overcome by shyness again and her velvety color deepened and she both wanted to run and to remain in the presence of this man who looked at her with such unrestrained gentleness and interest, as if he saw her as others never saw her.

Mr. Porter spoke then. "Have you ever heard the names of Sheldon and Widdimer, Ellen?"

She shook her head. "No, sir, never."

"Unbelievable," murmured Walter, shaking his head slightly.

Ellen moved back a step, feeling helpless and confused again. Mrs. Jardin was watching from the door to the kitchen, her eyes rapidly blinking as they moved from face to face. Then she said bullyingly, "Ellen, bring the gentlemen fresh coffee, and the strawberry pie."

Ellen ran, not walked to the kitchen. Mrs. Jardin, who felt herself in a privileged position, spoke to Walter Porter. "Ellen will be all right, I think, when she's trained. She's still raw; her first day here, or anywhere in service, a big girl like that! She should have been in service four years ago, and learning her place and how to be useful. But things are changing and not for the better, sir. Law here won't let a girl go into service until she's fourteen, and that's a scandal. Bringing up a useless lazy generation, ain't we? Ellen ought to be in a factory."

Walter gave his son a quick glance but Francis was laying down his knife and fork and had begun to speak. "I think it is a scandal to send very young girls into a factory, Mrs. Jardin." His light voice was precise and almost dogmatic. "Thank God this Commonwealth is beginning to realize that and has enacted a few tentative laws in the proper direction. I belong to a Committee—"

"May I trouble you for the rolls, Francis?" asked his father. "And save your elocutions for your professors at Harvard. I am sure Mrs. Jardin isn't interested in your opinions. Concerning child labor, at least."

Mrs. Jardin smirked at him knowingly. But Francis, his fair face animated at the mention of his favorite subject, could not be repressed. "When I am graduated from law school, Father, I am going into politics, much as they disgust me."

"Yes, so you have said before," replied his father, highly diverted. "But I think the stench will drive you out, in spite of your convictions. You see, I know politicians as you do not, my boy. Ah, well, have your dreams. You are still young and untouched, though you've gone through a war."

"Which was asinine," said Francis, and his eyes sparkled with anger.

"You didn't think so when you enlisted in Teddy's Rough Riders."

"Well, I think so now. And you know my reasons for thinking that."

"All imaginary," said his father with a wave of his plump hand. "It was an outright, and justified war. That's what Teddy said, anyway."

"To seize the Philippines and Cuba," said Francis.

" 'And the beginning of American imperialism,' to quote you, Francis, my boy."

"Certainly. We are now entering the Age of Tyrants."

Mr. Porter leaned back in his chair, smiling broadly and closing his eyes. "Where you get these notions!" he said.

"From reading, which you do not do, Father, and from history."

"Well, I was never a scholar, even in the university," said Walter, still good-humored. He lifted his hand in defense. "Please, dear boy. Don't bore me again. It's a fine day. Let's go for a ride. You still aren't well, you know. When you entirely recover your health you will also recover—"

"My mind, too."

"Now, now, my boy. Ah, here is fresh coffee and strawberry pie. An excellent breakfast, Mrs. Jardin. You are spoiling us."

"I just wish Mr. Francis would eat more," said Mrs. Jardin, her hands comfortably locked under her apron; she gave Francis a hypocritically false look of fondness. "All he had was a dish of prunes and figs, a few sausages and only two eggs, a slice or two of bacon, one small piece of fish and a little dish of potatoes, and four griddle cakes, and a couple cups of coffee and a teensy bite of pie. That's not a breakfast for a man, sir."

"It's enough for four breakfasts—for four men," said Francis, who did not like Mrs. Jardin and was not deceived by her jocular air and jaunty winking. He wanted to believe—it was a necessity for him to believe—that the "working class" was endowed with native nobility, virtue, and wisdom, and was exploited. However, his perceptiveness often refuted that theory, and Mrs. Jardin was one of those who refuted it by her very being. Therefore, he incontinently disliked her; she was an affront to his vehement idealism, an idealism which must be total and never conditioned by facts. He was beginning, lately, to accuse himself of lack of charity, or understanding, and a failure to "see deeply enough and grasp hidden factors."

Once his father had said to him, "Of course, there are a multitude of uncountable injustices in this world. But who said this world must be 'perfect'? Only an idiot would believe in the perfectibility of man and a Utopia where it would always be summer and no one would work very much but would wander around in an incorruptible garden singing. Who would carry out the slops, sweep the streets, and lay the crops? So long as we have bowels, and the air has dust in it, and we need to eat, we will have to work. Didn't St. Paul say, 'He who does not work, neither shall he eat'? Yes."

"Science is already prophesying that soon it will not be necessary for any man to labor," said Francis, flushing scarlet as usual when his theories were attacked. "In the meantime, labor must not be exploited; it must be given a living wage."

"I agree with that," said Walter Porter. "I pay my men well, far above what the new unions are asking. But man will never be freed from labor. Doesn't the Bible say that man must earn his bread by the sweat of his face? Yes. My boy, this is a realistic world, based on objective truths, and no dreams will change it. But dreams can destroy as well as create. Remember that."

"There are no objective truths," Francis had replied with heat. "All is subjective."

"Then let's have imaginary mills, factories, ships, crops, commerce, and God knows what else," said his father with exasperation. "In that way we'll let the world go back to a savage wilderness, for the world is not only subjective —in the minds of men—but brutally objective, too."

Walter had become alarmed after this conversation. Francis was not only his one child, but his son, and he expected much of him. He knew that Francis had an excellent mind and had had a sound upbringing. Where had he acquired these new and perilous ideas which he was expounding lately? Had the war tainted him? But thousands of young men had engaged enthusiastically in that war—as Francis had done originally—and they had returned to desk and bench in a normal fashion, though many of them had become afflicted with malaria as Francis had been afflicted. Was there some rotting flaw in his nature which demanded perfection in all things, in human behavior, in the very laws of existence? It was not for some years that he became convinced that such as Francis were dangerous to all men, for they brought the unstable atmosphere of dreams to the affairs of mankind, and not muscle, not realism. One must deal with things as they are, Walter would often ponder, not as we should like them to be. I am not against dreams, if they are possible, and God knows that without dreamers we should have no poetry, no justice, no Constitution, no order, and no civilization. It is only when dreams leave the realm of the probable, or even the possible, that we are threatened. When dreams exclude fallible human nature, then we are in trouble. Human nature is not mutable, in spite of the lacy philosophers.

He had tried, over and over, to impart his thoughts to Francis, but Francis was becoming more and more resistive. Worse, he would fall into a sullen silence when his dreams encountered the sawtooth edges of reality. As a believer in the subjective, he vehemently believed that reality itself could be changed. He did not blame his faulty theories; he blamed reality. He had become suspicious of nature itself.

There is plenty of room in this world for dreamers—if the dreams are credible—Walter would think, and room for absolute realists. We must have a mingling of the two —if that is possible itself!—and work together. The only danger to the world is in those who believe only in dreams, and those who believe only in brutish facts. Both are dogmatists, and if we do not watch out we will be destroyed by them. We must concede, all of us, that man is more than an animal, but that he is an animal also, and has appetites that embrace the spiritual, yet also must be fed and watered and sheltered as any other beast. I detest the noncompromisers!

On another occasion he said to his son, "When God became man He had to obey His own laws: Evacuation of the bowels, urination, itches, pains, lusts of the flesh, as the parsons call it, hunger, labor, sweat, dirty hands and face, the necessity to wash and sleep, to change His garments, to scratch His feet. He did not suspend the laws of being in order to make Himself more comfortable in the environment which existed. We must accept the human condition, as He accepted it, with all its miseries, discomforts and complaints and insect bites and toil. As man, as well as God, He became annoyed at His Mother when she demanded that He perform the miracle of the wine at the marriage in Cana. A minor matter—but He was annoyed. There is a deep meaning in this: We cannot escape our flesh. We can only control it to a certain extent, but we cannot obliterate our nature, and the weaknesses of our nature. We can only have compassion—when it is deserved. And a sense of humor, which you lack, my boy. Humor makes life tolerable. There is no mention of it in the Bible, but I am pretty sure that Christ laughed frequently and joked and told interesting stories. After all, He was a Jew in the flesh, and Jews are famous for their wry jokes."

Francis did not believe in any Deity, and he did not believe in Christ. But something in him was offended by his father's speech. It threatened his concept of the grim perfectibility of man. Once he said meaningly to his father, "There is a new spirit growing in the world," to which Walter had replied, "If it is what I think it is, then may God have mercy on our souls."

On another occasion, in order to conciliate his beloved son, Walter had said, "My boy, there is enough room in this world for both of us." He had looked pleadingly at Francis, but Francis had shut his face and had tightened his lips and had not replied. Consequently, and in increasing exasperation, Walter had begun to oppose any ideas of Francis', some of which he privately agreed were worthy. Such as my son would choke the theories which are probable, he would think, and set men like myself obdurately against what we know ourselves to be good. That is disastrous to everybody.

Today, on extra urging, Francis went with his father for a drive through the country. Francis was not interested in farms and fields and the exuberance of nature in flower and fruit and grain. He was an urban man, which Walter regretted. There were too many urban men in the world these days. They were bored by the obvious; they thought labor demeaning. Worse still, they thought it unnecessary, and an affront to something they called "the dignity of man." More and more, father and son were finding speech between them—honest and deep-hearted speech and self-revelation—impossible. Francis blamed his father. Walter was "old." He had no concept of the "new world." In his turn, Walter thought his son's ideas resembled a bowl of lusty oatmeal and milk prematurely rancid, and poisonous. Ah, well, he would think, when Francis becomes older he will find that there are laws to contain impossible dreams, the laws of God and nature. The only idea which has splendor is the bountiful mercy of God—and we surely need it in these days!

Mrs. Jardin said to Ellen, in the kitchen: "Now we'll go upstairs to do the bedrooms. The Missus makes her own bed, but there are the three others. Here is the mop and duster and the broom and the pail. Don't stare at them. You know what they're for, don't you?"

Ellen had been permitted the scraps from Francis' plate; she had devoured them with swift avidity, relishing every crumb. She had had a cup of coffee, which she thought delectable. She was surfeited; she was also sleepy, and it was only eight o'clock. "If you didn't romp around all night," said Mrs. Jardin with severity, "and behaved yourself like a Christian, you wouldn't be so heavy-eyed." As Ellen did not understand this, she could only accompany Mrs. Jardin in silence to the upper stories. Mrs. Jardin was a perfectionist for everybody but herself, something which would have interested Walter Porter, ironically.

The many bedrooms upstairs were as vast as the rooms below, but were so weightily populated with dark and corpulent furniture that they gave the impression of being thrust together in a small space, and even overlapping. As on the lower floor the light here was dun and shrouded, the air stifling. Every window was filled with shirred gray silk blinds, as well as lace curtains and dark-blue velvet draperies; the shutters were half closed. But here and there a ruddy needle of sunlight pierced a crevice at the choked windows and darted across a rug, or a wider bar made the edge of a mahogany arm redly incandescent. There were, in addition to beds with high corner posts and canopies, carved wardrobes gloomily closed and locked, dressers, chests, chairs, settees, tabourets holding bloated Chinese bowls in which a struggling plant fought for its life, and funereal pier mirrors. There was a dusty smell of lavender in each room, or clove, or bay rum or dead roses.

"Rich, ain't it?" said Mrs. Jardin, looking about her as Ellen labored. The girl's face was running with sweat; she licked it away around her mouth. I think it is terrible, she thought, with her very new rebelliousness. So she pretended not to hear Mrs. Jardin's complacent remark and dusted and swept and shook with feverish swiftness. She saw her first bathroom, in this house, and was genuinely awed by all that marble and whiteness and polished brass and taps. Still, it seemed to her not at all clean to have privies in the house, and she breathed as lightly as possible. She knew nothing of Bunyan's *Pilgrim's Progress* or its Slough of Despond, but she felt caught in something which dulled her soul while it terrified her.

She was sent to the cellar to iron, and here the air, though as still as stone, was at least cooler than the air upstairs. There were men's shirts damply piled in profusion in baskets, endless sheets, lace-edged pillowcases and shams, a woman's discreet and billowing underwear, napkins, tablecloths, "runners," and mounds of stockings, as well as corset covers and petticoats and aprons and lawn dresses and "wrappers," and men's drawers. The flatirons warmed on a hot plate, the first Ellen had ever seen, and she did not mind the rank odor of gas in her gratitude that the plate did not heat the cellar as a wood stove would have heated it. But the gas made her languid and faintly nauseated and gave her a headache. The hours passed in a semi-slumbrous way. For Ellen was indulging herself in her usual fantasy of wide lawns at sunset, with long golden shadows creeping over grass and roses, and of white houses with glittering free glass, of bright roofs and green vines, of soft music and peace, and somewhere, she herself, in a pale sprigged gown, walking serenely in the scented silence with a flower in her hand. And waiting. But for what or whom she waited she did not know.

"Ain't you done yet?" Mrs. Jardin's girlish voice shrilled down the stairway. "It's four o'clock. Need your help in the kitchen."

Ellen came to herself. She finished ironing a handkerchief; the cellar was pervaded now not only with the smell of gas but with the sweetness of beeswax. She was amazed to discover that all the ironing was finished, for she had moved automatically. She ran up the stairs and announced that the baskets were filled; she carried one, thrusting herself upwards and panting with the weight. Mrs. Jardin was skeptical; she critically examined the articles within the basket, and said with grudging, "Well, you're good for something after all. Wouldn't have believed it, a flighty miss like you."

Ellen was set to work helping with the dinner, which would be at half past five, for this was a weekday. Now she was aware of smarting eyes and pulsing arms and heaviness in her legs. Her hair was a shimmering and glowing mass of tendrils about her face, which had lost its color and had become ghostly with exhaustion. But she was not hungry; her nausea lingered. "You're all sweaty, and you smell, and you can't go into the dining room tonight looking and smelling like that," said Mrs. Jardin. "Better wear something clean tomorrow, I warn you." The pink cotton frock was stained with perspiration and cobwebs and dust, and Ellen looked at it with dim dismay. She wanted only to fall down and sleep in some lightless spot, and now she would have to wash and iron this dress tonight.

She faintly refused the scraps tonight; the odor of roast beef sickened her and she had to clench her teeth against a vomitous urge when she smelled the roasted onions and the hot apple pie. However, she concealed a wedge of pie and some slivers of fat and meat and a roll or two in her apron for her aunt. Something uneasily stirred in her at this pilfering which had never stirred before.

The sweltering streets seethed with people, as usual, when she left at nearly seven. She did not run this evening; she did not pause to look at the distant mountains drifting in a purple mist, nor was she exhilarated at the smoldering ball of the sun. She walked slowly, her head bent, painfully pushing one foot ahead of the other, and never heard the customary jeers and obscene whistles. Her hair fell like copper silk about her face; her lips were colorless. Her feet were not flesh; they were molten metal and each step was an agony.

May Watson was industriously sewing in the parlor, the treadle machine squeaking and protesting. The room was dusky, for kerosene was expensive. But she looked up, startled, when she saw Ellen, and blinked.

"Did they dismiss you, Ellen?" she cried. "You were supposed to work 'til ten!"

Ellen leaned against the settee and said in a voice so weak that May could hardly hear it, "No, Auntie. Mrs. Porter said from six to seven was all, and she's going to give me a dollar a week, not just seventy-five cents."

May was stunned by this magnanimity on the part of a woman she both despised and reverenced. She blinked rapidly, then rubbed her scorched eyes. "Well, then!" she exclaimed. "You must show your gratitude, Ellen! Go back at once and work 'til ten. You didn't leave Mrs. Jardin to finish up in the kitchen all alone, did you?" She was shocked and alarmed.

Ellen closed her eyes in complete despair. "No. We were all finished. Mrs. Jardin—she was pleased. She said I was better than Alice, and worked real fast and deserved the dollar. Oh, Aunt May! I can't go back, not even if they needed me tonight! I—I feel sick. I just want to lie down, somewhere."

May peered at her niece and her sense of what was "right" fought with pity. "You do look peaked," she said. "That's because you stayed up, chattering last night." She had another thought. "Did you get your supper? That was agreed."

Ellen whispered, "Yes. And I brought you something, the way you bring me things. It's in the kitchen."

She looked down at her frock. May uttered a sharp sound. "How did you get so dirty and wet? You're real careless, Ellen. Now you've got to wash and iron it right away, to wear tomorrow."

"Please," said the exhausted girl. "Let me wear the blue tomorrow. I—Aunt May—I just can't stand up any longer. I've got to lie down."

"A big strong girl like you! Wait 'til you get my age! Well, go along."

Drugged with weariness, Ellen moved with extreme slow effort out of the room and into her airless bedroom. She pulled off her clothes, not neatly as usual. She pulled on her wrinkled nightgown. She fell on the bed and was immediately asleep, curled up like a puppy.

Two hours later May Watson turned down the lamp in the kitchen, and with her own weariness she moved towards her bedroom. But she paused at the door of Ellen's room. The light from the distant streetlamp fell through the doorway and May saw the half-crouched motionless mound on the bed. There was something infinitely pathetic in the amorphous contour of the girl's body, and May, her eyes wetting, said to herself, "Oh, Ellen, Ellen."

Through her opened window May Watson saw the

moon, a huge fat white spider caught in a thin web of
drifting clouds, and now it was not only her body which
ached but her soul also.

4

Jeremy, the son of the Mayor, returned today from his
visit to the young lady in whom he had been interested.
A vital young man, a business administration student at
Harvard, he was both lusty and cautious, virile without
undo pugnaciousness, intelligent and cynical, pragmatic
and exigent. He concealed a formidable power of intellect
under an abrupt and offhand manner. He had no use for
fools, for the sentimental or the trivially expedient; his
particular hatreds were for the maudlin, the endlessly
smiling, the cliché-speakers, the average, the mediocre.
He had no love or mercy for "the people," which included, in his ruthless category, his own parents. Preston,
the village of some five thousand "dolts," appalled him,
and always had. The house of his parents revolted him;
their manner of living provoked him to execrations. The
Mayor had always considered his son "difficult." Mrs.
Porter adored him, though often he bewildered her with
what she called "crude remarks. They aren't nice, you
know, dear."

"Nothing is 'nice,' in this world, Mama," he would
reply. "It is ruled by the law of the jungle, 'The race to
the swift, the battle to the strong.' I don't intend to be
one of the weak. If we don't watch out the weak will
devour us, body and substance and country, and leave
only bones behind. They have such appetites!"

"You will learn," she would remark. "After all, dear,
you are only twenty-three years old, a mere boy." She
did not know that her son had never been a "mere boy,"
not even in infancy.

Once he wrote to a friend, "There are only two kinds of people in this world: Perpetual children, who are a terrible danger to civilization, and those who were born adult. When the 'children' take over this country and adults are in the minority, then it's the end for this country. I have known adults who were chronologically only ten years old, and children who were seventy-seven. One of these days we will have to face the fact that men are not born equal in intelligence—which is the only criteria for mankind—and act accordingly, or we'll all perish in a sweet swelter of sentimentality and brotherhood; what the Founders of this Republic established will be destroyed forever. America needs men, not diaperwetters, no matter their age."

He was an ardent advocate of the Malthusian theory.

Once a professor—whom Walter Porter would have called "lacy"—said to the young man, "We must have compassion for the weak, and help them."

"I think," said Jeremy, "that our semantics do not meet. If you mean the persistently poor, who do nothing to elevate themselves, and neither toil nor spin unless they are faced with starvation, and have no intelligence at all, and are determinedly stupid and whining and mendacious, then I say: Let them die off, and the quality of our populace will be improved. However, if you mean those of intelligence who were born poor, then indeed we must have some compassion for them, though they are proud enough to angrily reject compassion. We must help them in ways they will never discover. For on these depends the future of our country."

To Jeremy, his mother was the prototype of a "new spirit" in America: the rich who mawkishly bewail the "plight" of the poor, either for their own sinister reasons or to elevate themselves in the estimation of their neighbors. Agnes Porter was not intelligent enough for the first, whom Jeremy blackly and bitterly suspected, and so she belonged to the latter category, which Jeremy called simpletons, not as dangerous as the first but a power behind them. Both categories exploited "the poor," one for political purposes, the latter for public approval, especially the religious and social. "If anyone is the murderer of the helpless," he would think, "these are the guilty."

He had assiduously read all the works of Karl Marx and Engels, and was an intense student of the French

Revolution, which had destroyed France as a civilizing principle in the world. He had aroused the sly mirth of his professors because of what they called his "inconsistency." He spoke with contempt of the enormously rich: "They have only the cunning and greed of a weasel"; and he had spoken with equal contempt of the weaklings who depended on charity for their existence. "Let them prey on each other—but not on us," he would say. "When both devour our flesh, brothers in voracity, America will fall into the long twilight of bankruptcy, slavery, and despair. Somehow, these monstrous brothers will find a way to tax us into oblivion and chains. They are of one mind. But be sure *they* won't be taxed!"

He detested, above all, politicians. He had not enlisted in the war against Spain, but not for the reasons his cousin Francis cherished. He thought wars, except in self-defense, atrocious, though by nature he was a fighter.

Sometimes the complacent Mayor thought uneasily that he had begotten a bear cub, all powerful sinuousness and emphatic charges. He did not understand in the least what Jeremy asserted. He could only think that Jeremy was "young" and therefore too vehement. Once he had said to Jeremy in a grave and pious tone, "You must remember what Christ has said of the 'least of His brethren,' and that we must help them."

Jeremy had stared at his father in incredulous and caustic mirth. If there was anyone who was less interested in the "brethren" it was Edgar Porter, who treated his servants and his employees with contemptuous haughtiness and dislike, and was merciless and pettish in his demands on them. So Jeremy said, "God also condemned the lazy grasshopper who did nothing but sing and dance and eat all summer, while the industrious ant worked and prepared for the winter. 'Go to the ant, thou sluggard,' He said. Now, the Bible is not inconsistent. God permitted the gay grasshopper to die whimpering that fate had been unjust to him."

He found Preston intolerably boring, and his parents even more so. But as a conscientious young man he felt that it was his duty to endure them for a few weeks or so during the holidays. However, even then he found it absolutely necessary to escape occasionally, to New York or Philadelphia or Boston or even Pittsburgh. Here he found men like himself, of the same mind, who were already beginning to express fear for their country and its future. "The new Populism," they would say, and looked with a derision, not without fear, at William Jennings Bryan. "He'll go away, and his ideas with him," they had said to Jeremy. But Jeremy had shook his head. "Remember, we are not alone in this benighted world. Scandinavia, and to some extent France and Germany, have adopted a number of Karl Marx's ideas."

Jeremy had inherited, on his twenty-first birthday, a large estate from his maternal grandmother. With this— though he did not considerably deprive himself—he helped support orphanages in Scranton, and privately contributed to the salaries of various ministers. He kept these matters anonymous, however. Francis would not have understood this of a young man he called selfish and "an enemy of the people" and an "exploiter."

Jeremy had been amused when his father had run for the office of Mayor. "What for?" he had asked.

Edgar Porter had made a grave and pious face. "To help make the world better—in my small way," he had replied.

Jeremy had laughed uproariously, but had never explained his laughter. He was fond of his short and massive father with the sanctimonious eyes and the air of one who believed himself a servant of the public weal. "What this country needs is muscle, Dad," he had said. "Muscle and brains. They are not mutually exclusive." When Edgar had looked hurt, Jeremy kindly continued, "I am not speaking literally. We need the muscularity of intelligence, and not the flab of social reformers. I have never seen a reformer who was handy with his fists or who could express a sensible and realistic opinion. It is all tears and simpering and shrill and acid denunciations, and envy. Envy, above all."

When his son had diligently supported unions, the Mayor found this baffling and paradoxical. "Why?" demanded Jeremy. "I will support any union or organization which will protect the hard-working and the industrious and the proud. But I will fight to the death the weak who would prey on them, to fill their bellies without work. I think unions may eventually be the only things which will stand between America and despotism. If they don't fall into the trap of power, too." He shook his head. "The fault with humanity is that it is human."

To his parents, Jeremy was an enigma. To himself, he was of one sound piece—an American. He did not "trust" anyone, and especially not a politician. Once he had hoped that his cousin Francis would understand and be on his side, but Francis had disappointed him. "All air and foam and idealism," he had said. "One, at the last, must be pragmatic, and deal with things as they are." He found an ally in his Uncle Walter, who often secretly wished that Jeremy was his son. "No dowdiness there," Walter would say to himself. "Just common sense." On Jeremy's suggestion, Walter had bought many copies of Elbert Hubbard's pamphlet *A Message to Garcia,* and had distributed them widely.

Jeremy thought the self-styled intelligentsia hilarious. "Mediocres with pretensions of brains," he had called them. "There is no blood or vitality or reason or manliness among these little white worms. They are like the people they champion—witless, covetous, sniveling. And dependent, and poisonous. In more strenuous times, in this millennium, nature dealt with them ruthlessly. In circumventing nature we haven't been compassionate."

Many of the more milky by temperament thought him "cruel," though they were the most cruel of men themselves. Jeremy understood them at once; they were hypocrites and wanted a reputation for civic and humanitarian virtue. He avoided them when he could, but he found them increasingly prevalent in the universities. He would attempt to reason with them; they possessed no reason, and only emotion, which latter Jeremy suspected. He also suspected the zealous.

Though by character he was incisive and vivid and strong, he had no flamboyance nor was he ebullient. Yet in appearance he was impressive, being tall and sinewy; he had a look of stalwart vigor, invincible and potent. His mother was correct in considering him manly. Women, therefore, found him fascinating and completely masculine. He had no affectations, but possessed a hard and forthright look, not bold, if frequently challenging. His voice was vital and incisive, somewhat loud but never dogmatic. He invariably meant what he said.

He had not inherited his mother's pallid eyes, which often bulged like unripe grapes, nor her general fairness of coloring. His eyes were a forceful and penetrating brown, rather demanding and so very intriguing to women. They were fixed deeply in his swarthy rectangular face. His nose was bony and prominent, if well formed and aggressive, his brow square, his chin somewhat set, his mouth sensually full and skeptical, with the marks of quick humor about it. His dark hair was very coarse and plentiful, but never disordered. Women loved his hands, large and very male, with very clean square nails and big knuckles. As well as being exceptionally scholarly, he was quick of movement and of mind. He did not resemble either of his parents. "He looks like my dear papa," Agnes Porter would say with a fond simper. Jeremy was popular with most of his peers though anathema to those who considered themselves more temperate, or kinder, gentler, and, above all, more civilized. Those who prided themselves on their "tolerance" whispered sneeringly that he looked "foreign," even Slavic. In athletics, he had earned a prodigious reputation.

If he had one weakness it was his propensity for women, but he was very discriminating. He did not like vapidity and sweetness and pretenses of helplessness. But he admired spirit in a woman, self-reliance, courage, as well as beauty. Not for him the "common" and the unintelligent, nor even in a prostitute. He had, unknown to himself, a sense of delicacy and taste. He had not been the obvious reason for little Alice's dismissal, though the infatuated girl had more than hinted he was. He had never even noticed her in his father's house. He was not Mrs. Jardin's favorite gentleman, though she was obsequious to him, and it had been she who had spread the rumor, for, though he treated her with politeness, he had a way of looking at her which unpleasantly revealed to her, for an uncomfortable moment, her own character.

He had decided that the young lady from Scranton had her amusing facets but that she was not consistently bright. He was contemplating going to New York again before he had to return to Harvard. The thought of remaining in Preston until term depressed and bored him.

He arrived home the early evening of the Fourth of

July, to find the house empty. He had not been expected
for two more days.

"I'm going to the church picnic tomorrow," Mrs. Jardin
had informed Ellen on the eve of Independence Day.
"So you will have to stay 'til we all get back, after the
fireworks at night. Maybe nine o'clock. What are you
blinking for, like you was about to cry? Somebody has
to be here to lay out the late supper when we all get
back. That was always the way around here. Cold meats
and salad and hot bread and fried potatoes and them
pastries I baked this morning. Not much work, but you
kind of seem tired most of the time, and you bigger than
I am. You got such awful long legs."

Ellen had not replied to this, for she was afraid that
if she did she would burst into tears. For the first time
in her life in Preston she would miss the picnic, for which
May saved all year, and she would not see the fireworks
and, above all, she would not hear the band.

"There's no use crying," May said to her niece when
the girl returned home. She spoke firmly, for she, too,
was afraid of weeping. "That's the way things are, Ellen.
I'm sorry you won't get home until after nine, but—if
it'll make you feel better I won't go to the picnic, either.
I'll wait home for you."

But Ellen, momentarily forgetting her own misery—
and full of self-reproach—passionately protested. The
holiday was one of the very few occasions of entertainment for her aunt, and May looked forward to it for
months. Finally she persuaded May that there was "no
sense" in both of them being wretched, and valiantly declared that she did not mind at all. "The house will be
quiet, and maybe I can go into their library and find
something good to read," she said. "The park's not far
away, and I can listen on the stoop or through the windows when the band plays." She forced herself to smile,
and nodded her head, and May looked aside. It wasn't
fair, no, it wasn't, but when was the world fair? Ellen had
better learn that real quick.

Ellen hardly slept that night for her grief. When she
got out of bed at half past four it was dark, as usual,
though there was a cloudy pearliness in the east. Her
aunt still slept, for today was one of the days she would

not work. So Ellen dressed quickly and silently and stole out of the little house without a sound. She would eat breakfast at the Mayor's house, if Mrs. Jardin felt indulgent enough. Yesterday she had not felt indulgent at all toward Ellen and had waddled firmly out of the kitchen with the heaped plate of leftovers for the dog, making no comment while the girl looked after her longingly. The reason for Mrs. Jardin's displeasure was not Ellen directly. It was "that Mr. Francis." He had not accepted one of her offerings and had ignored her gestures and her urging. In truth, he was not aware of her. He was thinking of the tedium approaching him tomorrow; he found patriotic occasions irritating. Patriotism, to him, was mere chauvinism, a frivolous and egotistic emotion, and not an expression of a nation's pride in itself and its love for its heroes.

So Ellen had gone hungry until half past eleven yesterday. She prayed that Mrs. Jardin would be in a good humor today. Fortunately, she was. She even baked a fresh pancake for the girl and heated up the cool coffee. Ellen's gratitude made her swell with her own magnanimity. "After all, you're still growing," she said. "You'll end up being bigger than a house. Your dad must have been a giant, or something." She paused. Her little eyes narrowed craftily. "What was your dad like, anyways?"

"I don't remember him," said Ellen, licking her fork. "But Aunt May once said he was very handsome, and dark."

"How come you got the same name's your aunt—Watson?"

Ellen was surprised. "Didn't Aunt May tell you? She was married to Daddy's cousin, a very poor cousin. He and Daddy got typhoid fever the same time, in Erie, and they both died. It was very sad."

As this was the same version May Watson had given herself, Mrs. Jardin was disappointed. She was convinced that Ellen was not only ugly but stupid, and she had anticipated drawing some heinous information from her which would refute May's silly "lies," and expose the scandalous background of the young girl to the amusement of Mrs. Jardin. It would also give her a spicy tidbit to tell her friends. "Better clean up them dishes," she said sourly. "You're never ready to get down to work."

There was an air of holiday in this house and in spite of her dejection Ellen felt it. Mr. Francis had been exceptionally kind to her this morning; he had even touched her hand gently when she offered him fresh sausages and had looked up, smiling sweetly, into her eyes. She had felt such an urgent affection for him that she blushed and almost dropped the sausages and had been scolded by Mrs. Jardin for her carelessness. "Really, you are not progressing well in the girl's training," Mrs. Porter had rebuked her cook. "She is still very clumsy." Mrs. Jardin had wanted to hit Ellen right there and then but she saw Francis regarding her coldly and with full knowledge. Still, she let Ellen eat the scraps, and felt very generous and forgiving, and, above all, Christian.

It was a very hot blue and gold day and flags were waving from the courthouse staffs and smaller flags were planted before all the houses on Bedford Street, and even in some of the poor sections. Fireworks were cracking everywhere, accompanied by the shouts of children and their screams of excitement. Even the horses apparently felt the mood of holiday and their hoofs rang smartly on the cobblestones and those in the carriages exchanged hearty and laughing greetings with friends whom they passed. Somewhere someone was exuberantly playing "Hail, Columbia!" on a piano. Trees, luminous with light, sang merrily in the dusty wind. There was a scent of acrid punk and gunpowder in the sparkling air, and warm roses and freshly cut grass. The sky was a shining violet and seemed to pulse with heat. Ellen's dejection lessened. She thought of the books in the library, and quiet, and no Mrs. Jardin for long hours.

But Francis was gloomy. He could not offend his aunt and his uncle by pleading to be left behind. This was the Mayor's Day. He would be the speaker on the steps of the courthouse after the picnic. It was his occasion of open glory. He had written and rewritten his speech many times, sweating over it laboriously. He had ambitions, which he had not as yet told anyone, not even his wife. He hoped to be a State Senator, and he knew that several politicians from Philadelphia—potent men— would be here today, for Preston's sawmills were prosperous and were owned by Preston's few rich inhabitants. Preston might boast only a few thousand resident souls, but they were proudly of the Mayor's party and admired and liked him, for he had a genial way with him and an easy fashion of speaking—"democratic"—which inspired fondness in the voters. The gentlemen from Philadelphia were scrupulously not visiting in any of the rich houses in Preston, not even the Mayor's. They were temporarily residing in Preston's one hotel, the Pennsylvanian, which was not very lavish. In this manner they implied that they were not partisan and did not prefer the wealthy over the poor. After all, there were more poor voters than privileged ones.

Edgar Porter quite understood their reasoning, which was also his. But his wife complained. "I call it sheer unfriendliness, and after you delivered the votes for Congressman Meade yourself here in Preston." But Edgar had smilingly shook his head. "There are nuances, Agnes," he had replied. "It is all politics."

Somewhere lawn mowers rattled gaily; somewhere someone blew a trumpet. Dogs barked, alarmed at the firecrackers. Preston was noisier than usual today in the elation of holiday. Ellen's spirits rose. She remembered how she and her aunt had been sedulously isolated in the park on these occasions, and how they had been miserable at such treatment, and how often Ellen had heard snickerings when she walked to the fountain to get more water for May. She tossed her head. Even holidays were not pure enjoyment for such as Aunt May and herself. They had frequently felt downhearted afterwards, and could not bring themselves to offer cheer to each other. So she dusted and swept bedrooms, humming. I'm not sorry I'm not going, she told herself, trying not to think of the music and the escape from work. It'll be nice to be alone for once. Well, I hope everybody has a good time, though. Her young heart warmed. Love and trust. It was good to think of the enjoyment of strangers, even if one was barred from it. In a mood of joyous piety the girl hummed on as she worked, while Mrs. Jardin prepared the luscious picnic baskets in the kitchen. The cook began to sing in her immature voice:

"There'll be a hot time in the old town tonight!"

Ellen particularly detested that ballad. She quietly closed the door of the bedroom she was cleaning. She began to sing softly, without words, one of the most beautiful songs she had heard the brass band play one Sunday, the week before, in the park, and did not know it was from an opera and that it was called "The Vows We Plighted." She only knew that it was celestial, that it was at once mournful and haunting yet pervaded with tenderness, like a memory. Her voice filled the musty hot room with ardent melody, pure and yearning. Her eyes trembled with happy tears and again the promise came to her, of mysterious content, of the end of longing, of the completion of hope, of the fulfillment of love. Her new and imperative instincts rose in her and she could not understand them. She could only feel an anticipatory delight, but what that delight was, she did not know. Suddenly she lifted a small chair in her arms and hugged it tightly to her breast and felt comforted and assuaged.

Eventually the house was deserted by all but Ellen, and she ate her cold dinner in the kitchen, relishing every bite, though the gravy had congealed on the meat and the bread was flaccid. Feeling gleefully defiant, she went to the huge icebox and lifted a large jug of icy milk from its depths and poured a glassful for herself. She then attacked all the dishes with zeal. Her young body was soothed with food, and she began to sing again. She heard the slapping of screen doors as people hurried out of the houses for the park. Bells from the church began to ring with a rollicking sound. Footsteps ran on the pavement outside. Then it was very quiet.

Ellen went through the front door and stood on the veranda, listening. There was no one about; smoke from the last firecrackers drifted in the air. She strained for the band music. It came to her, faint but sure, and Ellen smiled richly to herself at the rousing marches. A trumpet note soared like a golden bubble and again she hugged herself with delight. Drums throbbed, and her heart quickened. The sky had never been so lighted; the trees hardly moved in the silence except at the tops, where they were illuminated and touched with fluttering gilt. The still façades of the houses across the wide street dreamed in the sun, spangled with the shadows of leaves. The sleeping lawns twinkled, for they had been recently hosed. The scent of water from the river came to Ellen, fresh and exciting. The sawmills were silent. All was peace. There was no grinding of phonographs, no beating of mechanical

pianos. Ellen knew the precious surcease from all that was
ugly and discordant. She did not as yet know the meaning
of harmony, but she felt it.

She went back into the gardens, where she had never
been permitted to go before, and marveled and rejoiced
at the multitude of tumescent flowers. She saw their color,
their succulent stems, their glistening leaves. There were
white and pink low borders enclosing summer lilies the
color of orange, and rose beds, and the last iris in tints of
copper and purple, and long pink and white sheaves of
gladioli, and coral bells and a low tree covered with huge
red flowers. There were birches and spruces and maples
and vaulted elms. She sat down in shade and leaned her
body against a trunk and it seemed to her that she could
feel a mystic life flowing into her own from the contact.
Fido, from the door of his kennel, panted and looked at
her with disfavor, and barked once. Sighing with a surfeit
of pleasure and content, she dozed, the sweetness of
breezes cooling her face. Her hair moved and was touched
with fire. Her sore hands lay simply and in childish re-
laxation in her lap. She did not know that she was the
most beautiful thing in that garden and that she looked
like a sleeping nymph. Drowsy birds in the tree peered
down at her and questioned. Bees blew about her and one
lighted on her hair for a moment. A white butterfly came
to rest on her knee, raising and dropping its wings.

It was there that Jeremy Porter found her. When he
had discovered the house empty he remembered that his
family went to the park on the Fourth of July and after
refreshing himself with his father's whiskey—the Mayor
was a strenuous teetotaler in public—he wandered out
into the garden. He had expected it to be deserted also.
He was interested to see the distant flutter of a light dress
near a tree and he went to investigate. He came upon the
sleeping Ellen and stood and gazed and could not believe
it.

The sun was sloping to the west and still Ellen slept,
dreaming of another garden she had never seen, and a
waiting, a waiting compounded of happiness and deep
yearning, a scented misty garden with no borders, and
groves of trees pearly-clouded with evening. She heard a
bird singing poignantly and knew it for a nightingale,
though she had never heard one before. She lifted her

dreaming eyes to the opalescent sky and sighed deeply and with felicity. Her apricot-flushed lips curved and smiled, the smile of a woman and not of a child.

Good God, thought Jeremy, where did this beauty come from? Who is she? He approached her nearer, and saw the whiteness of her throat and her arms, the perfect contour of her face, the flood of red hair which seemed to possess a life of its own, for it appeared to breathe, fluttering a little, moving. Jeremy studied that dreaming face, and he saw the intelligence in it, the profound innocence and peace. Not more than sixteen, he thought, and the loveliest thing I have ever seen. He studied her more acutely, and saw the blistered and calloused hands, the long slender hands with their broken nails, and then he knew that this must be the new housemaid who had replaced Alice.

Cautiously, he lit a cigarette and stood smoking and delighting his eyes. The soft and nubile breast rose and fell slowly; the lax legs were beautifully formed and were outlined under the dress which was too small and was almost ragged. Ellen had removed her shoes to rest her aching feet and Jeremy saw that not even the black cotton stockings could conceal their form, as slender and supple as the hands.

Jeremy reverenced beauty as much as he respected intelligence. To find the combination here in a little housemaid, stricken by poverty and work, was incredible to him. He also admired poetry. He was reminded of a verse from "Elegy Written in a Country Churchyard":

Full many a gem of purest ray serene
The dark unfathomed caves of ocean bear.
Full many a flower is born to blush unseen
And waste its sweetness on the desert air.

Damn, I'm getting maudlin, he thought to himself. A girl like this is surely not "blushing unseen," even in this desert of a town. He scrutinized her face more closely for any sign of wantonness, and was disbelieving on finding none. Why had he never seen her before, in this village in which he had been born and had spent the major part of his life? It was possible she was a newcomer. Ellen slept

and smiled. Jeremy came closer and his shadow fell over
the girl, and her gilt eyelashes fluttered; she murmured;
she moved restively and slowly opened her eyes and raised
them, bemused and startled.

5

Ellen's first frightened thought was that this stranger was
a "robber." She saw the tall young man before her, dark
and muscular, a stranger with amused eyes and a reassuring smile which showed his strong white teeth, and she
knew fear. She jumped quickly to her feet, paling, throwing back her hair; she looked about her for an open place
for flight.

"Don't be afraid," he said in a very gentle voice which
would have amazed those who knew him. "I'm Jeremy
Porter. I've come home early."

"Oh," said Ellen. Her fear left her, and shyness deepened her color "I'm sorry," she said. Her voice, he heard,
was musical and even resonant, and his delight increased.
"I—I didn't know—Mr. Porter."

She was confused. "They're all in the park, sir. You can
find them there." She forced herself to meet his eyes, and
tried to smile apologetically.

"I don't want to find them," he said. Her eyes widened
in more confusion. "What is your name?"

"Ellen Watson, sir."

The name was familiar to him, for he had seen May
many times before in this house. "Watson? Any relation
to May?"

"My aunt." Why did he stare at her like that? May had
mentioned that he was a "terrible" young man, very rude,
and disrespectful to his parents, and that he looked like
a "workingman, no fashion, no elegance. Rough and
ready." So Ellen had conjured up a man without manners,

a crude brute of a man, a man reputed to be cruel and uncouth, "with never a pleasant word to say."

The imagery disappeared and Ellen thought him very handsome, and not in the least like the other men in Preston. His clothing was not "sporty," but was dark and well tailored, and he stood with ease before the girl and smiled down at her with more reassurance. Why, he's really a gentleman, she thought, and a dim warmth came to her in spite of her shyness. Then, all at once, she wanted to run and the urge was delicious and exciting.

"I'll get you some supper," she stammered, and now all her face was pink. "Sir."

"Come to think of it, I am a little hungry and thirsty," Jeremy said. "And thank you."

Only Francis had ever thanked her before. Then she started and her face became alarmed. "Sir, please don't tell the Mayor and Mrs. Porter—and Mrs. Jardin—that you found me out here sleeping! That's awful. I should have been in the house, working. I just—I just came out to the garden, to see it. I hadn't seen it before. I was a little tired, and I fell asleep. Aunt May would never forgive me."

She tried to hide her trembling hands under her white apron over her dress, and her eyes, enlarged now and pleading, moistened with tears of shame and apprehension. What must he think of her, sleeping like this in his garden? He must think her lazy and worthless.

"You have a right to be tired," he said. "You have a right to see a garden—Ellen."

She was even more startled and did not know what to say. With a mumbled word of distress she bent her head and sidled very fast around him, then ran to the house like one pursued. He watched her go, frowning. He had seen her fear and he thought, Well, that's another example of my parents' solicitude for "the people." But what a beauty, what a voice, what a face! Wonder it doesn't all stir Papa up mightily. Jeremy knew all about his father's "official" visits to Philadelphia, where he allegedly consulted his fellow politicians of the party.

He followed the girl into the house and found her distractedly busy in the kitchen. He pulled out a chair and sat down in it. Ellen glanced at him in astonishment. None of the family ever visited the kitchen except Mrs. Porter, and she never sat down while giving her orders to Mrs.

Jardin. But Jeremy sat there at ease, one elbow on the kitchen table, and he was looking at her with an intensity she had never encountered before.

"Where do you come from, Ellen?" he asked. "And there's not all this hurry, you know. You don't have to rush around."

"I—I live here, in Preston, sir," she said. She felt quite breathless. "I was born in Erie. Aunt May and I have lived here since I was two years old."

"And how old are you now, Ellen?"

He saw her hesitation. "I'm fourteen, sir."

He lifted his thick black brows. He had thought her closer to sixteen, or even seventeen. Ellen moved swiftly and deftly about the kitchen, then ran into the dining room. He heard her there and said, "Ellen, never mind about that damned funeral parlor. I'll have my supper out here, in the kitchen. It's pleasanter."

She came to the door, more and more astonished. "The kitchen, sir? Nobody eats out here except me and Mrs. Jardin! And the gardener and handyman."

"Well, here is where I am going to eat," he said. "I like company, too. Have you had your supper?"

Ellen could not believe it. She stared for a moment before answering. "No, sir. I will have my supper after the family has theirs, about nine o'clock." She suddenly paused and lifted her head and a beatific smile raised her lips. The distant band was playing a German lied and the music was infinitely tender yet dolorous. Jeremy watched her as she listened, her hands clasped tightly together. She seemed far away, as if she were listening not only to this music but other music also, which blended together in one incomparable harmony. Jeremy smoked thoughtfully and did not move, for he was enchanted and curiously disturbed and aroused. He could not look away from the girl. She still seemed incredible to him.

She diffidently brought in the plates she had laid in the dining room and placed them on the kitchen table, which she first covered with a lace cloth. Jeremy began to watch her with rising amusement as she carefully arranged the silver. Her face was studious and grave and yet uncertain, as if she both deplored and could not understand his penchant for the kitchen, where the gentry never dined. "Where are your plates, Ellen?" he asked.

She turned to him, utterly shocked. "Mine, sir?"

"Well, yes. You are going to have supper with me, aren't you?"

She clutched her apron, then lifted her head with pride, and not servility. "That would be most familiar, sir."

"On whose part?" he asked, smiling. "Mine or yours?"

"Mine," she answered with firmness.

She stood there and he smoked thoughtfully, surveying her.

"You think I am condescending to you, Ellen?"

This was a new word which Ellen had recently added to her expanding vocabulary and she was pleased to be able to use it now. "Yes," she answered. "Sir."

"Well, I am not," and he was as pleased as she. "I happen to like company when I eat. I'm a gregarious feller. I especially like pretty company."

Ellen's face changed. She regarded him doubtfully. Was he mocking her? She rubbed her hands absently on her hips, looking at him with that gravity he found so delightful. "But," she said at last, "I'm not pretty. Everybody says I'm very homely, even Aunt May who loves me."

He thought, for an instant, that she was being coquettish, and then saw that she was not and his dark eyes with their polished whites fixed themselves upon her with new incredulity. "You? Homely?"

"Yes, sir."

He leaned back in his chair, still gazing at her. "Ellen, have you ever looked in a mirror?"

She sighed. "Often, sir. I don't look like anybody else, and I don't look like pretty girls."

He sat up and said with a gravity of his own, "Ellen, thank God every day for that. You don't know how lucky you are." He paused. He was still incredulous. "In most cases, people look almost exactly like other people and behave as other people behave and have the same sterilized thoughts and approved opinions. You can hardly pick one from another. To coin an aphorism, they are as like as peas in a pod, and their souls are cut out from the same pattern with the same scissors. Is that what you want to be like?"

She had grasped most of what he had said and thought it over, then suddenly a dimple flashed in her cheek and she said, "No, that's not what I want, sir. But if I was like other people, people wouldn't hate me so."

"Ah, so that's it," he said, and frowned. He narrowed

his eyes against the smoke of his cigarette. "Do you know why people hate you? You are different, and again you should thank God for that. People are like other animals; the unique is always suspect, always feared and hated, and, if possible, put to death. You have illustrious company, Ellen."

She pondered this and her red-gold brows drew together in reflection. Then she said, "Mr. Porter, it's very lonely, not having people like you because you're not like them, in looks, and other ways."

"You should congratulate yourself that they don't like you. Ellen, never try to conform. You'd only be assuming a masquerade, and lower animals are very cunning in their low natures, and will guess it is a pathetic mimicry after all, and they will ridicule you. Be yourself, child, be yourself, and let the identical beasts praise each other for never having an original thought and never a controversial opinion. Do you understand me?"

"A little, sir." She sighed again.

She looked at him swiftly and now her adolescent instincts quickened and her breath was short and she felt a warmth all through her body and a strange kind of comfort and protection. For the first time in her life she was experiencing the pleasure and ease of communication, of being understood, of being capable of conducting a conversation which would not be misinterpreted and would not bring forth sober-faced homilies, and startled reproof. She had been grateful to Francis for his kindness, and had felt a childish affection and devotion to him for that. But this was a new experience for her, and when she again looked at Jeremy the warm flush in her body heightened and she felt close to tears of joy. She wanted to touch Jeremy, to put her hand in his, confidingly and with complete trust, and laugh with him.

"I guess, though," she murmured, "that we got to have charity for people because they don't—know."

"That's silly, Ellen. Why should we suffer fools gladly? Now, don't tell me that that's in the Bible. I know it myself. I was brought up on the Bible. I think it really means we shouldn't oppress fools or dismiss them with total contempt, for they wear human garb as we wear it. So, in a way, it's really pity for them, because they are color-blind and deaf." He had chosen simple words carefully, so that his meaning would be clear to this young girl and not bewilder her. He said, "I'm not that charitable myself. Fools, being in the majority, have their place but it certainly isn't among the company of the intelligent, or in government. I can be as charitable as all hell if fools don't intrude upon me and insist on me noticing them."

He was surprised and pleased at Ellen's next words. "But, sir, Mr. Francis—I heard him talking to his father one night—he says all men are equal and if some people seem fools it is because they were deprived of an education. There's really no difference in people, he says. Just advantages."

"What do you think of that, Ellen?"

She looked dubious and uneasy. "I—I don't know, sir. I know he is very kind. I think he wants to believe what he says."

"Ellen, an appearance of kindness is a masquerade, too, unless it is accompanied by acts of kindness and not just words. I know a number of truly kind people, very few though, and they would seem to fools to be irascible—I mean, bad-tempered—and uncouth and brutally spoken. But I know hundreds of ostensibly—I mean, they appear that way—kind people. They use words instead of hard cash and real assistance. Are you following me?"

She gathered the import of what he had said though he had used phrases foreign to her, and she knew, for the first time, that import could be clearer than language. Unconsciously, she drew so close to him that he could have put his hand on her virginal body, and he knew that this was no lure, no invitation. It was as if she had come near to a friend.

"But, sir, Mr. Francis is real kind."

He smiled satirically. "No doubt he seems that way, and no doubt he thinks he means it. It gives him such a comfortable feeling of high-mindedness. That's very precious to the brotherly-lovers. Hypocrites are often deceived by their own hypocrisy. Now, don't scowl. I see you know what I mean by hypocrites. I'm not saying that your Mr. Francis is a liar; he has sterling qualities, which he would admit himself, and I think, sometimes, that he is an innocent. Like you, Ellen." Jeremy smiled. "Well, never mind. That ham looks delicious and I believe I am hungry. But I won't eat anything unless you do, too, and at this table with me."

"Aunt May, and Mrs. Porter and Mrs. Jardin, would say I am presuming, sir." She smiled at him uncertainly.

"Well, presume, my dear. I invite your presumption."

It came to her that she loved his voice, strong and even loud and touched with satire. The conversation had exhilarated her, though she could not have explained it. It was as if she had been starving all her life and had been given sustenance. He watched her as she neatly sliced the ham and arranged the salad on the table. He had never seen more exquisite hands or more graceful gestures. He had not been mistaken; the girl had intellect. When something moved in his loins he said to himself, "Now, now. She is only a child." He knew very well that men who approached children were not regarded with tolerance by the law, and he laughed at himself. Yet, she was far more intelligent and perceptive than the young lady from Scranton, who had deceived him that she had some brains. He was confirmed in his opinion that intellect was not the result of education or "advantages." It was native. All the education and "advantages" in the world could not transform folly into wisdom. The old aphorisms, which he usually scorned, were right in this instance: "You cannot make a silk purse out of a sow's ear."

He recalled what Aristotle had said: "Not everything that walks in the guise of a man is human." Ellen sliced bread and put butter on the table, and cups. The stove crackled and the coffee was bubbling. Jeremy watched the girl with an acuteness he had not known before, and then he was shaken by a new sensation. For the first time he felt a profound tenderness for a female, a gentleness, a cherishing, a longing to protect. This upset him. He confused his sensations with the stirring in his loins.

Ellen was trembling inwardly and yet she felt at peace, surrounded by understanding, by true kindness and comradeship. Joy seized her. Again she wanted to touch Jeremy and put her head on his shoulder, and she found nothing "improper" in this, as Aunt May would have said. There was a desire to surrender in her, to give herself wholly, to embrace, to be quiet and at rest. When she looked shyly at Jeremy again her smile was so brilliant that he was taken aback, and he could only watch her then in silence. He had never encountered absolute trustfulness before. The atmosphere in the kitchen became charged, even to Ellen. She wanted to cry out, to sing, even to dance.

Jeremy thought, There is breeding there, and good blood, and that can't be eradicated. I wonder what her background is. She certainly isn't common or ordinary. A face like that never came from the gutter; a mind like that isn't plebeian. He vaguely recalled what he had been taught when he was a helpless child confronted with the Bible every Sunday. What had Christ said? That beggars frequently rode on horseback while princes walked in the dust. Christ had been no egalitarian, and that was the reason, probably, why the new brotherly-lovers hated Him and sought to either distort His meanings or contemptuously refute them, or even, at the worst, denigrate them, and with hatred. However, to Jeremy, Christ was only as much a paradigm as He was to Francis, and was useful in the conduct of philosophical conversation.

Jeremy's wandering eye—he tried not to focus too intently on Ellen—saw a tattered book near the sink and he reached over and took it idly. Then he exclaimed, "Thoreau! Whose book is this?"

"It's mine, sir," said Ellen, and she was anxious, feeling that new twinge of guilt. But Jeremy was grinning at her, his mouth half open, as if he were seeing something impossible and humorous. "Good God," he said. "You and Thoreau. Now, don't look so miserable. Tell me, dear, do you understand what he writes?"

"Some, sir." Ellen wrung her hands in her apron. She said quickly, "An old lady, Mrs. Schwartz, gave it to me. Aunt May and other people say she is a witch, but she isn't." She paused. "I like to read, though I don't have much time."

Jeremy was still disbelieving. "I thought *Elsie Dinsmore* would be more to the liking of one your age," he said.

"I don't think I ever read any of her books," Ellen replied. She poured coffee for Jeremy. She could not understand the laughing brightness of his eyes, his wide smile.

"It's a book, *Elsie Dinsmore,* Ellen. All the nice little girls read it. Never mind. So a witch gave it to you, did she? I can believe that!"

More and more puzzled, Ellen said, "She called me 'Daughter of Toscar.'" She looked away from Jeremy shyly. "'Beautiful daughter of Toscar.'"

Jeremy scrutinized the girl's face. "Your Mrs. Schwartz

is no witch," he said. "Or perhaps she is. How much of this have you read, Ellen?"

"Only a little here and there, sir. I try to understand; sometimes I have to read a page over and over before it comes to me— Everyone says I'm very stupid, and perhaps I am," and her face expressed her depression.

Jeremy quoted, " 'Let not the poet shed tears only for the public weal.' Do you know what that means, Ellen?"

Ellen fell into thought. She slowly sat down, uninvited and absorbed. She began to rub her index finger over the stiff laciness of the tablecloth. " 'Public weal,' " she murmured. "That's what the Mayor is always talking about. It means good for the people, doesn't it?"

"Well, that's a fair translation. Go on, Ellen."

She pursed up her lips and gazed at a wall. "I think it means, what Thoreau said, that the poet should be unhappy about other—things, maybe more important ones."

Jeremy's big white teeth flashed in mirth. "Correct. What would you say was at least as important as the public weal?"

"Well. I think a single person, sir, just one person, is as important as millions of others. Maybe more. You can understand a person, and what he feels and—and—" She fumbled for a word. "His feelings, his thoughts, his—well, his sadness—are clearer and closer than just a mass of people. It isn't a matter, sir, I think Thoreau means, of a lot; I think he means that any one person, and his feelings, are—are equal—to what a million feel."

"In short, quantity does not increase importance. Is that what you mean, Ellen?"

She contemplated what he had said, then she nodded her head brightly. "Yes, sir. People are 'public weal,' but a person is a person, and so he is more important. I don't think I really know what it means."

"I think you do. In short, one man's agony is as great as the agony of ten thousand others. Multiplication adds nothing. Ellen, I think we've added a new dimension to what Thoreau said in this case. He went on to talk about dormice and hawks, which has nothing to do with what we have been discussing. Aren't you going to eat?"

Ellen hastily took up her fork as if she had unintentionally offended him. She sat awkwardly on the edge of her chair, half fearing she would be ordered from it at a new caprice. But when she saw that he took her presence

for granted, and that this was no mere pretension of kindness or condescension, she began to eat with appetite. It
seemed to her that the kitchen, with the red light of the
last sun at the window, was the most heavenly of places,
for it was filled with contentment and friendship and not
malice or discomfort.

Jeremy had become somber, and seeing the darkness of
his face, Ellen was not alarmed, for now she was full of
trust and she realized that this fine gentleman was not
bored with her and that, in fact, he was not thinking of
her at all. Gentlemen had many serious things to consider and one should know that and not be offended or
hurt or afraid when they subsided into thought. He knew
the awesome world she did not know, for his life was not
her life, and she was a stranger in his world though he
could enter hers easily. For a moment or two she was
wistful and again filled with longing. He would not remain in this house; he would go and she would be left
behind. He would forget, but she would not forget. Her
longing deepened to yearning and sorrow and a desire not
to be forgotten, not to be abandoned. She was not yet
fourteen, but she was in love as a woman is in love.

Where he went she could not go and she felt her first
true and adult anguish. He knew thousands of people like
himself, but she knew only him. He would laugh and talk
with them, but she had no one else. Her spirit put out
hands to hold him and she knew that he would not even
feel the woeful grasp. Jeremy looked up quickly and saw
the pain on her face. "What is it, Ellen?" he asked, and
she appeared older to him, for that was no childish expression in her eyes, which were now filling with tears.

"I was thinking," she said in a choked voice, "that sorrow is the very worst thing of all." She spoke freely, no
longer expecting ridicule or misapprehension or rebuke,
such as she always expected from others.

He put down his knife and fork. She was very young;
what did she know of sorrow? He had been about to say
that, then stopped himself. She knows well, he thought,
and if she hasn't actually experienced sorrow in her few
years she is aware of it, and all of its tragedy.

"What has made you sorrowful, Ellen?" he asked, and
his voice was full of compassion.

She was on the point of crying out, "Because you will
leave me and I will never see you again, and I can't bear

it!" But horror and full realization came to her of what this cry would mean to him. He would think her not only bold but impudent and he would laugh at her as a presumptuous minx. She struggled for inane words which would not betray her, and then to her greater horror and humiliation she burst into tears. She dropped her face helplessly in her hands and bent her head and grief swelled in her, a grief she could not fully understand except that it was enormous and she had never known such before in its intensity and despair.

Jeremy regarded her in silence. He did not know what to do. He did not know why she was weeping and with such adult abandon. But he sensed the barrenness of her young life, her hopeless estate, the loveless desert in which she lived, the misery of her future and her eventual insignificant death. He believed that she had suddenly realized that herself, and his compassion—the first true compassion he had ever known—made him almost physically ill and wretched.

He stood up, and stood near her as she cried. The light in the kitchen was dimming; there was a mournful bleakness in it now, for all the redness of the lids of the stove, for all the smell of good coffee and the lavish food on the table. He looked down at the bent head and the heaving mass of faintly glistening hair and at the rough and childish hands through the fingers of which tears were spurting. Her sobs were profound and heavy.

"Ellen," he said, and then he reached out and touched her for the first time, her shoulder and part of her soft white neck. It was as if he had touched fire. A huge tingling ran through him and he became rigid. Then desire struck him even while his pity and tenderness increased, and it was a desire greater than any other he had experienced before. He forgot that she was still almost a child; to him she had become the beloved and mourning woman whom he must comfort, and then take, not only with lust, but in consolation and love and protectiveness.

Ellen had become still at his touch. She had stopped weeping. Slowly, she dropped her hands and lifted her wet face to him, mutely, unashamed, piteously confident of understanding, helplessly waiting for solace. When he reached out and raised her from her chair she came into his arms at once. She was silent, but her tears still ran over her cheeks. He looked down at her. He felt his arms were filled with the whole world, rich and satisfying and infinitely inciting and adorable.

Instinctively, and with the passion of love, she pressed her face into his shoulder and her young arms rose and wrapped themselves about his neck, and all the suffering —nameless though it was—was swept away in an almost unbearable bliss. She felt the strength of his arms about her; it was as if she had reached an impregnable shelter, a home, which nothing could threaten, and that she was safe at last from the agony she had endured all her short life. When he gently kissed her lips she answered that kiss with fervent innocence and trust.

Jeremy held her gently, then with increasing passion, smoothing her long hair with his hand, pressing her closer to him, and she pressed in return. Then, though he longed to take her, he wanted nothing more than to lie down beside her in a soft dark place and hold her and speak soothingly and lovingly to one who had never heard these things before, and to take her somewhere where she would be secure and never menaced again, never hungry, never driven to labor and torment.

Neither of them in their perfect communion heard the door open and neither of them heard two simultaneous gasps.

Then a man exclaimed, "Oh, in the name of God! What is this?"

A woman cried shrilly, "Well, I never! I never, never!"

The gaslight flared up and Jeremy and Ellen blinked confusedly in the glare, and drew apart, and Jeremy said, "What the hell are you doing here?"

6

Francis had endured his uncle's long and incoherent though vigorous speech, which everyone but himself had applauded. He had endured the brass band through all its marches and was then too sluggish to enjoy the other music. Besides, he did not care for German airs; they conjured up suffering and death, both of which made him uneasy, restless and afraid. He was no man to face realities. He had a horror of grim actuality and confrontation with life as it is. It was his absurd belief that if it were not for "them" existence could be pure and simple and "good" and just and rich, but who were those who opposed this Utopia he was not quite certain. He was only certain they existed—somewhere, brooding over their heaps of gold. The fact that his father was a very rich man did not annoy him. Those riches provided for his ease, which he considered only his due. Had he asked to be born? The fact that the world had not asked him to be born, either, never occurred to him. Or, rather, if it did occur he hastily obliterated it. He preferred to consider himself a "victim."

Yet he was not a hypocrite in his convictions. He was entirely sincere, a fact which vexed his cousin Jeremy Porter, for Jeremy would often say that a hypocrite who knows he is a hypocrite is less dangerous than a man who does not know it, and acts accordingly. The fact was that Francis was also a gentle and kindly young man, who frequently had generous impulses, though these were conditioned by inner winces. He was penurious by nature, and in this he resembled his fellow "humanitarians." Jeremy considered him a disaster to the world, for Francis was more or less convinced, though secretly, that he was of the elite. He thought the manner in which the world was established was cruel and barbarous, heartless and unjust. Therefore, he was born to rescue mankind and deliver it from his version of injustice. He was not—though he insisted he was—truly egalitarian. Deep in his subconscious mind was the view—which he shared with his fraternity—that "one day" society would be rearranged in a new hierarchy—with himself and his brothers in absolute control.

It never occurred to Francis to help the "exploited" to a new dimension of existence, where they would have valid opportunities to improve themselves, and new horizons and new potentials for exerting their innate gifts. On the other hand, Jeremy was all for giving every man an opportunity to use his talents, unrestricted by poverty, despair, and evil circumstance, and to alleviate his hope-lessness. Francis wished to help "the oppressed" through better wages, more food, adequate shelter, and more leisure. That these were not complete fulfillment, and left the immortal human soul still bare and unsatisfied, did not occur to him. He believed that the "exploited" wanted only to be physically comfortable. Jeremy was, therefore, closer to the hoped-for liberation of mankind from dire existence than was Francis.

In short, Jeremy was concerned with the whole of man-kind, body and soul. Francis was concerned only with its animal appetites, thus relegating man to the level of well-fed domestic animals. (He excluded himself from this bestiality, of course, for was he not of superior birth and education?) Jeremy believed that the world had not yet taken full advantage of the endowments of men; Francis believed that the "proletariat" desired only mean gratifi-cations and pleasures, with firm punishment, certainly, if they dared threaten his own high position and sanctity.

Jeremy despised fools, whiners, the greedy, the lazy, and the incompetent. Francis thought the misfits "pa-thetic" and resented the industrious and the independent, who, he thought in his vague if-passionate way, were the "exploiters."

These were impassable differences between the cousins, and so they were always to be divided, and felt for each a strong hatred, and extended this hatred into situations which had no bearing on their philosophies at all. The fact that Jeremy had a profound respect for all that was truly human, and that Francis wished only to direct its destiny into dialectical materialism—with himself guiding that destiny—made them irreconcilable enemies, and af-fected their relations with others, in a very immaterial fashion. Their terms could never meet; their semantics were based on inherent character.

Their grim conflict rose to violent heights when Francis and Mrs. Jardin confronted Jeremy and Ellen in the kitchen of the Porter house. Francis had become so bored with the Independence Day proceedings that he had de-veloped a "fever." Mrs. Jardin, who was also bored, had wished to return to her beloved kitchen. So Francis had brought her home. (Francis had been bored because he did not believe in the Constitution of the United States and resented it. He considered it a "document for the oppression of mankind.")

Francis cried, "How dare you! What are you doing to that innocent girl?"

"Innocent?" shrilled Mrs. Jardin. "That thing, that strumpet, that trollop? Look at her! All rumpled and red in the face, but not with shame, you can be sure! There's no shame in her. Bad, bad, bad from the day she was born and I warned Mrs. Porter, but she—"

"Shut up," said Jeremy. He turned to Francis and his dark face became darker with contempt and repugnance. "What am I doing? I am trying to comfort an unfortunate girl who has been abused all her life. Sit down, Ellen," and he took her by her trembling arm and led her to a chair, then stood beside her with his protecting hand on her shoulder. She crouched on the chair, forlorn and silently weeping. She began to remove the tears with the back of her hand.

Francis took a step towards her, but Jeremy clenched his fist and made a threatening gesture with it. It was evident, by his expression, that he hoped his cousin would advance on him. Francis discreetly stood back, but his light-blue eyes glittered with hatred.

"Comfort her? Seduce her, you mean, don't you? A child!"

"Idiot," said Jeremy. "She gave me some inkling of her life, and I tried to console her, while thinking what I could do for her. You've been here for days, you mewling brotherly-lover, but have you given any thought as to how you could help her? I bet not!"

But Francis looked at Ellen, whose long hair fell like curtains nearly all over her tear-wet face. "Ellen," he said with gentleness, "did this—this man—hurt you?"

She shook her head. She was filled now with a sense of enormous guilt, inspired by Mrs. Jardin's attack, and disgrace, though she did not know why. She was only dimly aware of the exchange between the two men, and its implications. Nevertheless, she experienced degradation.

"Don't be afraid, Ellen," said Francis, trying to ignore the menacing Jeremy. "Tell the truth. Did he try to— Did he ask you to go up to his bedroom with him?"

Ellen slowly lifted her head and regarded him with bewilderment. Then she slowly shook her head and gave a great heaving sob. "We talked about Thoreau," she almost whispered. "And then, I was so sad, and I began to cry, and he put his arms around me and it was like—like—" But she had no words for the delirious happiness and content she had known, the surcease of misery, the rise of hope.

"Like what?" said Francis. But she could only shake her head dumbly. "Thoreau!" said Francis. "Oh, I am sure of that!" He looked at his cousin. "There is a law for men like you."

"I wish there was a law for men like you, too," said Jeremy. "God knows the country is going to need it. Now, if you'll get out of the way I'll take Ellen home and tell her a plan I have for her, which will rescue her from your kind."

Darkness stood at the windows and there was a distant cannonade as the first fireworks rose in stars and streamers of many colors into the sky. But no one in that kitchen heeded it.

"You mean, in one of your brothels?" asked Francis of his cousin.

"You talk like that once more and you'll need the tender attentions of your dentist," said Jeremy. He grinned at Francis with ferocious derision.

Frustrated, and trembling himself, Francis said, "Do you deny that you were attempting to seduce this girl?"

"I don't have to affirm or deny anything to you," replied Jeremy. "What are you, anyway?" He began to stroke Ellen's shoulder soothingly.

"I am a decent man, which you are not. I know all about you; I've heard the stories around Harvard Yard. And your women!"

"Don't be so envious, Frank," said Jeremy. "I have the wherewithal, which, I hear, you do not. Except, perhaps, for the ancient Greek caper?"

Francis was aghast, and now he felt the first pure rage of his life, and he wanted to kill. "You contemptible brute," he said in the hushed voice of outrage and anger. "If I had not come just now you'd be torturing this girl—"

"How do you know? Have you ever deflowered a virgin? Or are you still a virgin yourself? I shouldn't wonder. Ellen, dear, stop crying and don't listen to this indecent babble. I will take you home—"

"I will!" said Francis. "Not you! I wouldn't trust you a foot with her."

Ellen spoke clearly for the first time, and with fright. "But I can't go home! I can't go until it is after the late supper for the folks. I've got to stay here."

Francis was in a dilemma. He was also aware that he was hungry. "Of course, Ellen," he said. "After supper, I'll take you home. Now if you," he said to his cousin, "will leave the room Ellen will get at her duties."

"For your convenience," said Jeremy. "Isn't that always the way with your kind? You can love and love and love, and be a villain, to paraphrase Shakespeare. But not if it inconveniences to you. Dear me, no. Come on, Ellen."

The girl cried in desperation and fear, "No, I can't, Mr. Porter! I can't. I have work to do. I need the dollar a week I get here, I do, I do. If I leave now Mrs. Porter will discharge me."

"A dollar a week, and scraps," said Jeremy, with reflection. "That is truly a full life, isn't it? Well, Frank? Where is your famous rhetoric about the 'exploited worker'? Or don't you recognize an exploited worker when you see one?"

"She's only a young girl, and is being trained," said Francis, his fair face filled with congested color. "An apprentice." He returned to the attack on his laughing cousin. "I've heard all about you; I've heard about you and that unfortunate little girl, Alice, who worked in this house."

"What about Alice?"

"Surely you know."

Jeremy stared at him, then threw back his head again and laughed. "Why, you imbecile, listening to kitchen gossip! I never laid a hand on that wretched child, nor did I want to."

"Alice?" said Ellen, still weeping. "Alice got sick and she had to be sent away."

"And where did she go, Frank?" asked Jeremy. "Or didn't you ask, or care? But she wasn't one of your 'masses,' was she? She didn't stare into the future, with a heroic face, tramping to freedom and victory over the 'oppressor,' did she? She was just a homeless starving child, defenseless and alone, so she wasn't worthy of your damned brotherly love. Ellen, do you know where Alice is?"

This conversation had both frightened and puzzled Ellen and she stopped crying. "No, Mr. Porter. I heard she went to Scranton. She had no folks here, or any-where, I heard."

Jeremy turned on his cousin. "Why, you crawling thing! You knew about it and never offered any help! No doubt you just shook your head sadly, and sighed, and changed the subject. If ever I wanted to smash a man I want to smash you. Now."

"Why didn't you help her? She was yours!"

If Ellen, intent now on her work, had not suddenly moved between the two young men, Jeremy would have seized his cousin and punched him vigorously. In fact she and Jeremy collided for an instant and she uttered a small disconsolate cry and would have fallen had not Jeremy caught her. He looked over her head at Francis and said in an almost genial voice, "One of these days I will break your neck. I only wish it could be a collective neck."

Dazed by words and attitudes she did not understand, Ellen started to clear the kitchen table hurriedly. After a moment, Jeremy began to assist her. She was scandalized. "Oh, no, Mr. Porter! That isn't right."

"Why isn't it?" asked Jeremy. "I ate off these plates, didn't I? But then, I'm no aristocrat. Me, I'm just a brawny workingman full of beans after a good supper." He glanced at his cousin. "What? Are you still here? Why don't you go into the library and read a little Karl Marx, your favorite author?"

"I wouldn't leave this child alone with you for an in-stant."

"Tut, tut," said Jeremy, shaking his head. "I'm not that much of an ascetic. I prefer a softer place than a kitchen floor, though perhaps you don't."

No one had noticed the flurry of Mrs. Jardin's depar-ture. She had returned, running and panting, to the park and had found May Watson, sitting dolefully alone, as usual, her nearest companions sending disdainful glances at her, and tittering. Mrs. Jardin had gasped in her ear, "It's Ellen. No, I won't tell you now. We've got to find Mrs. Porter. Hurry along there. No, I won't tell you. No, she isn't hurt—or sick. But she may be worse, soon."

She dragged May along with her, and May's weary face was white under the glare and brilliance of the fireworks, and her ears were stunned both by the news she had just heard and by the explosions. They found Mrs. Porter, and

while May stood by, incredulous and shaking and horrified, Mrs. Jardin informed her employer that "that girl,
Ellen, she was—she was making up to Mr. Jeremy—yes,
he's home, sooner, and if me and Mr. Francis hadn't come
in, it would have gone on and on— Oh, it's shameful,
that's what it is! Don't ask me, ma'am, what I saw. I
haven't the words for it; I'd never let them pass my lips,
anyhow! I'm a good Christian woman, I'm a decent
woman—"

"Liar!" cried the distraught May, wringing her hands.

"I am, eh?" said Mrs. Jardin, and she actually made a
fist and brought it so close to May's face that May had to
throw back her head. "I never told a lie in my life! That's
left for your kind, and your dirty daughter, and everybody knows she's your daughter and don't you dare to
deny it any longer!"

She was filled with triumph, and panted again, her face
gleaming with gratified relish. May was appalled. She
seized Mrs. Jardin's arm, all her fear vanished, but Mrs.
Porter said coldly, "Let her go, May. And we'll all go to
my house, at once." She made a theatrically distracted
gesture. "I won't disturb the Mayor. This is dreadful,
dreadful. Jeremy and that girl! Oh, I should have obeyed
my intuitions. I knew she was wrong, and deceitful, and
bad, all the time, but my generous heart—"

"You are too kind, too innocent, for bad ones like her,"
said Mrs. Jardin, and the three women hurried off together, May sobbing drily, completely frantic. "Poor Mr.
Jeremy," said Mrs. Jardin, trotting beside her employer.
"You know what gentlemen are, Mrs. Porter. He's not to
be blamed. It was that one, holding and hugging him and
kissing him, and she wouldn't let him go, and she was asking him— No, I can't soil my mouth."

"Did Jeremy say nothing, nothing at all?"

"No, ma'am. He was just trying to get away from her,
and she clinging like a leech, or an alley cat, to him."

"To think I harbored such an ugly creature in my
house, such a shameless creature! Surely my poor Jerry
has eyes, hasn't he? He could see what she looks like."

Oh, Ellen, Ellen, May sobbed inwardly. Oh, my God,
my God. What wicked things these women are—what
liars.

But still, she had never understood Ellen or Ellen's
mother, Mary, for they had been "strange" to her, and

incomprehensible, and all her fears that Ellen "would go the way" of Mary returned to her with smothering force, so that she staggered as she tried to keep up with the other women. I did my best, she cried in her heart to the unanswering God. I did my best, my very best, to protect and teach her. My very best. My poor Mary, my poor Ellen.

She felt a convulsion of hatred and murderous fury against Jeremy Porter. The cannonading echoed the torment and discordant clamor in her own spirit. It was as if she moved through hell, as she pushed aside crowds with staring faces, with eyes and mouths black in the screaming light, and agape.

In the kitchen of the Porter house Ellen's shaking hands tried to cut fresh slices of ham. Jeremy took the knife from her and said, "I'll cut it, dear. You may finish setting the table in the dining room for the hungry horde, which has been stuffing itself all day. Afterwards, I'll take you home."

Francis had seated himself obdurately on a kitchen chair and was staring at his cousin with the old hatred they had had for each other since childhood. Jeremy wanted to laugh at Francis' posture of determined protection for an endangered damsel. What the hell, thought Jeremy. An ass is an ass and there is nothing one can do about it. I'm sorry for my doughty uncle, with a son like that. He should have been my parents' son. They are three of a kind.

Ellen, her eye on the kitchen clock, was sweatily running between the kitchen and the dining room, sometimes stumbling in her haste. When she dropped a saucer, and it shattered, she broke into wailing. "Oh, they'll take my dollar for that! Mrs. Jardin told me."

"Oh, surely not, Ellen," said Jeremy, as the girl began to pick up the small wreckage. "They are good, long-suffering, holy Christians, with palpitating hearts for the poor."

Ellen was crying again. "My dollar. Aunt May was going to buy a length of sprigged cotton and make a Sunday dress for me! And now I won't have it."

"Never mind, dear," said Jeremy. "Here, here are two dollars."

"In anticipation, no doubt," said Francis. "Girls in her

position must learn to be careful. When any money passes, it will be from me."

If Mrs. Porter and May and Mrs. Jardin had not entered just then Jeremy would have struck his cousin and there would have been a brawl. Mrs. Porter's eyes jumped to her son, and she saw the money in his hand, and cried out, not at first seeing Francis. "Oh, Jerry, Jerry!" she exclaimed. "The ultimate disgrace! And in my house, too!" She ran to her son and enfolded him in her fat arms and began to cry, while Mrs. Jardin gloated in the doorway and May looked over her shoulder in new frenzy and disbelief.

"Mrs. Jardin's told me everything, everything!" said Mrs. Porter. "My poor Jerry. Jerry, why didn't you send us a telegram? All this could have been avoided!"

Jeremy gave her a brief and impatient kiss, then disentangled himself. "What could have been 'avoided'? Nothing's happened, except that I got bored in Scranton and came home. I made up my mind suddenly."

But Mrs. Porter clutched him. "Mrs. Jardin's told me everything, about you—and this disgusting creature—trying to, trying to—"

"You didn't listen to that bitch, did you? Ma, that's too much even from you."

Mrs. Jardin gasped at that epithet and burst into loud tears. "That I, a good Christian woman, should have to hear that word with my own ears!"

But Mrs. Porter was staring at Ellen with loathing, looking up and down the length of the girl's figure. "Get out of my house at once, you shameless slut, you ugly revolting hussy, and never come back! We'll drive you out of town, you bold thing, you dirty thing!"

"Mother," said Jeremy, and now his indulgent voice was so terrible that his mother fell back from him, blinking. "Don't speak to Ellen like that. The girl has done nothing wrong, except she got my supper, because I was hungry." His dark eyes glittered at Mrs. Porter, and there was no affection in them.

"No," said Francis, "Ellen has done no wrong. It was your son, Aunt Agnes, who was attempting to seduce this mere child."

"Oh, you!" said Mrs. Porter. "I never did like you. I always suspected you, Francis. You were always sneaky.

Naturally, you would come to the defense of a filthy creature like this Ellen."

"Aunt Agnes," said Francis, "your opinion of me means nothing. I never liked you, either. But I was here before you, and I can swear that your son was attempting to—assault—this child. I am certain I arrived just in time—"

"To save her from 'a fate worse than death,'" said Jeremy. "You are wrong to despise my mama, Francis. You are two of a kind. Haven't you ever felt a throb at recognizing a kindred spirit?"

"This is intolerable," Mrs. Porter said, and began to cry. "Jerry, I never thought to hear such disrespectful words to your mother. I can't bear it. And all because of this wretch, this hideous wretch, a nothing, a streetwalker."

May had pushed Mrs. Jardin aside with a new strength, and had gone to Ellen, who had been looking, dazed and uncomprehending, at Mrs. Porter. She smoothed back her disheveled bright hair with quivering hands. When May put her arm about her, Ellen started and flinched, as if she had been struck. All the color had gone from her lips and cheeks. Her hand still held the fragments of the saucer, and she had been clutching them so convulsively since the arrival of the women that they had cut into her hand, and it was seeping with her blood.

"Don't try to defend her, please, Jeremy," Mrs. Porter whimpered, remembering her son's face. "It's just like you, of course. But she isn't worth it, she trying to do to you—she trying—"

"What, Mama? What was Ellen trying to do?"

Mrs. Porter glanced appealingly at Mrs. Jardin, whose face had become sullen and furtive. "Tell him, Florrie. Tell him what you saw yourself."

"Yes! Tell him your lies!" exclaimed May, whose cheeks were gray and damp. Her eyes shone with her fury.

"I told you, ma'am," the woman muttered. "I don't want to repeat it, here among mixed company. But I saw what I saw."

"You contemptible devil," said Jeremy. "You saw nothing except that I was trying to comfort this poor girl, this innocent little girl who does not know what all this is about."

"I saw what I saw," she repeated stubbornly. There was a red stain on her cheeks, and her expression was no longer jocular. She looked at Jeremy with enmity, but she said, "I know what gentlemen are, sir. I was married twice. It's your nature. And when a woman tries to—tries to—well, you know. It's your nature. You can't resist." She glared at Francis.

"You was with me, Mr. Francis. Tell them yourself."

Francis turned his pale-blue eyes on Mrs. Porter, who regarded him with total dislike. "He was trying to seduce her, Aunt Agnes. I've told you that before. I didn't hear what he was whispering to her, but I am sure that he was trying to get her to go upstairs with him."

Jeremy began to laugh. "Maybe you aren't as virginal as I thought you were, Frank. And I didn't really believe you had such an imagination. Maybe there's some hope for you, after all, when you grow up and put on spiritual long trousers." He turned to his mother. "Nothing happened, Ma. Nothing would have happened. I was only trying to console this poor girl for the awful life she has led —with you and others, too, probably. This money? She broke one of your damned saucers, and she knew that she would have to pay for it—out of her one dollar a week. Her one dollar. Here, take it." He threw the bill on the kitchen table. Any affection he had had for his mother was now obliterated, and he thought that she was too abhorrent for his hatred. "Well, aren't you going to take the blood money?"

"You can talk to your mother this way, Jerry, my son?" Mrs. Porter was stricken.

"Yes. Under the circumstances, yes. I'm sorry, but it is all you deserve. After I take May and Ellen home, I am going to leave this house, and go to the hotel, and then I'll go back to New York. I'm afraid that I should have done it long ago."

Mrs. Porter truly loved and even adored her son, and now she could not bear this. She swung on Ellen and slapped the girl's face heavily, and Ellen staggered back, and May with her. She lifted her hand again, but May intervened, putting her slight body between Mrs. Porter and Ellen.

"Touch my niece again, and I'll scratch your eyes out, Mrs. Porter. I really will! And take your clothes to someone else to be let out, after you get too fat to wear them. And don't ever expect me in your house again. I wouldn't dirty my feet—"

It was Francis who said sternly, "That's enough, Mrs. Watson. You are being insolent."

"Yes, indeed," said Jeremy. "The really exploited must never fight back. They must bend their heads meekly to their superiors, mustn't they? They aren't the 'masses.' They don't engage in the 'class struggle.' "

As Mrs. Jardin secretly hated them all, she began to smile, the jaunty expression back on her face. Oh, wouldn't she have a tale to tell her friends tomorrow!

The big kitchen was sweltering with crude emotions, and the gaslight hissed and spluttered. May said to Ellen, her voice shaking, "Don't cry so, love, don't cry like that. Nobody is going to hurt you. Let's go home, love, let's go home."

"To your unspeakable den!" Mrs. Porter shouted. "I've heard the tales!"

"And I've heard the tales about your husband, too," said May with her new dauntlessness. "He and his visits to Philadelphia. To the doxies, that's what. The difference is that you are lying, and I am not."

Mrs. Porter's eyes narrowed on her and her eyes scintillated. "You better get out of town, the both of you, May Watson. If you aren't gone in a few days you'll be arrested —both of you—for immoral behavior."

"With your son as witness against my niece, ma'am?" May was actually smiling, a smile of absolute contempt.

"May," said Francis reprovingly, and for the first time in his life Mrs. Porter regarded him kindly for all her rage.

"Now," said Jeremy. "Before we end this agreeable little confab, I have a word to say. May, I want to send Ellen to a good school I know of, a girls' boarding school, in Philadelphia, where she will be treated as a human being and not a slavey, where she will have good clothes and good food, and will learn to be the lady she really is. I will pay for it myself."

All in the kitchen were stunned, their mouths open. Ellen began to look at Jeremy and her face gleamed under its wetness. Then May stammered, "Why, Mr. Porter?"

"Because she deserves better from life, May. That's all."

Ellen said in a low voice, "I can't leave Aunt May. I could never leave Aunt May, not for a boarding school." But her soft features twisted. "Aunt May needs me."

"We're poor humble people," May began. "What would Ellen do, after that school?"

Francis interrupted. "You are quite right, May. I have another thought. I have an aunt in Wheatfield, my mother's sister, a wonderful lady. She needs a good housekeeper, and a maid. She will pay you both well, May, and you will be very comfortable. She is a very kind lady, my Aunt Hortense. Her name is Eccles."

May's wan face glowed. "Oh, that would be wonderful, Mr. Francis! I hate this town. I thought it would be good for us, but it hasn't. When can we go?"

"I will send her a telegram tonight," said Francis, and his own face glowed. "You could go day after tomorrow. I am very fond of my aunt; she has been like a mother to me. You couldn't find a more generous lady, and she will be like a mother to Ellen, too. You have only to do your duty."

Ellen had been listening to this, and only Jeremy saw her young despair. "Spoken like a true elitist," said Jeremy. "Let the masses struggle, but never, but never, let them rise out of the rank and file. May, do you realize what these two offers mean? I want a better life for Ellen. If you take my cousin's offer Ellen will never reach her potentialities. She will be a servant for the rest of her life. Do you want that?"

May had no idea of what "potentialities" meant. She had only the memories of her own life, and her sister's. Then, she did not trust Jeremy, though she trusted Francis, for he was always soft-spoken and gentle with her, whereas Jeremy had a "bad reputation" and his voice could be harsh and ugly. Look at the way he had talked to his own mother—even if she had deserved it! Confusion swept May for a moment. Conviction also came to her that had not "God" intervened Jeremy would indeed have "taken advantage" of Ellen.

She spoke with firmness. "I'm Ellen's legal guardian. So I must make the decision for us both. Thank you, Mr. Francis. We'll take your offer, and get out of this town forever. Never did like it."

She glanced at Jeremy. "We are servants, sir, and we aren't ashamed of it. Work is work, if it's honest. Ellen will be a good servant, after she's trained. She's already good. I'll teach her to cook real well. Being a servant isn't bad. Ellen," and she turned to her niece, "it's late. Let us go home."

Ellen turned on Jeremy such a look of anguish, such a look of longing and yearning, that he took a step towards her, pushing his mother aside. But May seized the girl's hand and pulled her out of the kitchen, out of the house.

Jeremy did not sleep that night. He had refused to listen to his father's somewhat hysterical upbraidings. He had seen his Uncle Walter's sympathetic eyes, and had winked at him with affection. He had not comforted his mother. He had not spoken again to Francis. He was done with them all, with the possible exception of his uncle.

There was but one thought in his mind as he gloomily tossed and turned: He would never let Ellen go. When she was old enough he would rescue her. It would be three or four years—but he would never let her go.

"What are you crying about, Ellen?" asked May the next night as she and her niece prepared for bed. "Such a wonderful thing to happen to us! You ought to get down on your bended knees and thank God. Ellen?"

But Ellen did not answer.

"And Mr. Francis is going to pay our fare! Such a good young man, a real saint. To think what he is doing for us, only servants in his aunt's house, though I'm a dressmaker, too. Ellen?" But Ellen did not answer.

"To get out of this town!" said May, sighing blissfully as she put on her clean if ragged nightgown. "Forever. And Mr. Francis thinks his aunt will pay me eight dollars a month, and you four dollars a month. It's a fortune! We can even save a little money, because we won't have to buy food."

She paused. "I'm selling this furniture tomorrow. But, Ellen. You must stop reading books. They can weaken a female's mind. Besides, Mrs. Eccles wouldn't like it. You've got to settle down, Ellen. I'm going to boil black-walnut shells tomorrow and wash your hair in the water, to tone down that color. Then maybe you'll look almost pretty."

She paused again, and faintly blushed. "Tell me the truth, Ellen. I'm your flesh and blood. Did that—that bad man—touch you—there?"

Now Ellen's own white face blushed. "Aunt May! No! He only kissed me."

May nodded grimly. "He'd have done worse, if God hadn't been watching."

Ellen went to bed. The guilt and shame she had been feeling for so long overcame her. She cried tonight as she had cried all last night.

But worst of all was the sharp and terrible yearning, the desperate longing, for Jeremy, for the touch of his hand, the touch of his lips. She would never see him again. Mr. Francis had promised Aunt May that he would "see to that," and that he was writing his aunt, "warning her."

Never to see Jeremy Porter again, never. It was more than the girl could endure. She bit her pillow to smother her cries. For one brief moment she had glimpsed another life, another dimension, a glorious hope, a devastating love.

It was gone. Perhaps, she told herself, it was all she deserved. In some way she had forgot to "love and trust." But she did not know in what way. She only knew she was being punished.

7

Walter Porter looked about Jeremy's suite in the Waldorf-Astoria Hotel with urbane pleasure. "Yes," he said, "you've done yourself proud, Jerry. I never come here without feeling solid pleasure and a sort of reassurance."

"You haven't been here for nearly a year," said Jeremy. "That's a long time to go without 'pleasure and a sort of reassurance.' Why don't you come here more often?"

Walter's face changed and became subtly older. His short massiveness had increased, his square and ruddy face was more sober, his white hair had thinned in four years. His hands, in contrast to his general bodily substance, were small and pale and elegant, as were his feet. He resembled Jeremy's father to a remarkable extent, but whereas there was something meretricious in the Mayor of Preston's appearance, Walter possessed an air of integrity and sincerity. His eyes had a candid directness and not the fraudulent sweetness of a politician's.

He answered Jeremy with a question of his own. "Why don't you see your parents more often, or at least invite them to visit you?"

"I've told you. There is just so much I can take from them. We usually end up quarreling. For instance, they are all for William Jennings Bryan, though his ideas are the absolute opposite of what *they* are, intrinsically. They think by agreeing with him and praising his Populist ideas, they lend themselves a certain style, a certain tolerance. They exhibit themselves as Good. Oh, I know, my father is a politician and has to pretend to be quivering like aspic with tender solicitude for the People, and my mother wants to have the cachet, among her friends, of being a lady full of the most Christian sensibility and compassion. But now they are beginning to take their public hypocrisy seriously, and that is what sickens me. A hypocrite who knows in his heart that he is a hypocrite, is often a likable rogue, and you can wink with him. But a hypocrite who believes his own self-advertising is despicable. If their pretensions changed the intrinsic rascality of their characters it wouldn't be so bad. But my parents are still the same greedy and exigent people they always were, inside. They are still arrogant and grasping—What's wrong? Did I say something you don't like, Uncle Walter?"

"No. It's not that, Jerry. I'm thinking of something—someone—else. Arrogance. Yes. It's funny, though. Arrogance isn't solely the sin of the crafty and the hypocrites. It's also the sin of those who call themselves humanitarians; it's their besetting sin. Behind it is the ancient lust for power, the very dangerous lust for power over other people."

He stood up, his thick belly protruding, and he walked slowly to one of the large arched windows which were smothered in lace and velvet. He held the draperies aside and looked far up Fifth Avenue to the white and gray mansions of the exceedingly wealthy, with their tiny green lawns shimmering in the summer heat and surrounded by wrought-iron fences, and with their polished bronze doors. The Avenue seethed with lacquered carriages, with wagons and drays and even horsemen on fine horses, all fuming under the hot whitish sky and the glaring sun. He saw the distant church steeples, still the highest elevations in New York.

Without turning, he said, "You didn't enlist in the Philippine War, Jerry."

"No. And not for the reasons your son Francis opposed it. He could only mouth—I am sorry—about 'war profits and imperialism.' But I know, and I think you know, what was behind that most shameful episode, up to now, in American history. I said—up to now. But we know it is part of the conspiracy by the elite, the international elite, to consolidate the world under their own control and subjugation. I'm surprised that Frank didn't know that, too, considering he's ostensibly one with them. But then, he was always an innocent, and there's nothing more perilous than an innocent who is part of a conspiracy of men who aren't innocent at all."

"They recruit and use men like my son, to give them a façade of respectability and nobility."

"I haven't a doubt. In fact, I know it. Have you tried to enlighten Frank?"

"Hundreds of times. It's no use, Jerry. He can't, won't, believe that men who employ the very elevated and ethereal words he does are sinister, and use the very appearance of disinterested concern to deceive, and for their own purposes. It would seem as if he thinks that the very usage of his own terms, and the honorable appearance he himself has, are credentials of simple magnanimity and love of mankind, and couldn't possibly be used by murderers, true imperialists, and potential slave masters."

Still, thought Jeremy, in his conceited way Frank is really one of them, though he hasn't the intellect to understand what it is all about. He said, "Uncle Walter, Frank, too, believes in a one-world government, under the elite. 'The Parliament of Man,' as Tennyson called it, and Tennyson has been called, by his most eminent peers, a very stupid man, though they acknowledge the lyricism of his poetry and the purity of his ideals. The only difference between Frank and the powerful conspirators is information, and, I am sorry to say, intelligence. I'm sure that if Frank really understood he would be as aghast as the rest of us are."

Musing, Walter said, "Isn't it strange that the most

noble ideals can also be the most dangerous? 'An excess of virtue,' I think someone called it. Zeal. That's the trouble. Remember what Talleyrand said at the Congress of Vienna: 'No zeal, gentlemen, for God's sake, no zeal!' Yes. It's the zealots you can't overcome easily, for they believe. 'True Believers.' With public enlightenment and exposure, the cynical conspirators, who aren't zealots at all, could easily be overcome. Yes. I can see why they use men like Francis. Perhaps men like Francis invented the ringing phrases the conspirators have adopted. Well, God help us all, that's all I can say." He added, "I'm glad I'm not a day younger. I can't stand the thought of what is going to happen in the near future to my country."

"The only hope is that the American people will eventually catch on, Uncle Water."

But Walter shook his head. "No hope, Jerry, no hope. People can understand wars and oppose them. But when it comes to high-souled slogans, no."

"Well, the United States Supreme Court did declare the federal income tax unconstitutional, Uncle Walter, in spite of all the high-flying rhetoric in behalf of it, and all the appeals of evil men to the emotions of the American people. So perhaps we can have some faith in what is called the good common sense of the average citizen."

Walter shook his head and slowly turned from the window. "When did common sense ever triumph over greed and envy? Common sense is a civilized latecomer into the spirit of mankind, but greed and envy are intrinsic in human nature, and primal. No, there's no hope."

"Have some whiskey and soda," said Jeremy. " 'Eat, drink and be merry, for tomorrow we die.' "

Walter smiled somberly and took the glass. He sighed, then looked about the spacious suite as if searching for comfort. All six rooms had been furnished by Jeremy himself in the slender refinement and grace of the Louis XV style; beautifully turned chairs and tables, glistening and serene, with upholstery in light yellows and greens and dim rose, and sofas of elegance and lightness, and marble pedestals of alabaster surmounted by delicate bronze figurines. His paintings were few but distinguished, Van Gogh, Manet and Monet, and others of similar celebrity. There were also cabinets of intricate and lovely Chinese design, black and scarlet, filled with objets d'art Jeremy had collected from all over the world. Walter's smile became less somber. He looked at his nephew, and thought: He resembles a stevedore in appearance, a roughneck, as it is called, and yet he has all this discernment and discrimination which Francis, astonishingly, does not. Nature does not believe in stereotypes, it would seem. Yes.

A shaft of hot sun struck through the western window of the parlor of the suite and brought into brilliant prominence the rose damask wall. Walter appeared to be studying it, though he was not.

"I confess I was surprised that you took up law, finally, as well as business administration, Jerry. You never told me why."

"Oh, I may go into politics. I took up international law, you know, not merely corporate law, and civil and criminal law. Who knows? I may end up in the Supreme Court myself." He laughed.

"Francis has that idea, too."

"Well, if it's only a matter of 'the race to the swift and the battle to the strong,' I'll make it first. Sorry, Uncle."

Jeremy, too, had changed these past four years. He was leaner and tighter in appearance, and travel had darkened his already dark face; the lines in it were new, and defined, and he appeared older than his twenty-seven years. His body was still the body of a vigorous athlete, and he treated that body as a tool which must be kept honed and clean. His black hair was neater and shorter; his eyes were less gay when he laughed or made a joke, though they still had their earlier forthright and piercing regard, skeptical and disillusioned.

"Your concern making money?" asked Walter, the businessman and industrialist.

"Babcock, Smith and Kellogg? They certainly are. There are hints they may make me a partner—one of these days. How's your business, Uncle?"

"Not so good, Jerry, not so good. I think we're going into a panic. Panics usually follow wars, don't they? Yes. This one is on the way. I give it only three to four years to arrive. But we are all feeling the uneasiness and doubt which precedes panics. Bryan and his screams that we should go off the gold standard! The idiot doesn't know that when that happens in a country the government issues fiat money, which has no intrinsic value at all, and ultimately leads to disastrous inflation and economic collapse. But you can never convince a zealot. Bryan's one of your innocents, too."

"There's one hope. Teddy Roosevelt, our President, isn't a zealot, except for wars, and he's no innocent."

Walter said, very suddenly, "I wish you were my son, Jerry."

"And I wish you were my dad, Uncle Walter. Frank is more to the taste of my parents. Incidentally, my father never got over not being appointed by the Pennsylvania legislature to the Senate. Now he's all for having Senators elected by the People, and he's working with an organization for an amendment to the Constitution to that effect, as well as for an amendment to bring about the federal income tax."

"That's what the international conspirators are after, Jerry, as you know. They know that those amendments, if attached to the Constitution, will mean the beginning of the end of America as a sovereign free country. She'll become part of their wanted 'Parliament of Man,' and be just another enslaved nation, bankrupt and dependent on her masters. Well. Let's change the subject. It's depressing. I know you want to know about the little girl, Ellen Watson."

Jeremy looked into his glass. "I know considerable. I've employed investigators, who often go to Wheatfield. But the only thing I've been able to find out definitely is that she is well, more beautiful than ever, and is apparently content as a servant, and that she dresses, as they call it, in a manner becoming her station. That is, drab if wearable, and extremely discreet and modest. Fitting to her class, as Frank would say. I even know where she takes her walks on her few hours off, at her mistress's discretion. And that isn't very often."

"Well. My sister-in-law, Hortense Eccles, is really a good woman, Jerry. Quite intelligent and shrewd. Since she became a widow she has managed her husband's estate remarkably well, and increased it considerably. She has the respect of her brokers and bankers. She can turn a keen penny, believe me. She advised me on some investments and I took her advice and they're the only ones paying substantial dividends. She is sometimes kind, and I think she is truly interested in Ellen, that is, in making her an able and competent servant. And Ellen's become ex-

actlv that. Since her aunt, May Watson, was stricken with
arthritis, poor soul, and stays in bed most of the day,
Ellen has taken over entirely, almost entirely, except for
the cooking, which May does. Yes, indeed, a very competent servant."

"Now, isn't that jim-dandy," said Jerry, with a hard
look settling on his face. "A girl like Ellen—a servant."

"I never told you, Jerry, but I had a friend when I was
young, a John Widdimer, of Philadelphia, very good old
family. His father had married a beautiful girl, an Amy
Sheldon, of even more distinction than the Widdimers.
She died when Johnny was very young. There was a
portrait of her, as a young woman, in the Widdimer
drawing room. Ellen resembles that portrait amazingly.
I was struck by that when I first saw the girl, and even
your father, who doesn't have too much imagination, also
was. I've often wondered—"

"The resemblance could be coincidence," said Jerry, but
he was interested.

"I don't know. If it was an ordinarv kind of beauty, the
accepted standard of beauty—which it isn't—I'd believe
it was coincidence. But how often do you see hair like
Amy's and Ellen's, and eyes of such extraordinary brilliance and color, and such molding of the face and mouth?
Amy was a tall woman, and so is Ellen. Even the figures
are almost identical. The hands, the throat, the shoulders,
too. And the lovely innocent expression, the simple
sweetness, the innocence above all. John's father said that
Amv believed everything she heard, and had the utmost
charity of spirit. An angel, he called her. Innocent as a
lamb, he said. And very intelligent, which is almost unbelievable in the innocent. I've never seen anyone like
Amy, that is, anyone so like her portrait, except Ellen.
Do you know? There were many people who didn't
consider Amy a beauty; some even thought she was
homely."

"Um," said Jeremy. "Tell me more about your friend
John."

"Well, he was a womanizer. Like you, Jerry." Walter
smiled. "A discreet womanizer. No coarse random females. So, perhaps—"

"If he was so discriminating, how could he have tam-
pered with a servant? Presuming Ellen is his daughter,
which I can't believe. May Watson is a servant; therefore

her sister must have been one, too. I must investigate this. But somewhere I heard, probably from my mother, that Ellen was born in Erie, and so was May, and so, apparently, was May's sister. Very humble people, to quote Frank."

"Ellen's mother could have been a servant in the Widdimer household. And if she had been beautiful and gentle and fairly intelligent, John wouldn't have balked at a servant. He never married, incidentally. And he was at least thirty-eight when he was killed by a horse. I don't know."

"I'm going to investigate this," said Jeremy. "It would be interesting, at least. By the way, does Frank see Ellen often?"

"Quite often. Perhaps every month or so. But not with coupling in mind," and Walter laughed, not very heartily. "Purely altruistic, he tells me. He also tells me, with approval, that Ellen has become a very able and trustworthy and respected servant."

"Of course, he would think that is fine," said Jeremy, and his face changed dangerously. "I wanted to send Ellen to school, to bring out her potentialities as a lady, and an educated lady. Then it was my intention to marry her."

"No!" said Walter in surprise.

Jeremy nodded. "It is still my intention. That is, if Frank doesn't snatch her for his kitchen before I can accomplish it. No sign of his marrying yet?"

"No, though he has his own house in Scranton now. We were both quarreling too much. A very modest house, even if he has quite a fortune of his own, of which he will spend hardly a cent." Walter paused, and his expression became somber again. "Did I tell you that he has joined that Marxist society, called 'The League of Just Men'?"

"No, you didn't tell me. But it is just like him, isn't it? The international conspirators, the 'elite,' aren't Marxists. They just use some of Marx's ideas, and are trying to bring more and more countries into Socialism, for their own ends." He stood up. He repeated, "I am going to marry Ellen, and very soon, even if she's forgot all about me, which I doubt. By the way, what's Frank's house like?"

"Very modest, as I said. You won't believe it, but it is

furnished in odds and ends, some secondhand, and I don't mean antiques. Very spare."

"You mean cheap."

"Well. Yes. Fill my glass again, Jerry. And again, I wish you were my son." He added, "You know, Francis is doing very well as a lawyer. And he charges very well. Even his beloved 'poor.' "

The Eccles house in Wheatfield, while not the mansion the mistress believed it to be, was a square Georgian house of yellow fieldstone, substantial and dull and heavy, with four white pillars outside on four wide stairs facing double oak doors. It had many small windows and many rooms. The third floor was reserved for servants, of which there were two, May Watson and Ellen, her niece. The gardens were severe and the grass apparently cut with scissors. The furniture of the house was almost as ponderous as in the Porter house but somewhat more expensive, and the draperies were heavy, of dark blue and brown. The servants' quarters were bare and contained only the necessities, for Mrs. Eccles, who was a worthy woman in the estimation of her friends, herself, and her pastor, did not believe in "pampering the lower orders." It disrupted discipline, and Mrs. Eccles heartily believed in discipline for others, except for herself. She was a short stout woman, with a round plump face, shrewd brown eyes, and a sleek mass of brown hair. She was also very stylish and knew, secretly, that she had obtained a bargain in May Watson, who was not only an excellent cook, when she could painfully crawl down to the kitchen, but an experienced seamstress into the bargain. Therefore, Mrs. Eccles had brought herself, in spite of her convictions and her desire not to "corrupt" the "servant class," to give May an extra dollar a month for each of the four years she had served her mistress. She had also given Ellen an extra dollar a month, and advised saving.

Nevertheless, she was in her keen and alert way a just woman almost most of the time. She would praise an especially fine dish, and would sometimes smile sweetly at Ellen, though deploring her hair and her height regularly. ("One must keep them humble, for the sake of their souls.") She would sometimes express solicitude for May and her pains, and on one occasion had called her own physician to attend her. "But one must be strong, my dear," she often lectured May. "One must not give in, you know. That is weakness." Mrs. Eccles always "gave in" to her appetite and devoured twice the amount of food her dependents ate. However, she never forced them to eat scraps from her table. She was, in her partially tolerant way, also a martinet. Nothing must be out of order or disarranged, and she regularly inspected her house for dust, and once a week she also inspected the servants' quarters. On Christmas Day she would give May two dollars, and Ellen one. May thought her mistress a veritable benevolent queen, and constantly praised her to her niece.

Since May had become afflicted with arthritis—"I can't send the poor thing off," Mrs. Eccles would say to her admiring friends—the burden of keeping the house clean and in order was left to Ellen. May sometimes painfully crept downstairs to prepare dinner and to teach her niece the art of cooking and to adjure her to be grateful for the "lovely rooms we have," and to honor and respect Mrs. Eccles at all times. Did not Mrs. Eccles insist on Ellen attending church every Sunday, and did she not insist on Ellen studying a chapter of the Bible daily? Yes. Did she not leave pamphlets of a very evangelistic kind on their tables regularly? Yes. She was anxious for their salvation; she worried about their immortal souls. Mrs. Eccles was an accomplished pianist and played many hymns on Sunday and insisted on May and Ellen standing in the doorway of her parlor while she performed and sang in a very trembling voice full of sensibility. Too, they knelt on the threshold every night while Mrs. Eccles knelt in her parlor and implored God to bless her household, "and all therein." "All" also included her four cats, to whom she was passionately devoted, as she was a childless widow.

May found this overwhelmingly kind. "Compared with Mrs. Porter, Mrs. Eccles is a saint, an angel, Ellen. We should thank God hourly for our good fortune." Sometimes she was a little uneasy with Ellen this past year or so, for Ellen would make no comment. This was partly due to Ellen's chronic exhaustion. Her only recreation was an hour or two off a week to walk in the very pretty little park near the house, and to listen furtively to Mrs. Eccles playing a sonata in her parlor. She would creep near the door of the immense and crowded room to saturate her spirit with the resonant sounds, and she would remember what Thoreau had said about music, its tranquillity which bound together the past and the present and the future, and translated the soul into peaceful ecstasy. Sometimes at night, when May was asleep—after her nightly cup of hot camomile tea for her pains—Ellen would silently slip down the stairs into the library with a lighted candle, there to browse over the excellent library the late Mr. James Eccles had gathered. She would shield her light of the candle with her palm and enter a different world of grandeur and nobility.

Otherwise, the seventeen-year-old girl had no other recreation, no other outlet for her rising passions and vague longings and the sorrow that was now her constant misery. Once Mrs. Eccles had said to her with kind severity, "You know, my dear, I do not permit my dependents to have followers—not, of course that you with your—ah, appearance—would ever attract followers, and for that you should be thankful. But do keep it in mind." Ellen had finally discovered that "followers" meant young men, and she had colored and had said vehemently, "You need never worry about that, ma'am!" Mrs. Eccles had smiled with satisfaction. She feared losing Ellen, who was the best housemaid she had ever employed, but she also remembered that "inferiors" had base natures and were inclined to produce offspring without "the benefit of clergy," and were congenitally "flighty." "I guard the modesty and decorum and morals of my dependents as I guard my own," she would proclaim to her friends. "My Ellen is only a young servant, but I have impressed on her that she must do nothing demeaning to her person, and that always Duty comes before Pleasure, and Christian living before self-indulgence." She also had another fear: That her friends, observing Ellen and her deftness and grace in serving and her instant obedience, would entice the girl away from her house. So one day she said to Ellen, "My dear, I love you as my very own daughter, and I think you know that, and I should like to warn you not to be led astray by false promises on the part of—others—and lured into the worship of filthy lucre. You know that the Bible warns us not to put Mammon before God." This had puzzled Ellen, and she had replied only with a slight shrug, a new habit of hers which vexed Mrs. Eccles. Ellen had investigated that phrase in the Bible, and she had laughed a little to herself. She had inwardly commented that Mrs. Eccles served Mammon assiduously, and then had regretted the improper reflection. But often she found it hard to "love and trust" Mrs. Eccles.

Ellen's dreams, all distressful and full of anguished yearning, centered on the memory of Jeremy Porter. This was in spite of the fact that May, at least once a week, impressed on her niece that she had indeed escaped a fate worse than death in Mrs. Porter's household, and that only God had rescued her out of His boundless love and mercy. "Such men are like the beasts of prey the Bible talks about, and Satan, looking for who they can devour, Ellen. What a bad man he is, what a scoundrel, a man without a conscience, to attempt to—well, you know what I mean."

Only in the past two years had Ellen come to understand what May had hinted, and still hinted, and she had been ashamed. However, her shame did not decrease her hunger, sometimes too painful to endure, for the sight of Jeremy, or to hear any news of him. The memory of those few moments in the Porter kitchen, which grew more vivid every day, was enough to make her moan in her pillow. Now she knew the meaning of the garden of her fantasies, and for whom she had been waiting as she walked among mist-wreathed trees and the lusty scent of roses, with a flower in her hand. But all that was gone; there was nothing for her, except her memory and work. Sometimes, consumed by an amorphous passion she did not understand, but which was rising more powerfully in her every day, she felt a sharp if wordless rebellion and agony. She always repented this. God had ordained her lot; she must be content. This thought never stopped her tears. On several occasions lately she had had rapturously licentious dreams of Jeremy—though the dreams, due to her innocence, never became specific—and she had twisted on her narrow bed in hot ecstasy. On waking, and panting and covered with sweat, she would get out of bed and kneel beside it, praying for forgiveness, and then would bathe her palpitating throat and reddened face with cold water. Such dreams were wicked, though she could not control them. However, she never prayed that she would be delivered from them. Had she been more sophisticated she would have wondered why.

Francis Porter, who was his aunt's particular favorite, and whom she loved as her son—she had made him her heir—came at least once a month over the weekend to visit Mrs. Eccles and to see how Ellen was progressing. He was very kind and sweet and gentle with her; he would praise May's cooking and the expert way in which Ellen cooked also, and the polished cleanliness of the house. He was never too condescending, and was genuinely fond of Ellen. It was not for some time that he realized he was in love with her. Thus far, he had not reached this disturbing conclusion. He only knew that he felt warm and comforted when he saw her, that he delighted in her appearance and would follow her with his eyes, and that when she left a room it felt colder and dimmer than when she was present. Last Christmas he had bought her a pair of black kid gloves, the first she had ever owned, and she had been overwhelmed by his thoughtfulness. But she was becoming timid with him, not only remembering that night in Mrs. Porter's house, but seeing also that he became more austere, more abstracted, and tighter of fair face and brow, each time he visited his aunt. Sometimes his speech was abrupt, and a resentful expression would make his open features lowering. He often appeared secretive and suspicious, something which only Ellen discerned, and this would baffle her.

Mrs. Eccles always teased him about his bachelor state. "After all, dear one, you are twenty-six now, and you should think of a suitable wife, with your expectations. No young lady has caught your fancy yet?" Often Francis would think this might be desirable—if the young lady had a fortune of her own. Then he could employ Ellen himself, to be his housekeeper. Aunt Hortense would not begrudge him this. The thought of Ellen in his house often came to him when he was in Wheatfield, and he would smile at the girl radiantly and the recent cloudiness would leave his face and he was a handsome blond young man all glowing and gracious and even affectionate in his manner when he encountered Ellen. May Watson frankly adored him; he would invariably ask about her health, commiserate with her over her pains, and compliment her on the soundness of her rearing of her niece. She would thank him fervently, over and over again, for what he had done for her and Ellen, which invariably heightened his self-esteem and made him expansive.

He had forgotten that he had once thought Ellen's face noble and aristocratic. If the thought ever intruded into his mind now he shook it away, for it was not credible to him that a girl of her station could be anything but what she obviously was: a menial. To him, servants were not "labor." They were not part of "the toiling masses struggling to be free." This fine distinction never failed to make his father stare at him with a smile of mingled disbelief and satire. Francis was still intrinsically kind, as Walter would admit, if inconsistent. He was very much like his aunt, Hortense Eccles, who gave willingly enough to the Missions, and had a genuine concern for Ellen though she never considered that the girl was of human flesh and driven to the point of collapse many times in her service.

Walter would often think that his son's concept of "labor" was puerile. He had never really seen "labor." He had never met a workingman. The father had some hopes that when Francis was admitted to the bar and encountered others outside his class he would "come to his senses." But his humbler clients were only poor: clerks, tellers in banks, shopkeepers, owners of butcher and grocery stores. They were not "labor." They were petite bourgeoisie, and so he had a disdain for them, as if they were not flesh and blood and full of misery.

Wan, shriveled, and stricken with unremitting pain, May lay on her bed and looked at her niece reprovingly. "Are you going out again, Ellen?"

"Aunt May, I haven't been out of this house for a week. It is only for two hours. I just have to go out, to breathe, to think a little, to be alone."

"Ellen, you are a very strange girl. Sometimes I can't understand you." She had a terrible thought. She sat up in bed, uttered a faint moan, and cried, "You aren't meeting somebody outside, are you—all this gallivanting?"

"Aunt May, I know nobody in Wheatfield, nobody. You know that. I hurry home from church on Sundays, and no one speaks to me." Ellen smiled, and the rare dimple in her cheek flashed. "Are you comfortable? I won't be long."

May fell back on her bed and sighed deeply. "You

know Mrs. Eccles wouldn't stand for you having a follower, Ellen. I hope you don't talk to strangers in the park."

"No, Auntie."

"It don't seem right to me, Ellen, for you to leave the
house. There must be something for you to do here. Did
you polish all the silver today?"

"Of course. I do that every Thursday."

"Well, if you see Mrs. Eccles, ask her if it's all right
for you to go out." She sighed again. "There's nothing
too good for her. Look what she has done for us. You've
got fifty dollars saved, in the bank, and I have a hundred.
Due to Mrs. Eccles."

Ellen went slowly down the stairs, dressed in a "decent"
brown wool dress, a black coat which was ill-fitting, as it
had once belonged to Mrs. Eccles, a battered wide black
hat on her coiled and burnished hair, Francis' gloves on
her hands. She wore a new pair of black-buttoned shoes,
cheap but stylish. She looked, as May called it, "respectable," and she also superficially looked what she was,
a servant. But a close scrutiny of her face and her coloring, the perfection of her features in spite of her broad
cheeks, often startled passersby and those who came
wearily to the little park nearby for momentary refresh-
ment.

The house was warm and very quiet, except for the
distant clank of the furnace and the booming echoes in
the big rooms. Mrs. Eccles sat at her desk in the library,
facing the door, and frowned as she went over her ac-
counts. She was alarmed at the cost of food since the
Philippine War. Butter—twelve cents a pound! Milk—
seven cents a quart! A roast of beef—sevent-five cents!
Outrageous. She smoothed her sleek brown pompadour
in exasperation. These prices were enough to bankrupt
even the rich. Her plump cheeks were quite pink with
indignation. She pulled at the second of her chins, and
thought. There was a pile of gold coins on the desk at
which she sat, and to cheer herself she touched them with
tenderness. She was glad that winter was approaching;
she would no longer have to pay her gardener and handyman ten dollars a week. There was the snow shoveling,
of course, but there was always a little boy from the poor
section of the town to do that for twenty-five cents. When
I was young, she thought, they were glad to do it for a
meal.

Ellen tried to slip past the door without being seen.
Then Mrs. Eccles spoke to her. "Out again, Ellen?"

Ellen paused. "Just for an hour or so, Mrs. Eccles.
You know I do that every Thursday. I like to sit in the
park, and winter will soon be here and the park will be
full of snow."

Mrs. Eccles frowned again. "Did you study a chapter
in the Bible, Ellen?"

"Yes, ma'am. I do that every day, when I first get up."

Mrs. Eccles leaned back in her chair and looked severe.
"Ellen, I didn't like the way you roasted the chicken last
night. Not the way May does it, with a touch of tarragon
and thyme. I thought by now you'd be equal to May, in
cooking."

"I'm sorry," said Ellen, feeling that now very familiar
stab of guilt and embarrassment. "I thought you said last
week, ma'am, that you didn't care for those herbs too
much."

"May's very subtle in her seasoning. There's a difference. Did you put more coal in the furnace?"

"Yes, Mrs. Eccles. Half an hour ago."

"And did you give the cats their afternoon cream?"

"Yes, ma'am." Ellen looked anxiously through the far
window. The blue shine of October was dimming a little.
It would soon be dark.

"Very well. You may go, Ellen. But do be discreet.
Keep your eyes down, like a proper girl. Never look at
people directly. It's bold, for one of your station."

Ellen pulled open the heavy oaken doors and walked
out into the blessed cool and spicy air of an October afternoon. There was a fragrance of leaves burning, mingled
with the acrid odor of fresh horse manure. A few carriages
moved sedately over the cobbled stones on the streets,
filled with ladies in furs and gloves and with plumed
hats, their knees covered with warm robes of wool or fur.
From somewhere came the exciting scents of boiling
ketchup and grape jam and roasting meat. The sky was
an intense blue, with here and there a mounting white
cloud. It looked cold and distant, for all its color. The
street was lined with big houses similar to Mrs. Eccles',
the windows polished and richly draped, the knockers
bright as gold. Trees lined the walk, scarlet and yellow
and russet brown, contrasting with the occasional sharp
green of a fir tree. The lawns were a more vivid emerald

than in summer, due to the recent heavy rains, and seemed almost artificial. The last salvia and red calla lilies burned closely in flower beds. A slight keen wind blew, and the drying leaves on the trees crackled and a drift of them raced before Ellen in swirls, as if they were still alive.

The air was chill on Ellen's cheeks, and she moved with briskness, her long legs gliding and sure. She saw, in the distance, the hazy blue of a leaf fire rising up in the shining air, and heard a child shout. She came to the little park, which was enclosed in an iron fence, and she walked through the gates. Here were narrow paths of gravel winding through the trees, and a scattering of wooden benches. The park was patronized mostly by nursemaids with their charges in perambulators, covered with rich plaid blankets. In the center was a large rose bed, but only a hopeful bud or two shivered among the fading leaves and the bent stems. It would soon be winter. A squirrel ran before Ellen, raced halfway up a tree, and looked eagerly at her for nuts. She had purloined a few from the kitchen and she threw them on the ground and the squirrel, chittering, hurled himself down and snatched at them, sitting up on his haunches as he cracked a nut and ate it. A thin dappling of light came through the trees and moved over Ellen as she went on.

She found a bench. She saw she was almost alone in the park, except for a woman walking her dog and two women, obviously servants, who sat on a bench and furtively cackled together. No one noticed Ellen as she sat down on her bench, and placed her cheap imitation-leather purse on her knee. The wind blew a little stronger and tendrils of her flaming hair came loose and curled about her cheeks and forehead. She settled her black hat more firmly on the coiled mass. All May's concoctions of black-walnut shells boiled in water could not dim the luster and glow of that hair, nor all the rice powder obliterate the apricot stain on cheek and mouth.

Ellen sat, conscious of her weariness. She had risen as usual at five, was in the kitchen at six, or before. She never climbed up to her bed until long after ten at night. The heat of the furnace never rose to those cold bedrooms which she and May occupied, and the blankets, if adequate, were coarse and dark, the harsh linen prickly. So Ellen always hastened through her prayers, shivering in her flannel nightgown, and then crept under the blankets, there to lie for a long time gazing through the high narrow window which boasted no curtains and no draperies. When she finally fell asleep it was only to dream distressfully, and to awaken fitfully several times.

She had no hope for anything. She would grow old and wrinkled and wan in service, until she was no longer of use. Then, with her meager savings she would go to the "poor farm," or perhaps, if she was lucky, she would supervise children in another strange house, or do needlework or mending in some cold upper back room for a pittance, her body arthritic, her hands crooked with labor, her feet forever chilled and aching with corns and bunions, her back bent with years of toil, her skin furrowed and parched, her hair white.

She was accustomed to desolation now, and melancholy haunted her always. But it was deeper today, as the year died, and it was like a heavy battering pain in her heart.

For what was I born, and why was I born? she asked herself. There seems to be no reason, no answer. Aunt May says we are all born to suffer meekly, for it is the will of God, and we live only to please God; we cannot aspire to heaven if we neglect the duty He has assigned to us. But, dear God! I don't want any heaven! I want a little joy, today, tomorrow, a little wonder, a little anticipation, a little hope. I want to see something of this beautiful world, to be free, if only for a short time, to be idle so I can think, to laugh, to sing, to be young as I was never young. For a brief while, before I die, I should like my own fire and my own bed and my own walls. I know I can never be like the girls who come with their mothers to call on Mrs. Eccles—the beautiful girls in their pretty summer frocks all lace and silk, and their furs in the winter, and their carriages, and their happy laughter, and the pearls at their ears and their throats. I know I shall never wear their flowered hats in the summer, their plumes in the winter, their fur-lined gloves, their lustrous muffs, their dainty shoes. I was not born to that; I was born to be a drudge, and so I must not envy, not for an instant, those girls my own age, so carefree, and with such pleasant futures.

But just for an hour, a day, a week, of peace and aloneness, of freedom from fear and dread, of time to read a book by a fire, to listen to music, to go to a theater, of time to walk in woods and by rivers with no pressing duties hurrying me along, and away, from all that is lovely! I would gladly die for that hour, that day, that week, and would ask no heaven and would petition no God for anything more. I would sleep—O God, to sleep!—never waking again, afterwards, and it would be enough. It would be more than enough.

But there was no hope for such as she, nor for countless millions like her, laboring like trolls in the dark mountains to forge and to contrive treasures of gold and gems for those who lived and laughed in the light, and rejoiced in the sun.

There was no bitterness or envy in Ellen, but only sadness that she would never see the splendor of the world in which she had been born, never see new skies or mysterious islands swarming with many-colored dancing birds, never see the ocean or the great white sails of ships, or mountains draped in snow and glaciers, or mighty cities throbbing with voices and music and the thunder of mills. She would never see the stone lace of cathedrals, or listen to the silence in their incensed vaults, or hear a choir, or walk through exotic bazaars. Of all these things she had read—she would never know them, no, not even for an hour.

She fell into fantasy, her one refuge from reality. She thought of Jeremy Porter and her lips were suddenly afire with the memory of his kiss, the enfolding strength of his arms, the pressure of his body against hers, the feel of his chest against her breasts, the stroke of his hand on her hair, his murmuring, his half-heard words of consolation and tenderness, the warmth of his flesh.

The heat at her lips spread through all her body until it tingled and yearned and urged against the poor clothing. She could see and hear and feel him so acutely that the pain in her heart rose to an inner groaning and weeping. The yearning was so fierce that it became almost unbearable. She wanted to get up and run, run into the approaching twilight, run into his arms. She could see him so intensely that it was as if he were there with her and calling to her.

She dimly heard the crunching of gravel under someone's feet. And when she looked up, her eyes full of tears, and saw that it was Jeremy himself, clad in a heavy wool chinchilla coat and dark trilby hat, she was not surprised. In silence, she immediately got to her feet, and as he came closer to her she held out her hands, then ran to him, and she was in his arms, her face buried in his shoulder. I am dreaming, I am only dreaming, she thought incoherently, and then he was kissing her lips and a deep quiet came to her, a fulfillment, a joy she had never known before, a peace, a safety, a surcease, and the air sang in her ears.

8

They sat on the bench in the cold twilight, and Jeremy's arm was about her waist and her head lay on his shoulder, and she was sheltered and secure.

"How did you find me?" she asked.

"I never lost you," he answered, and smoothed away a small curl that was blowing into her eyes. "I knew you came to this park, on Thursdays. Never mind how I knew, love, my dear love."

She leaned against him and felt wave after wave of the utmost tranquillity and happiness flowing over her, stilling even the remembrance of pain and wistful longing and despair. She was complete, in a refuge, protected, and, incredible though it was to her, loved. Her diffidence was gone, for the first time in her life, and she talked to Jeremy with delicious confidence, and a naïveté he found pathetic, and a trust which was entire. She questioned nothing; it was sufficient for her that he was here, as she had dreamed thousands of times, and though the air of the increasing twilight had become very cold she felt warmth all through her body, and a comfort so profound that it was both physical and spiritual. At moments she was frightened that this, too, was fantasy, but a glance into his face above her, reassuring and tender, made her sigh with rapture.

She had confided to him all the wretchedness of these past four years, all her fantasies of him, and her yearning, all the hopelessness, all the inability she was experiencing to "love and trust." "I feel so guilty," she said, "for my rebelliousness, when all this time you loved me and knew where I was, and were waiting for me." She had told him of the "kindness" of Mrs. Eccles, who had "taken Aunt May and myself in," and the solicitude of Francis Porter, who came to Wheatfield at least once a month to see if she was faring well. Ellen did not see that Jeremy's face had darkened at this, though he made no comment. He only looked down into her eyes and her face, as he listened, and he saw that maturity had brought more beauty to her even though there were shadows of sadness around her mouth.

She did not ask about the future, nor did she think of it. She only knew that Jeremy was there, that he was no dream, that he had not really abandoned her, that he had thought of her always. In her timid voice she asked him, over and over, to repeat this, and then she would sigh with delight and solace. But she mourned, again and again, that she had not "loved and trusted" enough.

At this his mouth became wry and he glanced away. Finally he said, " 'Love and trust'? My darling, there is no one you can really love and trust in this world, not parents, not brothers and sisters, not even husbands or wives, and especially not friends. Haven't you found out yet that this is an ugly and evil world, the seven-story mountain of hell, where only malice and envy and treachery flourish?"

She drew away from him for a moment, and then he laughed slightly and pulled her to him again. "I'm a cynic," he said. "And a pessimist, and I got that way from associating with the brotherly-lovers and the optimists." He did not want her to realize the full hideousness of living; her shyness and innocence were part of the touching qualities which had made her adorable to him from the first. So he said, "Well, never mind. Maybe you can—er—trust in God. You do trust in Him, don't you, my love?"

Her face became downcast and sorrowful. "Not enough, as I did when I was a child. I have been so rebellious! I hope He forgives me."

" 'Beautiful daughter of Toscar,' " he said.

"Thoreau," she said, comforted again. "At night, when everybody is asleep, I creep down to Mrs. Eccles' library, with a candle, and read some of her marvelous books—"

"And the books I sent you every month?"

She was startled. "Your books? I never saw them— Jeremy."

He was silent for a minute or two, while she looked up into his face anxiously. Then he said, "I see. Yes, I see. The dragon at the gate, warned by another dragon."

"I don't understand, Jeremy."

"Never mind. It's bad enough that I understand. And what do you read in that library, Ellen?"

"Hobbes. Edmund Burke. Montaigne. Kant. Erasmus. Spinoza. Shakespeare, all Charles Dickens' books, and Thackeray. History. Adventure. Many other things."

"It's very kind of Mrs. Eccles to let you read her books." He waited for the reply he was sure he would get.

Ellen said, "Oh, she doesn't know. She and Aunt May say that books weaken a female's mind. Mrs. Eccles reads only business journals; she is heavily invested, she says."

"And all that business doesn't 'weaken' her mind, does it?"

Ellen laughed gently. "Mrs. Eccles is a very strong-minded lady."

"I bet. And very religious, too, no doubt."

"Yes. She makes Aunt May and me kneel down with her every night for prayers. She is the one who prays aloud." Ellen felt a thrust of betrayal, and said, very hastily, "She believes absolutely that God guides our every movement."

"Especially to the bank," Jeremy said. "I'm sure that Mrs. Eccles believes more in banks than she does in her God, and that is very sagacious of her."

Ellen felt vaguely uneasy, though she did not entirely comprehend. However, she said, "God brought you to me, Jeremy. He answered my prayers." There was something like a plea in her beautiful voice, and he could not resist it.

"If it gives you consolation to believe that, love, go on believing." He drew her tighter to him. "Now that you are eighteen—we have plans to make."

He felt her pull away from him, and he glanced down at her. "What is wrong, Ellen?"

She looked frightened, then gazed at him beseechingly. "I'm not eighteen."

He smiled indulgently. "Frankly, I thought you were older. Nineteen? Twenty?"

"No." He could hardly see her face now in the dark. "I'm only seventeen. You see, I had to work, in Mrs. Porter's house. We needed the dollar a week, and then I got two meals in that house, and Aunt May told me I should say I was fourteen, and not thirteen, as I was. If we had told the truth the law wouldn't have let me work full time, over twelve hours a day."

Now, that's a damned contretemps, thought Jeremy. Her aunt is still her legal guardian. Then he reminded himself that in New York State laws were somewhat different, and that children were permitted to work in factories and in shops as young as the age of five or six, and considered "a female" after puberty mature enough to marry, at her own desire, at any time.

Darkness now filled the little park and a shivering icy wedge of moon rose over the loud crackling of the trees and stars danced through the leaves. In her entrancement and joy Ellen had forgotten the time and her Duty; she was elevated into a world where all was consummation and serene perfection. She did not see the darkness or the moon, or the slowly lighting windows of the houses across from the park, nor did she feel the bitterness of the rising night wind on her face. Jeremy could see her eyes, as sparkling as the stars, even in that duskiness, and he thought that in these four years Ellen had acquired an immaculate charm and a powerful magnetism, of which she was obviously unaware. He did not know if this was because of her innocence or because no one had ever told her, surrounded as she was only by women, and especially by women who found charm and magnetism only in the prettily average. At any rate, mingled with his tenderness, his solicitude for her, his genuine love, his desire to protect and rescue, was a growing lust. He bent and kissed her lips again, in a prolonged encounter, and she opened her mouth and gently returned the kiss. He almost lost his self-control; he touched her breast, then held it, her rich young breast, covered by harsh wool. She did not flinch or draw away; in a natural surrender and still incomprehensible return she pressed her breast more firmly into his palm, and sighed, long and profound,

and in absolute trust. It was this trust, this innocence,
which made him hastily release her, then pat her cheek
in what he hoped was a paternal gesture.

A silence, deep and content, fell between them, while
Ellen nestled against him like a lost child who had come
home to love and light. He reflected that even while she
was telling him of the most dreary moments of these past
four years she had shown no resentment, no self-pity, no
petulant wonder as to why she had been chosen for this
misery. He found this even more pathetic than her recital.
She had obviously been assured that this was her ordained
station in life and that to protest, except feebly on occasion, when driven, was "wrong" and an affront to God.
Had he not been convinced years ago of her intelligence
he would have thought her stupid, and his love for her
would have been infinitely less.

A church bell stridently struck the hour of seven, and
Ellen came out of her encompassing dream of joy with
a start and a little cry. "Oh, I forgot! It's seven, and I
should have been home two hours ago! Oh, Mrs. Eccles
will be so angry; she will scold Aunt May, and perhaps
she will discharge both of us! What shall I do?" She
looked at Jeremy with terror and dismay, and smoothed
her clothing and resettled her hat. He drew her tightly
to him again.

"Dear love, but I came to take you away, and to marry
you as soon as possible. Didn't you understand that?"

Her enlarged eyes, as she stared at him, became stupefied; her mouth fell open. "Marry?" she murmured,
faintly, and he shook her with fond impatience.

"Of course. That's why I came for you today." He
laughed at her stupefaction. "What did you think I came
here for? Just to hold you and talk with you? Ellen,
haven't you any sense at all?"

She gripped her hands together, still staring at him with
disbelief. "I—I didn't think, Jeremy. It was enough that
you were here."

"And you thought we'd spend the rest of our lives
sitting on this bench in the park, and no doubt be covered
eventually by leaves and snow? What a goose you are,
Ellen."

"But you can't marry me! You are—Jeremy Porter—a
rich man and a lawyer, and I am only a servant girl!"

"Well, then, haven't you heard of King Cophetua and

the servant girl, or Cinderella and her prince? Or, in your heavy reading have you neglected the dear old myths?"

"I didn't think at all," she whispered, and closed her eyes and squeezed them together to shut out the glory that was suddenly visible to her: a life of bliss, with Jeremy, in his own house, in New York! She suddenly began to cry, deep shaking sobs, and he was alarmed, and then he understood that she was crying because she was overwhelmed with joy and could not bear it. He drew out his handkerchief to wipe her streaming face, and then she convulsively tore off the gloves Francis had sent her, and she spread out her swollen and reddened and burned and callused hands vehemently, to show him, in the gaslight which was now burning yellow in the park, what she believed he must see. "Look at them." She faltered. "Are these the hands of the wife of Jeremy Porter?"

He took them in his own and kissed them. "I hope they are indeed, you little fool."

Confused and shaken, but glowing, she pressed her hands to his lips. "I don't believe any of this. How could I believe that a man like you would want a girl like me?"

"You should look in the mirror occasionally, and hear your own voice, too."

She was bewildered, and blinked at him. Then she had another thought, and her face became distraught. "But I can't leave Aunt May here, Jeremy. I can never leave her."

"Who said you should leave her? She will come with us." This was a new aspect of the situation he had not as yet considered. "Or if she wants her own place, in a quiet hotel, we will let her have it. God knows, she deserves what little pleasure she can get from life now, with her arthritis and her whole life of suffering."

Ellen grasped his arm with an impetuous strength and he could see her enraptured face, beautiful again with happiness. "You mean that, Jeremy, you mean that?"

"Certainly I do. And now we'll go to Mrs. Eccles' house and break the glad news to your aunt. I am at the Hitchcock Hotel, and you and your aunt will pack as soon as possible, and we will all leave together, for New York, where we will be married."

She uttered a great cry of delight, and they stood up, and hand in hand hurried towards the house. Ellen, to

Jeremy's half-amused compassion, began to skip like the child she still was, murmuring little sounds of ecstasy and anticipation. When he saw her face it was shining brighter than the moon, and he was almost unbearably touched, and he held the hand in his tightly. She glanced at him with total adoration.

Lamps were burning in the lower windows of the house and it was Mrs. Eccles herself who came to the door, her plump cheeks darkly flushed with anger, her eyes jumping with fury. "Ellen, this is shameful!" she said. "You are two hours late—" Then she saw the dark shadow of Jeremy behind the girl, and she was more furious. So, the young sneak had a "follower" after all, and she would plunge this house into scandal, and would have to be sent away, and Mrs. Eccles would then be deprived of the cheapest, and best, cook and housemaid she had ever employed. "Oh," she gasped. "Who are you, young man?" Her voice was full of contempt and umbrage.

He took off his hat and said, "Mrs. Eccles, I am Jeremy Porter, the cousin of your nephew Francis."

Her mouth fell open and she stared at him idiotically, and for the first time she noticed his clothing. She stepped back. She recalled what Francis had told her, that this man had tried to seduce Ellen and that Ellen must be guarded from him and all letters confiscated and destroyed, and that his name—the name of a very bad and licentious man—must never be mentioned. "Best it be forgot by Ellen and May," Francis had said. "They must be protected from a born womanizer and seducer, who tried to take advantage of a poor girl in my mother's house." Mrs. Eccles had thought that this had shown Francis' wonderful heart and charity, and his concern for "the lower classes," who all had propensities for vice and indecent behavior and were flighty and full of low passions, and never considered the results of their irresponsible acts.

She had read of Jeremy in the New York newspapers. "A rising young lawyer of considerable brilliance, who will make his mark in the world," one account had read. So Mrs. Eccles did not know what to do. Jeremy was above her in station; Francis had informed her, with some gentle envy and resentment, that Jeremy was rich in his own right and was certainly becoming richer. He was also a gentleman, and anyone in Wheatfield would have been honored to entertain him. Her training urged her to obsequiousness and hospitality; on the other hand, she was still enraged at Ellen, and the direful thought came to her that today Jeremy had accomplished his obscene purpose. She wanted to strike the girl for this dilemma, for her morals impelled her to upbraid Jeremy, and her realism impelled her to welcome him with gratification and pride, and fawning.

She tried to make her voice severe, as the two still stood on the threshold. Ellen had become white and she was trembling. "I am amazed—Mr. Porter—this girl, a servant in my house—where did you meet her today? What is she to you, a servant, a housemaid, and you—a gentleman of New York?"

"I came," said Jeremy, "to marry Miss Watson. Have you any objections? And may we come in? It's very cold just now."

"Marry—marry—" she stuttered. "Why, that's impossible. I just don't believe it. Ellen—and you, Mr. Porter, after all— Oh, do come in! Please forgive me for making you stand there. And Ellen"—her voice was stern and cutting—"please go at once to the kitchen. Your aunt is so distracted over your absence that she has taken a turn for the worse and can't come down to get my supper, and you will have to get it yourself, and please, for once, remember not to brown the onions for the roast too long. Go at once to the kitchen, Ellen. I will deal with you later." She gave the girl an accusing and threatening look, one of the most ominous Ellen had ever received, and the girl trembled so much that she almost fell over the threshold. Jeremy caught her arm and steadied her, and then she fled, tearing off her coat and hat, her face frightened and drawn.

He entered the hall, and Mrs. Porter, all sweet and welcoming smiles, took his hat and coat. "You must really join me for supper, Mr. Porter, if that—that girl— doesn't ruin everything. You have no idea about servants these days—incredible. Shiftless, dowdy, without any self-respect or humility or responsibility. Such a trial. I am in the library, where there is a nice fire. A glass of sherry perhaps?" She added, with a sigh, "I have been like a mother to that girl, a true mother, and now she repays—" She looked at Jeremy, remembering his words, and her eyes and smile were full of significance. Of course, he

intended to steal the girl away, to New York, and to "take
advantage of her," and then to, to use the current phrase,
"discard her like an old glove." Well, gentlemen were
gentlemen after all; the late Mr. Eccles had taught her
only too well. But that shameless girl, that wanton and
conniving girl—she was a different matter. Marry, indeed! She had been betrayed by an enticement, but that
was to be expected. Dear me, what deceivers men were.
However, it was the girl who should be blamed, after all
the careful teaching in this house, and not a man of Mr.
Porter's station in life.

While Jeremy, who had forced a genial expression onto
his dark and somewhat taciturn face, followed Mrs. Eccles
into the library, she felt a twinge for Ellen, of whom
she was vaguely fond, for she was a fairly just woman
in her heart. She was determined to protect Ellen, who
must be told that a man's promises were only his schem-
ings to "have his way with a girl, my dear. You mustn't
believe him for an instant—for all he is a gentleman."
What had the Psalmist said about his inability to comprehend "the way of an eagle in the sky, the way of a dove
on her nest, the way of a serpent on a rock, and the way
of a man with a maid"? Ellen must be reminded of that,
with calm severity, so that she would be "warned." (Mrs.
Eccles had taken the word "maid" literally, and in the
modern meaning, and so a servant.) Peremptory though
she was, and unbending when it came to duties, she was
no Agnes Porter. Still, she remembered what her darling
Francis had said of this man. But he was really charming
and very courteous, in spite of his rough look and very
authoritative voice. He was a very naughty gentleman, indeed, to deceive that miserable housemaid, Ellen, like this,
and Mrs. Eccles felt very coy and arch toward him, and
very worldly.

Jeremy sat on one side of the very welcome (to him),
fire, and Mrs. Eccles sat on the other, and they sipped
sherry together. Jeremy was quietly studying Mrs. Eccles,
even while they engaged in pleasant chitchat on the
weather and on mutual acquaintances in Philadelphia and
New York. It took Jeremy only five minutes of scrutiny
to know all about this short plump woman in her black
silk dress with the lace ruffles about her throat and her
heavy wrists. He saw that she was very shrewd and
knowing and probably considerably brighter than his

mother. Her eyes had a merry twinkle which he suspected did not come from her soul but was deliberate and contrived. She had a certain vivacity, also contrived. From the conversation he was having with her he knew that she spoke mostly in clichés, the origin of which she probably did not know in the least. Those who spoke in clichés, he had discovered, were not very intelligent, no matter their education. Original speech testified to an active intellect, and it was manifest in simple phrases and lucid words, and never involved. But Mrs. Eccles could not complete a sentence without a cliché, or a platitude, and she wore an air of erudition while doing so. He might have been amused by her if she had not spoken to Ellen in a bullying tone, and if she had, indeed, treated Ellen "as a daughter."

He also saw that she believed his remark about marrying Ellen a sheer frivolity, with masculine and sinister undertones.

He stood up to throw more wood on the fire, and she watched him with open admiration now, and conceded to herself that he was really very handsome, if one were a connoisseur of masculinity, which she thought she was. He had none of his cousin's delicacy, either in speech or manner or in appearance. He had a ruthless and dominant look, totally male, from his black coarse hair to his cynical eyes, to his prominent jutting nose and hard and unbending mouth and square dimpled chin. Ah, if I were younger! she sighed deliciously to herself, and felt a very improper thrill. She stared at the firm and inflexible planes of his face, somewhat concave, and she knew him to be inexorable. She glanced at his hands, square and thick and large, and she was thrilled again, and felt very naughty.

She said in a coquettish tone, "I do hope you are visiting for a little while in Wheatfield, Mr. Porter. I should like to give a dinner for you. After all, in a way, you are part of my family. Your uncle, Walter, is my brother-in-law, you know. He was married to my sister."

"Yes, I know," said Jeremy, seating himself again and crossing his big and heavy legs, which were covered with large-checked trousers of an excellent and expensive cut and material. "But, I am taking the afternoon train back to New York in a day or two." He paused and looked at her straightly. "And I am taking Ellen and May with me."

She was so taken aback that she paled and then she stuttered, "But Mr. Porter, that is not to be believed! They are my servants; a week's notice, at least— Surely you are joking, sir. Ellen! A housemaid! Agnes Porter had written me; what she endured when the girl was in her house! Your mother, Mrs. Porter—"

"My mother," said Jeremy in a cold and deliberate voice, "is a liar, Mrs. Eccles."

She was shocked. Her eyes widened so that the whites were all about the pupil. "Your mother, your sainted mother! I can't believe my ears, Jeremy. It is Jeremy, isn't it? Why should she lie about a wretched creature like Ellen, whom I am trying to train to be a good servant? It is beneath your mother to lie about such. But I forgave Ellen; I believed I could subdue, direct her, make her realize her station in life, make her properly humble, and I protected her morals, no followers, you know, nothing questionable. She lived here as in a convent; I give her a chapter of the Bible to study every night, and send her to church, and admonish her frequently, all for her own welfare, you see, and to preserve her soul—"

"Very good of you," said Jeremy. She did not hear the irony in his voice, and the condemnation. Therefore, she subsided and even smiled a little.

"Thank you," she said, preening. "I do my best for these poor creatures; it is only Christian." Now she shook an arch finger at him and shook her head also. "Mr. Porter—Jeremy—do you think it is fair or kind to delude Ellen like this, with a promise you couldn't possibly fulfill?"

"But I do intend to fulfill it," he said. "I've been in love with Ellen since she was a child of thirteen, in my mother's house."

"Oh," she said, with a knowing look, remembering what Francis had told her. "Let us be honest, do, Jeremy. You want May and Ellen for your own establishment in New York, as cook and housemaid. Ellen as housemaid," and she almost winked at him. But his expression was tight and immovable.

"I want Ellen for my wife, and she has agreed to marry me."

She was more shocked than ever. "Jeremy! A low servant, of doubtful origin—I have heard stories, though I never held it against that poor girl. I have heard that—"

"Yes," said Jeremy, "I know what you have heard, that Ellen is illegitimate. Quite true." His manner was calm and quiet. "I have investigated, because my Uncle Walter told me a very interesting story. I didn't investigate merely out of curiosity; I wanted to verify something in my own mind. And I did. Ellen is the illegitimate daughter of John Sheldon Widdimer, of Philadelphia, of a very prominent family, and very rich, too. Ellen's mother, and May, too, were housemaids in his father's house, and the mother, Mary, was small and beautiful. It's an old story, isn't it?"

Mrs. Eccles was astounded. "Ellen! Of the Widdimers? I know—well, I know of them, at any rate. Oh, it isn't possible!"

He nodded his head. "I assure you it is not only possible, but it is true. May took her sister away to Erie; she was older than Mary and felt responsible for her. It was in Erie that Ellen was born, and Mary died shortly after her birth. And there's something else: John Widdimer left a curious will. I can quote one paragraph in it verbatim: 'To each, if any, of my natural heirs, and surmounting any legal difficulties, I leave the sum of two hundred thousand dollars.' He must have known that Mary was— shall we say, in a delicate condition? I also discovered that he tried to find both the young women, May and Mary, and failed. He probably wanted to marry Mary, as I want to marry Ellen."

"I heard, yes, I heard, that he was killed by a horse," Mrs. Eccles said faintly. "Two hundred thousand dollars! Ellen! But then, the law won't allow it—"

"Oh yes, it will. I am a lawyer, Mrs. Eccles. No one quite knew what he meant in that will, not even his father, who had had some suspicions, though. Ellen, by the way, is an almost exact replica of her grandmother, Amy Sheldon Widdimer. My Uncle Walter saw her portrait when he was a young man, and he was very startled when he saw Ellen."

Mrs. Eccles sat upright in her rose wing chair and clenched her hands tightly together. "Are you going to tell Ellen?"

"No. She doesn't need that money; she is marrying me.

I want her to continue to believe whatever May has told her about her parentage, and I am sure that you, as a well-bred lady, won't mention what I have told you to either May or Ellen."

"Oh, you can be sure of that!" Mrs. Eccles considered. "It seems unbelievable, yes, truly. Well, I always suspected something like that, not that I condemn the poor unfortunate girl. Your mother wrote that Ellen was really the daughter of May and some low fellow—"

"As I mentioned before," said Jeremy with deliberate ease, "my mother is a liar and likes to believe the best of herself and the worst of others."

"How disrespectful, sir, of your poor mother, who sheltered—"

"She never sheltered anyone in her life, and took from all the unfortunate people who worked for her the very means of their survival. That is, she underpaid them and starved them as much as possible. Yes, indeed, she is a good Christian woman, full of lovingkindness. I've met hundreds like her, all diarrhea of goodwill in the mouth, and constipation of the purse."

Mrs. Eccles blushed at these crude words, and Jeremy smiled at her winningly. She turned her head aside, modestly, as if offended, but she was an earthy woman and after this one gesture to breeding and her sex, she looked at Jeremy again.

"But Ellen! You, sir, are a handsome man, of position and profession. You could marry anyone, and not just a—"

"Bastard," said Jeremy.

She fluttered her hands before her face, as if to protect it. "Oh, let us not be so uncouth— I am speaking of Ellen herself, not her parentage. A very homely girl, not in the least pretty or prepossessing. A very homely girl of no name. I consider it most improper, Jeremy, most improper, for one of your station. I don't know what your parents will think—"

"And I don't give a damn," said Jeremy. He had another thought. He had to make matters as smooth and pleasant for Ellen as possible, when she spoke to her aunt. He knew the sad Mays of this world, with their obdurate convictions of impropriety and their obstinate belief in classes. In a way it was a sort of self-protection, as well as a matter of pathetic pride. So he made himself look embarrassed and even a little pleading, and he leaned towards Mrs. Eccles and said, "I should like to ask a great favor of you, Mrs. Eccles, a very great favor, but I hesitate to ask it."

She preened again. "Do, please, sir."

He bent his head with such an affectation of bashfulness that only those like Mrs. Eccles could be deceived. She leaned at him avidly. "Mrs. Eccles, you know what poor May is, a very sick woman, prematurely old, and very tired. And you know the obduracy of her—class—and their ideas of what is appropriate; God knows, it's been drilled in them from birth, for very cunning reasons, indeed. I have really two favors to ask of you. I should be most grateful if you went now, very quietly, up to May and explained the situation to her—"

Mrs. Eccles smiled at him shrewdly. "I understand. You are afraid that May will become hysterical and forbid the marriage—after all, she is Ellen's guardian—and refuse to go with you to New York, and then Ellen won't leave, either. May has a very keen awareness of the proprieties."

Jeremy nodded. "Exactly, Mrs. Eccles. And now, for the larger favor. I suppose—no, I don't think you would even consider it—but I should be in your debt forever if you would accompany the three of us to New York, and be a witness to my marriage to Ellen. I have a large suite at the Waldorf-Astoria, and I will rent, if you consent, another for you, and a nice room for May. No, I am sure you won't consent—"

She was overwhelmed, then clapped so sharply that Jeremy frowned. But she cried, "Of course, I should be honored, Jeremy! Honored—that you should ask me. And I will be the perfect chaperone for dear Ellen, and help her to buy her trousseau." She put her fingers to her lips. "But she has no money."

"Let it be a secret between us, Mrs. Eccles. I will give you all that you need for Ellen."

"But that would be most unseemly—"

He smiled. "Very well. Let us put this in another way. Another secret. You will tell Ellen that it is your gift to her, and later I will write you a discreet check, but first you will spend your own money, openly. Very seemly, that, isn't it?"

Mrs. Eccles loved intrigue, like all her kind, and she

was enchanted. "You naughty boy, you! You would have me lie, wouldn't you? But then, it wouldn't be a lie, really. It would be my own money, from my own purse—"

"And I will reimburse you afterwards. It is our secret. And now, please, would you speak to May?"

She rose, and just then Ellen appeared at the doorway and said, "Supper is served, ma'am, if you please." She was very white and resolute, and her look at Mrs. Eccles was neither meek nor servile and Jeremy knew that she had iron in her soul, something he had always suspected. She had had time to calm herself in the kitchen, and to renew her faith in Jeremy, and her huge blue eyes glanced at him briefly and in utter trust.

But then Ellen started when Mrs. Eccles fell upon her with cries of deep affection, forgetting that Ellen was only a housemaid in her house. She enfolded Ellen in her plump, black silk arms, and Ellen, stupefied, looked down at the sleek brown head which hardly came to her chin, and then she turned her astounded eyes on Jeremy, and her mouth fell open.

"My dear, dear child!" cried Mrs. Eccles. "Dear Jeremy, the impetuous boy, has just told me everything! Everything! Oh, how wonderful it is, and what a secretive minx you are, and how lucky you are, oh, I am just out of breath! It is too much, entirely too much—"

She hugged Ellen to her broad bosom and the girl almost staggered with the energy of this embrace and the words she had heard, which had stunned her. She was agape, limp in Mrs. Eccles' fervent arms, and she accepted the kiss on her cheek with more stupefaction. She looked at Jeremy, beseechingly, and he wanted to laugh, but kept his face grave. He nodded at Ellen and said, "Yes, my love. And Mrs. Eccles is now going to tell your aunt, and everything is splendid."

Then Ellen began to cry, and Mrs. Eccles began to utter cooing sounds like a tender mother and wiped away Ellen's tears with her scented handkerchief, and kissed her again. Now Jeremy turned abruptly, for he thought it was an inauspicious moment to laugh.

"Let us go up together!" exclaimed Mrs. Eccles, concluding the work on Ellen's face and eyes, and she caught Ellen by the hand like a gay schoolgirl. "We will tell May together! Oh, how happy she will be! I can hardly wait to see her face when I tell her!"

That's a sensible idea, thought Jeremy. The hysterics will be just for once, and not double, and May will certainly be intimidated by my artful Hortense, who does have common sense, at least. So he nodded at Ellen and said kindly, "Yes. Go with Mrs. Eccles at once—and give May my love."

Mrs. Eccles literally dragged Ellen from the room, enthusiastically gripping her hand, and to the last Ellen looked back over her shoulder at Jeremy in a daze, dumfounded, unable to utter a single sound, her hair tossed and muddled about her petrified face. It was as if she had been confronted by a miracle, and was unable to comprehend it. There were tears still on her cheeks and her mouth quivered childishly.

All this emotionalism, thought Jerry, highly pleased with himself and his dubious dexterity in manipulating Mrs. Eccles. And I'm damned hungry, too. I hope the tears and the hysterics and the cuddlings won't last too long.

He found his way to the kitchen and saw the luscious beef and onions which Ellen had completed roasting, and he idly cut a juicy slice and devoured it, and hummed a little hoarsely. He licked his fingers, then helped himself to some of the browned onions. Excellent. He would permit Ellen to cook occasionally for him, the little love. All in all, he was satisfied that he had put a somewhat sticky situation into Mrs. Eccles' very competent hands. He must remember that he must buy her a very substantial gift, in gratitude. Very substantial.

That night Mrs. Eccles sent her nephew Francis a discreet telegram.

9

Jeremy had been able to procure a very large, warm, and luxurious stateroom on the train which left Wheatfield

two days later, and which then would proceed to Pittsburgh and Philadelphia and after that to New York. May,
hobbling on two canes, was tenderly assisted by both
Ellen and Mrs. Eccles, who was as bright as a bird, and
as full of euphoric chatter. When May saw the stateroom
she stood on the threshold and stared, her eyes gazing
suspiciously at the couches, the chairs and the tables and
the big windows draped with damask, and at the carpets
and mirrors. She could not believe it; she gulped and
blinked. She had the air of one who had been deeply
deceived and tricked by some malignant magician, and
that at any moment she would be greeted by raucous and
derisive laughter for her gullibility. She looked helplessly
at Mrs. Eccles, who said vivaciously, "Isn't it beautiful?
And all for us. And very expensive, too."

May mumbled in distress, half turning, "It's too—rich.
Not for Ellen and me, Mrs. Eccles. We will go in the
coach."

Mrs. Eccles was all archness. "And leave me alone with
that naughty, adorable, delightful Jeremy Porter!" She
looked at May's derelict clothing, her wan and shriveled
face, her bent and trembling body, thin and emaciated,
and she felt a new wonder, a new contempt, and even a
little anger that such as this, and her niece, could now
dare enter this magnificence. Dear Jeremy was surely out
of his mind!

Therefore, in her resentful exasperation, she pushed May
quite roughly into the stateroom and forced her to sit in
one of the large soft chairs. She glanced over her shoulder at Ellen and said with her old impatience, "Ellen, for
goodness' sake, stop staring around and help your aunt
take off her hat and coat and make her comfortable. We
must be settled before Jeremy has taken care of the luggage, and not look like overwhelmed gawks who had
never seen anything so splendid before."

Ellen said, "Well, we haven't. It's all new to Aunt May
and me. Perhaps it would be best if we were in the coach."

"You—Jeremy Porter's fiancée—in the coach? How
absurd you are, Ellen. Do hurry, stop fumbling." Mrs.
Eccles was no sentimentalist. She did not believe in Cinderella and the prince, or, if she had ever thought of it,
she had considered the prince quite mad. Her resentment
grew, for all of her bright smiles. Ah, if only she had had
a pretty daughter, demure and accomplished, to give to

Jeremy! Yes, he must be insane—wanting to marry this homely girl who had no graces and no education, and had such chapped red hands and chipped nails. Look at her figure, now that she had discarded her coat: Not at all stylish, not at all enticing. That big bust, now, and that long thin waist and the narrow hips, and those long, long legs! Hideous. Her skin was entirely too white, except for that color on her cheeks and lips which I dearly believe, in spite of everything, is some sort of paint that won't rub off, though I've tried it a few times.

Ellen did not really wish to go into the coach with its cold fetidness and straw-covered floor and rattan benches. She only felt compassion for her trembling aunt as she affectionately removed the mildewed hat and darned black coat and cheap black cotton gloves. She was filled with pity and love; she smiled down into May's pleading eyes. She's very frightened, and not reconciled, thought Ellen, and she thinks this is all wrong and that we are out of place, and she suspects and fears Jeremy and can't believe it, even now, in spite of two days of arguments and pleading and reasoning. She thinks it is some sort of wicked deceit, that we will be abandoned, all alone, in New York, with our meager savings in our purses and nowhere to go. She can't believe that Jeremy actually wants to marry me.

Ellen thought of how her aunt had implored her and had wept, crying that she did not believe it, could not believe it, and had begged Ellen to "come to your senses and behave yourself and try to see that this is impossible, it isn't for our kind, and you should have more humility. We have a good home here with Mrs. Eccles, who has been so wonderful to us and who took us in, and this is ingratitude, Ellen, pure ingratitude, to desert her. We are stepping out of our class."

Mrs. Eccles, who had heard this in May's bedroom, heartily agreed with her, and hoped that the poor woman could convince her niece to remain in Wheatfield. She hoped that May would refuse to go to New York, and May did that a moment later. How had that ungrateful girl responded? She had said in a newly resolute voice, "Well, then I will go alone with Jeremy." Such brazenness, such outrageous boldness, such lack of respect for elders! May had been horrified. She had clutched Ellen's hand and had cried, "But that's just what he wants, you alone with him!"

"Jeremy?" said Ellen, and her great blue eyes had misted with joy. "I would go anywhere in the world with him, marriage or not."

May and Mrs. Eccles had been appalled, and May had put her hands over her face and had groaned. "To think you have come to this, Ellen, so shameless, so—so—and with such immodest words in your mouth! I think I will stay here." She looked miserably at Mrs. Eccles for support, but Mrs. Eccles had no intention whatsoever of keeping May without Ellen; after all, charity should extend only so far, and one should take care of oneself. May, crippled and increasingly ill, must not become her pensioner. She, Hortense, had too much business to attend to herself, and she was not running an almshouse, nor was she inclined to pay for services she did not receive in full.

So Mrs. Eccles, seeing Ellen's resolution to go, had soothingly patted May's shoulder and had said, "Do not spoil Ellen's happiness, my dear. That would be so— unchristian. To reject God's good fortune is quite sinful, I am sure."

Mrs. Eccles had been able to procure, very hastily, a new cook and housemaid for her house, and Ellen and May had exhausted themselves in teaching them the ways of the kitchen and their duties. Mrs. Eccles had one satisfaction: She would be paying the newcomers two dollars fewer a month, each. "A penny saved is a penny earned."

Divested of her hat and coat and feeling more alien and unworthy of this grandeur every moment, May said to Ellen, "Where are your manners, dear? Help Mrs. Eccles with her own things and take her bag and put it—somewhere." She looked about her weakly, and shivered, and clutched her aching elbows in her hands. Mrs. Eccles graciously permitted Ellen to make her comfortable, and said, "I will sit on this couch with dear Jeremy. It is only seemly, while you sit with your aunt, Ellen, in those two chairs near the window."

Ellen was slightly amused, and then she rebuked herself for her lack of charity. Mrs. Eccles meant well; she had really been very kind and solicitous these past two days, and very lively with anticipation. Mrs. Eccles was one of the very few people whom Ellen was to suspect and understand thoroughly, yet she never looked with clarity at the woman without a sense of anxious remorse, and an eagerness to make amends for her ungenerous thoughts.

Jeremy entered the stateroom then, saw May's meek hostility and suspicion, Mrs. Eccles' complacency, and Ellen's serene expression and the sudden brilliance of her eyes when she encountered his again. He was both amused and vexed to see Mrs. Eccles occupying the place he had intended Ellen to occupy, and he sat down and regarded the ladies pleasantly. "Well," he said, "the luggage is all taken care of and we leave in five minutes." He glanced at his watch.

May said in her flat yet shrill voice, "All this space here, Mr. Porter. We could've had our bags here. Things get stolen on trains." She made a nervous if aimless movement with her hands.

"Not from first-class passengers," he said, and May winced and glanced almost frantically through the window. Steam hissed from wheels; a trainman was ringing a bell; the platform was filled with people waving to passengers, and the engine suddenly roared. May had a desperate impulse to rise, put on her hat and coat, and seize Ellen by the hand and drag her from the train as if she were a threatened child. All wrong, all wrong, for people of our station, she wailed inwardly, a sentiment with which Francis would have agreed with a grave nod of his head. Jeremy saw the poor woman's tremblings and apprehension and he was sorry for her, if impatient. Mrs. Eccles also saw these manifestations and she winked at Jeremy, who turned away, thus discomfiting the lady and causing her to bridle.

The train began to move and May's hands clasped themselves convulsively and painfully together. Ellen, near the window, saw this and she put her own warm hand over those chilled and crippled fingers. May wanted to cry. She had had such a safe haven with Mrs. Eccles and Ellen, such comparative peace, but the willful girl had ruined this for a precarious if not actually dangerous future. Lured away, thought May Watson, deceived by a man like this! She glanced through the corner of her eye at Ellen, whose face was almost incandescent with love as she gazed at Jeremy, and May thought of the bridal night and screamed within herself.

May had never known a man; she was a virgin. She

knew nothing of the mechanics of sexuality, except what had been darkly hinted to her by her late mother, who had rolled up her eyes and had shuddered and then had covered her face. So May had come to consider "congress," as her mother had called it, shameful, horrible, degrading and agonizing to a woman. To think Ellen, that innocent girl, was to be subjected to this dreadful thing was more than May could endure. Had she later married the elderly farmer of May's dreams and hopes, he would have preserved her as a daughter, while she dutifully, and virginally, labored in his kitchen and on his land and in his chicken yard, and fed his pigs. May was vaguely of the opinion that sexual desire ended for a man when he was forty, and women never possessed it at all. Mary had succumbed to the dirty and evil "wiles" of a man, and look into what an abyss she had fallen! Tears began to gather at the corners of May's eyes and she blindly fished for a handkerchief in her worn purse. No, she could not bear it, she could not bear it.

Mrs. Eccles was coquettishly engaging in conversation with Jeremy, who had become taciturn if polite. He was looking at Ellen and she was looking at him, and she was smiling radiantly, and he wanted to hold her and love her. The thought made him move, embarrassed, on his seat, and again he glanced at his watch.

"The dining car is crowded," he said, "so I have ordered our dinner to be served in here. What wine do you prefer, Mrs. Eccles? A sauterne or champagne? We are having lobster and then pheasant under glass."

Mrs. Eccles preened, then thought. Then she said archly, "Why not both? Sauterne with the lobster, and yes, a sparkling Burgundy with the pheasant, and then" —she clapped her hands like a delighted girl—"champagne with the dessert! After all, there is a wedding approaching." She looked at him with loving brightness.

May listened to this conversation, then she forced herself to speak. "Mrs. Eccles, I made some sandwiches with the last of the roast beef—Ellen did it well this time— and the last of the pound cake. It's all in my black bag there. Wrapped in napkins, which you can take back, ma'am."

To Mrs. Eccles' horror and fury Jeremy appeared to consider this suggestion soberly. Mrs. Eccles glared at May, and Ellen kept back a smile. She pressed May's hand again and said with her usual gentleness, "Jeremy has ordered the dinner, Auntie, and you and I know nothing of wines."

"There's wickedness in strong drink," May said.

Mrs. Eccles nudged Jeremy but he said to Ellen, and the polished whites of his eyes glinted in the sunlight that flashed through the windows, "Have you any objections to sauterne, sparkling Burgundy, and champagne, Ellen?"

"You know very well, Jeremy, that Aunt May is right: we know nothing about wines. You must order for us." She turned to her aunt and said, "There is no 'wickedness' in wine, Aunt May. Jesus, through a miracle, changed water into wine at the marriage in Cana, and He drank it regularly, as did all the people in Israel. It is the abuse of a good thing which is wicked, and not the thing itself."

Hear, hear, thought Jeremy. My love is not as unsophisticated as others believe, and she has read wisely and well.

"I won't drink it," said May with the stubborn sullenness of her convictions. "And neither will you, Ellen."

Ellen sighed, feeling that sickening thrust of guilt which she was never to overcome. But Jeremy said, "Surely, a glass of champagne, Ellen. And a little of the others. As my future wife, and hostess, it would be very uncivil of you to reject what my friends will drink. They would think it rude of you."

May could hold herself back no longer. "You are dragging my little girl into a den of iniquity, sir! A den of iniquity, mingling with shameful people, godless people, drunken people."

Mrs. Eccles nudged Jeremy again and smiled at him maliciously, as if to say: There! And you are going to marry one of that kind!

"People who never go to church, who are doomed to Hell," continued the distraught May.

Jeremy was not in the least a patient man, and he never or rarely had patience with ignorance. He had restrained himself these past days from replying to May's wails and anguished suspicions with brutal harshness, because he both pitied May and did not want to hurt Ellen. Nor did he want, just now, to force Ellen into choosing between him and her aunt, and distressing her. Again that stab of desire for the girl came to him, and he regretted that he had included May in this journey and had promised to care for her the rest of her doleful life in New York. He knew, now, the profound love and passion Ellen had for him; he was sure that he could have persuaded her to let him put May into the Hitchcock Hotel in Wheatfield, where she could live in great comfort and under the care of physicians. He foresaw a future in which Ellen would have to either placate her aunt or defer to him, and he did not want that for his love. She had suffered enough.

He tried to keep the natural roughness out of his voice, and leaned towards May with a kindly air, which did not become his features. "Mrs. Watson," he said, "I assure you that my friends are good and respectable people, even if they drink wine with their meals, as do tens of millions of other people like them, all over the world. Many of them are even Christians, too, and some are Catholics."

This horrified poor May even more and she clapped her hands to her cheeks. "Romans!" she cried, and glared with terror at Ellen. "Ellen, he will drag you into the midst of Romans, and you know what they are!"

"What are they," asked Mrs. Eccles with malevolent kindness and glee. "To be sure, they aren't well thought of in America, especially the Irish, but I have a Catholic friend in Wheatfield—English—or maybe it's High Church, and she is an exemplary person. May, you shouldn't be bigoted." She hoped that Jeremy "was beginning to realize." Certainly his expression indicated that, in her estimation.

But his voice was restrained when he said, "Shall we leave, then, the question of wine for you and Ellen, today, at your own discretion?" He looked at Mrs. Eccles and could not help saying, "You drink wine at dinner or supper, don't you, Mrs. Eccles?"

"Quite regularly, Jeremy, and May knows that only too well. Are you implying, May, that I am a dissolute and wicked woman?"

May's gray and tortured face flushed with a sickly crimson. "Oh, no!" she cried. "I know you are a good Christian lady. I know only too well! You must excuse me."

Mrs. Eccles became all graciousness and leaned back enough to touch Jeremy's shoulder with her own. "Well, then," she said. "You and Ellen do as you please, but Jeremy and I are going to enjoy our dinner." She now decided that neither Ellen nor May had been tippling in her wine cellar, though she had been suspicious at the disappearance two weeks ago of a half bottle of her cheaper wines, though all her wines were cheap. It was probably the handyman, she thought darkly. I will discharge him at once when I return.

Having won this small and pathetic victory, Mrs. Eccles sat back in her velvet crimson chair and looked at Ellen almost with pride. Ellen merely seemed sad and uncomfortable. But Jeremy gave her a cheerful smile, and as cheerfulness was not one of his more prominent virtues, this was quite a victory for him, too.

Daughter of John Sheldon Widdimer, indeed, thought Mrs. Eccles, tossing her head. I don't believe a word of it, though obviously Jeremy does.

The train was passing rapidly through the autumn landscape, and Ellen, looking through the window, was suddenly absorbed in the wild burning of color everywhere, in the trees, on the scarlet-laden grass, on the rising plum-tinted hills in the distance. The western sky was a deep pellucid green, remote and awesome, over the far mountains, which had turned to bronze iridescence in the sunlight. She was conscious only of beauty, except for the insistent awareness of Jeremy's presence, and that awareness only enhanced the tranquillity and grandeur of what she was seeing. In his turn Jeremy was watching her profile and again he marveled at such immaculate perfection, and felt the charm and the magnetism of it.

Two waiters in long white aprons to their ankles came in with a number of tables, all steaming, and Mrs. Eccles, sparkling and avid, leaned forward to look at them, and at the glistening white linen and silver and flowers in a silver vase, and the silver ice-filled tubs of wine.

"Oh, lobster! Don't you adore it?" she asked in the groaning voice of ecstasy. "I haven't tasted it since I was last in New York a year ago." She inspected the pheasant under glass and groaned again, and Jeremy said to himself that she sounded as if in the midst of an orgasm, which, come to it, he thought, is probably happening to her, but in her stomach this time. May looked at the lobsters, red and glossy with butter, and at the huge claws, and she was nauseated and put her hands to her middle and turned her face aside. Then when she saw the pheasant under glass she rose abruptly and said to Ellen in a weak voice, "Please—take me to the lavatory." So Ellen led her into the corridor, her face pink with embarrassment, and to the lavatory, where May promptly vomited, while Ellen held her head and was almost ill with sympathy and self-reproach. When May had finished she sat down in a state of collapse on the toilet seat, her face coldly sweating, her damp hair falling down her scorched neck, her whole body trembling.

"To think they eat *that*," she moaned. "I can't go back there, Ellen, while they are eating such stuff. I just can't. And the smell!"

"The lobster just smells like fish, Auntie," said Ellen, "and the pheasant is just another fowl like chicken. Please, Auntie. I know how you feel, but this is the way rich people eat, and there is nothing disgusting about it."

May seized Ellen's wrist frenziedly in her twisted and swollen fingers. "Ellen! Let's get off the train at the next stop. Let's tell Mrs. Eccles we are going home—"

Ellen spoke quietly. "Home? To where, Auntie? We never had a home. Mrs. Eccles will be only too glad to have us back—at a lower wage. I don't like her, I never did, and please don't look at me like that. She has taken our labor for a pittance over four years, and we owe her nothing. Besides, I will never leave Jeremy. I'd die if I did; I almost died a few times, thinking of him, over those long years. I am going to be his wife."

"We are not his kind, Ellen," said May, beginning to weep. When Ellen offered her her own handkerchief, while May fumbled for hers, May pushed Ellen's hand away almost savagely and glared up at her through trickling eyes. "No, we are not his kind. What will you do among his friends, Ellen? They'll laugh at you, a servant girl, putting on airs. They'll know you are only a servant no matter how grand he dresses you, in silks and satins and laces and furs and ribbons. You'll look like a lady clown in such clothes, Ellen. Look in that mirror; see yourself as you really are, only a servant girl, trying to rise out of the station to which God has called you. Pride cometh before a fall, the Good Book says, and it's true, it's true. I thought you had better sense, Ellen."

Ellen pushed up her large and lustrous pompadour, looked briefly in the mirror, and she wondered, as she had wondered many times, what Jeremy saw in her and why he wanted her. Then she said, "Jeremy is going to hire a tutor for me, Aunt May, to eliminate the gaps in my education, or, I should say, to give me the education I never had. He wants me to be at ease with his friends." Her beautiful voice faltered. She smoothed down the gray flannel skirt, of cheap wool, which May had made for her, and she eyed the little pearl buttons on her cotton blouse to see if any of them had opened indecently over her full high breast. Then she studied the rainbow glitter of the large diamond ring Jeremy had brought for her from New York, and it seemed to her that the rainbows in it danced for her alone, with gaiety and promise. May, sobbing, saw the girl's sudden bemusement, and she said, "Look at that ring! Do you think it's right for you to have such a costly bauble, Ellen? I just can't believe you'll have anything but misery if you marry him. If he marries you."

"He will," said Ellen, and her voice was rich with passion and love.

"If only it had been Mr. Francis," said May, desolated. "Though he has better sense, Mr. Francis."

Ellen thought of Francis Porter with affection. Yes, he had been kind and good, and he had done his best for two homeless servants, and Ellen was grateful. But at the absurd thought of marrying him she could not help laughing. She took her aunt's arm. "You are all right now, Auntie. Let's go back; it's very impolite to stay away this long, and Mrs. Eccles will be only too happy at our—our —discomfiture. She would just love it if we turned tail and ran, and came slinking back to her."

"How can you talk that way about such a lovely lady, who has been like a mother to you! A mother! God will punish you, Ellen, for such ugly words."

Ellen took her aunt's arm with loving firmness and raised her from the seat. "Aunt May, you don't need to look at that food. You can eat your own sandwiches, which you brought, and have some hot tea." She was wildly impatient to be back in the stateroom with Jeremy; it was as if she had been away for hours; he might have disappeared.

"You can't eat that horrible stuff either, Ellen. It will poison you; you're not used to it. Poison you."

"If it doesn't poison Mrs. Eccles it won't poison me," said Ellen with an ambiguous smile. May tottered with the swaying of the train and her real illness and distress, but

Ellen guided her strongly into the corridor and into the stateroom. Jeremy rose, looked sharply at May and then at Ellen, who smiled into his eyes. The stateroom was filled with delicious odors and Ellen discovered she was very hungry.

While Jeremy still stood, Ellen put her aunt into her chair, and Mrs. Eccles watched with complacent malice and smugness, her mouth dripping with melted butter. Then Ellen calmly picked up her aunt's bag and opened it on the neatly arranged cold beef sandwiches and pound cake. She glanced at Jeremy over her shoulder and she could not read his expression, for he was trying to control both his vexation and his pity. Had he been alone with May and Ellen he would have brought himself to the limit of his capacity for solicitude, but Mrs. Eccles was there, gloating, laughing inwardly at Ellen. Smirks meant nothing to Jeremy, for himself, and he had seen them thousands of times on the faces of the meager men like Francis Porter, the greedy, cruel, bloodless men who called themselves the intelligentsia. But smirks for Ellen were another matter. He wanted to hit Mrs. Eccles.

He rang for tea for May, then took Ellen a little unceremoniously by her arm and led her to a seat at the table, and when she would have drawn back, to stay with her aunt, he gave her his first formidable look of command and masculine force, and she sat down. She knew now that she could never successfully oppose him, but—it was strange to her—this only increased his fascination for her, and she gave him a submissive uplifted glance and he saw the deep blue shining of her eyes and was touched.

Ellen ignored Mrs. Eccles and tried the lobster and the fowl and discovered they were delectable. She ate with her natural delicacy of gesture and plainly showed her enjoyment; her eyes kept returning to Jeremy and he smiled at her with compassion and amusement and approval, and she felt the now familiar warmth flowing over her, which made her breasts tingle and her breath momentarily short.

May, sniffing occasionally into her handkerchief, nibbled at the sandwiches she had made, and drank the hot tea with lemon, and pretended, in her wretchedness, to gaze through the window occasionally. But she was again desolated; Ellen had become someone she did not know, through pride and vanity, both heinous crimes against God. She had always been very lonely, in her deprived life, but never this lonely before. She longed for her bare chilly room and the rough blankets and the hot bricks Ellen would bring her, wrapped in flannel, for the pain in her ankles and knees. She longed to be "home." She was like a half-starved bird driven from its wintry nest and terrified at its eviction.

Ellen, whose back was to her aunt, drank some of the wine and it gave her a delightful sense of elation and excitement, and her cheeks turned a deeper apricot and so did her lips. Forgetting both the other women in the coach, she talked with her naïve confidence to Jeremy, and it seemed to him that the stateroom was filled with melodious music, so full of cadences was her voice. He had never seen her so beautiful, so animated, and he thought of his wedding night and his dark face colored and became hot.

When Mrs. Eccles suggested, after the meal, that May go with her "for a little walk, for our circulation, dear," May got painfully and meekly to her feet and went with the woman she still feared and who she still felt was her mistress. They went to the lavatory, where May became abject and tearful and clutched Mrs. Eccles' arm. "Take us home, please, Mrs. Eccles, please. We want to go home."

Mrs. Eccles, who had been examining her own sleek brown pompadour with pleasure, stopped her patting and looked over her shoulder at May, and her expression became alert. "Do you mean that, May? With Ellen, too? Ellen wants to go back to Wheatfield?"

May stammered, "Ellen will do whatever I say, Mrs. Eccles. I think."

"You've talked to her about it?" Mrs. Eccles gleefully considered Jeremy's face at this announcement. She had nothing against Jeremy; she had become very attached to him these past two days, and admired him greatly, especially his money and his manner. But she was by nature full of intrigue, and loved mischief for its own sake, and this had induced her to send Francis a telegram with the incredible news. Moreover, she deplored Jeremy's "infatuation" for a servant girl, a girl hardly higher in station than a trollop, a streetwalker. Then, the magnificent engagement ring had inspired her with umbrage and envy.

"Yes," said May in a doleful voice, "I talked to Ellen about it, right here, ma'am."

"And what did she say?" said Mrs. Eccles eagerly.

May hesitated, and dropped her head. "She didn't say much, ma'am. But she didn't say no, either."

Mrs. Eccles regarded her shrewdly. "Well, I reckon that means no, May. I know Ellen. A deceitful puss, with a close mouth, and bold, and disobedient and willful. She will have her way! We can only pray for her, I suppose, and she will very probably need our prayers."

May still clutched her arm, and her suffering wet eyes, with their red rims, were desperate. "Mrs. Eccles, after the—wedding—if it happens, and I pray it won't, take me back to Wheatfield with you. I've worked for you a long time—"

Mrs. Eccles disengaged her arm. (Take you back, indeed, you hapless cripple! A whining invalid in my house, useless, a drag on my affairs. You must think me mad, or something, throwing away money on you.) She gave May a sweet, affectionate smile. "Now, now, May, you must be sensible, even if Ellen is such a determined and ignorant and uppish little hussy, and doomed to misery, I can tell you that, after he's tired of her. Ellen—and Jeremy Porter! It's ridiculous. It's insane. I agree with you. But you must stay with Ellen. It's your duty, and we must do our duty no matter our tears and our sighs, isn't that so?"

May had been too wretched to hear the epithets Mrs. Eccles had called Ellen; she only received the import of her words, that she must stay with Ellen, and she laboriously got to her feet, stroked her white hair with both her moist palms, and went back to the stateroom with Mrs. Eccles, walking so feebly that Mrs. Eccles freshly despised her and thanked Heaven she was rid of this creature.

Mrs. Eccles, who often cried copiously when her minister pleaded for the Missions, and had waved her scented handkerchief and had been conscious of the tender smiles of her friends about her, had no pity for May Watson. Mrs. Eccles could weep over the minister's eloquent stories, and especially when he spoke of the dolorous state of Chinese women, who hobbled about on bound feet. But she had no compassion for a woman who had become disabled in her arduous service. The Chinese

women, and the inhabitants of "godless jungles," were
very far away. May was near, and "a burden," and that
was a different matter. Mrs. Eccles was a very pragmatic
woman.

10

May had been benumbed at the clamor and roaring of
Fifth Avenue, in New York, on this dusky autumnal night
spitting with rain. But Ellen leaned forward, entranced,
dazed, at the sight of all this traffic and the crowds, and
she would wipe off the steaming carriage windows and
feel an almost unbearable excitement and ebullience. Why,
she thought, I've been here before, I know it so well! I
know it's silly, but it seems so familiar to me, all these
burnished victorias and glossy landaus and the glassy carriages with the charming flowers painted on their sides,
and the white and black and sorrel and dappled horses
prancing on the glistening wet cobbles and their silver
harnesses singing like bells, and the coachmen, and all
these yellow mist-wreathed gas lamps dancing like veiled
butterflies, and the shopwindows lit up like Christmas and
full of beautiful jewels and dresses and objects of art, and
the pounding streetcars and the endless throngs with their
wet gleaming umbrellas and the gentlemen with canes,
and the ladies in furs, on the walks, and the laughter and
the voices and the grinding of wheels and all the side
streets choked with impatient vehicles and the piercing
steeples and huge buildings running with bright rain which
shines like falling gems in the lamplight, and the noise
which is really like fast and galloping music full of importance and gaiety, and the theaters with their brilliant
white lights and the arcades, and the sense of thundering
activity—I know it all, all.

But I do not know these automobiles, bellowing and

smoking, though I have seen a few in Wheatfield. No, they are not familiar to me as all the rest.

She looked across at Jeremy and could not stop her exclamation: "I have seen it before," and her face beamed with delight and he reached to her and he pressed her hand tightly with understanding. But May said, almost in a whimper, "How can you say that, Ellen? You were never in New York."

Jeremy pointed out to the girl the mansions of the Vanderbilts, the Astors, the Belmonts, and all their kin and she looked with astonished awe at the white or gray marble houses with their pillars and lighted windows and the coming and going of laughing and greeting guests. But, I have seen it, she thought, and remembered what the poet Rossetti, had said, "I have been here before." Above the odor of wet dust and wet trees and wet stones she could smell the sea. The leaves of the trees were dripping liquid scarlet and brown and gold light and bowing and swaying in the autumn wind. Mrs. Eccles said, "I love New York. Always such liveliness," and she yawned and looked at Ellen and May with fresh ridicule and resentment. They are nothing but menials and peasants, she thought. All this magnificence for such as these! Yes, dear Jeremy must be out of his mind.

"I must see the opera," she said.

Jeremy said to Ellen, "Yes, I do believe *Aïda* is here this week."

They arrived at Jeremy's hotel, and the doormen and bellboys in crimson and gold livery ran out to meet Jeremy's carriage and flung open the doors with lordly gestures. May shrank, clutching her poor coat together, but Ellen took Jeremy's hand and jumped out eagerly, looking about her with overwhelming happiness. Mrs. Eccles alighted more sedately, smoothing her sable capelet regally about her plump shoulders. They entered a red and gold lobby full of soft warm air and perfume and gentle music, and saw the distant vast dining room with its scintillating chandeliers and white napery and the bustling of black-clad waiters and the crowds of women with pale shoulders and furs, and their rich escorts. Ellen could not see enough; she shivered with a new access of delight, unaware of her shabby servant's garb and her wilted black hat. The doormen and bellboys surveyed her with furtive astonishment, and looked offended at the sight of May.

Even for servants, they thought, they are poor specimens. Still, the girl is uncommonly beautiful, like an actress with that hair and face. "Yes, Mr. Porter, thank you, Mr. Porter, and this is the luggage, sir, and we shall notify the stable for the carriage, directly."

"We shall dine in my own dining room," said Jeremy, well aware that he could not take Ellen and May into the great glittering room beyond. "My man, Cuthbert, has everything ready for us."

Neither May nor Ellen had ever been in an elevator before, and May was terrified and shut her eyes against the sight of falling floors through the gilt bars. She was also nauseated and stunned. No, it was not right, any of this, for her and Ellen.

They passed down a corridor paved with soft crimson carpet and lighted by wall lamps of bronze twisted into intricate shapes, and May appeared to grow smaller and smaller as she tiptoed along in growing dismay and stupefaction. They saw carved closed doors and heard the sound of laughing voices beyond them. Then another door opened and they entered Jeremy's suite and May halted on the threshold, unable to move. Mrs. Eccles pushed impatiently past her, chattering vivaciously, and Ellen followed. Jeremy took May by the arm and forced her across the marble step of the doorway.

A very tall and slender and distinguished elderly gentleman greeted them, bowing, and May, in her bewilderment, thought that he must be a prince at the very least, so majestic was he in striped trousers and black long coat and black cravat and pearl stickpin and polished white cuffs and shirt. She dipped her knee in a small curtsy, and peeped timidly at the grave lined face and smooth white hair. Oh, he would order them out, all of them, or perhaps call the police! Jeremy said, "Mrs. Eccles, Mrs. Watson, Miss Watson, this is my houseman, Cuthbert."

"Good evening, ladies, Mr. Porter," said the first butler May had ever seen. She almost cowered at this condescension, but Mrs. Eccles said brightly, "Good evening, Cuthbert," and Ellen stared at him mutely, and with curious frankness, and smiled, and the butler thought: So, this is the young lady, Mr. Porter's lady, and she is lovelier than any actress I have ever seen, or any other lady who came to this suite.

Ellen looked about her with candid avidity, and saw

the luxury and grace of the large living room and again she said to herself, I have seen all this before, long before. She wanted to run about the room, touching the furniture, the silken walls, the cabinets of treasures, studying the pictures and gazing through the tall arched windows. Her heart was jumping with excitement and almost unbearable exhilaration. She looked at Jeremy like a bewitched child discovering enchantments, and he smiled at her, sharing her pleasure.

When Cuthbert lifted a bag May found her voice and it issued with apologetic shrillness and stammering loudness. "Oh, no, sir! I will carry my own baggage, thank you so much, sir, if you please." Cuthbert raised a discreet eyebrow and murmured, "Oh, no, madam. I am just putting it aside for your own suite, later. The boy will deliver it." He bowed again to the ladies and said, "Perhaps Mesdames would like to freshen up a little before dinner?"

May blinked, her mouth opening palely; she was dazzled by the lamplight and the chandeliers, and then she looked about her stupidly. Ellen took her arm and they both followed the sprightly Mrs. Eccles, who was all sparkles and worldliness, to one of the marble and gilt bathrooms which Cuthbert had indicated with another bow. Here was all scented soaps and white soft towels. Mrs. Eccles laughed gaily and said, "A bidet! Oh, the naughty boy!" She trilled like a young lark, and looked at herself in one of the long gold-framed mirrors, watching her two companions in it with a face gleaming with spite. May hobbled about the room like a blind and crippled hen, seeking its way, until Ellen caught her arm and sat her down on a plush stool and touched her cheek gently and reassuringly. "Let me wash your face and hands, Auntie," she said. "We are very sooty, aren't we?"

What a swindler she is, thought Mrs. Eccles, now swelling with her umbrage. She pretends this is nothing to her, when she is just as flabbergasted as that deplorable May, who can do nothing but whimper and wave her hands about like an idiot. All the kindness Mrs. Eccles had once felt for aunt and niece had long since evaporated in the fury of her indignation. Now she experienced animosity towards them, and outrage that they should be tolerated here, where she was so much at home and so knowing. They'll probably try to use the bidet instead of the toilet behind that door, she thought, and waited maliciously. But Ellen led her quivering aunt to the door and opened it for her, and then washed her hands serenely. As if unaware of Mrs. Eccles—as she was—she let down the long abundance of her hair and it caught fire in the lamplight and the waves shimmered and undulated. Ellen shook it out; it lay over her shoulders and breast and back like a burning mantle. Mrs. Eccles said, "You must really, my dear, do something about that rough hair of yours. A nice hairdresser perhaps, to tone down that awful color. Quite vulgar, I assure you."

But Ellen was thinking only of Jeremy as she pushed up a fresh pompadour and coiled her hair over the back of her head.

Jeremy was pouring a glass of whiskey and soda for himself, and he thought gloomily: I should have left that damned Eccles woman home. I wonder what she is saying to Ellen. I bet it is something unpleasant.

The ladies emerged into the living room, and Jeremy felt a wild surge of felicity again when he saw Ellen, and he went to the three women, smiling. "Cuthbert is a remarkable chef," he said. "Will you all have a glass of sherry before dinner?"

May was unable to speak, and visibly shaking, but Mrs. Eccles cried, "Of course, dear Jeremy! Bristol Cream, my favorite?" Ellen said, and she took his hand like a confiding child, "I don't know anything about sherry, and neither does Aunt May, though we have seen it in your aunt's house, and Mrs. Eccles'. Is it good?"

"If you like sherry," he answered, and made a wry mouth, and Ellen laughed, and the sound to him was again entrancing.

"No strong drink for me and Ellen," whispered May, but no one heard her, not even Ellen, who was gazing at Jeremy like one astonished and illuminated by magic. He led the girl to a chair and seated her, then bent over her, almost eye to eye, and she colored and looked aside, shyly. But her young breast lifted on a fast hard breath, and she was bemused, stormed by emotions which were both delicious and frightening.

Cuthbert brought the sherry in tall crystal glasses, and Mrs. Eccles accepted with a coy gesture and a flirtatious look towards Jeremy as if archly admonishing him for this temptation. Ellen also accepted a glass. May took one, afraid of vexing this stately man whom she still could not accept as a servant like herself, if indeed it ever occurred to her to think of him as a servant. Again, fearful of offending him, she put the glass to her chattering teeth, but the smell of the brownish liquid sickened and affrighted her. She looked about her, a little wildly, then put down the glass on the table next to her and behind the lamp. She had never seen an electric lamp before; she became fixed at the sight of it and clung to the illumination as if it would save her, and Ellen, from a most terrible disaster. Her eyes became glassy like the eyes of a sleepwalker. She could hear voices about her but they were as far as a dream. She wanted only to sleep and wake up in her barren cold room in Mrs. Eccles' house, with the rough blanket against her chin. She wanted to weep in her despair and her fear and against this strangeness, this dazzle of color and crystal and silk.

Cuthbert indeed proved himself an excellent chef, with his delicate mushroom soup heavy with cream and fragrant with white wine, brook trout stuffed with crabmeat and truffles, lamb chops with fresh mint, potatoes in a delectable sauce, late peas, the new Porter House rolls, and a salad with a cheese dressing and wine vinegar and a dainty touch of garlic. With this, in the small dining room sparkling with a chandelier and the brightest silver, he served various chilled wines and little cups of coffee, and a chocolate mousse.

May, benumbed again, would not have eaten this "heathenish food" if Ellen, for the first time, had not frowned at her pleadingly. But the meal revolted her, she who had known nothing before but the grossest of "hearty" workingman food and the coarse and heavy meals of the people for whom she had worked in Preston. She ate every small morsel with the direst suspicion and a feeling of persecution. Each morsel, she was certain, would poison her. Her "stomach was not fit for it." She was only sure that if this was to be Ellen's diet in the future, then her very life was in danger. She did not know the word "effete," nor did she know "decadent," yet she knew the import. No, this was not for Ellen or herself, and again she felt such a passion to "go home" that she almost burst into tears. She would glance imploringly at Mrs. Eccles, her benefactor, her protector, and Mrs. Eccles was again amusedly disgusted. She did not join May in timid sly derision at these delights, as May had hoped. As for Ellen, she heard and saw nobody but Jeremy, at whose right hand she sat; she was not even conscious of what she ate, nor the silver bowl of pink roses on the table, nor the lace, nor the warm luxury. It all became part of her love for him, and her absolute trust and sense of harbor and peace. At moments she reproached herself humbly that she had ever doubted the beneficence of God, who had heaped her hands with such joys. Love and trust. How had she ever forgot?

Jeremy saw her weariness after the journey, for all the large and shining blue gaze on him, and he saw her utter innocence and pliant air of yielding, and he wanted her desperately, not only bodily but spiritually. He felt that total communion with Ellen would restore his clouded hopes, lighten his cynicism, make him less grim and full of foreboding for his country, less involved in his work— and would give him again a measure of his youth and guarded optimism. A world which could produce such as Ellen must have produced silent multitudes like her also, and in them was his reassurance that dedicated men could protect American freedom from all its enemies: the violent white-faced hysterics who talked of "social justice," the hidden and powerful international plotters who wished to efface his country and fatten on her flesh and bring her to slavery for their own aggrandizement and rule and wealth, the Populists, the Socialists, and all the other vileness clothed in human flesh which would make of America only a soft ruin and send her people "eyeless in Gaza, at the mill with slaves." What we need here, he would think, are a few of the ancient Hebrew prophets who thundered at tyrants and admonished their people to remember what Moses had said: "Proclaim liberty throughout the land, and to the inhabitants thereof!"

Liberty was a rigorous state, uncomfortable for most of the hordes of mankind who preferred to be "guided" and led. But liberty, it had been said, was the unalienable right of men. However, men had to be true men to appreciate and even die for it. The hoary enemy had already surfaced, in the persons of Marx and Engels, to relieve men of the onerous burden of being free, and to be "protected" from all of life's vicissitudes and be reduced to placid domestic animals. Except for the "elite," of course, who would rule them "lovingly" but sternly, and milk them always, and devour their souls and blind them to the light. (Where had he read, in the Bible, "Fear not those who would destroy the body, but those who would destroy your soul"?)

For the first time in his life Jeremy considered the ortho- dox view that there was, in full reality, Satan, bent on destroying man in the persons of man's primordial enemies. He smiled to himself. If there was a Satan, then his servants were those who passionately asserted they "loved" mankind and knew what was best for it.

Ellen whispered to him urgently. "Aunt May is very tired," she said. "Would you excuse us after dinner, soon?"

Jeremy glanced at May, who was sunken in a gray and exhausted reverie, her plate almost untouched. "Certainly," he said. "In a few minutes." He put his hand over Ellen's and a charge of something powerful and beautiful rushed between them, an empathy which suddenly made them one.

He courteously rose and bowed when the ladies in- dicated that they wished to retire. He hoped, he said, that they would be pleased with the quarters which had been assigned to them. Accompanied by Cuthbert, they left the room, but at the last Ellen's blue and luminous eyes smiled at him with ardent love and trust.

Mrs. Eccles was exceedingly pleased with her small and luxurious suite. The one for May and Ellen looked out upon the Avenue, and was larger and even more sumpt- uous. May was now completely stunned. A maid came in to turn down the silk damask bedspreads, to unfold the puffed quilts, and to draw the golden satin draperies. May watched her in a humble and apathetic silence, though once she made an ashamed and protesting gesture when the maid swiftly unpacked their two small bags and hung the dreary and wilted clothing in a vast mahogany ward- robe all carvings and gilt handles and embellishments. A steam radiator hissed warmly; the sounds of traffic below reached the room in a subdued blur of sound.

"Isn't it all too wonderful, too unbelievable?" asked Ellen in a soft ecstatic voice. She gazed about her with innocent and almost childish glee.

"It's not for us," said May. There were heavy gray lines of weariness and confusion and denial and pain about her eyes.

But Ellen said, with that deep gentleness of hers, "I'll

get your pill, Auntie, and a glass of water—from this beautiful crystal bottle here on the table—and you will sleep well, and cozy, too."

May began to cry. "I want to go home," she said, sobbing drily. "I want us to go home. Please come home with me, Ellen, please." She reached out and took the girl by her round forearm and raised a desperate and pleading face to her. All the feeble dauntlessness she had occasionally felt some years ago had gone. All the stubborn tenacity and determination of her kind had dwindled with her increasing pain and incapacity. But she still had the pride of her class, the obdurate pride of her "place," which was at once a defense and a defiance.

Ellen said in a quiet contented voice, "I am home, Aunt May, home at last."

She began to undress, carefully stroking out the long gray flannel skirt, the cheap imitation-leather belt with its brass buckle, and the cotton blouse, now stained with soot. She hung them up, and sniffed the cedar-scented interior of the wardrobe with pleasure. May watched her in a prolonged silence, and between those intent glances she also gazed about the room. She could not bear the splendor.

Then she said, "Ellen, there's something else. Have you ever thought what you are doing to Mr. Jeremy, you marrying him?"

Ellen looked at her aunt over her shoulder, in astonishment.

"I don't know what you mean, Auntie."

"Ellen, dear, think again, remember, you are only a poor servant girl, born to be a servant, by God's will. And he's a gentleman, and rich. You don't know anything, Ellen. You're as ignorant as I am. You're out of place here, and in his life even more, my poor little girl. He has important and wealthy friends; think what they will say about him and how they'll laugh at him, and he's a very proud man, you can see that. They'll make him ashamed, they'll make him realize— Ellen, if you—if you—like him, you won't marry him, for his sake. You will rise above your own selfishness. Don't make a man like him miserable, Ellen, and you'll make him miserable and ashamed if you marry him. You can't do this thing to him, Ellen, you just can't, not if you care a fig about him. It isn't fair."

This was an aspect Ellen had never considered. She stared blankly at her aunt and her face slowly paled and became rigid. May leaned forward eagerly from where she sat on the voluptuous bed, for she saw Ellen's expression and her hopes rose.

"He'll go far, Ellen, as Mrs. Eccles has told us over and over. Maybe even to Washington. Or at least Governor. That is, if you don't marry him. But people'll think, big people, that if he could bring himself to marry a little servant, a nobody, then he isn't the man for them, and they'll turn away from him and find a man with better sense. Don't you see, Ellen? He's the kind that wants to do great things, to amount to something. And you'll be standing in his way, dear, and he'll come to hate you, and himself, too. How could you possibly be his hostess? Even if he gets a tutor for you? You can't make a silk purse out of a sow's ear."

Ellen sat down on her own bed and dropped her head on her chest. She said, "Aunt May, you truly think I could hurt him, by marrying him?"

"Oh, yes, dear! I've talked to Mrs. Eccles, she is a wise woman in this world. And she said, 'Poor Ellen, she will find out when it is too late.' I know you don't like her, but she knows this world, and she is sorry for you and Mr. Jeremy."

Sudden waves of desolation and anguish rushed over Ellen. Compared with this agony, the misery of her short life was as nothing, not even the past four years. How could she live without Jeremy, how could she go away and never see him again? Her throat became thick and breathless, and she gasped. But—how could she ruin his life by marrying him, by making him a pariah among his powerful friends? Love had taught her his strength, his ambition, his forcefulness. She had recognized these things instinctively. He would never be satisfied to be obscure, a mere pedestrian lawyer, not even if he was rich. Was she a barrier to his nobler and more distinguished life? Would her love for him eventually be nothing, and only a smothering of his aspirations? Would he be despised? Yes, it was very possible.

But I can't live without him, she thought, in her suffering. Then another thought came: But how dare I stand in his way? What am I, compared with him, Jeremy, my darling? I am nothing. He is all there is.

May was watching her acutely. She saw Ellen despairingly run her hands through her hair with such violence
that it fell about her in rippling folds and heavy lengths.
May did not consider herself cruel, and a destroyer. She
loved her niece; she sincerely believed that she could save
Ellen from wretchedness, from the torment of "rising out
of her station in life." Had she not taken Mary away
from the man who had wanted to marry her, that John
Widdimer? Had she not truly saved Mary from such a
disaster? It was sad that Mary had died of sorrow and
childbirth, and that Mr. Widdimer had been killed by a
horse. But better that than a lifetime of grief and dis-
sension and ultimate unhappiness and sorrow. In the end
both of them had attained peace, even if it was in the
grave. May, like many of her kind, believed that as the
grave was always the fate of man it was better than laboring in regret and fevered affliction. Her entire life had
been centered on hymns and aphorisms about death and
cemeteries. Though no longer religious, she was convinced
that the grave was superior to existence. Whenever she
had had leisure she had haunted graveyards, sighing senti-
mentally, and touching stones with a wistful hand. Her
girlhood had been full of paeans to death, and one of the
songs she remembered most lovingly had proclaimed:
"Cradle's empty, Baby's gone!"

Had Ellen died when Mary had given her birth May
would have had a singular consolation, a sentimentality
to remember, to cherish, with deep luxurious sighings and
uplifted tearful eyes and hushed confidences to acquaintances. But Ellen had not consented to die with her
mother. Unknown to her simple self, May had unconsciously resented this robust defiance, this determination
to survive. Now, unconsciously again, she even more
resented Ellen's prospect for happiness. In some way it
was not "proper." Ellen had robbed her aunt of a dismal
reason to live, herself, with tender memories. She had
robbed her of emotional riches. Ellen had no way of
understanding the complexity of her aunt's motivations.
She sat, drooping, on her bed, a tragic figure of devastation.

May felt victorious and uplifted, and her sadness was
almost sexually exciting. Misfortune, and its wailings and
panoply, was the supreme dignity of the poor.

"Let's go home tomorrow," she pleaded. "Back to

Wheatfield, on the train, back to Mrs. Eccles and her lovely house. We were so happy there."

"Happy?" murmured Ellen. "I wasn't even alive."

She contemplated her whole dolorous life, her famished longing for love, for protection, for contentment, for a little beauty, a little surcease, a little quiet, a little privacy. She had never understood the resignation of such as her aunt, the self-righteous acceptance of wretchedness and poverty. She did not know that there was a perverse satisfaction in this, a sensual gratification, a sense of importance in being selected for submission to ordained fate. Once she had dimly guessed this, and it had outraged her. Jeremy had recognized in her an iron of the soul, a refusal to be cowed by circumstance, though in her youth she had not recognized this herself. She only knew that her very spirit had stiffened at May's servile platitudes, and rebellion had made her smart. But that very rebellion had filled her with remorse and penitence, for she had hurt May. The girl's thoughts became black and whirling and chaotic, suffused with her growing anguish.

"I haven't long to live, Ellen," said May piteously. "For your sake and mine—let's go back where we belong. We are poor and simple people; it never does to try to get out of our place."

Ellen was saying over and over in herself, in a stricken convulsion: No, I can't hurt him. Jeremy, Jeremy. He took pity on me and tried to help me. How can I repay him with ruin? Jeremy, Jeremy.

She stood up, trembling and distraught. Her hair fell about her white face and quivering cheeks and lips. But she said quietly enough, "Did you take your pill, Auntie?"

May, knowing her victory, nodded almost with cheerfulness and placation. "Yes, dear. And now let's go to bed and go home tomorrow. It's all settled, isn't it?"

"Yes," said Ellen, and helped her aunt undress. For a single moment, watching her niece, May experienced a pang. The girl looked like death itself. "Yes," said Ellen again. "It's all settled."

At peace at last, and sighing deeply, May fell instantly asleep, and Ellen stood by her bed, watching the lines of pain recede on her aunt's face. What was her own life worth compared with her aunt's tranquillity and Jeremy's triumphs? Nothing. Exhaustion suddenly swept over her, exhaustion of the spirit and the mind, and the awful hollowness of prostration struck her middle and made her dizzy and weak. She was forced to collapse beside her aunt's bed; she leaned her head against the mattress, powerless to move for a long time.

The baroque room was filled with bowls of late roses and chrysanthemums and ferns, and the scent made Ellen retch as she half lay beside May's bed. The rumor of traffic reached her; now it sounded like a diabolical chorus, mocking her. The satin draperies at the windows swayed a little; they had the shapes and distortions of agony. The very furniture taunted the girl, creaking over and over, "You do not belong here. You are an intruder—in his life. Run away!"

May began to snore under the influence of the narcotic. Ellen pushed herself to her feet. She mechanically rolled up her hair. She put on her flannel skirt and blouse, her hands feeling thick and clumsy. Then, without a sound, she left the room and climbed up the five flights of stairs to Jeremy's suite, her face set and passionless and full of resolution, for all the bending of her knees under her, and for all the icy sweating of her body. It had not occurred to her to take the elevator. There was a jeering in her mind, "Beautiful daughter of Toscar!" She uttered a faint sound of self-contempt.

11

Jeremy Porter was sitting in his small library, in his silk nightshirt and a magnificent Chinese robe of black and gold, and sipping a nightcap, when he heard the knocking on the door. He glanced at the ormolu clock over the mantel and saw it was after eleven, and he wondered who was there. Cuthbert had left an hour ago. Rising and stretching, but wary, Jeremy went to the door and

cautiously opened it on its chain. Then he exclaimed,
"Ellen!"

He removed the chain and flung the door open and
reached for the girl and took her cold hands and pulled
her into the room, disbelieving and excited almost unbearably. Then when she was in the room he saw her
deathly pallor, her wide eyes, her roughly tumbled hair,
and he felt the moisture on her palms and saw the trembling of her colorless lips.

"What is it, love?" he asked, and drew her against him.
She did not resist. She even lay against his chest like one
who had been terribly wounded and must rest a little. He
smoothed her hair and held her and knew that she was
nearly fainting. She was heavy in his arms and her head
had dropped and he could not see her face now. But his
arm, about her very slender waist, could feel its vibrations,
strong and uncontrollable, as she fought down her inner
weeping. He became alarmed. He took her to a chair and
forced her down in it, then he knelt beside her and again
took her hands and held them tightly, warming them with
his own. "What is it, my darling?" he demanded, and his
voice aroused her from her crouch in the chair, the feeble
turning aside of her head.

She looked at him and he saw the naked anguish in her
eyes. Her white face seemed polished and taut as marble,
and it had the calm of despair and renunciation.

She spoke with that calm, which was also lifeless as
well as resolute. "I am going away tomorrow, Jeremy,
back to Wheatfield, with my aunt."

He frowned, and the frown was formidable. "So?" he
said. "May I ask why?"

"Because I can't marry you, Jeremy."

He stood up and lit a cigarette very slowly and carefully. She watched him, and could feel a wild tearing and
splintering in herself. He was a stranger to her now, someone she had never known. She only knew that he was
coldly and blackly enraged, and she shivered. Everything
in the room became acute to her, and threatening, the
walls of books, the little fire, the lamps, the thick carpets.
The paneling gleamed at her with hostility. The ormolu
clock struck and it seemed to her that it was tinkling
derision.

Then she saw that his dark eyes were fixed on her, no
longer with love or desire and understanding. They were

the eyes of an enemy, a prosecutor. Yet he spoke quietly
enough. "You haven't told me why."

She looked aside and whispered, "Because I love you."

He began to walk up and down the room, stopping occasionally to adjust a toppling book or to straighten out a
paper on his desk. He was as if he had forgotten her. She
felt that should she get up and leave he would not even
be aware of it. Now the tearing and splintering became
intolerable to endure. She compelled herself to speak
louder.

"You see, Jeremy, if I married you it would ruin you."

He stopped in his pacing and looked over his shoulder
at her as if she were a curious object, not to be taken
seriously.

"Who told you that?" he asked. "Mrs. Eccles?"

"No. No." She hesitated and then began to wring her
hands tightly together. He saw the writhing fingers, the
whiteness of the knuckles. "It was my aunt—she made me
see it was—impossible. That it would be disastrous for
you. That I was selfish, and never considered you at all,
and your career." Her voice was strained and almost indifferent in intonation. "My aunt is right. I never thought
of it before."

His face swelled, became engorged. He came closer to
her.

"And you believed that stupidity?"

Now she came out of her apathy and said with passion,
"It isn't stupidity! What am I, compared with you? Your
friends, the people who could help you, will laugh at you
for marrying me, a servant, a nobody— They could harm
you, Jeremy. You could marry some woman of distinction,
a lady, a beautiful woman, and not I, who haven't even
any good looks to please your friends. A nobody."

While he still stared at her, aghast at this ingenuousness, she showed him her worn and scarred hands, as she
had shown them to him in the park in Wheatfield. "Look
at them, Jeremy! The hands of a drudge, a slavey. Look
at my face, my hair, my—well, at my big feet, my—figure.
People will laugh and wonder and ask—" Her lovely
voice, with all of its mellifluous cadences, faltered. She
could not bear the strange intensity she saw in his eyes,
the incredulousness. He saw the immaculate innocence of
her suddenly averted profile, the spasm in her throat under
the cheap imitation cameo brooch.

He drew a chair close to her and leaned forward without touching her. "Ellen," he said, "I've discovered something just now about you and it isn't flattering. You are a fool, my girl, a fool, and there's nothing I despise so much as a fool."

She winced and shrank, but did not answer.

"I thought better of you, Ellen. I thought you were intelligent, and had some reason."

She shook her head slowly and heavily, like a pendulum. "No, no," she said. "I am stupid, to think I could really marry you and perhaps make you happy."

He was silent. He watched her closely. Then he began to smile. He stood up and took one of her hands. She tried to resist, but the warmth of his hand, the strength of it, shattered her and she began to cry, slow and soundless tears, and she dreaded the moment he would release her and take from her the comfort and security she was feeling again. She could not help it; her head dropped against his thigh and she believed she was dying.

He looked down at her glowing hair, at the dimpled whiteness of her chin. Then he laughed a little. He pulled her almost roughly to her feet. He said, "Come in another room with me." She followed him helplessly as he literally dragged her. He took her into his large bedroom, with the dark and shining furniture and the crimson draperies and the Aubusson rug and the silver articles on the huge dresser. There was a full-length mirror here. One lamp burned. He turned on another, and then another, until the room was vivid with light. Then, with that new roughness, he took her flimsy blouse in his hands and rudely unbuttoned it.

She stood numbly before him, not fully understanding what he was doing. Like an imbecile, unaware of what was transpiring, she saw him expertly push the blouse from her shoulders, then drop it. His hands moved very fast and she watched them in a sort of stupor. They almost tore the corset cover, with its faded blue ribbons, from her body. Then he was contemptuously removing the belt, and let that drop, and then he stripped the flannel skirt from her waist, her legs, and then her three petticoats, one darned wool, the others coarse cotton. He bent to pull off her shoes, her black ribbed stockings and garters, and then he laughed softly and kissed her navel. She started, drew back, trembled, and a flood of fiery heat and delicious weakness fell upon her. She put one arm across her breast and one hand over her revealed sex, in the ancient gesture of a virginal woman, who was at once appallingly afraid and surrendering.

He took her by the shoulders and pushed her with hard force before the mirror. She stared at her reflection, all her bare flesh shrinking, all her loosened hair flowing over her shoulders. She caught a strand of it and pulled it quickly over her breasts.

He stood off from her a little, and surveyed that white perfection of her tall young body, and the roseate shadows in every curve and hollow. She was far more delightful and lovely than he had suspected, and now he was filled with tenderness.

"Sweet love," he said. "Look at yourself. Haven't you ever looked at yourself before? Are you blind? Wouldn't any man want that, you idiot?"

Now she blushed and was abject with shame at her nakedness, and could not look either at her reflection or at Jeremy. She stiffly bent, trying to hide herself, and began to pick up her clothes. But he unceremoniously kicked them from under her hand. She cried out faintly, and squatted on the rug, covering herself with her arms. She was suddenly terrified of both herself and Jeremy.

He looked at her for a moment or two. Then he lifted her to her feet, pulled her across the room, and threw her upon the damask-covered large bed with its carved posts. His face was congested, thickened, and the sight of it frightened her while it excited her, and she did not know why she was excited and why the touch of his hands burned her and thrilled her. He rolled her aside to pull the bedspread from under her and lifted her long legs to release it, and he pushed her into the soft puffiness of the pillows and the creamy blankets. She closed her eyes, shivering and mute, cowering under her long hair and desperately trying to cover herself with it.

"Look at me!" he said, and she could not recognize his voice, because he was panting in quick gasps. She opened her shut eyes and saw him above her, as naked as she was herself. Her ears began to ring, her flesh to quiver.

"Ellen! Do you love me? Do you trust me?"

She could only look at him with stretched and fearful eyes and he saw the answer in them, timid and helpless, yet surging.

"My wife," he said. "My dear, stupid, ridiculous wife. My dear little fool."

The lamps were still lighted, but to Ellen the room darkened, became hot and thunderous, without light or form. She fumbled upwards and took Jeremy in her round arms and drew him down upon her. There was a sudden stab of startling pain, which was also blissful, and a murmuring in her ears, incoherent, and she surrendered, overpowered by an incomprehensible joy, and an alien passion.

Mrs. Eccles comfortably ate her breakfast, happy because of the contented sensation in her stomach and belly, the gurglings of sensual satisfaction. She could give, and usually did, her whole attention to the voluptuousness of eating, beyond any other hunger of her body. Except for money, she loved excellent food the most, and this was excellent. Her doctor had warned her of her gallbladder, and so she had been prudent, ordering only stewed prunes and figs (for "elimination"), a small order of broiled kidneys and bacon, two eggs, a basket of heavily buttered muffins, a delicate little broiled fish, marmalade, plum jam and guava jelly, and a large silver pot of hot chocolate "with just a teensy dab of whipped cream," and plenty of sugar. There was also a small flagon of brandy, for "stimulation of the circulation." Sipping the brandy luxuriously, and daintily wiping up the last crumbs of the sixth muffin and jam with an arched index finger (admonishing), she leaned back in her velvet chair and gave herself up to tranquillity as her stomach slowly began its arduous task of almost lewd digestion. So as not to hinder this very valuable labor she had not put on her whaleboned corset, and her plump figure sprawled peacefully under her embroidered morning robe of deep-blue silk.

She pondered on the pot of chocolate. It was very "healthy," chocolate. She mused whether she should order another pot. Her full face was flushed and pleased, and she forgot Ellen and the miserable creature, May Watson, as she argued lovingly with herself. After all, it had been a very ascetic breakfast. She was about to pull the bell rope, while she smiled with affectionate admonition and shook her head slightly, when she heard a sharp knocking at the door. Ah, the waiter was here; she would give her order and she gave herself up again to that affectionate reproof. "Come in," she almost sang. (No whipped cream;

on that she was sternly determined. The chocolate was rich enough.)

The door opened, but it was not the waiter. It was Francis Porter. Mrs. Eccles sat up abruptly, with some consternation and surprise and dismay.

"Good morning, Aunt Hortense," he said, and gave her a slight smile. He was clean of face and hands, but his clothing showed the stains of recent travel. "Did I surprise you?"

"Oh. Francis," she said. It was one thing to plot naughty mischief, out of high spirits and malice. It was another to confront the result, and she felt a stab of resentment at this unexpected appearance. What in God's name was Francis doing here?

He entered the room and closed the door behind him, and she regarded him almost with dislike as her resentment increased. How like a priggish professor he looked! Strange she had never noticed that before. He wore pince-nez now, and his blond hair was thinner and brushed severely, and his mouth had a tight and intolerant expression. His thin nose was sharper than in his youth, the tip like a needle, and the well-defined earlier flush on his high cheekbones had dimmed. He was much paler; his skin had a bleached look, rigid and unbending. All at once Mrs. Eccles was not fond of him. He really looked very prim.

He gave her a dry kiss on her red cheek, to which she did not respond. Alarm took her now. What would Jeremy, that dear boy, say to this, when he learned that Francis had come here apparently in response to her mischievous telegram? Much as she loved Francis it was in her nature to disconcert, when she could, even those for whom she felt fondness. It elated her. Now she felt quite cross and moved restively in her chair.

"What on earth are you doing here, Francis?" she asked in a petulant voice.

He himself was surprised. Her eyes were regarding him with displeasure.

"But you sent me a telegram, Aunt Hortense! What did you expect me to do? You telegraphed me that my cousin Jeremy had induced poor Ellen to come here with him, for marriage—marriage! Of course, he doesn't intend to marry her! You must know that. I thought you did. I thought that was why you sent me the telegram, so that I would come here and prevent the—the—ravishment of an innocent servant girl at the hands of a seducing brute. And take her, with you, back to Wheatfield."

She was almost glowering at him. "I reckon you misunderstood, Francis. Would I be here, as Ellen's chaperone, if that was what he wanted? Her aunt is here, too. I—I just thought you ought to know, seeing you sent her to me. I felt like a mother towards her. I just thought you should know. Not that I approve of any marriage between Jeremy Porter—he's your cousin, after all—and a servant. I just thought you should know, as you've been so kind to her."

"You honestly think he intends to marry her?" Francis was astounded and incredulous.

She shrugged her plump shoulders, lifted her hands, and dropped them. "I'm not a man. How could I know what goes on in a man's mind? At least, that's what he told me he has in mind. But perhaps"—and she was quickly animated—"he will fraudulently marry her. You understand? One of his friends pretending to be a minister or a justice of the peace. Or something."

She laughed and shook an arch finger at him. "You men! But that's all that girl deserves, impudently trying to rise out of her class. Not that I don't pity her, and her ultimate fate, which will probably be the streets, as your Aunt Agnes Porter wrote me over and over."

Francis considered. "Where is this famous marriage supposed to take place?" His light voice was harsh and bitter.

She waved a negligent hand. "In City Hall, four days from now, when she has a decent trousseau. Then they are going to Europe for the honeymoon."

Francis stood up, put his slight hands into his trouser pockets, and began to pace the room, his "professor's" head bent, his facial muscles twitching. "If it is City Hall, and you and her aunt are to be there, and officials, then it won't be fraudulent. May is clever enough to demand both a license and what she would call 'marriage lines.' No, if it is City Hall, it will be actual."

"Oh," said Hortense Eccles, with disappointment. "Well, if you came in response to my telegram, what do you intend to do about it?"

"Stop the marriage, of course." He stood before her tensely. "I've brought his mother with me. I thought that best. He might listen to her."

"To Agnes Porter? Why, he hasn't seen her in a year, and she's brokenhearted. She writes me he is avoiding his parents! He won't listen to her."

"We're registered here in this hotel. We arrived only an hour ago, together. Perhaps Ellen will listen to me. I'm sure she will. She knows how I have cared for her welfare over these years and did what I could for her. I thought she was a sensible girl, in spite of her innocence and ignorance and her native simplicity. And her lack of worldliness. After all, her background—" He shook his head. "I don't think it will be hard for me to convince her that she is doing a very wrong and stupid thing—rising out of her rank—as she probably thinks she is doing. Or he is deceiving her. I know him well, and his cruelty and his hardheartedness, and his contempt for the unfortunate. And Ellen is a very unfortunate girl, and deluded. I intend to persuade her to return to your house in Wheatfield where she properly belongs. And May, now that she is incapacitated, must go to the county infirmary. I will make Ellen see these sensible things."

She looked at him contemplatively. "Well, that would be best, for Ellen. But as she has been so ungrateful to us, and so obstinate, she can return to my house only at a reduced wage, as a proper punishment. What else can she do? She hasn't any money. Stupid though she is, she must realize that her place is under my care, in my house, and your care, where she will be protected. Otherwise the streets are her only alternative." She had, for a few moments, forgotten that Ellen was to marry Jeremy. She now remembered, and frowned. "Unless your cousin marries her, and I still think it is a fraud."

"It's no fraud. But what a frightful life she would have with him, after he tires of her ignorance. She can hardly read or write, can she? He would discard her like—"

"An old glove," said Mrs. Eccles. "Yes. Well, that is all she deserves. I don't know why we worry about her, really I don't, dear Francis. You must be very stern with her, and not talk to her with your usual solicitude and kindness. She will obey you." Her eyes sparkled with anticipation.

Francis lifted his hands in a rare vehement gesture. "He must be out of his mind, he a rich Porter, and a servant girl! I can understand Ellen a little. She longs for luxury, for her kind, sad to say, are vulgar and avaricious and don't understand the niceties of propriety, and want to strive to elevate themselves above their status. Yes, vulgar. I'm disappointed that Ellen has shown the vulgarity of her sort; I thought better of her."

Mrs. Eccles suddenly thought of what Jeremy had told her of John Widdimer and the dead Mary Watson. She leaned towards her nephew again, with new mischief.

"Do you know what poor self-deceived Jeremy told me? No, no! I mustn't tell you. I promised. But it has something to do with Philadelphia. But I gave my word."

Now Francis actually blushed. "I know all about that, Aunt Hortense. I, too, did a little investigating. I'm afraid it is quite true. I've even thought of telling Ellen myself, in order to show her what fate lies in wait for servants who presume to rise above themselves."

"It's really true, Francis?"

"Of course it's true." He was impatient. "I spent several hundred dollars finding out."

"Why?"

"Because of something my father said, a long time ago, in Preston, about a portrait of John Widdimer's mother. I wanted to disprove it. I confess I was taken aback when I found out it was true. However, that doesn't negate Ellen's position. She has inherited all the faults and failings of her class, her mother's class, and her aunt's. Avarice. Unrealistic hopes. Presumptions. Yes, I'm disappointed in Ellen."

"Did you know about the nearly quarter of a million dollars John Widdimer left his 'offspring,' legitimate or illegitimate?"

Francis was stunned. "No, I didn't."

"Well, Jeremy does. He told me. But he didn't tell Ellen. He says he never intends to."

Francis was incredulous again. "Why not?"

Mrs. Eccles shrugged. "I don't know, really. He did say something, but I don't remember."

Francis could not believe that anyone could be indifferent to money, however rich he was himself. "He intends to collect that money, Ellen's money, for himself, after they are married!" His voice, usually gentle and restrained, took on a note of viciousness.

"Are you going to tell Ellen, when she goes back with us to Wheatfield?"

He almost wrung his hands. "No. That would only

make her bold, and she would demand the money, forgetting she is only a servant, and then she would waste it in—in—riotous living, and then be impoverished again." But he was thinking rapidly, and his thin and transparent eyelids fluttered as he stared at the carpet.

"She wouldn't have a chance to waste it if she marries Jeremy. You Porters are very careful about money."

Francis was thinking more intensely. He became even paler. He stared about him, his thoughts running like mice through his mind. Wildly, he came to a certain conclusion, and he moistened his lips. Ellen, and all that money! Beautiful Ellen, and that money. Any man would be anxious to marry her.

There was another knock at the door and Mrs. Eccles said impatiently, "Oh, come!"

Agnes Porter lumbered in then, extremely agitated, her bloated fat face quivering, her very pale eyes twitching. She was in total disorder, and panting, and she gave every impression of fright. The years had been cruel to her. She was enormous and shapeless, her light hair almost totally gray. Her two fatty chins had increased to three. Her pompadour wavered. Her dress, of crimson merino with many flounces and much drapery, bulged over great breast, about huge girth and vast hips. She had no contour at all except swollen formlessness. The plump Mrs. Eccles was almost svelte in comparison, and certainly in more control of herself, and neater and prettier and younger.

"Agnes!" she exclaimed. "Dear me, you are in a state! Francis, put your aunt in a chair; she is about to faint, poor dear one."

Agnes Porter was gripping her hands together; she had burst into tears. She looked about her as if she did not know where she was. She said no greeting; her hands now flung themselves out as if she were drowning.

"Dear God, dear God!" she groaned. "Where is my son?"

"Oh, sit down, Agnes, do, and control yourself," said Mrs. Eccles, avid again for misfortune and drama. "Sit down, and tell us. Jeremy has probably gone to his office. After all, it is nearly eleven o'clock."

Mrs. Porter slumped into a chair Francis had pushed against the back of her knees. "No, no, he hasn't gone to his office." Her voice rose in hysteria; her eyes bulged at Mrs. Eccles, and then at Francis, frantically. "I called there, after I went to his rooms and found him gone. I—I wanted to talk to him about that slut—I couldn't believe it when Francis sent me a telegram— I couldn't believe it! My son, and a streetwalker, everybody in Preston knew she was a streetwalker, a bad creature, and ugly as sin, and lewd. Everybody knew it; she used to, she used to meet men in the woods and fields at night—everybody knew it. I have to talk to my son, my poor son. What did she do to him? Did he get her—"

"In a delicate condition?" asked Mrs. Eccles. "It could be. I know that she had been meeting him regularly, in the little park across from my house. Oh, they said they had just met, for the first time in four years, but I knew it was a lie, all the time. She'd been meeting him regularly. I know that. Men! But then, men will be men, and servants will be servants, wanting to better themselves any way they can. I don't blame Jeremy. I blame Ellen. I was like a mother to her."

"She can have her brat on the streets!" shouted Mrs. Porter, now beside herself. "That's where she belongs, the filthy thing, and that's where I'll send her! I'll see that she goes to the prison farm, too, for her crimes."

Francis said with some sternness, "It was your son who seduced poor Ellen."

She doubled her fist savagely and struck him on the arm, and the blow was so fierce that he staggered back and began to rub his arm through his black sleeve.

"Oh, you!" she exclaimed through clenched and exposed teeth, like a fat aged lioness. "I wouldn't put it past you that you didn't sleep with her yourself!"

"Let's not be vulgar," said Mrs. Eccles, thoroughly enjoying herself. "I know Francis. He wouldn't condescend to—well, that was very nasty of you, Agnes—to a servant like Ellen. He's most fastidious, though he was very kind to her."

"Kind! Oh, I know all about that! Fastidious! No. He's as bad as the other men she was meeting in Preston. But not my son, Jerry, not my son! He's just trying to be an honorable man."

"Honorable!" said Francis. "He doesn't know what the word is."

Agnes surged forward furiously in her chair and again would have attacked him had not Mrs. Eccles said with hard severity, "Agnes, control yourself. You are acting like a low washerwoman. Let's be calm. Let's discuss this reasonably. We must come to a proper solution. Francis and I have been discussing it. What do you mean, Jeremy wasn't in his office? You called, you said?"

"I did! From my room. And his employees said he hadn't been there this morning, and had called to say he wouldn't be." Agnes was panting and groaning and flexing her hands. "Where is he? I went to his rooms—I talked to his man, that Cuthbert. And he said that Jeremy had left two hours ago. Where is my son? Is he with that dreadful creature?" She paused a moment. "That Cuthbert! He's very sly. I swear he was grinning under his nose. He knows something."

"Jeremy and Ellen have run away together," said Mrs. Eccles, with satisfaction. "That's it. He persuaded her, or she persuaded him. So they're not getting married, after all, so calm yourself, dear Agnes. He'll have his way with her, then pack her off, and so be grateful and relieved."

Agnes subsided, still weeping, but her face was calmer. "You believe that, Hortense? You think it's so?"

Mrs. Eccles nodded energetically. "I do believe it."

"I don't," said Francis. "Ellen's with her aunt, isn't she? Her aunt wouldn't let her leave, in a strange city, with a strange man."

"May Watson?" said Agnes incredulously. "She's as bad as Ellen, if not worse. She's that girl's mother, not her aunt. Everybody knew that. Illegitimate scum, that girl. Everybody knew it." She glared at Francis, and said in a hushed voice, "Yes, you're as bad as all the rest of the men she had in Preston, and she was only fourteen then. You ought to hide your head in shame, Francis Porter, associating with sluts like that. But your father is a very coarse man, not a gentleman at all. What's born in the bone comes out in the flesh." She was not the only one who spoke in clichés.

Francis shrugged, and turned away and went to a window, where he looked out. He felt sick, shaken.

"Marry her!" said Mrs. Porter, infuriated again, but smiling wildly. "So that's what she thought, did she? Well, she knows better now, thank God. But how could he bring himself even to touch her? My son."

Mrs. Eccles spoke soothingly. "Well, it's over now. Jeremy, poor darling, will get what he wants, and that girl will be sadder and wiser. Not that I'll take her back after this. It would be a scandal." She thought of John Widdimer's will, and was dismayed. Jeremy would tell Ellen of the money, and Ellen would never come back to the Eccles house. It was the least Jeremy would do for the miserable young thing—telling her of the money. It would be a gentlemanly gesture, after he had had "his way with her." She was the best cook and housemaid I ever had, thought Mrs. Eccles with fresh resentment. I'd have taken her back, yes, I would. It would have been only Christian. Now she was angry with Jeremy, who had deprived her.

The door was violently thrown open, and May Watson, despite her crippling arthritis, scuttled into the room, moaning, her thin bent body trembling. She hardly saw Mrs. Porter and Francis. She cried to Mrs. Eccles, hobbling towards her, "Is Ellen here? Is my niece here with you, Mrs. Eccles?"

Mrs. Eccles smiled widely, and looked with significance at Agnes. "No, May. She isn't. She hasn't been here at all. Where in the world could she be?" She raised her eyebrows knowingly, but managed a concerned expression.

Francis turned alertly from the window; Agnes Porter was breathing heavily through her mouth, blinking her eyes, and relief flooded her. She nodded her head silently. It was all over, thank God. Hortense had been right. It was all over. She felt weak and faint with her relief, and subsided fatly in her chair.

May was crying again, her voice cracked and broken. "Her bed hasn't been slept in. She undressed last night; I saw her. I took my pill—she promised to go back home, to Wheatfield, today." May pushed back her thin white hair, distraught. "And then I woke up, just a little while ago. Her bed hasn't been slept in. Just the sheets and blankets turned back, like the maid did. Her skirt and blouse—they're gone. And her coat and hat. Oh, my God! Where is my Ellen? Where is Mr. Jeremy? Does he know she's gone? My girl, alone on the streets, with white slavers everywhere. My poor child. Oh, tell me! Where can she be?"

Francis said in a hard voice, "May, Mr. Jeremy has gone, too. Nobody knows where he is, no one in his office, and not his houseman. He says. He's taken Ellen somewhere. He's ruined Ellen. You should have watched her every moment. And you, too, Aunt Hortense. You were supposed to be her chaperone."

"I couldn't sleep with the damned girl!" said Mrs. Eccles with anger. "Who cares where he's taken her? Good riddance to bad rubbish, I say. Who cares what happens to her?" She turned to Mrs. Porter. "Agnes, you were right about her all the time. But don't worry about Jerry. He'll be back—alone, as I told you."

"He's taken Ellen away?" groaned May Watson. "My Ellen? She's run away with him? But he wanted to marry her!"

Mrs. Eccles laughed with delicate cruelty. "Yes, I know what he said. I know what she thought. We were all so foolish, believing it. We were children! And all the time the naughty boy had this planned." She wagged her head, obviously amused. "The naughty boy. Well, Ellen has got just what she deserved, and don't look at me like that, Francis. Jeremy and Ellen!"

A man spoke from the door. "Are you all talking about me? About us?"

They stared at the doorway. Jeremy and Ellen stood there, Jeremy smiling wolfishly, and Ellen beside him, Ellen as beautiful and as stately as a spring morning in a new gray woolen suit with a short sable cape, Ellen with a plumed hat of velvet, and with gray leather gloves and a sable muff, and dainty French shoes and silk stockings.

"You scoundrel," said Francis, and then he knew, with total knowledge, and total anguish and total frail passion, that he loved Ellen Watson and had always loved her, from the moment he had seen her kneeling and ecstatically examining a little daisy on the street in Preston. He wanted to kill Jeremy Porter, as he had wanted to kill him before, but now with an intensity and rage he had never known in all his contained life.

"Jeremy!" screamed Mrs. Porter in a frenzy. She tried to push herself out of her chair, but her bulk held her back, and a vague terror.

May hobbled towards her niece, holding out her shaking hands, her face pitiable, her features working. Ellen saw her come, and she took one of those pathetic hands and smiled like an angel, and she held her aunt's fingers tightly. A sweet perfume came from her, compounded of joy and expensive scent. The diamond Jeremy had given her blazed from her glove, and below it was a circlet, plain and new. May did not see that, however.

"Ellen, Ellen," wept the poor woman. "What has he done to you?"

Jeremy held Ellen's arm, and he was still grinning. He had not even looked at his cousin. He glanced at Mrs. Eccles, then at his mother. He did not seem surprised to see Mrs. Porter, nor Francis.

"Ladies," he said, and bowed, then for the first time looked fully at Francis, "and gentleman, I presume: My wife. We were married an hour ago, in City Hall, and the Mayor of New York himself was one of the witnesses."

Only Mrs. Porter made any sound for long moments. Then she screamed, the scream loud and piercing. She fainted away in her chair.

Mrs. Eccles was calm. She could not help it, for she was mischievous: She smiled gleefully; she clapped her hands. Those faces! She would never forget them. "Someone get smelling salts for poor Agnes," she said, and then she laughed.

Francis turned away. He was full of tumult, of agony. May leaned helplessly against her niece, and Ellen held her and bent her head and kissed the wet cheek. "I am so happy," she said. "So very happy," and her face glowed and she closed her eyes for a moment.

12

Walter Porter was admitted to Jeremy's office, and he was dusted coldly with snow and his full face was ruddy from the wind. He shook off his hat and hung up his walking cane and coat, then went to the rustling bright fire to warm his hands. Jeremy brought brandy and whiskey from a cabinet and two glasses. It was four of a stormy February afternoon and the sky was nearly dark.

Walter sat down before the fire and looked about the large paneled office and nodded with silent appreciation, as he always did. "Well?" he said at last. "And how did you enjoy your lunch with the lads of the Scardo Society?"

"It was about what you've already told me," answered Jeremy, sipping at his brandy. "I still don't see why they want me to be a member. I'm not that rich, or important."

"Ah," said Walter. "But they think you will be, and they already suspect you have political ambitions. They wanted to look you over, as they told me when they approached me six months ago. Wanted me to join years back. No. They couldn't understand, no, sir. Here I am, one of the richest industrialists in Pennsylvania, and I couldn't get interested in the banker boys, or the politicians. Too lazy, I said. What do I need more money for? I asked them. They thought I was mad, and kindly informed me that in 'ancient days' land and territory were the roots of power. Today it's money. I agreed. I further baffled them when I said I wasn't interested in power, either." Walter laughed shortly. "I have an idea they think I've been castrated, or something. Money is power and women, to them, and control of governments. I've had them all; I don't want any more."

He peered inquisitively at Jeremy. "Are you going to join them?"

"Yes. But not for the reasons they think. You never told me. Why haven't they invited your son, Francis? He's one of their kind, the self-elected elite."

Walter stared into his glass. "I thought you understood. They don't trust him; that is, they trust him only to the extent of believing that he is sincere. But they are not sincere about the things he believes they are. They looked him over. They are cynics. While they nodded their heads solemnly over his pronouncements, and heartily approved of him, his sincerity makes them laugh. They say all the things he says, in trumpet notes which are widely quoted in the press, but they themselves speak only for public consumption. What they say privately is an entirely different matter. While Francis also wants to be one of the elect who will rule this world, he unfortunately believes what he clamors. So the Scardo Society can't trust him. They regret that, knowing he is my son, and one of my heirs."

"I think I fooled them about my own opinions," said Jeremy. "I sang the 'compassionate' songs they sang, and they never heard a false note. I'm a real actor. I should be on Broadway." He made a sour mouth. "I'm joining so I can be aware of what they are doing, and plotting. I must constantly remind myself of that. Otherwise, they'll probably have my throat cut."

Walter did not smile. He nodded his head. "They are experts in *coups d'état,* all over the world. Well. If you receive their full endorsement they'll introduce you to the Committee for Foreign Studies, which, as I've told you, are about to instigate a world war in the near future. Perhaps 1910, '15, '20. They'll succeed, too, through their chaps in London, Paris, Berlin, Rome, St. Petersburg, Washington, Tokyo—everywhere."

Jeremy studied his uncle curiously. "And you don't care very much, do you, Uncle Walter?"

Walter slapped the arm of his red leather chair sharply. "No, son, I don't. We've sent rumors whispering all over the world, and strong warnings. We've had consultations with kings and princes and the Kaiser himself, and the Czar, and King Edward, and God knows who else, including our raucous boy in Washington, Teddy. What good has it done? Nothing. We're a world at peace, and every nation is getting more and more prosperous, aren't they? And don't all the members of academe at large sing today of endless love among various countries and 'the rising tide of popular concern with the poor and downtrodden'?

"We've tried to tell them of the conspiracy of international men who want to rule the whole damned globe, to control its industry, economics, currencies, governments —people, for their own use and their own power, and to reduce every nation to the status of slavery under their whips. Power. Power. We've offered proof. We've shown our own government in Washington the plot to have Senators elected directly by the electorate, so that those Senators can be controlled and made as impotent as the Congress is going to be made. We've shown them proof that the conspiracy is going to push through a federal income tax—despite the fact that the U. S. Supreme

Court has ruled such a tax unconstitutional at least half a dozen times. We've quoted Lord Acton to them—'the power to tax is the power to destroy.' We've quoted Thomas Jefferson until we were hoarse: once a national tax is levied on the people, that country is doomed.

"Yes. What have all our efforts and money achieved? Nothing. If the American people allow the direct election of Senators and the imposition of a permanent federal income tax, then, son, the hell with them. The hell with the whole —— world."

He raised his glass. " '*Ave, Caesar, morituri te salutamus.*' "

"You don't think we have a chance to stop these would-be Caesars in their tracks?"

"No, son, I don't."

"If it's all futile, why did you want me to join the Scardo Society?"

Walter stood up abruptly and began to pace up and down on the Aubusson rug in the office, his head bent, his face brooding. "I'm not a young man any longer. I hope young men like you will fight for a delaying action. I want to live out the rest of my life in comparative peace. And there's always the preposterous possibility that we can arouse the people in time, though I doubt it."

He shook his head. "By the way, did the boys talk of that private banking plan of theirs, a Federal Reserve System?"

"Yes, they spoke of it. Taking away the power of Congress to coin money, as the Constitution directed. Who are Congressmen? they asked me in fatherly tones. Many of them are ignorant farmers from the Midwest, small pols who once ran grocery stores or butcher shops, former mayors, and insignificant lawyers. Who are such, they asked me, to be given the sole power of coining our currency, when we are a rapidly growing nation? We need educated bankers, shrewd men who understand the international and national currencies, to 'guide our economic future.' "

"Yes," said Walter in a grim voice, "they are quite right. They are going to do it, son. The people believe in slogans, with the assurance that their 'betters' know more about their needs and wants and aspirations than they do. Well, Rome died that way, and Greece and Egypt, not to mention Ninevah and Tyre."

"Caesars never die, do they?"

"No, son. The ancient lust for power was born in the human race. It is in our blood. As Solomon said, there is nothing new under the sun. Human nature never changes; it never will. That is our curse."

The winter sky was almost black now and the winter storm was screaming and hissing at the windows. The fire roared suddenly on the hearth, as if distressed and aroused. Walter and Jeremy sipped their drinks in a short silence, pondering. Then Walter said, "I am afraid Americans have lost their manhood and their valor. Oh, here and there there are still some signs of it, but we are getting womanish. The small comforts and cozinesses of life are now beginning to be of the utmost importance to us, and the little amusements. I have heard that there is some talk of 'love' in the schoolrooms of this nation, instead of duty and responsibility. That is fatal. There was never much love in this world, but cowardice is growing. At one time in our history the humblest farmer and small shopkeeper avidly read the *Federalist Papers,* and understood them. Now college students can hardly interpret them. Are we growing more stupid, Jerry? Men have forgot how to be brave, stern, masters of their government, their families, and their lives: willing to die for their country, their God above all. Now men want safety and happiness."

"Perhaps we should support the solid strength of the workingman, who still controls his government, his wife and his children, and should halt growth of what I call the lumpen intelligentsia," said Jeremy. "The sterility of the so-called 'intellectuals'! Who listens to them?"

"The rabble," said Walter. "The rabble that destroyed Rome."

"Yes," said Jeremy. "Yes, they will destroy us as well. Didn't Lincoln prophesy this? Yes."

"But governments will use them—the sort of men you met today, Jerry."

"It's an old story, Uncle Walter. Nations never learn."

"When you were an assistant to the District Attorney," Walter continued, "you succeeded in prosecuting those bomb throwers, although Frank opposed you with tears and sobs for 'the poor workers,' as though he knows anything about workers."

"He mistakes the workers for the street rabble. But the

boys at the Scardo Society don't! They congratulated me on my prosecution. What bastards they are! They have no particular race, no nation, no allegiances. They told me they think exactly as I do about 'the people.' I could have given them an argument then, saying their semantics were not mine, but I refrained. I wanted to know more about them. You are right. They despise men like Frank. But they use them, the lumpen intelligentsia."

"Who were those bomb throwers, anyway?" Walter asked.

"Who knows? But someone hired them. You can be sure that they were not the real workers of America. One was given the death sentence for murder; the two others were sent up for life. Frank is going to appeal."

"I suppose so," said Walter in a tired voice.

"Frank won't win. The judge is hard-nosed, and a respected man."

He looked at his watch. "It's time to go home, Uncle Walter. I have to dress, and so do you, for the dinner party."

Walter turned slowly from the fire. "How is my dear Ellen?"

"Well, she's pregnant—"

"Should I congratulate you or commiserate with you, son?"

Jeremy laughed. "Ask me that in twenty years. This is a hell of a world to be bringing children into." He became serious. "I worry about Ellen. Her trustfulness, her naïveté, sometimes alarm me, though they are the qualities which I most admire. My will is drawn so it will protect her from the wolves. As you know, she is really extremely intelligent, but her intelligence is sometimes clouded by what she calls 'love and trust.' She isn't afflicted with that new disease which some people call 'compassion.' She knows what the world is, God knows. But she has pity, and she has strength, and some iron in her soul. Let's hope 'love' doesn't betray and destroy her, as it has done so many others."

"Your friends like her?"

"The men do. Their wives don't. They don't understand simplicity and honesty. Few women do. So they think Ellen is either a fool or a hypocrite. Or her bluntness outrages them when she detects some falseness. Women are very devious and elliptical, aren't they—the majority?"

"Indeed," said Walter. "They're agitating for the vote now. I'd do the same to them, if they ever get the vote, as I'd do to male voters today—demand they prove some intelligence and objectivity when it comes to politics."

Jeremy called for his carriage, and they wrapped themselves in their furlined coats and put on their heavy gloves, and went through the warmth of offices to the street. Walter said, as wind and snow assaulted him and his nephew, "I'm sure you're convinced now, Jerry, that no President of the United States of America can henceforth be elected without the agreement of the Scardo Society and the Committee for Foreign Studies. If he opposes them he will be assassinated or impeached or otherwise be driven from office."

"I wonder if President Teddy knows who got him his office?"

"Perhaps. Perhaps not. I only know he is beginning to sound like them, especially when it comes to execrating Kaiser Wilhelm of Germany, whom he once greatly admired and visited. I have heard that the Kaiser knows, but who can tell?"

Ellen's music teacher said to her, "Madam, you have a genius with the piano, but you must practice."

Ellen said, with the note of apology in her voice which was habitual and guilty, "I know I am very stupid, but I am trying. I hear such sounds from the piano—when I am not playing on it. Such sounds!" She sighed and looked at her teacher with eyes so luminous that he was deeply touched and felt tears in his own eyes.

"Madam Porter," he said, "that is the soul of an artist, to hear and see and feel and taste and touch that which is not evident to grosser minds and souls. Sad it is that an artist cannot speak of these things to others, except to those of his own kind, and they are very few. What we hear and see in silence is much greater than what others hear and see in actual sight and harmony. Sometimes it is too much for the spirit to bear, for we are isolated in a desert of the mediocre. We are only grateful if they do not ridicule us. Is that not so?"

But Ellen's humility interposed between her understanding and what her teacher, Herr Solzer, had said. She became depressed. "I just want people to like me and accept me," she murmured. He threw up his hands in despair.

"The only understanding and acceptance is with the *Gross Gott,* madam! Let Him be your comfort. He is the one Refuge."

"My husband is my refuge," she replied, and smiled with tenderness and joy.

"He is only mortal, madam."

"And so am I." Her cheek dimpled. "I don't aspire to anything, Herr Solzer, except pleasing him."

He looked at her intently, and turned away. What a waste it was to give women talent or genius! They submerged these things in a dedication to a man. But did not St. Paul and Bismarck urge such an attitude for women? Herr Solzer did not agree either with St. Paul or Bismarck. He believed that gifted women should never marry, though they should have lovers. This lady—how beautiful, how gifted! She should live in a gilded palace and not in a brownstone house in New York. She should be adulated by multitudes both for her loveliness and for her perceptions. Instead she was only a wife. Herr Solzer might be German, with a Prussian's rigidity, but he worshipped art, which was also a German trait.

He suspected that Ellen was pregnant. What a waste, too! Genius never bestowed its brilliance on offspring. It was a great mystery. Physical attributes and characteristic features—yes. But never genius, never talent. He had known many geniuses in the sciences and arts and philosophy, but their children were drab and unendowed, if envious and resentful of their parents, and sometimes alarmingly dangerous out of their jealousy. Many a genius had been exploited and defamed by his children, and even murdered. Humanity was something to be feared more than a tiger, or even governments.

He said with severity to conceal his agitation, "Madam, you will now practice Debussy's *Nocturne,* and you will not play by the ear but the music. Tomorrow, I expect much better than today."

"I will try," said Ellen, and he was more despairing than ever. "I never touched a piano, Herr Solzer, until four months ago, and you must be patient with me."

He kissed her hand and left, shaking his head.

Ellen looked at her piano in the great dim music room, which was all brown and gold and ivory paneling with large arched windows suffocated with lace and pale blue velvet, and Aubusson rugs and mirrors. She was tired. She had spent hours with her tutor this morning, and he was very rigorous and had left her considerable work to be done tonight. If he found her naturally gifted in the matter of French and German, and swift of mind in other subjects, he never praised her. "Mrs. Porter," he had said once, and ponderously, "there are vast discrepancies in your education."

"I know," she said with regret. "I know very little. But I am really trying. I must be a proper wife for my husband."

Sometimes she felt hopeless. She was so stupid, no matter her efforts. Jeremy praised her and was delighted with her, but she believed that was so because he loved her. She lived in a constant tension of hoping to gratify him and when he fondled her and found her delicious she was afraid that he was only being patient with her out of natural charity. He was even tolerant of her "condition," no matter her morning sickness, and she could not be thankful enough for his solicitude. When he told her he was overjoyed at the thought of a child she wanted to cry; he was so good.

She went listlessly to one of the windows and looked down at the street, which was swirling with gray snow and the winter wind. There were few carriages about, and fewer pedestrians, and they scurried quickly along the pavement. It was twilight, and the gaslighter was scuttling up and down lighting the streetlamps, which burst into blowing golden light. Then her volatile spirits rose; she loved New York for all she had never known a city before. There was something infinitely exciting here, something always in movement, and electric. The tall ebony clock on the upper landing boomed five in silver notes, and she ran downstairs to the basement kitchen, which was warm and bright and huge, with walls of red brick and brick underfoot. The kitchen was full of fascinating odors and steam. Cuthbert was poised over the iron-and-brick stove, with a fluttering housemaid in attendance; she was peeling vegetables under Cuthbert's stern surveillance.

He looked at Ellen and his grave elderly face became suffused with pleasure and affection. "Mrs. Porter," he said, "do you not think it is time to put on the roast beef?"

"Yes, of course," she said, in that tone of apology which always touched him with its poignancy. "And the roast onions, sliced, underneath, a thick layer of them, and lots of butter and thyme and a little garlic rubbed on all sides."

"No one," said Cuthbert, "can roast beef as you do, Mrs. Porter. I think the oven is hot enough now, and I will turn down the gas a little."

"Yes," said Ellen, examining the beef seriously and touching it lightly with one finger. "It is very tender, isn't it? Do you think it is enough for eight people, and the rest of the household? I think, three hours?"

Cuthbert looked judicious. "Only twelve pounds. Two hours and a half, Mrs. Porter. That should do. And no salt or pepper until half roasted?"

"Yes," said Ellen. She looked about the kitchen and sighed blissfully. "Mr. Walter Porter is coming for dinner, as you know, Cuthbert. Why do gentlemen always like roast beef so much? I prefer lamb or chicken. Are the oysters good? And"—she looked apologetic again—"would you please put a dash of powdered cloves in the tomato bisque—just a dash?"

"Very good, Mrs. Porter. And the oysters? How do you prefer them?"

"Just with lemon juice, on a bed of ice, Cuthbert. But you must select the wines. I know so little. Are the lobsters very fresh? Good. And the melons from Florida? Imagine, fruit in the winter in New York! What will there be for dessert?"

"A chocolate mousse, an angel cake, a chestnut glacé, parfait, and assorted pastries. A little austere, perhaps, but you prefer simple dinners, do you not, Mrs. Porter? Yes. I have prepared the sauce, green and pungent, for the lobsters, according to your suggestion. They are rather small, only three pounds apiece, but after the appetizers of oysters and the bisque with the sour cream and sherry, and the salad, the lobsters should be enough before the rest of the dinner, the meat and roasted potatoes and brussels sprouts and asparagus and artichokes and hot rolls and gravy. Perhaps we should have had some cold shrimp, too? They are in the icebox."

Ellen considered. She was always fearful that her dinners were too restricted, too plain. "Perhaps the shrimp with the lobsters? Yes, I think so. Gentlemen are always so hungry."

"And the ladies, too," said Cuthbert with a smile. "They all want to resemble Miss Lillian Russell, who is somewhat plushy." He looked at Ellen's slim figure with approval. She wore an afternoon tea gown of apricot velvet, which matched and enhanced her cheeks and lips, and it flowed about her, glistening, revealing glimpses of delicate lace at the throat and wrists.

Ellen became depressed again at the thought of the ladies. Gentlemen were much kinder to her, but ladies were wary and had sharp critical eyes which were not deluded by her. She knew that they considered her vulgar in appearance, even tawdry and garish. No matter how much French powder she patted on her face her color intruded, like a peasant's. Her hair was deplorable, too, always rioting out from her pompadour into little curls and tendrils, in spite of her maid's efforts. Jeremy would frequently and teasingly pull those curls and tendrils, even at the table. It was evident, to her, that he considered them childish and unsophisticated.

Seeing her downcast face, Cuthbert said, "Mr. Diamond Jim Brady would enjoy this dinner, Mrs. Porter."

All at once Ellen was nauseated and bile rose in her throat, and she caught at Cuthbert's arm, while the housemaid stared curiously. "I think I am a little dizzy," said Ellen. Cuthbert led her to a kitchen chair and watched her with sincere concern. He motioned to the housemaid. "A little brandy, Mabel," he said. He returned to Ellen; he knew she was pregnant. "To settle the stomach, Mrs. Porter. You study and work too hard, perhaps."

"But I accomplish nothing," Ellen gulped in a dismal voice. "I am such a disappointment to Mr. Porter."

Cuthbert raised his eyebrows. "You are a joy to him, madam, a joy. I have known him a long time, and I perceive what he thinks."

Ellen accepted the brandy, which she loathed, and sipped at it, holding it in a shaking hand. But it warmed her and the nausea began to retreat. She thought, distressfully, of the coming child. Would it be as unattractive as she was, and as stupid? She could not endure the thought of Jeremy's dismay. She hoped for a son who would resemble his father. "You are very kind, Cuthbert," she said. She stood up, somewhat weakly. "And now I must visit my aunt. Did she eat her supper?"

"Yes, Mrs. Porter. It was only a small cup of broth and a broiled fish and browned potatoes and a salad, and some mashed turnips and cold ham and tea and some pound cake with the caraway seeds she likes. A small supper, but she seemed to enjoy it."

"Thank you, Cuthbert. You are so kind." Ellen moved towards the kitchen door with an anxious expression, thinking of her aunt. The doctor visited May every week and was very comforting to Ellen. "One must remember her pain," he had told her. "But that new Aspirin is very helpful. One must not listen too much to the complaints of women her age; it is too melancholy. We can only console, endure—" But his comfort invariably disappeared when Ellen entered the tiny elevator which would lift her to the fourth floor, where May had a warm and pleasant suite of her own, with a nurse in attendance day and night, and a fireplace always filled with crackling red embers, and a fine view. There was even a phonograph with wax cylinders and ballads, wistful and sentimental and sorrowful—May's favorites.

By the time the elevator had creaked to a halt on the fourth floor Ellen was guilty again, and despondent. She had caused Aunt May so much unhappiness, so much discontent, by marrying Jeremy. Nothing pleased her; nothing assuaged her misery. She felt deprived of her normal estate, which was suffering and labor and meek acceptance of fate. In that estate she had experienced a kind of exaltation, even if it had sometimes been touched by angry rebelliousness. In her class she had been important in wretchedness. Now she was not important at all, and had no genuine status. She was only the dependent of a man she still feared and distrusted and disliked; she believed he considered her a nuisance. Her memories of Mrs. Eccles' house were her only pleasure. Oh, if Ellen had been sensible! But Ellen was as heedless and flighty as had been Mary, and May never doubted that the girl had a disastrous future which might descend at any moment, bringing calamity to both of them. It just wasn't "natural" for Ellen to pretend to be a great lady in this house. Half with terror, half with anticipation, May awaited the day of rout, when she could say, with tears, "I told you so, Ellen, I told you so!" The girl's obvious bliss did not delude her or disperse the terror. In fact, May resented that bliss. She felt robbed, and frustrated. Each morning she thought forebodingly, "Perhaps this will be the day." When the "day" passed serenely, she was chagrined, and even more foreboding. She would sometimes hear Jeremy's distant laugh and she thought it derisive of Ellen. She would hear the murmur of men's genial voices as they spoke to Ellen and she was convinced they were mocking. Ellen, in that great dining room all glittering crystal and elegant mahogany and silken rugs and silver and enormous chandelier and glowing velvet and lace—May cringed for Ellen. She would often whimper in sympathy. When Ellen could not understand her aunt's remarks May was angered at the girl's obtuseness. After all, Ellen was eighteen and a woman, and she should not be so dense! But then, Mary had been a fool, too, and had dreamed of being a fine lady.

When Ellen would appear, for her aunt's approval, in some gorgeous creation of Worth's, May would say, "It's not for you, dear, not for you. You're not gentlefolk, Ellen. And that diamond necklace! It looks like paste on you, really it does. It needs good blood to set such things off, and you don't have it." When she would see that Ellen became melancholy under this criticism she would feel, not self-reproach, but sadness. She dreaded, if hoped for, the day when Ellen would "realize, and come to her senses." She never relinquished the happy thought of returning, chastened, to Mrs. Eccles' house.

At times she would say to her niece, "Have you and Mr. Jeremy been quarreling? I thought I heard him speaking real mean to you last night on your way to bed." Ellen had replied, "Oh, Jeremy was speaking about one of our guests; an odious woman. He had overheard her say to another woman that I looked like a chorus girl." Ellen had laughed but May had said with significance, "You see?"

"Her husband, though, was very kind and attentive and the other gentlemen persuaded me to play a little Chopin and Jeremy was very proud. I made only one mistake."

"I heard you bellowing last night while you played on that piano."

"I know my voice isn't very good, though my teacher says it is; he is very nice. But the gentlemen applauded.

I'm sorry I disturbed you, Auntie. You should tell the nurse to keep the door shut."

May did not know that she was attempting to destroy Ellen. She truly believed she was rescuing her, or "hardening" her for the inevitable catastrophe. Then she also deplored Ellen's "looking for the limelight." It wasn't "proper" for a girl like Ellen, who was only a servant, no matter the draped Worth gowns and the jewels and the perfumes and the scented soap and the beaded slippers, not to speak of the gemmed combs and earrings and bracelets. It was even less "proper" for Ellen to have servants of her own, Cuthbert and the housekeeper and two housemaids, and a carriage with two splendid black horses. When Ellen appeared in a long sable coat May had shuddered and had said, "That would keep us for years, Ellen, years. You'd better be careful of it; one never knows."

"Oh, I don't think Jeremy will ever go bankrupt," Ellen had said, smiling. She never suspected her aunt's pathetic motives, though Jeremy did, with an anger he did not express to Ellen. Ellen often repeated these conversations to him, with her gentle humor, explaining that "dear Aunt May just cannot accustom herself to all these dazzling things. We must be patient with her, my darling." Jeremy usually understood, for he was subtle and was aware of human nature, and did not, even to himself, accuse May of a malice she did not honestly feel. He knew that it was only fear for Ellen that impelled her, and he often, obliquely, tried to reassure the poor woman. That only made her mistrust him more. "He's trying to pull the wool over my eyes," she would tell herself. "But I'm not dippy, as he thinks." She would stare at him with sullen suspicions as he spoke.

She was sitting, huddled, by the fire in her small sitting room, clad in a very expensive dark-blue woolen robe, when Ellen entered tonight. She had never explored the Bible before, but now Ellen's old Bible lay on her emaciated knees, open. She constantly searched for hortatory passages to read to Ellen, especially about "the daughters of Jerusalem," happy damsels (though condemned by the severe prophets) who arrayed themselves in silks and bangles and earrings and cosmetics, and "walked haughtily" with bells on their dainty ankles. On hearing these passages Ellen puzzled why the grim

prophets were so stern in denouncing joy and beauty. Did
one have to live in sackcloth and ashes and wear a somber
face to gain the approval of God? Ellen had begun to
doubt that, for was not God the Creator of all loveliness
and had He not demanded of Moses the utmost embellishments for His Temple, including music? Had not
David said, "Make a joyful noise unto the Lord"? Had
not Christ remarked on the splendor of the lilies of the
field? Ellen, though she said nothing to her aunt, had
begun to doubt the Puritan imperative of dullness and
lack of grace and charm. This doubt was immediately
followed by a surge of guilt, and a conviction of wickedness. Ugliness and lightlessness, it would seem, were
marks of holiness.

Once she timidly mentioned her guilt to Jeremy, who
had laughed and kissed her and had told her to "consider"
the gorgeousness of the peacock and the elegance of the
swan and the bursting redbud trees and dogwood in the
spring, and the happy laughter of winter-released brooks
and rivers. "All things laugh and rejoice in their beauty,"
he had told her. "And so should you, my sweet conscience-
stricken imbecile." He reminded her of the ascending
cathedrals of Europe, the temples of God, and the fire of
gems, and the glory of the mountains and the color of
seas and skies. "Does your aunt consider them, 'works
of the Devil'?" Ellen sometimes thought it was possible.
But still, when reproached by May for "ostentation" and
"fine arrayal," she became dejected again.

She wondered, this evening, what adjuration May had
prepared for her from the Bible. May looked up sourly
when Ellen entered her sitting room, and said, "Ellen,
that apricot color isn't nice on a married woman all of
eighteen. You should wear more 'sober garb.'" She
looked dissatisfied and ominous. "And you're looking
washed out lately, too. Is there something the matter?"
she asked, almost in a tone of hope.

Ellen had not told her aunt of her pregnancy. She was
not certain why. Would it be indelicate? She had a vague
intuition that May would disapprove, as she did herself,
for Ellen never forgot the evil and vindictive natures of
children, and their instinctive viciousness and cruelty. She
had not blamed it on their parents, when she had lived in
Preston, for even the most slatternly had shouted at their
offspring in anger when they had persecuted Ellen too

much on her way home from school or church or employment. Besides, did not the Bible admonish that man was evil from his birth and wicked from his youth? So Ellen, remembering, was often filled with disquiet concerning her own child now stirring in her womb. Would it become the enemy of Jeremy? Would it attempt to destroy and exploit him, as so many children did to their parents? Would it bring him unhappiness? When the doctor, to whom Jeremy had taken her, told her kindly that she was pregnant she had burst into tears. In her innocence she had not quite understood how marriage often led to children. Both Jeremy and the doctor had been astonished at her response to the news, but she could only stammer, "I hope—I hope—it won't hurt my husband." "You should be happy," the two men had informed her. But Ellen, remembering her childhood, was not happy. Once she even fiercely thought, "If it injures Jeremy—I will kill it!"

"I'm feeling quite well," said Ellen, tonight, to her aunt. "Quite well. How are you today, Auntie?"

The nurse, a Miss Ember of more than lavish proportions, and a woman of about forty, said with heartiness, "We are doing very well, Mrs. Porter! We ate a good supper, and enjoyed every morsel."

"You mean, you did," said May, and then was frightened, for Miss Ember was "superior to" her in station, so she said with apology, "I didn't mean that, ma'am. I did like my supper, though I have no appetite." Miss Ember continued to beam but she felt inner scorn. May had confided too much to her, in her search for consolation for leaving Mrs. Eccles' house. So Miss Ember also felt some condescension for Ellen, too, and was less polite than customary. May had repeatedly mentioned to Miss Ember—in that pathetic search for understanding—that Ellen was "only a servant, really, and out of her station, and someday she will regret it." Consequently, Miss Ember was often impatient and overweening when Ellen questioned her about May's condition. "I am sure, madam," she would say with hauteur, "that me and the doctor know what her condition is, and we need no other advice."

To Jeremy she was obsequious. But she snickered about "the mistress," in Cuthbert's absence, to the other servants. Had Cuthbert not been a disciplinarian and in charge of the house and had he not had a strict knowledge of "dependents," the household would have degenerated into chaos, with the servants in arrogant authority, and their mistress in terror. Cuthbert, fortunately, knew very much about human nature and its tendency to exigency and malice, and so did Jeremy.

May set up her usual complaints of pain and sleeplessness before Ellen, as her niece sat near her, somewhat fixedly smiling. "I suppose you'll have a lot of noise downstairs tonight, when I am trying to sleep," said May.

"You must keep your bedroom door shut, Auntie," said Ellen. "We'll try to be very quiet. After all, it is four floors below."

"And you'll be crashing on the piano again," said May. "Such horrible noise! You shouldn't try to attract unbecoming attention, Ellen, from your superiors. That's vulgar." Miss Ember smiled nastily, and preened, as if in agreement.

May said, "Hasn't Mrs. Porter accepted you yet, Ellen?"

Ellen said, with her gentle humor, "Jeremy hasn't accepted his mother, Aunt May."

"How sinful! His mother! 'Honor thy father and thy mother that thy day may be long in the land which the Lord thy God hath given thee.'"

"I think parents should honor their children, too," said Ellen. "That is, if the children are worthy of being honored." She added, somewhat forlornly, "But most children aren't worth honoring are they?" She had spoken softly, as if to herself, fearing again for Jeremy and fearing the enmity of his child. She continued, "Jeremy says his mother must now make the second move, as he has made one before."

"But Mrs. Porter is quality, Ellen! And you're not. You should humble yourself, and beg her pardon."

"For Jeremy loving me?" Ellen's usually controlled voice rose a little.

"You know exactly what I mean, Ellen," said May with severity. "For you marrying him, against his parents' wishes."

"Jeremy asks no one's permission," Ellen replied. She was suddenly very tired. The snug room almost suffocated her; the fire was too hot and close. She wanted to leave but her conscience would not let her. She was nauseated again and she felt heavy and weak. Miss Ember was watching her with smiling animosity. Such a gaudy thing! She's used less from the paintbox today, it seemed.

"I hope you are wearing something in keeping, and respectable tonight," said May, with that ever-present reproof in her thin voice.

"My black spangled velvet, and my diamonds. Jeremy wishes it."

"You look like a cheap actress in it, Ellen! Why not your nice brown wool, draped quietly, your day dress, and a little brooch?"

"Jeremy would disapprove," said Ellen.

"At your age, and married state, Ellen, you should dress more seemingly."

Ellen pushed herself wearily to her feet. "I try to please Jeremy," she said. May looked at her a little slyly. "I had a nice letter from Mrs. Eccles today, Ellen."

"Good," said the girl, drawing her apricot velvet gown about her.

"She's delighted that Mr. Francis is now established in New York."

Ellen was silent. May sighed, "If only we had stayed in Wheatfield, where we belong! Contented, peaceful, doing our duty. And Mr. Francis watching over us."

Again Ellen felt suffocated. She had not told Jeremy of Francis' visit to her yesterday, and she had asked Cuthbert not to mention it, either. She knew that Jeremy would not have liked it in the least, and her chronic guilt made her nervous. Why Jeremy would have been annoyed she was not quite certain. But in some way she intuitively guessed that Francis had relied on her keeping silent concerning his visit. She had sensed it in his lowered voice and the significant way he had of glancing over his shoulder, as if afraid of eavesdroppers or of Jeremy himself suddenly appearing.

As she went down to the third floor to her rooms to dress—in the warm and dusky twilight enhanced by softly lighted lamps here and there—she thought of that visit. Her maid had laid out her gown for the evening and her jewelry, and the snow hissed against the windows and the wind savaged the glass. A fire danced on the black marble hearth. The rooms were large and well proportioned and beguiling with delicate furniture in the French style and with mirrors, and with thick oriental rugs underfoot.

Usually Ellen rejoiced 'n such luxury, in gratitude and delight. Tonight she did not see it.

She had been practicing on the black and gleaming grand piano which Jeremy had bought for her when Cuthbert came in with Francis' card, and a scribbled message on the back: "Please see me for a few moments, Ellen." Ellen's first emotion was pleasure that he had remembered her out of his kindness. Her next was uneasiness, as she thought of Jeremy, who detested his cousin. But surely he would not resent Francis' remembrance of his protégée? So Ellen asked Cuthbert to show Mr. Porter into the library, where they would have sherry and biscuits. She remembered that Francis abhorred whiskey and preferred only wine.

She went into the library in her afternoon tea robe of pale-blue velvet and lace, holding out her hands in shy welcome to Francis. The dun winter light, glowering through the windows, made him appear very austere and rigid as he took her hands and bowed a little over them, stiffly. But his eyes, smaller now behind his pince-nez, studied her with sharpness and she became uncomfortable and bewildered.

"How kind of you to come, Mr. Francis," she had murmured, indicating a chair for him. "I am happy to see you."

"I am happy to see you, too, Ellen," he said in a tone that indicated mysterious reproach. She was suddenly a presumptuous servant again in the Porter house. She stood in the middle of the beautiful rug, not knowing what to say next—while Cuthbert discreetly poured sherry, arranged small napkins, and put down the silver salver of biscuits. Then Cuthbert, who saw so much and understood so much, drew out a chair for her near the fire. She sat down, feeling helpless and out of place, and looked at Francis earnestly.

"I have heard you are now living and practicing in New York, Mr. Francis," she said. "I am glad—if you are glad."

I am here because you are here, he thought, and because I must protect you. His expression became more severely pompous as he sipped his sherry. He said, "I, too, have ambitions, Ellen."

"No doubt," she murmured. "All gentlemen are ambitious, aren't they?"

"Not always in the right direction," he said in a sentи tone, and she knew at once, to her dismay, that he meant Jeremy, and then she was vexed. She had never understood the hostility between the cousins, nor did she know that she was the cause of the old hostility becoming malign and full of absolute hatred. Jeremy had, some months ago, guessed that Francis was in love with Ellen and he had laughed to himself with angry ridicule, and even umbrage that "such an anchovy, such a hypocritical fraud," had even dared to look at Ellen. To Jeremy, this had been an insult, not a compliment, to his wife.

For some reason the gentle-spirited girl felt a sudden irritation with Francis, and had to remind herself vigorously of his solicitude to obliterate her exasperation which had arisen because of his new pomposity and intimations of baffling criticism of herself. Why, too, did he look at her so strangely, with a mingling of affection and rebuke? More and more she was beginning to feel like an intruder in her own house, an insolent intruder whose very presence was obtrusive and unacceptable.

Acutely perceptive of others' emotions towards himself, Francis saw that the girl was gazing at him with those lustrous blue eyes of hers in a most peculiar fashion. He smiled placatingly. "I came because I wanted to see that all was well with you, Ellen. My aunt, I am sorry to say, is very concerned. She had a letter from your aunt which was slightly odd—"

"In what way?" Ellen said, astonished.

"Well, I am really breaking a confidence—I saw the letter myself. Your aunt thinks you are homesick for Wheatfield, and not too happy in New York. She also wrote that she, too, is homesick, and longs for my aunt's house."

"Good heavens," said Ellen, and colored with annoyance. "That is really too bad of Aunt May. She has the most wonderful care here, with a private nurse, and has her own suite of rooms and everything she could desire."

"Perhaps she prefers something else," said Francis. When Ellen only stared at him, her beautiful lips tightening somewhat, he added, "After all, New York must seem very alien to her. Does it seem alien to you, Ellen?"

She never really detected condescension in his voice and manner towards her, she only knew discomfort. "No,

Mr. Francis. I love New York. I am exceedingly happy here, and my days are busy with tutors and music teachers and I am learning to dance, and I have a teacher of voice, also."

He raised his pale eyebrows and smiled with slight superciliousness, as if he were highly if politely amused. "And you like all that, Ellen?"

"I love it." She disliked sherry but now she sipped it to escape that intimated amusement. Why should I feel so gauche? she asked herself.

"You look a little pale, even wan. Too much confinement perhaps?"

"Indeed not, Mr. Francis! I go for long drives almost every day, often to the art galleries, the museums, the opera, concerts—with a new woman friend, the wife of one of Jeremy's attorneys. And Jeremy and I go out frequently to dinner, and entertain."

"But you seem somewhat subdued, Ellen." Again, that faint amusement, tinged once more with implied rebuke.

She could not tell him she was enceinte. That would be most indelicate. "I am not in the least subdued," she said. "But, after all, I am now eighteen, and no longer the child you knew, Mr. Francis."

Now he was annoyed; he truly thought her saucy and was speaking out of her "place," to him, who was a gentleman. Why, the girl was actually being impertinent! So much for those who rise out of their station, when they should have been happy in their proper milieu. His thoughts became confused; he wanted to reproach her meaningly and he also wanted to take her in his arms and kiss and fondle her and tell her of his love for her. The very thought that Jeremy Porter embraced her intimately sickened him both mentally and physically. He shut his eyes for an instant, to banish the lascivious vision, then he opened them to look at her pliant body, the new swelling of her breasts, the outline of round thigh; for a second or two his eyes lingered at her pelvic area under that flowing velvet. He imagined her in bed with him, and his face changed so eloquently that she said in haste, "Is there something wrong, Mr. Francis?"

"No. No, nothing, Ellen. It is just that I have been worried about you. After all, you were, in a manner of speaking, in my care in Wheatfield. I wanted to be sure you were—contented." (Her breast rose and swelled softly with her breath. He had an almost uncontrollable urge to go to her and enclose one of those breasts with his hand, to reveal, to kiss it.)

Ellen was smiling with deep tenderness, for she thought of Jeremy. "I am very contented, Mr. Francis. And thank you. More sherry?"

"No, thank you, Ellen." He spoke very graciously as one speaks to a young and appreciated servant, who was being very attentive, even if with "exaggeratedly genteel airs." He hesitated. "Ellen, I should like to visit you occasionally, in the afternoon, in confidence, so that I can reassure my aunt."

Ellen spoke with new directness. "You mean, Mr. Francis, that you do not want me to mention your visit, or visits, to my husband?"

Above all things Francis detested open confrontations, directness, and unequivocal approaches. He thought them crude and even barbarous. Then he reminded himself that he must be patient with this ignorant girl who came of such a coarse and plebeian background. Tutors and teachers, indeed! How ridiculous.

He said, with a dainty dropping of his eyelids, "You know, Ellen, that Jeremy and I do not have anything in common, in sympathy, though we are cousins. He would not understand why I was concerned about you, which I am. He is a very blunt man—"

Again Ellen had to remind herself strongly that he had always been so kind to her, and that she had some fondness for him, and that he was only anxious about her. He had been the first person in her life, with the exception of her aunt, who had shown her solicitude. He had given her her first pair of kid gloves; he had been like a brother to her.

"I don't like to deceive Jeremy," she said. She paused and considered, while he watched her and lusted for her young body and urgently desired to kiss her soft open mouth. "Well. I don't want to disturb him, either, though I don't see why he should object to your kindness towards me, Mr. Francis. I don't think he would; he might even be pleased. Still, if you'd rather I'd not mention it—"

"I'd rather you would not, at least for now, Ellen. Later, perhaps. Jeremy and I sometimes encounter each other in the courts; I am hoping we may become more congenial as time goes by."

Ellen nodded, though with a certain disquietude and the old guilt. Love and trust—she was always forgetting. Mr. Francis certainly deserved both love and trust and here she was, nearly insulting him in spite of what she owed him. Francis had an almost feminine perceptiveness, though he customarily disliked women. He caught the import of her expression, and so he said, "You must remember, my dear, that it is only my concern for you, and the concern of my aunt, which brought me here."

"Yes, I know, and I can't thank you enough. Please tell Mrs. Eccles that Aunt May is much better than she was in Wheatfield, and that most of the time she is without pain, and that I am very happy. Aunt May has every attention that money can buy, and affection give her." He noticed, with fresh vexation, that her diction and manner had greatly improved, almost miraculously so in these few months, and he thought it all pretension.

He stood up and she stood with him, guiltily thankful that he was leaving. She gave him her hand, and then he could not help it: he leaned towards her and kissed her velvety lips and the contact with her mouth almost made him cry out. But he spoke in a tight and restrained voice. "Goodbye, Ellen, for just now. I will call again soon, if I may."

"Please do," she said. She had been taken aback by the kiss, and then again reminded herself that he felt towards her like an elder brother, and she was touched. He left her for the waiting hack outside; the street was gray and leadenly shining with sleet, and he shivered. He detested New York. The long rows of brownstone houses revolted him; he thought they frowned on him with hostility. The door shut gently behind him. He went to his small and inexpensive apartment on West Twentieth Street, also in a brownstone house, which had recently been converted from a private mansion to "gentlemen's establishments," much to the consternation of neighbors. After seeing Ellen, and feeling still the heat of contact with her, the prospect of returning to his apartment was singularly bleak and lonely, and he ached with an unfamiliar despair.

Cuthbert had been discreetly listening and watching in the background, and he had been smiling a little to himself. He was not deluded. He came into the library, where Ellen stood aimlessly before the fire, and he said, "Is there anything else, madam?"

"No. No, Cuthbert. That gentleman is Mr. Porter's cousin."

"So I gathered. There is not much resemblance, is there?"

"No, indeed," Ellen replied with such fervor that Cuthbert smiled under his nose. She hesitated. "Cuthbert —it seems—well, it seems—that Mr. Francis Porter, and my husband, are not—are not—"

"*En rapport*, madam? I guessed that, in some manner. You do not wish me to mention that you had a visitor today?"

Ellen felt somewhat soiled. "That is it, Cuthbert," she said, and hurried from the room, almost running.

She remembered that as she absently dressed for the dinner she and Jeremy was giving tonight. She thought of Walter Porter, Francis' father. She did not know why she experienced such a sudden uplift of relief, such a happy anticipation. She was so very fond of him, and he insisted that she call him "Uncle Walter," and he would look at her with an admiration she could not understand, and a deep affection.

"Madam is looking very beautiful tonight," said Clarisse, the maid, fastening the last button on the black velvet gown. She took up the bottle of Worth scent and sprayed Ellen's arms and throat with it.

Ellen laughed. "Madam is feeling a little confused, Clarisse."

She heard Jeremy's step on the stairs—he rarely used the elevator. She ran to him joyfully and threw herself into his arms and said, "Oh, my darling, how happy I am to see you, how happy!"

"Well, I haven't been away for years," he said, holding her tightly and rubbing his lips over her blazing hair. "Why are you so exuberant?"

"It's just—it's just that God is so good to me, as little as I deserve it," she said. She thought of Wheatfield, and she shivered, and clung tighter to Jeremy, looking up in his taut dark face with adoration.

"You must really let me go, Ellen," he said, and wondered at her unusual excitement. "Uncle Walter is down in the library waiting for us, and drinking up my best Scotch whiskey. And I have to dress. As always, you look divine, and I'd rather go to bed with you this instant than entertain guests."

She blushed and whispered in his ear, "And so would I." She looked about her beautiful boudoir and sighed with rapture.

13

The youngish woman who had become Ellen's best friend in New York was the wife of a partner in Jeremy's law firm. She had long been in love with Jeremy Porter, a fact he had soon discerned and, being a gentleman, had affected to be entirely unaware of, and so had spared the lady's sensibilities. He hoped that in this case the old aphorism of "hell hath no fury like a woman scorned" would not apply in his case. Her name was Mrs. Jochan Wilder, and she was nicknamed Kitty. Though Jeremy had always been a womanizer, Kitty repelled him, for she was like a dark little sinuous cat, constantly vivacious and in movement, with a narrow and very small lean face, a distinctly olive complexion, round staring eyes the color of agates, and enormous flaring white teeth. The teeth were startling in that tiny countenance, and when she laughed or grinned they seemed to fill that countenance from side to side, and worse, up and down. (She was proud of them.) Her features were rarely in repose, and even then they had a feline alertness and impatience as she waited for others to cease talking so that she could pour out a rush of words so shrill, so insistent, so vehement, as to irritate her listener. Then she would laugh noisily, the teeth would engulf her face so that the other features sank into minor significance and were almost obliterated. To make the teeth even more conspicuous—predatorily glistening and glaring and wet—she would redden her thin wide lips, and she had a way of inserting her crimson tongue between them. She thought this irresistible.

She was a small woman, hardly five feet tall, and so very thin that she had to wear additions to her meager bosom and her backside, and her hands were even darker than her parched facial skin, and always rapidly gesticulating. When she was not screeching with laughter—she considered herself to have a devastating sense of humor—she was murmuring while others spoke. However, she was very stylish and animated and lively, and very knowing, and could also purr like the cat she so closely resembled. Her sophistication was complete: She was cunningly aware of human nature in all its aspects and exploited it when she could, sometimes for a profit for herself and sometimes sheerly out of malice.

Ellen, for some reason baffling even to the astute Jeremy, found Kitty fascinating. But Ellen said, with gentle pleading, "She is very *soignée, distingueé,* as M. Penserres would call it. She has elegance and wit, and is so very kind. She teaches me so many things I should know about New York, and the people, and takes me everywhere during the day, to see everything I should see so that"—Ellen hesitated—"you won't be ashamed of my ignorance."

Your dangerous innocence, you mean, my pet, Jeremy thought.

"She teaches me how to select clothes, too," said Ellen, pleading for her new friend. "You do admire my new clothes, don't you? Kitty chose them all, especially that gray velvet with the little yellow topazes on the bodice, which you particularly like, and the earrings and bracelet and chain to match. There is nothing Kitty doesn't know, just about everything. Her taste is perfect; you must admit that. I wanted to buy a scarlet dress, and she refused to let me, with my hair. She chose my maid, Clarisse, for me, and Clarisse is excellent, not that I know anything about ladies' maids. She has been tireless in helping me, so very kind. I don't know why she does it; I am not much of a companion to her."

But Jeremy knew, to some extent. Kitty Wilder was a very rich woman in her own right, and her husband was almost as wealthy. Kitty, however, had ambitions. She was a consuming woman, never satisfied, always reaching avidly for something she considered more important, more befitting her hungers, her aspirations. She had no patience for the plodding, the conscientious, the content, the dutiful. She had long discerned that Jeremy Porter had the talent for power, over and above money, and that in many ways he was as restless as she was herself. However, his restlessness was masculine; hers was feline, if voracious. Her less than delicate pursuit of him earlier had not been mere physical lust (though she was a lustful woman and often too demanding for her husband, who believed that females indicated no pleasure in bed, if they were ladies). Her desire for Jeremy was for his potential as a ruthless leader, a powerful man in all ways, who would never be satisfied, as she was never satisfied, even though she was considered a reigning socialite. She smelled success about Jeremy, and she adored success.

She detested Ellen and laughed inwardly at her "country bumpkin ideas and ways," but she was very careful in concealing that, attending sedulously to the girl. (She was thirty-three herself.) Through Ellen, she believed she would either seduce Jeremy by being so constantly in his house, or she would be able to attach herself also to his star, or rather, she would attach her husband. She would have liked both, but would be delighted with either. She was beguiled insatiably by his potent qualities; she loved the very sound of his voice. Her husband's voice was somewhat high and he had a deplorable habit of giggling, and was tall, thin, extremely fair, and a total gentleman. Kitty was not a lady for all her birth and antecedents and money and the fine finishing school she had attended, and her demure and proper relatives who were invariably correct in their conduct and their conversation, and, she suspected, in their thoughts also. Propriety was not admirable to Kitty Wilder. Only a few suspected her wild scheming nature, and her husband was not one of them. He thought Kitty vital and amusing though her sallies at him held the venom of a cat's teeth. He loved her even when she was most grinningly obnoxious. He believed she was simply full of high spirits and vivid sprightliness.

That she was very intelligent, not even Jeremy denied. She was a patron of the arts, the opera. She lived with her husband in a gray stone house on Fifth Avenue, decorated in the most superb taste, with not a single hint of vulgarity. Her refinement and discrimination were famous in the city. She had no children, for which she was thankful.

Her devoted friends—and they were multitudinous,

being attracted by her constant air of humor and good
nature and worldliness, and her family and money—believed her to be beautiful, though Jeremy Porter thought
she was one of the ugliest women he had ever encountered, so "scrawny" was she, so apparently made of tight
tendon and dark skin and drawn ligaments. "She never
sits quietly for an instant," he once complained to Ellen.
"She wears me out, just watching her." To which Ellen
had replied, "Oh, Jeremy, she is just so full of life, that's
all. Not dull and heavy like me." "You are so restful
love," he said, and she answered smiling and sighing,
"So is a feather bed."

Kitty always angrily wondered why Jeremy had married
"such a dolt, such a big huge thing, so unpleasing in her
face and her figure. She is like one of the young laundres-
ses my mother employs. She reeks of harsh soap, at least
in temperament, and new-cut grass and starchy clothes."
Kitty was very urban; she was not fond of the country,
of simplicity, of sunshine in long golden shadows on green
lawns at sunset. Though her family had an enormous
"country cottage" on Long Island facing the ocean, surrounded by bountiful and glowing flowers and trees, she
disliked the place and rarely visited it even in summer.
The heat of New York in July and August pleased her,
for she was averse to cold or even to the apple-scented
autumn. She would laugh gaily at herself when speaking
of this to friends. Let them desert the city in the summer
if they wished. She found no place on earth more delightful than New York at any season, and was happy when
summer departed and all her friends either returned from
abroad or "from the country." She avoided all lakes,
streams, and the ocean as much as possible, for she had
a catlike aversion for them.

"Her head is too large for her body, and she empha-
sizes it with that gigantic black pompadour of hers,"
Jeremy said once to his wife when she had expounded on
Kitty's beauty.

"She has the loveliest black hair, dear," Ellen said,
"so sleek, so shining, so straight and always in order. Not
even a high wind can ruffle it."

Jeremy did not try to discourage the incongruous
friendship between the worldly and sophisticated and, he
suspected, evil woman, and Ellen. He was conscious that
Kitty was polishing Ellen in her manners and was giving

her poise and some assurance, which all his love could not do, for Ellen believed it was only love which made him praise her and not truth. But when Kitty sometimes affected to admire her she was overwhelmed with happiness, and believed the falsities. Had not Kitty told her over and over of her affection for the girl?

"I wish, sometimes," Jeremy said, "that you'd be a little more cautious about people than you are, Ellen. It's all right to 'love and trust,' provided the few persons you encounter are worthy of it."

"Kitty is worthy," said Ellen with conviction. "Why else could she endure me?" Jeremy did not laugh at this, as he would have some months before. He only looked at Ellen with somber apprehension while he wondered what more safeguards he could put for her in his will, in codicils.

Kitty was always very careful not to let Ellen suspect she thought her gauche and "impossible," and "a disgrace to poor dear Jeremy." Ellen had confided in her utterly, and this Jeremy deplored, though he had never found a way of successfully intimating to Ellen that her background and earlier employment as a servant were not the best tactics in attracting admiration in the society of New York. He had tried, as delicately as he could, to advise her. He had said, "No one, my darling, is really concerned with anyone else, and a little air of mystery about you, and your origins, would perhaps be more interesting."

But Ellen, with her acute sensitivity, had immediately cried, and with tears, "I know, I know, you are ashamed of me and that's always been my deepest fear!"

He had sworn at her then, for perhaps the first time, and had said, while he alternately embraced and shook her, "What an idiot you are, really, Ellen. I am just trying to protect you from the malice of cruel people, and most people are cruel." But she did not understand, and only cried the harder. It took him several exhausting nights to reassure her that he adored her, would never have married another woman, and that she was the joy of his life.

May was more direct. Ellen had made the error of taking Kitty upstairs to see her aunt, and though Kitty had been all solicitude and bantering vivacity and grace and perfume and impeccable manners, and had told May of her "devotion to your charming and delicious niece," May had hated her immediately and had mistrusted her. But she was "quality" and therefore entitled to obsequiousness and open respect. She said to Ellen later, in her dark and warning tones, "Mrs. Wilder is a lady, Ellen, and she don't show that she don't think much of you, but I know. I can tell. She wants something, and it isn't you, Ellen. Her airs aren't put on, like yours, dear. She comes by them natural—family, schools, money, blood. But she hides what she thinks under those manners. All the real quality do that, but you weren't in service long enough to learn. A lady like Mrs. Wilder isn't nice to somebody like you, Ellen, without a reason, and the reason isn't that she thinks you're worth it, for yourself."

"Oh, Aunt May, what on earth could be the reason?"

May shook her head. "That I don't know, but I don't think it's good for you, Ellen. I have a feeling—"

Miss Ember, the nurse, also had a "feeling." She, too, had not been deceived by Kitty Wilder, though she had been properly awed by her, recognizing her class immediately. She wondered what a lady like Mrs. Wilder could "see" in a lumbering hulk like young Mrs. Porter, with all that awful red hair and the too colorful face and the lack of sophistication. Miss Ember, having seen a great deal of life, shrewdly suspected that it was "the master, Mr. Porter, who's the attraction." Miss Ember smiled lewdly to herself. She hated "people of quality" while she served them with true devotion and humility.

Kitty did not gossip about Ellen to her friends or make fun of her. She was far too shrewd for that, for even the best of friends had a way of repeating tidbits, not out of malevolence but for the pleasure of it, and without a sense of betrayal at all. She well knew, also, that gossip had an unpleasant way of reaching the object of it sooner or later, with sometimes disastrous results. So, though she smiled when others wondered about Ellen and her origins, she merely shrugged and said, "Well, who knows? There's many a skeleton in everybody's closet, to coin a brand-new cliché."

"But one does like to know about someone's family and background," a lady had once said to Kitty. "It is only proper, to know."

"We all know that she came from some little godforsaken town in Pennsylvania, of a poor but respectable family of some consequence. Jeremy has said he knew them well, and even hinted to a very illustrious ancestor."

"She is very well behaved and deferential to her elders," admitted one elderly lady, "and has refinement and a natural aristocracy, though most of you younger women do not credit that. I can tell good blood. And she has an excellent mind, if a little timid. It is such a mystery."

"Let it remain so," said Kitty, who had no intention of having Jeremy belittled by her friends and made uncomfortable. Though, I suppose, she thought, he wouldn't give a damn. No, they couldn't make him uncomfortable. He is too assured in himself, too potent in himself.

Jeremy noticed her more when she was with Ellen and that was temporarily sufficient for her. She felt she was making progress in both her aims. In the meantime her husband was becoming more and more tedious and hesitant with her, and she would lie beside him thinking it was Jeremy there, and her whole meager body would glow.

"What! You are enceinte?" exclaimed Kitty Wilder when Ellen shyly told her. "What a contretemps! How unfortunate! With the season at its highest now."

"Unfortunate?" said Ellen, and all her apprehensions about her child came acutely alive again.

"Yes. Just a bride still. How old did you say you were, my dear?"

"Eighteen. But what—"

Eighteen, very, very plus; I can trust my observation, thought Kitty. But her sort always lies. They think youth is everything; she's at least twenty-four. Kitty said, "I know a very fine, discreet doctor, and I'll be happy to have a word with him in your behalf."

"What for, Kitty? I have a very good doctor of my own, a friend of Jeremy's. He thinks I am in the most perfect health. I—it is my fourth month now."

"Not too late," said Kitty with briskness. "It can all be managed." Her polished, round agate eyes glittered on the girl. Then she saw that Ellen had totally misunderstood her and her dislike and contempt quickened. She leaned towards the girl and whispered, "I mean—it can all be eliminated. I have had it done three times."

Ellen stared at her, confused. Then suddenly she colored deeply and turned aside her head, vaguely comprehending. She was sick with horror. "I—I couldn't," she stammered, and felt overwhelming shame because she now understood. "Jeremy—wants—it."

Kitty was very quick, and she laughed and all her monster teeth flared out in the lamplight of Ellen's boudoir, wet as a tiger's.

"But you don't?"

"I—don't know," said Ellen. "You see, I am afraid of children, remembering how they were when I was a child. They weren't 'angels' at all, in spite of what a lot of women say. Many of them were devils."

"Then, do as I suggest, dear."

Ellen shook her head. "Jeremy would never forgive me. Did your husband forgive you?"

"I never told him." Kitty reflected. A child might bind Jeremy closer to Ellen, and then again it might not. Men like Jeremy were not fatuous fathers. They frequently found their children distasteful or boring, and fled their milky wives, who usually preferred the nursery to their husbands' company. Ellen was just the kind to be such a wife, with that great breast of hers. Kitty made a slight mouth of disgust.

"Well, perhaps you are right," she said, patting Ellen's hand. "You will make a wonderful mama."

"I don't feel like a mama," said Ellen. "I am only Jeremy's wife, and that is all I ever wanted to be."

Have a few brats, and he won't be much of a husband to you any longer, sweetheart, Kitty thought, and smiled with satisfaction in herself. Her husband, Jochan, was becoming more friendly day by day with Jeremy, and admired the younger man greatly. Kitty believed this was her own doing, for had she not deftly arranged it so that the Porters dined at her house at least twice a month and she and her husband dined with the Porters that many times, too? The four were becoming very "intimate." Jeremy was being spoken of as the next Congressman for this constituency, where he was highly respected. Once she had had hopes that Jochan would show some political acumen and ambition, but he did not possess the ruthlessness of Jeremy Porter, nor the disciplined intelligence nor the potency. He would also never risk anything; he was caution itself, admirable in a lawyer but fatal in a politician. He loved his money more than Jeremy loved his. Kitty, a gambler herself, had recognized a gambler when she had met Jeremy.

But a successful politician had the power of distinguished appointments, and Kitty was determined that her husband would have one of them, through Jeremy. After New York, Kitty was fond of Washington, where her father had once been a Senator. The family had often been entertained at the White House.

When spring came Ellen knew it was no longer possible to conceal the bulge of the child in her belly, no matter what swirling house robes she wore. Moreover, she suspected that Miss Ember, her aunt's nurse, had already guessed and was waiting malevolently for May to receive the news. She had her suspicions that Ellen believed her aunt would not rejoice in the coming child and that Ellen was sparing her as long as possible.

One day Ellen asked Miss Ember timidly if she would leave the room for a few moments, and Miss Ember left promptly but took up a convenient spot near the door. She heard Ellen inquire about May's pain and what the doctor had said this morning and May petulantly answered, with sighs. Then Ellen began to murmur and stammer a little and Miss Ember smiled to herself and leaned her ear to the door. There was a small sharp silence, then May exclaimed as if in mortal anguish, "No! Oh, dear me, no, Ellen! How did that happen?"

I could tell the old bitch, thought Miss Ember, laughing to herself. She could visualize Ellen's embarrassment, the clasping of her hands on her knee, her wretchedness.

Ellen was sitting with her aunt before the perpetual fire, but the windows were open to the bright spring air and the curtains blew and the traffic below and on Fifth Avenue came clearly and buoyantly to them. Ellen said, pleadingly, "People usually have children when they marry, Aunt May, don't they? And Jeremy is so happy about it. I don't understand why you think it is such a tragedy, a misfortune." The spring wind raised her ebullient hair and brushed it across her cheek, and her face was full of anxiety for her aunt, who was more than distressed.

"Yes, he'd be happy, wouldn't he?" cried May, sitting up in her chair and trembling. There fled from her her final hope that she and Ellen would be banished and would return to Wheatfield and the house of Mrs. Eccles, and tears began to roll down her dried gray face. Ellen went to her at once and knelt down beside her like a penitent child, but one also baffled and confused. She tried to take May's hand, but May pulled it away from her and covered her face with her hands.

"I don't understand, Auntie," said Ellen. "Of course, Jeremy is happy."

"Have you no shame, Ellen?" May demanded from behind her hands, using the very phrase she had used to the wanton Mary.

"Do women usually have shame when they are going to have a child?" asked Ellen, more and more bewildered.

"Yes, they do! They know—they know—what started it!"

Ellen's cheeks felt hot, but she smiled faintly with remembrance. "We are all born that way, Auntie. There's no shame in it."

May dropped her hands and glared wetly at her niece. "A lady feels shame, Ellen, but then you are not a lady, as I've always told you, and that's why you don't feel any shame."

Ellen stood up slowly and went back to her chair and considered her aunt with gentle candor. "I know three ladies who are going to have children, too, and they aren't ashamed. They talk together about it—and to me. Of course, they don't go out in public or to parties any longer, but neither do I. I just take walks with Jeremy in the evening, as the doctor advises, for fresh air and exercise."

But May was back some nineteen years ago when her young sister had confessed to her "shameless condition." It was Mary whom May addressed now, and not her niece, and it was in piercing agitation.

"What shall we do? What can we do?"

Ellen was amazed. "I don't understand what you mean, Auntie. There's nothing we can 'do.' " Was her aunt hinting what Kitty had hinted? "I'm a married woman; I am Jeremy's wife. This is our child, and I am so pleased that he is happy over it."

May cried, "Children are a curse! It is terrible to have them!"

As Ellen was always assailed by fear of what his child would do to her husband, she turned pale. But she said sturdily enough, "Not everybody feels that way. Jeremy doesn't." She thought to herself, with compassion, that her poor aunt had never been able to please her own husband that way, and she tried to take May's hand again but was repulsed.

"What will you do with that—that child?" said May, thinking of her sister. "Where will you go?"

Ellen's beautiful face became blank. "Why, this is my home, Aunt May. I won't go anywhere else. Jeremy and the doctor have already engaged my nurses—"

But May interrupted her wildly. "He'll throw you out when he knows!"

Ellen's confusion grew. "But he's known from the beginning, Auntie. Why should Jeremy throw his wife and child 'out'?"

"Men are all alike! It's all love until they get a girl in trouble. Then it's out with them!"

Again Ellen was amazed. "But, Auntie, I am not 'in trouble.' I am a married woman. And Jeremy is my husband, and this is my home."

May was sick and trembling. She struggled to focus her eyes on her niece, but overshadowing that brilliant face was the face of the beloved sister, Mary. "We can't stay here any longer." She paused, then saw Ellen clearly. She began to stutter. "We should never have left Wheatfield and Mrs. Eccles. I warned you, Ellen."

Now the iron that lay so far beneath Ellen's gentleness and innocence momentarily emerged. Her voice was still kind and patient, but she said, "I think you are unwell, Auntie. I'll call Miss Ember," and she stood up. May grasped her hand, and the thin twisted fingers were feverish.

"You never listened to me, Ellen! You were always willful and determined on your own way, and look what has happened to you, as I knew it would. Ruin." She cried again for her bare little cold room in Mrs. Eccles' house, where she believed she had been safe, and at peace. Nothing was "right" in her present world; all was chaos and uncertainty and suspicion of fate, and the conviction of catastrophe.

Ellen said with great quietness, "I am not in ruin, Auntie. I am the happiest woman in the world. I adore Jeremy; he is, as it says in *Romeo and Juliet*, 'Lord, lover and friend.' That is how I feel about him. I know he loves me, too. Why else did he marry me? No one forced him to do that. He came for me in Wheatfield, and took me away from misery and hopelessness and gave me—bliss. I never told you all that I felt in Mrs. Eccles' house. The misery and despair. The blackness of my existence. I've tried to tell you, but you refused to understand. If for nothing else I would love Jeremy, that he took me away from there, and married me."

But May was hardly listening. "You can say all that about a lady who was so good to us? Gave us shelter when no one else wanted us?"

Then Ellen spoke her first harsh words of anyone: "She is a hateful woman, Mrs. Eccles, as bad in her way as is Mrs. Porter!"

She was immediately stricken by guilt and felt quite ill. She turned towards the door but again May grasped her. "Mrs. Porter! What can she possibly think of this— this— She'll never speak to you again, Ellen, and it is all you deserve. The shame—"

Ellen said through lips cold and stiff, "She already knows. I wrote her a month ago."

"And what did she say in return?" May leaned eagerly towards her niece.

"You know very well she wasn't—pleased—by our marriage, Aunt May. But she answered, not me, but Jeremy. He never showed me the letter, but he did say that she hoped for a grandson."

"He never showed you the letter! I wonder what she really said!"

"It doesn't matter in the least to me, Auntie. Jeremy and I have each other. And there will be—our family."

Now she went to the door, but before she could open it May exclaimed, "Have you thought of the pain, the agony, every woman has? And women often die when they have children!"

"I don't intend to die, Auntie." Ellen was moved, believing her aunt was concerned for her. "The doctor says I am very healthy and should have no trouble at all. Pain? I've heard of it, but nothing is too painful if it pleases Jeremy. Now, I must really go. We are having a few guests. Do try to rest, dear Aunt May. I know this must be a shock to you, and you've always been afraid for me."

She opened the door. Miss Ember had already retreated to a discreet place in the hall. Ellen said to her, "I think

my aunt, Mrs. Watson, needs you, Miss Ember. Maybe
an extra one of those pills which quiet her sometimes.
And a very light supper, if you please."

Without waiting for the woman to reply—she had
spoken very firmly, which was also new for her—she went
down the stairs in the bright spring evening. Her knees
felt somewhat weak. She had been more disturbed by her
aunt's inexplicable remarks than she had known. Cuthbert was entering the lower hall from the library. "Mr.
Porter, Mr. Francis Porter, is calling, madam."

Ellen felt a new vehemence and impatience. She had
wanted to consult Cuthbert about the dinner—one of the
few she would be giving until after her confinement—
and she was suddenly very tired and wished to lie down.
She hesitated on the stairs. She would have run up again
if she had not known that Francis must have heard Cuthbert.

"Very well," she said with an unaccustomed weariness
in her young and lovely voice. "Please bring us sherry
and biscuits, Cuthbert."

Francis had not visited her for a month and she had
hoped that he would not again, and when she had known
that hope she had been ashamed and again guilty. She
remembered, too, that Jeremy had defeated Francis in
three more cases. She went into the library smiling, but
the smile was less radiant than usual.

He was standing near the library fire, and he turned
when she entered, and she held out her hand and greeted
him as shyly as always.

"I have been away, dear Ellen," he said, certain she
had missed him. "That is why I haven't called in so long."
He still spoke to her with that kind condescension of his,
but this time she heard it and resented it.

"Please sit down, Mr. Francis," she said. "It is getting
chilly after the nice warm day, isn't it?"

He heard the unusual note in her voice, and frowned
slightly as he sat down. It was unlike Ellen to be "presumptuous," and suddenly unaware of her lowly class.
He waited until she had seated herself, then sat down near
her.

"Did you miss me at all, Ellen?" he asked.

Ellen said, "Miss you?" and she spoke with a kind of
wonder. But immediately she thought herself discourteous
and once more was guilty. "I—I did think—I have been

very busy, Mr. Francis. So many things. Time passes so fast, doesn't it?"

"Especially when you're happy?" His voice was pouncing.

"Yes," said Ellen. Something was wrong but she did not know what. She only knew that she wished he would leave so that she could lie down. She had still not told Jeremy of these visits, and had hoped that she need never tell him, if Frances remained away.

She watched Cuthbert pour the sherry from its gold-and-crystal decanter, and was conscious that her head had begun to ache. "I am very happy. And you, Mr. Francis? How have you been?"

He had always thought Ellen considerably stupid. Was it possible that she was unaware of his three defeats at the hands of that brute of a husband of hers? But naturally, his cousin knew that she understood very little of the world in her blandness and ignorance. She is a woman, he thought, but she has never matured. Is that part of her charm? Why did he sicken for her when he was away from her—this beautiful young servant?

"I have been very well, Ellen," he said with formality. "My aunt, Mrs. Eccles, sends her regards."

"That is very kind of her," said Ellen. "Please give her mine also."

Francis was taken aback. Ellen was being impertinent again, and he was deeply annoyed.

"I also saw your mother-in-law, and Mr. Porter, when I had occasion to visit Preston two weeks ago."

Ellen was silent. She sipped her sherry and looked over the rim of her glass at him. He thought she was pretending to be inscrutable. What airs she had learned! Then Ellen was studying him and she was thinking: Did Jeremy's parents tell him of our child?

She said, "How are Jeremy's parents?"

"Well enough," he said in a tone of kind severity. "They are still hurt by Jeremy's—disaffection." He added, "Disaffection? You know what that means, Ellen?"

Ellen could not help smiling. "My tutors are very good, Mr. Francis. And I have always read very much from the time I was a young child. Yes, I know what disaffection means. It's not Jeremy's fault. He has—approached— them several times. If they choose to keep their distance that is their own affair, isn't it?"

She waited for his next remark. Then she saw that he had not been told, and she was mortified and distressed. Or was it that gentlemen did not refer to these things to ladies?

"He is their only son, their only child, and naturally—"

It was Ellen's headache which made her answer with a little sharpness, "Naturally what, Mr. Francis?"

"You must know that they hoped that he would marry the young lady in Scranton, Ellen."

"One can't help disappointing people sometimes, can one, Mr. Francis?" The full blue tea gown she wore enhanced the intense brilliance of her blue eyes, and they were sparkling though she was not smiling.

His pomposity, always evident, had become more so over these months. His self-control, usually very strong, suddenly was swept away and he leaned towards Ellen and said, almost blurting, "Your welfare has always been of the utmost concern to me, Ellen. You must know that."

She weakened, remembering again how kind he had always been to her, and she wondered why she had been so acerbic to him, and the guilt was upon her. She said, "Yes, Mr. Francis. I've always known. I'm really very grateful."

He saw that he had "reduced" her again to her proper position, and was pleased. She leaned forward to him to offer him the salver of biscuits and her gown drew tightly about her and he knew what he had not known before. He thought, for an instant, that he would be violently ill, there and then in that warm firelit library.

"Is there something wrong, Mr. Francis?"

He could only mutter in a thickened voice, "No. No, not at all, Ellen. It is just that I've been very busy myself, and this was an unusually warm day." Sweat had come out on his forehead; he could feel its trickling and stinging.

Ellen stood up and opened the window near him a little wider and looked down at him with solicitude. She was so close to him that he could smell the scent of her young body, and her eau de cologne, which was of a light sweet odor. He could feel the warmth of that body, its innocent sensuousness, of which she was not aware. He wanted to seize her, to hold her, to weep on her breast, which he saw was much fuller now. He wanted to tell her of his sense of her degradation, of his longing, of his love, and desolation. He trembled with that desire.

"That feels much better, thank you, Ellen," he said.

She drew her chair a little closer to him and said, "You gentlemen often work too hard. I sometimes tell Jeremy that. It makes me very anxious. Perhaps you need a rest. Jeremy and I—after—I mean, this summer, we are buying a house on Long Island, for the summertime, and I hope he will rest then for a while." Her eyes were a blue shine in the rising dusk.

The desolation was an anguish in him; he experienced a loss almost too terrible to endure. He knew now that he had always secretly hoped that his cousin would tire of Ellen very soon—that womanizer!—and that she would come to him for comfort and shelter.

"That will be nice," he muttered incoherently. He wiped his forehead with his handkerchief. Ellen was filled with that old weakening contrition. She had hurt his feelings in some manner, and he had been good to her and her aunt. She said, "Mr. Francis, you do not look well at all! Would you prefer some brandy?"

"No. No, dear Ellen. It has been so warm—"

But she stood up and went to him and put her gentle hand on his forehead. It was hot and wet. She bent over him, scrutinizing his face. Her eyes were full on him and he saw the pupils dilating anxiously. It was too much for him. He put his arms about her waist and drew her down closer to him and kissed her mouth over and over, passionately, while she stood, dazed, in his embrace, her lips parted in astonishment and some fear. She tried to release herself but his grip was too strong.

"That is a very tender scene," said Jeremy Porter from the threshold. "How long has this been going on, if I, a mere husband, am crude enough to inquire?"

Ellen and Francis both started. Ellen pulled away from Francis, and Francis stood up, white and trembling. They both looked at Jeremy in the doorway, stupefied. His face was tense with anger and his eyes were gleaming in the dusk. When Ellen could recover herself she went to Jeremy, but he put her aside with some roughness and looked only at his cousin, who still could not speak. Ellen took his arm.

"Jeremy!" she said. "Mr. Francis was taken a little ill, and I was trying to help him, to see if he had a fever."

She could not understand her husband's very apparent rage; she thought it was because he had found Frances here. "I am so sorry—I should have told you before. Mr. Francis sometimes comes to see me—he knew me before you did, Jeremy. He has always had my welfare at heart—"

"I haven't the slightest doubt," said Jeremy, still not looking at her.

Francis finally could speak. "It is not what you think it is, Jeremy."

"And what am I to think, a strange man clutching my wife?" His voice was one Ellen had never heard before and she was frightened more by the tone than the words, which she could not comprehend at all.

"I should have told you," she repeated. "But I knew— I thought—that you did not really like each other, and Mr. Francis suggested—"

Now he looked at her. She could not endure his stare, and shivered. "What did Mr. Francis suggest, my dear?"

She put her hand helplessly to her aching head. "I don't think I quite remember." She turned pleadingly to Francis, who appeared to be on the edge of collapse. "Didn't you say, Mr. Francis, that perhaps it would not be well to tell Jeremy you came to see me, because you don't like each other? Yes, I think that is it." She was now more alarmed at Francis' appearance than she was by Jeremy's. "I should have told Jeremy from the beginning, Mr. Francis. It is all my fault."

Jeremy said, with some savagery, "It is always your 'fault,' isn't it, Ellen, when people take advantage of you, deceive you and exploit you? I am beginning to think you are right, in a way. Well, Frank, can't you speak?"

"Ellen has told you the truth—"

" 'The whole truth and nothing but the truth, so help you God'?"

Francis was silent again. "Yes," said Ellen, "it is the truth, Jeremy. Yes, I should have told you. I've felt so guilty, but I thought it was for the best."

Francis said, "You have an evil mind, Jeremy, just as you are an evil man. Now, I think I will go. Ellen, I won't trouble you with my visits any more. I only wanted to be sure you were happy—and safe."

"Of course," said poor Ellen, thinking all was settled agreeably now. But Jeremy was still standing stiffly with his fists clenched at his sides. He said, "If you ever bother my wife again I will kill you. Do you understand? Kill you. I've known you've been slavering for her a long time."

"Jeremy!" Ellen cried, terrified now. "What are you talking about?" She looked from one man to the other, and swallowed against the sickness in her throat.

"Kill you," said Jeremy again.

At this moment Cuthbert discreetly appeared, carrying Francis' coat and hat and cane. Jeremy looked at the cane, but Cuthbert deftly gave it to Francis and helped him on with his coat. Ellen took a step aside and sank into a chair, shivering heavily. Jeremy still stood in the doorway. It was Cuthbert who expertly pushed him aside so Francis could pass him, which he did very quickly. Cuthbert led him to the door, then disappeared again.

Ellen, very pale, looked up at her husband and her eyes were severe as they had never been before. "Jeremy, you were most rude to poor Mr. Francis. He has known me since I was a child; he did all he could for Aunt May and me, when your mother threatened us with the police, and everything. He only wanted to know if I was well. I'm so sorry. I should have told you from the very beginning, but he thought it best not to. And you've repaid his kindness to me with cruel words and abuse. I am very vexed with you."

He looked down at her, and relaxed. It always came to him with fresh wonder, at every new experience, how little Ellen knew of people, and how vulnerable she was. But he was still enraged. He took her by the shoulders and pulled her upright, almost against him, and looked down at her. He did not know what to say to her; he did not want to destroy her innocence, but he was infuriated also. He began to shake her, though not roughly, and she timidly tried to smile, for often he shook her this way.

"Ellen, listen to me," he said. "I've told you about many of my cases, and my court appearances. I thought you were listening, that finally you were beginning to understand that this is a most terrible world, and that you must be on your guard against it. But you never understood, or believed me, did you?"

"It's also a very good and beautiful world, Jeremy. There is more goodness in it than wickedness."

"Is that so?" he said. "Well, I've also told you something of world affairs, too, haven't I? It was all for your protection, Ellen, for it is possible that I will die before you."

"Oh, no, I could not live then!" she cried, and the child in her womb leapt in answering terror. She put her hand over it, as if to quiet its fears.

Jeremy said, with new gentleness, "You must face life, Ellen. You won't die if I die. You will have children. Never mind. Listen carefully to me, my love. I want to tell you something about people like my dear cousin. He is of the kind which will approach anyone insidiously, for one reason: conquest and control. With you, he has used your gratitude, your pity. That is one of their big weapons, and they have others. I thought, when I have been telling you many things, that you did understand a little, and that it might be possible, in the future, that you will be on guard not only against Frank's kind, but a thousand other predators. Yes, predators. He is one of the very worst sort, the most ruthless and merciless, as well as contemptible. You don't understand, do you?"

"Not quite," she said. He was now holding her lovingly, and that was enough for her. "Mr. Francis is not in the least ruthless and merciless. He is a very kind man. I know that myself."

"I really give up," said Jeremy, releasing her. "Ellen, you're not stupid. You are really a very intelligent girl. You can understand music and literature and poetry and philosophy, sometimes better than I can, for you are intuitive. But your intuition doesn't work with people, does it? Only in abstract matters, in things which can't protect you. I'm not sure that I want you to be another Kitty Wilder. God forbid. But surely she has been telling you of this world, hasn't she?"

"She's very witty," said Ellen, and felt a pang of jealousy for the first time in her existence. "But I know she is really just being funny when she talks of people; she isn't malicious."

"Good God," said Jeremy. "Yes, I really give up. Ellen, listen to me. When I talk to you, really listen. When Kitty talks, really listen. I don't want you to become hard and cynical. I just want you to be aware of what this world really is: a den of wolves, red in tooth and claw. Even the saints knew that, but it didn't embitter them or turn them against humanity. It only saddened them, I've heard. So listen, Ellen. Be sad if you must, and you will. Awareness doesn't necessarily destroy innocence; it only arms it, when necessary. What in hell am I going to do with you?"

"You can kiss me," said Ellen. But he shook his head, sighing. "Let me tell you of a case which came to me today. A lady of great wealth. She has four adult children. She adored them all their lives, and believed they loved her, too. She is a woman something like you, though considerably older. Her husband died six months ago and left all his fortune to her. Do you know what her loving children have done to her? They have robbed her of every penny, in those short six months, her two daughters, their husbands, and her two sons, their wives. Now they are evicting her from her house. She loved and trusted. Are you listening?"

"Yes," said Ellen. She thought of her unborn child and what that child might do to Jeremy, and her lips went white.

"She was brought today to me, by a friend who loves her, a man. She was all tears, all misery. And all bewilderment, too. She couldn't understand why and how her devoted children could do this to her; she still couldn't believe it, the poor woman. She desperately tried to make excuses for them, with the facts right there on my desk, before her. Her children meant no harm, she said. She was sure of that. I was so exasperated when I failed to reach her that I wanted no part of that case. I could see her blubbering in court and persuading the judge that it was 'all a mistake,' as she said in my office. Then I had to show her not only the eviction notice but a petition they had signed—those loving children!—to have her declared incompetent and confined in some private mental hospital —a cheap one, too. She fainted."

"Poor thing," said Ellen in a dim voice.

"Oh, God," said Jeremy again. "Now, what do you think of that case, of those children, and that fool of a woman?"

Ellen considered, hoping to please him. "I think she should not have let them—take—from her. Perhaps they needed the money, though. But she should have consulted someone, such as her friend who brought her to you."

"Excellent," said Jeremy, patting her shoulder. "I think I am finally reaching you."

"But a mother loves and trusts—"

He clenched his fist and put it gently but firmly under her chin.

"If I ever hear that sickening phrase again, my pet, I'll beat you. I'll beat some sense into you."

She smiled. "But what has all this to do with Mr. Francis?"

"Everything. Her swinish children appealed not only to her love and her trust, but to her compassion, and if there was ever a disgusting word it is 'compassion.' No one uses it but predators, for their own purposes. They are always declaiming it, while they prepare to loot, subjugate, and control. Remember that, Ellen."

"It would be a terrible world, Jeremy, if no one trusted or loved anyone, or had compassion."

"But it *is* a terrible world, in spite of the poisonous pink jelly such as my cousin spreads around to disarm others, and persuade those innocent others that they have only their welfare at heart. They are all heart, the bastards, all steamed up with a desire for social justice and the 'welfare of the toiling masses,' and what not. I think I've told you before."

"Yes, but Mr. Francis is not like that. He really cares about my welfare."

"Let him come here once again, about your welfare, and there'll be one fewer dangerous man in the world," said Jeremy.

Cuthbert appeared on the threshold. "If Madam would like to look at the birds—"

"Yes, of course, Cuthbert. Jeremy, it is time to dress, isn't it? I will just go into the kitchen for a moment."

Jeremy looked after her as she left him, and he was filled with the grimmest forebodings. Who had corrupted Ellen's mind long ago? he asked himself. Innocence was wonderful, but it should not be folly. The saints had been innocent, but they had not been fools. He hoped, someday, to teach Ellen the difference.

Part Two

This, indeed, is at once the hallmark and the justification of an aristocracy—that it is beyond responsibility to the general masses of men, and hence superior to both their degraded longings and their no less degraded aversions.

—H. L. MENCKEN

14

On July 4, 1904, Ellen Porter's first child was born—a son, who was named Christian Watson Porter.

The day was hot and fetid and blowing with a gritty wind and glaring with unshaded sun, which penetrated even the trees along Fifth Avenue and the house of Jeremy Porter in the East Twenties, and threw brilliant black shadows on scalding pavements.

Ellen awoke, sweating and restless beside her husband, and she recalled that it was on such a holiday that she had first seen Jeremy and for a happy moment or two she could lie on her damp pillows and smile in memory. It was eight o'clock, and though the shutters were closed and the curtains and draperies drawn across the glass of the windows, the tormenting sun shot through any chink or little opening it found to blaze on rug or wall or arm of a chair or on the high carved mahogany of the head-board of the bed. Ellen blinked against the daggers of the small beams, closed her eyes and saw a redness as of blood. She turned on her side but there was no escape. Jeremy slept, his face tired and somewhat somber and tense, and Ellen looked at his dark profile and a vast sweet melting ran through her in spite of her discomfort. Her hand crept to touch his white silk nightshirt, a touch as light as a moth, and as tenderly soft. She sighed deeply. She was afraid to move for fear of disturbing Jeremy, who needed to rest after his long hot days in the city courts and in his offices. The house on Long Island was already bought, and Ellen thought longingly of the cold gray Atlantic waves collapsing in foam on the sand near the house, and the strong sea breezes and the warm lashings of trees over cool green grass. The house awaited them, and they would go there in less than a month.

Ellen inched her way over the heated linen of her bed to lay her mouth against Jeremy's arm. Her child was not due for another two weeks, but she was strangely uneasy. She panted a little and wiped her damp face cautiously and lifted the heavy weight of her hair from her wet neck. She wanted to get up and sit in a chair. The child in her belly moved restlessly and strongly, and seemed to burden her body with its pressure. She struggled against her fear of it; she already loved it, for it was Jeremy's, but still she was afraid. She had spent an almost sleepless night because of the heat and her pervading apprehension, which had increased these past weeks. Boy or girl— would it become the enemy of her husband? She had never recovered from her fear of children and the monstrous things of which they were capable, the thought of which terrified her. Once Jeremy had thoughtlessly said to her, "It is the oddest thing, but the most cunning and clever crimes are committed by children under the age of ten, and are the hardest to detect."

"I know," Ellen had said, remembering. He had looked at her, amused.

"And how would you know that?" he had asked.

"I don't know. I just know." She was thinking of the children of Preston who had persecuted her and had despised and ridiculed her. She saw their gleefully beaming faces as they had chased her when she was as young as four, and their vicious catcalling, and their flung stones. She remembered the children in her school who had pointedly refused to sit near her, and had pushed her aside in the aisles and in the dusty corridors; the pushing had sometimes been so violent that she fell. She had finally decided that it had been because her aunt and she had been so poor and her clothing had been so patched.

Jeremy had remarked, "What is it that Solomon had said about children? 'Man is wicked from his birth and evil from his youth.' What's wrong, Ellen?"

"There must be some good children," Ellen had replied. "Children who love and trust and are not vicious."

Now, this morning, the fear was sharp upon her. She argued against it. The world, surely, could not endure if all was wickedness and evil. Perhaps all the ills of the world arose because of a lack of love and trust on the part— of a few. She calmed herself, temporarily, and tried to think of the blessed quiet and coolness of the house on

Long Island, with its wide white porches and white clapboards and its great gardens and open windows where the
lace curtains floated like wings in the freshening winds.
The thought momentarily overcame the sounds of the
street outside, the rising explosions of firecrackers, and the
busy rattling of carriages and the human laughter and
the quick footsteps and greetings below. The clock struck
half past eight. This morning they would not have breakfast in her bedroom until nine, for it was a holiday and
New Yorkers did not rise as early on a holiday as did the
people in the small towns of Pennsylvania.

There would be a parade at twelve down Fifth Avenue.
Ellen had never seen an impressive parade, and she had
cajoled Jeremy into taking her in their carriage to see it.
Even now there was the distant sound of a band and
Ellen could almost see the fierce gold circles of light on
the trumpets, and she became a little excited.

It was then that her first pain came to her, sharp in the
small of her back, and penetrating. A dull wave of spasmodic pain also washed over her belly, and she was
alarmed. The wave subsided and retreated, and she closed
her eyes and thought she could see it leaving her. Fresh
sweat broke out on her face and breast. Then she saw that
Jeremy had raised himself on his elbow and was looking
down at her with quick anxiety.

"It's nothing. It's just a little pain, and it's gone now,"
Ellen said, and lifted his hand to her lips and kissed it.
He lay down again and took her into his arms and kissed
her wet forehead and then her mouth and held her gently
but tightly against his body and she was at peace.

Cuthbert knocked at the door, then entered discreetly,
as stately and magnificently aristocratic as usual. He
carried a large silver tray which he deposited on the
round table nearby and said, "Good morning, sir, madam." He unfolded white linen and put it on the table.
He moved deftly in the hot gloom and added, "It is a
very warm day." Carefully, as always, he avoided looking
directly at the large bed, as he laid out covered silver
dishes, a silver coffee pot and a silver platter of fresh cold
melon and a rack of savory toast. Then he gave Jeremy
his robe and assisted him into it. Ellen waited until he had
left to move heavily to the edge of the bed, where Jeremy
could help her to rise. She felt heavier than usual and
more clumsy, and now the pain struck her in her back

again. But she was determined not to alarm Jeremy, for this was a holiday and he enjoyed the rare opportunity to rest and eat a pleasant slow breakfast with her. She went into the gold-and-marble bathroom, then sat abruptly on the short lounge. She began to gasp; the sweat on her face and body became cold and she shivered. It finally took all her power of will to wash her hands and face with the scented soap and to comb her damp and tangled hair. She saw her face in the mirror, very pale, and there were sharp lines about her nose. The pain was subsiding again, and she forced herself to smile and returned to the bedroom, where Jeremy was holding her chair.

"Is something wrong, Ellen?" he asked as she lowered herself painfully in her chair.

"Nothing," she said. "It is the heat. And it is almost time, you know."

"Not for two weeks. Should I call Dr. Lampert?"

"Oh, he isn't in town. Don't you remember that he said he would be in Boston for this holiday and the weekend, visiting his daughter? And my two nurses have gone to Newark for the holiday, too. No one expects the baby for at least fourteen days." Ellen made herself gay and smiling. "Do sit down, dear Jeremy, and have a nice breakfast. Those lamb chops look delicious." But the sight and smell of the food suddenly sickened her.

"And the housekeeper, Mrs. Frost, has the day off, and one of the housemaids, and your damned silly Clarisse, for the holiday, and there's nobody here but us and Cuthbert and one of the maids, and your aunt and Miss Ember."

"They have very few holidays, Jeremy," said Ellen. "I must talk with you about that sometime. They deserve more." She changed the subject and said with assumed exuberance, "And you've promised to take me to the parade today, at twelve." A deep numb languor was beginning to overtake her. She looked at the plate which Jeremy had filled for her and nausea rose in her throat.

"I don't know about the parade," said Jeremy. "You don't look well."

He waited for her cry of disappointment and was alarmed when she said nothing.

"Well, it is very hot," she said finally. "This is my first summer in New York, and it is very much warmer than Wheatfield. But you must go, Jeremy."

"I've seen many a New York parade," he replied. He lifted the morning newspaper, and frowned at one of the headlines. President Roosevelt had remarked, in view of the Day of Independence, that "our manifest destiny is to confer upon the world the civilization of our race, our form of government, our Anglo-Saxon spirit, by persuasion if possible, by force of arms if necessary." Idiot, thought Jeremy. Doesn't he know who has inspired him to talk such dangerous imbecilities? Or does he? Jeremy thought of the events of the Panama Canal not long ago, and Roosevelt's part in the matter and his smug remark when congratulated: "Some people say I fomented insurrection in Panama. No, I simply lifted my foot!" Jeremy also thought of the offer Roosevelt had made Colombia for the perpetual use by the United States of the territory for the Canal: ten million dollars in cash and an annual rent of two hundred and fifty thousand dollars, for three hundred square miles. When Colombia had appeared doubtful Roosevelt was infuriated and exclaimed, "Bandits! Corruptionists, blackmailers—we'll have to give a lesson to those jackrabbits." To Secretary of State John Hay he wrote, "Those contemptible little creatures in Bogotá!" He had considered sending American troops to occupy the Isthmus.

But, oddly enough, this had not been necessary. An ambiguous lobbyist named Bunau-Varilla entered the very intricate spiral of negotiations and threats. There was also William Nelson Cromwell, who represented the rights of the French Company which had begun the work of the Canal and then had abandoned it. Congress had authorized the creation of the Canal through the hot jungles, and had consented to pay the "French Company" forty million dollars for their rights. Cynics might have questioned —and some did, futilely—that the French Company and the United States totally ignored the very real "rights" of the Colombian government, which governed the land, and that neither France nor the United States had absolute rights there at all, except that France had originally leased the land for two hundred and sixty million dollars.

Then entered the mysterious Bunau-Varilla, who, less than a year ago, on October 14, 1903, had met with a number of Panama "secessionists" in the Waldorf-Astoria Hotel in New York, and there had decided that the area of the Canal must be a separate and independent republic, apart from Colombia itself. So the new Republic of Panama was born. The Colombian garrison in Panama had meekly submitted—after considerable bribery on the part of the United States—and had withdrawn, and the new President of Panama had exclaimed joyfully, "President Roosevelt has made good! Long may he live!"

On November 6 Secretary Hay formally recognized "the free and independent Republic of Panama." A week later the two countries signed a treaty which "gave" the United States the Canal Zone, and Panama accepted ten million dollars. The J. P. Morgan Company of New York received the forty million dollars originally offered by the United States to the French Company, but who finally got that money was never fully known. It was known, however, that the representative of the French Company, William Nelson Cromwell, the corporation lawyer, received eight hundred thousand dollars.

There had never been any doubt in Jeremy Porter's mind that the Canal was necessary, not only for the United States but for international trade also. But the method of taking the Zone was something which aroused his intense suspicions. He was always being accused of being an exigent man, but he despised expediency, especially when it involved arrogance, force, threats, bribery and corruption, and the veritable seizure of land which did not belong to the United States or France. Roosevelt, he once said, was the real bandit, not Colombia. The fact that good relations between the United States and all South America had rapidly declined into sullen enmity on the part of the southern countries had not disturbed Roosevelt in the least. He had only repeated his epithets contemptuously concerning America's southern neighbors, including "jackrabbits," and worse.

On reading the paper this hot Fourth of July, Jeremy tried to be objective. One must not always be on the alert concerning the Scardo Society and the Committee for Foreign Studies; the matter of the Canal was a small thing —wasn't it? Or did it imply that the "road to empire," about which Roosevelt had once remarked approvingly, was already embarked upon by America? If so, who was behind it? It was not the plan of the Scardo Society and the Committee for Foreign Studies that America become a world empire all by herself. This Jeremy had learned. Rather those mysterious and invisible and powerful men wanted a world government, for themselves, with absolute despotic regimentation. Was the Canal part of the "conspiracy"? The Canal benefited all nations— Still, Jeremy thought, and rubbed his chin. He had a low opinion of President Roosevelt. It was most probable that he had no part in the conspiracy, for his intelligence was not remarkable, and at the very least the conspirators were men of extraordinary intellect and would not be inclined to include among them a man of Roosevelt's limited cerebral capacities. He was also a chauvinist, and his patriotic perorations were obviously sincere even to the suspicious ears of Jeremy himself. Roosevelt loved his country with overwhelming pride and passion. No, he was no man for the Society and the Committee.

But someone had given him orders or suggestions in a very subtle manner which could not affront his devotion to his country, and his zeal for her. There was the matter of the "liberation" of Cuba, for instance, and the seizure of the Philippines and Hawaii, only recently. Only one thing could have moved him deeply, the insinuation that America must become an imperialistic and dominant empire, even if she retained the form of a republic. The fact that he was most probably not part of the conspiracy did not make him the less dangerous. Foolish if potent heads of state could be easily manipulated through their egotism and even their virtues, whereas wiser and more astute men would resist, for they were cynical. Roosevelt was conspicuously free of cynicism, which made him more of a menace, as all fervent fools were menaces.

He was up for re-election this November. His opponent was the gentleman Roosevelt was distinctly not, a modest Democrat named Alton B. Parker, who had been known to shudder at the mention of the incumbent President. The Democrats had some very knowledgeable, clever, and virile men among them. Why had the Democratic Party chosen as its candidate for the Presidency a man who could easily be defeated by the exuberant, shouting, howling, and belligerent Roosevelt?

The average American appeared to adore Roosevelt. Did the Democratic Party, the conservative party in America, truly believe that it was now time to offer the people a less rambunctious man, a more thoughtful and reflective man? If so, they were making a deadly error, for America was still a frontier country, vital and noisy and active as Roosevelt himself. Surely the Democratic pols knew that. Was it possible that they had been subtly influenced to offer a colorless gentleman as opponent to Roosevelt so that the latter would win the election?

It had always been Jeremy's intention to rid Ellen of what he considered her "damned young sentimentality and vulnerability," while at the same time not inciting cynicism and hardness in her, and that depraved sophistication which marked Kitty and her kind. He had met a few, a very few, ladies of both elegance and sweetness, and a gentle worldliness, and he hoped that Ellen would become one of these. Yet he had a hard suspicion that it was Ellen's very innocence which made her so dear to him, an innocence which did not distort, however, a certain astuteness and intuition; on rare occasions, she had revealed a native iron steadfastness of character which was not worldliness at all but rose out of her innocence. For she could not endure cruelty, hypocrisy, or treachery of any kind, or any falseness. (Though she seemed curiously blind to these things in her friend Kitty, which mystified Jeremy.) At last he had come to the conclusion that she could not recognize those traits if they were covert and concealed with smiles and amiability, and this dismayed him, for he never himself went unarmed.

On mornings like this, leisurely and slow and pleasant, he would not only read his newspaper without hurry but would have Ellen read the more important news as well, and would encourage her to express opinions, which often surprised him with their clarity and common sense and even subtlety. So now he said, "Ellen, read this about our bouncing President."

He looked at his young wife and because of the radiance of her smile he did not at first see how increasingly white she had become, nor the lines of suffering about her beautiful lips. As always, her beaming adoration for him startled him as if he had been struck with light in the midst of darkness, and he thought, as he often thought: No one should love another human being as Ellen loves me. It is dangerous, deadly. Yet with this thought came a passionate tenderness as well as fear for her.

She took the newspaper from him, but first poured him a second cup of coffee, and he saw how delicate her once scored hands had become, and, in a touching way, how newly fragile. She read the President's words, and a faint frown puckered her forehead. She put down the paper and looked at Jeremy with a long thoughtfulness. "Well?" he said.

"He's not a very intelligent man, is he?"

"No one ever accused him of that, Ellen."

"He seems to forget that this country is not entirely Anglo-Saxon," said Ellen, "but is composed of many other races which have made America strong and increasingly powerful. I wonder, for instance, what the Poles, the Jews, the Hungarians, the French, and all the rest of the non-Anglo-Saxons think of such silliness?"

"I don't think they are laughing," said Jeremy. "If the Democrats had nominated someone of character and strength instead of that poor fish Parker, I think they could have beaten Teddy Bear. Maybe they didn't want to."

Ellen's face became anxious, even brooding. "I just thought of that myself," she said. "I often think of what you've told me about the Scardo Society and the Committee for Foreign Studies. It's very hard to believe in such villainy."

"You may believe in it," said Jeremy.

"What is it that they want? Yes, you've told me. Power. But it must also be something else—"

"It is. Hatred of the human race." When he saw that her face had saddened and that she had looked away from him, he lightly touched her hand.

"There is nothing a girl like you can do about it," he said, to comfort her. Then she raised her eyes and he saw that their large blueness had become almost piercing.

"But you are trying to do something about it, aren't you, Jeremy?"

He had never told her about his election to the Scardo Society. He said, "Now, what can I possibly do? Nothing."

"I don't believe that, darling."

He became serious. "I hope you haven't talked to Kitty or her friends of what you do believe, Ellen, about me?" His concern almost reached alarm.

She smiled at him slightly. "Jeremy, our talks together are just that—our talks together. Besides, I am afraid that most of the ladies I know are under the impression that I am very stupid." Her smile widened. "Possibly they are right."

"I've discovered that an appearance of stupidity can be a very fine safeguard," he said. "Against this damnable world. Some of the cleverest and wisest men I know often pretend to be stupid. It's surprising what they learn and hear by simply grunting and keeping their mouths shut."

Ellen laughed a little. "I don't hear much, except gossip, and discussions of styles and domestics and dinners, and something called the 'new woman,' and the suffragettes. I sometimes think this bores Kitty, too, and she usually changes the subject. She is a great reader of *Everybody's* magazine, and just a short time ago she quoted an article in it. 'We'll find ourselves cheering on the working woman who chooses to be a supporting rather than a supported wife. Why shouldn't a married woman work if she chooses and can?' "

"And what did the ladies say to that?"

Ellen laughed again. "They were horrified."

"I bet," said Jeremy. "Such a lot of coddled and useless females. Do you offer them any opinion of your own?"

"Occasionally. Not that they listen to me."

Cuthbert came in to take the breakfast tray, followed by a disgruntled and surly housemaid who resented working today. She desultorily drew Ellen's bath, then returned to the rooms to make the bed and dust with small jerks of her cloth. Cuthbert began to leave the bedroom, then glanced at Ellen. "Is there something wrong, Mrs. Porter?" he asked.

Jeremy acutely looked at his wife and saw that her pallor had increased and that her face gleamed with sweat and that her lips were white. He started to his feet with fresh alarm.

"Ellen! What is wrong?"

But suddenly Ellen could not speak for the intense agony she was suffering. Cuthbert gave the tray to the maid and motioned for her to leave. He came to Ellen's side and studied her intently.

"I believe the time has come, Mr. Porter," he said.

Jeremy bent over his wife and he saw that her eyes were filmed over and dilated. The hot air of the bedroom now resounded with the strident and triumphant clamor of the marching bands on Fifth Avenue, and footsteps raced down the street and voices rose in louder laughter and excited exclamations. Ellen's lips moved, but the noise shut off her voice. She could only look at Jeremy in mute appeal.

"Help me, Cuthbert," he said, and together the two men lifted Ellen and carried her to her bed. "Damn, damn," said Jeremy. "And Lampert's out of town and so are the nurses, and we're alone except for you, Cuthbert, and one maid." He was very frightened.

"I believe Dr. Lampert has an assistant," said Cuthbert. "Shall I ring him, sir?"

"At once. Please." Jeremy bent over the stricken girl, who now held his hand in her wet and slipping fingers. She began to writhe feebly and draw up her legs in a spasmodic reaction to her anguish of body. It was unusual for Jeremy to feel helpless, but now he was overcome with a sense of impotence and weakness. He drew a chair to the bedside. "Ellen, Ellen," he said, knowing the most intense fear of his life. "Are you in much pain, my love?"

She tried to halt her agonized movements and tried to smile. "Just a little," she said. "Please don't worry, Jeremy."

Cuthbert returned, in a state of anxiety. "The assistant himself is in the hospital, with that new disease, appendicitis. Is there anyone else you know, in the medical profession, Mr. Porter?"

"There's old Dr. Parsons, but he's full of arthritis and is practically crippled. There's Dr.— No, he told me he was sailing on the Long Island Sound for this week. I don't seem to have many physician friends, damn it. And we're all alone here."

"There's Mrs. Watson's nurse, Miss Ember," said Cuthbert, frowning. He did not like Miss Ember, who was both tall and stout with a very small head and cruel little eyes; she had a thin knot of black hair on her skull, and a twisting sly smile as if, as she often said herself, "I could tell a tale or two, if it wasn't unprofessional. Medical Ethics, you know."

At the mention of Miss Ember's name, Ellen became momentarily still. Her glazed eyes opened wide. "No, no," she muttered. "Not Miss Ember, not ever."

"Why not? She's better than nothing, Ellen."

But out of the deep pit of her pain Ellen felt an irrational terror, and did not know why she felt it. She was only invaded by a nameless dread and shrinking. "No, no, not Miss Ember," she pleaded in a dim voice. "I don't know—I just don't want her near me, or even in this room."

"That's foolish," said Jeremy, trying to sound stern. "She's a nurse. She's competent. She must have attended dozens of births." But Ellen was shaking her head feebly on the pillow and her grasp on Jeremy's hand tightened. "Please," she whispered, and her terror quickened, for some primal instinct was clamoring in her.

Then Jeremy had another distracted thought. "Your friend Kitty, Ellen. She must know some doctor we don't know." He told Cuthbert to call Kitty's home, and the elderly man literally ran from the room and down the long hall to the upper telephone.

In the meantime, Ellen gave herself up to her suffering though she did not release Jeremy's hand. Her fingernails cut into his flesh. She was struggling against the pain, and was gasping and moaning deep in her throat. Jeremy released his hand and went into the bathroom to wet a cool cloth for that hot and contorted young face, and he tenderly wiped it while murmuring distraught words of comfort and reassurance. The bands had swung into one of Sousa's most thunderous marches and it seemed to Jeremy that the very walls of the large bedroom were vibrating with the shouts and trumpets and the turbulence of drums. There were also explosions, and the smell of gunpowder invaded the room on gusts of hot air. The light had become dazzling.

Cuthbert returned. "The lady is much concerned, Mr. Porter. She will call one or two doctors she knows. Then she will come here herself, as soon as possible." He hesitated. "Would you consider a hospital, sir, in this emergency?"

"Good God," said Jeremy. "Not one of those pest-houses for the poor!"

"Some are excellent, sir, and more and more people are going to them."

"Not for my wife," said Jeremy. "She doesn't need an operation, nor has she some disease. I won't permit her to go to one of those dens of infection."

Out of his fear he felt a wild impatience for Ellen, who would not have Miss Ember with her. He did not like the woman himself, but at least she was a nurse. In this extremity she was far better than nothing.

Then Ellen had a sudden cessation of her anguish and

she subsided on her pillows with a deep quivering sigh. She closed her eyes and fell into a sodden doze. But the sweat was heavier on her face. Jeremy watched her, while Cuthbert stood near the door almost as frightened as the husband himself. He did not like the "look" of Mrs. Porter. Her silence, her immobility, disturbed him. Her swollen body raised the sheets over her. Her face had dwindled, become sunken.

Jeremy was thankful that Ellen slept, if only for a little while. This might pass. Dr. Lampert had told him that very often, especially in the case of a first child, there might be occasions of "false labor," and this was not to be alarming and would fade away.

Long moments moved into half an hour and Ellen still slept, though occasionally her head moved restlessly. There was a bead of blood at the corner of her mouth. Jeremy did not wipe it away, for it might awaken the girl. He sat by the bed and heard nothing of the noise outside, for all his attention was fixed on Ellen. He did not even hear the doorbell ring, but Cuthbert went from the room with agility. He returned with Kitty, who was all soberness, though very smart in her mauve silk suit and straw hat filled with mauve and pink flowers. Her big teeth glistened ferally, through her silvery veil, though she was not smiling now. She tiptoed to the bed, laid her hand on Jeremy's shoulder, and stared down at Ellen. What a blowsy, overblown creature! she thought. She looks more like a peasant than she did before. Kitty bent and whispered to Jeremy, "Is the poor child in much pain?"

"Not just now," he whispered in return. "Could you get a doctor, Kitty?"

Her hushed voice was mournful. "I've sent my servants scurrying all over town. I called a few doctors myself, especially my own, but they're either out of town or incompetent to help Ellen. Many of them don't even have medical degrees—they are old and are the products of 'diploma mills.' I wouldn't have them for one of my cats!"

She had, in fact, called but one physician, and to the end of her life even her lucid mind could not explain to her why this had been so, though she asked herself the question frequently, not out of shame or regret, but out of curiosity. She did not like ambiguities, especially concerning her own motives. She only knew that on this morning she had experienced a leap of hope and exultation, to which she would not give a definite name.

She only remembered that as she looked down at the dozing girl she was seized by a passionate hatred, and despised her, and so fierce was the emotion that she herself had been momentarily startled. She also remembered that she had become conscious of some intensity in the air of the bedroom and she had glanced over her shoulder and had encountered the steady stare of Cuthbert, where he stood at his post near the door. There was something in that stare that intimidated her, she who was never intimidated by anything or anyone.

"What the hell shall we do if this is real labor?" Jeremy asked her, and she started and pressed her hand more firmly on his shoulder, then patted it.

"Well, I'm no authority on childbirth, Jerry. But there's that nurse of Ellen's aunt."

"Ellen won't permit her even in this room, Kitty. She begged me not to allow her to come in. I don't know why."

A sharp gleam touched Kitty's agate crinkled eyes. "How silly," she murmured. "Ellen often speaks of the woman's competence in caring for her aunt. One mustn't listen to whims of women in her condition." She thought of Miss Ember, who had shown her the obsequiousness due to her station, but who had manifestly detested Ellen. Kitty's hand patted Jeremy's shoulder rhythmically but with a quickening tempo. Darling Jerry, she thought, to be caught in this abominable situation by this gross dull creature! How ugly Ellen looked, sweating on her pillows, her disordered hair streaming about her and darkening with sweat. How graceless, how vulgar. A cow, she thought, a young cow. How could Jerry have stooped to this? If anything—happened—he would be well rid of her.

Jeremy continued to sit by his wife's bed, leaning close to her as if all his world lay there and there was nothing else. Kitty saw his expression, and her own features shriveled and she was furiously jealous, enraged and disgusted, and then sick with her own deep pain. She removed her white silk gloves, and then her hat, and laid them on the table. She did not know why she was trembling. She smoothed the great shining black pompadour which loomed over her small parched face and which heightened the scarlet thread of her lips. What if the child died, too?

Then Ellen suddenly shivered and uttered a loud gasping cry and opened her eyes, which were misted with the water of renewed and more savage agony.

"Oh, Jeremy!" she cried. "Jeremy, Jeremy, help me!"

He took her in his arms but she struggled. Kitty looked at Cuthbert and said, "Call Miss Ember down here, at once."

The stench of hot stone filled the bedroom, and the odor of animal urine, and the blinding blaze of sunlight. A fine yellow dust compounded of street sweepings and dried horse manure blew through the windows, coating everything on which it settled, and drifting in the air, chokingly. Jeremy held Ellen to him and sweated. Someone leaned over the girl and wiped her face with a cool wet cloth, and Jeremy glanced up to see the grave and kindly face of Cuthbert. The houseman then stepped back a pace and stood there, as if on guard. Miss Ember came into the room, stiff with white starch. She and Kitty looked sharply and meaningly at each other and understood each other at once. There was a sudden emanation of pure evil now in the room and Ellen, even in her agony, felt it, as did Cuthbert.

"Well, well," said Miss Ember, as if amused. She looked down at Ellen, and she wet her lips and her eyes gleamed and her small topknot of black hair caught a shaft of light. Her apron rustled. "Seems like the time has come. Mr. Cuthbert told me there is no doctor. Never mind, Mr. Porter. I think I can take care of things. Now, if you gentlemen will just leave the room—" She picked up Ellen's writhing hand and felt her pulse, and nodded with satisfaction. The pulse was erratic and pounding.

Ellen's eyes flew open and fixed themselves wildly on the face of Miss Ember, and she shrank. "No, no!" she cried. "Go away! Please go away!" She clutched Jeremy's arm with desperate fingers. "Send her away. Jeremy, send her away." Her mind filled up with dread and fear and she forgot her pain for a moment or two. She felt as if death itself had touched her hand. Cuthbert moved nearer the bed, his own instincts aroused and alert.

"I think," he said, looking at Miss Ember with a quietly

terrible expression, "that Mr. Porter and I will remain, if
you please, Nurse."

"Really," said Kitty, "I think it most improper, Jeremy,
for you to remain. And very embarrassing." She clucked
with loving sympathy and advanced to the bed. "Ellen,
dearest, I know you are suffering, but it will soon be over.
Tell Jeremy to leave, do. There are things to do which
gentlemen should not see." Shaking her head with affectionate rebuke, she covered Ellen's sprawled and trembling
legs with the sheet, and lowered her glittering eyes as if
shocked, and she made a moue.

"Don't leave me, Jeremy," said Ellen, through her gasps
of torment. "Something will happen—don't leave me."
She caught his hand in a revival of terror.

"I won't, love," he said.

A glance like the edge of a naked knife flashed between Kitty and Miss Ember. Neither had any thought
they dared put into words in their own minds, but the
urgency was there and the primeval malice and desire.
Neither asked herself, "Why do I hate this girl, and why do
I wish her to die?" For there was no answer; even their
wicked souls recognized that amorphously, but their self-
esteem and self-love would not permit them to face it
honestly, and know themselves for what they were.

Cuthbert said in a loud clear voice, "I have seen children born before. I know what should be done, though
I cannot do it myself."

"Really," said Miss Ember, obsequiously echoing Kitty.
"Most improper."

"Birth and death are," said Cuthbert, and Jeremy looked
at him with chaotic astonishment. Then Ellen saw Cuthbert and she groaned, "Don't leave me, please. Don't
leave me."

"Of course not," said Cuthbert. "Mr. Porter, if you will
just move your chair a little aside so Miss Ember—
Thank you. Mrs. Wilder, towels if you please. They are
in that chest near your elbow." He held Ellen's hand
strongly and smiled down at her. "Courage," he said.
"We are brave, aren't we?"

Ellen suddenly smiled at him from her wet pillows.
"No, Cuthbert," she said in a faint voice. "We aren't.
Not a bit."

All at once she screamed, for Miss Ember had roughly
inserted her large thick fingers into the birth canal.

"Gently, gently," said Cuthbert. "This is not a mare you are delivering, my dear woman. This is a young girl, a human being, if you please."

Kitty jeered in herself. She laid the towels on a pillow and pushed up her sleeves. Miss Ember extended Ellen's legs, as far apart as possible; she was enraged at Cuthbert, who was watching her every move. Old fool, she thought. I'd like to kill him, and the thought so relieved her that she ministered to Ellen less rudely and brutally. The fury could be expressed in her mind, and she was almost assuaged, as well as frustrated. She projected her hatred upon him and so it was like a catharsis. She looked over her shoulder at Kitty and Kitty looked aside. "Don't we have boiling water at a time like this?" Kitty asked. "I think I heard that somewhere. Cuthbert, will you—"

"I'd prefer not to leave, madam," he said with the greatest courtesy. "Will you be so kind as to get a large jug of it, and a bowl?"

Miss Ember felt the child's small head in the canal, and the most horrible impulse came to her to crush it in her strong fingers. Then even she was appalled at that impulse, and her nurse's training mechanically asserted itself. For an instant only she had experienced a deep nausea and her body shook very hard and briefly. A gush of blood poured from Ellen's body, and again she was screaming. Miss Ember said, "So big a girl, but the pelvic area is uncommonly small. Mrs. Porter, bear down quickly. Can you hear me, Mrs. Porter? Stop screaming! You must help me, if you want your child to be born alive. I think the cord's caught. Mrs. Porter! Hold Mr. Porter's hands with both your own and push. There now."

Jeremy thought he would vomit at the sight of Ellen's blood. Her wet hands clenched his. Her eyes were so distended that the glistening whites circled the pupils, and her mouth, not screaming now, was open and panting. He cursed himself for inflicting this on Ellen. Acid tears gathered in his own eyes. He kissed her mouth and murmured incoherently, as Ellen pushed down. She saw the top of his head so sharply that she was conscious of a poignant compassion for him. "Yes, yes," she murmured. She must hurry, she thought. Jeremy could not stand much more of this. She was filled with a storm of love in spite of the fiery anguish she was enduring.

Kitty had left the room and now she returned with a

maid and a copper kettle of steaming water. The maid looked distastefully at Ellen and was pleased at her raw pain, for Ellen had always been kind to her, and considerate. She smirked and affected a delicate shudder, and poured hot water into a bowl and held it nearby.

Miss Ember was giving Kitty orders, and, averting her eyes as much as possible, Kitty assisted under the unmoving watchfulness of Cuthbert. The smell of sweat pervaded the room. Faces dripped and itched. Jeremy rubbed his chin on his shoulder; he never released Ellen's slipping hands.

"Ah," said Miss Ember, with genuine gratification. "There is the head!"

The child's head had emerged, streaming with blood. The tumult of the bands on Fifth Avenue seemed to increase their volume in triumph, and the whole room was thunderous with the sound of drums and trumpets and flutes. Ellen uttered such a great cry that the music of the bands was almost obliterated. She writhed and screamed again, over and over, and now she was only a primitive female animal, mindless with her unendurable travail, forgetful even of Jeremy. She threshed on the bed; Miss Ember appealed to Cuthbert and Jeremy to hold the girl down. Ellen bent her head and bit her own arm, groaning. "God," said Jeremy. "Oh, Christ!"

Slowly now the child's body presented itself. "There!" exclaimed Miss Ember. "Another minute— There, there is the baby! And a boy, too!"

She was exultant. She had forgiven herself and so had forgiven Ellen. "Scissors, please, Mrs. Wilder. Mr. Cuthbert, that big towel, please, to wrap the baby in." She tore a smaller towel into ribbons, as Ellen's child lay between her thighs. The nurse tied the severed cord and to Ellen's renewed screams she delivered the placenta. Jeremy retched. Through a haze he darkly saw someone lift his son and wipe him with damp linen which steamed and became bloody. It was Cuthbert now who was wrapping the child in a large soft towel. The room palpitated with relief and a kind of hysteria. Ellen was no longer screaming. She lay limp and white and dwindled, her eyes shut, her mouth gaping and silent. Jeremy felt as if he himself had passed through childbirth, and he was prostrated.

Someone was giving him brandy, and he looked up and

saw, through that trembling haze, the smiling grave face of Cuthbert. "Congratulations, sir," said the older man. "It is a fine boy—your son. A very fine boy."

But Jeremy looked only at Ellen and as he looked she opened her eyes and like a child she whimpered and then began to cry and she moved into Jeremy's arms, bloody and wet though she was, and she fell asleep, uncaring about her child. Again, she had reached surcease and comfort in her husband.

Kitty Wilder peeped at Miss Ember, and then both women looked aside sheepishly, and wiped their faces. Each felt an aversion for the other, though nothing had ever been said, and each believed the other unspeakably guilty and detestable. In this way they absolved themselves. But they also felt a stronger aversion for Ellen, the source of their guilt.

Shouts came from Fifth Avenue and a higher crescendo as the colors passed, and all America sang in naïve exultation and a passionate and simple love of country, uncomplicated by doubt or bitter cynicism or troubled questioning. It was noon, one of the last peaceful and hopeful noons America would ever know again. Her enemies were moving.

15

Ellen went up in the elevator to see her aunt, accompanied by a nurse carrying Ellen's son in an embroidered shawl dripping with lace. May had not as yet seen the child, nor had she asked about him. She had "cried" day and night, said Miss Ember, and her arthritis had become worse. Ellen felt guilt; she had neglected Aunt May because she herself had still been confined to bed for several days after the birth. The doctor, coming belatedly two days later, had expressed concern for the girl. "If I did not know better, sir," he said to Jeremy, "I would believe the difficult birth—due to certain abnormalities of the—er—pelvic regions—was the result of malnutrition in childhood and severe manual labor when the bones were in the process of development. Rickets, if you will pardon me. It is rare for one to see this deplorable and painful condition in a lady like Mrs. Porter, who had, no doubt, a pampered and cherished and well-fed childhood, and all the care sedulous parents can give a little daughter. Very rare, indeed." To which Jeremy had said nothing, though the doctor waited inquisitively.

Ellen was still weak and pale, but she put a resolute and cheerful smile on her face as she entered May's quarters. May was sitting, huddled in shawls, near the window, though she rarely, for lack of interest, looked through that window. She seemed older and more withered, and Ellen felt a pang of self-reproach. "Dear Auntie," she said, "I am here at last, and with my baby, who will be christened in two weeks! Christian Watson Porter." She motioned to the nurse, a nice young girl all rosy cheeks and starch and fair hair and efficiency. She had taken a deep fondness for Ellen, who was near her age. "Miss Burton," added Ellen, indicating the nurse, who was peering with a sad lack of sympathy at May.

"It's about time you came," said May, sniffing in a watery fashion. "Never a word from you, Ellen, except for the messages you sent through Miss Ember." Miss Ember was standing nearby like a fat grenadier, her thick arms folded across her breast. She tossed her head and stared inimically at Miss Burton, who returned her stare, for a moment or two, with a slight sneer on her full pink mouth.

Ellen sat down near her aunt and the nurse placed the child in her arms. Ellen leaned towards May. "Look at him, Auntie. He has my red hair and eyes. Jeremy says he looks exactly like me. And eight pounds! Such a big boy." She tried to make her voice gay and light. May glanced at the child, then averted her face and wiped her eyes. "Yes. Looks like you. Too bad. But you never did have any looks, Ellen. Well."

Ellen was immediately depressed. She felt a wave of prostration. She returned the child to Miss Burton, who said in a determined voice, "Mrs. Porter is the most beautiful lady I've ever seen, and this boy here is going to be a lady-killer when he grows up, and big too. He's already bigger than most babies his age, and plump. Look at those pretty curls he has, and only nine days old. He wasn't wrinkled and red, monkey-like, like all the others I've seen. A real killer."

May sent a half-glance at the baby over her shoulder, and her gray face became sullen and offended. She avoided Ellen's placating and pleading eyes. She said, "Children aren't no bargain, Miss— What did you say your name was? Burton. I don't know why Ellen wanted a child; she ought to know better."

"And Mrs. Porter's doing fine," said Miss Burton, who needed no long explanations of human behavior. She had seen a great deal of it. "I'm glad you're happy she is feeling better every day."

"What?" said May. "You still look awful sick to me, Ellen. That's what women pay for having children. I still can't understand why you wanted—And a boy, too." Her frail voice reproached Ellen. All her former deep concern for Ellen had vanished. Ellen had been willful; Ellen had betrayed her; Ellen still insisted on pretending she was a lady born; Ellen refused to feel sorrow at deserting Mrs. Eccles, "who was so good to us, and we was happy with her. You had no right, Ellen." Pain and resentment had completely changed May, and she lived now in a state of self-pity and tears, and in an aura of pungent ointments and lotions for her disease. A table nearby, a beautiful piece of authentic Sheraton, held all her medicines in a disorderly array. Some had spilled and had ruined the finish of the surface. Her Bible held the most prominent space on the table, and a none too clean handkerchief marked the pages. Miss Ember had twisted one curtain at the window into a rope, "for air." The delicate lace and silk were grimy. The housemaid had refused to "do" the rooms; "It's that nurse's job." So the rooms were dusty and had an odor of must and decay. May, once so insistent on cleanliness and order, no longer cared. She pined for Mrs. Eccles' house, and daily her resentment of everything increased, and Ellen was the source of that resentment. I never thought, May would say to herself often, that Ellen'd turn out this way, so mean and selfish, and never thinking of anybody but herself, and never a thought for her poor aunt.

Ellen looked at her earnestly, leaning forward in her

pretty house robe of mauve silk and lace. "Is your pain better, Auntie?"

Much you care, thought May. She said in a whining voice, "No, it ain't. Worse every day. It's this heat; can't bear it. Wheatfield was nice and cool, even in July. Never hot like this, and so dusty. Bad for my arthritis. Can't sleep at night, mostly. Hardly walk, now."

"We'll soon be going to our house in the country, on Long Island," Ellen pleaded. "For weeks, right on the ocean."

"All that water! No, sir! Water'll make the rheumatism worse. Miss Ember told me, didn't you, Miss Ember? We're going to stay here."

Ellen was dismayed. "But, Auntie, we are closing up the house! The staff is going with us, too."

"We'll manage, alone, Mrs. Porter," said Miss Ember, tossing her head again. "It'll be quiet here, too; good for Mrs. Watson."

Ellen felt helpless. "I talked to Mr. Porter last night," Miss Ember added, with triumph. "He said it was perfectly all right, here, with a maid and a temporary cook. He's arranged it."

For some reason—and for which she was immediately guilty again, Ellen felt a profound relief, and a deep gratitude to her husband. Miss Ember smiled with victory, and with contempt for Ellen. "Nothing to worry about," she said.

If I was Mr. Porter, thought Miss Burton, I'd pack them off to some hotel and forget all about them. She felt no compunction at all. Her fondness for Ellen became stronger. She was concerned about her. The poor beautiful dear, even paler now, and so thin, and so sweet and kind, and trying to do the best for everybody: why don't she think of herself once in a while? Only yesterday Ellen had said to her, in response to some cynical remark by Annie Burton, "But you know we have to love and trust, Annie." Miss Burton had stared at her for a moment, in incredulity, and had then replied, "Who says so, ma'am? The parsons? What do they know about people?" She had then commented to herself with compassion: The poor dear thing talks so foolish, about people, when anybody knows what they are. She's going to be in bad trouble, one of these days, with all that "love." Annie had had a long talk with Cuthbert about this and

Cuthbert had nodded and had shaken his head. "We've got to take care of her," Annie had said. "I'm staying for a long time; Mr. Porter asked me, and that's one good thought. That Miss Ember! And that old aunt!"

Ellen and Annie returned to the nursery, where the nurse busied herself with the child. Ellen watched all this; her breasts were aching with milk. She said to herself: I wonder why I don't feel the way other women say they feel about their children? Why am I always so frightened, like a premonition? I do love the baby; I'd die for him. But there's really no one for me but Jeremy. He is always first, all the time. It seems to me far more important to be a good wife.

While she nursed her son Ellen's thoughts were engrossed with Jeremy, and she smiled, and Annie thought with tenderness: Her face shines like the sun. Never saw anything like it before. It's her goodness, that's what it is. Hope her kids appreciate that later, but you can never tell with kids. Serpents, mostly, that's what, when they grow up and smell their parents' money. Wish I could put some sense in her, poor darling. The good get all the kicks in this world, and all the hate and robbery, and mostly from those they love, too.

Ellen's face changed. Suddenly she was crying, and Annie came to her and put her firm plump arm about her shoulders. "There, there," she said. "Every new mother feels like this for a couple of months, dear. After-birth melancholy. There's no need to feel sad. This'll be the first dinner you've had downstairs with Mr. Porter since the baby was born. We want to look pretty, don't we?"

Ellen tried to laugh, then was depressed again. "It's just—I'm afraid. I don't know why, but I am afraid for Mr. Porter, and in some way for myself, too."

"Don't you worry about Mr. Porter," said Annie in a sturdy voice. "By the way, I don't like that maid of yours, Clarisse."

Ellen was surprised. "Why not?"

But Annie was discreet. She could not tell Ellen that every day Clarisse had a hushed conversation, accompanied by derisive giggles, with Mrs. Wilder, whom Annie despised. It was all about Ellen, and Annie knew that though they spoke in French. Annie's young face tightened and she pressed Ellen's shoulder with more protectiveness. "Oh, I don't know," she answered. "Guess we're not fated to be friends. Anyways, I wouldn't trust her too much if I was you. Don't talk to her so sweetly, and so kindly. Don't chatter to her about what you think and feel all the time, and confide in her."

Ellen gave Annie an indulgent smile. "Oh, Annie, Annie," she said. "What a cynic you are. I'm very fond of Clarisse."

All at once Annie felt helpless. How did you warn the good—they were so uncommon—that their very trustfulness was destructive to them, dangerously destructive, and often fatal? If they listened, and they very seldom listened, God help them, it might change them and they would be as wicked as the general run of mankind, and in some way the world would be poorer after their full knowledge and their loss of innocence.

Maybe, thought Annie, God will reward them someday, but I doubt it. She was an agnostic, something which shocked Ellen, as did Annie's lack of idealism. Annie's pink and pudgy face, with the pert upturned nose and shining gold eyelashes and eyebrows, and forthright gaze, would change and harden when Ellen talked of the "innate nobility of mankind," and her expression would become old and withdrawn, and her sense of dismay for Ellen would increase, and her incredulity. She knew Ellen's history by now, received from Cuthbert, Clarisse, and Miss Ember, and it seemed incomprehensible that one who had endured so much, and with such loving candor, could be so naïve and so defenseless and so ominously vulnerable, and so incapable of drawing grim and obvious conclusions. There was a certain stupidity in innocence, and Annie sometimes suspected it was this that aroused the ridicule of others.

Thank God she has a husband who is no fool, Annie would think. But what of the day when she doesn't have him? If there is a merciful God, and I don't believe there is, He will let her die before her husband does. She has no idea how to protect herself. She doesn't know how to be careful. Once it came to Annie, dismally, that if everyone "watched" each other, and there was no trust or love anywhere, misery and despair and hatred would overwhelm the world of men and there would be nothing but death. Ellen, in her own gentle insidious way, born of blamelessness, had given Annie her own doubts and uncertainties about her robust view of life, though Ellen was impervious to Annie's common sense. Neither girl understood that there must be a balance between love and trust —and realism. The ultimate in each destroyed the world as effectively as any plague. Christ was the God of wrath as well as the God of love, Ellen had yet to learn. But an absolute realist deprived the world of fantasy and beauty and mystery, and the immanence of God. Annie did not know that now. Still, in her generation she was wiser than Ellen, and much better armed against her fellow man.

Kitty Wilder affected to be overwhelmed by the "honor" bestowed on her and her husband on being godparents of the baby. "Oh, how adorable!" she would croon over the infant's crib. "How beautiful he is, Ellen, just like you! Imagine you choosing us for this darling's godparents! You know I don't like children much, but I am simply mad over this precious little one!" She would regard the child with secret detestation. How ugly he was, resembling his mother. He had none of Jeremy's handsomeness, Kitty would think. And what an awful name—Christian, which Ellen had chosen.

Ellen and Jeremy, remembering Kitty's forced helpfulness at the birth of the child, had given Kitty a bright diamond lavaliere in gratitude, and Kitty's little eyes had actually glowed, for she was not only rich but avaricious. "Ellen selected it," said Jeremy. Kitty did not believe it; it was so very tasteful—and expensive. She kissed Ellen rapturously. She looked at Jeremy with an almost abject adoration, and he smiled in himself.

The weeks on Long Island were blissful for Ellen, though she saw Jeremy only at the weekend, for it was too far and too long on the train from the city. She walked over the lawns and on the beach, and helped in the garden, and regained her vitality. She slept happily every night, waiting for Saturday and Sunday. Her hair took on its brilliant sheen again, and her blue eyes were radiant with light and joy. She ran like a child, and played tennis with neighbors, and cuddled her son. Watching her, and hearing her free and melodious laughter, Annie would feel old and battered by life, despite her own youth. Sometimes the girls would throw a ball to each other and shout and laugh, and Annie became rosier.

She could not, however, rid herself of a portent of disaster.

The neighbors became fond of Ellen, and indulgent, but it was a fond indulgence which inevitably became wryly amused and somewhat ironic and touched with disbelief at her ingenuousness. Seeing this, Annie once said to Ellen, "Mrs. Porter, dear, don't be so outspoken and kind and affectionate to these people. They don't understand you. They think you are a little—foolish."

"No," said Ellen, with her own indulgence, "they are only very good and pleasant to me, and why should I distrust them or think nasty things about them?"

Annie shrugged. "People are all the same. These neighbors of yours are no better than the Mrs. Eccles you told me about, or Miss Ember, or even Mr. Porter's father and mother. I know, believe me!"

Agnes and Edgar Porter had come to the christening in the nearby Episcopal church, and so had Walter Porter. Ellen tried to please Jeremy's parents, and had been overcome with shyness and awkwardness, and a deep old sense of inferiority, for they treated her with offended superciliousness and Agnes remarked on the lack of resemblance between the child and his father. So Ellen felt guilty in some manner, and Jeremy said, "He is beautiful, like his mother, and not an ugly monster like me."

The meeting had been constrained, to Ellen's suffering. She was glad when her guests departed. She said to Jeremy, "I don't think Mr. and Mrs. Porter care for me much, even now. Perhaps they are right. I am really nothing, you know."

"You are all the world," said Jeremy with some impatience. "At least, to me. Now then, smile like the silly angel you are."

His fear for Ellen was increasing. He was not alone. He had the company of his uncle, Walter Porter, and Annie Burton and Cuthbert. They circled the girl with protectiveness and hoped that time would make her less trusting, more cautious, and less intense in devotion to anyone who showed her the slightest acceptance and kindness. To Ellen the world now was a place of joy and delight and love, filled with friends and honor and spontaneous affection.

She was forgetting to be afraid of her child, in her happiness. She would rock him on the wide white porches

and look at the sea, marveling over its changefulness.
There were sunsets when the water resembled hammered
gold under the golden light, or it would be running brass
or whitely flowing beneath a white sky. Even the storms
entranced her. She wanted to cry in ecstasy. She would
sing, and her marvelous voice would echo in the wide
and tranquil evening silence, and Annie would listen and
tears would smart her eyes. Dear God—if there is a God
—the older girl would pray—don't let her know. Never
let her know what the world really is.

For Ellen had almost forgotten her wretched childhood
and girlhood. She was even forgetting Mrs. Eccles and
Wheatfield. If she remembered Mrs. Eccles at all it was
with pity, for Mrs. Eccles, Ellen would think, had lacked
all joyousness. In her way, she had been kind, Ellen
would force herself to believe. This was Ellen's method
of coming to terms with the years of her persecution
and labor and hunger and despair: If people really "understood" they would love and trust each other. It was
sad if circumstances forced them to be wary and malicious
and greedy, and even cruel.

Ellen, who had never had a childhood, became a child.
May complained to Miss Ember: "I think Ellen's lost her
wits, I really do."

16

"Well, how does it feel to be a Congressman?" Walter
Porter asked his nephew.

"You ask me that every time you see me, Uncle Walter.
Do you expect a different answer each time?"

"Of course," said Walter. "Who can stand Washington?
Terrible city. White sepulcher of rotting bones, stinking
with liars and thieves and charlatans and the endlessly
exigent. Does Ellen still dislike it?"

"Yes. She's never complained, but I know, even though she professes to be delighted with our house in Georgetown. I think it's the commuting between New York and Washington that really bothers her. She never had a home until she married me, as you know, and so New York, her first home, is the place where she lives, and Washington is only intangible and temporary. There's something she seemed to be afraid of there, too."

"I shouldn't wonder," said Walter Porter. "It scares the hell even out of me whenever I visit you there. Ellen's very sensitive; she doesn't know what is going on, but she senses it, intuitively, I sense it from observation and objective knowledge; Ellen knows the presence of evil subjectively, and it frightens her, as it would any other innocent. Is she getting along any more comfortably with your colleagues and their wives?"

Jeremy hesitated. "Well, yes and no. The men admire her, but are amused by her lack of sophistication. Most of them are kind to her, though, as one is kind to a child who is also beautiful and unaffected. But—their wives! When they're not snubbing her they are covertly ridiculing her, out of envy or malevolence, or patronizing her. The poor girl still hasn't learned why, and so she shrinks or hides or says nothing. I've never seen anyone so lacking in self-esteem, and I worry about it more and more. I've done my best, and I've had hopes, for under all that gentleness and genuine magnanimity there is a core of iron. I've seen it glitter a few times. But the hell of it is that she's always so confoundedly contrite afterwards and makes a fool of herself trying to conciliate and placate."

"Her grandmother, Amy Widdimer, was exactly like that, so you can't blame Ellen's childhood for her shyness and timidity. They're aristocratic traits, sadly lacking among American women, especially the suffragettes and the 'new women.' We're a plebeian country. Ellen's a lady, and what's a lady doing down there in Washington?"

Jeremy laughed. The two men were sitting in Jeremy's office in New York on this bleak and brown autumn afternoon. The sky was a sullen saffron, the streets were sepia crevices, and a dull ocher light lay over everything. The street traffic had a somber flat note, subdued and cheerless (like the Panic which had overwhelmed America this year), sometimes rising to a frenzied clatter, then subsiding again to a listless monotone, as if resigned.

Jeremy found it very depressing, even more depressing than Washington. He said, "I wonder why the people keep sending such clowns to Congress and the Senate, and even to the White House. If they're not naïve and as mindless as puddings, though usually hysterical, too, they're vicious and corrupt scoundrels. Present company excepted, of course." He smiled. "They bore me to death," and now he was not smiling. "Especially since I've found out what is going on among the 'quiet men,' nationally and internationally." He paused. "I can't understand the general public, which is comparatively intelligent and decent and hardworking, with a sense of honor and patriotism."

"It's because the rascals, and the fools, are such good actors, so earnest with their constituents, echoing what their constituents say and demand. Then behind the backs of those constituents they do whatever their foolish or black hearts prompt them, out of exigency. I wonder if we'll ever again have the kind of government we had following the Revolution. I doubt it."

"So do I." Jeremy drank deeply of his whiskey and soda. Walter said, "Any regrets?"

Jeremy hesitated. "Well, no. I know damned well I can't do anything about what is going on down there, and now I know that if I should open my mouth and shout it from the Capitol I'd either be kicked out of Washington or murdered. Or, worse yet, laughed at. I've tried to hint it to a few newspaper correspondents, and they just stare at me incredulously. Well, I shouldn't blame them. No politician is ever honest with the newspapers. He's either afraid, or prudent, or just a liar. No, you can't blame the newspapers. But a lot of the newspapers have good fun lampooning many politicians, and I'd like to tell their editors that they'd better make the most of the freedom they have now. It won't be long before they're regimented and threatened or browbeaten into submission to politicians, and government."

Walter pondered, then shook his head. "I'm counting on editors to insist on freedom of the press, one of our most important freedoms, and to fight every blackguard who intrudes on it in the name of 'public virtue' or 'national safety.'"

"Editors," said Jeremy, "are men, and men are human flesh and blood, and men have families, and men need to eat and have shelter and clothing. Their very humanity makes them vulnerable to mountebanks and malefactors. Also, many newspaper mortgages are owned by politicians and their very potent friends."

"We need a few heroes," said Walter, and then both men laughed cynically. After a moment or two Walter said, "Frank's never forgiven you for beating him twice in your mutual race for Congress. Candidly, I think he'd be delirious with happiness to be in Washington. He's made for Congress, born for it. They'd love him down there, and he'd love it, too. Of course, some would call him a dangerous radical—and some would call him a fool, and I think both designations are correct." His square and manly face became bitter. "Of course, he's an hysteric, but the whole damned town is hysterical, led by Teddy himself."

"And the whole country's hysterical, and terrified, with this Panic, and that's understandable. But how many of us know what caused that Panic?"

"Quite a lot of us. But who'd believe us? And the deadly men know that, and they laugh at us and know how impotent we really are. We don't have the money, we don't have the importance, we don't have the power to be heard by the country. When a few of us speak here and there, or write about it, we're called insane or crackpots, for our voices are puny. It's not that the people are apathetic. It's just that they would not believe there is a certain terrible destiny planned for them; they just don't believe in that much evil. We're still a trusting and simple-minded country, and the politicians, and those who control the politicians, intend to keep us that way as long as possible. What would the people say, if they really listened, when the true cause of this Panic, which is starving them to death and terrifying them, was explained to them, and they believed it?"

"There'd be another Revolution," said Jeremy. "But the malefactors aren't worrying. The people will never believe it, until it is too late."

"Well," said Walter, in a somewhat hopeless tone, "so long as we are able to keep Washington weak and small, and we have strong local governments in the jealous states, we'll have decentralized government, and so a measure of our freedom. But God help us if Washington ever becomes big and overpowering, with a swarm of harassing and arrogant bureaucrats who would rule by fiat and not by law. Then will come the man on horseback, attended by the bureaucratic vultures and hyenas, and that will be the end of America as it was the end of Athens and Rome, and God only knows how many other civilizations now lost to history."

"Washington was able to put through its antitrust laws, which will destroy productive advance and efficiency, in order to 'protect' the backward and hidebound smaller industries, and all in the name, too, of 'promoting competition,' which our politicians detest, being weaklings themselves—and 'fair practices.' We can shout to heaven that government protection of the inefficient and weak will destroy the strong, who are the builders of a nation, and it will do no good, for our enemies know that the coddling of the inferior will eventually eliminate the strong and bold and the way will be open to absolute uncontested slavery of all our people. So, the 'elite' use men like your son Frank, who are vociferous and hysterical and emotional, to inform the public that punitive measures used against the strong are all in the name of 'justice' and humanitarianism. Not that," added Jeremy with some ruefulness, "that I trust what we are calling the 'oil trust.' I've had the pleasure, if you can call it that, of meeting John L. Bellows, at a meeting of the Committee for Foreign Studies."

Walter sat up alertly, his white hair glinting with red shadows from the fire. "It would seem, then, that they are confident you are with them."

Jeremy frowned. "I don't know. Maybe they just like to have me with them to keep an eye on me, though I've been very circumspect, as you know. Very potent fellers. I knew all about them before, but just having knowledge is an impotent thing. You have to be in the actual presence of these men, and listen to them when they speak in confidence, to get the full impact of what they are up to. Cool and smooth as cream, and as lethal as cyanide."

"Did they say, during their last meeting, about the coming war?"

"I think they've moved up the date. I doubt it will now be 1917, '19, '20. I think it is imminent, perhaps in the next few years, and no later than 1915. Their timetable for Russia has been moved up, too. They are very confident, now, of instigating a Communist revolution in

Russia, with practically no opposition. They are showing fierce concern because Russia is getting more and more prosperous, and the Czar has abdicated much of his absolute monarchy, and the Duma is gaining in influence and is insisting on more and more freedom for the Russian people. If they let Russia alone for too long she will become a constitutional monarchy, like England, and there will go their long-laid plots to invade every country with Communism, or its sister, Socialism, and then seize power for themselves. There are constant meetings with bankers, including the Bellows clan, and other enormous financiers and industrialists and 'intellectuals' and high-placed politicians all over the world."

Walter closed his eyes wearily. "Yes. I've heard rumors, too, but nothing as definite as what you have just told me. Again, thank God, I won't live long enough to see the destruction of my country. I'm sorry for men your age, and your families. You'll have nowhere to turn; you'll have no hope, no refuge, no new continent to which to run and set up a new nation. Our last frontiers are vanishing, literally and figuratively. Where will men go, say, forty or fifty years from now, if they wish to be free? Religious oppression was bad enough in old Europe, but they had a young open land to flee to and make a fresh life for themselves. But the coming oppression will be universal and there will be no place for a man to hide and draw a free breath."

Jeremy saw the profound depression on his uncle's face, and he knew there was just reason for that depression. But he tried for cheerfulness. "Well, let's not be too pessimistic. Remember, we are not alone. There will be millions of men, being born now and in the future, who will fight for the right to live in freedom and in peace."

"Yes," said Walter with heaviness, "but the chaos first, and the wars, and the tyranny and the death! The four horsemen of the Apocalypse. Why do men wait for total ruin and destruction before they act?"

"Why don't you ask God?" said Jeremy. "He's seen this happen scores of times for millennia. If He has any angels, why aren't they whispering to mankind now?"

"Maybe they are, maybe they are," said Walter. "Who knows? Yes, I am glad I am old. I may see the beginning of the end, but I won't be around when the end comes."

"And you won't see men like your son Frank holding

enormous power over his abject countrymen. That should really cheer you up, Uncle Walter."

Walter grimaced. "I should never have let him go, for that year, to England, to listen to the Fabians, and come back all trembling with intensity and with shrill, savage, and vindictive hatred for manly men, men of patriotism and strength and honor. Not that I sent him to the Fabians, of course. He just wandered into their company. They're always recruiting men like my son, all over the world. Yet, he wouldn't have been so attracted to them if the disease wasn't waiting for a catalyst to explode in his mind. He was born that way. He's a born zealot, and you know what Talleyrand said about zealots."

Jeremy said, "I suppose millions of fathers look later at their adult children, and wonder how in hell they ever begat such sons, and what they had done to deserve them."

"I hope that won't happen to you, Jeremy, concerning your own children. How are Christian and Gabrielle? Has Ellen fully recovered from the birth of the little girl?"

Jeremy's face subtly became somber. "Yes. But she'll never be able to have any more children. It seems that her early poverty and deprivation and heavy work did something— She's healthy enough now, of course, but there's a malformation of her pelvic bones, the doctors say. As you know, she almost died this time. Considering everything, myself and Ellen and what's waiting for us, I'm really glad there'll be no further additions to the family."

A brown autumnal rain began to surge against the windows, and Walter stood up. "We Americans are becoming as concerned with soft sweet animal cozinesses and comforts as the British are also becoming. We all want to be let alone to suck on our sugar tits and have Mama sing us soothing songs, and tell us fairy tales about the wonderful future about to be granted us—by our dear friends in our government. I see that attitude creeping on deadly little feet, everywhere, even in stalwart Germany. The warm fireside is becoming more and more important to all of us, more than the heroic men who fought to make us a nation, and who gave us our liberty. Children! Where are our men now?"

"I have a faint hope they are still here. That's the only hope we have. I'm bringing up my children to love their country." He smiled, though not with paternal sentimentality, as if the thought of his children not only pleased him but amused him. "Christian's only three, but he is already shouting the words of Patrick Henry, which I taught him, and his enunciation is very good, too. As for little Gabrielle, I am teaching her a few words, at her elderly age of one, and she's already proficient. Pity she's such an ugly little wench, resembling me."

"On the contrary, she's very interesting in her appearance, I think," said Walter, with the fondness of a grandfather and not that of a mere great-uncle. "All that dark hair and shining dark eyes. Yes, very interesting and provocative, and intelligent. Full of mischief, even this early, and very knowing. You have two beautiful children, Jeremy. God grant they'll be—safe."

"Now, that's a word I detest—safe—Uncle Walter. The world's never been a safe place and it never will be. No, I don't want my children to be 'safe.' I want them to be strong, to have moral stamina, to be able to fight. Ellen once or twice suggested that I was a little too rigorous with them and demanded too much of them. Probably remembering the hardships of her own childhood. It is useless for me to point out that Christian can be sullen and resentful at times, and disobedient. When I punish him, she almost cries, though she doesn't interfere. That's one thing I won't allow from her—any dispute about how I am bringing up the youngsters. I think she's forgot how natively wicked children are—how wicked the whole human race is, and always was. Thank God I have the nursemaid, Annie Burton, still with us. There's a girl with rare common sense, and a hard hand on the kids. It's very baffling, when I think of her and Ellen, for Annie had a very rough time of it, too, when she was a child, almost as bad as Ellen did, and it's made Annie sturdy and cynical and realistic, whereas Ellen is a little Mrs. Rousseau, all by herself, even once suggesting that man was innately good and that it is 'society' which distorts him. I think your son Frank can be blamed for that foolishness of hers."

"Perhaps," said Walter with considerable glumness. "After all, he was the biggest influence in her life for the three years she was with my sister-in-law in Wheatfield." He sighed. "Francis is becoming more and more pontifical all the time—my only son. He resembles a priggish spinster, and his intolerance grows, as does his mawkishness about something amorphous he calls the 'masses.' He has a look about him when he rants which makes me suspect he is thinking of you. You epitomize, for him, a world he both fears and detests, and would have vengeance on, a strong just world which neither gives quarter to nor takes quarter from—fools. He is babbling even more vociferously about 'compassion,' which he really doesn't possess at all. But it has a nice pure-in-heart sound. Good God, why did I ever have such a son?"

Jeremy laughed. "Maybe he had a great-great-grandfather who was hanged. There's such a thing as heredity, you know, though the pure-in-heart—I love that designation!—are beginning to deny it. They're shrieking about 'environment' now. Pure Karl Marx. Maybe Marx resents his own heredity, and if he does, then perhaps his screaming followers will follow his example."

He thought of Ellen again, and looked aside. "I've tried to tell Ellen that her absolute lovingkindness and generosity tempt people to exploit and ridicule her, for they know secretly exactly what they are, and that makes them feel guilty; because they are made to feel that way by Ellen, they get infuriated, and worse. She—corrupts—them. Why hasn't someone yet written that some of the grossest corruption is caused by tender and unselfish people? Ellen brings out the worst in others, by her very nobility. She causes them to be more vicious than they'd ordinarily be, and even more cruel, and they hate her for it. Yes, I've tried to tell her, but she doesn't understand."

"Her grandmother was like that," said Walter gloomily. "Maybe the old boys who used thumbscrews and the wheel and the rope and the fire on the saints had some justification. Don't laugh. Her grandfather said to Amy, 'Dammit, girl, you make me want to beat you!' At least I heard he said that."

"Sometimes I feel that way about Ellen, too," said Jeremy, and he chuckled with some ruefulness. "It's hard on a man to have a wife like Ellen, at times."

Walter regarded him shrewdly. Many women, he thought, drive their husbands to more worldly and naughty women by their sheer virtue. It's a relief for the poor men. He thought of Kitty Wilder, and frowned. Well, it was none of his business.

Jeremy said, "You haven't met my associate yet— Charles Godfrey, though he's been with me for a year.

He takes over when I'm in Washington. One of my class-mates at Harvard." He smiled widely and his large white teeth flashed in the dusk. "I think he's more than a little in love with Ellen, and that's good. He is one of my executors." Jeremy touched a bell on his desk, and sent for his friend. Walter waited with interest. Charles God-frey entered almost immediately, and Walter was instantly impressed by him.

The young man was shorter than Jeremy, but as firm and muscular and as masculine in appearance, and he moved with quiet and sure authority. He possessed a solid square face, grave and certain, though there were humorous trenches about his large mouth. All his features expressed strength and an enormous intelligence. He had a short, powerful nose, and his gray eyes were quick and thoughtful. He is a man, thought Walter, and could think of no greater accolade. He is a man as Jeremy is a man, and God knows we need such men in these days and in the days to come. Why in hell couldn't I have had a son like either of them?

"I've heard a lot about you, Mr. Porter, from Jeremy," said Charles as the two men shook hands. His voice was resonant with command, though agreeably respectful, and Walter's admiration increased. "I think you knew my father slightly, Charles also, in Boston?"

"Why, yes, I did," said Walter with pleasure, and his tired face brightened. "Old Chuck. A devil on campus, too. And off campus. With the girls. I often wondered how he settled down with just one of them."

"Mama's a very masterful lady," said Charles. "You knew her?"

"Yes. Very handsome; a fine figure of a woman, as we used to say. Geraldine Aspenwall. Yes. I remember dancing with her. I think she led me instead of vice versa."

"She doesn't lead Papa," said Charles, and as he smiled his face became amused and excellent to look at, even charming. "Though she is a suffragette. Heaven help our poor Congressmen if Mama, and ladies like her, ever get the vote. She even dominates her pastor, unfortunate Father Malone, though the Sisters are less cowed. Mama would like to rewrite the liturgy. Outdated, she says. Very formidable, Mama. I think she could set the Pope running if she made up her mind to it and could get entrance to the Vatican."

The three men sat in warmth and comfort, drinking their whiskey and smoking and listening in peaceful contentment to the traffic below and the rustling of the fire, and watching the sparks blow upward.

Perhaps, thought Walter, enough of these men now and in the future can save my country. Perhaps.

Then he shivered. Perhaps not enough, not enough. He felt a sick presentiment.

17

Earlier that day, when a faint sun set its feeble flickerings over the buildings and the street, Ellen went upstairs to see her aunt before accompanying Annie Burton during the children's daily airing.

"I thought you'd come earlier," May complained.

"I'm sorry, but I have to lie down after lunch, Auntie," said Ellen. "You know that. But it won't be long before I have all my strength back, the doctor says. May I bring the children upstairs tomorrow? You haven't seen them for a week."

May threw up her crippled hands and shook her head. "No, please, Ellen. They give me a headache; all that shouting, and the way Christian runs about. So restless."

"Well." Ellen smiled. "He can't do that when Jeremy's home. He's a very active little boy, and the weather's been so bad that we couldn't go out the last couple of days or so, and he finds the nursery very confining."

"The little girl's as bad, though she's only a year old," May whimpered. "Children in my day—seen but not heard, and seldom seen, either. You're too indulgent, Ellen."

As Jeremy also said that to her repeatedly and with

sternness, Ellen answered nothing. Then she changed the subject, and tried for brightness. "You look very well today, Auntie. Did you sleep well? Did you enjoy your lunch? Cuthbert ordered it especially for you."

"Well, tell him not to do it again," said May with a glance at Miss Ember, who was standing nearby, her heavy arms crossed over her big breast, as if with defiance. "Miss Ember didn't like it, either. The broiled chicken was overdone, and the cauliflower had such a horrid sauce on it, cheese or something, and the potatoes—*au gratin*, do they call it?—had a very funny taste, and the soup had mushrooms in it, and you know I don't like mushrooms, you should have watched, Ellen, but you never have time for anybody but yourself, and the good Lord knows I didn't bring you up that way. It had wine in it, too, strong drink, and the fish was too crisp and the rolls too hard, and I don't like that sweet butter, and the coffee was too black, and the salad had a perfectly horrible dressing—the girl said it was Italian, heathen, I call it. Thank goodness I'm never very hungry, anyway."

But you ate it all with relish, you old bitch, thought Miss Ember, and grinned and nodded. "I agree with Mrs. Watson, Mrs. Porter. Revolting. Maybe you should supervise that Cuthbert, him and his terrible cooking. Or let the regular cook do it. Good American cooking—that's what we like, isn't it, Mrs. Watson?"

"Yes. Just good plain food. That what I like best, with my poor appetite. Do try to spare a little thought now and then for others, Ellen. You do get more selfish every day."

Ellen's face became sad and depressed. She said, with apology, "I'll tell Cuthbert, Auntie. What would you like for dinner? We're having guests, I'm afraid, and there's partridge, and I know you don't like it. Does a thick bean soup appeal to you, and some steamed cod with cream sauce?"

Miss Ember was vexed. It was quite in order to criticize the resented Cuthbert's excellent menus, while secretly enjoying them with intense satisfaction, and it was quite another thing to have to eat "plain food," which Miss Ember had grown to dislike. May said, with a sullen downward glance, "All right, Ellen. Anything will do, except those fancy dishes. Maybe a wing of that partridge? I hate being so much trouble, and I know you get impatient with me, with all your fine friends and having to bother about me. I know I'm a burden." She gave Miss Ember another enigmatic glance, and Ellen uneasily was aware of it. She felt an air of conspiracy in the dusty and untidy sitting room.

"You know you're not a burden, Auntie," she said. "You'll never be a burden."

Good, thought Miss Ember. Hope you holds to it. "I think," said the nurse, "that your aunt has something to tell you."

May hesitated. She folded a section of the shawl on her knee and stared at it with a martyred and melancholy expression, which made Ellen feel acutely at fault. "I've been writing to Mrs. Eccles," said May, and glanced up sideways at her niece and there was a triumphant exultation in her red-rimmed eyes. "Yes?" said Ellen, more and more uneasy. "I know you write her, dear."

"I've been writing to tell her how miserable I am."

"Oh, no," said Ellen, distressed. "How could you do that, Auntie?"

"So," May went on, as if she had not heard, "she is willing to take me back."

Ellen's blue eyes stretched and widened in disbelief. "Take you back?" she exclaimed. "You, Auntie, who can hardly walk to the bathroom? Take you back!" She put her hand to her head, dazed.

"I don't mean to work for her," said May, not able to meet Ellen's confused and aghast eyes. "I mean—well, I wrote her how I long for our lovely rooms in her house, and Wheatfield, and I said I remembered how good she was to us—how really good!—and I want to live in peace and quiet, away from those little children and all the noise they make and all the noise your friends make, and your piano playing and singing—well, she understood. I hate New York, and always did. You and me, Ellen—we got no right to be here at all, and you know it in your heart. Yes, you do!"

Now she stared at Ellen with bitter accusation and open hostility. "It's all your fault, Ellen, and someday God will punish you for your hardheartedness—no consideration for others. Everything just for yourself—greedy, greedy, greedy. Your airs, and everything, just as if you was a lady born. I told you from the beginning, and someday you'll admit it, on your knees, when it's too late.

Well, I'm not the one to judge you. God'll do that—vain, conceited, proud, due for a fall."

Ellen had heard these accusations before, but never before had they struck her so painfully. She shrank visibly; her sense of nameless guilt made her feel quite ill. She moistened her lips, but could not speak. May thought her crushed, and she experienced a happy thrill of vindication. Ellen's long convalescence had dimmed much of her color and she was still thin and even her hair was less radiant and her eyes less lucent. Now her cheeks and her lips were pallid. "I think," said May, "that you're beginning to understand—when it's too late."

To the incredulous Ellen her aunt's ugly words had no meaning at all, but Jeremy would have understood at once: Ellen had corrupted her aunt's integrity with undeserved love and kindness and trust and devotion. May only knew, and without shame, that Ellen's increasing grayness of cheek and lip pleased her, and exonerated her, for since uttering her accusations she believed she was justified and that they were true. Ellen's very silence assured her of this. She had, in Ellen's childhood, lifted her hand to the girl only once or twice. Now she longed to do it again, but with vigor and emotional outrage, and her drawn and sunken face flushed with righteousness. She raised her voice and spoke with emphasis.

"So, I had to think of myself, Ellen, just once, though you think only of yourself all the time. Well, anyway, to make a long story short, and after many letters, Mrs. Eccles replied graciously, out of her Christian charity, and has agreed to accept seventy-five dollars from me, a week, for those two lovely rooms and my board. And she wrote—I showed it to Miss Ember—that she'd be willing to let Miss Ember come, too, and ask her for only a few hours a day's work, maybe four or five, and let her have your old room, and board. And Miss Ember will help me, too."

Still speechless, Ellen looked at Miss Ember, her eyes glazed with shock and her mouth dropping, so that she appeared, to the nurse, to be more "foolish than usual." May continued: "I said I'd help pay for Miss Ember's keep. I'd give her four dollars a week. You can afford it."

Now Ellen, swallowing drily, was able to answer. She said to Miss Ember in a tight and dwindled voice, "And you—you think—you want to do this?"

Miss Ember's bulk appeared to increase, to swell, to fill half the room. "What do you take me for, Mrs. Porter? An imbecile? Of course I don't want to do that and I won't do it! Never heard so much crazy nonsense in my life! I think your aunt's lost her mind, indeed I do."

May regarded her with blank horror and amazement. "But," she stammered, "only this morning when I got the letter—I showed it to you—you said, you said, you thought it was the thing to do, and you said you'd go with me, and you'd help Mrs. Eccles—I told you what a wonderful Christian lady she is, and you said—"

"I was just humoring you," said Miss Ember, giving her a terrible and inimical smile. "Just as any nurse would do."

Her voice was rough and cruel. She tossed her small head, so like a ball perched atop her enormous frame, and regarded both aunt and niece with smiling contempt. "What should I have done, Mrs. Porter, when she told me about it this morning? Called for a straitjacket? I did my best. I soothed her, calmed her down, best I could, promised her anything, she was like a kid, clapping her hands—so silly. I did my best; I always did my best. I thought she ought to tell you herself."

It was very rare for Ellen to see anyone with a clarified vision, to see another in all her ugliness, without gentle-hearted illusion, and with total recognition. The sight made her ill, caused an actual physical pain in her heart, and actual dread and loathing, as if she had encountered something unspeakably vile, beyond mortal capacity to be vile. It shattered her, made her want to run away wildly, and not to see at all, for the encounter of innocence with human evil was unbearable to her and violated her. She could not remember being so frightened before.

Now her innate fortitude returned to her, high and clear and condemning, as she looked at Miss Ember with brilliant eyes. "You know you lie," she said. "You wanted my aunt to believe you, so you would have the opportunity to hurt her, she who had never hurt you. You wanted the opportunity to make me wretched, too, though I have always been kind to you. You are a hateful woman, a wicked woman, and I give you notice now. A week's notice, with pay, and I want you out of this house by tomorrow morning."

Never had she spoken like this to anyone before, and

Miss Ember gaped, astounded. Then her small eyes glinted cunningly. May had begun to cry and whimper like a sick child, her face in her hands. "You'll pay for this, madam," said the nurse, in one of the ugliest voices Ellen had ever heard, and one of the most intimidating. "I know all about you, my fine madam. Everybody does. I don't know why I've stayed so long, in the same house with a shameless creature like you. Everybody knows. I know what really made you so sick when you had those kids. After all, I am a nurse. You'll pay me for a month, and give me a good reference or—"

"Or what?" asked Ellen, freshly stricken. She felt as if she would faint. The woman appalled her.

Miss Ember nodded and smirked. "I'll tell the whole town about you. You won't be able to lift your head again in the high society that laughs at you behind your back, anyway."

What could she possibly say about me? thought Ellen dimly. But it came to her then, for the first time in her life, that lies and calumnies are accepted joyously by the majority of people, and the truth is ignored or denied. Jeremy! she thought. His enemies will believe anything that would discredit him, even though it is just about his wife.

Her fear rose to terrified heights; her heart lurched and pounded in her throat. Miss Ember watched her with pleased exaltation and hatred, seeing the girl swaying and trembling. "A month's pay and a good reference," she repeated.

Then suddenly the iron which underlay Ellen's magnanimity and genuine solicitude for all that lived flashed visibly into her face. She clenched her thin and delicate hands at her side. She looked at Miss Ember and her eyes were dark with anger and disgust.

"You utter one lie about me, and this household, or anyone in it, and I will have you arrested," she said, and her voice hardly shook. "Who are you? You are nothing, nothing. My husband is a respected Congressman, and a lawyer. Pack and go at once or I'll call him, and you'll spend a considerable time in jail, for dangerous threats. Threats. Get out! There'll be no recommendation from me. But I will be merciful enough not to expose you to the hospital who sent you here. Go, before I lose what little patience I have left."

Then May uttered a high shriek. "What about me, Ellen? Who'll take care of me? Why are you doing this thing? Miss Ember—she didn't mean anything wrong. She was just trying to soothe me."

"That's true!" cried Miss Ember, whose face had turned to the color and texture of lard. "I'm only a poor woman, a nurse, trying to do my duty by my patient, and you turn on me—turn on me—Mrs. Porter, like a snake! But that's just like you rich people. No heart for anyone but your purses."

Ellen went to her aunt and put her hand on the older woman's shoulder. She bent and said, "Annie will take care of you tonight and until we can get another nurse for you, Aunt May. We'll get a good nurse for you, to-morrow."

"I don't want anyone but Miss Ember," moaned May, turning her head away from Ellen, as if Ellen had struck her. "I don't want that—girl."

"I should think not!" exclaimed Miss Ember, realizing for the first time the enormity of her conduct, but immediately blaming Ellen for it. "She's nothing but a hussy, and incompetent." She breathed heavily and loudly. She had thought that since May was an invalid, and Ellen "soft in the head, and weak," she could abuse both without caution. Over these years she had insulted Ellen covertly and overtly, and the girl had merely looked depressed and had not replied, and so the nurse had become bolder and bolder with her sneers and innuendos, and had told herself that as aunt and niece "weren't any better than me, and lower," she could speak and act with impunity. Not until today had Ellen ever challenged her, and she was outraged. Who did the red-haired nothing think she was, anyways?

Miss Ember was shrewd. She saw Ellen's white and strangely obdurate profile as she bent over her aunt. She knew all about Ellen's character, so she resorted to tears, sobbing convulsively. "Here I am, faithful and loyal all these years, day and night, doing everything, on call all the time! Loyal as a slave! Nothing was too much for me to do for my patient—"

"Only too true," May wept. "Loyal and faithful—that's Miss Ember. And now you make her leave me, all alone, with no one to care, maybe dying up here by myself. I won't have that girl, or anyone else, Ellen. Send me to the poorhouse; that's what you want, you always did, and that's the payment I get for taking care of you all your life."

Ellen looked at Miss Ember, whose reddened and swollen face was running with tears, and who was sobbing in long hard gulps. Her treacherously compassionate heart began to overcome and drench the iron in her nature. Where would this poor woman go if ejected from this house, without a recommendation, disgraced and alone? Yes, she had been impudent. But so deep was the self-betrayal in Ellen that she forgot the woman's cruelty and insults for a moment. Her eyes began to soften and Miss Ember saw this and sobbed more vigorously. "Loyal, faithful," she groaned. "But what else could I expect, a poor and defenseless creature at the mercy of rich people?"

Ellen thought of the Sermon on the Mount: "Blessed are the merciful, for they shall receive mercy." She could see the sunlit drab little church in Preston, and could hear the pastor intoning. She opened her mouth, even as she began to accuse herself of hardheartedness, when Cuthbert's voice, cold and grave, came from the open doorway.

"May I assist you, madam?" he asked. All in the room started violently, and turned, to see Cuthbert and Annie Burton on the threshold. Never had Ellen seen Cuthbert so harsh of countenance, and never had she seen the lively Annie with so enraged an expression.

"I—I don't know," said Ellen helplessly. "It was just a little disagreement— I think everything is all right now—"

"No, madam," said Cuthbert in a strong severe tone. "It was never 'all right' from the beginning. You've endured too much from this woman." He looked at Miss Ember, and the nurse cowered. "You will pack at once and leave this house, with no extra pay and with no recommendation. I've known your kind before, bullying, exploiting the kindness of others, offensive, overbearing, and extremely bad. I will give you half an hour to leave."

Miss Ember shouted, her face contorted with such hatred that Ellen involuntarily stepped back. "Who do you think you are? You're only a servant like me, and that girl, too! It's what Mrs. Porter wants, not you, and Mrs. Watson!"

"Get out," Cuthbert said, and advanced on her formidably, and Miss Ember shrank at his look. "I'll go, I'll go," she muttered, wiping her wet face with the back of her none too clean hands. "I was only doing my duty. I get paid like this."

"Don't leave me!" screamed May, and for the first time she looked at Ellen with glittering eyes of actual hatred, and Ellen was again appalled. "I have a say in this, too."

"I'm sorry, Mrs. Watson, but Mrs. Porter has the say," said Cuthbert. "She discharged this woman. Go," he said to the nurse, and took out his watch and glanced at it. "I will call the police if you have not left within the hour. Threats and attempted intimidation. My patience is running short."

"But," Ellen began timidly. He looked at her with affection but also with severity, and her lips closed. "Please let me manage this as Mr. Porter would manage it," he said, and his voice was not too gentle. "I will take the responsibility. You have endured too much."

Annie spoke for the first time, and to Miss Ember. With briskness, and a determined wave of her rosy hand, she said: "I'd like to throw you out personally." She sniffed. "This room's dirty. Edith wanted to come in a few times and clean up, but you wouldn't let her, and besides it's your job. 'Faithful and loyal!' People like you always say that when they get caught."

"I won't have you near me!" May wept, and so distraught was she that she could force herself quickly to her feet. Her white hair was disheveled about her face, a face now passionately alien and tight. Ellen took a step towards her but Cuthbert caught her upper arm and held her as a father would. Then Ellen, distracted, said to her aunt, "Don't look at me like that, Auntie. I can't stand it. Please don't."

May turned to her almost savagely. "I will, I will. You deserve it, Ellen. You're as bad as your father, maybe even worse. I knew it when you were a child. Willful, always trying to get your own way, never caring for anybody but yourself. And what are you, anyway? You are a—"

Cuthbert lifted his hand commandingly. "Mrs. Watson, I have heard the whole conversation in this room. I will have a word with Mr. Porter myself, tonight. Now, if you please, would you sit down?"

But May was beside herself, all the years of her frustration rushing into her mind, all her imagined abuse, all her resentment. She spoke only to Ellen. "You haven't any shame! You spent the night before you got married with that man! Like a slut! You was lucky he ever married you. He didn't want to, but I was there to protect you. Like a slut you was, Ellen, and maybe you're no better now."

Ellen averted her head so that no one could see her tears. Her love for her aunt was still too strong for her to completely comprehend what had been said to her. She only knew that she felt deprived, alone, vulnerable, abandoned, by someone who had loved her and cared for her; now her aunt was an enemy who despised her, and perhaps with reason. Her aunt had cherished and fed her and had worked for her for many years—if Aunt May rejected her like this the fault was probably her own. Worse still, she felt degraded, lewd, and unworthy.

Annie had moved threateningly on Miss Ember, and Miss Ember dodged her outstretched hand and ran heavily from the room to her own, where she began to pack. Cuthbert looked at May, who was still standing, but holding the back of her chair and glaring at Cuthbert. "You're only a servant! I'll talk to Mr. Porter tonight. I'll tell him all about you."

"I'm sure you will," he replied courteously. "As you don't want Annie, I will send up one of the housemaids to be with you, Mrs. Watson." Again he took Ellen's arm. "Isn't it time for your walk with the little ones, madam? Yes. You need the fresh air, before it rains. Remember, your health has not been completely restored, and Mr. Porter will be displeased if you don't take your walk."

At the mention of Jeremy, Ellen immediately became submissive. She allowed Cuthbert to lead her to the door. But she looked pleadingly, desperately, at her aunt, who returned her look with obdurate rejection, and so Ellen dropped her head and went downstairs with Annie, who assisted her with tenderness though her light-blue eyes were flaring. Annie said, "The kids are all ready, waiting for us. Let's hurry, before it rains. You got to take care of yourself, Mrs. Porter, for Mr. Porter's sake. Dear me, you look very ill."

"I haven't any mercy," said Ellen in a low voice.

Annie smiled at her. "People forget," she said. "God's a God of wrath as well as a God of mercy. And we should be like that, too, or we've got no self-respect as a human being, and no pride. Just keep in mind what that bitch said to you. She's been talking like that, more or less, to you and your aunt, for years, and you never said a word back! You got to have pride and discipline, Mrs. Porter, or everybody will think you're a poor thing and kick you. I'd like to have given that woman one!" she added wistfully. "I've been wanting to bash her for a long time."

Ellen was still pale, but more composed, as she left the house with Annie, her little son walking beside her impatiently, her infant daughter tucked into the perambulator. Her light-green wool walking suit set off her fiery hair, and her green felt hat with golden plumes was very becoming. Her white silk shirtwaist was held at the collar with a diamond-and-ruby pin. Her gloved hands were still trembling, and she tried to control them. Annie pushed the perambulator briskly and made gay conversation, to which Ellen tried to reply, as she also tried to smile. But she could not forget the stare of malignity which her aunt had given her, and her throat would close with repressed emotion.

Annie was an attractive little figure in her white nurse's clothing, half covered by its long blue wool cape. Her white cap perched on top of her curling yellow hair and the sharp wind brought strong color to her round pert face with its tilted nose. When Christian tried to pursue a random dog she called to him sharply, and he returned to her side with a rebellious expression. But Annie could make him obey as Ellen could not. At the age of three he already had a clear idea of his mother's gentle character and exploited her in Annie's absence with shouts of defiance and tears, so that she would inevitably give in to his shrill demands. However, he feared and respected Annie, and would actually become docile in her presence. Annie had a hard swift hand, which she used on Christian in spite of Ellen's feeble protests. Christian respected his father even more than he did Annie, and Jeremy had only to give him a stern glance to enforce his discipline.

He was a handsome little boy, strikingly like his mother in appearance, and with her own mass of glistening red hair, and her own beautiful blue eyes and large carved lips. But his expression was not hers. It was ruthless and defiant, even at his young age, and his chin was obstinate.

He walked proudly and arrogantly, as Ellen did not, very charming in his sailor's blue suit and short little trousers, and with all those bright brass buttons, a sailor's hat cocked at a challenging angle on his head, his small hands gloved, his black boots shining. Ellen watched his marching pace with mingled apprehension and love. Such a lovely child, she thought, and smiled involuntarily.

The little girl, in her white wool coat and lacy bonnet, was a vigorous child, sitting upright in her carriage and watching everything with great and intelligent dark eyes, her dark curls fluttering about her pink cheeks and clustering around her neck and over the collar of her coat. She kept up a constant strong babbling, pointing here and there and bouncing on her cushions. She was very insistent, but Annie could give her a quelling look which would cause her to subside for a moment or two. In Jeremy's presence she was so engaging and so bewitching that he was almost persuaded she had a honeyed disposition. To Ellen she was as rebellious as her brother, and her elfin face, with the pointed chin, would become, even as an infant, hard and calculating, and she would watch Ellen alertly for signs of weakness. She and her brother were excellent friends, for they understood each other with certitude.

"You've got to teach 'em, once and for all, even the first day, who's boss," Annie would tell Ellen. "Let 'em out of hand, even one single time, and you've got monsters on your hands." Then she would grin.

"Children don't need punishment. They need love," Ellen would suggest, forgetting the children of her childhood.

"Sure, they need love. Who don't, Mrs. Porter? But everybody's got to learn there's limits, or there'll be pain. Kids are like puppies. They got to be trained by a master, or they're all over the place and shitting on everything, even when they grow up. I've seen plenty, believe me!" Ellen, after a moment's shock, laughed.

Today, as they all walked together, Annie slowed her usual brisk pace to accommodate Ellen's exhausted movements. She prattled, though she was deeply concerned over Ellen's pallor and her listless expression. She saw Ellen was not really listening, and the girl felt some impatience. She's thinking of that aunt of hers, thought Annie. Never saw such looks in my life! Fit to kill. And for what? Because Madam is so kind and so sweet and gives in. I'd pack that aunt off, that I would, if it was me. She isn't good for that house.

The earlier sunlight had vanished. The brownish clouds moved lower in the sky, and there was a chill wind blowing, filled with dust and fine manure and flakes of soot. The air was permeated with the stench of coal gas. The small trees along the street clutched the last of their bronzed leaves tenaciously. Those fallen flew before pedestrians and carriages and trolleys and drays with a crackling sound. The whole scene fitted Ellen's mood, which was bleak and dreary and filled with anguished sorrow. She shivered, and drew her sable stole closer over her shoulders. The little parade turned into Fifth Avenue, where the windows of mansions were already flittering with the lamplight within.

A young man came towards them with a swaying but priggish stride. He was tall and thin rather than lean, dressed in rich black broadcloth which enhanced his appearance of fleshlessness, his black vest brocaded, his black derby hat half concealing his fair hair. The pin on his black cravat was a black pearl, and he carried a walking stick in a gloved hand and he wore square steel-rimmed spectacles which did not hide the cold and rigid fixity of the light eyes set straight ahead. He had a rigorous pale complexion, a tight compressed mouth that showed no sign of humor or laughter. He moved swiftly towards Ellen, Annie, the carriage, and the prancing little boy, as if he did not see them and as if he would collide with them, and Annie halted in alarm and made a slight warning sound. Ellen looked up from her sad contemplation of her feet, and then she flushed and halted. "Mr. Francis!" she said.

The young man stopped abruptly, then also flushed. He lifted his hat, then stood squarely before them, the hat in his gloved hands, the wind lifting his fine fair hair. "Ellen," he said, and a slight tremor ran over his face.

Annie regarded him inquisitively. So this was the "Mr. Francis" of whom Ellen had spoken of a few times, and with hesitant affection and gratitude. Well, he was a stick of a man if ever she saw one, though a gentleman. Good-looking, too, in a bloodless way, if you liked the kind. Annie did not.

Ellen had not seen him for nearly four years. She smiled

at him timidly and extended her hand, and he took it. Then she tried to withdraw her fingers but he held them so hard that they immediately began to ache and a ring cut into her flesh. Neither Jeremy nor Walter Porter mentioned him in her presence, but she often read about him in the newspapers. "The lawyer of the workingman." Some papers lauded him; others were derisive, and their cartoons were "quite unkind," Ellen would comment to herself. His nose was not that sharp and thin, like a stiletto, nor his expression that grim and venomous. Otherwise the likeness was only too true, if a little cruel, and exaggerated, like all political cartoons. Francis was also designated in hostile papers as a "muckraker."

As she looked at him now she could not help thinking that time had not gentled him or softened the outlines of his face. His air of pomposity had increased, but as he looked at Ellen there was a bitter if yearning warmth in his eyes and he even smiled a little, with unusual uncertainty. She brought his attention to her children, and his expression changed and it was even tighter than before, and colder, though he shook hands with Christian and affected to examine the baby with interest. Why, thought the astute and curious Annie, looks as if he hates the kids, and I wonder why. But he sure likes Mama, if what I saw in his eyes was really there.

Ellen was embarrassed at this meeting, remembering their last one and Jeremy's somewhat violent attitude towards his cousin. What had Jeremy said? "Kill, kill you." The flush deepened on her face, and her manner became both nervous and conciliatory as she asked about his health. "You do not look too well," he commented, and his tone was significant.

"Oh, I am getting better every day," responded Ellen. She thought of Francis' father, who would be dining at her house that night. She wondered if Walter ever mentioned her to Francis.

"You've been ill?" His tone was genuinely concerned.

"Well," Ellen said, and was helpless. The sturdy Annie said, "Mrs. Porter had a hard time with this last baby, Mr. Porter."

"Annie!" Ellen exclaimed, and did not know where to look. But Francis forgot that they were standing in the middle of a busy street, with pedestrians pushing impatiently around them, and he saw only Ellen and thought

of Jeremy with fresh cold fury. So the brute had reduced
her to this haggard and unbecoming slenderness, his beautiful Ellen. He had never forgotten her, not for a single
day; seeing her in person moved him as he was rarely
moved and if he had been a woman he would have cried,
and would have taken her in his arms. He wanted to do
both.

He said, to lighten her embarrassed confusion, "How is
your aunt, Ellen?" He looked at her very keenly now,
for his aunt, Mrs. Eccles, avidly kept him informed and
he knew of May's abject letters.

"You know she has arthritis," said Ellen, and the sound
of her voice moved him again, stronger than before, for
he heard pain in it. "Otherwise, she is as well as can be
expected." She was in acute discomfort, and a slight hot
sweat broke out on her forehead, and she wanted to go
away as fast as possible.

"She should never have come to New York," he said,
and it was as if he were again blaming Ellen.

"But where should she have gone?" said Ellen. "I am
—I was—the only one left in the world to her. She
wouldn't have stayed behind."

"No?" said Francis, and at his tone her discomfort
quickened, and he tilted his head and looked at her cen-
soriously, as at a servant who had questioned his judgment, and once again Ellen felt inferior and gauche.

Still she said, with a little firmness, "No. She had no
one else."

"She had my aunt," said Francis. Ellen regarded him in
silence. A few drops of dark rain began to fall, for which
the girl was thankful.

Christian had been staring at his father's cousin with
the open and unabashed blankness of children, and as he
was still primitive he felt the tension between this man
and his mother. Annie briskly turned the perambulator
about and said, "It's raining. We'd better hurry home before it pours."

"Yes," said Ellen fervently. Again she held out her
hand to Francis and he took it and held it. He said, and
his voice dropped, "I think of you often, Ellen," and his
self-control wavered.

"I—I think of you, too," said Ellen. "Good afternoon,
Mr. Francis. Remember me to Mrs. Eccles." She caught
little Christian's hand and tugged at him urgently. Annie

moved on, and Ellen quickly followed, and Francis stood there and watched them go, and the old passion was on him again, the old despair. He was jostled, and he did not feel it. He followed Ellen with his eyes until she had turned the corner and his face was no longer rigorous. It was tremulous with longing and desolation, and a deep and shaking pain.

That night, after the guests had gone, Cuthbert accosted Jeremy and said, "May I have a word with you in the library, sir?" Jeremy raised his black eyebrows and nodded, and Cuthbert followed him into the golden warmth of the room, where a fire blew and snapped in the windy chimney. Cuthbert said, "Mrs. Porter has not told you about a certain—episode—which occurred today in her aunt's quarters, sir?"

"No." Jeremy looked more intently at his houseman. "She seemed very tired tonight, and asked to be excused half an hour ago. Is something wrong?"

So Cuthbert told him with quiet precision and a tone that held no judgment. Jeremy listened, and his expression was harsh with dark anger. "You must pardon me, sir," Cuthbert concluded, "and not think me impertinent, but I thought you ought to know, for Madam's sake. She looked like death after the—episode—and looked even more distressed at dinner, if possible."

"Thank you, Cuthbert." Jeremy turned quickly about and went upstairs to May's quarters. Her door was open as usual, and Jeremy saw that Edith, one of the housemaids, was with her. May's gray face became furtive when she saw Jeremy, and she turned her head and stared at the fire, but not before he saw her red and swollen eyes. He motioned to Edith and the girl rose and left the room, closing the door behind her, a forced act she regretted, for the news was all over the house.

Jeremy sat down and regarded the sick woman without mercy. There were times when he felt pity for her, though he rarely visited her. He then looked about the musty and cluttered room, and his anger grew. He said, with no casual opening words at all, "Mrs. Watson. I have just heard that you would like to return to the house of Mrs. Eccles, in Wheatfield, though she has asked an exorbitant sum for your board and room. Seventy-five dollars a week! She must really be suffering from the Panic. I will offer her thirty, and knowing Mrs. Eccles, she will take it without quibbling. I will also arrange for a nurse to attend you there. In fact, I will engage one tomorrow who will conduct you to Wheatfield and remain with you."

May turned her head impetuously to him and he saw that she was desperately dismayed. She said, "Ellen! What lies did she tell you?"

"I haven't spoken to Ellen. She did not tell me anything." He was trying to control his temper. "Cuthbert informed me, just now."

"Oh, that man! He would tell you anything! Did he tell you how cruel Ellen was to poor Miss Ember and how she drove her out of this house, leaving me alone, and not caring a thing about me, who took care of her since she was a baby and her mother died? I was more than a mother to her—how has she repaid me?" May began to cry, sobbing fitfully, but Jeremy only sat in silence and watched her.

Then he said, "Mrs. Watson. I know you are ill, and so I don't want to trouble you much longer. I know your illness has changed you these past years. Once you loved Ellen; once you cared about her. She loves you and always protects you and is concerned about you, even in her present condition. I am not going to ask you why you are now so estranged from her, even though she is not estranged herself. I think I know. Never mind. But I want you to know that Ellen is heartbroken, and I will not—I repeat—will not, have her made to suffer any longer. It is too much for her. So"—and he stood up—"I will send you 'home,' as you've called it many times, and I will telegraph Mrs. Eccles tonight that you have accepted her offer, and will soon arrive."

"No!" May cried. "I don't want to go! Not without Ellen. Tell Ellen I want to see her at once." She wrung her twisted hands in agony and with vehemence.

"I will not," said Jeremy. "I am taking her to Washington with me tomorrow. You will be gone before she returns. So I will say goodbye for her, here and now." Then he said, "Just for my own curiosity. Why did you write Mrs. Eccles that you wanted to share her house with her?"

May chewed her wet lips. She put her hand to her forehead and slowly shook her head from side to side. "I—I don't really know," she whispered. "I'm a sick woman—you don't realize."

"I think I do, only too well," said Jeremy, and the deep

anger was back in his voice. "You wanted to hurt Ellen. You wanted to make her miserable and guilty. When you told her, you really had no intention of leaving my house. It was a vicious fantasy of yours—to crush Ellen."

"No, no. How can you say such things? I thought—I truly thought—that it would be the best thing. I even asked Miss Ember; she can tell you herself. I think I really wanted it. I've thought about it all the time I've been here, an unwanted guest, a burden. Ellen always made me feel I was imposing, that I had no right here. An unwanted guest. She never thinks of anybody but herself and her own comfort. We should never have left Wheatfield!" and she looked at Jeremy with recrimination. "You did the wrong thing, and you know it. God will—"

"Suppose we keep God out of this," said Jeremy.

But May was now wild with fear, and excited. "I keep telling her that she'll regret it one of these days, and then she'll have no place to go but to me! She'll come to her senses, I can tell you that, and the sooner the better! She wasn't made for this kind of life, and she's sick because she's started to realize. In her heart, she wants to go home, too, and be what she always was, and your fine clothes and jewelry will never change her, make her happy—"

Good God, thought Jeremy. His anger was mingled with pity for this stupid woman, for this obdurate woman whose love for her niece had changed to resentment, and perhaps even to hatred. He made himself think of her crippled condition, and her real suffering, and so he said, "You're not yourself, Mrs. Watson. Illness affects the mind, I know. When you feel better, later, write to Ellen as affectionately as you can. She deserves it, and you know that, in spite of everything."

May beat her emaciated knees with her fists, and she glared at him through her tears. "She'll be glad when I'm dead! That's what she wants, me to be dead. As for you, sir, you'll learn what Ellen is, in time, and I pity you."

He turned and left the room and all down the stairs he could hear her wretched wailing, and now he had no compassion. He went into Ellen's bedroom and found her lying, prostrated, on the bed, her hair floating on the pillows. She was not asleep. She sat up when she saw him and her eyes were dripping tears, and she held out her arms to him, mutely. He sat on the bed beside her and took her in his arms, and his anger deepened. He said,

"As you know, love, we leave for Washington tomorrow at seven o'clock in the morning." He did not ask her why she was crying. He wiped her eyes and smiled down into them.

"Oh, I forgot! I can't, Jeremy! I can't leave Aunt May. There's something I must tell you."

"I know all about it. Cuthbert told me. He thought it best, to save you from having to tell me. Now then, don't look like that, my sweet. Your aunt will be perfectly all right. Edith is giving her her sleeping draught. She will sleep late. So don't disturb her. She needs all the rest she can get, doesn't she? There'll be a new and better nurse with her tomorrow."

"She wants to go 'home' to that awful house in Wheatfield. Imagine," and Ellen smiled even as her eyes ran, and her nose.

"Yes. Imagine," said Jeremy. "Now, lie down, my love. Would you mind if I lay down with you, too?"

She became almost gay and her beautiful face colored with delight. It had been a long, long wait, all those months of her recovery. She put her soft white arms about Jeremy's neck and drew him down to her. She did not quite know why, but Jeremy's very presence sheltered her, surrounded her like a wall. They made love for the first time in months, and it was like the first night.

18

Kitty Wilder's husband, Jochan, an associate of Jeremy's in his law office, had lost the major part of his fortune in the year or two before the Panic of 1907, and he was now comparatively poor. He had been optimistically invested in the market to a dangerous extent. Kitty, the shrewd and astute, had been more conservative. However, she too was suffering, and this both frightened and outraged her.

Jochan was still a shy man, somewhat lissome, to Kitty's increasing disgust, and she no longer thought his fair and candid face, a face which expressed a gentle naïveté, handsome, nor did his light and fluttering eyes intrigue her. He had retained his thick golden hair, waved and overly long; but Kitty did not like fair men. The transparency of Jochan's delicate features, his elaborate and sincere courtesy even to servants, his engaging smile, all seemed to her to be covertly feminine. Moreover, he had long fled her bed and he kept his bedroom door locked, to Kitty's acrid amusement. She was more like a little black cat than ever; she did not know that Jochan now found her horrendous and that, to him, she had a feral odor. She did not know that he had a complaisant and tender mistress, who loved and admired him. Had she learned about the woman, Kitty would have been incredulous and would have made a lewd remark reflecting on his manhood. Once she had said to a confidante, "Jochan is really a masculine Ellen Porter," and had laughed gaily. "But perhaps I am exaggerating when I use the word 'masculine' in referring to Jochan."

Jochan was distressed at the loss of the major part of his fortune, for now he could not spend as much on his mistress. She assured him it did not matter. But it mattered to Jochan, who adored her. So when Jeremy, after his first year in Washington, asked him to be his assistant there at a more than generous salary, Jochan was overwhelmed with gratitude. He felt, for Jeremy, the devotion and admiration the less assertive feel for the man who possesses great personal authority, and never doubts his puissance. Jochan doubted his, for Kitty had been very frank on the subject over the years of their married life, and he had a deplorable habit of self-deprecation. Jeremy, who knew Jochan's dedicated character, was fond of his friend.

So Kitty, elated, and Jochan, anxious to be of the utmost assistance to Jeremy, moved to Washington, and settled in a small but charming house in Georgetown very near to the Porter's larger and more elaborate establishment. Kitty, the socialite, soon made friends among Jeremy's colleagues and their wives, and they were fascinated by her, as they were not by Ellen. Her worldliness, her startling wit, her original bons mots, her gracious desire to please—she was an expert at this when it was to her advantage—and her obvious sophistication, made her very popular almost immediately. Moreover, she had acquaintances in many of the embassies, and often spoke of her father, "the Senator." She had ease and grace, gaiety and captivating manners, and her taste in clothes and jewelry and furnishings soon became famous, and she was consulted on dress even by the wives of Senators and ambassadors, and once the First Lady had asked her advice before a ball.

Kitty was jubilant over all this. She felt herself to be in her rightful milieu, among the potent and influential people of America. She loved the strong scent of power; it was more exhilarating to her than wine or fine dinners. She often regretted that women could not vote, and believed that if they were given the vote she would herself be a member of Congress.

She never stopped assiduously courting and deferring to Jeremy, who was, at last, becoming amused by her and more tolerant. She was now, more than ever, the confidante, guide, and devoted friend of Ellen, who was frightened by Washington and felt uneasy in assemblies, and trembled when invited to a large party in the White House. Ellen relied on her more and more, a trend which Kitty carefully cultivated. Kitty happily spent half her time in Washington, and half in New York, and could not understand Ellen's dislike of the capital. "My dear," she would say, "here is the very heart of the law of America. How is it possible you are not excited by all this?" Ellen was definitely not excited. She would look about her in strange fear during churning parties, and she rarely spoke, while Kitty moved about sinuously and rapidly, exquisitely arrayed, her conversation glittering and full of humor. She was a great favorite with the gentlemen, but she was very careful to bewitch their wives, too. No one noticed that she was really ugly; her vivacity even overcame the enormous white teeth which usually filled her small dark face. There were some who, first calling those teeth "horse's fangs," came to admire them and consider them very attractive. Ellen would watch and listen to her with awe, and would feel crude and clumsy and stupidly mute.

Kitty had been deeply tempted, at first, to guide Ellen in the purchasing of unbecoming clothes, clothes too tawdry and "actressy," so that Ellen would be even less popular than she already was, and would be severely criticized. Then Kitty's clever mind dissuaded her. She knew that Jeremy would be the first to notice and would blame her at once. Jeremy's good-will was the most vital element in her existence, both for her ambition and for her lust. However, most skillfully, she was undermining what little self-confidence the girl possessed, so that Ellen could hardly endure her brief visits to Washington, and came to believe that her presence there was detrimental to Jeremy's career.

When Ellen was absent, in New York, especially during the months of her second pregnancy, Kitty would give faultlessly appointed dinners for Jeremy in her Georgetown house. Even Jeremy was astonished at her range of acquaintances and friends. She was careful to flatter him and admire him in the presence of others, who would otherwise have been alienated by his "queer ideas" and his brusqueness, and as her flattery and admiration were quite sincere, and she daintily avoided fulsome obsequiousness and servility, even Senators began to approve of him, if with some caution and reservations. Because of Kitty—and this also amused Jeremy—he was invited to houses where he otherwise would not be a guest, and he was grateful to her for this. He, too, had ambitions, not entirely for himself but for his country. When President Roosevelt singled her out and called her "Kitty," Jeremy thought that she deserved some little cultivation from him, if only in gratitude.

After the birth of little Gabrielle, Ellen's health remained precarious for several months, and she spent those months almost entirely in New York under her doctors' anxious care. Jeremy was very busy in Washington, during the Panic, and Jochan found himself being sent to New York for extended periods to manage Jeremy's affairs there. Kitty was secretly overjoyed. She knew all about Jeremy. She knew that Jeremy had been faithful to his wife during the years of their marriage, with only one or two lapses, and those transient. She also knew that Jeremy was more than ordinarily attracted to blithe and amusing women, and that his masculinity and sexual urges were greater than in most men, for all his fastidiousness. She knew, too, that he felt obligated to her, and she easily guessed, from what Ellen had timidly confided to her, that marital relations between Ellen and her husband had been forbidden by physicians until Ellen's health had been restored. Kitty's elation became almost unbearable. Her passion for Jeremy was now total; as much as she could love anyone she loved Jeremy, and lived for the sound and sight of him.

The inevitable, of course, happened, five months after Ellen's last child had been born, and Ellen was confined at home in New York, listless and in pain and suffering long weaknesses, and Jochan himself was in New York on Jeremy's business. Jeremy, during those austere months, had indulged in some meaningless affairs in Washington, with random women, carefully avoiding any entanglements with the wives or daughters of his colleagues. He did not consider that he was betraying his beloved Ellen, for the women were of no significance to him, and he hardly remembered their names when he was tired of them. He knew he was a full-blooded man, and that he could not do his best work when plagued by powerful urges, and he had never been abstemious even from puberty. He was a man, and women were women, and he enjoyed the pleasurable encounters and never felt guilty, for he was never deeply involved with his women and never felt more than a passing affection for them. He also tired of them regularly, and looked for others and for variety. It never crossed his mind that Ellen would be devastated by his activities, for he loved her more now than ever he had done, and his women were only necessary substitutes for her until she recovered. Besides, he was a man and Ellen was a woman, and she would not understand, he once thought, when he gave the matter any thought at all. As with all lusty men, women were a necessity to him, and were as much a hunger as any other physical hunger, and it must be satisfied. Moreover, he observed that his colleagues, the majority of them, were almost as actively engaged in sexual pursuits as he was, and so long as they were discreet no one was offended.

So Kitty quite casually became his mistress. He was not very much tempted by her, but he knew her well and was distracted by her, and she was intelligent and diverting and collected all the gossip of the city, and her observations were acute and frolicsome and lively. She

did not bore him, as other women bored him even before
he was done with them. She was invariably interesting and
her sharp wit made him laugh at the very times he was
the most disgusted with Washington. Kitty had well
learned the art of pleasing, even when she had been a
young girl. She had polished it to fine accomplishment,
and her love for Jeremy gave it extra luster.

He began to look forward to the lighthearted and
merry dinners she had prepared for him, with all his
favorite dishes, for with the sensitivity of love Kitty had
long noted what he most preferred, and the wines he enjoyed. After a wretched and frustrated and enraged day
in Congress, he felt relaxed and contented in Kitty's
house, and did not feel that he was betraying his friend
Jochan. Kitty had delicately made it plain that she and
Jochan had "nothing in common any longer. We are just
friends—and have been so for a long time. It is a—
platonic—relationship, and I am still quite fond of Jochan,
in a sisterly way." So Jeremy, in the most casual way
possible, availed himself of Kitty's unmistakable invitations. When, in her bed, she had been transported and
had whispered ardently of her love for him, he thought
it only amiability and a momentary ecstasy. He had
heard the word "love" too many times from too many
other women to give any credence to Kitty's honest and
blissful avowals. Had he actually believed that Kitty did,
indeed, love him to despair, and only him, he would never
have come to her again for solace and entertainment. He
believed that with the exception of Ellen the majority of
women used the word "love" as a gay and self-exonerating
password to the rompings in a mutual bed. It was just a
rapturous and complimentary exclamation under the
blankets and sheets, and really meant nothing. He was
well aware that Kitty felt a most urgent attraction to
him, but he was convinced only that she was a light
woman of many secret affairs, and had much of his own
importunate lusts. The affair would only last until Ellen
was well, he would say to himself. Kitty would feel no
stronger ties to him than he felt for her, and they would
part, grateful for a pleasant interlude but nothing more.
He had not robbed Jochan and Kitty had not robbed
Ellen. He and Kitty temporarily enjoyed each other, and
that was all.

Kitty, however, was now overwhelmed by her love for Jeremy. She was certain that Jeremy loved her in return, and that the affair would become permanent. Any other alternative would have been unendurable to her. We belong together, she would think in joy and surfeit. We are the same sort of person, my darling Jeremy. Fulfilled, she began to bloom and even acquired a sort of dark prettiness, and her spirits were so elated, and so ardently engaged, that she became more and more fascinating to her friends. She literally gleamed, as she had never gleamed before.

19

The Speaker of the House rose in pontifical majesty and surveyed the crowded ranks of Congressmen, and his appearance was forbidding and ominous. He looks, thought Jeremy Porter, like a hanging judge about to pass sentence, with sadistic relish half concealed by a menacing piety. Jeremy had never admired the Speaker, whom he considered an old fraud, always mouthing aphorisms tinged with evangelistic fervor, and frequently calling upon "Almighty God." He usually gave the impression that he had just emerged from a long and secret colloquy with the Deity, and he would often cast down his eyes humbly as if listening to a divine prompting audible to no one but himself.

He was a small thin man but his voice was like that of a bass drum and so he was called, irreverently, the Fart. He invariably wore black, summer and winter, and always of the same dull broadcloth. "If he sweats at all," Jeremy once said to some of his colleagues, "he does it through his bladder." His laughing colleagues most naturally and eagerly informed the Speaker of this small witticism and in consequence of this, and other witticisms concerning him from Jeremy, the Speaker hated Jeremy with the venom possible only to a hypocrite who considered himself a man of God, and a lover of his fellow man.

After calling the House to order the Speaker stood in silence, staring at his lectern. His wrinkled face was very solemn and judicious and expressed a deep sadness tinged with stern resolve.

He said, and his voice boomed through the Chamber, "We are called here today in a preliminary investigation of allegations made against the Congressman from New York City, Congressman Jeremy Nathaniel Porter. It is our unquestionably terrible duty, imposed on us by the Laws of the Land. We are empowered by conscience as well as by law to conduct this investigation, and to answer the demands that the Congressman be censured, if not impeached."

Jeremy sat back on his seat and his expression was grimly amused. He folded his arms across his chest. His colleagues carefully avoided looking at him, even his few friends. It was a hot May day, as only Washington can know such a day, humid and dusty and unbearably heavy. The windows of the Chamber were open; a white hot sky blazed beyond them and everything glittered outside, from the harness of the horses to the pavement itself. Great fans moved sluggishly from the ceiling of the Chamber, which disturbed clouds of flies and moved the dust about in golden whirlpools where the sun struck. The assemblage wiped its collective rows of faces, all of them wet and red, and sometimes there was a discreet fluttering of papers as some fanned themselves. Those inclined to favor Jeremy, the very few, were irritated by the fact that it was because of him that they were confined here when they longed to be home in cooler places or resting in their gardens, or napping in the shadowed beds of their mistresses.

The Speaker continued, "Congressman Porter of New York City has been impugning this Congress to the press. It is beneath my dignity as the Speaker of the House to repeat the canards, open accusations, and direct calumnies Congressman Porter has incontinently uttered to the press, without regard for truth or verity or courtesy towards his

colleagues, whom he at one time castigated as 'bought' "—
the Speaker cleared his throat, let his voice drop dolorously—"whores or country jackasses who would not
recognize a bandit even with guns pressed to their heads,
or conspirators against the People of these U-nited States.
These are the very least of his accusations, blurted to the
yellow press. No newspaper with any sense of decorum
or respect would repeat his charges. One would ignore
these charges had they not been picked up by various
irresponsible journals throughout our country, and had
they not caused malcontents to gather in city halls to
discuss them.

"Congressman Porter has also disparaged the President
of these U-nited States, implying that he is the creature of
what he chooses to call 'the international conspirators
who are determined to subjugate the whole civilized world
for their elitist purposes' He has actually said that no
President of recent times has been elected without the
advice and consent of these so-called conspirators, and
that none will so be elected in the future without the
approval of this nameless body of men. He has denounced the august Body of the Senate, also, which has
finally and openly protested.

"Every responsible gentleman here present has heard of
these matters to the point of nausea. Our sense of outrage,
therefore, has gone beyond our Christian forbearance, our
legislative restraint, our honor as gentlemen chosen by
the great people of these U-nited States to represent them
in this Chamber. Therefore, before we begin our discussions—there are excerpts of his speeches and rantings
on the desks before you—we will permit, in our justice,
Congressman Porter to give some slight explanation of
his conduct, which has aroused the indignation of sober
men throughout our country."

Jeremy uttered something obscene, half under his
breath, and several Congressmen near him could not
suppress their quick smiles though they continued to
regard the Speaker with gravity. For several reasons no
spectators had been permitted to occupy the gallery.

Jeremy rose languidly, tall and broad, expressing indifference. He said, "Point of order, if it pleases the
Speaker of the House. Is this Congress in solemn session?"

The Speaker hesitated. A hot silence filled the Chamber. Then the Speaker said, "Not as we usually deem it, Congressman Porter. This is merely a preliminary discussion of the charges brought against you, and to allow you to deny or affirm them."

"Oh," said Jeremy, "there need be no discussion of that. I affirm them, every word. The only trouble is that the press did not quote me in full, and deleted several expletives, no doubt in order to preserve public chastity. I told the press that I had resigned from both the Scardo Society and the Committee for Foreign Studies because I can no longer keep silent. I have learned all I need to know, in this year of Our Lord 1908, and in the midst of the continuing Panic. The electorate will this year vote again for the man they will choose as their President. I believe it is my duty, as a citizen of this country, to inform as many of the people as possible, so that they can judge who are their enemies. Though God knows," he added, "it is much too late to do anything about it, I fear."

The silence in the Chamber became more intense; there was an air of total concentration in it, and stirrings of secret alertness. Jeremy's voice had been quiet, almost indifferent, almost casual, yet it had carried power and conviction and an undertone of despairing bitterness.

He continued, "As the eminent Speaker of the House has informed you, gentlemen, you have before you, on your desks, some of the material which I have given the press, and of which you have already heard from me. No doubt you are well aware of what I have broadcast. There is no need at this time to go into every detail, every sentence, every grave accusation I have made. I have put myself in jeopardy not only with this Congress but with the cold but violent and dedicated men who are determined to destroy the existing order of things among nations and then, in the chaos which will result, they will become the Men on Horseback, the monstrous dictators they aspire to be. It is not just their lust for power which impels them. It is also their innate hatred for humanity, and their desire to oppress it, and to bequeath to their sons and their sons' sons that same rule of death and oppression. They believe they are superior in intelligence to the average man, and that they are of superior birth and talents. While they prate of egalitarianism, to serve their purpose, they detest equality of men even under the law, as promulgated by our Constitution. They talk of social justice and even Populism, and urge a federal income tax 'to help redistribute the wealth' in order to 'abolish poverty' and bestow benefits on 'the workingman.' It is no paradox that they are excessively wealthy men themselves.

"They know very well, and believe it, too, that as Lord Acton said, 'the power to tax is the power to destroy.' That is why they are working for a Sixteenth Amendment to the Constitution, a federal income tax, which repeatedly, in the U. S. Supreme Court, has been declared unconstitutional. Their desire is to eliminate the rising middle class all over the world, for the middle class is their supreme adversary and the frustrater of their desire to subjugate all men to themselves. Once the middle class is taxed out of existence, the masses will have no defender, and they will become the silent and docile slaves of the elitists. It is as simple as that. That is why they are 'informing' the working people of the world that it is the bourgeoisie who are their oppressors, and arousing the envy and hatred of the proletariat against their very friends.

"It is not a very complicated plot. Lucius Sergius Catilina of ancient Rome attempted that, for he detested the common people and more than that the rising middle class of ancient Rome. He wanted power, and the opportunity to rule the people of the Republic with absolute authority, to assuage his malignant detestation of them. Fortunately, Rome had Marcus Tullius Cicero, the Consul of Rome, to preserve law and order and justice and freedom for Romans. At least for a time. Sadly, however, evil is far stronger than good, in spite of what churchmen say, and, sadly, the Roman Republic soon was destroyed and Caesarism rose, and the rights of Romans were abrogated and even free men were enslaved. The middle class of Rome had been eliminated. There is no reason at this time to belabor what happened to the Republic when the middle class was taxed to death and Rome reduced to dictatorship and Caesarism. I am sure all you gentlemen"—and he threw a sardonic look at his fellows—"remember your history."

The fans overhead stirred up the heat and increased it. The Congressmen stared at the papers on their desks and some of them mouthed the words, scratched their cheeks, and moistened their lips. Some faces remained obdurately blank; eyes blinked. But now a few of them turned their heads and gazed at Jeremy with mingled admiration and respect and full knowledge. They were but a few. The Speaker piously studied his hands.

Jeremy resumed in his calm and emphatic voice: "This Panic, which we are still enduring, to the despair of the people, is just one appalling move of the conspirators. Their object is another amendment to the Constitution: the so-called Federal Reserve System, which will put control of the country's currency into their own hands. In that way they can manipulate the currency and the flow of money. They tell the people that if the amendment is passed that will be the end of national panics. Under it all is their determination to take America off the gold standard—and place the power of gold in their own hands. Once our currency is not backed by gold they will have the absolute power, through their bankers, to control not only our money but the people themselves. Yes, gentlemen, I have heard them say this themselves in their secret conclaves.

"Only two years ago, one of the most powerful bankers in America, Jacob Schiff, said that if our monetary system was not reformed, through a Federal Reserve System— mark that—America would 'get a panic compared with which the three which have preceded would be only child's play.' Mr. Schiff is one of the urgent and influential bankers who desire a Federal Reserve System. Need I say more? For months before the Panic, call money on the Stock Exchange had been moving up and down between 10 per cent and 125 per cent. Mr. Schiff has said, 'This is a disgrace to a civilized community.' He is correct. But who invented those excessive rates? Mr. Schiff, among many others, knows the answer, and so do I."

The Speaker rose and in a loud shrill voice exclaimed, "Mr. Schiff is a great, respected, and patriotic American, concerned with his country!"

"Indeed," replied Jeremy. "To quote Shakespeare's Mark Antony, 'Are they not all honorable men?' Yes, indeed."

The Speaker spluttered a protest, then sat down. He said, with a gathering glance at the Congressmen, "How did Shakespeare get into this discussion?" Not one laughed, but most of the Congress nodded sage heads in amused agreement, though many of them had never heard of Mark Antony.

Jeremy, after the amusement had subsided, continued, and now his voice was bitter and pejorative again.

"The conspirators, the holders of tremendous wealth and the savage entrepreneurs, the financial wielders of power all over the world, the enormous industrialists everywhere, have recruited a front army to deceive and delude and arouse the envious people: the so-called intellectuals, feeble men in their own right, weaklings, feckless, men who recognize their own inferiority and hate the robustness and strength of others. They are impelled by a desire for revenge on the more intelligent and effective, and they, too, desire power. They are Fabians, to the man, and express admiration of Karl Marx and his League of Just Men. They are all for the people—whom they secretly loathe and despise. Do not underrate them!

"The pseudo-intellectuals have substituted mad ideologies for the calm and philosophical abstractions of true intellectuals, which are the mark of civilized men, and which have created art and religion. *Their* ideologies are incubating revolutions and public disorder, wars and massacres, hatred and destruction. We will soon see the results in a devastating war, worldwide, which has been planned to overthrow existing and orderly governments."

At this a shout arose: "What war? War! Ridiculous! What do you mean?"

Faces were flushed and angry and incredulous. Jeremy waited again until his colleagues subsided, and until the last mutter of "War!" had died down.

"The pseudo-intellectuals are very effective, in the service of their masters. The true intellectual dismisses them as raving radicals, and therein is our awful danger. The true intellectual avoids controversies and public disputes, whereas their pseudo-brethren court the press. They are so noisy and vehement; they froth and declaim; the press finds them colorful. They rely on the fact that no politician ever tells the press the truth, or dares to tell the truth. You have shown disbelief in the approaching war. But I tell you there will soon be a universal war. I have heard it being plotted, and who the adversary will be. They are not certain just now whether it will be Russia—as yet immune to Socialistic Communism—or Germany.

France and the British Empire have been discussed, in my presence. They will soon decide. It is all the same to the conspirators.

"First of all, they say, Russia must be invaded by Marxism, and this is progressing at a merry rate. When the world is devastated by war, the Russian Communists will come into their own, and with power. There are some amongst you who will later say that Communism is the enemy of the world entrepreneurs and the bankers and the capitalists. You will be wrong. The conspirators are the power behind Communism, as you will see too late. The Communists will be financed by the international bankers and their allies, and will be hailed by our pseudo-intellectuals, who are already inventing slogans cunningly tinged with humanitarianism. I cannot really say that the pseudo-intellectuals are a whole part of the conspiracy. They are too stupid. That is why they are being recruited.

"If I tell you that William Jennings Bryan and the other Populists are part of the conspiracy, I would be wrong. They are too innocent, too naïve about human nature—and too silly—to be conspirators. But they are being manipulated by our enemies.

"I tell you, gentlemen, that the Apocalypse is upon us, and from this time henceforth there will be no peace in the tormented world, only a programmed and systematic series of wars and calamities—until the plotters have gained their objective: an exhausted world willing to submit to a planned Marxist economy and total and meek enslavement—in the name of peace."

He let an impressive silence fall and there were some who even in the heat of the day felt a sharp thrill and chilliness and foreboding. Then Jeremy said in a lower but still carrying voice:

"As for me, gentlemen, and my kind—who are unfortunately few—I will quote Josiah Quincy: 'Under God, we are determined that wheresoever, whensoever or howsoever we shall be called to make our exit, we will die free men.'"

Again he let a pause develop. Finally he quoted, "Hail, Caesar! We who are about to die salute you!'"

Then, without permission of the Speaker, and without speaking again, he turned and left the Chamber.

He was neither censured nor impeached, to his amazement, and a little hope. But neither was he again quoted by the press. This did not surprise him. The press was impotent before the conspirators. Jeremy was effectively silenced. He was not re-elected in November. But Francis Porter was, and Jeremy again was not surprised.

20

There were times when Jeremy felt that his wife, Ellen, exemplified America herself, guileless, naïve, and unwilling to believe in evil and plotters, unwilling to believe that man was imperfectible, destructive, and malicious. The cult of Rousseau was not only rampant among the innocents like Ellen, but had invaded the professed beliefs of the pseudo-intellectuals—that man is born good and is ruined only by "society."

Cynic though he was, and suspicious of organized religion, Jeremy began to reflect on the Godhead, and even found himself reading the Bible. He began to discover ineluctable truths, ageless and pertinent to contemporary life. He happily also discovered that the Bible was not completely composed of unqualified sweetness and light, but was full of wrath and warning, and a certain terribleness and doom. The world was charged not only with the grandeur of God, but with His inevitable anger.

Somewhere he had read, "A Mighty Fortress is our God!" But if the Fortress was undermined by deliberate evil, who could save the dwellers in the Fortress? He repeatedly read in the Bible that God would always triumph. But God counted in centuries, whereas mortal man had to count by hours and days. Man's present misery was hardly alleviated by the fact of eventual victory, far in the future. He had to endure hourly despair, and few men could contemplate the final success of coming generations with complacency. He lived in the

immediate, did man, and his hungers and terrors were
more pertinent to him than the remote conquest of evil by
those yet unborn. There were few saints with a universal
vision. Millions of potentially good men, and saints, were
overwhelmed by present wickedness, and undone by it.
So they compromised, comforted by a spurious hope, and
the meretricious belief that life was too short to take up
arms and fight.

Jeremy tried to enlighten Ellen, without making her as
cynical and despairing as himself, and without making her
as worldly as Kitty Wilder. It was useless. Though she
was still being tutored, her innate innocence prevented
her from fully comprehending Jeremy's exhortations.
Again Jeremy was convinced that the innocent stood between man and his victory over evil.

"But Christ," Ellen would say, "was innocent and good
and without stain."

"You forget how He drove the money changers from
the Temple, dear, and how He castigated the exigent
Pharisees and the scribes. You forget the Revelations of
St. John."

To this Ellen replied, with a rosy smile, "I am so glad,
my darling, that you are beginning to study the Bible."

This only increased Jeremy's sense of impotence, and
his fear for her future if he should die before her. He
consulted his executors, Charles Godfrey and Walter
Porter. Walter was dismayed that his son was now a
Congressman and was frequently quoted, and with approval, in the press.

Jeremy was agreeably surprised that his practice of law
had not been endangered by his defeat. Jochan Wilder,
relieved by not living in Washington any longer, was
proving himself more and more competent, and aware,
though Kitty was devastated at leaving her friends in the
capital city. However, she was consoled by Jochan's
mounting income, paid by Jeremy. She had feared that
once leaving Washington Jeremy would also leave her.
But Jeremy, more and more surfeited by Ellen's trustfulness—though it did not affect his love for her—still
found some skeptical amusement in Kitty's company. She
was like tart wine in contrast to Ellen's resemblance to
the new pink Jell-O. He still did not like Kitty. But she
was a relief.

He was not in the least surprised when the British

Parliament declared its "troubled reflections" on the growing intrusion of Germany in "our heretofore unchallenged dominance in world trade." So, he thought, Germany is going to be our adversary. Germany, apparently, was also concerned, for an entirely different reason. The Kaiser began to expand his army and cavalry. This was called, in the press "Germany's sudden warlike activity." The conspirators, thought Jeremy, with a new fatalistic attitude, are on the move. When he read that Russia was sternly prosecuting Communists and had exiled Lenin, and that this was regarded in the world press as "unconscionable," he knew that the end was near.

But America was newly exuberant. William Howard Taft had been elected. The new President's pronouncements of "more and greater peace and increasing prosperity" were fully quoted in the press. The Panic had passed. Jeremy had considerable respect for President Taft, a sound and reasonable man endorsed by Theodore Roosevelt, but Mr. Taft was amiable and willing to compromise, and Jeremy was suspicious of this. When Mr. Taft tentatively expressed his approval of a federal income tax, the direct election of Senators, and a Federal Reserve System, Jeremy joined the more conservative Democratic Party, which was denouncing Mr. Taft as a Whig.

May Watson wrote to her niece Ellen, under the date of June 3, 1911:

"It has been six months since you visited me here in Wheatfield, Ellen, and two weeks since I've had a letter from you. I thought you'd listened to me last December when I told you how inconsiderate you are, thinking always only of yourself. I hate to bring this up again, at this late date, but you were most uncivil to my dear Mrs. Eccles, who is like a sister to me. You scarcely spoke to her, though she had invited you, kindly, to stay at her house as her guest. But no, you stayed at the hotel, with that awful maid of yours, Clarisse. What a heathen name. Well, Mrs. Eccles is still hurt. She got me a new nurse a week ago, a very good one now, not like the one your husband got for me. He never thinks of me, either. The nurse he got was impudent to Mrs. Eccles and refused to help out in the house a few hours a day. Here I am, a burden to Mrs. Eccles, though she never says a word, being a good and patient Christian woman. She is sweetness itself. The new nurse helps out as she should do. Please send me ten dollars, I need some new shawls. And I think your husband should pay Mrs. Eccles more for me. Tell him so.

"Your letters just chatter along about your husband and your children, when you know what pain I am suffering and need cheering up. I suppose there is nothing I can say, though, to make you more concerned about me, or caring for anybody but your parties and your clothes and your family. When I think how happy we could both be now, safe in Wheatfield in this lovely house, I just cry."

May's letters invariably smeared Ellen's day with despondency. She no longer showed Jeremy those letters because of his spurts of anger. He seemed obliquely to blame Ellen for the letters. Once he said, "Why the hell, Ellen, don't you write that old—I mean, your aunt—and try to get some sense into her head? Give her a few facts, that I am paying for her lavishly to live with Eccles in Wheatfield, and paying for her nurse, and where the devil would she be now if you hadn't married me? In the poorhouse, or dead. You might remind her, too, that I am paying her doctors' bills, and other things. For God's sake, don't cry! And while we are at it, I want you to stop being Lady Bountiful with those increasing charities of yours. Yes, yes, I know there are the Poor, as you say in capitals, and I have no objections at all to helping the worthy poor, but in some damned way you always pick out the charities for malingerers who refuse to work and think the world owes them a living just because they had been born, for God's sake! Where they come from these days only God knows. Confine, if you can, your charities to the Salvation Army and other religious organizations, who help but also expect people to help themselves, too. Ellen, if you don't stop crying I'll go to my club tonight."

So Ellen, out of her housekeeping money, surreptitiously sent her aunt the ten dollars May had demanded, and from the same funds sent Mrs. Eccles five dollars extra a week "for my aunt's care." She confided all this to Annie Burton, the children's nurse, and Annie said bluntly, "Mrs. Porter, as I've always said, you are a dear wonderful lady, but sometimes I think—"

"Think what, Annie?"

"Well, you know what I think, and I worry about you."

"Annie, I couldn't live if I believed everything you say about people. I just couldn't endure living, truly. What would be the point?"

There isn't any "point" in living that I can see! thought Annie. You've just got to take care of yourself; nobody else will, and the more you trust people, the more they think you are a fool. Annie knew all about Kitty Wilder, as did the rest of the staff. If Annie prayed it was a prayer that Ellen would never know.

Once Annie, in a burst of wild desperation, said to Cuthbert, "Mr. Cuthbert, if I ever had any religion at all the Madam has cured me of it! Don't people like her ever realize—realize—"

"That they corrupt people, Annie? Yes. It is all very well to help others who deserve it, and to help with prudence. But unthinking lovingkindness is a grave disservice not only to yourself but to those who receive. Generosity and charity are very exemplary virtues, yes. But one should use judgment, too, and be certain that those assisted are worthy of being assisted, and have courage and self-respect and will soon stand on their own feet. To help the unworthy, the whiners and the lazy, is to corrupt them irretrievably, and enslave them to their own bad natures. However, Mrs. Porter is one of those people who will never understand that, unfortunately."

He paused, and his white brows drew together and he rubbed his rheumatic elbows. "One time, when I was employed by another very saintly lady, I heard her tell her little son that we were all born to help 'others.' The little boy asked his mother, 'And when we're helping others, what are the others doing?' His mother thought about it and said, 'They too are helping others.' Now, children often have a lot of wisdom, Annie. The little boy said, 'Wouldn't it be better for everybody if they just helped themselves, instead of waiting for others to help them?' " Cuthbert laughed a little hoarsely.

"And what did his mum say to that?" asked Annie.

"I am sorry to say that she punished the little lad severely and called him unchristian. I was always afraid that she would eventually corrupt him, too." He sighed.

"Well," said Annie, "the Madam will never corrupt Christian and Gabrielle. They are born hardhearted devils, and they laugh at their mother behind her back. They think she is silly. And sometimes," Annie exclaimed, throwing out her arms helplessly, "I think so, too!" The young woman almost cried. "They think more of that awful Mrs. Wilder than they do of their own mother. Wicked people do seem to understand each other, don't they? Those kids are real wicked, Mr. Cuthbert, and if I didn't hit them hard once in a while they'd be worse. At least they don't dare to laugh at the Madam to her face. I warned them."

"The master keeps a hard hand ready, too," said old Cuthbert with grave approval. "No nonsense there. Sometimes I think that all that love the Madam bestows indiscriminately on her children helped to corrupt them. It is certainly very sad."

Ellen did not know it was "sad." She now believed, with happiness, that her children would never injure their father. They appeared devoted to him, and competed with each other to please him, in spite of his sternness and his insistence on manners and discipline. They never screamed at him as they screamed at her, nor did they dare to dispute his word. They listened to him with respect and open affection, a respect and affection they did not give their mother. She was not to know until much later that once eight-year-old Christian said to Kitty, "Mama's very stupid, isn't she?" Nor was she to know that six-year-old Gabrielle had giggled and said, "Mama's dippy. Everybody knows it. Nobody pays any attention to her."

To Ellen, their frank insolence to her was only "high spirits," and their disobedience "independence." Did not these new alienists warn parents not to inflict severe punishment on their children, but to pour out lavish love on them? Yes. Jeremy laughed at them and wondered why they did not return to Vienna and let American parents alone.

"But Americans," he would say to Ellen, "are beginning to listen humbly to every foreign charlatan who insults them. I think Americans are now starting to feel guilty because of their own good fortune, which is the result of worth only." Ellen did not understand why he had suddenly looked at her sharply and not with his usual tenderness, and then had shaken his head. If she ever recalled the cruel children of her childhood it was with the thought that they had been "unfortunate" in some manner, possibly their poverty. Hence her reckless charity and her unquestioning generosity.

Ellen blissfully lived her life, protected by Jeremy, Cuthbert, and Annie, and now Charles Godfrey, who was a frequent guest at dinner and had a way of gazing at her which both embarrassed and pleased her, though she did not know why. Always, he spoke gently to her, even when Jeremy had expressed his impatience at some remark of hers. It never occurred to Ellen that Charles both pitied her and loved her, and was afraid for her.

Her beauty had now matured and Charles, rather inanely, thought that she resembled a rose. But Charles was not an original poet. He was not a poet at all. He only knew that he loved this immaculate and charming young woman. He also knew that she was friendless, except for himself and the domestic staff. And, of course, her husband, and his uncle.

While Jeremy cherished his wife more than ever, he rarely spoke to her any longer of the things which were troubling him and driving him to despair. Her happiness had clouded the sun of her comprehension and perceptiveness. Prolonged happiness, Jeremy would think, is also an enemy in its own way. It leaves us unguarded and open to attack. We need occasional unhappiness and misfortune as much as meat needs salt, or as nations need arms. Sharp crises added pungency to bland and sunlit existence, and nations needed to defend themselves.

21

In January 1912, Jeremy's mother wrote to him, as she did once a week. He was always impatient with her letters, and with his father's, too, and they depressed him, for there was always a covert insinuation about Ellen despite the sending of "love to Ellen, too, and the Babies." (Babies, hell! he thought. One is nearly eight, the other six.)

His mother wrote: "I have been reading so much lately in *The New York Times* and other papers about your cousin Francis, whom I never liked but who seems to have improved in the past few years. He has so much compassion for the People, and so eloquent! I read his speeches in Congress closely; what a Heart he has! It is even hinted that the New York legislature will name him a Senator!"

Good God, thought Jeremy. Francis and his kind can talk without stopping, in Congress and the Senate and in other political situations and in their colleges and in the newspapers. They must have auxiliary bladders. They can never shut up.

"Ah, if women could only vote!" exclaimed Jeremy's mother in her letter. "Francis endorses votes for women. Francis believes that a wonderful Change would come over America if we could vote. There would be no more wars or national upheavals, no more unemployment or misery, and the Children would be cared for sedulously and women would be Elevated in society, and future eras would be tranquil and everyone joyous. This, with the thoughts of noble men like Francis, and their new laws, would indeed usher in a new Golden Age."

Jeremy sighed wearily and shut his eyes for a moment in his library on this cold winter day.

"Francis does so hope Mr. Roosevelt will be elected this year and Mr. Taft ousted. Mr. Taft, as you know, has shown much ingratitude to Mr. Roosevelt, who was really responsible for Mr. Taft being President. (You see, Jeremy, I do Read, and am not a stupid Woman, as you always think women are.) I do not blame Mr. Roosevelt for refusing to visit Mr. Taft in the White House—really such ingratitude on the part of Mr. Taft, and, as Mr. Roosevelt has said, he is guilty of 'the grossest and most astounding hypocrisy,' and disloyalty.

"Francis thinks we need a Fighting Man for President, and so he will support Mr. Roosevelt. Wasn't it wonderful what Mr. Roosevelt said recently? 'I stand for the Square Deal for the People of our Country. My hat is in the ring. The fight is on and I am stripped to the buff.' (A rather Indelicate Phrase, I thought, but he is such a virile

man and one knows how Gentlemen talk when overwrought.)

"Francis says we must really wait to see who the
Democrats nominate. He talks vividly of a Professor
Wilson—Richard? William? Woodrow? One never knows
these names, though it is not important. Mr. Wilson,
Francis says, is a man of Compassion, too, and talks of a
new world of peace and justice and prosperity."

Jeremy thought of what Thoreau had written: "For
what avail the plow and sail, the land and life, if freedom
fail?" Jeremy thought of his children who would live in
the future. He shrugged. Paraphrasing Christ, he said to
himself, "Sufficient unto the day the generation thereof."

"If only you had been more discreet, dear Jerry, and
so had been returned to Congress! How Proud we should
have been! But no, you antagonized your constituency,
in your blunt and ruthless way, and made enemies. You
were always a somewhat difficult child; your teachers did
not love you. You were always in an argument, against
something you called, when you were only ten years old,
'sweetness and light.' I hate to give Francis praise, but he
is more attuned to people than ever you were, my dear."

That's the best compliment you ever gave me, dear
Mama, thought Jeremy.

"I do wish, my dear son, that you would now refrain
from writing articles for the magazines and newspapers
which Francis calls 'reactionary.' This will only make you
more enemies. I do read those articles, and your father
and I are often distressed by them. You simply seem to
lack Charity and Hope, and your words are bitter and
offensive. After all, we don't live in the Age of McKinley
any longer. We are Advancing."

Yes, we certainly are, thought Jeremy.

"Enough of politics," wrote his mother. "We were so
hurt that you and Ellen and your dear Babies did not
come to Preston for the Holidays. Could it be that Ellen
does not love us enough, and Influenced you? I hope not.
No woman should Influence her husband against his
devoted Parents, and break their hearts. I have suspected
for some time that Ellen is not in Accord with your
mother and father, though we have been most kind to
her and accepted her into the family. Could you not
have come alone with your adorable Children, if Ellen

wished to decline? Francis was here, with his father, and Mrs. Eccles. Mrs. Eccles is a most lovely Person and speaks nothing but good about Ellen, and how devoted she is to Ellen's aunt, in Wheatfield. Such Charity!"

Thirty dollars a week, and nurses, thought Jeremy. Charity comes high these days.

"Mrs. Eccles, whom you do not like, I have observed, always defends Ellen."

He stood up and carefully drew aside the heavy draperies at the library window. I am seeing shadows, thought Jeremy. That "skulker" across the street is only a man waiting for his assignation. He returned to his mother's letter.

"Our only son, our only child! And he would not come Home for Christmas and New Year's! Who has turned you from your Loving Parents? Who has made you Indifferent to them?"

Jeremy remembered that Ellen had implored him to visit his parents at some time during the holidays. He had brusquely refused. He had learned that Francis was to be there, and his stomach, a little uncertain these days, had caused him to decline. Francis and Mrs. Eccles were too much for his constitution. Besides, he had been engaged in articles for *The New York Times* and various magazines, not to mention some acute court cases.

His parents had sent very expensive gifts to his children, and to himself. To Ellen, they had sent four linen handkerchiefs, for which she had been pathetically grateful. Jeremy clenched his teeth. When would Ellen stop being grateful for the slightest kindness or consideration, as if she were unworthy even of notice? Jeremy looked at the telephone. Then he reached for it and called Kitty Wilder.

He needed a good dose of sound cynicism tonight, something to take the sweet smell from his nostrils. Ellen had put greenhouse roses in the library. He lifted the vase and dropped it in the hall. Roses in their season were excellent. When not in season they were cloying. Jeremy was beginning to find the whole world cloying, though he knew that disaster was imminent.

He reached for the bell rope and when Cuthbert came in he said, "Please inform Mrs. Porter I will not be here for dinner tonight. I have a business arrangement I must attend. Unfortunate."

Yes, thought Cuthbert. Unfortunate. He said, "Yes, sir. I will inform the Madam—after you have left." They exchanged glances, and Jeremy turned away. Cuthbert removed the roses from the hall.

As Ellen had no frame of reference concerning the rearing of upper-class children, she sedulously read every new book pertaining to this subject. Jeremy thought this hilarious. He said, "There's nothing to beat your precious Bible's injunctions about sparing the rod and spoiling the child. And isn't there something also in the Bible about a father who 'chastens' his children if he loves them, and pampers them if he hates them? Yes. Even better, the old saying 'A dog and a kid and a walnut tree —the more you beat 'em, the better they be.' I don't agree with that concerning a dog and a tree, but a kid is different."

"Oh, Jeremy," Ellen replied, smiling. "You don't mean that. Our children adore you."

"That's because I thrash them thoroughly when necessary, and so does Annie. They adore her, too."

This tactless remark dimmed Ellen's bright face. Seeing this, Jeremy said quickly, "They treat you, love, as just one of themselves."

"Yes," she said with an eagerness that made him both impatient and tender towards her. "They do, don't they? You should read what Horace Mann said about that. You must be friends with your children, teach them to confide in you and love them without any restraint or mental reservations, give them all your attention, treat them seriously, play with them, reason with them rather than punish them, give them choices in conduct, respect them—"

"I've read Horace Mann, too," said Jeremy. "He's a blithering ass, as our English cousins would say. If ever his theories take real root in America we are going to raise generations of selfish, greedy, self-adoring, whining, demanding, wild brats. Remember, love, what Solomon said about children, 'Man is wicked from his birth and evil from his youth. . . . The heart of a child is deceitful.' There is nothing in your Bible which demands that parents honor their children, remember."

Ellen said in a very mild and smiling protest, "Horace Mann says children are born pure and blameless, and how they develop is due only to their parents."

"There are times," said Jeremy, "when I really do believe in Original Sin. Children reek of it, from the day they are born." He became thoughtful and studied Ellen. He was understanding more and more about her as time went on, and he knew that she was attempting to alleviate the suppressed memories of her own childhood; in giving to her children she was not only giving because they were his, and so entitled to adoration, God help her, she was also giving to the little hated and derided child she herself had been. Her old pain was assuaged and soothed in the tending of Christian and Gabrielle. He knew that she delighted in the belief that never would they be stoned on the streets, never despised, never cold or hungry, never treated with contempt and jeering laughter. So now he only bent and kissed her and said with a dark gravity, "Don't be overzealous, dear. Remember, our children are venal human beings who need constant correction and stern guidance, and must be taught respect for authority."

"Oh, they understand that, Jeremy. They are very intelligent."

Jeremy had personally selected his children's governess, a Miss Maude Cummings, who had no illusions about children, and who treated Ellen with kind attentiveness and a gentle wonder and perhaps a considerable compassion. She was a thin little woman of about twenty-two, and highly educated, and English and a daughter of the proverbial vicar; she was a born spinster, and Jeremy often thought of the Brontë sisters when he saw her. She had an oval reflective face, smooth and pale and with delicate features, and straight black hair parted severely in the center and drawn back, in an old-fashioned way, into a round knot on her nape. She dressed severely in black silk, summer and winter, and she might have seemed an anachronism had she not had large and flashing black eyes that were never sentimental but were acutely humorous and steadfast. Had Miss Cummings ever had "carnal knowledge" of a man? Jeremy doubted it, in spite of her sparkling gaze at him and the faintest subtle smile on her colorless lips. There was something of a Mona Lisa about her, when she was silent, and she was usually silent at the dinner table. She wore a signet ring on her little left hand, which she never explained, though it was very unusual. Her voice was quiet, yet filled with authority. Jeremy's children did not like her and often complained of her to Ellen, but they held her in a respect which even Jeremy found remarkable. She would listen to Ellen's expoundings on the vaporings of Horace Mann with kindness and good manners, and would say, "There are so many new theories these days, aren't there, Mrs. Porter? One has to be judicious about accepting them, and putting them to test."

Ellen found Miss Cummings to be a little disconcerting, for the governess made her feel somewhat jejune though that was not Miss Cummings' intention. Kitty said of her, to Ellen, "That young woman is quite snobbish, isn't she, and superior—at least in her own mind. Probably poor as the mythical church mouse. The English are very haughty; I never did like them. They are always forgetting that we overthrew them in America."

Kitty disliked the governess with her usual malice and suspicion. Miss Cummings was the very essence of politeness, but her enigmatic repose seemed to reject Kitty's constant vivacity, loud laughter, thrusts of cruel wit, and restless movements, as if Kitty were a parvenu. Then, there was too much awareness in those undeluded eyes, too much scrutiny, too much thoughtfulness. "Secretive," Kitty would say to Ellen. "And sly, too. I know her sort."

As Ellen did not find Miss Cummings congenial for all her elegant consideration and manners and kindness, she did not immediately come to the governess's defense. Then she said, "Oh, I just don't know. The children don't like her, either, Kitty. Well, let's be charitable. She's really excellent, as a tutor. And wouldn't she be pretty if she were a little more stylish?"

"Nothing could help her appearance," said Kitty. She thought of the way Miss Cummings watched her when Jeremy was present, and the way her long dark lashes would quiver with the calm intensity of her regard. *I wonder*, thought Kitty, *if she's ever hinted anything to that stupid Ellen?* One night when she and Jeremy were alone, she said, "I just can't endure that governess, Jerry. She's crafty, and seems to see—everything. Your children dislike her, too. It isn't fair to impose such a woman on such young little creatures, who are so sensitive."

"Sensitive, hell," replied Jeremy. "Children are as sensitive as calluses, and Cummings knows that, too. A fine understanding woman, and I'm lucky to have found her. She has private means, too, as the English say. She teaches because she likes to teach, though God knows why anyone would pick such a profession. There are no rose spectacles on Cummings; she knows all about kids and I have the feeling she doesn't particularly love them, either, which shows she is a woman of profound sense. Now, Kitty, you don't like children either, so don't make such a sad mouth to me as if you are consumed with maternal passion all at once."

Kitty laughed. They were enjoying one of her delightful dinners in her house, as Jeremy had sent Jochan to Philadelphia to consult a client. She said, "Well, I fear she suspects something between you and me, and might confide that to Ellen."

"If she does suspect she'll keep it to herself. British reticence, you know." He considered, then winked. "Do you actually think she knows I tumble you in bed?"

"Don't be coarse, Jerry. I really love you, you know, and I'm available only to you." She spoke with the deepest honesty she had ever known, and for the first time Jeremy heard it and was uncomfortable. Perhaps, he thought, I should be seeing Kitty less and less, until it is all over. Besides, there's that little Mrs. Bedford, who's a toothsome mite and intelligent, too, and entertaining, and very knowing, like Kitty, but in a less sharp way, and as young as Ellen. Those hard lines between Kitty's eyes are getting heavier all the time. Come to think of it, what did I really see in her?

The astute Kitty saw something on his face which frightened and chilled her. She said quickly, "Let us discuss something more pleasant than your Cummings, who seems to have an eye for you, too." Kitty knew very well that no woman who loved a man—if he was not her husband—should annoy or dispute him. Nor bore him. The beasts were undependable, and had a way of skittering off immediately if any demands were put upon them, or given hints they did not appreciate. What they would endure in a wife they would not endure for an instant in a mistress. They could not easily, and forever, dispose of a wife, but mistresses were expendable. Too, wives, however detestable, were their property, and men guarded their property. Women, thought Kitty with a new compassion strange to her nature, do not have the best of lives in this world, particularly if they do not have a legal hold on a man. Kitty had never liked her sex; men to her were indispensable, and Jeremy particularly so. Her fear grew, and she drew on her best witticisms to amuse Jeremy tonight, and was angry with herself that she had even momentarily annoyed him.

Ellen read to her children every night. She had been advised to in the new grave books about the rearing of children. No matter the attentions of devoted servants, nursemaids, or governesses, the books urged, children needed the tender ministrations of their mother at bedtime, and "an improving and lovely story from some selected book." When Ellen had told this to Jeremy he said, "Read to them from *The Three Musketeers*. Children love blood and thunder and murder and sin. Yes, dear, they really do. You are only twenty-seven, and not too old to remember what children are like."

"Twenty-six," said Ellen. "I won't be twenty-seven until January. I know you are not serious about *The Three Musketeers*. I am just starting on *Grimm's Fairy Tales*."

"They're grim, all right," said Jeremy. "That is, if they haven't been bowdlerized by now by the new child-lovers, who spare kids the gory facts of life. Why should they be spared? Besides, they are born fully equipped with those facts. Then they are taught hypocrisy, and pretense that life is really a beautiful dream, and all men are brothers. Kids know that's a lot of damned nonsense, and it does something harmful to them later if they are taught lies. Politicians are prime examples."

Ellen did not know that she was a source of intense amusement to her children, who mocked her behind her back to each other, and often to her face. They would listen to her in the nursery at night when she read to them and would exchange less than affectionate winks at Ellen's expense. Christian was a great handsome lad now, and Gabrielle more Latin in appearance, and lively. They were both unusually intelligent, and both were without kindliness or illusions. To Miss Cummings they were even "worse" than her last American charges, though she could control them with ease. Like Cuthbert and Annie, she feared for their mother.

Ellen had selected one of the brothers Grimm's less "gory" stories to read to her children this wild March night, with the snow hissing at the windows and the wind screaming in the chimneys. The nursery fire was warm and red and chuckled to itself, safe from the storm. Then, remembering what Jeremy had said, she took up another book, by Hans Christian Andersen. "The Little Mermaid" would do splendidly. She read it with deep feeling and understanding, and there were tears in her eyes when she concluded the touching story. She looked at her children, Christian in his nightshirt and blue wool robe, and Gabrielle in her silk and lacy nightgown and red robe.

"I always loved that story," she said. "It always made me cry."

"Why?" asked Christian. "I think it's silly."

"In what way?" said Ellen, dismayed.

It was Gabrielle, the pert pixie, who answered her. "The prince was too stupid to fall in love with the mermaid, and she was stupid to love a man who was more stupid. Why did she decide to give up the long life she'd have had if she'd not had her tail cut into legs and feet? She should have found a merman to love, if she wanted love that bad, and lived a long, long time. But now, with feet and legs, and all that pain when she walked and danced, she had nothing."

"She acquired a human soul," said Ellen, more and more dismayed.

"What made her think she or anyone else has a soul?" said Christian.

Ellen was horrified. "But, dear, you know we have souls."

"No, Mama, I don't know. I know what you say, and the minister and the Sunday-school teachers say, but that doesn't prove anything. It's only something they want themselves, and because they want it they believe it is so."

Ellen regarded him with distress. "But the Bible says so, too. It's something we should believe."

"Why should we believe something you can't prove, Mama dear?"

Ellen did not hear the taunting in her son's voice, or

the contempt. She thought she had heard only a serious question. "It is a matter of faith, dear," she explained. "We should accept certain things on faith."

"Why?" asked Gabrielle.

"Because God and Our Lord and the prophets said so, Gaby." Fresh tears came into her eyes. She had a thought. Jeremy was always talking about the corrupting of children. Was it possible that Miss Cummings had taught them these upsetting ideas? Ellen had already suspected that Miss Cummings was a skeptic, for all she dutifully took the children to Sunday school and insisted on that, and quieted their protests.

"Whoever gave you these awful ideas, Christian, Gaby? Miss Cummings?"

Christian's large blue eyes, so like Ellen's own except for the expression, lighted up. Now here was a chance to get rid of that prig! Then he reconsidered. Mama was a fool and had no authority in this house. She would immediately report to Papa, and Papa had a way of asking very keen and telling questions, and he would question his son with no mercy. Christian remembered his last thrashing, which had been the most painful he could remember. "You've got to stop lying, Chris," Jeremy had said. "The next time you'll get double, if I catch you in it."

So Christian, with a sullen anger perceptible even to Ellen's doting eyes, said, "No, Mama, she didn't. It's just some things I asked of myself. Gaby and I often talked about it."

"You never talked with me about it, Christian, and I'm your mother."

More's the pity, for Gaby and me, thought the boy. He looked at his mother with wide innocence. "We will, next time, Mama. After all, we are only little children, aren't we?"

Gabrielle had listened to this with a dark sparkle on her pointed face, and with eyes that leapt in their sockets with hilarity. Christian was really very good, she thought, better than any of those silly actors in that dippy play last Christmas, *Peter Pan*. When Ellen looked at her, almost imploringly, Gabrielle said in an affectedly sweet voice, "You must bear with us, as Miss Cummings says, Mama."

"Yes, darling," said Ellen, relieved. "And now we will say our prayers together."

That night, as usual, Gabrielle crept from her room to Christian's. She sat on his bed and they talked of their mother and shrieked with laughter into pillows, so Miss Cummings would not hear. Tonight, their laughter was more prolonged.

22

Miss Cummings had a splendid regard for Cuthbert, whom she considered "quite a gentleman." For Annie she had a special fondness, for, like all the English, she respected common sense and an acquaintance with reality, and had an innate disgust for sentimentality. (She had a special liking for the Brontës for this reason.) For Clarisse, Ellen's maid, she had cold contempt and suspicion; Miss Cummings disliked any invasion of privacy and eavesdropping, but she had overheard, without trying, some of Clarisse's muffled and derisive remarks, in French, to Kitty Wilder.

Miss Cummings' favorite spot, even above her delightful quarters on the third floor, was the big brick kitchen with its fireplace. There she would sit, on cold or dank and chilly days, near the fire, thoughtfully sipping China tea and nibbling at Cuthbert's shortbread, which she admitted was as good as any she had ever tasted in England. ("A little more butter perhaps, Cuthbert, and have you tried a drop or two of vanilla bean? Just a touch; not enough to be identified, but it does give it a certain something.") The housemaids liked her calm presence and admired her smooth oval face and the old-fashioned way she dressed her hair. A lady, they would remark to themselves. Cuthbert especially liked her to be in the kitchen, to sip his court bouillon critically, watching her for a nod of her head, or his shrimp ("prawns") dressing for lobsters. "Mr. Jim Brady admired it also," Cuthbert said once. "I was not impressed, however, Miss Cummings. A vulgarian."

Miss Cummings remarked wryly, "Diamonds are always an excuse for bad taste, I've discovered."

Miss Cummings was becoming more and more concerned over Ellen's children. "I well know," she said, this brawling late March day, "that children are born wicked and intransigent, but Christian and Gabrielle seem to have few if any compensating virtues, except, perhaps, unusual intelligence. However, the evil are much more formidable when intelligent than the stupid. Despite Mr. Porter's discipline, and Annie's and mine, and my exhortations and their Sunday school, they have a peculiar bent of mind. They are utterly ruthless, lacking the slightest inclination to Christian charity or kindness, or remorse, or gentleness of thought. They seem to find these exemplary traits risible. It is as if they were born without—what shall I call it?"

"Without humanity," suggested Cuthbert.

Miss Cuthbert sighed. "Well, I do not have the highest regard for humanity, Cuthbert, even at its best. No. It is something else. Like a defect of the spirit—a blindness. This is not new to me." She hesitated. "Before I accepted this post it was my misfortune to have a young lad, a little older than Christian, under my guidance and care. He, too, had a defect of the spirit, a confirmed cruelty, even more so than Christian's. A fine boy, too, handsome, beguiling, ingratiating, when it suited his purposes. I am certain he killed his little brother, though no one suspected besides myself. He resented the child's presence and his parents' affection given also to another."

Cuthbert, who was inserting slivers of garlic into a leg of lamb, paused and looked at her with intent gravity. "They were out in a boat, Cuthbert, on a large pond. The little one, about three years old, could not swim. The boat overturned. The older boy declared over and over, with tears, that he had tried to save the child, and his sorrowful parents believed him. I did not. No, there was no direct evidence, but I had watched him over many months, and so I knew. He was capable of anything that interfered with his own gratification. I left abruptly. I could not bear to look into his beautiful serious eyes when he spoke of the dead child. I could not bear to see his tears. I was afraid"—and her voice dropped—"that if

I remained I might confront him—with disastrous results. I am not a meek person."

Cuthbert continued his delicate work with somber thoughtfulness. "I have seen such myself," he finally said. "Yes. Well, I fear you are quite correct, Miss Cummings, in your opinion of Master Christian and Miss Gabrielle. They enhance each other's wickedness. Mrs. Porter speaks with fondness of how 'close' her children are. The wicked recognize and know each other at once, and complement each other. Let us be thankful, however, that they are not enemies."

"It would be interesting to know their ancestry," said the governess. "I do not believe in this new insistence on environment; I believe bad blood leaps over the generations, and is born in the flesh, and nothing can eliminate it. Mrs. Porter is the soul of gentleness and tenderness, and Mr. Porter is a gentleman of integrity for all his fierce glances and abrupt manners at times. Their children are nothing like them at all, in spite of the physical resemblances. It is strange, but beauty is often the delightful garb of the evil; it is as if Satan bestows that on them, to be a menace to others."

"Yet, Mrs. Porter is very beautiful," said Cuthbert.

"Extraordinarily so, yes. And Mr. Porter has his moments of handsomeness. Ah, well, who understands these things? We can only be perceptive and wary. I try to convey warnings to Mrs. Porter, whom her children mock and taunt, but she gazes at me in a puzzled way. I fear she dislikes me."

"Mrs. Porter does not dislike anyone, I am afraid," said Cuthbert. "One wonders about Mrs. Wilder—"

The two exchanged deep and significant glances, and Miss Cummings sighed again and Cuthbert poured another cup of tea for her. They listened to the rumbling of the fire and the hissing of snow against the leaded windowpanes. "I am not particularly sensitive," said Miss Cummings, "but I have an ominous presentiment of tragedy."

"So do I," said Cuthbert. "I have felt it for a long time, even from the moment I first met Mrs. Porter. There are those who are marked for doom, are they not?"

"It makes one think," said Miss Cummings. "It is very

strange that the clergy talk of God loving all His children, even the most dangerous. I doubt that the Almighty has no discrimination. We are exhorted to have compassion on all things. I have not read that in the Bible. Forgive your enemies, yes. But do not weep over them."

Jeremy spoke angrily to some of his politician acquaintances. "Why Wilson?" he demanded. "No, I will not be a delegate to the convention. That is final."

The politicians looked at each other, and several lit fresh cigars. They were gathered in Jeremy's office. "We need a fresh view of government," one said.

Jeremy gave them a cynical stare.

"Such as Wilson's 'new progress,' as he calls it? I have mentioned, over and over, what you already know, that he established a Communist cell in Princeton. The man is not very bright; I've had a series of conversations with him. But then, no Communist has any brains; he has only the lust for power. However, I doubt Wilson has even that. But he is a man who can be easily manipulated, for all his erudition. Am I correct?"

"Jerry, damned if we know what you're talking about."

Jeremy studied them, and carefully lit a cigarette. "Perhaps you don't, perhaps you do. What about his friend Colonel House? Or don't you know anything about him, either?"

The politicians were silent, studying the glowing ends of their cigars. Jeremy said, "I see. You've had your orders."

"Now, what the hell do you mean by that? We've selected the man we feel is best for the office."

"But what about the country?" Again they were silent. Jeremy threw his match at the fireplace with a curse. "We've had Roosevelt, who was a blusterer, and we have Taft, who is amiable and has some intelligence and is a prudent man. They are, at least, men who have a regard for America, though words have been put into Roosevelt's mouth quite often. Neither would betray his country."

"And you think Wilson would?" The politicians chuckled, but Jeremy did not.

"In one way or another, yes, perhaps without intention. He is a very weak man. And there is Colonel House, who is not weak, but a very insidious gentleman."

"I know some of his ideas, Jerry," said one politician. "He thinks it is about time that America took an active part in the affairs of the world. We are no longer an isolated nation; the world is at our doorstep; we can't, any longer, be insular."

"And why not? What is reprehensible about a man keeping his doors and windows locked against wolves— or international criminals? What is wrong with Washington's warnings against foreign entanglements?"

"Times change, Jerry. This modern world is different."

"Times always change, and the world is always different, from day to day. But there are certain verities, which never change, and are never different. Such as minding your own business, for one."

"All very vague, Jerry."

"I don't think you believe that. Wilson's a cloistered man without a deep measure of intelligence. Were he actually intelligent he wouldn't have founded that Communist cell. I doubt he has a very clear idea of what Communism means. But the Communists are hellishly clever in finding men like Wilson, and putting them in power. I know. My cousin is one of the idiots himself. He calls Communism a 'system of Love.' I've heard that Wilson remarked that, too. Frank Porter, my cousin, babbles just like Wilson."

They did not answer. Jeremy stood up with grim intentness. "The new child-labor laws— Children have worked for centuries, in factories and fields. I don't like it, I don't approve of it. But why can't their fathers earn enough money to keep their children out of factories and industries? You know why. The government taxes all materials so heavily that it is an impossibility for free enterprise to pay adequate wages to their workers, and make the slightest profit. In the meantime the people are being incited against capitalism. You know it, I know it. What is the object? You know what it is—the alleged destruction of capitalism in behalf of Socialism or Communism; they are both the same, as any intelligent man knows. Then the middle class will be eliminated; it is part of the general design."

They looked at him and said nothing, though one or two indulgently shook their heads.

"The Scardo Society," said Jeremy. "Ostensibly just

good sound financiers' and bankers, meeting in quiet closed spots all over the world. Just excellent gentlemen concerned with the soundness of currency and investments, yes? Now, boys, you know better than that. And the Committee for Foreign Studies, on Fifth Avenue. 'Studies' don't require armed guards, do they? Or barred windows and doors?"

He was aware of a sudden sharp stillness in the room, though a few of the politicians seemed honestly puzzled. Jeremy looked from one to the other with a cold savagery. "I see some of you understand me perfectly. When is the great war coming? Next year, the year after, or the year after that?"

"You belonged to the Committee for Foreign Studies once, didn't you?"

"Ah," said Jeremy, "and how did you know that, sir?"

"Oh, come, Jerry. It's not a secret. Nothing criminal about it, is there? Some of the most powerful men in America belong to it—"

"True. And has any one of you any idea of what is discussed among those 'powerful men'? I do. War."

"With whom?" asked one of the politicians who was genuinely baffled. "And why?"

"Ask your friends here. They know."

"What are you smoking, Jerry? Hashish?"

They all laughed loudly. Jeremy watched them, and suddenly he was weary. He threw up his hands, while some regarded him with half-hidden hostility and watchfulness. "Politicians," he said. "It doesn't matter if you are Democrats or Republicans. Politicians are all alike. As Aristotle said, 'Politicians are not born. They are excreted.' "

No one was amused. One man said, "Why don't you return to the Republican Party, if you're so dissatisfied?"

He replied, "There is no difference between you."

"You might join the Populist Party out West."

Another said, "Jerry, you and I know that enormously rich men belong to the Committee for Foreign Studies. They know that Socialism would eliminate them. So they can't be for it."

Jeremy looked at the speaker in disbelief. "Are you out of your mind? Socialism will not destroy the great rich, otherwise they wouldn't secretly advocate it. Again, they want to destroy the middle class, which stands between them and the exercise of the tyranny they want."

He paused, then said, "There is just one thing I want to know: Who paid you off?"

They rose as one man in honest or simulated indignation. They said nothing more. They left his office.

23

Maude Cummings dined with the family during intimate dinners when only one or two old friends were present. Ellen had often invited her to the large parties, but Maude had gently declined. "They are strangers," she said. "And I am a stranger." On these occasions there had been a far and startled sadness in Ellen's eyes and she had turned away, her head bent. Maude had watched her go and she had thought, "My dear, you too are a stranger, and always will we be, you and I."

Maude never declined when Charles Godfrey was present at small dinners. She had early detected his love for Ellen. She knew, with her perceptiveness, that he was also a man to be trusted. Still, she hesitated. She was English, and she had the English love of reserve and privacy, the English dislike of intrusion and subjectivity. Also, though a governess, she was only an employee of the household. She doubted that Jeremy would approve of her "interference," especially one so delicate as the one she was considering. But her urgent desire to help Ellen overcame her reticence, and one morning she quietly called Charles Godfrey. Jeremy was in Philadelphia.

"Mr. Godfrey," she said in her soft but firm voice, "I should like a conference with you, if you please, and at your convenience, preferably today."

He was surprised. He could see Maude's face before him, smooth, pale, composed, and he wondered, for the first time, why he had not seen before that she possessed a certain distant beauty of her own. He had admired her from the beginning. She was a lady of "sense." He also knew that Ellen had an air of uneasiness when the governess was present, as if she knew she should listen but did not wish to do so. It was as if some warning instinct was trying to speak to Ellen, and she denied it out of fear.

"Certainly, Miss Cummings," said Charles. "Would you lunch with me? Delmonico's, perhaps?"

"A smaller, less conspicuous place, perhaps, sir? Besides, I do not have the proper dress."

He named a discreet little restaurant near Delmonico's where he frequently took his women friends. He wondered if the air of discretion would embarrass Miss Cummings, then he no longer wondered. The girl was worldly, he thought, and he wondered, again, why he had not seen that before. Ellen might be abashed, but certainly not Miss Cummings. So he gave her directions on how to reach the restaurant. "Perhaps it would be best for some conveyance?" he said.

"No, thank you. The trolley will be quite sufficient."

It was a sweet mild day in April, sweet even in reeking New York with its streets littered with garbage and random filth, which made walking, except for the main avenues, somewhat difficult and dangerous. There were always rowdies about, and the sinister loiterers who followed women alone, with abusive language and obscene gestures. Charles was worried, then not worried. Miss Cummings was a young lady who could cope with almost anything, he decided, with fresh admiration. It would be a doughty wretch who would press her.

Miss Cummings' wardrobe was small and not fashionable, though the materials were excellent, as Charles had noted before, and were doubtlessly expensive. She is a very mysterious girl, he had often thought, watching her at the table. Today she wore her customary black silk dress, plain in bodice with a white lace collar, handmade and weblike, and fastened with an opal brooch, the skirt slim and only slightly draped in front. Her black shoes were polished and well made, her black kid gloves impeccable. Over this she wore a black cloak of fine broadcloth. Her wide hat was of black felt, with subdued silk roses in a maroon color. It was always her desire to be inconspicuous, and so she was in her clothing, her severely dressed hair, her quiet face. She carried a purse of black leather, old but not shabby or poor.

Yet, on the trolley she had immediately attracted curious glances and speculations as she sat serenely on the rattan seat, alone. Her expression was withdrawn, though not secretive. She looked through the dusty windows at the seething streets, and her thoughts were as composed as her face, but clear and determined. She knew exactly what she intended to say, without any maidenly coyness or hesitations or pretended shyness, or fluttering protests that she knew that she should not be speaking thus, but she was compelled— No "forgive me, please." A person must do as she must, thought the daughter of a vicar.

The shops were bustling, though the Panic had not been over long. The walks were crowded with hurrying men and women. The spires of churches reached up towards the warm and whitish sky. On each corner were ragged women selling violets, and there were many men trundling hot-roasted-chestnut carts. The trolley clanged and swayed and rattled. Why did everything in America seem so noisy? Miss Cummings reflected. Even the omnibuses roared. It was like a fever; everyone rushed, even those obviously not going anywhere in particular. The trolley banged its bell incessantly, when drays and carriages and automobiles impeded its way, though it moved hardly faster than these. Not English, thought Maude, then laughed at herself for her light snobbery. Her laughter was mainly reserved for her own foibles, for she was innately too kind to laugh much at others. Yet, for the dolt and the unworthy, the lazy and the stupid, the ignorant and the impetuous, she had nothing but a silent contempt which would gleam in her splendid dark eyes.

She found the restaurant without any wanderings and Charles met her at the curb. She thought, and not for the first time, how handsome he was in a compact and masculine fashion, and how genuinely strong and capable was his face. He did not have Mr. Porter's restive vitality, of course, nor did his eyes flash and appear to crackle, as did Mr. Porter's. Yet, he had an equal strength and a quiet alertness. She looked at him with pleasure as he took her hand and led her into the restaurant, with its discreet curtained booths. "We can talk easily here, Miss Cummings," he said, "without interference or curiosity." She knew at once what all this prudent richness implied, and smiled a little, hearing the subdued voices behind the crimson velvet curtains, voices mainly of women. She saw Charles' sidelong glance at her, and she was somewhat amused. Did he think her naïve?

The headwaiter bowed to them and led them to a booth, and before he drew the curtains together he had given Maude an admiring glance and knew instantly that she was a lady and that this was no rendezvous. The round table had a glittering white cloth upon it and heavy silver and an exquisite epergne, with violets in a polished bowl. Charles, after seating Maude, looked at her again. No, he thought, she does not resemble these violets, for all her appearance. A carnation, perhaps, and he was surprised again. Yes, possibly a carnation, though certainly she did not outwardly resemble that pungent and sensual flower. He had not thought to enjoy this meal with the governess; now he was full of anticipation. "Wine?" he said, and knew instantly that her choice would be perfect. "A Chablis, if you please," she said. "I do not particularly care for sweet wines."

He liked her English voice, which did not, however, have that warbling high treble so many Englishwomen affected, which made communication difficult for an American. There was a stateliness about her voice, which indicated breeding. He glanced at her clothing and thought of Shakespeare's "rich, but not gaudy." She was composedly removing her gloves. Her hands were superb, he thought, and delicate. The signet ring on her left hand glowed in the soft gaslight.

He consulted her about the menu, and was pleased with her taste. He wondered again why he had not seemed to see her as beautiful before. She did not possess Ellen's incomparable and dazzling beauty, of course, but she had a distinctive charm born of worldliness and unclouded knowledge. Though younger than Ellen by several years, she yet gave the impression of profound maturity. A fine woman, he thought, a truly fine woman, and her eyes were remarkable, like black sapphires.

Maude noticed his furtive evaluation of her and she felt a stir of gentle elation. This was going to be less awkward than she had feared once or twice. She mused, for a moment, on the pleasure she was beginning to feel. All at once Charles was no stranger to her. There was a warmth of confidence between them. They talked pleasantly during the meal of many idle things, and Charles discovered that she had a wit of her own, not sharp and raucous like Kitty Wilder's, not cruel, not darting. Nor did- it have the insistent personal quality about it, like Kitty's. Personalities were not for Maude Cummings. She did not crave attention, as Kitty did, nor was she feverishly animated. Charles disliked Kitty Wilder intensely, and knew all about her.

It was not often that Charles found a woman's company so pleasing as he found Maude's. She was restful; her gestures were small and few. She had absolute control of herself. As they ate their dessert and drank their coffee, however, the still light on her face began to subside, and her expression was increasingly remote and abstracted.

Now she was raising her eyes with total candor and looking at him directly. She said, "I am considering leaving my position in the house of Mr. Porter."

"Indeed," he said, as if they were speaking of the weather. "May I ask why, Miss Cummings?"

Now she hesitated for an instant. "There is nothing I can do for Mrs. Porter, sir, though I have tried my best. She is so vulnerable. I am afraid for her. If I could do anything at all I would remain." She hesitated again. "I know you are a friend as well as an associate of Mr. Porter's, and that you—that you are most kindly drawn to Mrs. Porter. You are concerned about her as I am concerned."

Charles sipped his coffee in a short and reflective silence. Then he said, "Have you discussed this with Mr. Porter?"

"No. I fear he already knows—much. About Mrs. Porter. But he does not know, fully, about his children."

"I see," said Charles. "But you do."

"Yes. I know children well, perhaps too well. That is why I never married. I did not wish to have children."

He looked at her quickly. His gray eyes were very bright, she noticed, and very intent. He slowly moved his hand over his thick light-brown hair, but did not turn his eyes from her, and now she could not read them, though a faint tingle ran over her body.

"Not all children are wicked," he said.

She sighed and relaxed in her chair. So, she thought, I do not need to tell him anything more. He knows about Christian and Gabrielle. She said, "Quite right. But one

never knows, does one? Then it may be too late. I wish"
—she paused and looked at her hands—"that Mrs. Porter
did not love her children so much. That is very dangerous.
Still, I sometimes feel she is afraid of them. Instinct, perhaps."

He thought about this, and frowned, again rubbing his
hair. At last he said, "You must not leave that house,
Miss Cummings. I think it needs you."

She knew he meant Ellen, and all at once she was name-
lessly despondent. "I will consider it," she said. "Cuthbert and Annie want me to stay, also."

"Yes. Well, they are both very intelligent, Miss Cummings." He drank a sip of wine. "There are people in this
world, Miss Cummings, who need protection against themselves, trusting and artless people."

Again, she knew he meant Ellen, and she caught the
corner of her mouth in her small white teeth. She glanced
at her watch, which was pinned on her bodice. "I will be
missed," she said. "Thank you for your understanding,
sir."

"I will drive you home, Miss Cummings. It looks like
rain now."

"Thank you, but you must let me off a street away. It
would look very odd otherwise." She thought for a moment, then said with unusual passion, "There is Mrs.
Porter's maid, Clarisse. I know it is none of my affair,
but she calls Mrs. Wilder frequently, speaking in French,
concerning Mrs. Porter."

Charles became freshly alert. Miss Cummings lowered
her voice. "The maid speaks very—disrespectfully—of
Mrs. Porter. I have considered telling Mr. Porter, though
that might be an impertinence."

"I don't think so. Would you rather I told him, without
quoting you?"

"Oh. If you would."

They looked at each other, thinking of Kitty. Miss Cummings said, "I fear Mrs. Wilder has a bad influence on the
children. She seems very fond of them, I must admit, and
I am afraid they prefer her to their mother. She is very
quick and clever, Mrs. Wilder. The children seem more
like her own."

"I have observed that myself," said Charles. "Strange,
isn't it?"

"Not really," said Maude. "People who are alike in personality are drawn to each other."

They stood up, while Maude drew on her gloves. Again their eyes met in awareness. "You will not leave, then?" said Charles.

When she did not answer he went on: "More than one person would miss you, Miss Cummings."

Her pale cheeks flushed, and he touched her elbow gently and led her through the curtains, and then outside, to where his Cadillac waited. The sky had darkened, the street had grown dim, but it seemed to Maude that everything was flooded with exhilarating light and when she smiled at Charles now her whole quiet face was illuminated. "I will stay, sir," she said.

"Good."

The next day, with his card, he sent her a box of hothouse carnations, and she slept that night with the flowers beside her on a table, and the card under her pillow.

Two days later, over the protests of Ellen, and without explanation, Jeremy abruptly dismissed Clarisse. Kitty was dismayed when the tearful Clarisse came to her, saying, "Madam, it is that foolish woman, Mrs. Porter. She must have overheard me, though I was always discreet." Kitty sympathized, but as Clarisse was no longer of use to her she gave her a five-dollar gold piece and patted her arm and dismissed her.

A little sly probing on Kitty's part brought the news to her, with relief, that Ellen did not know why Clarisse had been discharged by Jeremy. Moreover, Jeremy looked at Kitty with blankness when she mentioned Clarisse's absence to him. "Oh," he said, "I never did like the woman, and she antagonized the rest of the staff. One must have harmony in the house, isn't that so?"

"You are quite right," said Kitty, and missed the hard gleam in his eyes. "I never liked her myself. I advised Ellen long ago to discharge her, but you know Ellen."

"I do, indeed," he replied, and she was pleased. So he knew Ellen for a fool himself!

Ellen did not know why she felt so depressed and melancholy at the beginning of summer when the family moved to its house on Long Island. It was true that Jeremy was more and more engaged in "business," and that their circle of friends seemed to become smaller in consequence. (Ellen did not know that this was because many of them had become wary of what they called his "extreme notions," with which they disagreed, though this did not prevent them from engaging his potent services when needed and his apparent power in Washington despite the fact that he was no longer a Congressman.) Jeremy traveled more and more, and Ellen concluded this was "business" also, and even the speeches he gave all over the country and the articles he wrote in various journals, including law journals, she considered were part of the mysterious world of men. That Jeremy was frequently discussed in the White House was unknown to her.

Even when he was home Jeremy spent several nights a week away from his family, either with Kitty, from whom he was gradually disentangling himself, or with little Mrs. Bedford, who was scandalously divorced, though not socially avoided for that reason, as she was enormously rich in her own right and of an impeccable family. Emma Bedford was much of what Kitty was, but in addition she was kind and affable and had a broad and charitable view of humanity which was not stained with sentimentality. ("What the hell, Jerry," she would say in her light and merry voice, "we can't help being human, can we, though some of us are more human than others, such as bitches and bastards. Who was it said that life is a tragedy to the man who feels, a comedy to the man who thinks? Yes, I think it is a great comedy, in the dramatic sense, and so long as one does not take it too seriously one is not in too much danger from his fellow man. Yes?")

Unlike other men, Jeremy carefully concealed all signs of his infidelity from Ellen, for he loved her too much and was too solicitous of her, and his tenderness grew steadily. As for Ellen, had she known, it might have literally killed her, for her knowledge of humanity was still more instinctive than objective, and therefore not to be defined, and infidelity to her would have meant that Jeremy no longer loved her and had rejected her for some deadly fault of her own. She had not the slightest idea about the nature of the male sex and its irresistible bent for polygamy and desire for variety in women. When Kitty had once said to her, "It is totally unrealistic for a woman to expect her husband to be faithful to her," Ellen was aghast. She had replied, "Kitty, you are exaggerating and being naughty, as usual. I would no more suspect Jeremy of being unfaithful to me than suspecting that of myself. It is an insult to Jeremy, and to all good husbands."

Ellen never listened to gossip, or, if she could not avoid hearing it, she honestly believed that the stories were intended only to amuse, or that they were false and malicious. The very thought that a woman could be attracted to a man not her husband was not only repugnant to her but beyond belief. She was not unaware of the world about her, of the Lillian Russells and the Diamond Jim Bradys, but these existed in an incredible theatrical world and even so she was half convinced that this, also, was "exaggeration." She read novels both in English and in French, but after all, they were "only novels," and romances. That there were many Madame Boverys about her she did not know, and as for Don Juans, such did not exist in Christian America. In this area Jeremy conspired with her innocence to keep corrosive knowledge from her, for her innocence, however irritating it might be to him at times, would have made her less endearing to him and his love for her might have been destroyed had she lost it.

"Ellen's a true believer in the sanctity of the hearth and the purity of the marriage bed," Kitty had once laughed to Jeremy. "Really, my love, she is like a child still, and," Kitty added hastily, seeing Jeremy's dark expression, "I think that is lovely, in a way." When he did not answer she went on, somewhat recklessly, "Why it is, my love, that men consider chastity in women the one complete virtue, especially in their wives, when chastity is mostly lack of temptation or opportunity? Or fear of pregnancy?"

Jeremy had laughed, in spite of himself. "I suppose it all goes back to the rights of inheritance. Men want to be sure that their sons, who will inherit their property, will really be their sons, and not woods colts. And women are men's property, too, which they don't want to share with another man. Too messy."

Kitty did not consider this paradoxical, though Ellen would have thought it bewilderingly so, and incredible. The love between a man and his wife was impregnable, in her conviction. Though she was far wiser than her contemporaries in many fields of knowledge, and more intelligent, Ellen's knowledge of the true nature of humanity and its motivations remained fragmentary and disturbing. When she had a sudden insight it devastated her and she quickly turned her thoughts to something else.

Ellen hardly gave it words, but Jeremy's long and frequent absences, and his late homecomings, left her lonely and bereft. She was a patron of the Metropolitan Opera Company and the Metropolitan Museum and various art galleries, and had begun to collect art for her houses. She had learned to paint, originally and delicately. Her days were taken up in lunches with ladies like herself, and she spent hours at her piano, playing and singing softly to herself. Her house was meticulously managed. Her children absorbed all her thoughts when she was at home. But there were long weeks, and long nights, when Jeremy was not at home, and she would feel the old sickening ache and longing for him which she had hopelessly felt from the time she was thirteen until she had married him. The weekends were the worst of all, for even the most marauding husbands considered it their duty to spend those days with their families. Ellen was too frequently alone, then, with no company, except for Sunday-afternoon calls for tea, which were brief, and so she was thrown more and more into the company of her mocking children, whom she would never be able to understand.

That Ellen could have easily taken a lover by a mere glance of her eye did not occur to her, though her beauty increased with time and many were the long and thoughtful looks which gentlemen gave her, and many were the tentative overtures, which she never recognized. Kitty recognized all this, however, and she raged inwardly with jealousy and hatred. What could men see in this blowsy creature, this overripe pear, this mindless fool? Kitty had detested Ellen for her youth and captivating charm from the beginning, but as Kitty was now middle-aged her resentment and derision sometimes tormented her for hours, and made her fantasize on disfigurements and calamities descending on Ellen, or even death. But the only revenge which seemed close at hand and realizable were Ellen's children. She knew all about them; at times she felt a curious affection for them. Therefore, she cultivated them; too, they were Jeremy's children. Never overt, Kitty was able, by smiles in her eyes and certain cockings of her head and certain writhings of her painted mouth, and certain intonations of her voice, to influence Christian and Gabrielle in their contempt for their mother. It did not need much effort. The contempt was already there, almost from birth. By this summer of 1912 both the boy and the girl had lost whatever affection they had ever had for Ellen, and they thought her incurably ridiculous and so a legitimate target for their mockeries, disobedience, tauntings, and disregard.

Once or twice a year, though Jeremy objected, Ellen took her children, and Annie Burton, to Wheatfield, "to visit poor sick Aunt May." The children hated these excursions, and found May Watson even more contemptible than their mother, and Mrs. Eccles' pampering of them did not give them much enjoyment. When Christian once complained to his father, Jeremy had said with his stern coldness, "There are many things in life, son, which we must do, even when they aren't very interesting or pleasing to us, and you'd better learn that as fast as possible. We weren't born just to have what you call 'fun.' We have responsibilities to others, too, and loyalties, and, as human beings, we have duties."

"Yes, Papa," Christian had replied, but Jeremy continued to frown. There were things about his children which often disturbed him, but as they were beguiling with him, and obeyed him implicitly, and honestly admired and loved him and never whined or wheedled him, he would only shrug and forget them. They never teased or vexed Ellen in his presence, for it was their intention that in this case their father must also be deluded, if only a little. Moreover, he was always very ready with drastic punishment, and so they feared him, and being what they were, their fear only increased their affection and respect.

Ellen's innate perceptiveness and sensitivity were particularly alert this summer, and there were times when her loneliness was intolerable. She knew that Jeremy was deeply engaged in politics, a mysterious entity to her, and that his absences were "unavoidable." Now, her loneliness, on Long Island, though surrounded by apparently affectionate friends, took on a certain restlessness and uneasy premonition. She painted little vignettes of her beautiful surroundings. She walked on the beach at sunset and even at sunrise. She stared at the long reaches of the ocean and listened to its hissing and growling voice or its small lappings, and she would look at the horizon and feel a terrible sadness and nameless melancholy. Her only anticipations were letters from Jeremy, and if one did not appear she was desolate and her restiveness increased unbearably. Sometimes Kitty arrived for a weekend, a real sacrifice for her, and Ellen would weep weak tears of gratitude for this beneficence. "I don't know," she once confessed to Kitty that summer, "what is wrong with me. I've always loved it here, and the children are with me, and the staff, and"—she hesitated—"Miss Cummings. I told Miss Cummings that she had a month's holiday due her, but she refused to take it, saying she had nowhere to go and she loved the sea, and this house. And Christian and Gabrielle. It was most kind of her, and yet."

"Yet, what?" asked Kitty avidly.

Ellen sighed. "I feel Miss Cummings thinks she has a duty to be here with us in the summer. It's absurd. She says she must continue tutoring Christian all summer, for his entry into boarding school in the fall. I don't want Christian to go, and neither does Gabrielle, but Jeremy insists on it. Oh, I'm rambling. I think I just miss Jeremy."

"He has business, Ellen. You must realize that."

"I know, I know. I don't know what's the matter with me! If I were superstitious I'd say I have a premonition about something wrong."

Kitty knew all about Mrs. Bedford, whom she also hated. "Perhaps," she said with forced levity, "Jeremy has a lady friend. That would be normal for any man with a family. Men do get bored, you know, with their wives and children."

"Jeremy!" exclaimed Ellen. "Oh, don't be silly, Kitty. And it's disrespectful and insulting to Jeremy." She looked at Kitty with her great blue eyes under the mass of her shining red hair, and laughed. "I know you just intend to amuse me, and I already feel less despondent."

Oh, God, thought Kitty. She had had the vague intention of arousing Ellen's suspicions and had been prepared to hint about Emma Bedford. She guessed that under Ellen's sweet submissiveness and trust lay a blade of fire, or iron, which, once revealed, could be very damaging indeed. When she had first discerned this some years ago Kitty had been disturbed. Her natural astuteness had warned her that if Ellen ever was forced to confront treachery and absolute evil the results would be awesomely unpredictable. Could she arouse this sleeping fierceness in Ellen with regard to Jeremy and Emma Bedford? This was very tempting. But Kitty was self-protective and cautious. She might unloose the uncontrollable and it might destroy Kitty herself.

Ellen then tried for a lightness of her own. "I shouldn't say I am lonely, or anything, though I do miss Jeremy. My neighbors invite me for tea and dinner, and the weekends are always gay. And Charles Godfrey comes nearly every Saturday and stays to Sunday night. Jeremy asked him, and he is so kind. He tries to entertain Miss Cummings, too, and takes her for long walks, and he plays with Gabrielle and Christian. I often wonder why he never married. He's very eligible."

That very evening Charles, walking with Miss Cummings along the beach with the children racing ahead, said to the governess, "Maude, will you marry me?"

She took his hand and smiled up into his eyes and her calm face was suddenly pink with the sunset. "Of course," she said, in the most natural voice in the world, as if she were merely affirming what she already knew.

24

In spite of her most determined efforts Ellen could not shake off her oppressive despondency. She often went into New York to help with her many charities, but it was with listlessness. She would have herself driven to her house, now attended only by a caretaker and a temporary housekeeper, who cooked for Jeremy when he was in town. It had a dark and musty smell in the heat. She opened windows, talked with the housekeeper and her assistant, examined the larder and pantry, and wandered about aimlessly. She would lunch with Kitty and shop and discuss the newest plays to be shown in the autumn. But the crowds and Kitty and her other city-bound friends could not alleviate her strange mood. Finally, she went to a new doctor Kitty had recommended, for she was beginning to lose her color. The doctor examined her closely, then, as he was a young man with all the new certainties of the year, he said with some severity, "Like most ladies, Mrs. Porter, you do not have enough to do. I suggest charity work, serious undertakings, the personal care of your children, an interest in the affairs of the world."

Guilt turned Ellen's face red, then all at once she felt her rare indignation. "Doctor," she said, "I do all these things until I exhaust myself, and it is no use. I need my husband—"

"Possessiveness," he said in a dismissing voice. "A preoccupation with self. Cultivate your mind, my dear madam. One of these days women will vote, and you must not come unprepared into the new world."

Suddenly Ellen was smiling. She said, *"Plus ça change, plus c'est la même chose.* At least, that is what my husband is always saying and I agree with him. Occasionally, though, it does get worse."

The doctor was startled and oddly affronted. This beautiful young woman, in her gray linen and lace dress and yellow straw hat, had annoyed him from the start, for he had recognized her, he had thought, as one of the idle, rich, and pampered women who had known no anxiety or despair in her life and so had little awareness and no "compassion for the toiling masses." Yet her eyes now were not only gently amused but brilliant with intelligence. He did not like having his conclusions challenged, and so he did not like Ellen. She left him, and her amusement lasted for several hours and lifted the depression.

The next day she received a telegram from Hortense Eccles in Wheatfield. "Your aunt quietly passed away this morning. Your presence necessary for funeral arrangements."

Annie was out with the children for their morning walk, and Miss Cummings was in the library preparing material for Christian's afternoon lessons. She heard Ellen, who was in the long hall, gasp and cry out, and she went to her at once. Ellen stared at her blankly and then, without speaking, gave the governess the telegram. "Oh," said Maude. "I am so sorry. We shall go at once to Wheatfield. I will find out about the first train."

"No," said Ellen in a dull tone. "That is, I will take the children and Annie. That's all I need. But thank you." Miss Cummings' composed face and fine eyes expressed no hurt. She only said, "We must send Mr. Porter a telegram, then. He would not want you to suffer this alone."

Ellen shook her head slowly. "No, he is in Chicago. It is very important that he be there. He is delivering a speech at a political banquet this evening. He—he has not seen my aunt for years, though he has taken care of her. No, he must not be disturbed."

"Then," said Maude in a firm voice such as she used to children, "I will certainly go with you. Annie will have too much to do with Christian and Gabrielle to be of much assistance to you in this emergency, Mrs. Porter. I will ask your maid to pack you a bag, and then will pack mine. Please sit down, Mrs. Porter. You look quite ill."

Ellen suddenly sat down in the long wide hall which stretched from the front door to the rear. She stared at the leaves of a shaking willow and at the climbing rose trellis near it—scarlet against chartreuse fire. But she did not see the beauty. She began to whimper deep in her throat. All at once she was a child again, listening to May's peremptory and weary voice in the little cottage in Preston. She could see her aunt's face, gray with exhaustion and glistening with summer sweat, as she sewed. A sharp odor of cabbage and boiling beef came to Ellen's nose then, and it was in her aunt's kitchen that she was sitting now, hearing May's affectionate reproaches concerning her carelessness.

"Oh, Aunt May, dear Auntie," she whispered, and there were no years between of alienation and estrangement and guilt. She forgot that May was in her late fifties, and that she had led a comfortable life, because of her niece, for a long time, comforted by good care and attention. Ellen could only feel guilt for that alienation. There had been weeks when she had not thought of May at all, so engrossed had she been with her family and her occupations and Jeremy. She had written but once a week to her aunt; she forgot that May rarely answered those letters except to compain and rebuke and accuse. (The letters had actually been written by Hortense Eccles or May's nurse, for May's hands were almost totally crippled.) She could only whisper, in the sweet warm silence of the hall with but the ocean murmuring at a distance, "Oh, Auntie, I am so sorry, so sorry. I should have done something for you— I should not have neglected you so much for so long. I should have seen you more often, given you a little pleasure in your pain. All alone there, in Wheatfield, with no one to comfort or help you." Ellen began to cry and was overwhelmed with remorse.

Miss Cummings returned with a glass of brandy, an anxious Cuthbert looking over her shoulder. "Come now, Mrs. Porter," said Maude. "You must drink this. Your maid is packing a bag for you for two days and mine is almost ready. May I suggest that the children not go with you?"

Ellen's wet eyes flashed at the governess now with open dislike. "Not take my children to the funeral of their aunt! How outrageous, Miss Cummings, for you to suggest that!"

Miss Cummings sighed and gave the empty glass to Cuthbert. She said, and again in her quietly firm voice, "Mrs. Porter, the children have seen your aunt, Mrs. Watson, only on scattered occasions. They have no affection for her. That is only natural. They never speak of her, and that is natural, too. Children are only concerned with themselves. Too, it is a long hot journey, and Gabrielle's summer cold is just now subsiding. It would be better for you to go alone with me. The train for New York leaves in one hour—"

"I don't want you with me!" cried the distraught Ellen. "It is my children's place to be at the funeral! Oh, please, let me alone!" She jumped to her feet, in a turmoil of grief and anger. She had never like Miss Cummings; she had been daunted by her, for there was something in the younger woman's character which had abashed Ellen and had made her uneasy. Miss Cummings had poise and certitude and was of a piece, and women of her sort had invariably intimidated Ellen and had made her feel inferior and incompetent.

Miss Cummings said, "Very well. Shall I call Mrs. Wilder, then? She may wish to go with you."

Ellen clasped her trembling hands tightly together. "Kitty, Kitty? Yes! No. She is visiting some friends—I don't know where. I don't think she told me. Philadelphia? Boston? Oh, I don't know. She went last night."

The slightest flicker appeared for a moment in Maude's eyes, and there was also a flicker in Cuthbert's. Ellen put her hands helplessly over her face. She murmured from behind them, "Oh, dear God. You are right about the children. Too long a ride, and too hot, and there is so much infantile paralysis about. No, they can't go with me. I am afraid I will have to accept your offer, Miss Cummings." She dropped her hands and her eyes were streaming again. "And please send Mr. Porter a telegram, too, so if he should try to call me he will know where I am. I am so confused."

She saw Miss Cummings clearly for the first time and then was ashamed of her outburst. "I am sorry, Miss Cummings. It is just that I am so upset. Now I must change."

Miss Cummings watched Ellen run up the stairs, and she shook her head. She was glad that she had persuaded Charles not to press for an announcement of their coming marriage in October. Mrs. Porter disliked her enough as it was, and that was open now. She suspected that she was one of the very few people whom Ellen had ever resented. Maude was not hurt by this. One never knew what deep undercurrents lay beneath human behavior and human loves and hatreds, not even those who loved or hated. Life was a very complicated matter, indeed.

Ellen barely spoke to Miss Cummings on the long, hot, and sooty ride to Wheatfield. The compartment was so stuffy that it was necessary to open the train windows, and so smoke and noise poured in and made conversation almost impossible. Composed as always, outwardly, Maude was deeply concerned over Ellen. She studied Ellen's pale profile with the tremulous lips and the wide, almost unblinking eyes, and she was full of pity. The red hair made the pallor even more intense, and the stretched eyes had crimson edges and were swollen. How she punishes herself, thought Maude, and most unjustly. This is not mere grief she is suffering, but self-chastisement, a weakness of those who are not guilty at all. The truly wicked feel no guilt, or, if they do, they blame it not on their own actions but on others who are blameless.

Maude was several years younger than Ellen but infinitely more mature and worldly. She believed, with Spinoza, that to feel remorse is to be twice guilty. To this

she had added an addendum: The innocent were always
in a state of self-reproach. She wanted to say some words
of consolation to Ellen but knew that she would be fiercely
repulsed, for Ellen desired her self-punishment, which in
some manner lessened her sorrow. Literal flagellation,
mused Maude, can assuage emotional torture. Maude
smoothed the black silk of her gloves and serenely surveyed the passing landscape between bouts of coughing.
As usual, she wore her discreet clothing with elegance.
Ellen had found a black suit to wear, too heavy for this
weather, and a black silk shirtwaist with a boned collar,
and a black felt hat. Sweat dripped from her temples and
wide white forehead but apparently her mental suffering
was greater than her physical, for she did not wipe away
the drops of water and did not seem conscious of any
physical discomfort.

It was twilight when the train arrived in Wheatfield and
waited, puffing impatiently, for its next run to Pittsburgh.
Mrs. Eccles' carriage was waiting for the two ladies, an
expensive brougham, Miss Cummings noticed, driven by
a man who was obviously not employed solely as a coach-
man. But it was cooler here in this small city. So anxious
was Ellen that she tripped on her long black skirt and
Maude caught her arm to steady her. Almost wildly, Ellen
shook her off and ran to the carriage, Maude following
her more sedately. Ellen was already seated when Maude
climbed the carriage steps, and was wringing her hands
and leaning forward feverishly, as if to wing the vehicle
to its destination. "Hurry, hurry, please," she murmured,
as though her aunt were still alive and she must rush to
save her from death. Maude frowned. She had adored her
father, the vicar, and had been his housekeeper and hostess
after her mother's death, and had quietly made his life
bearable and even rich. When he had died suddenly, in
his pulpit, she had believed that her own existence, at
nineteen, had come to an abrupt end, and she had not
desired to live. Yet, she had shown no outward evidence
of mental anguish, as Ellen was now doing, and had displayed a commendable restraint at her father's funeral,
a restraint which was most admired. But then, she thought,
Americans are much more emotional than the British, and
it was at once their weakness and their strength.

Maude surveyed the green arches of the elms over the

streets with approval, and the wide lawns and the evening light illuminating the roofs of large houses. She heard the rattle of lawn mowers and could smell the scent of cut grass and water and dust. So this was America, beyond New York, the only American city she had ever known before. It was quite a different America here, and the people on porches and sidewalks seemed more placid and content, and even the automobiles made less noise and appeared less in a hurry. There were no trolleys. The town was too small. "Hurry, hurry, please," Ellen was still murmuring, her hands clutched together.

When the carriage, a very old-fashioned one, stopped before Hortense Eccles' house, Maude glanced at it and decided it was in very bad taste, indeed hardly more tasteful, if larger, than its neighbors. But the lawns were wide and there were sharply colored flower beds and a very pretty small park at the end of the street, filled with playing children and their ringing calls in the twilight. The carriage had hardly stopped when Ellen, not waiting to be assisted to alight, jumped from the step and ran to the house, her black garments fluttering, her head craned forward, her hat tilted over her hair—in complete disarray. Maude, again, followed more sedately. The door was opened by Hortense herself, plump and older but still sleek, and clad in a gray silk dress and wearing a most mournful expression, at once accusing and somber. Ellen fled past her. Maude mounted the steps, gave Mrs. Eccles —whom she immediately disliked—a calm hand and a slight cool smile. "I am Maude Cummings," she said, "and I assume you are Mrs. Eccles. I am governess to Mrs. Porter's children."

To Mrs. Eccles a governess was only a mere servant. She said coldly, "Yes, I am Mrs. Eccles. Didn't Ellen have a *friend* to accompany her?"

Maude said, "I am her friend."

"Indeed," said Hortense, thinking that this young woman, a servant, was behaving in a very saucy and insolent way. She added, "Maybe you'd like a cup of tea, or something, while I talk to El— I mean, your mistress. The kitchen is back there, at the end of the hall, and my cook will give you your supper there." She said this with deliberate contempt—servants must be put in their place at once—and besides, Maude's manner and her English accent vexed Hortense. Superior-like, and impudent.

Maude held back a smile at this woman's vulgarity, and said, "I should like that very much, indeed. Thank you. I see our luggage is being brought in. No doubt you have assigned us rooms."

"You can share my housekeeper's bedroom," said Hortense, despising and resenting Maude even more. "Mrs. Porter will have the bedroom next to mine, on the second floor. I assume—what is your name again—"

"Maude Cummings."

"I see. All right, Maude, I must leave you now. You know the way to the kitchen. My housekeeper will appreciate your help in serving dinner and washing up afterwards. My nephew, the Congressman Francis Porter, is my guest here also. In this emergency my maid will appreciate your help, too, so please take care of the Congressman's bedroom beginning tonight."

Maude Cummings, whose father had been the younger son of an Earl, and who himself had been the Honorable Gerald Cummings, and an alumnus of Magdalen College at Oxford, and a very rich man, went with composure to the kitchen, highly amused by Hortense Eccles. She found the housekeeper to be much more of a lady, and much politer. Really, thought Maude, the American working class is very commendable, and very kind. The housekeeper recognized Maude's distinction at once, and made the girl as comfortable as possible in the hot kitchen.

In the meantime Ellen had plunged upstairs to the third floor, where May and her nurse had small sweltering rooms under the roof, but rooms comfortably furnished via Ellen's purse some years before. Ellen only too well had remembered the mean furniture and the bleakness of those rooms, unbearable in summer, dankly cold in winter. The newest nurse, a tiny and smiling and amiable girl in white starch, greeted Ellen warmly, for Ellen was a lavish tipper in behalf of her aunt. But Ellen ran past her, in the little sitting room, which had once been her bedroom, and into May's room. May had been "laid out" carefully by her nurse, and she lay on her white pillows with hands folded on her breast, her face gray and still, her hair neatly combed, her best brown silk dress on her motionless body, her features small and withered yet strangely lofty. The lines of pain had softened, and she wore the majestic peace of death. A low lamp had been lit, and its yellowish light flickered over the bedroom. Someone was sitting in a chair nearby, but Ellen did not see anything but the body of her aunt.

She fell on her knees beside the bed and put her hand over the cold stiff fingers and burst into wild sobs. "Oh, Auntie, Auntie!" she groaned, and her hat fell from her head. "Oh, why did I leave you, or you leave me? Oh, Auntie, Auntie, I am so sorry!" She kissed May's cheek, and wailed desperately. "I am so sorry for being so inconsiderate. You were right. I never thought of anybody but myself. What shall I do? What shall I do?" Her hastily pinned mass of red hair tumbled down her back. Her body shook with her sobs. Her face ran with tears, and sweat. The black shirtwaist was damp and twisted.

Someone touched her shoulder, and she glanced up despairingly to see Francis Porter beside her, his face stern, his spectacles glittering in the lamplight. "Control yourself, Ellen," he said. His voice was muted but condemning. "It is too late for self-reproach now. Too late, too late."

She had not seen him for years. Now he seemed to her to be her conscience, her nemesis. He was so tall, so thin, in his dark clothing, so pale, so rigorous, that she wanted to grovel before him and beg him for forgiveness, too, though for what she did not know. "Too late," she muttered. "Yes, too late."

As if imploring his compassion, his absolution, she pressed her wet cheek to the fingers on her shoulder. She did not feel their sudden trembling, the sudden heat of lust that ran through them. She did not even feel the sly movement of his other hand over her racked body, nor its pressing and searching. When the hand moved to her white neck, and then down under the unbuttoned collar, even touching her bare breast, she did not feel that either.

"Forgive me," she whispered. "Oh, forgive me."

"Not yet," he answered, and his voice was hoarse. "Not quite yet. Oh, Ellen," and his voice dropped to a lower intonation. "Oh, Ellen." Her breast was soft and white. She had fallen into a dim faintness.

"Jeremy," she whispered, not even aware now of where she was. She leaned against Francis' hip, in that

chamber of death, and he shook with desire. He kissed
the tumbled red hair, and still she did not know. He
thought she did, and was elated.

25

Maude came into Ellen's bedroom at eight the next
morning, carrying a breakfast tray. A doctor had been
called last night to give Ellen a sleeping draught, for she
had been obviously dazed and distraught. Now she lay on
her pillows, white and mute and listless. Maude drew
aside the heavy maroon draperies to let in the brilliant
morning sunlight.

"Now, Mrs. Porter," Maude said in her tranquil voice,
"I have made this nice breakfast for you, and you really
must eat it, or you will be very ill. You had no dinner
last night. What would Mr. Porter say to that? By the
way, we have received a telegram that he will be here
tonight. Unfortunately, he will not arrive before the
funeral this afternoon."

Ellen sat up quickly. "Jeremy!" she cried. "Oh, thank
God." She began to cry, but not with the wild agony of
the day before. "I do need him." Her cheeks flushed
faintly. "But what about Chicago?"

"I am sure," said Maude, "that he delivered his speech,
and then planned to arrive here as soon as possible. Now,
you must really eat this breakfast. Mr. Porter must not
find you in this state. It will only distress him, and we
do not want that, do we?"

"I dreamt," said Ellen, "that he was right there with
me when I knelt beside my aunt's bed." The flush deepened on her cheeks. "I must have fallen asleep there. I
was so tired." Her tears ran faster, but they were calmer.
She looked at the tray. "Thank you, Miss Cummings. It is
very kind of you. The funeral? Yes. My aunt loved Wheat-

field so much; she was at home here. She was never at home in New York. I can't forgive myself for taking her away."

"You have nothing to ask forgiveness for," said Maude very gently.

But Ellen immediately stiffened, and she looked at Maude with remembered dislike. "You don't know, Miss Cummings." Her beautiful voice was actually sullen. "Thank you, again. Yes, I will try to eat my breakfast."

It is very hard to forgive ourselves, thought Maude, especially if we have nothing with which to reproach us. Ellen tried to eat the stewed figs and prunes. "Did I dream it, or is Mr. Francis actually here?"

"He is here," said Maude in a peculiar tone. She had left the kitchen last night to look for Ellen and to console her, and had found her clothing in what is discreetly called "disarray," with Francis leaning over her avidly. Maude's hard aloof look at him, her open scorn when she had appeared at his bent shoulder, had not only vigorously startled him, but had angrily shamed him. They had stared at each other in a terrible silence, and then Francis had turned away, his face slightly contorted. It was Maude who had led Ellen to her bedroom and who had called the physician.

Ellen said, "Jeremy doesn't like Mr. Francis, though Mr. Francis was really the only friend I had for years. I am glad he is here." She sipped the tea on the tray. Her tears slid down her face.

"Yes," said Maude. "Now do try these scones. I made them myself. This strawberry jam is excellent." She sat down near Ellen and regarded the older girl seriously. "Mrs. Porter. I lost my dearest father when I was nineteen years old. He was all I had in the world. I do not count uncles and cousins and aunts. I had to reconcile myself. I had to accept things as they are. I came to America, alone, to see myself clearly and what I must do with my life. Death is as common and as natural as birth, and is part of our lives. Once we understand that, we are invulnerable, in spite of grief."

Again Ellen's dislike for the younger woman quickened. "You don't understand," she said. "My aunt, Aunt May, worked and sacrificed for me for many years. She went hungry so I could have food. I was an orphan, and she became my mother. But I was ungrateful; I did not consider her. I—deserted her." She turned her cheek to the pillow and began to sob. "I thought of nothing but my husband, and myself, though my first duty was to my aunt."

Maude frowned with impatience and a faint disgust. "Mrs. Porter, a woman's first duty is to her husband, and her love. I have heard you did everything possible for Mrs. Watson; you should not reproach yourself—"

But Ellen cried, "You don't know! Oh, please, do go away and let me alone, this day of her funeral!" She pushed aside the tray and cried convulsively. In silence, Maude picked up the almost untouched tray and left the room, shaking her head. Ellen sobbed, over and over, "Jeremy, Jeremy. Come quickly, or I'll die."

It was Maude who dressed Ellen for the funeral, in the bedraggled black she had worn. It was Maude who had firmly led Ellen away from May's bedroom, so that the undertakers could do their last duties and place the body in a bronze casket. It was Maude who had firmly informed Hortense Eccles that a shabby parson would not "do," and who had called an Episcopalian priest. It was Maude who had called for flowers, though Hortense had an outraged comment. "She was only a servant, like Ellen. The flowers are not necessary. No one will be at the funeral, except my nephew and myself, out of mercy and consideration."

"The flowers," said Maude, "are for the living. They will comfort Mrs. Porter."

"Much she needs comforting for," Hortense had said. "She left her poor old aunt to my Christian compassion."

"Which I am sure you gave her," said Maude. Hortense did not miss the irony and was freshly outraged. "How dare you speak to me like that! You, only a servant, and presumptuous!"

The granddaughter of an Earl looked at Mrs. Eccles, and in that exchange Hortense felt "lowered." "Only a servant," she muttered. "You take too much on yourself. I never did like the English. They get above themselves. I will have a talk with my darling Jeremy. He doesn't like insolence, either, in servants, though how he overlooked Ellen's station and married her I just don't know."

"I do," said Maude. "Mrs. Porter was never a servant. She is a gentlewoman."

Hortense turned on her incredulously. "How could you

possibly know anything, you only a servant yourself! I will talk to Mr. Porter. He will give you your notice at once. I will make sure of that myself. Then you will be on the streets, where you belong." She smiled in satisfaction as she bustled away.

What an odious woman, Maude commented to herself, not in the least perturbed by the encounter. She went into the parlor, where the casket had been placed on the undertaker's trestle. It stood open, and May's hands held a bouquet of white lilies and white roses covered her feet and twisted legs. Draperies had been drawn; candlelight flickered about the coffin. Ellen was seated by her aunt; her hand lay on the dim, neatly combed hair; the girl was in a state of semi-stupefaction again, but tearless. Her red hair flamed in the candlelight; it had been Maude who had arranged it, and every bright wave and curl glistened. Ellen's fixed eyes shimmered in the gloom; her pale lips were parted as if for air. Her black garments seemed more funereal than the dead woman herself. At her right shoulder stood Francis Porter, and he looked only at Ellen, and for a single moment Maude felt pity for him, thinking that a man does not fondle a woman sensually in the presence of death—and certainly not a man like Francis—except for some extraordinary and uncontrollable emotion in himself.

Mrs. Eccles stood decorously at the foot of the casket, her hands clasped together as if praying, her expression solemn. There were strangers present, friends of Mrs. Eccles, and they too stood decorously and glanced with affection at their friend. Their glances at the silent Ellen were not so kind. Here was a young woman who had deserted, unfeelingly, her lone relative, and had neglected her shamefully, and had it not been for Hortense, who, out of her large heart, had taken this unfortunate creature into her house and had attended her like a sister, only Heaven knew what would have become of her, May Watson. The poor farm, without doubt, or some back-street boardinghouse full of vermin and the stench of cabbage and coal gas, there possibly to starve to death, alone. In the doorway of the parlor the house servants were gathered, avid for drama.

To think, Mrs. Eccles' friends whispered to each other, that a Congressman from Washington, a real Congressman, Mrs. Eccles' nephew, had condescended to attend

the funeral of a servant. What a gentleman he was, what
kindness, what humanity. Maude, who had much perception, and very keen hearing, was amused. She knew now
what had brought Francis Porter here, and again she
pitied him.

The priest arrived, with his secretary, and he was in
his clerical garments, a rosy little man with twinkling
eyes. He did not consider death a calamity; he had seen
too much of life to deplore dissolution. Ellen did not hear
the brief service. She had sunk into a numb apathy, in
which she relived the years of her childhood, seeing not
the dead woman but the aunt who had loved her and had
stolen food for her and had admonished her and guarded
her. She did not feel herself raised to her feet; she blinked
in the raw hot sunlight outside while Francis and Maude
led her to the waiting limousine. She looked about her
blankly, her black-gloved hands folded weakly over each
other. She was conscious of none of the living about her.
She gazed through the windows of the limousine at remembered streets in which she had walked and in which
she had cried. A loosened curl, vivid and lustrous, had
escaped a pin and lay on her shoulder. Francis could not
look away from it; he remembered how soft such a curl
had been against his lips the night before, and how fragrant and warm and living, and he was full of pain. He
avoided glancing at Miss Cummings, whom he considered
a drab servant, lifeless and meek, for all the cold disbelief
and condemnation that had shone in her fine eyes the
night before.

The hearse went before, slowly, and other automobiles
followed, and people on the walks looked curiously at
the procession. Ellen felt nothing; she was like one
drugged. When she sagged against Francis' shoulder and
lay there, it was as if that shoulder were wood. Francis
caught a breath; he could hardly breathe. It was the
sweetest moment of his life, and he wanted to hold Ellen
in his arms. But he saw the glimmer at the corner of
Maude's eye, and hated her. Still, it was ecstasy to feel
Ellen's weight against him, to see her cheek pressed into
his shoulder, and to experience the irregular breathing
against his chin. He did not want the ride to end; he
wanted it to go on forever, even with others present. The
poor man, thought Maude, who had heard much in
Jeremy's house on the Congressman, from Cuthbert. As if

she were reading his mind Maude knew that Francis was thinking of his fondling of Ellen last night; he was recalling the white velvet of her breast, her neck and throat. She had not resisted, he was thinking. She knew he was there. She had been aware of his hands on her body, and she had not shrunk away. Ellen, Ellen, he thought. What shall we do, you and I? It did not seem odd to him, and out of character, that he had lost control of himself last night. He remembered with rising joy and heat. He contemplated himself as Ellen's lover, when she had recovered from her grief. No. Better still, his wife, for all she was only a servant. He would cherish her, always, gently condescending her and keeping her in her place, humble and docile, grateful for his patronage, thankful to have been delivered from that brutish cousin of his, who was not even present to comfort his wife.

At the cemetery Ellen heard, as at a great distance, the prayers of the priest. She was swaying. Now Francis could put his arm about her with even greater joy, to steady her. She had a dying sensation. When the priest threw a handful of soil on the casket she uttered one single faint cry. Someone was saying like a far echo, "I am the Resurrection and the Life—" Then someone was lifting her in his arms and carrying her away.

"Really," Hortense whispered to her friends, "one would think she had cared for poor May. Quite the contrary, I assure you. But how good it is of Francis to carry her to the limousine. He always had such Heart, such sympathy for the Masses, even the most insignificant. Look at my darling. One would think she was his wife, instead of a servant girl who had waited on him hand and foot in my house. He was the soul of consideration for her, and he and I were her only friends, and still are."

Hortense Eccles had used the occasion of her "servant's" death to honor her Congressman nephew with a tea after the funeral, calling it, "you know, the cold meats for the dead." So, in a hushed voice, she informed Miss Cummings of this and suggested that she help Ellen "tidy up" for the occasion honoring her aunt. Miss Cummings said with composed coldness, "Mrs. Porter is very ill and is suffering from shock. I feel she should stay in her room and rest, and so be excused."

Mrs. Eccles said, and her voice was less hushed, "You

are presumptuous, Maude! Inform Ellen at once that she must appear, in respect for her aunt, and for Congressman Porter, who condescended to come for this occasion—a great honor for Ellen. It would be most reprehensible if she did not come to my tea; an unpardonable impudence."

Maude hesitated. She looked at Francis, who was standing in the background, and at the two friends who had accompanied Hortense to the funeral, and the priest. Francis gazed at her with a most censorious expression and hauteur, and Maude remembered that Ellen always spoke of him with gratitude. She went upstairs to Ellen's room. Ellen was lying in a half-stupor on her bed, her eyes fixed on the opposite wall, her clothing wrinkled, her hair bedraggled, her face still and white. Maude said very gently, "Mrs. Eccles wishes you to go down to her tea, in remembrance of your aunt. I would advise—"

Ellen sat up stiffly and suddenly. "Of course. I was thinking only of myself, something which Aunt May was always scolding me about. How kind of Mrs. Eccles." She swung her long silken legs over the edge of the bed and despairingly began to fumble with her hair. Her reddened eyes were more swollen than before, though she was not crying.

"I would advise," said Maude, "that you rest in preparation for our return to New York tomorrow night."

Ellen gave her an unusually angry glance and her lips quivered. "It is the least I can do, now. I do wish you would stop interfering with my private affairs, Miss Cummings. Besides, I have to discuss certain financial arrangements with Mrs. Eccles." She stood up abruptly and swayed, and Maude caught her arm. Ellen, with a new gesture of despair, shook her off.

The guests were already arriving, speaking in low voices, while Maude combed and coiled Ellen's hair and brushed out as many creases as possible in the black suit. She was full of pity for Ellen, and an extraordinary impatience. When would the poor young woman be able to distinguish between friend and enemy, and understand, in the slightest, the crude and cynical behavior of people, and so protect herself? While several years younger than Ellen, Maude felt infinitely older, and very tired. The room was reflected in three mirrors, and in all of them Ellen looked exhausted and haggard and ill. The windows blazed with the last sunlight and it was very hot. When

Maude tried to hold Ellen's arm as they descended the stairway, Ellen again shook her off, clung to the balustrade, and feebly moved downstairs. There was a smell of steeping tea in the hall below and strawberry jam and ham and freshly baked bread and cakes. Ellen paused on the stairs, dropped her head, and gulped. But Maude did not touch her again, though she paused also.

Downstairs Hortense was solemnly playing "Lead, Kindly Light," and singing in accompaniment, and the guests joined her in religious tones. What execrable taste, thought Maude, and she saw a wincing on Ellen's white and averted face. They were met below by Francis, who tucked Ellen's arm in his and led her into the large room, now filled with at least a dozen people, men and women. Maude stood on the threshold. She knew she was not welcome, and knew she had not been invited, but she lingered like a servant, full of solicitude for Ellen, who was being seated by the Congressman. He bent over her like a tall black bird and was now murmuring to her. She tried to answer, but her lips only moved mutely.

Mrs. Eccles saw Maude and came to her briskly from the piano, and said in a peremptory tone, "Go into the kitchen at once and help the housemaid serve my guests. Be careful of my china; it is very old and very expensive and a family heirloom. And the spoons will be carefully counted afterwards. By me." She looked forbiddingly at Maude, who wanted to laugh. Mrs. Eccles continued: "I think it is disgraceful that you didn't pack Mrs. Porter's bag with an extra black dress. But servants these days—!"

Maude somewhat lost her customary composure and said, "Madam, I am not a servant. But I do not expect you to discern that." She went serenely down the hall to the kitchen, where she knew she would be more politely treated, and with kindness. Hortense stared after her, furious and panting. Really, she must tell Ellen to discharge this impertinent creature, and at once.

Francis brought Ellen a cup of tea himself, a most gracious gesture, thought Hortense, whose plump face was red and swollen with anger at Maude. Francis, it was, who insisted that Ellen drink the tea, which she did, humbly. But she turned her head aside at the sight of the food, which was being heartily devoured by the guests, whose voices, after sherry, were a little less subdued. The late evening light poured through the tall thin windows, which were ajar, letting in the fragrance of pine and flowers and grass. In the meantime, Maude came in with fresh tea and edibles, grateful for this opportunity to observe Ellen unobtrusively. Hortense pettishly criticized her and ordered her about, her tone sharp and peremptory. But some of her guests thought the English maid had "style" and was deft, and wondered if they could lure her away from her mistress with a promise of a higher wage. One of them, a lady, very portly, whispered to her, "Are you a good cook, my girl?" To which Maude demurely replied, "Excellent, madam," and moved gracefully away with the teapot in her hand.

Everyone came to Ellen to express condolences in a stilted and patronizing fashion, for several remembered her as a servant in this house. The girl only nodded her head dumbly. Her hair caught one of the last rays of the sun and set it afire, and made her face, in consequence, appear dwindled and ghostly. The guests now began to leave, kissing Hortense's cheek, and nodding, and informing her, with admiration, how excessively kind she was to have honored a servant and the servant's niece so lavishly. Hortense stood up taller, in self-congratulation.

When the last guest had departed and the room stood in pale light, Hortense sat down near Ellen and her nephew and said in a no-nonsense voice: "Now we must be sensible, Ellen, and discuss certain matters. Are you listening? Dear me, how dull you look. Do listen, please. You are leaving tomorrow night and, hard though it may be for you now, things must be settled."

"Yes," Ellen said, and fumbled with a fold of her black dress.

"The cost of the funeral—I have the bill—is eight hundred dollars. It was in the best of taste, and the casket is bronze. There are certain gratuities, too. And the flowers your maid ordered, against my wishes. And the gift to that priest—not of your aunt's religion, but your maid insisted. A most unsatisfactory servant, in my opinion, and one you must discharge for her insolence to all of us. All in all, I think one thousand four hundred dollars will cover all expenses. Do you have that amount with you?"

"No," said Ellen, and Mrs. Eccles glanced at her nephew with exasperation and pursed lips. "I—I didn't think. We left so suddenly. I have only about one hundred dollars with me."

"Well," said Hortense, "you can write a check, surely."

"Yes," said Ellen. The fold in her skirt had become a sharp line under her fingers.

"I hope you are grateful to me for everything," said Hortense. "I have gone to a great deal of trouble for you, Ellen, and considerable personal expense. I am asking you nothing for that. But I do think I should be paid for the balance of this month."

"Yes," said Ellen. Francis nodded in approval, austerely.

"As for your aunt's personal belongings—my church will be grateful for them. The blankets, sheets, pillows, towels, shawls, and clothing. I will be glad to relieve you of the responsibility of sorting them out."

"Yes," said Ellen.

"There is also the small table clock you sent her two years ago, and a mirror over her chest, and some minor jewelry and knickknacks. May I dispose of them, too?"

"Yes," said Ellen.

"Good heavens," thought Maude from the doorway, where she was standing in a deliberate parody of menial meekness.

"And there is the matter of May's last medical bills and medicines. I will tell the doctor to send you the bill."

Ellen sighed. Now her eyes filled with bright blue water. Seeing this, Hortense said with severity, "I know you feel conscience-stricken, Ellen, though it is far too late for that now. You neglected your aunt shamefully. Perhaps, in extenuation, you'd like to give a donation to my church. Say, about one hundred dollars."

Ellen began to sob, dropping her head. Francis put his hand on her shoulder, feeling the warmth of her flesh through the black silk, and he was again deeply stirred. Maude smiled sardonically. She happened to glance through the tall windows on each side of the oak front doors and saw, to her glad relief, that the man coming up the walk was Jeremy Porter. She ran to the door so that he should not ring, and quietly opened it, while the pillorying voice of Mrs. Eccles continued to thrust behind her.

Maude soundlessly swung aside the doors, and drew Jeremy aside. "I must speak to you, Mr. Porter, and

quickly. Mrs. Porter is in quite a state and her—friends—
are doing nothing to alleviate it. The Congressman, Mr.
Porter, is here."

Jeremy's face was tight and grim. He listened while
Maude continued to whisper. His expression became
formidable, and his hands clenched. He was tired and
travel-stained from his long journey, but the forcefulness
of his character came with welcome to Maude. "I would
suggest," she said, "that you remove Mrs. Porter from
this house to a hotel for tonight."

"Of course," he said. He looked at the girl with hard
gratitude, understanding everything. Then he followed her
to the parlor, and saw his wife crouched in her chair
like a stricken thing, with Francis' arm about her, and
Mrs. Eccles leaning forward severely to Ellen, and still
talking.

"Nothing can relieve your guilt, Ellen," said Hortense.
"You must live with the memory of it, and pray for
forgiveness. I did all I could, like a sister, for your aunt.
I ask no recompense. I leave that to Almighty God. I can
only say that you had no right to desert your aunt. You
should have remained with her, in consideration of your
station, in my house. But you were never grateful for the
care I gave you, a mother's care. You insisted on running
away, like a bad girl, heedless of others' feelings and the
duty you should have felt for them."

Jeremy entered the room, and came at once to his wife,
and Francis and Hortense glared up at him in stupefaction, and Francis hastily removed his arm from Ellen's
waist. But Jeremy looked only at his wife. She saw him
at last and stood up, shaking, and threw herself into his
arms and burst into wild sobs.

"I came as fast as I could, my darling," he said. "Now,
I am taking you out of this damned house, to a hotel.
Miss Cummings is packing your bags."

Francis stood up, his pale thin face flushing. "You
insult my aunt, Jeremy. She has relieved Ellen of a great
burden, by arranging everything. You were not here,
naturally. You were delivering one of your inflammatory
and subversive speeches in Chicago! But my aunt, in her
maternal way, did all things for Ellen on this sad occasion, sparing her grievous details—"

"Shut up," said Jeremy. "One of these days I am going
to deal with you, once and for all, Frank." His dark eyes

flashed in the deepening dimness of the room, then he made a dismissing gesture with his hand. He held Ellen to him strongly, for she was shaking and wilting against him.

"There is a matter of bills," said Hortense, speaking for the first time. "I have detailed them for Ellen."

"How much?" said Jeremy over Ellen's shoulder.

Hortense licked the corner of her mouth. "I think two thousand dollars will cover everything."

"How kind of you," said Jeremy. "I will write you a check for the whole thing before we leave."

"I don't think Ellen is in a state—" Francis began. There was a red stain on each of his thin cheekbones, like a splash of blood.

"Shut up," said Jeremy again.

"How can you be so offensive to the only friends Ellen has?" cried Hortense. "The only friends in the world! I thought highly of you, Jeremy, until just lately. Now I know you for a brutal and ruthless man, with no regard for anyone."

"Good," said Jeremy. "I hope your nephew remembers that."

But Ellen was now feverishly pushing herself away from her husband. She stood before him, trembling, her white face lifted and condemning, her swollen eyes actually blazing.

"It was all your fault, Jeremy, that she died here alone, without me! You sent her away, when I was with you in Washington! When I came back you told me she had wanted it this way, to spare me the parting, but I know now it was not true! She wanted to stay with me, in New York."

"Who told you that damned lie?" Jeremy said, with no softness in his voice.

"Mrs. Eccles. She told me that poor Aunt May often cried and said you had driven her away, to get rid of her from your house." Ellen's voice was hoarse.

"Don't be an idiot, Ellen. You know very well she wanted to leave, as she told you, that day. She insisted on it. Surely you remember. Ellen, for God's sake, face reality for once. Your aunt wanted to come back to Wheatfield; she cried about it a thousand times, as you told me yourself."

"That is true," said Ellen, and her voice was weaker

than before. "But she wanted me to come back here, with her, to this house, and I wouldn't."

"Good God," said Jeremy. "You really are an idiot, Ellen." He wanted to say something more merciless, but restrained himself. Ellen was too distraught. He reached for her, but she sprang away, the tears flooding her face. "It was wrong, from the beginning," she stammered. "It was always all wrong."

"Good God," said Jeremy again. Francis and Hortense exchanged significant glances, nodding to each other.

"I was never anything but a servant!" Ellen wailed. "If I had remembered that, Aunt May would still be alive."

"You are out of your mind," said Jeremy. "Sometimes I think you always were, you infernal innocent. Now, collect yourself. I see Miss Cummings is at the door, with your luggage, and your hat and coat. We are going to the hotel at once."

"No!" exclaimed Ellen, out of her confused and suffering anguish.

"Yes," Jeremy said, and took her arm roughly. "I've been too patient with you, Ellen, for too long. I have a car waiting. Wipe your nose and your face, for God's sake."

It was as if she were seeing him clearly for the first time, and she flung herself into his arms, crying, "Take me home, Jeremy, take me home!"

"Yes, dear," he said. He pulled her to the door, where Miss Cummings was waiting. For some reason the younger woman suddenly epitomized, for Ellen, all her grief and anger and pain.

"I don't want her with me any longer! Miss Cummings. She has turned my children against me. I know it, I know it, I can feel it! She has been very rude to me, and Mrs. Eccles, since yesterday. She is arrogant and overbearing. I refuse to have her in our house any longer. Jeremy, send her away!"

Jeremy smiled, very darkly. "You needn't worry about that, sweetheart. She has somewhere more interesting to go, haven't you, Maude?" Charles Godfrey had already told Jeremy of his intention of marrying Maude in October.

Maude only smiled in answer. They went out into the hot twilight and got into the waiting car. Hortense and her nephew looked at each other a long time in the parlor.

"I think," said Francis, "that Ellen has come to her senses at last, and realizes, finally, what she really is." He was elated.

"Just a servant," Hortense agreed. "What's born in the bone comes out in the flesh."

26

Ellen remained in a stupefied condition for a considerable length of time, listless, almost unspeaking. So Jeremy had recourse to Kitty, Mrs. Bedford, and sundry other women, for relief. Kitty was most sympathetic, and delicately so. "Let her recover slowly," she said. "One must remember her background, my dear. It intrudes. The alienists from Vienna say that one's childhood is the most emphatic influence in one's life. I sadly don't believe that Ellen yet realizes her position as your wife. But you must give her time. That is the kindest thing to do."

Mrs. Bedford, who was very fond of Jeremy though not in love with him, was less mendacious. "Poor Ellen. She is always accusing herself of crimes she never committed. I had a sister like that, with a very tender conscience. It has nothing to do with Ellen's earlier life. She was born that way; I understand. One of these days, perhaps, she will come to herself, and laugh, and all will be well. It happened to my sister, who now lives in Chicago, a very healthy and vital woman who loves life, finally."

Ellen recovered sufficiently to be matron of honor at the wedding of Charles Godfrey and Maude Cummings, though she once said to Jeremy, "How Charles can do this, marrying Miss Cummings, is beyond me. She is so unsympathetic."

"She has common sense," said Jeremy. But Ellen never could come to a liking for Maude and distrusted her.

Charles had taken his bride to a brownstone house he owned not far from the brownstone where Jeremy and Ellen lived. Maude knew that Charles had for her an entirely different love than he had had for Ellen, a comfortable and confiding and companionate love, full of trust and mutual amusement and understanding. Ellen, for Charles, had been a rosy and romantic dream, teeming with almost adolescent fantasies. Men were instinctive poets, she would reflect. But a warm fire and a warm serene love were what they eventually desired, a love that did not unduly conflict with their romanticism, and was always stable and steadfast. Poetry is beautiful, she would think, and often contains profound wisdom and nuances. However, at the last, a good dinner, intelligent conversation, and tender sympathy were the foundations of men's lives. Poetry was moonlight, but one had to deal with the day. Maude knew all about the masculine character, and she would listen to Charles' excursions into poetry, though somewhat banal, with a gentle and loving smile, not contradicting or obtrusively inserting common sense into the discussion. Men were very suspicious of female earthiness, and resented it. So Maude rarely suggested anything that might shake the fanciful castles of her husband's soul. She only insinuated, when necessary for Charles' benefit, and then he would believe it had been his own idea from the beginning.

Once Charles said to Maude, "I am really worried about Jerry's political activities and his polemics all over the country. He makes enemies."

"Because he tells the truth?" said Maude. "Yes. But a man must do as he must. He must never compromise his integrity for expediency. When he does he becomes a scoundrel, a hypocrite, a liar, for he is false to his nature. Sometimes he may die for his integrity, but it is a noble death—unless when one remembers what King David said: 'Better a live dog than a dead lion.'"

"I think," said Charles, "that I'd rather be a live dog than a dead lion."

Maude looked at him shrewdly, and with love. "I think not," she said. He touched her hand with gratitude. She thought: How men delude themselves, which is not true of women, the original cynics. But a world devoid of men's romanticism would be a very drab world, indeed. We complement each other, men and women. If that ceases, we will have a brown existence.

"It may be that it is because I am getting so old that I am frightened," said Walter Porter to his nephew. "For you, Jeremy."

"Oh?" said Jeremy, refilling his uncle's glass as they sat together in the gloomy dusk of the early October day in the library of Jeremy's house. "You never were before."

"Well, as I said, I am getting on. But there is something in the air that smells of danger. I have no fear for myself, but I have for you. You are like a son to me, and fathers fear more for their sons than they ever fear for themselves. Now, your article in the *National Gazette*—"

"You don't approve of it?"

Walter hesitated. "I approve of it highly. I only wish you hadn't written it."

Jeremy laughed, then stopped. He said, "I thought it about time to stop hinting to the American people. The *Gazette* is not only the most popular magazine in the country, but it is also both courageous and controversial. An editor or two had doubts; the others did not. I was able to give specific dates of meetings of the Scardo Society and the Committee for Foreign Studies' discussions, and the names of those present, when the plans were laid and worked out for wars, revolutions, incendiarisms, racial conflicts, bankruptcies, panics, treasons, assassinations, the overthrow of governments, riots, the subversion of heads of state, the subordination of politicians, disorders and chaos in all the nations of the world, the destruction of currencies, and the final subjugation of the world to Communism—under the tyranny of the 'elite,' the powerful, the gigantically rich. The *Gazette* agreed with me that the time had come to name names, and not merely societies and committees, and so I did."

When Walter did not answer, Jeremy continued. "Societies and committees and organizations are vague and diffuse, and therefore appear to be not imminently dangerous, like rumor or gossip, without names and facts and dates. Conspiracies sound exciting. Wasn't it Disraeli who said that anyone who does not believe in the conspiratorial theory of history is a fool? So, I gave the names and facts and the dates, and was able to repeat discussions almost verbatim; I memorized them when I was a member of both conspiracies. I also made notes immediately after the meetings, so I would have an accurate record. You may have noticed that no one I mentioned has disputed what I wrote."

"Yes. And that's what is worrying me, Jerry. Had any of them denounced you as a fraud, a fantasizer, a muckraker, a laughable liar, and denied everything, or had ridiculed you, I wouldn't be alarmed."

"Maybe they think that if they ignore me I will go away, or that what I wrote will soon be forgotten by a ragtime-loving public."

Walter shook his head. "I'd feel less worried if so many magazines and newspapers hadn't carried editorials about your article. You've stirred up national speculation, and demands that the conspirators be exposed once and for all, before it is too late."

"I'm not worried. In fact, I intend to attend many political gatherings, both Republican and Democratic, to elaborate on my article and give more incisive information. My offers of speeches have already been accepted, especially by the Republican Party. Uncle Walter, Wilson must not be elected President. I doubt he has any idea of who is manipulating him, and will manipulate him, if he is President. He was chosen because he is an innocent idealist with no notion of how a country should be governed—and who really governs it. Taft, I have heard, has already more than an inkling concerning the conspirators, and so he is dangerous to them. Teddy Roosevelt, too, is gradually becoming dimly aware. So both are scheduled to be eliminated, via the election of Wilson."

"Jerry, I think you may be in danger. I'm frightened."

"Oh, come, Uncle Walter! You don't think they would confirm my accusations by murdering me, do you?" Jeremy laughed again. "They're delicate, and will move delicately, especially at this time. They move in the dark; they would not want photographic flash powder suddenly illuminating them. So you need not worry. Besides, they save their assassinations for heads of state, not mere lawyers like me."

Walter changed his tact. "Everything you've written, and spoken, Jerry, did nothing to help prevent Wilson from being nominated. What if Roosevelt is elected, and his Progressive Party comes into power?"

"I admit he would be worse."

Walter sighed heavily. The years and anxiety had dwindled him. He watched the lamplighter skipping down the street; there were brilliant bluish arc lights, however, on the corners, spitting and blazing at shadows. "And my son is one of them," he said in a dim voice.

After a silence, Jeremy said, "I have been reading the opinions of Freud and his brother alienists, or psychiatrists as they are beginning to call themselves. I am beginning to think that men like Frank are mentally sick. Remember what Thoreau said: 'I believe that what so saddens the reformer is not his sympathy with fellows in distress—but his private ailment. Let that be righted and he will forsake his companions without apology.'"

"Perhaps that is true, Jeremy. I wonder what Francis' 'private ailment' is."

"He had too strong a father for his fragile temperament. He both hates authority and secretly longs to be submissive to it. There's something very female about male reformers. They really want to be raped by someone more powerful, so they can adore the rapist. But if they are treated like reasonable and responsible human beings, they become arrogant and tyrannical."

"And you think I made the mistake of treating my son as if he were a reasonable and responsible man?" Walter turned from the window and Jeremy saw his pain and was regretful.

"Well, it's an interesting hypothesis. Yet, no man can ever know what another man is, or why he does and thinks the way he does. It is impudence to believe that this is possible."

The dinner bell rang. Walter looked at Jeremy, seeing the increasing strength and resolution in him, the hardening maturity, and the white streaks at his temples, and Walter wished again, with a kind of despair, that the younger man were his son.

Because of Ellen's agitated state of mind over the death of her aunt, Jeremy permitted his son, Christian, to remain at home until the following January, rather than sending him to boarding school—Groton—in September. Ellen clung to her husband and her children as to a despairing refuge against what she considered her "guilt." Jeremy understood that she must be occupied if only in her house, for she had given up her music and language lessons, her visits to the museums and to the opera. She accepted dinner invitations, and gave dinners, only at Jeremy's insistence. "Good God, Ellen," he would say, "are you trying to bury us in your aunt's grave?" But when he looked into her eyes he saw an irrational but powerful fear. She was terrified that if she relinquished her hold on those she loved or forgot them for even a moment, they would be taken from her, as her aunt had been taken. She must watch them incessantly. She had seen death for the first time and had known its irrevocable terror. Jeremy understood, but his impatience became vivid, for Ellen insisted that if he were to be late he must call and explain so that she would not be seized by a frantic anxiety.

Her children knew, and thought their mother's state of mind hilarious, and their ruthless taunting of her, and their demands, became more overt. She now could deny them nothing, in the vague but passionate belief that to deny them was to invite eternal separation. She would try, haltingly, to explain this to Jeremy, and while he sympathized he also would become angry. "Why do you try to order the lives of others?" he would ask her. "Ellen, we have lives of our own to live. You never understood that, even concerning your aunt. She made her decision; we make our decisions, too. You can't clutch us forever, you know." But this remark only made poor Ellen more frantic.

Her children had their own phonograph in the nursery, and Ellen bought records for them constantly, though Jeremy deplored their taste. They loved ragtime and would dance together for hours to the rollicking tunes, while Ellen watched them with a yearning smile, sighing over their happy childhood. But they were very careful not to play a certain maudlin song when their father was present:

> *She's only a bird in a gilded cage,*
> *A beautiful sight to see;*
> *You may think she's happy and free from care,*
> *She's not, though she seems to be.*
> *'Tis sad when you think of her wasted life,*
> *For youth cannot mate with age,*

And her beauty was sold for an old man's gold,
She's a bird in a gilded cage!

While this record was moaning from the phonograph Ellen's children would watch her acutely, winking at each other and sometimes pressing their hands against their mouths to restrain their cruel laughter at her. Ellen would wince at this song, and others like it, but would determinedly smile. After all, were they not just children with unformed and indiscriminate tastes, the tastes of innocent ones? That her children were not innocent, and had never been innocent, did not occur to Ellen. After a prolonged session with such maunderings she would take them downstairs to the music room and play arias for them, and sing in her entrancing voice, or run through a sonata, particularly the Moonlight Sonata, and various nocturnes. They would listen, grinning at each other. They did not think their mother had an enchanting voice; they told each other she "bawled like a calf." They did not care for her music, finding it boring and not in tune with their endlessly restless temperaments.

They now had a male tutor, a delicate young man with a perpetual cold, pale watery blue eyes which stared pathetically, a long pallid face and a mass of straight almost colorless hair. It was soon evident to Christian and Gabrielle that Sydney Darby was in love with their mother, though Ellen was not aware of this in the least. When she appeared during their lessons, standing on the threshold just to fill her eyes with the sight of them, poor Mr. Darby would turn a bright crimson, and would begin to stammer in his weak voice, much to the children's delight. They would purse up their mouths in maudlin moues, roll their eyes in mock agony, and whimper under their breath. If Ellen did not see this, the unfortunate Mr. Darby did, and so he hated the children with a passion which would have awed them had they known; they would have respected him. If they could have guessed at his desire to slaughter them, even they would have been intimidated. Annie alone saw and knew all this, and on several occasions she would discuss Christian and Gabrielle with the tutor.

"They're monsters," she would say. "But all children are, honestly, Mr. Darby."

"Yes," he would reply, sighing. "It's very strange, but I like to teach, even though I know all about children. I still have the hope that in some way I can make children less terrible, less formidable. Sometimes I know it is hopeless, Annie; children merely grow up to be perilous adults. One wonders what happened to Christianity."

"Nobody ever tried it," Annie said once in her sturdy way. "They call us a Christian country. I don't think any country was ever Christian. It's against human nature to be good and decent. Except for a few. Like Madam and Cuthbert, and you, Mr. Darby." She looked at him fondly and he returned her look, startled and pleased, noticing for the first time how pretty the nurse was and how intriguing her tilted nose and how charming her smile. Annie had become somewhat plump, and rosier, with the years, but Mr. Darby did not find this a fault. He liked robust and tender women. He suddenly wanted to kiss her, and she saw this in his shy eyes, and she wanted to respond heartily. But for Annie there would be no casual encounter. She had experienced that once and was determined that her fixed goal was the altar. In the meantime she affectionately if covertly encouraged Mr. Darby.

"I only stay here because of Madam," she said to him. "The kids don't need me any longer, if they ever did, except when they were babies. But Madam needs me. I guess you don't understand that, Mr. Darby."

He nodded his head vigorously. "Oh, but I do, Annie, believe me," and Annie glowed. That night she sang a melodious song she had heard on the children's phonograph: "I never knew—what love could do!" She followed this with another song: "When Irish eyes are smiling—!" It no longer mattered to the exuberantly loving Annie that Mr. Darby was not only Irish but a Catholic, too. Pragmatic Annie, suddenly remembering her Bible, could smilingly, and with secret tears, repeat to herself, "And thy people shall be my people, and thy God my God." She bought herself a rosary, and instructions. One Sunday, in early October, she appeared at Mr. Darby's side as he descended the brownstone steps. She was dressed in her newest garb, a light-blue wool suit and a large dark-blue felt hat, new black button shoes and black gloves, her golden hair quite radiant, her cheeks quite pink, her lips red and full. She said to Mr. Darby softly, "I thought

I might go to church with you this morning. If you don't
mind."

Mr. Darby, looking down at the round and shining face
and the love-filled blue eyes, became, in his sensations, at
least a foot taller and very virile and aggressive, and he
manfully tucked Annie's gloved hand in his arm and
strode off with her to Mass. She blessed herself when he
blessed himself, and genuflected and rose when he did so,
and she was very moved by the candles and the organ
and the statues and the ceremony, for it was all transfigured in the ineffable light of love. However, being
astute, Annie knew that at heart Mr. Darby was very
timid and gentle, and an open chase of him would send
him flying, so she waited.

In November 1912, Woodrow Wilson was elected President of the United States of America. It was not a surprise to Jeremy Porter, even though he was embittered.
It did not surprise him, either, that in the month of
January 1913 Mr. Wilson signed into law the ominous
amendments to the Constitution: the federal income tax,
the Federal Reserve System, and the direct election of
Senators. It had been inevitable for decades, in spite of
constant rulings against such sinister innovations by the
U.S. Supreme Court, which had declared that these were
unconstitutional. Jeremy said, "Well, the mad Emperor,
Caligula, made his horse Consul of Rome. So does the
American voter."

"It will become increasingly evident, I am afraid," said
old Walter Porter to his nephew, "that we shall soon be
governed by men and not by law."

"That is always the fate of republics," Jeremy answered.
"What was it Aristotle said? 'Republics decline into
democracies, and democracies into despotisms.' Yes. There
is much to be said in favor of monarchies and Parliaments.
They do exist longer, and are stable."

In March 1913, a strange and virulent ailment known
as *la grippe* began a tentative invasion of the whole world.
It had a different characteristic than the familiar influ-
enza. It caused more deaths and stronger and longer
disabilities. It would soon be known as the Spanish In-
fluenza, losing its more dainty and pseudo-French earlier
designation.

Walter Porter died of it in late March, and very
suddenly. Jeremy was his main heir. He had left his son,

Francis, but a fourth of his large estate. Francis, driven almost mad by this "injustice," fought it through the courts, and lost. If he had hated his cousin before, that hatred was nothing to what he now felt for Jeremy. The old enmity became malign.

Ellen, deeply saddened by Walter's death, could not understand her grim husband and his frequent expressions of detestation for his cousin. "Jeremy," she once said, "the money isn't important, is it? Why not let Mr. Francis have it?"

He had looked at her incredulously. "How can you be so silly, Ellen? Uncle Walter left that money to me. Should I insult his memory by rejecting it? It's a matter of principle, too, which you would not understand. Don't mention it to me any more."

Ellen had cowered at the look on his face, for it was the look of a hostile stranger and never had she encountered it before, and she cried until he took her in his arms and consoled her. He had seen the fear in her eyes and though he did not guess the reason he knew the fear.

Jeremy's parents were elated by Walter's will, and Agnes, forgetting her late approval of Francis, said righteously, "Walter had a right to leave his money to whom he wished. He must have had a very good reason, indeed!"

27

When Woodrow Wilson became President he sonorously, in the best Princeton accents, declared his "New Freedoms" for America. He approved the Underwood Tariff, which reduced duties on foreign importations. This cheap competition with American industry threw tens of thousands of American workers out of jobs, and induced a depression, and widespread despair. There was no longer any protection for American workingmen against foreign labor, and so starvation and misery became universal.

"Things," said Jeremy Porter with bitterness, "are right on schedule. The next step is war." But few listened. He was not surprised that he was no longer invited to speak, though he offered to do so without a fee. Nor was he surprised when Mr. Wilson denounced President Victoriano Huerta of Mexico as a "desperate brute," because Huerta had restored law and order to his country after it had been in a state of chaos and anarchy under the "reformer" President, Madero, who had incited the mobs in what was euphemistically called a "class struggle." "Right out of Lenin's mouth," Jeremy had said. "Now, when will Wilson take military action against Huerta? Almost any day now."

The State Department, under Wilson, spread the rumor that German ships were unloading arms for Huerta in Veracruz, and the Department declared its indignation. "Anti-American!" it shouted, though what was "anti-American" about this private agreement between Mexico and Germany, paid for with Mexican money, was not quite clear. "So," said Jeremy, "we are beginning to interfere with the legitimate rights of foreign nations to conduct their own policies for profit or self-protection. We are on the road to American imperialism—as planned." Jeremy's friends were still incredulous and laughingly accused him of "seeing conspiracy in every move in Washington." They were somewhat sobered when, on April 21, 1914, Wilson hysterically gave orders to "take Veracruz by storm." American warships were ordered to bombard Veracruz, and American sailors and marines seized various government buildings. Greatly alarmed, and justly so by this American, and unique, intrusion into Spanish-American governments and internal affairs, Brazil, Argentina, and Chile quietly protested to Washington and discreetly offered to mediate between the United States and Mexico, and the offer, given silkily but with determination, was reluctantly accepted by an excited State Department. Jeremy was delighted. "It is about time," he said to his friends, "that foreign governments begin to look coldly and realistically at our government, that is, if they don't want to be submerged in radical conspiracies which will destroy them." But under his delight was a cynical pessimism. Again, it

was justified. President Huerta mysteriously resigned—
and retired to Forest Hills on Long Island, New York—
he who had protested American intervention in the
internal affairs of Mexico! "He must now watch proceedings with agony," Jeremy said, as a Communist revolu-
tionary named Venustiano Carranza became President of
Mexico, with the high approval of Washington. Huerta
was oddly silent, and under severe surveillance in his
"exile" in the United States, an exile imposed upon him
by Washington itself. "It is not an exile," said Jeremy
to his stunned friends. "It is an imprisonment. He was
forced into that imprisonment in America by our very
'concerned' government."

The innocent American people, struggling to survive
in the depression induced by Washington, were too engrossed with their immediate predicament to note the
ominous and intricate policies of their government. They
had never heard of the secret Scardo Society or the
Committee for Foreign Studies. Nor would they have
believed in the existence of these sinister organizations
which had long ago plotted the abrogation of their
liberties as Americans, and the conspiracy to reduce
America to a mere membership in an international organization busily and softly at work in The Hague under
the title of "World Peace." It was a working title. The
ultimate name would be given later.

Jeremy went to the German Embassy in Washington
in May 1914. He knew the Germans to be elaborately
courteous and polite and rigid in protocol. He had been
agreeably surprised to be invited on a mere cryptic letter
he had written to the Embassy. The Ambassador himself
received him and conducted him to private chambers.
"Your Excellency has heard of me?" Jeremy asked the
Ambassador. The Ambassador smiled grimly under his
mustache. "Herr Porter," he said in German, "we have
indeed. And we have listened."

He introduced one of his attachés, Herr Hermann
Goldenstein. "I worry," said Herr Goldenstein, who was
a young and intense man.

"Jews," said Jeremy, "always worry, and with excellent
reasons. But all of us should worry, too." He turned to
the Ambassador. "I am sure Your Excellency knows of
the international plot against your country."

"Yes," said the Ambassador. "Unfortunately, His Majesty, the Kaiser, refuses to believe in this infamy. We have given him copies of your speeches, Herr Porter. He calls it nonsense. But someone more—shall we say, aware?—has induced him to increase our very small military forces. Sad to say, Mr. Theodore Roosevelt has suddenly become hostile to Germany, he who admired us."

"You are not astonished, sir?"

The Ambassador sighed. "Nothing astonishes me." They looked at each other with significance.

"Bismarck," said Jeremy, "was quite a Communist. He drove out the sound German middle class to America, and to other countries. It has been to our profit, though a loss to Germany. No country can afford to lose much of its middle class, the bourgeoisie as it is now being disdainfully called in America."

"Tyrannies," said the Ambassador, "are always at war with the middle class. It is an ancient story, from Egypt to Athens to Rome—to modern Germany, to France, to Spain—and now to your unfortunate America. What will be the result? As you have written, and spoken, a worldwide despotism under the self-elected elite. The straw men, the impotent, the hysterical, and the insane, the feeble creatures who know their own inherent emasculation, and so would take revenge on a world which recognizes their impotence, rejects them, and laughs at them. The so-called intellectuals, who are not intellectual at all."

"And who are being used by the international conspiracy, which is employing Communism itself to destroy freedom in all the world. Cynically, they are using Socialistic Communism for their own rise to power, and are as much the enemy of Communism as they are of individual liberty. What shall we do, Your Excellency?"

The Ambassador threw out his hands. "Governments are powerless against those who control the monetary policies of a nation. You have said that yourself."

"Yes," said Jeremy. "We now have a private banking organization, the Federal Reserve System. The American people are deceived, in that they believe the word 'Federal' means government. *Gross Gott*, Your Excellency, have you any thoughts about this frightful situation and what we can do about it?"

"Herr Porter, you can help by persuading the American people not to engage in any foreign entanglements."

"Your Excellency does not appear to be optimistic."

"It is not the function of a diplomat to be optimistic," said the Ambassador, and now for the first time he smiled. "We take the view that anything catastrophic is entirely probable. We are never disappointed. I have heard about the book you are writing. Tell me of it."

"I have a book, *America, Beware!* I have just finished it. It will be published very shortly. What good it will do, I do not know. Possibly no good. You see, I am as realistic as Your Excellency."

The Ambassador sighed again. "In a world where fantasy is dominant, realism is suspect. Mankind loves to dream. It will not face facts, even in the very face of its own imminent destruction. *Sic transit mundi.*"

"The world deserves its destruction," Jeremy said, and was despondent. "If it will not listen to truth—it should die."

"Herr Porter, it will surely die. I am older than you, and filled with dire premonitions. It grieves me, however, that I have sons."

"I also have a son," said Jeremy.

"Accept my condolences, Herr Porter." He added, hesitantly, "There is always the *Gross Gott.*"

"I do not believe in Him," said Jeremy.

Just before they parted the Ambassador said, and with sudden gravity, "Herr Porter, you do not realize your own influence. May I give you a warning? Trust no one. Look for entrapments."

"Your Excellency means assassination? I am not that important."

The Ambassador was silent for a few moments while he studied Jeremy. Then he said, "Have you consulted with the French Embassy?"

"I asked for an interview. I received no answer."

"So," said the Ambassador, "it is very ominous. *Ja?*"

On May 24, 1914, Jeremy's book was published, with all its warnings. The American critics were incredulous, though they admitted its wide scholarship and comprehension of international and internal affairs. The critics asked, "Are we not acquainted with George Washington's advice not to engage in foreign entanglements? The American people would not permit such involvement. Mr. Porter is pursuing dragons which do not exist." The book sold widely.

Congressman Francis Porter denounced it as "absurd."
"The author is obviously mad." His denunciations were
included in the *Congressional Record*. "I wonder," said
Jeremy to his friends, "who wrote that for him. It is very
forceful, and he has no forcefulness at all. He is just an
hysteric, and incoherent, as are all radical hysterics. *You
will notice that he attacks me as a person, and not my
ideas, and that is typical.* Here is one review: 'Ex-
Congressman Jeremy Porter is noted as a womanizer. He
is also very rich.' What the hell has that got to do with
the facts I have written in my book? Nothing, of course.
The same reviewer just loves Wilson and his 'New Freedoms.' That, too, is typical. The self-styled intellectuals
have limp penises, and that is their trouble. If physicians
would concentrate on alleviating the difficulty we'd have
no screaming saliva-dripping 'reformers.'"

On June 2 Jeremy's Cadillac suddenly exploded and
burned furiously on Fifth Avenue. He died in the flames.
His last thought was: "Ellen! Oh, Ellen!"

The German Ambassador was sorrowful. But he was
not surprised. Nor was he surprised at President Wilson's
agitation concerning Germany in early August 1914. "He
is an innocent," he said to his associates. "But are not
the American people all innocents? Alas."

President Wilson was unequivocally aghast at the furious rush of events. He said to his friend Colonel House,
"At all costs, we must be impartial." The Colonel smiled
and regarded the President with a strange expression.
Unknowingly quoting the German Ambassador, he
thought: He is an innocent.

28

On the day before Christmas 1916, over a month after
Mr. Wilson had been re-elected to the Presidency with the
slogan "He kept us out of war," Ellen Porter was released

from the Rose Hill Sanitarium on Long Island. She was
hesitantly pronounced cured of the desperate mental illness she had suffered as a result of Jeremy's murder. The
physicians said to Congressman Francis Porter, "She is
still somewhat dulled and chronically depressed and
usually very listless, in spite of the best treatments, but
we have hopes that the return to her children will have a
salutary effect. For the first six months of her—residence
—here—she never spoke of her son and daughter. In
fact, she rarely spoke at all, as you know, Congressman,
and appeared not to be aware of her surroundings or her
visitors. Dreadful, indeed. We all pray that eventually
she will be restored to full health and regain an interest
in life. We have done our best."

"I am sure you have," said Francis. With the aid of a
nurse, who would live with Ellen until her complete
"restoration," he escorted Ellen to his waiting limousine.
She had become very frail and unsteady; though wrapped
in furs she shuddered as the wintry wind off the ocean
struck her, despite the fact that her face remained vacant,
her eyes aimlessly staring. However, she said to Francis
in a faint and toneless voice, "I must think of my children." It was as though she were repeating a lesson by
rote she neither understood well nor knew the meaning
of. She looked up at Francis with those stretched and
lightless eyes which were hardly aware of him.

"Yes," he said very gently. "They need their mother,
Ellen."

Just before entering the limousine Ellen glanced about
her, and for an instant she appeared startled and confused, as if not knowing where she was. She stared at the
large red-brick façade of the sanitarium, and her confusion grew. It was obvious that she did not recognize
the building. One lock of her still brilliant hair escaped
from under her hat and fluttered on her very white gaunt
cheek. She repeated Francis' words in her deathly voice,
"They need their mother."

She strained piteously towards him like a child in a
nightmare and her dry and wasted lips were tremulous
and pleading. "Yes," he said, and she nodded obediently.
Snow was falling. Flakes fell on her gloves and pursued
her into the car. Francis and the nurse covered her with
a fur robe, for she was trembling violently. The nurse,

Miss Evans, a plump and cheerful middle-aged woman, said, "Tonight we must decorate the Christmas tree! What fun, home at last."

"Yes," said Ellen. She blinked, sightlessly. She sat between the nurse and Francis, and Francis held her hand tightly. There was no warmth in her fleshless fingers, and no response. "The children will be glad to see their mother again," he said, and his light voice was moved. Ellen nodded with that empty acquiescence. Her profile was very sharp and resembled white stone, and there were deep lines about her mouth though she would not be thirty until January. Her face was both curiously old and wizened and as expressionless as a very young child's. She was no longer the Ellen he had known so many years ago, Francis reflected. But he still loved her. In a few months, he told himself, her beauty and vitality would return and she would begin to forget. He had hopes that she had already begun the process. Not once had she spoken of Jeremy since his death. She had not been able to attend his funeral. Francis wondered if she thought often of her dead husband, whose death had been caused by a very sophisticated bomb which had been placed in the interior of his automobile, and whose murderer or murderers had never been known and apprehended.

Ellen did not speak on the long drive, though she smiled spasmodically once or twice when the nurse touched her arm and made some lively remark on the passing scenery. The nurse suspected that the unfortunate young woman had not even heard her, and that the smiles were merely automatic and more like grimaces. But she continued to chatter brightly. Suddenly Ellen closed her eyes and fell instantly asleep. "She is tired, sir," said the nurse to Francis. "So much excitement, getting ready for Home, and the dear little ones."

"Christian is not very little," said Francis in his pontifical voice. "He is twelve now, and home for the holidays from Groton, and Miss Gabrielle is ten. Still, they are but children, and very lively. I am their cousin, once removed, and they call me Cousin Francis. I am very fond of them, Miss Evans," and his voice contained a hint of severity, as if she had questioned his word. Miss Evans regarded him shrewdly. She was not awed that he was a Congressman, for she had been employed by Senators and once by a

Governor. What a stick he is, to be sure, she thought, and like a skeleton in all that black and that derby hat. You can almost count his bones. His eyes are the color of cold oysters, too, and seem to glare behind those spectacles of his, as if scolding the whole world. Forty or so, I'd guess, and his hair is either very light or is getting gray, and thin. Poor Mrs. Porter, to have no one to turn to but this cousin of her husband's. Except, of course, that nice Mr. and Mrs. Godfrey who visited her often. As for that Mrs. Wilder, she's nothing but a middle-aged cat, and no friend to this poor lady. Nor are the others who came, probably out of curiosity or a sense of duty.

Miss Evans compassionately squeezed Ellen's other hand. There was no response. The nurse sighed. It was true that Ellen had never spoken of her dead husband, but the nurses had heard her wailing and calling for him during her drugged sleep, and they had seen the rivulets of unconscious tears running down her sunken cheeks. She had been brought to the sanitarium in an ambulance, as stiff and rigid as a corpse, and more than half moribund, her face and eyes without cognizance. It had been six months before she had been able to dress herself with assistance. She was still emaciated, her once beautiful figure no longer evident.

Francis said, "I hope you remember the red roses I sent you every week, Ellen." His tone was admonishing, like a male teacher's. Ellen awoke, dimly.

"Yes," she said. The nurse thought: She doesn't have the slightest idea of what he is saying. But Francis nodded with approval. The brown furs and the brown silk dress Ellen wore were like garments on a mannequin, for they did not stir. Her breath was just faintly visible in the icy interior of the vehicle, and it came and went very slowly. Again she slept, while the white and black landscape rolled past them. Then to Francis' dismay large shimmering tears began to run down Ellen's cheeks from under her shut lids. Miss Evans wiped them away. "She often cries in her sleep, sir," she said. "It's like her soul remembers, even if she doesn't when she is awake."

"Of course she remembers when she's awake!" said Francis, his words heavy with rebuke. "It is just that she controls herself."

The nurse shrugged. "Yes, sir," she said. "She is a lady."

Hardly that, you chattering vulgar fool, thought Francis, with his quick and pointless anger. He glanced coldly at the nurse, and saw her round red face and sparkling brown eyes and somewhat thick lips, and he was filled with distaste. Her big breasts welled under her white uniform, and his aversion increased. Her brown hair was neatly combed under her white cap, but without luster, and she had a coarse double chin. To others, her appearance was both reassuring and comforting. To Francis, she was almost disgusting. He found overt health distasteful and plebeian. Just a farm woman, he commented to himself. But Ellen will soon be entirely well, and we can get rid of her. He was already thinking of himself and Ellen as "we."

On his Aunt Hortense's death a few months ago, as a result of a virulent attack of "Spanish flu," he had inherited her entire estate, which was very considerable, and he thought of it now with pursed-lipped satisfaction. He was almost as rich as Ellen herself. He considered Jeremy's executor, Charles Godfrey, with intense resentment and something close to hatred. By all that was decent, he should have been co-executor, despite the enmity between the cousins. But what could one expect of such as Jeremy Porter, who had had no family feeling? The fact that he himself had little if any "family feeling" did not occur to him, for always he had been dutiful to the parents of Jeremy, who were now old and still shocked by their son's death. They had dwindled in appearance and seemed almost as vacant and listless as Ellen. Francis expected that they would not live long, and he thought of the fortune which Ellen's children would inherit. "We" would administer it until the majority of the children. Francis pursed his lips again and slightly nodded. The lawyers in Philadelphia would not give him much trouble. They respected him as a Congressman and a New York lawyer. He knew them well and made it a point to visit them occasionally.

He thought of Ellen's children as he often thought these days. He was diffident with them, but they treated him with effusive affection, which he appreciated. The notion that they secretly laughed at him never entered his mind.

He believed that they had not cared overly for their father. They had almost forgotten him, in the urgent exigencies of children. In the last few months they had not even mentioned their mother or inquired about her health. They had visited her but three times, on Charles Godfrey's command. "Children should not be exposed to these—things," Francis had told Charles, who was their guardian. Charles silently agreed with him, but not for the reason Francis gave. Charles had no illusions concerning Christian and Gabrielle. He thought them detestable. He had a child of his own now, a little girl of three, a sweet and intelligent child who had almost convinced her father that it was possible that some children were not entirely wicked. Maude had not been too happy when she had discovered she was pregnant. She was a stern if loving mother, and Charles had begun to hope and to forget his earlier forebodings. He had seen too many adult children who had exploited widowed parents for their money, too many children who were ruthless and greedy, and who waited impatiently for the death of a mother or father. Years of law had convinced Charles that humanity was not an admirable species even at its best.

Jeremy's children had long ago understood Francis, for they were very intelligent as well as "detestable." Christian, in particular, had confidently come to the conclusion that he would be able to "handle" Cousin Francis easily, and with this his sister, the only creature Christian loved since the death of his father, concurred. Their mother had never been a force in their lives, and they did not expect that she would ever be. If they thought of her at all it was with amused disdain. They had not been at all enthusiastic when they heard she would be coming home permanently before Christmas this year. "She'll spoil things," said Gabrielle. "She's so awful silly."

"I hear she's still dippy," her brother commented. "She won't get in our way, not that she ever did."

"I think she's just like that stupid mermaid she used to read to us about," said Gabrielle, and brother and sister laughed together. "Dancing on feet that felt like daggers."

"And getting herself a human soul," said Christian, and they laughed again as at something risible.

"I bet Cousin Francis will marry Mama," said Gabrielle.

This annoyed Christian. He was already thinking of money in large quantities. For an instant he thought of his father with a lurch of his heart.

There was no governess in the house now, with Christian at Groton and Gabrielle attending a fashionable girls' school during the day in New York. Annie Burton had married Mr. Darby a year ago and had moved to a small upstate town where Mr. Darby happily taught at a well-disciplined private school for boys. His wife knew that she was no longer needed at the house in New York, and "that Congressman" had told her that it was doubtful that "Mrs. Porter would ever regain her senses." With this Annie did not agree. She had visited the unseeing Ellen several times, and had always returned in tears. But she was a nurse. She had seen recognition in Ellen's eyes on occasion, and once Ellen had even smiled at her. However, she knew that it would be a long time until Ellen was normal; that she would return to health Annie did not doubt.

The car wound its tedious way through drays and wagons and automobiles and streetcars and pedestrian crowds blown before the winter wind. Shopwindows began to glow in yellow lights and the lamps on the street woke to a white illumination. For the first time Ellen seemed to rouse feebly and she looked at the familiar avenue and blinked drily. Her pale lips quivered but she said nothing. "We're almost home," said Francis.

"Home," repeated Ellen, very faintly, and she frowned slightly as at an alien word she did not know.

"A nice warm fire and a good dinner and your own bed," said Miss Evans with encouragement. "And your children, Mrs. Porter."

"The children," said Ellen. Her once resonant voice was dull and uncertain. Then her throat worked and she gasped and strained her face upwards, as though seeking breath. Miss Evans tightened her hold on Ellen's hand, which was trembling, and the nurse nodded her head in satisfaction. The poor lady was beginning to feel "something" at last. Miss Evans was annoyed at Francis' open consternation. "Does Mrs. Porter need air?" asked the Congressman.

"No, no, not at all," said Miss Evans. "She is coming to herself, a little. She is beginning to 'feel.' "

But Francis opened his window a little and Ellen immediately quaked when she felt the icy wind on her face. "There, that's better," said Francis. "Very airless, in a shut vehicle, isn't it?"

"I don't advise it," said the nurse with some sharpness. "She hasn't been out before, all this long time. Please, sir, close the window."

Francis was outraged at this request from a "menial." He glared through his glasses at Miss Evans, but she was not intimidated. She said, "It would be too bad if Mrs. Porter got lung fever."

"You mean pneumonia," said Francis with aloof contempt. He looked down at Ellen, who was shuddering. "Are you cold, Ellen?" he asked.

"Yes," she whispered. "I am cold, very, very cold." He closed the window, somewhat affronted. He had thought the brisk wind "refreshing, bracing." Ellen repeated, "Very, very cold," but only Miss Evans knew that she was not referring to any bodily discomfort. The nurse gripped the flaccid hand more strongly, and Ellen leaned against her shoulder.

The car turned into the street where Ellen lived. The brownstone fronts of the houses were streaked and dappled with snow; chimneys poured out clouds of acrid black smoke; lamplight fell on crusted and dirty ice. The darkening sky had a reddish tint in which floated a pallid ghost of a moon. "Here we are," Francis said, and patted Ellen's shoulder. He did not feel her shrinking. The car door opened and Francis alighted and reached in for Ellen. But she sat and stared at her house, and her face was one white anguish, and she gasped again.

"Now, now, Ellen," said Francis pompously. "We must not be foolish, must we?" He took her arm and pulled her towards the open door.

"No, no," said Ellen, and Francis nodded. Miss Evans said, "Let her wait a minute until she has strength to get out, Mr. Porter. I know what she means."

"Do you, really?" said Francis. He tugged at Ellen again and she uttered an inhuman cry and struggled with him. Miss Evans said as loudly as possible, "Let me, if you please. Mrs. Porter is my patient." She said to Ellen very gently, "You must face things, Mrs. Porter, no matter how hard. I know it is terribly hard, but it must be faced, and you are a brave lady. I know that myself."

Francis was about to rebuke her and "reduce her to her station," but to his discomfiture he saw that Ellen was nodding piteously and was making an effort to rise. Very stiffly Francis moved aside a little and let Miss Evans assist Ellen from the car. Once on the gritty sidewalk Ellen swayed, but Miss Evans' grasp was strong and reassuring. It was Miss Evans who guided her charge up the brown and slippery steps, while Francis, angry again, followed closely. The door opened and there was the aging Cuthbert, whose faded eyes blurred with tears when he saw Ellen. "Welcome home, madam," he said. "Welcome home."

Ellen looked at him and could not speak but he saw that she had recognized him. He helped Miss Evans bring her into the vestibule, and then into the hall, which was warm and lighted with a subdued electric chandelier. There were voices from a distance. Then, as Miss Evans helped remove Ellen's coat and hat and gloves, the voices came nearer and people entered the hall: Kitty Wilder, Maude and Charles Godfrey, and Christian and Gabrielle. Ellen looked at them, and seemed to dwindle, and she shivered. She looked down at the spot where she had fallen soundlessly when she had received the news of Jeremy's death. She looked at it as if fascinated, her head bent, as one looks at a new grave.

Kitty, withered and parched in her mid-forties, and even thinner than ever, thought with intense bitterness: Oh, you fool, you mindless fool, who was not capable of loving him! What do you know of grief and sorrow? Did you love him as I loved him, you blank-faced imbecile? No, you ran off in your mind to escape facing his death, to be pampered and cosseted in a pretty sanitarium, while I was here, I was here, suffering and almost dying. He loved me, not you.

Her large white teeth flashed in her sallow face, and she came to Ellen and embraced her, murmuring, "Darling, darling, how wonderful you are home at last. And how well you look!" Her emaciated arms, in black silk, closed about Ellen.

Maude and Charles came forward. Maude took Ellen's deathly cold hand in hers, without a word, and Charles stood at her side. He thought: The poor girl. I wish that damned prig hadn't insisted that he go alone in his car for her.

Then Christian came forward gravely, elegant in his black knickerbockers and black jacket and tie, his red hair like flames about his healthy face. Gabrielle came, too, in her crimson wool frock, her dark curls surmounted by a huge crimson ribbon, her mischievous olive-tinted face, with its pointed chin and black eyebrows, appropriately sober.

"Welcome home, Mama," said Christian, and Gabrielle echoed him. Their behavior was exemplary and dignified, with a proper shading of concern. Ellen looked at them, and looked for a long time. They came to her, waiting for an embrace, and Kitty stood aside, as did Maude.

Then Ellen's eyes, alive and filled with horror and despair and torment, flew to the stairway, and she cried out, "Jeremy, oh, Jeremy, Jeremy!" Before anyone could stop her she had raced to the stairway and was climbing it, crying over and over, "Jeremy, Jeremy! Where are you, Jeremy?"

She stumbled on her skirts, she staggered, but Miss Evans was now with her, and Maude, and they drew the agonized woman the rest of the way up, while that awful wailing continued and was not muffled until it was shut behind a distant door.

"Well," said Francis to the silent Charles Godfrey and Kitty. "I didn't expect that, I am sure. I thought she was —cured. How very distressing."

"Yes," said Charles.

"She didn't say a word to her children, who were waiting impatiently for her," said Francis in a cold voice. "That was hardly maternal."

Charles eyed him curiously. But he only said, "It will take a long time. Jeremy was Ellen's whole life, her whole reason for existing."

Kitty sighed. She looked at Ellen's children, whose faces were very calm. "Poor little ones," she said. "Such a disappointment."

Gabrielle burst into tears and came into Kitty's arms, and Christian was very serious. "Perhaps Mama should go back to that place," he said to Kitty.

"I don't think she should have ever left," said Kitty,

putting an arm over the boy's shoulder. "But we must be brave, mustn't we?"

Charles looked at the touching group under the chandelier and his face was very cynical, but it was obvious that Francis was moved. "Very sad," said Francis. "And very unnerving to the young. Ellen should have controlled herself. After all, it's been over two years."

"I've heard that grief has no fixed schedule," said Charles, and he left them and walked into the library and stood before the fire.

Kitty was comforting Ellen's children. "Now, dears," she said, "one must understand. Mama is not a very—strong—character, you know. She didn't have the advantages and disciplines you have had, nor the training in—correct—behavior. You must make allowances."

Francis did not like Kitty, with her little agate eyes and feline expression. He thought her extremely ugly, and was somewhat afraid of her acidulous tongue. But now he regarded her with approval.

"Mrs. Wilder is quite right, Christian, Gabrielle. Your mother lacks your background, your breeding, and self-control, all of which you have been taught. As Mrs. Wilder has said, you must make allowances."

Ellen's physician had been called and he had given her a strong sedative. He saw Miss Evans' competence at once, and was relieved. "I will arrange for a relief for you," he said to the nurse, but she shook her head.

"I've taken care of Mrs. Porter almost completely the last few months. She knows me and trusts me. A stranger would be hard for her to get used to."

Ellen lay on her bed where for many years she had slept with Jeremy, and she was in a drugged stupor. Maude sat near her. Maude and Miss Evans had undressed her and put on one of her silk-and-lace nightgowns. Maude had been shocked at the frailty of Ellen's body, its bony thinness, its transparent lifeless skin. She wanted to weep in compassion, and she stroked the bright long hair which streamed over the pillows, while Miss Evans unpacked Ellen's bag.

"She'll be all right, Mrs. Godfrey," said the nurse. "She's broken through, at last. Look. She isn't crying in her sleep now. She's accepted things."

"I'm glad she has you, Miss Evans," said Maude. The nurse was pleased. What a pretty lady this was, and so understanding.

"It'll take some time, Mrs. Godfrey," said Miss Evans. "We mustn't be discouraged. I was waiting for just that —her screaming and crying. Sooner than I expected." She hesitated, and met Maude's fine dark eyes. "Her children. They didn't seem very happy, did they, that their Mama was home?"

Maude, in her turn, paused. She had been about to make some cool and conventional remark, and noncommittal, about Ellen's children and their most apparent lack of distress. She said, and very quietly, "No, they didn't seem very happy. They are that sort— They prefer Mrs. Wilder. Miss Evans, Mrs. Porter has few friends. She really had no one but her husband."

Again the eyes of the two women met, with sadness and comprehension. Miss Evans said, "She has you, Mrs. Godfrey."

Maude averted her head. "But she never knew that, I am afraid. We must help her all we can."

They both looked down at the sleeping young woman, whose face was slack and expressionless, and Miss Evans was relieved that it no longer was twisted with anguish and tense with despair.

It was Christmas Eve. After dinner Maude and Charles and the children decorated the Christmas tree, which, for all its splendor, seemed forlorn to Maude's eyes. It stood in the living room, twinkling with candles and tinsel and colorful balls and delicate glass trinkets, with a star upon its highest point. Yet, it was forlorn.

Maude thought of the frightful war exploding all over Europe, and the men in trenches and dying in the scarlet lightning of guns. God have mercy, she thought, dear God, if You exist, have mercy.

Gay carols were ringing through the cold black night from the churches, and church doors were opening and streaming with the candlelight within and people were already beginning to drive up in automobiles for the midnight services, and the street was noisy with honkings and distant laughter.

God have mercy, thought Maude. That is all we can ask of You now. Mercy. We do not deserve it—but have mercy.

A group of carolers had gathered in the street, speckled with snow.

> "'*Tis the season to be jolly,*
>   *Tra la la*—"

29

On a particularly wild day of blizzards and gales Francis Porter visited Charles Godfrey in the latter's offices. There was a natural antipathy between the two men, an alienation of personalities. Charles greeted his visitor with cool courtesy and shook hands briefly with him, while his probing gray eyes expressed their curiosity at what Charles could only call "a visitation." It seemed incredible to Charles that this man was the cousin of Jeremy Porter, who had tremendous vitality and convictions and profound realism.

It was a January afternoon of storm; snow was plastered everywhere on the sides of buildings and on doors, and windows trembled under the assault of the wind. "A very nasty day," remarked Charles, as the two men sat down before the fire in the office. "Brandy? Or a scotch, Francis?"

"I do not drink," said Francis with an offensive formality which implied that Charles was a drunkard. Amused, Charles went to a cabinet and helped himself to a whiskey and soda. He sat down again, slowly, and wondered again why Francis had come to see him. Francis sat straight and stiff in his chair, his thin white hands clenched on the arms, his manner unbending and severe. His spectacles glittered in the mingled firelight and lamplight, and his mouth was a pale and ascetic slash in his lean face. His expression, as usual, was severe and condemning. I wonder if he ever had a mistress, Charles thought. I doubt it.

No woman could lie easily in a bed with this man. He has no blood, no real life, for all he is an hysteric.

"I will not take up much of your time, Charles," said Francis in his toneless voice, which, however, always threatened an impending violence. Charles inclined his head politely, and waited. "I know what it is to be a busy lawyer."

He paused. He looked about the large warm office, his face expressing his disapproval of the luxury of it, paneled walls and Aubusson rug, walnut and mahogany and framed pictures, and rich draperies. Then he said, "You are the guardian of my late cousin's children. You and your office are the executors of his estate."

"True," said Charles with a quickening of interest. "Your late father was also an executor, and would be now if he had lived."

"Jeremy should have named me also," said Francis, glancing at Charles as if the latter were to blame. Charles said nothing; he waited.

"I am not here to question your administration of Jeremy's estate," said Francis. "I am here to consult you about it, however. With the exception of their grandfather, Edgar Porter, I am their sole remaining male relative. Naturally, their welfare is of importance to me. Their mother, of course, is incompetent to judge what is best for them, their future, and their inheritance on her death. You have, no doubt, discovered that for yourself."

"Ellen is an inexperienced lady, I admit," said Charles. "Few ladies understand law and the administration of estates, and that is unfortunate—for them. But we are doing our best for Ellen, and her children. We have become heavily invested in munitions—though it was a little against my conscience."

Francis' rigid face quickened. "Then you know we will soon be at war with Germany?"

"I hope not. That would be a calamity for America, and for all the world, for that matter. Without our interference these past two years, such as sending munitions to England against ethical international law, and violating all the laws of neutrality, the war in Europe would have been over months ago. Was it not Wilson who practically forbade the King of England and the Kaiser to meet and settle on peace terms? Yes. And did he not say openly that it would be himself who would conclude the war?

Yes. Extraordinary, for a neutral American President. One wonders who directed him." He studied Francis keenly.

Francis stared at the fire and his spectacles glittered fiercely. He said, "You are forgetting the *Lusitania*."

"No, I do not forget. Who induced those hundreds of American tourists to sail on a British ship loaded with contraband, despite the pleas of the German Embassy? Yes, military contraband, for England. Against all the laws of neutrality. It is just a conjecture, of course, but who wants America to engage in foreign entanglements, despite our traditions; and for what nation's benefit? I do not think, as Jerry did not think, that it was for the benefit of either England or Germany."

Francis smiled superbly. "I am sorry, Charles, but your thoughts are as fantastic as were those of my late cousin. I myself know the President well. I have often dined at the White House. He is all for peace—"

"Such as practically forbidding the King and the Kaiser to meet openly and define terms for peace?"

"He has excellent advisers. They certainly know what they are doing."

"Oh, I am sure of that!" said Charles.

"They know all about the ambitions of the Kaiser and the bestiality of the Germans—"

"And no doubt the bestiality of the Allies, too, who have committed their own atrocities, and worse. As for ambitions—there is something not yet shown which has its own terrible ambitions."

Again Francis quickened. He turned partly in his chair to face Charles, who was looking at him with a formidable expression. "Mysteries!" he said. "Who could possibly gain—from all this?"

"I have an idea," Charles said, and rose to fill his glass again. His usually steady heart was beating with rage and hate. He said, as he poured the whiskey, "Millions of us are doing our best to keep America out of war. Whether we shall succeed or not, I do not know. I am afraid we don't have much influence." He turned back and sat down. "We were speaking of Jeremy's estate?"

"Yes." There was a stain of sharp scarlet on Francis' cheekbones. "There are certain extravagances which I think should be overcome, for the sake of the children's inheritance."

"Such as what?"

"The big house on Long Island. The number of servants in the house in New York: a houseman, Cuthbert, a cook, three maids, and a handyman. This is all a waste of money. Ostentation. It is necessary for Ellen to have some supervision, but why a registered nurse? One of the house-maids could do as well. It is not as if Ellen were bed-ridden. And there is Groton—very expensive and class-conscious—for the boy. He would do as well in one of our New York public schools, as would Gabrielle, the girl. There is also a permanent staff at the Long Island house. And a chauffeur. This is now no era for a vulgar display of riches, and the heedless spending of money. It antagonizes—"

"Who?"

"The American people. These are new days—"

"Ah."

"I do not understand you, Charles. You are supposed to be a prudent administrator."

"Let me put this clearly, Francis. Jeremy was a rich man. His estate is very large. His family is living as he desired them to live. The people in the employ of his houses are paid well. What if they were thrown out of work?"

"They could be more valuable, as workers, in other fields."

"Such as factories, no doubt. And on the land. They might object to that."

"Not if they were educated to believe that their labor is more worthy in other occupations. Besides, their present work is demeaning, degrading, without social significance."

Charles gave a short laugh. "No honest work is either demeaning or degrading."

"Certainly some work is. A woman who washes a rich man's dinner dishes would have more dignity in a factory."

"Why don't you ask Ellen's servants for themselves?"

Francis flushed again. "The people do not know what is best for them! They must be guided, taught, for their own best interests, and to serve their country."

"What country?" asked Charles. "Or what system of government?"

Francis clenched his hands on the arms of his chair. "You speak in riddles."

"Now, Francis, you and I know we do not speak in riddles, so don't try to diddle me. By the way, what do you mean by 'social significance'?"

"Working for the welfare of all, of course."

"That is against human nature, and against sanity. When a man works well for himself he benefits everybody. But to force him to work for others is an insult to his human integrity, his individuality, and his innate drive for excellence. It is also involuntary servitude, and I believe there is a constitutional prohibition against that. We have become a great and prosperous and free nation because the multitudes have worked for themselves, competing in all fields. Competition is the machinery for prosperity for all. Surely you don't want to abrogate prosperity?" Charles smiled.

When Francis did not reply, Charles asked, "What do you mean when you say the people do not know what is best for them?"

"History has proved that."

"On the contrary, history has proved, by way of America, for example, that the people well know what is best for them, and that is why they suspect politicians—and others. I hope to God they will continue to suspect."

A sudden flash of vindictiveness passed over Francis' thin features. Charles said, "You think that you, for instance, know what is best for the American people?"

"I am an educated man and a sociologist and a student of government. The masses are ignorant and debased and stupid."

Charles laughed. "You tell your constituents that! I know."

"My constituents," said Francis with a flush of cold anger, "are not the masses."

"I know," said Charles. "And that is the danger. We are getting nowhere, however, though I see we understand each other. As the executor of Jeremy's estate I will not consent to eliminate what you call 'extravagances.' "

"I must protest. These are the days for prudent humility, not display."

"In short, the days for drab equality and pretense of moral concern." Charles glanced at his watch. "I'm sorry, but I have a client almost immediately. When do you return to Washington?"

Francis said, "Soon. I have been invited to hold a prominent position during Mr. Wilson's next inauguration in March."

They shook hands formally, and parted. Charles puffed at his pipe for a few moments, frowning. Then he went to his desk. He glanced at his calendar. January 22, 1917. He put in a call to Washington, for a certain Senator, not of New York. While he waited he leaned back in his chair and thought.

Eventually the Senator answered, and very cautiously. "The gentleman," he said, referring to the President, "addressed the Senate today in a mood of belligerency, directed not exactly to the Senate but to other—certain—nations, if you understand me. Yes. He arrogantly demanded a 'peace without victory.' He intimated American force if the—antagonists—did not comply at once with his orders. He said it was not to be a 'private peace.' America must participate and lay down the terms."

"Good God," said Charles.

"Indeed, Charles. There's worse to come. He spoke in imperial terms, almost like a conqueror. He spoke of a pet idea of his, 'the League to Enforce Peace,' his own invention. He seemed to believe that both the British Empire and the German Empire were naughty territories of the United States, small fiefdoms who must not question the King's edicts. You can imagine how this will be received by the two empires. He implied that he was to be the super-peacemaker, the enforcer, all by himself. If not — The threat was there—directed mainly to Germany—that if his terms were not met he would sever diplomatic relations with Germany, which will delight England, of course, and cause the war to continue."

"Which is the general program," said Charles. "What was the reaction of the Senate?"

"High approval from those we both know of, and anger from those who are beginning to get a vague idea of whom is behind all this, the many whoms. But the gentleman, naturally, has no suspicion of them; he is only their mouthpiece."

"So, despite the true sentiment of the American people, we will be in the war."

"As you said, Charles, that is the program. By the way, I have some more news for you. Lenin is very active in Switzerland now, feverishly active, consolidating his Marxist forces. His next plan is to go to Germany, almost immediately, where, as an aristocrat and an intellectual and a linguist, he will be most welcome by certain— 'groups.' If I were the Kaiser I'd order his assassination. But the Kaiser, too, is an innocent, as is Franz Joseph. It is sufficient for the Kaiser that Lenin has denounced the war as 'a trade war.' It is amazing how these intellectuals can combine truth with lies, and make the lies effective. Your New York bankers, as you know, are financing Lenin; he moves with a rich entourage."

"And the bankers are financed by others infinitely more powerful."

The Senator sighed. "There is nothing we can do except oppose our entrance into the war—which will be futile. 'There is a tide in the affairs of men,' and nations. I wouldn't be a day younger, Charles."

"Nor I." Charles brooded. "Well, it seems we are to have a series of Genghis Khans and proletariat imperialists and powerful 'elite' planners. God help the people of America. Yet, perhaps we deserve it with our complacency and our optimism and our belief that this is the best of all possible worlds. If I had any power I'd force the optimists to face reality in its bleakest aspects, but that is something the optimists refuse to do. They shrink from it."

After the conclusion of his call he thought with gratitude that he had no sons. He considered Francis Porter, who was now very influential in Congress and who had delivered many speeches, placed in the *Congressional Record*, concerning the "monstrous imperialism" of the German Empire, and America's lack of "courage and fortitude" in not "confronting the dragon at once." He had many supporters.

Charles also thought of Jeremy Porter, who had died because of his knowledge and his attempted exposure of the enemies of mankind. Charles winced. He had no desire to die as terribly, and as futilely, as Jeremy had died. He turned his attention to the work on his desk as the day darkened and the storm increased.

Ellen cowered before the fire in the library this cold February day, with its shining white sky and brilliant air. Kitty Wilder sat near her, busy with the tea tray and pastries which Cuthbert had brought. Kitty's appetite was enormous; she could devour food in vast quantities all

day long and never attain flesh. Her spirit consumed it,
feverishly. Her dark face was lined and avid. She bent
over the tray, voluptuous murmurs in her throat, considering every delicious morsel like a woman in love, her
clawlike hands hovering. Her agate eyes were desirous.
"Um, um, good," she crooned. She licked a finger delicately. "Really, Ellen," she said, "Cuthbert, though he is
very old, is a wonderful pastry cook. Why don't you
have one of these?" But she snatched at another cake and
thrust it eagerly into her mouth, as if Ellen had threatened
to take it first.

"I'm not hungry, Kitty," said Ellen in her dull voice.

"Um," Kitty said, and pounced on still another cake.
Her eyes glistened with lewdness and she raised her eyes
in ecstasy. She was always hungry; nothing could satisfy
her avarice. Her lips were white with cream. "Would you
like me to stay for dinner, dear?"

"Yes," Ellen said, and pushed a lock of her hair from
her thin cheek.

"What have Cuthbert and your cook in mind?"

"I don't know," said Ellen. Kitty looked at her with
contempt. Bread and cheese and a slice of salt pork and
a cup of weak tea—that was Ellen's preference, no doubt.
"Ellen, you must really try to eat and regain your strength.
You owe that to your children. What would Jeremy think
of you now? You refuse to get well." She paused. "You
make me very sad, Ellen. You must strive to live again."

Ellen was silent. She thought of what Kitty had said,
and her old guilt returned. Her eyes filled with tears, and
the thick agony in her heart was like an iron fist. She
looked at the large, almost demolished tray of sweets
and for an instant she was disgusted by Kitty's greed. She
immediately quenched this thought and her guilt increased.
Kitty said, her eyes fixed on the tray, "Why don't you ring
for Cuthbert and find out what he and the cook have
prepared? You really should take an interest, Ellen."

Ellen pulled the bell rope and Cuthbert entered. "Cuthbert," said Ellen, "Mrs. Wilder would like to know what
we have for dinner."

Cuthbert glanced at Kitty with restrained distaste, and
then at Ellen with compassion. The poor lady's mind had
returned, but she ate very little and was always very listless and exhausted.

"A shrimp bisque, a cold lobster salad, fresh broiled

trout, a joint of veal with herbs, vegetables, hot French rolls, white wine, fruit, and a torte, madam. An Austrian torte, with warm apricot marmalade, and whipped cream and a chocolate icing."

Kitty's eyes again glistened. Ellen had heard with apathy. "Very good, Cuthbert," she said.

"In one hour, madam?"

Kitty coquettishly hugged her stomach and leered at Cuthbert seductively. "I may starve before then!" she laughed. Cuthbert withdrew. "It's this weather," said Kitty. "It makes me so hungry, I could eat everything in sight."

So I see, Ellen thought, and once more quenched the uncharitable thought. The fragrance of the tea and the cakes made her ill. Kitty seized still another cake after first regarding it with smiling pursed lips as though she thought herself naughty. She no longer wore the pompadour of her youth. Her lightless black hair was puffed out in immense clusters over her ears. She said, "I am thinking of having my hair bobbed like Irene Castle. Do you think it's extreme, Ellen?"

"I never thought about it," said Ellen. She wore a thin black wool dress from Worth with a string of pearls which Jeremy had given her. She wore but one other piece of jewelry, her wedding ring. Kitty was wearing red velvet with a tight long skirt, a "hobble skirt." Rubies shone in her ears, to match her painted lips. As she chewed, her huge white teeth glittered and clamped. She said to herself: Do you ever think about a single thing, you vulgar idiot?

"Is that Maude Godfrey and her husband coming to dinner, Ellen?"

"No, their little girl has the Spanish flu. They have a bad time getting servants these days, Kitty. The people are all in the factories working for Preparedness."

Kitty sighed happily. "Well, that's prosperity, preparing for war. We'll soon be in it, you know."

Ellen said, and for the first time showed animation, "Jeremy knew it was coming. He fought terribly—it did no good."

"You can't go against fate, Ellen. Besides, we must overthrow the Kaiser and all that he represents. Just a beast."

She added, "I detest that Maude. So sly. Whatever possessed a man like Charles Godfrey to marry a mere servant?"

Ellen's sunken cheeks suddenly flushed. "She wasn't exactly a servant, Kitty. She was a governess, and a lady."

Kitty shrugged. "I thought you didn't like her."

"I—well, no, I never did. But it is not her fault. There is just something about her—"

"Sly," repeated Kitty. "I know her kind. Servants watch everything; they have no minds of their own and so are interested in the affairs of those they serve. It fills up their empty souls, and their malice." She glanced cunningly at Ellen. Ellen still had Miss Evans and a personal maid, yet her red hair was always disordered, Kitty thought, and she never used paint for her lips or cheeks. She looks like a corpse, thought Kitty with satisfaction, and shows her years. Why does she lie about her age? She's almost mine. Kitty refused to believe that Ellen was only thirty.

Kitty's husband, Jochan, was highly regarded by Charles Godfrey, and was still a member of Jeremy's law firm. For all his gentleness he was a shrewd lawyer. His kind mistress had presented him with a son five years ago, and he was proud of the boy. Moreover, his good fortune had returned, and Kitty thought of that with contentment. Then she said, "You're very lucky, Ellen, to have Francis Porter so concerned with you, and so helpful. I hope you appreciate him."

"Oh, I do," Ellen replied. "He's very thoughtful. The children are fond of him, and he of them. When he's in town he visits us often. He's quite a comfort." She moved uneasily in her chair. "But he wants Christian and Gabrielle to attend our public schools in the city. Jeremy would not like that."

"He is thinking of saving you money, Ellen, and that's not wrong."

"Charles says I don't need to save money. He knows what Jeremy would want."

Kitty and Francis were *en rapport*. Kitty cultivated him sedulously. One never knew. And Francis was a powerful Congressman. The fact that Jochan absurdly disliked him was of no consequence. One must court the powerful, something Jochan still did not understand.

A few months ago Kitty had given Francis a long and serious consideration. He was rich; he was powerful; he was frequently quoted in the New York newspapers, though the *Times* found him slightly ridiculous and had implied this in sedate prose. It was rumored that he would soon seek the nomination of his party for the Senate. He was not married. He was thought to be a "great catch" in the society news. Though not physically attracted to him, Kitty had attempted a very subtle and skillful seduction of him, for her own purposes. He had not responded. She had some obscene thoughts about him, then, for Kitty knew all the darknesses of the human soul. She directed an attack on him in another direction: She pretended to support all his policies and idealisms and ideas. She agreed with him heartily when he spoke, though she laughed inwardly. She was enthusiastic when he was palely enthusiastic. She was grim when he was grim; she denounced what he denounced. She insisted she had always been a feminist. As much as possible he began to warm towards her. A lady with intelligence was a rare phenomenon.

When Francis asserted, at a dinner party she and Jochan gave for him, that America must go at once to the rescue of the embattled Allies, most of the guests looked at him coldly and condemningly, including the amiable Jochan. But Kitty cocked her head and said in her insistent and emphatic voice, "Francis does know what the sentiment in Washington is; he is privy to counsels we never hear of, and he has Importance and is a Leader. We only know what we read in the press, and it is cautious. But Francis Knows what he Knows, so his opinion must come from a source hidden from us."

Jochan, who had never been noted before for sarcasm or bitterness, said, "Perhaps that is the trouble." His usually kind eyes had hardened on Francis. Kitty pretended to meek dejection at her husband's words, though the guests smiled amusedly. Francis had not been amused. But he saw Kitty's sympathetic eyes and was grateful. Thereafter, whenever he encountered her he felt that he was in the presence of an understanding friend. A little later Kitty mused on marrying him. Divorce was not quite the stigma it had been in her youth, and she despised Jochan. She now knew all about his mistress and his son. At first she had laughed when Jochan had hinted at divorce, for it pleased her to thwart him and make him miserable and prevent him from marrying the woman he loved, who had been a pretty member of the Floradora chorus.

She might not be able, she would think, to seduce Francis into her bed, for he had the austere tight air of a Puritan. (She even suspected that he was a virgin.) But marriage? That would be a holy and sacred thing to him, or at the very least "proper." She had long ago discovered that the "reformers" were not full-blooded men with the sexual power of most males. They were priggish, in the main, inclined to a womanishness under all that icy violence they often displayed in their conversations and their writings. They had the innate and relentless brutality of the Puritan, but it was mental and not physical, though Kitty had no doubt that if the opportunity ever came to them they would enforce their ideas with death and oppression, and these without a single qualm, and only a conviction of righteousness. At heart, they were sadists, and Kitty had read enough to know that sadists were usually impotent men and if they possessed any voluptuousness at all it was closely allied with cruelty and hatred, and not buoyantly of the flesh.

As their friendship increased, Kitty thought more and more of marriage to him. A Senator's wife! Perhaps, later, even a First Lady! She began to hint to him of her own political influence and how she had been much admired in Washington and often invited to the White House. Francis had listened with increasing interest, and made pompous and approving remarks and had even flattered her, not only with his attention but with comments on her astuteness and knowledge. Once he had actually said, "You are a charming lady," and had colored as if he had made an improper remark.

There was one thing Kitty did not know, that he was in love with Ellen Porter and wanted to marry her. For did he not speak always with disapproval and criticism of Ellen? He confided to Kitty that Ellen really needed a guardian herself. She was unworldly; she was naïve; she was not truly educated and had no real intellect. But, after all, one must remember her Unfortunate Background. She needed Guidance. ("Guidance" was one of his favorite words, and he used it often in referring to the Masses.) He approved of nothing Ellen did or timidly said. He thanked Kitty for her affection for "that poor young woman," and expressed his hope that Kitty would never desert her. Kitty could Influence her for the better, and soften her gauche manners and give her some Character, a trait she obviously did not possess in spite of all the tutors she had had and all the Advantages for many years. Kitty had bowed her head humbly and had whispered, "I try, I do truly try, Francis, though sometimes—" He had actually touched her thin arm in consolation for an instant.

She had some thoughts about his potency in bed. She doubted not only that he was potent but was capable of potency. It would be like being in bed with an icicle, she would laugh to herself. No matter. It could be endured and there were always other men. That Francis was capable of wild passion she did not believe, for all his secret intensity was reserved for Ellen, and was waiting.

So, while dining with Ellen tonight, and lovingly savoring the excellent dinner, Kitty continued with her conversation about Francis.

"I do wish, Ellen, that you would listen to Francis more. He has only your welfare at heart."

"I know, I know," said Ellen with humility. She had hardly touched the fine food and her chronic look of exhaustion increased. "He has always been so kind to me. He was the first person, outside of my aunt, who showed me any interest and concern. But I've told you that very often, Kitty. I can never forget it. But why should the children of Jeremy Porter go to a public school in the city?"

"It's more democratic," Kitty said, and again laughed in herself at Francis.

For the first time Ellen actually smiled spontaneously. "Jeremy did not believe in democracy. He thought it pretension on the part of the rich, and a trap for the poor, who were envious and resentful. He used to say that democracy was like the beds in Sodom and Gomorrah."

Kitty was puzzled. "Are you joshing me, Ellen? What in the world does that mean?" She was annoyed that Ellen had made a reference alien to her.

"Well, it seems that in Sodom and Gomorrah they had beds of only one length, and when they caught a stranger in their midst, or an enemy, they would cut off his head, or his feet, to make him fit their beds."

"How uncivilized," said Kitty.

"That's what Jeremy said of democracy," and Ellen was smiling again. "In some ways I think Jeremy was a monarchist. He said republics never endured; he was quoting

Aristotle. They declined into democracies and degenerated into despotisms."

"How un-American," said Kitty with tartness.

"No. Jeremy was a realist. And to many, he was a dangerous realist. That is why he was killed." Her eyes filled with tears; she was not conscious of them. One or two slowly rolled down her white cheeks. She stared into the distance and her throat underwent a spasm.

"And what, may I ask, was his idea of an ideal state?" asked Kitty, making a mouth.

"He said it wasn't possible, for men are not and never will be ideal. The most we can do, he would say, was to follow the Constitution and outlaw anyone who violated it."

As Francis was always denouncing the Constitution as "an enemy of the Masses," and a hindrance to perfect justice, Kitty began to reflect. Of course, Francis Porter was an obvious fool, she thought. But—he was rich and powerful and that overcame any folly. She said, "How extreme of Jeremy. Ellen, you should listen more to Francis. He is a very brilliant man."

Ellen moved restlessly in her chair. "I suppose so," she said in her lifeless voice. "But I am a woman and am not really much interested in politics. That is a man's province, not a woman's."

Kitty looked at her curiously. "What do you, Ellen, really live for, if you lack interest in so much?"

"I live for Jeremy's children," said Ellen.

Who despise you, thought Kitty. And why should they not? "Very exemplary," she said aloud. "But you should have a life of your own, Ellen."

Ellen looked at her, and her great blue eyes were stark with anguish.

"My life died with Jeremy."

"Now, that—" Kitty began. But Ellen was struggling to her feet, her face stark with suffering. "Kitty, please forgive me, please excuse me. I—I must go upstairs. Forgive me. I am not feeling very well." She pressed her hand over her mouth and ran from the room, while Kitty stared after her.

Well, thought Kitty, that was a low-bred demonstration, my girl! But what else could I expect from a menial?

Alone, she devoted herself to the delicious Austrian torte and her reflections of Francis Porter.

In her bedroom, Ellen threw herself upon her bed, clutching an old coat of Jeremy's to her breast, soundless with grief and despair. It took some time for Miss Evans to soothe her, induce her to relinquish the coat, undress, and take a sedative.

30

In early February 1917, Charles Godfrey visited his friend the Senator, in Washington. Charles had gone reluctantly; he constantly remembered what had happened to Jeremy Porter. He, Charles, had no desire to be either a martyr or unpopular, for he had the Boston Irish cynicism, though he possessed the Irish tendency to belligerence and indignation. Moreover, though he was married to an English lady he adored, he did not like the Sassenach in general. But Maude was different; she believed with him that it was to America's advantage to stay out of the European war, and she had no passionate attachment to the politics of England. Wise and without illusions, she understood that it was only on the surface that this was a trade war. It had deeper and more terrible implications. Often she said, "If Jeremy had not been so reckless he might have lived to have had a greater influence than mere rage and disgust. Leaders must exercise prudence, too."

Charles, who was unusually prudent, said, "In war there should be no prudence, that is, if you expect to win." To which Maude had replied, "In love and war all things are permissible." Then she had added, "In the real revolution that underlies this war only bravery and agression and courage will prevail. Prudence, a euphemism for self-interest, makes cowards of us all."

Charles had said, "They are too strong for us. We have been sleeping, and we'll continue to sleep."

Maude said, "I am thinking of the old poem of Horatius

on the bridge. A handful of Romans was powerful enough
to defeat the whole army of the enemy."

Charles had laughed with some bitterness. "I'm afraid
we have no 'old Romans' in America any longer. If we
do have they have internecine quarrels. But there are no
quarrels in Hell. And that is its strength."

"It seems to me, Charles, that after the French Revolution, Hell indeed had its quarrels. They were always guil-
lotining each other in their fight for power. When Hell
falls out humanity can profit."

"If there's any humanity remaining to profit. Usually,
there comes the Dark Age of chaos and anarchy, and the
whole horrible business starts up again."

"Well," said Maude, "there is nothing anyone can do
to change human nature. That is the one immutable, in
spite of the idealists, and Rousseau. For better or worse,
we are what we are."

Charles thought for a while and when he spoke Maude
did not consider his remark to be irrelevant: "In the old
Roman religion—or was it Greek?—Justice was the last
goddess to leave the world and left it to its own destruction. She never returned."

He went to Washington to talk with the Senator. It was
a grim and stormy day of blizzard and wind, and Charles
remembered an old Irish saying that when nature was
convulsed man was convulsed also. He had never seen
such a storm in Washington before, so vicious and formidable; it was also a city in which the Spanish flu appeared
to be more virulent than anywhere else. He saw ambu-
lances and hearses everywhere, crowding the streets.
Through the gray-white swirling haze of snow the looming monumental buildings appeared mere trembling
façades, with nothing behind them, and he gloomily wondered if the illusion were not true. Union Square, in that
shivering haze, was populated with a multitude of little
black figures which scurried, bent against the power of
the storm. There was such a sinister activity in the city
now, Charles thought, and it appeared subterranean, and
curiously feverish. All my imagination, he told himself,
but there was an aura here, pervasive and dangerous. His
Irish soul perceived it, for were not the Irish strangely
perceptive? They could smell snow long before it appeared
and disaster impending in an atmosphere of tranquillity.

Charles had difficulty in the storm in finding a taxicab

and had to wait a considerable time. The trains were vomiting out streams of avid-eyed men, all with brief-cases, all craning their heads forward with the searching expressions of men who were almost unbearably excited. Many reminded him uneasily of Francis Porter; their faces had zealous gleams discernible even in that shifting haze of snow. He no longer deluded himself that it was all his "imagination." Scores of voices, muffled partly by the gale, came to him in bursts of fervency. Though it was only three o'clock in the afternoon the streets and the square were dark and lamps were already beginning to pour their blurred lights on the hurrying throngs. Charles, finally snaring a cab, with numbed hands tightly fastened some loose buttons which held the canvas curtains of the vehicle. He was driven to the Senator's office in the Senate Office Building, after long and considerable sliding on the fast-freezing snow. Washington, always crowded with automobiles, appeared far more crowded than usual.

The Senate Office Building's corridors and rooms were filled with milling politicians and lobbyists and men who were obviously financiers and businessmen. They talked with vehemence in the halls, waving cigarettes and cigars and grasping the latest newspapers which carried very large black headlines. They caught each other, engaged in loud or furtive fast conversations, nodded, went on to other groups. If any felt dismay or anxiety or despair or appre-hension, it was not evident. It is like an uproarious fiesta, thought Charles with bitterness. He had to push his way determinedly through the mass, and many glanced at him, but then, not recognizing him, glanced restlessly away, waiting to pounce on friends or acquaintances. A blue fog of smoke hung over everything.

Charles' friend the Senator seemed strangely isolated in his very quiet offices. His staff was subdued, wore gloomy expressions, and spoke in hushed voices as if something direful had happened. There were no military men swarming here, as there were in the rest of the build-ing. "I am being ostracized," said the Senator as he shook hands with Charles, and he smiled faintly but without amusement. An aide brought them whiskey and soda, then left the gentlemen alone. "Did you hear the latest about our valiant President? He not only wants to name the terms of any peace, but will demand a superstate, a world union of 'all nations,' no doubt with himself or the

American government presiding with absolute power. Sometimes I think he has lost his mind."

"No," said Charles. "He is just a radical, and from what I've overheard in this building just now, the whole damned place is teeming with radicals."

"All rich, too," said the Senator in a dry hard voice. "Well, we know what we know." He gave Charles a cigar and lit it thoughtfully, his handsome face tight, his silken white hair slightly ruffled, his eyes exhausted. "Charles, we're not all exigent criminals here in this building, among the Senators. Many know what we know, and are resisting. But now the corruption of the sound middle class has begun, they who are always idealistic, somewhat simple, believing in the innate good of humanity. They are being aroused by the hugest propaganda machine I've ever seen, aroused against Germany. Millions are demanding the 'end to the Hun.' They're that simple, in spite of all they have been told about this war. But the working class is not that deluded, thank God. Still, it is hopeless —you and I know that."

"I thought you could tell me something I can do myself."

The Senator shook his head, then smiled again. "What, you the prudent Irishman who doesn't want to be a martyr? What changed your mind?"

"Thinking, a little, about Jeremy Porter. I don't want to pledge my 'life, my fortune, and my sacred honor' in any useless attempt to save my country. But I want to do something."

"Any ideas of what that something should be?"

"I've heard of various organizations who are working against American participation in this war. Which one, of the largest, would you recommend?"

The Senator considered him. "There is our Church. The Church, which is the wisest of all, understands what is behind this war, and is, as diplomatically as possible, opposing it."

"Too diplomatically, Senator. But then, the Church has to be careful. America is no longer a mission country, but the Church is still widely hated here. We want no fresh outburst of violence against her in America."

"Prudence, prudence," murmured the Senator with satire. "Sometimes, in the name of God and humanity, there has to be an end to prudence."

" 'He who fights and runs away, will live to fight another day,' " quoted Charles.

"Sometimes he runs too far, and the battle for survival has already been lost when he returns to fight again. Remember, from Shakespeare, when a general ran away and then returned to congratulate his king on a victory? 'Hang yourself, brave Crillon,' said the king, 'we fought—and you were not there!' " The Senator's voice rose, now impassioned. "I think we should say that to the prudent—when they return, softly smiling. But then it will be too late, even for hanging."

He stared down at his desk. "I will tell you the latest developments here, but in confidence, though." He laughed abruptly. "There I am myself using 'prudence'! As you know, Germany has been recently using unrestricted submarine warfare against our alleged 'merchant ships,' which are carrying contraband to England, arms and such—though we are still supposed to be a neutral country. Our government is as 'neutral' as Satan! The Kaiser has said that if Wilson wants war—as he truly does—he can have it and let him make it. We will make it, and very soon, Charles. Within a few days Wilson will sever diplomatic relations with Germany and arm our so-called 'peaceful merchant ships,' all carrying munitions to England. I often wonder if the British King has any idea himself of what is behind all this. I doubt it. The conspirators in his own government keep him uninformed, I am sure. Still, he did try to make a peace with Germany, and would have succeeded if Wilson had not arrogantly interfered. But that is now history."

"I have noticed," said Charles, "that when any prominent man suggests an international conspiracy is at work, actively now, politicians jeer at him and suggest—what is the term the alienists are now using?—yes, paranoia. The American people don't want to believe in conspiracies; they want just to be 'happy,' and things kept simple and comprehensible. They want their nickelodeons and their 'full dinner pail,' and a car, if they can afford it, and a little cozy house and contented wife and children, and their beer and their card games and their sports and their firecrackers and their occasional slut, and something they call 'fun.' "

"It wasn't Nero who 'fiddled' when Rome burned," said the Senator. "It was the populace who did, until their own homes were afire."

"The common people are still more excited about Mary Pickford's romances than they are about the arsonists who are setting fire to their houses," said Charles.

The Senator laughed abruptly. " 'Bread and circuses.' It is the old story. It was designed that way. Keep the people's minds on their bellies, and their genitals, and you can eventually enslave them. Never let them think. Never let them know the truth. The politicians, and others, know that. Besides, I really don't believe they want to think or to hear the truth. Remember Cassandra? She tried to arouse her people in Troy, and I believe she met an unpleasant martyrdom. Well, again, there is nothing we can do, Charles."

"Christ also met an unpleasant end," said Charles. "Still, He aroused a whole world—"

The Senator shook a finger at him, and his face was grave. "Let me make a prophecy, Charles. The next war will be against Judeo-Christianity, though it won't be called that. Religion, as you know yourself, stands between man and his oppressors. Ergo, religion will eventually be attacked, ridiculed, and rendered impotent. Perhaps not in my lifetime, but certainly in yours."

"I know, Senator. Marx called religion the opiate of the people."

The Senator sighed. "Well, I think it is practically over, unless we can make people realize who their enemies are. The conspirators. Lincoln knew that. I have his whole quotation here. Let me read it to you. The conspirators were beginning to be very active, even in his time:

" 'When we see a lot of framed timbers, different portions of which we know have been gotten out at difficult times and places and by different workmen—and when we see these timbers joined together, and see they exactly make the frame of a house or a mill, all the tenons and mortises exactly fitting, and all the lengths and proportions of the different pieces exactly adapted to their respective places and not a piece too many or too few—not omitting even scaffolding—or if a single piece be lacking, we can see the place in the frame exactly fitting and prepared to yet bring such piece in—in such a case we find *it is impossible to not believe the conspirators all understood one another from the beginning, and all worked upon a common plan drawn up before the first lick was struck.*' Well, Charles, the people will never 'believe.' "

Charles stared somberly at the snow-painted windows of the Senator's office. "Still," he said, "we have the Constitution—"

The Senator's laugh was both derisive and despairing. "The coming attack of the conspirators will be on the Constitution. Jefferson? Yes, he said: 'In questions of power *then let no more be heard of confidence in man but let us bind him down from mischief by the chains of the Constitution.*' The trouble is that the Constitution will soon—perhaps even in my own lifetime—become the target of the conspirators. It will be interpreted by wicked men, in the U.S. Supreme Court, to the advantage of the conspirators and the corruption of the American people. And what will the American people do? Whimper a little, then go back to their nickelodeons and their beer. Perhaps, in the long run, slavery is what they deserve. Why kill ourselves desperately trying to inform them? They just don't want to be disturbed in their animal comforts."

"That is what such people as Francis Porter believe, too, Senator."

"That is one thing we patriots and the conspirators have in common, Charles. We understand human nature. We would save it from itself. The conspirators would use it for themselves."

He looked again at his desk. "I don't know what good it is to tell you something else, Charles. Russia is now being infiltrated by rich and active American agents of the conspiracy—to overthrow the Czar and bring Communism to Russia. It should succeed in the near future. The Russian Communists are fully financed by our American bankers and financiers. You aren't surprised? Of course not. We have known about this for a long time. Russia will soon make a separate peace with Germany, and then all hell will be let loose."

"I think," said Charles, "that I will go into a monastery."

"You won't be safe there, either. No. Teach your children what it is to be an American. Perhaps they will learn. Perhaps, they too will be corrupted. All we can do now is to oppose evil as much as possible, and to pray."

He groaned. "Do you know what Wilson is now calling men like you and me? 'Willful.' In short, we oppose the conspiracy and love our country and would preserve our independence and our liberties."

"And he is against all that. He wants America to be

part of a superstate, as you've said yourself, Senator. Men like him hate independence of thought and valor and defense of country. Yes, I think he is mad. He wants an end to nationalism and pride and hegemony."

"I don't think he even knows what he wants. There is the deadly Colonel House, his friend and adviser, you know, who is part of the conspiracy. To be innocent is to destroy yourself. Man must always be on guard against his fellow man, and never believe in his avowed 'love and trust.' Those are the passwords of the conspirators, who neither love nor have concern, themselves, for their fellow men, but just for their own plots against humanity."

"We are a very nasty and dangerous species, aren't we?"

"Christ, and His Church, never denied that, Charles."

Charles dined with the Senator that night but both men were wretched, knowing what they knew. The Senator raised his wineglass and said with somberness, " 'Eat, drink, and be merry—for tomorrow we die.' "

The impotence Charles felt haunted him the rest of his life. The issue remained with the American people, and the people all over the world. They would not assume their responsibility as men. They wanted comfort only and desired not to be disturbed. The end was inevitable: slavery. But how many wanted freedom, with its arduous demands? Slavery was death in life; it was also peace, as an animal has peace, with its daily ration of food and servitude and mindlessness and dependence on its masters. As Aristotle had said, "All that walks in the guise of men is not human." A human being, in the full sense of the word, was very rare in this world, and was also persecuted by the multitudes who "walk in the guise of humanity," yet are not men.

They were being taught to "love and trust." Yet Christ Himself had advised mankind to sell its cloak and buy a sword. The ancient Jews had understood that centuries before Christ. They protected themselves and their country and their families—with the sword, against oppressors. They knew that governments were not to be trusted, as Samuel the prophet had told them.

We could take a lesson from them, Charles would think. But no one listened. One heard hardly any truths now; but truth was not accepted. The people listened to the lumpen intelligentsia, the pretenders to intellect, bursting with fury and zeal, and spluttering with saliva.

Charles remembered his early school days when his copybooks were headed by aphorisms and platitudes in script (mostly admonishing), and all polished by time, and all shining with verity. But Rudyard Kipling remembered the "copybook headings," and only two years ago had published his poem about them. Charles recalled the ominous last stanza:

As sure as water will wet you, as sure as fire will burn,
The gods of the copybook headings with terror and
    slaughter return.

They were returning, one by one, and the skies were darkening with their looming presence.

Many Senators and Congressmen were aghast when President Wilson asked for authority to arm American merchant ships, which were carrying munitions and other contraband to "the Allies." Many protested that the American people were in no mood for any war, or overt actions inevitably leading to war. Angry debate began. But, also inevitably, Congress, in the lower house, passed a resolution, 403 to 13, the bill for arming merchant ships. The Senate, however, debated, led by eleven indomitable men, they themselves led by Senator La Follette. Before the end of the session, they filibustered, with the aim of delaying all action on the authority.

This enraged the majority of the Senators, who wanted war. (After all, some of them reasoned together, there was a depression increasing in the country; war would bring prosperity. Therefore, with adjournment threatening, and with adjournment a long if not permanent postponement of the desired authority to arm merchant ships, eighty-five of the ninety-six members of the Senate, simulating wrath and public virtue, signed a protest against the eleven Senators who stood in the way of war. Mr. Wilson joined in the protest, and so did Mr. Roosevelt—joyfully.

But the Senate was forced to adjourn, on March 4, 1917, for it was the end of the session. The authority had not been given. Mr. Wilson flew into a passion of invective, and cried: "In the immediate presence of a crisis unparalleled in the history of the country, Congress has been unable to act either to safeguard the country or to

vindicate the elementary rights of its citizens! More than
five hundred of the five hundred thirty-one members of the
two Houses were ready and anxious to act. But the Senate
was unable to act because a little group of willful men,
representing no opinion but their own, had determined
that it should not. They have rendered the great government of the United States helpless and contemptible."

He asked the Attorney General if he, the President, had
the right to call for the arming of merchant ships without
authorization from Congress. The Attorney General, smiling, assured the President that he did, indeed, have the
power. On March 9, this was done, to the confused dismay of the majority of the American people, and their
dread. German submarines promptly attacked.

Like a man newly rejuvenated, and full of elation and
hatred for Germany, Mr. Wilson summoned an extraordinary session of Congress, which would meet on April
17. But before that session three American merchant ships,
heavy with contraband for "the Allies," were destroyed
by German U-boats. With gleeful drama, Mr. Wilson, feeling vindicated and advised by Colonel House, called for
a special session of Congress "to receive a communication
concerning grave matters."

He was not happy to discover that Washington was
suddenly inundated by pacifist armies from all over the
country. They surrounded the Capitol, and cried for
peace. "This is outrageous, subversive," said Colonel
House. An escort of cavalry swept about the President's
vehicle to protect him from these anxious and frightened
crowds of men and women, who might, said Colonel
House, "annoy our President."

The Supreme Court, arrayed, solemnly occupied the
seats in front of the rostrum, Chief Justice White in the
center. Behind the court crowded the Cabinet. Behind
the Cabinet sat the diplomatic corps, among them M. Jus-
serand of France and Mr. Spring-Rice of Great Britain.
They, too, showed countenances of much solemnity, but
their eyes radiated their own elation.

Wilson stood before the momentous gathering and
said:

"The present German submarine warfare is a warfare
against mankind! It is a war against all nations, a challenge to mankind! . . . There is one choice we cannot

make, we are incapable of making—we will not choose the path of submission."

Chief Justice White leapt to his feet, openly smiling and weeping, and the entire Senate rose with him, applauding like thunder. And the tender spring rain rustled softly outside, remote and impersonal, unconcerned with human madness.

Within a few days the now turbulent country was faced with conscription. The rapture suddenly subsided when it was realized that the approaching war would not be fought solely with Mr. Wilson's grandiloquent phrases and passionate accusations, but with arms, and those arms would be carried by young American men, and those young men would die. But long before the actual conscription the machinery for its operation had been built and established, in secret, long before the people had even imagined that this was being done, almost completely without the knowledge of their representatives in Congress. It was a secret known practically only by the President, his Secretary of War, Mr. Baker, and Judge Advocate General, Enoch Crowder. Millions there were who wondered, confusedly, how such a vast system as the draft could come into being almost overnight, without any publicity whatsoever in the newspapers or any rumors. They believed, until the very last, that if there were a war it would be fought by a volunteer army.

Angry questions were raised in the House against conscription. Many exclaimed that they would not vote for the Draft Act. "Autocracy!" some Congressmen cried, and others denounced the draft as "Prussianization, the destruction of democracy, involuntary servitude, slavery." There were those who said that there would be riots all over the country—and several of those who declared this had been vociferous for war. They were overwhelmed with telegrams and letters from terrified constituents who were against the draft, and they had no answer. At the end they could only use the President's soothing phrases:

"The necessary men will be secured by volunteering as at present, until a resort to a selective draft is desirable, which possibly will not occur." He would then murmur, "Let us say that it is a personal obligation to serve your country, which no American will reject."

But the idea of a draft became increasingly unpopular. It was one thing to "denounce the Hun and his atrocities," and quite another to take up arms against him, in spite of the fact that America had declared war against Germany. Zeal and excitement and large black headlines in the newspapers, and "extras," and public shouts and millings in public places, and enthusiasm and denunciations and passionate wavings of the flag, and bands, and banning the German language in the public schools and renaming sauerkraut "liberty cabbage," and accusing neighbors of German ancestry of being "barbarians" and "subversive," were one thing. But it was quite another to have one's sons conscripted and sent to die in European trenches. "Victory gardens" in one's little meager backyard—accompanied by grinning at neighbors and jovially waving rakes and hoes, and laughter and a beer on the porch afterwards, were splendid and invigorating, and singing patriotic songs in the warm evenings of early summer was exciting and made people jubilant. But to watch a son or a brother or a husband forcibly marched off to war—probably to be slaughtered—was a bewildering and outrageous violation of traditional American independence and choice.

The President took counsel with Colonel House, that quiet and ambiguous man. He issued a public statement:

"I am exceedingly anxious to have the registration and selection by draft conducted under such circumstances as to create a strong patriotic feeling and relieve, as far as possible, the prejudice which remains to some extent in the popular mind against the draft. With this end in view I am using a vast number of agencies throughout the country to make the day of registration *a festival and patriotic occasion.* Several Governors and some mayors of cities are entering already heartily into this plan, and the Chamber of Commerce of the United States is taking it up with their affiliated bodies."

For the first time in their history the American people were subjected to a strictly foreign blandishment; propaganda by government. But millions of wives and mothers protested angrily, and in public. The Subversive Act was hastily passed. Those who objected to the draft, and foreign entanglements, were called "enemies of America, traitors, malcontents, cowards, and secret German sympathizers." The moving-picture industry almost overnight produced films depicting American wives and girl children being forcibly raped by monstrous German soldiers in the tender peace of their own households, in the cities of America, while their menfolk wallowed in their blood in the streets. Many were the newspapers who raised angry ridicule at all this—but, strangely, they were soon silenced. A Chicago newspaper did mention, in an editorial: "The day of freedom of the press is over. The press is now the creature of the government, to be used at will. Who is behind this real atrocity, this violation of American liberty, is known, but we dare not name them any longer." The newspaper soon went into bankruptcy.

The President, speaking of the draft, proclaimed: "Carried in our hearts as a great day of patriotic devotion and obligation, when the duty shall lie upon every man to see to it that the name of every male person of the designated ages is written on these lists of honor—"

The proclamation was signed and sealed by the President on May 18, 1917. As "honor" had always been the pride of Americans, very few were not bedazzled by words unctuously spoken and delivered with fervor. Those were threatened—and many arrested.

On June 5, 1917, a day called by the President "a joyous pilgrimage," every American male between the ages of twenty-one and thirty was required to register for the draft. The American spirit was now numbed by propaganda and overpowering and ceaseless exhortations from Washington. For the first time in its history the American people became terrified of its government, and that government's means of violence against objectors. The Europeanization of America, and Europe's oppressiveness and control of public opinion, had begun with a fanfare by suborned politicians and their secret masters, with much passing of gold and with coercion. "Liberty Bonds" issued by the government were sold in great quantities, and those who did not buy were accused of "hampering the war effort." Businessmen who did not conform were called "slackers." A War Industries Board suddenly appeared to force businessmen to observe certain restrictive regulations. Food, overnight, became "scarce." Those who objected, in the case of businessmen, were attacked in the newspapers and were punished by government.

It was not notable, at first, that those who understood what was taking place were furiously assaulted in print, and often in person, by the men who had a Socialist-Populist background in government, and in private life where they were influential, especially in New York and in Washington. When it was finally discovered it was far too late.

Tens of thousands of American women still objected and wept. They were called "mad," and many were incarcerated. But the majority of women walked and bustled about with stars in their eyes, and their young daughters were used as shameful and "patriotic" bait for hesitant young men to "show their manhood" and convince them the war was a tremendous adventure.

The American government, as designed by the Russian Communist Lenin, became the enthusiastic servant of the international conspiracy against the people of the world, and delivered them happily to their enslavers. Francis Porter made many eloquent speeches in Congress, and many of those speeches were incorporated in the *Congressional Record*. He was honored by the White House. This war, he said, was "an adventure of freedom against ancient enemies." He quoted Karl Marx profusely—without naming Marx. President Wilson said he was a magnificent patriot. He was beyond the draft age. He toured the country, selling Liberty Bonds, as did many other Congressmen and Senators. His face was constantly flushed with fervor, so that he appeared feverish, and his eyes behind their spectacles, glowed. He posed for newspapers. He was given a special aide who wrote his speeches. That aide was a secret member of the Communist Party. He thought Francis "a poor thing," but a weapon against the people of America. If he laughed at Francis, the laughter was behind closed doors where the enemy gathered.

"We have American politicians in the palms of our hands," the American aide, who was a very rich man himself, confided. "The prospects are limitless. We are on the way! As the Germans say, *'Der Tag.'*" Thinking of Francis again, he said, his thin face alight with gleeful malice, "What an innocent! But he and his kind serve our purpose. This autumn—"

That autumn of 1917 Russia withdrew from the war and the Bolsheviks savaged the Russian people—numbed, themselves, by war and desperation—into total slavery. The Russian people had never voted for Communism. It took only a few and cynical men to impose it on them, with the help of international financiers.

"But we," said the historical enemy, "will not have to force Socialism on other nations, as we did in Russia. They will vote for it, under the heroic phrases of 'equality and fraternity,' and 'social justice,' which sound so noble though they are only abstract ideas unequated with reality."

Charles Godfrey understood this as well as did the enemy. He said, quoting Jeremy Porter, " 'Sic transit America.' " But, he would think, perhaps that is all America deserves, after all. A nation is guilty of her own death. He decided that in no manner would he be a martyr. "A man has to live," he would remark defensively to himself. "Governments come and go, but men must survive, though why I don't know! What was it the Holy Bible mentioned? The strong tree was thrown down in the gale—but the meek grass bent uncomplainingly and lived."

However, though the expedient grass survived it was eaten by voracious cattle. The valiant fallen tree scattered its viable seed and new forests rose to defy new gales, and to shelter the earth and fertilize it. Had the Bible really spoken ironically? The Church proclaimed that it grew stronger with the blood of the martyrs. Charles had no desire to replenish his country, though his conscience tormented him. Like too many other Americans, he compromised. But at the end of his life he thought: "To compromise with evil is to sell your soul to death." Nations did not reach a détente with Hell—unless they desired to live in Hell. They usually did.

(It was not surprising, Charles would think years later, that on his deathbed President Wilson mourned, "I am a most unhappy man. I have ruined my country.")

31

As Francis Porter was incapable, by nature, of honesty with regard to himself, to others, to reality, he did not think: "The best and quickest access to Ellen—and her money—is through her children. Therefore, I must set out to cultivate those children, who will then help me to get what I want."

That, however, was the cold and pragmatic core of the matter, which he never faced with valid cynicism or brutal candor. He had always prided himself on his "frankness," though he possessed no true frankness at all. He was also incapable of admitting this even in his deepest reflections; he was a classic case of self-deceit. He was his own mirror, in which he saw an image of uprightness, honor, sobriety, "compassion," justice, and "concern for humanity." He was not able to judge himself, or indulge in the slightest self-criticism or doubt or uneasy guilt, or humor. All that he did was impeccable, based on what he considered humanistic impulses. That he was a Grand Inquisitor, really at home with the auto-da-fé and the thumbscrews and the wheel and the lash and the gallows, never occurred to him in nightmares. As all mankind possesses the latent instinct for cruelty and vengefulness, he possessed this also, but to a larger extent. To be contradicted was to him a personal affront, an affront to his superior intelligence and endowments and judgments and convictions. Excellence should never be challenged, was his subconscious reasoning, and that he was in all ways excellent and above confrontation he never questioned for a single moment. Those who questioned should be, at the very least, condemned; at the worst, punished severely.

He was the new and sadistic man who had begun to emerge into the startled awareness of the world after the French Revolution. He was the fanatic, the "reformer," the champion of the Common Man, the warrior engaged in a battle to the death against all the powers of reason, judiciousness, tradition, Western Judeo-Christian culture, established religion, law, order, pride, patriotism, temperance, philosophy, balance, and civilization.

His father, with alarm, had guessed this even in Francis' childhood, for Francis had always been too fervid, too obstinate, too enamored of his own conclusions, too inflexible, too vengeful when opposed, too convinced that he was inevitably right. His teachers had found him difficult, though an excellent scholar. He had plunged into the Spanish-American War with intensity, believing it just. But after that war a phenomenon happened, strange and alien to his nature: He had actually changed his opinion. Walter suspected that the change had come about when his son had been brought rudely to confront reality, and had recoiled in self-protection. Or, perhaps, Walter would think, it was Francis' first experience with raw humanity, among the soldiers, and he had retreated from it with disgust and hatred. He never really examined this experience with honesty, otherwise he would never have become a Fabian Socialist or developed his own enormous fantasies concerning mankind.

Naturally, he had voted to declare war against Germany, and had made a coldly impassioned speech in favor of such a declaration. In some manner Germany had now become the focus of his frightful hatred for his fellow human beings, and he could use invective against the Germans which was simply invective against all that lived in the form of man, which would not pay obeisance to him and his kind.

So, while the dread war against mankind increased, Francis gave long thought to the "welfare" of Jeremy's children. It was obvious to him that their mother was too weak in character to "care" for Christian and Gabrielle in a true maternal fashion, or she was, doubtless, too stupid and ill-bred and ignorant. They "deserved better," these fatherless children. Their characters needed to be "molded" along wider perspectives, their "compassion" stimulated, their duty made evident, their horizons "encouraged" to extend beyond their mere existence. ("Stimulation" and "encouragement" were favorite words of Francis'.) So Francis set out to stand in loco parentis to the children of Jeremy Porter. But subconsciously he guessed that they had an enormous capacity for evil, which did not revolt him. In fact, the more he saw of those children, the more rapport he felt for them, for in Christian he recognized—though subconsciously—his own capacity for ruthlessness, his own detestation of challenge, his own will to power, his own lack of noble love. He liked Christian more than he did Gabrielle, for Gabrielle had a wicked sense of humor, a sharper aversion for delusion than did her brother, and she was also more clever in dissimulation and pretense. Had Francis ever liked Kipling—in fact, he detested Kipling—he would have quoted, "The female of the species is more deadly than the male." Too, Francis was more inclined to favor Christian because the youth, in physical appearance, resembled his mother.

Francis became as amiable as possible to Christian during the Easter recess in 1918, in spite of pressing business in Washington. Christian would never respect him, for Christian was far more intelligent than his cousin. But the boy had considered how best he could use Francis for his own advantage, and pretended to a great affection for "Cousin Francis." He early understood that Francis had a relentless determination to marry Ellen, and Christian gave long thought as to how this could be manipulated. The youth hated Charles Godfrey, who was a stern guardian and not open to cajolery or charm; nor could he be diddled. He refused great increases in allowances; he could never be deceived by such as Christian. Therefore Christian, while he hated and sullenly resented Charles, respected him. But Charles was an impediment to the enjoyment of life, and it was obvious that he had no burning love for the younger members of the human tribe. He was also a disciplinarian, and could persuade Ellen not to grant the more lavish desires of her son. He had only to say, "Jeremy would not approve," to get Ellen to do what he wished. Christian knew that Francis detested Charles Godfrey, and that Charles despised Francis.

A stepfather, in the person of Francis Porter, would be more amenable, and his wife would be less docile with Charles. Christian knew the sensitivity of his mother, her timidity, her susceptibility to dominance, her guilty desire to please and placate at all costs. She would be helpless before Francis Porter, and Francis Porter, Christian believed, would be helpless before subtle adroitness in Ellen's children. Gabrielle, after some reflection, heartily agreed. The two children set out to woo Francis as avidly as he was now wooing them. They pretended to agree with all his opinions; they looked at him, with open mouths, when he exhorted them, and would seriously nod their heads. That they laughed even more hilariously at him than they laughed at their mother, he never suspected.

They enlisted the assistance of "Aunt Kitty," though they well knew that she wanted to marry Francis Porter herself. They carefully concealed from her their knowledge of her own schemes. They merely desired her "help" against Charles Godfrey, who was very oppressive and was no doubt paying himself a large fee as administrator of their father's will, thus robbing two innocent children. As Kitty greatly disliked Charles Godfrey and his "upstart wife," the children found no opposition in their dear "aunt." They found an enthusiastic ally. With immense art Kitty began her campaign to get Ellen to mistrust Charles, and as Ellen still did not like Maude, and found Charles somewhat stringent, this was not difficult to accomplish. "You should listen more to Francis, dearest Ellen," Kitty would say. "He has your best interests at heart, and he adores your children. Such a greathearted man." She reminded Ellen constantly of the "debt" she owed Francis, to which Ellen somewhat uncomfortably agreed. There were times when Ellen felt guilt that she did not "appreciate" Francis as much as he deserved, and so she forced herself to be very attentive to him in contrition, and listened to him more and more when he reprimanded her—though the reprimands were always delivered in an austerely kind manner, and with a patronizing tenderness. Ellen found herself depending on his advice. He did so cherish her children, she would tell herself, and they needed a man's guidance, and the children obviously loved him, too. They would tell her so, on endless occasions, their eyes big and trusting.

In the meantime, Francis was busy in Washington. The draft, he said, should be extended to include able administrators, even in their forties—such as Charles Godfrey, he would say to himself. In September 1917, Charles, seeing the inevitable, enlisted, was immediately made a colonel in the War Department. This was not to Francis' liking, but at least it removed Charles from the constant supervision of Ellen, Christian, and Gabrielle for a considerable number of months, thus placing them more and more under the influence of himself.

Francis did not know that Kitty Wilder was determined to divorce her husband, Jochan, and marry him as soon as possible. He found in her only a devoted assistant in the matter of Ellen and Jeremy's children, and he forgot his former dislike of her. As for Jochan Wilder, Francis considered him a pleasant nonentity, with no social conscience and no intelligence. Francis did not know of a closed codicil in Jeremy's will: If no executor named in the body of the will survived to the children's majority, Jochan Wilder and the law firm were to be executors.

"The sweet smell of money," Jeremy Porter had once said, "has driven millions of good men to the most appalling heights of treachery, madness, betrayal, and greed. It has turned potential saints into devils, and has more crucifixions in its name than have ever been recorded."

"I wish," said Christian Porter to his sister in October 1918, "that this war would go on for years and years. Such fun. I wish I were old enough to enlist."

Gabrielle laughed derisively. "Oh, yes, for the gay uniform and the leather leggings and the cane and the salutes from the ranks, and the new wristwatches for men—for men!—and all the bands and the dancing and the heroism. You're not of the stuff of heroes, Christian. You just like the stage."

"You're a brat," said Christian, laughing himself. "A thirteen-year-old brat. I could, though, run away and enlist and say I was eighteen instead of fifteen."

Ellen had opened her house on Long Island for wounded soldiers. Though Francis primly approved he did not honestly like it. One knew what these raw men would do to a fine house, when it was used as a convalescent home, and that lowered property values. Ellen so brought herself out of her apathy that she spent almost all summer in her house, rolling bandages, wearing a gray-and-white uniform, and singing and playing a piano for the suffering young men. Francis had assured her that this was exemplary. Her children, however, no matter her gentle reproaches, would not join her at the house, whose present inhabitants they forthrightly loathed. They preferred the city and their friends and the excitement of the war days.

"They're old enough to be by themselves," Francis would say. "You have a good housekeeper there, and even that old Cuthbert, who is becoming very useless, I must say. An ancient pensioner; you should really discharge him, Ellen. Didn't Jeremy leave him fifteen thousand dollars? Yes, and he has always been paid large wages. No doubt he is financially independent by now."

"Jeremy would want him to stay with the family the rest of his life, Francis." Ellen spoke with her usual timidity, but there was that disagreeable echo of iron under her words, an iron which Francis both mistrusted and resented. Who was Ellen, by birth or breeding, to dare assert herself against his better judgment? It was insolence. He had, however, prevailed on her a year ago to discharge Miss Evans, who had promptly enlisted as a nurse in the Army and had gone overseas with the troops. She wrote quite regularly to Ellen, and was pleased to hear that her patient had roused herself from her listlessness and had joined "in the war effort," a new phrase culled from English phraseology. (America had become excessively loving towards England by this time. No longer were Fourth of July celebrations filled with tauntings and fervid denunciations.)

Francis had entered the primaries in his campaign to become a United States Senator, and had been defeated. However, he had been re-elected Congressman by a significantly lower majority than in his last campaign, and this had enraged him. Moreover, the mood of the country was changing, and this was also infuriating. There had been a vast decrease in élan and elation as the war had progressed, and especially since the Draft Act had been amended on August 31, 1918, to lower the draft age to eighteen. The war fever considerably cooled when the wounded returned, and the death lists grew longer and longer. There was a new sullen feeling in the national air, and a new anxiety since Russia had fallen to the Bolsheviks and had withdrawn from the war. People, and the newspapers, spoke apprehensively about the Communists. Sometimes there were even blacker and larger headlines in the papers pertaining to Russia than news of the Front. Confused indignation was expressed in behalf of the Czar and his family. Articles began to be printed in national magazines concerning the annihilation of tens of thousands of Russians who opposed the new regime, of peasants hideously slaughtered on their farms and in the little villages, of the mad murder of the middle class and the confiscation of their property.

"If it were not for the Spanish flu decimating this country, and taking up some of the public's attention, we'd be in difficulties," said Francis' friends. "We must pursue our work with deeper attention and dedication. We have come a long way. It is now time to end this war and pursue our objective ruthlessly."

Consequently, the war did end, and with suddenness,

on November 11, 1918, to the innocent jubilation of America.

It was on that day of excitement and delirious relief that Francis proposed marriage to Ellen. He had, quite inadvertently, been forced into this (despite his suspicion that Ellen would refuse him) by Kitty Wilder herself.

A month before, Kitty had received her divorce from her husband, Jochan, naming his kind mistress as co-respondent. (Jochan promptly married his lady the next day, in spite of some unkind remarks from the judge who had granted the divorce to Kitty.) Kitty had received a large divorce settlement, which, combined with her own fortune and her canny investments in munitions, was very comforting to her. The time had come for her to assault the "virginal" battlements of Francis' bachelorhood. She was convinced not only that he had much affection for her as an ally and a clever woman who could advance him, but that he was weak and vulnerable. Moreover, she had long ago guessed that he loved money, and she had a quantity of it, and she, very artfully, had mentioned this on numerous occasions to him, and he had shown a sincere and gratifying interest. He had advised her on investments and she had expressed her gratitude effusively and with admiration for his astuteness. They saw each other regularly when he came to New York. At his earnest request she had supervised the household in the city when Ellen was away on Long Island, and she had followed all his instructions, with overt docility, which pleased him.

She was more sprightly than in earlier years, in spite of her age, though the effort frequently exhausted her. No gray appeared in her hair; it was expertly dyed. She was increasingly chic and fashionable, if quite gaunt by now. Her big teeth flashed constantly. She had spoken eloquently at bond rallies, in the company of Congressman Porter. She knew that Francis was admiring her more and more, especially since she informed him that his political prospects "were only just revealing themselves. There is nothing you cannot accomplish, dear Francis." That he regarded her only as an audience, and a useful person, and not as a woman, she did not believe for an instant. (She had been very active in the work for Votes for Women, to Francis' approval. She did not suspect that under that approval lay a subconscious aversion to women, and a cold dislike for them. Nor could she guess that there were certain episodes in his life with his male masters which would have horrified her, and that the only woman he had ever desired was Ellen Porter.)

Two days before the Armistice Francis had occasion to return to New York and Kitty invited him to dinner in the brownstone house which was now hers alone. She had discovered that Francis did not care for gourmet food, nor did he particularly like meat any longer. In fact, he was almost a vegetarian except for an occasional breakfast of bacon and eggs. "Plain food," he would say severely, "wholesome food, is the best. There is no room in America any longer for Diamond Jim Bradys and their ilk, nor for Lillian Russells. Profligacy!" Kitty would laugh in herself while she eagerly agreed with him, and forced her outraged cook to prepare dinners of stewed or boiled vegetables laced sparingly with butter and cream, and rice puddings, and meatless soups. Francis would deign to partake—as he called it—of "a little sip of light wine, the sweet variety." He constantly accused Americans of "eating entirely too much. The money could be used for the Poor." Kitty had no illusions about the man she was determined to marry.

The dinner was, as usual, horrendous, but Kitty pretended to enjoy it while she listened attentively to Francis' pejorative remarks against "America's threatened intervention in Russia, at a time when the Russian people have finally, after centuries of oppression, freed themselves from tyranny." He also denounced the "bourgeois mentality in the United States." Kitty sipped at the detestable wine and nodded gravely. Then came a pause in the conversation. She leaned towards Francis and said, with a serious face, "I never asked you before, dear Francis, but why did such a personable, handsome, and suitable man like yourself never marry?"

He preened, then studied his pudding, which was filled with raisins. "Frankly, Kitty, I have always been so busy, working for my country—"

"I know, I know," she murmured with sympathy. "But you must think of yourself, too. Self-sacrifice is commendable—but a man must live also."

Francis suddenly thought of Ellen and his long lean face colored and Kitty saw this with delight. He avoided her eyes. "Kitty, I have been considering marriage for some time. For several years, in fact."

She regarded him with elation and cocked her head coquettishly. "And who, may I inquire, is the fortunate lady?" Her eyes gleamed on him. He suddenly looked at her, and saw her drily dark and ravaged little face, the deep lines about her smiling mouth, her coy expression, her tilted head, her wet exposed teeth, and he understood at once and was immediately horrified and filled with revulsion. His cheeks became stained with scarlet. He pushed aside his pudding. He wanted to flee. Good God, he thought. What made her think for a moment that I would consider her, or any other woman, except Ellen? I never gave her any encouragement. I never noticed before how really ugly she is; a black twig, in spite of her stylish clothes and her jewels. If she were to touch me now I would scream!

He said in a tight, half-choked voice, "I don't know how fortunate the lady would be—that is, if I have even considered any particular woman, which I have—" He paused abruptly. This woman had been his ally, had obeyed his every suggestion regarding Ellen and her children. She had much influence over Ellen, he had observed, and over Christian and Gabrielle. She would make a formidable enemy; he was quite aware of her vindictive and cruel nature. So, he considered, his thoughts flying confusedly but warily. He coughed, as she waited and leaned towards him, her huge teeth glittering under the electric chandelier. He tried to smile, shyly.

"I don't know," he repeated, "how fortunate the lady would be."

"No particular lady?" she asked with archness.

He began to sweat lightly. He knew he could no longer delay in approaching Ellen, no matter his dread that she would refuse him. So he smiled again. "You will be the first to know, Kitty, the very first. I promise you that—in the eventuality—"

What a stick, she thought. But a rich stick, and a powerful one. "You are too modest," she said. "Any woman would be honored by your proposal."

Though he was a politician he had never learned the art of dissembling. He was not capable of deception, except as concerned himself, nor had he ever been consciously a hypocrite. He believed his own words; he would have perished for his convictions of his superiority, and what was best for the People. He was too much of a fanatic, too convinced of his own truth, to lie or deliberately deceive. In that lay his terribleness and his danger to his country.

"You are too kind, Kitty," he muttered, and the scarlet stain on his cheeks deepened. Her elation grew; she saw how he tried to avoid looking directly at her. He was sweating quite visibly now. "Kitty," he said again, "I give you my word: You will be the very first to know."

She studied him, the two sharp lines between her eyes drawing together. "I should be very hurt, dear Francis, if you did not tell me—at once. You know how fond I am of you; you have no better friend."

She burst into a volley of gay forced laughter, high and shrill. "A June wedding, perhaps?"

"Oh, no," he said with sudden vehemence, "much sooner, I hope—if the lady is willing. But she may not be willing."

Ah, Kitty thought, relieved. He just needs a little encouragement, a little nudge. "Ask her!" she cried.

"I will, I will," he answered. He was more frightened than he had ever been before in his life. He began to tremble, and Kitty almost hugged herself.

"When will you ask her, you naughty boy?"

"In a day or two—when I have the courage."

"There is no time like the present."

In this he fervently agreed with her. He compelled himself to meet her eyes as she said, "Do I know the lady?"

"Oh, very well, very well indeed! None knows her better than you, Kitty, none better."

There's no one else, she said to herself. He never has courted a woman in his life, neither here nor in Washington. I'd know immediately. He drew out his watch and his hand shook slightly. "You must excuse me, Kitty. I—I have some telegrams to send tonight, some speech I must finish."

She saw his intense nervousness and lightly bounded to her feet. She led him to the hall and assisted him with his coat. He repressed a shudder when she touched him, flirtingly, on the arm and peered up into his face. He felt profaned by her proximity. He found himself breathing with difficulty. A sooty November rain was falling and the wind was keen and nimble. He plunged into the night

412   *Taylor Caldwell*

without another word. Kitty watched him go, exultant. I have him, she thought. But not in my bed, if I can help it. I doubt, though, that I'd encounter that contretemps.

Driven by his fear of Kitty Wilder, Francis visited Ellen unexpectedly on Armistice night, while New York frolicked and danced deliriously in the streets and sang, "It's a long way to Tipperary, it's a long way to go—," and "over there, over there—!" and, with open tears, "Smile the while you bid me sad adieu, when the clouds roll by I'll come to you—" and various other popular war songs. Impromptu brass bands appeared out of nowhere. Confetti blew in blizzards. Strangers embraced, kissed each other, laughed in each other's eyes. Every street and alley echoed with songs, shouts, bursts of hysterical mirth, and hurrying feet. Soldiers were hugged, swirled into dancing. Streetcars clanged in happy chorus, automobiles roared, shopwindows lighted up, children yelled. Newspapers were snatched from clamoring newsboys who caught a rain of coins thrown exuberantly into the air. Saloons glared with electric light and their doors swung and the bars were crowded to the doors. Throngs filled the sidewalks, overflowed before traffic. Restaurants almost burst with endless lines of celebrants. Police, on horseback, could not restrain the people and they did not try overmuch, though they blew their whistles valiantly.

"I am so happy the war is over, Francis," said Ellen as they sat before the fire in the library and sipped sherry before dinner. "I was so afraid, thinking of Christian—if the war were to last a few years longer. When I think of the poor boys in my house on Long Island—well, I would think of my own son. I am so happy it is over."

But the real war has just begun, Francis thought, the war for the liberation of mankind all over the world. But he nodded soberly at Ellen. She sat near him in a simple black velvet gown, and though she was still thin she now possessed an air of quiet composure and maturity. She looked up at the portrait of Jeremy over the fireplace and sighed. "It would be such a happy night for Jeremy," she said, and if her large blue eyes filled with pain and grief her smile was gentle. She had not cut her hair in the new fashion; it was braided and heaped over her head and it caught threads of fire from the spluttering coals in the grate. The old purity, the old immaculate serenity, had returned to her translucent face. She played with the pearls at her throat, and forgot Francis. She sighed again, and her lovely rounded breasts pressed against the shimmering velvet over it. Francis could not look away from her. Ellen, Ellen, he said in himself.

The clock in the hall struck eight notes. Dinner would soon be served. "I suppose they will give the children a holiday tomorrow," said Ellen. "Christian from Groton, Gabrielle from her day school. I think I will take them for lunch at Delmonico's. A very special treat."

It is now or never, thought Francis, trembling. He leaned towards Ellen urgently. "Have you ever thought, Ellen, that your children need a man's guidance and counseling and solicitude?"

She glanced at him quickly, puzzled, then smiled. "They have you, dear Francis," she said.

"But I have no real position of authority, Ellen."

"They adore you, you know that. As for myself, I wouldn't know what to do without you—and Charles. You and Charles—you are like fathers to my children, even though Christian, that bad boy, often complains of Charles." She laughed a little and shook her head.

"Perhaps he has reason to complain," said Francis, with meaning. Ellen was surprised.

"Oh, no, not really, Francis. Besides, Christian has you, too. The boy almost worships you, and so does Gabrielle. They are fortunate."

"They might not always have me, Ellen." His hands were shaking and he had to clench them. "I may marry— and leave New York."

Ellen uttered an amazed cry. "You are thinking of marrying, Francis?"

"Yes. I am. After all, I am not young any longer. I want a family of my own."

Ellen was intrigued. "Is it someone I know?" She had never thought of Francis marrying and leaving, and she had a faint sensation of loss and regret.

"Yes, Ellen. You know—her."

She waited. She saw how tense he had become; she saw the drops on his forehead; she saw that his hands were clenched together.

He said, "Again, Ellen, you must think of your children, and a father's strength behind them, to admonish, to inform, to guide. They impress me as somewhat unruly at times—a little bold, especially Gabrielle. You are too lenient with them—and they need authority. A man's authority." He caught his breath, while she stared at him innocently. "Ellen, have you ever thought of marrying again?"

She was freshly amazed. "But I *am* married!" she exclaimed.

"What?" A thundering confusion came to him, an icy throb of horror. "You are married?"

"Yes, of course. To Jeremy. I am his wife."

The dreadful hammering of his heart slowly subsided; he moved his neck against his stiff white collar. "Ellen, my dear. You are Jeremy's widow. You have no husband."

The apricot color, fainter than in her youth, faded from Ellen's cheeks and lips. She averted her head, and was silent.

"And your children have no father, and they desperately need one. Surely you can see that for yourself. You are too timid, too—inexperienced—too submissive, to be a force in their lives. This is very bad for them. Forget yourself for a moment, and think of the welfare of your children. They are at a very vulnerable age, and have no father to protect them even from themselves. You must marry again, Ellen."

She shuddered and dropped her head. "How could I do that, loving Jeremy?" she whispered.

"He is dead, Ellen, dead. He can no longer help you, and your children. Think of how worried he would be now—about Christian, who is almost a man, and Gabrielle, who is approaching womanhood. They have only a mother, who is not strict enough, I am afraid, and is too unworldly. This is a new age, Ellen, and it will become hectic very soon. Your children need protection. How can you deny them a father?"

The old sick guilt washed over Ellen, the old shrinking, and he saw this. Her face was very white and taut and her lips had dried. He went on, relentlessly, "You must give this immediate thought, Ellen. Your children must come first, and not any lingering sentimentality concerning a dead husband and father. You must face the truth, Ellen, and the sooner the better. Christian is almost out of control as it is; I sometimes have to rebuke him sternly. As for Gabrielle—does she listen to you?"

Ellen's head began to move from side to side, in deep pain.

"A new father would control Christian, a new father would give Gabrielle a steadfast governing. With affection, of course, and a personal influence. Fatherless children are always in danger. Christian and Gabrielle are in particular danger, for they are rich and have been denied nothing, and do not have, I fear, much in the way of principles and ideals. You are not strong enough to give them these, Ellen. You never were. They are very spirited, and often rebellious. Let me be honest with you, Ellen. They have no particular respect for you. Don't you see how dangerous this is for them? They must respect somebody. Charles Godfrey? He has a family of his own; he has no authority over your children, except to deny them undue extravagances."

Ellen said in a weak voice, "My children—they would not like me to marry again." She was pleading with him, and now she turned to him and he saw the stark fear and irresolution on her face. "And how could I marry again, remembering Jeremy?"

"There you are, Ellen! Thinking only of yourself, as your poor aunt used to accuse you, with some justification. One must not be selfish in this world, Ellen. One must think of others occasionally, something, alas, which you do not do often."

"I think of my children all the time! I live for them!"

He shook his head. "No, you do not, Ellen. If you did, only once, you would recognize the truth of what I have told you. You would see yourself as a sentimental soft woman, who believes her children are still little children, and not adolescents in desperate need of a father's guidance, protection and care and authority. They are in peril, Ellen, desperate peril. It is almost too late as it is. I can see that for myself. I worry about them constantly." (He actually believed this.)

He went on as she began to wring her hands together in her lap. "I have known you since you were very young, Ellen, even a little younger than Gabrielle. I know your yielding character, your inability to control your own feelings, your—again I must say it—your selfishness, your preoccupation only with your own desires and impulses. You forgot your poor aunt readily enough, and she died alone and in sorrow. Then, as now, you put yourself first. Don't you think it is time to consider others, and especially your children?"

When she did not answer and only displayed cringing and self-reproach, he leaned even closer to her and took her hand. It was cold, but the very touch of it thrilled him unbearably. She did not shrink from him; she let her hand remain flaccidly in his. There were tears in her eyes.

"Ellen? You have been listening to me, I who have a profound regard for you, more than anyone else has? There are times I am desperate—"

She said, with faintness, "But who would marry me? I know no unattached men."

He let a deep stillness come between them. His love had its own wisdom. When she looked at him slowly and imploringly she saw the fervor on his face, the flash of light behind his spectacles.

"You have me, Ellen," he said, and his voice quivered. "You have me, who has always loved you. Ellen, will you marry me, and give your children a father, one who shares their own blood?"

"You, Francis? You?" She was stunned. Her mouth fell open.

"Is that so frightful a thought, Ellen? I love you; I have always loved you."

She could not believe it. She felt dazed, removed from reality, strange, alienated, floating, whirling in a confusion that made her numb.

"I have always loved you," he repeated. "From the moment I saw you, kneeling on the summer grass in Preston. You do remember Preston, don't you, and the Porter house? Or have you forgotten that, too? Jeremy's parents? They are old, and forgotten. They see their grandchildren rarely. Whose fault is that, Ellen? I know they have said disrespectful things about their grandparents, who have no one else now, and you have never corrected them. Oh, Ellen. You, too, need guidance and care, as well as your children."

Her eyes were stretched and wide, and there was a wildness, a shifting in them.

"I love you," he said. "I want to be your protection; I want to help you. I've always wanted that, Ellen. I've always stood near you, in thought if not in physical presence all the time. Surely you remember that I helped you many times. That was because I love you. You were never out of my thoughts. Did you never know that?"

She shook her head. She was crying silently, the tears running down her cheeks. He let her cry and still held her hand. Then she said in a far and shivering voice, "You don't know, Francis. I—I can have no more children. I would not really be a wife to you."

"Let me be the judge, Ellen. Let me be your husband —to care for you and be your strength."

He drew her gently towards him and slowly put his arms about her. He bent his head and kissed her mouth, but with the artfulness of love he did not let her guess his passion for her and the urge he felt to take her lips fiercely with his own, and his overwhelming desire to stroke her breasts and kiss them.

She was suddenly conscious of a powerful exhaustion, even a prostration. She felt herself being torn away on a dull wind that would not release her. Her will was torpid. She closed her eyes and wanted only to sleep, be nothing, and forget.

"Ellen? Will you marry me? Tomorrow?"

"Yes," she whispered to the hollow darkness before her eyes. "Yes."

Cuthbert, frail and old, came to the door to announce dinner. Ellen never remembered if she ate that dinner or not. She did not remember even going to bed. She slept that night in a sort of stupor, comatose, unfeeling, and without a single thought.

They were married hurriedly the next morning in City Hall, by a judge hastily summoned by Francis, while the city continued to rejoice and celebrate the end of the war. That night the newspapers carried, on their front pages, news of "the quiet marriage of Congressman Francis Porter, to the widow of Jeremy Porter, once a Congressman himself, and a notable lawyer, who was murdered by persons unknown, four years ago, in New York. The Congressmen were cousins—"

Kitty Wilder read the paper that night. She could not believe it at first, and then her friends began to call. Her maid was told to inform those friends that Mrs. Wilder was out of town, briefly, for a few days. Kitty took to her bed, overcome by rage and hatred and mortification, frustrated as she had never been before in her life. She

wanted to kill. She could not decide whom she hated
the most—Francis Porter or Ellen. She decided later that
night that Francis was the most hated by herself, after
he had called to tell her, politely.

He had kept his promise.

32

"I still can't believe it," said Maude Godfrey to her
husband, Charles. "How could Ellen have brought herself
to marry that man?"

"God knows," said Charles glumly. "Francis Porter, of
all people! I see he whisked her off to Washington fast
enough, to let the dust settle, I suppose. Poor Ellen. He
must have given her drugs, or something. I suspect she
didn't know what she was doing. Well. I'll soon be out of
this uniform, love. I'll try to find out where they are
staying in Washington, when I go back."

But Francis had taken his bride to Baltimore, to a
secluded hotel the management of which was discreet.

Ellen remained in the dusky if luxurious suite for the
entire week after her marriage to Francis, and could not
be persuaded to leave it even for the dining room. She
moved in a semi-stuporous state as if her vital forces had
been suspended. She thought of nothing; she could repeat
only over and over to herself, "I did this for my children." There were dim nights when she was briefly
aroused to a vague aghastness and cowering at the lascivious violence Francis displayed towards her in their
marriage bed. He had become a total stranger to her, a
man she had never known. Sometimes she was brought
to an obscure awareness of his sweaty probing and searching of all her body, his loud panting, his gripping hands
on her flesh; he would bury his face in her breast, hurtingly, and would groan over and over, "Oh, Ellen, Ellen!"

Driven by desire and love, he could not have enough of her; he seemed to have lost his mind. She endured all this flaccidly, like one in a drugged dream, sometimes weakly trying to avoid kisses that cut and bruised her mouth, her neck, her legs, her arms, even her feet. He would light the lamps the better to see her and examine her; sometimes she would protest faintly, conscious of shame, but this only increased his avidity. He seemed to want to devour her; there was a ferocity in his breathless love-making, a savagery. It was as if he hated and adored her simultaneously. He would wind his fingers in her hair and shake it, then, when she moaned and tried to free herself, he would soothe her incoherently, crushing her body to his, half smothering her.

"You don't know, you can't know, how long I've waited for this, my darling, all these years! You can't know how I've dreamt of it through the long, long nights! Give me your hand; I'm your husband, give me your hand! I love you, Ellen, I love you! Do you understand? I love you!"

He was insatiable. He would rouse her several times at night from a heavy and sodden doze. His body appeared to loom over hers without surcease. His lean face was constantly red and swollen out of recognition. At times she would feel a fleeting but intense fear of him, for not even Jeremy had displayed such wild abandonment and passion for her. Mute at last, she would lie supine, not resisting, no longer alert as to whether it was day or night. She was like one given up to immolation and she would think: For my children, my children.

Had she been less innocent and naïve she would have come to pity him, to feel a deep compassion for this overwrought man who loved her with so much brutal ardor and treated her with such barbaric hunger. She would have understood that only a man of intense rigor, a man who had denied himself for so long and had held himself in such cruel restraint for too many years, could bring himself to these excesses, these gasping, almost insane, exclamations, these shameless explorations. Her pity, then, would have evoked a kind of profound tenderness and perception in her, for all her profaned body. She would not have felt so ravished and degraded. She might even have arrived at a deep affection for him and would have soothed him, comprehending, and would have been moved by his frantic excitement, his violent and painful activities, his tireless hands and mouth. She might even have been flattered, a little later.

But she was innocent and inexperienced; she could not understand such self-abandonment in a man she had considered excessively controlled and aloof. She could not imagine such love, such impetuous lust which seemed to be a terrible force apart from him while it drove him. Had she understood, even mildly, their future years might have been entirely different, both physically and mentally, their lives transformed.

She could feel only fear and repulsion and disgust, and a confused desire to escape him and never see him again, and forget him forever. Therein lay their mutual tragedy. Totally depleted, she could not resist, could not speak to him, not even when they dined together. She was conscious, always, of his eyes seeking out her flesh; he was always lunging at her in the midst of a meal, dragging her back to the disordered bed, while the food cooled and congealed and the wintry light was subdued by shutters which never opened. There were times, in the midst of her submissive silence and surrender, when she longed to die, to remember nothing, not even her children, not even Jeremy. There were other times when she would have recoiled from him. But she no longer had the strength, or the will.

They had no conversation together in the midst of the storm, no exchange of smiles, no remarks on the weather or their future. There were only brief dozes, then renewed and frenzied copulations. There were a few times when, momentarily depleted, he would look at her with beseeching eyes and say to her almost timidly, "Ellen? Ellen?" But she would not and could not meet his eyes and was incapable of answering that pathetic plea, and he would be silenced, seeing her white face gleaming expressionlessly in the gloom of the large bedroom, her still hands, her collapsed body. Then he would take her to the bed again, in a bewildered effort to get her to respond to him by the slightest gesture, the slightest shadow of a smile, the smallest word. But she never did; he was bereft and did not know why, and anxiously hurt, and could not understand.

On the last day, after a night that was endless to Ellen, he said, "We must leave this afternoon, at four, for New York. Ellen?

She nodded mutely and docilely began to pack. She had the appearance of one who was gravely ill and broken. She seemed to have retreated to the day when she had left the sanitarium. He watched her, and could have wrung his hands. He had given her all of which he was capable, and she was like a woman who had been violently assaulted, then thrown down. She did not speak to him on the train. Lifelessly, she stared through the sooty windows. He took her gloved hand in his and her hand was dead. I don't know, I don't know, he thought to himself. There is something wrong—and I love her. Surely she knows that now.

Christian and Gabrielle were delighted, and laughed gleefully together while their mother was on her honeymoon with their stepfather. Gloating, Christian said, "Now I can have what I want. My dear new papa will be under my thumb."

Gabrielle was more discerning. Her piquant dark face glimmered with mirth and her black eyes glinted. "I hope so," she said in her light and pretty voice. "We'll be so sweet and nice, won't we? Let him think we admire him and will obey him. Never let him know what we honestly think of him. He's such a fool, isn't he? He's even more foolish than Mama. Or maybe he isn't. We'll see."

"I wonder how dear Aunt Kitty is taking this, Gaby."

"Her maid still says she's out of town. But I'd bet anything she is pounding her pillows in bed and chewing her claws off and cursing Mama. I'd love to peek into her room right at this minute! She should be quite a sight. Such fun."

"I have a feeling," said Christian, rubbing his hands through his brilliant red hair, "that we should still continue to cultivate Aunt Kitty."

"Of course. I have a feeling, too, that she'll be even more valuable to us now than she was before." Gabrielle twisted one of her black curls about her finger, and looked thoughtful. "She's hated Mama enough. This is much worse. We must plan how to use her." She laughed. "Did you notice how miserable Uncle Charles looked when he told us we must be 'kind' to our stepfather? And that awful old Maude of his, who sees a lot more than she seems to see. Well, they are out of our lives now, and let's be thankful."

Christian said, "Now I must start working on Papa to let me out of Groton. I can't stand it much longer."

"I hope," said Gabrielle, "that Mama won't oppose him, not that she ever did very much. I hope you won't laugh at this, Chris, but there's something deep down in Mama that can't always be moved."

"Oh, the stupid can often be stubborn, like mules. I know that myself. But Papa is even more stubborn. He thinks he owes it to himself and his convictions. So we'll just have to convince him that what we want is his own decision and not ours. It should be easy. He thinks he's an intellectual when he's really only a fanatic and chews other men's thoughts. I don't think he ever had an original idea of his own during his life. He gave me a book on Engels, and when I innocently asked the meaning of something Engels wrote Papa looked confused and changed the subject. I understood it, all right. We're not going to have any trouble with dear new Papa, Gaby."

"Nothing is simple," Gabrielle replied, frowning. "Nothing is direct and clear. We only fool ourselves when we think it is. You can say that Papa is an idiot, even worse than Mama, but an idiot can be dangerous and slippery. Let's be careful."

"I'll be careful," her brother promised. "I have to go back to that damned school on Monday, before Mama returns with her beloved. I think we should pay a call on dear Aunt Kitty and cry in her arms."

Gabrielle considered this in her usual shrewd and thoughtful manner, then her lively face lighted and she nodded. She put on her dark-red wool coat with its beaver collar and her broad beaver hat, while Christian tugged on his school coat and cap. They set out gleefully together, to Kitty's brownstone house, so like their own. Snow was swirling fitfully along the windy street, setting up small ground blizzards on the sidewalks. A holiday air still enlivened the city. The sky was darkening and streetlamps started to blaze out in the early dusk. A red two-decked bus roared down Fifth Avenue, marked "Riverside." Shopwindows began to shine, and the crowds thickened.

Kitty's maid hesitated when Christian politely asked to see her mistress. "I don't think she's to home," said the girl. "I'll see." She reluctantly let the children into the small warm hall with its gay wallpaper, stripes of red on a white background, and went up the narrow steep stairs. A few moments later she returned, nodded, and led brother and sister into the long and narrow living room where often they had visited Kitty. A low fire was burning here and a lamp or two was softly lit. Gabrielle always appreciated the taste with which the house had been furnished, a taste which was elegant but not intimate. She thought the house much quieter here than the house of her mother, though it was not the quiet of repose. It had an expectant aura, like Kitty herself. It seemed to promise some latent excitement.

Kitty entered the room, wrapped in a dark-blue gown of rustling silk. She had hastily applied rouge and powder and lipstick which made her yellowish pallor more intense. But her huge smile filled her face, almost obliterating the dark marks under her eyes and her reddened lips. "My dears, my sweet dears!" she cried, holding out her extremely thin arms, from which the silk sleeves fell like a kimono. Gabrielle ran to her at once and buried her face on Kitty's shoulder, while Christian advanced with a sober expression and kissed Kitty's cheek.

"What a shock this must be to my darlings," Kitty said. "Do let us sit down and have tea together, and we'll have a little talk." She sighed significantly. "What a shock," she repeated. "And young people are so sensitive."

"Mama never said a single word," Gabrielle wailed. "Cuthbert had to tell us. It was the cruelest thing. Christian and I feel so—so betrayed. We don't think we like Cousin Francis any longer. We just can't believe it!"

"We can't believe it," Christian affirmed.

Kitty had come to the conclusion that Ellen was not only stupid, as she had always believed, but sly also. What else could explain this sudden and incredible marriage, if not cunning? Ellen had expertly deceived everyone, and Kitty was mortified that she had not detected that slyness in Ellen long ago. Those empty blue eyes of hers were really an ambush from which she had craftily watched others, laughing in secret. Kitty moistened her thread of a scarlet mouth and her own eyes narrowed vindictively. She listened with pleasure to Gabrielle's tearful accusations against her mother, and she watched the slow and somber nodding of Christian's head. She sighed over and over as she patted Gabrielle's hand.

"Well," she said at last, "we mustn't judge, must we?

But not even to tell me, her best friend! Her most loyal friend. The things I hear others say— Never mind. What's done is done, and we must make the best of it. Francis— it was all so precipitate, so unlike your cousin, who never struck me as an impulsive man. Rather too controlled, I thought. I sometimes wonder—"

"Mama must have promised him something," said Christian. Kitty gave him a sharp look and he faintly colored. "I mean," he added, "that she persuaded him she would be a fine wife for him, and perhaps she will be. He's very simple, in a way. I do hope he is a little fond of Mama, and will make us a good stepfather. But it wasn't a very kind thing to do to Gaby and me—not to tell us but to leave a message with an old servant."

Kitty regarded him sorrowfully. "There must be an explanation, dears. We must wait until your mother returns. Then in a day or two I will call on her. One must forgive, you know."

When the children left, Kitty felt some satisfaction. She would never be able to marry Francis, but she would have her revenge, someday. She poured a second cup of tea for herself and hummed under her breath. Yes, she would have her revenge.

When she learned that Ellen had returned to New York with her new husband, Kitty waited three days, then called on her friend. She was not too surprised to discover that Francis had hurriedly left for Washington that morning. She was delighted to see that Ellen appeared to be in a state of lethargy and dull confusion, all her color vanished and her hair less dazzling and somewhat in disorder. Those great blue eyes which Kitty so detested seemed to be filmed over, like the eyes of the very old, and she hardly was aware of Kitty's presence.

"You naughty thing, running off like a delicious school-girl with no warning to your friends!" Kitty exclaimed, grasping the limp arms of the younger woman. Her vivacious voice rose a pitch. "The whole town is talking and twittering over it all. Such speculations! No one ever believed that Francis would marry anyone. And all the time, you sly things, you were plotting this! Naughty, naughty." She held Ellen off at arm's length and was happy to notice that Ellen was wearing an old brown wool frock, very unbecoming, and no jewelry except for the gold wedding band. She seemed very ill and distracted and kept pushing back locks of her loosely pinned hair, and glancing aimlessly about her. Kitty's curiosity became avid and she stared at Ellen eagerly. But Ellen sat down in her chair near the library fire as if she had crumpled in herself and all life had seeped away from her. She had, as yet, said not a single word.

The fire crackled. Cuthbert came in with tea and cakes and sherry, and glanced at his mistress with shadowed eyes from under his white brows. Kitty waited until he had left. She waited for Ellen to serve her, but Ellen merely gazed emptily at the fire. At last she spoke, without turning to Kitty.

"I did it for the children," she said in a toneless voice. "They need a father. That is what Francis said: They need a father. He—he made me feel so guilty, and I was. I haven't been much of a mother to them. It was always—" And she looked up suddenly at Jeremy's portrait over the mantle. Her pale face contorted, and she threw her hands over it and rocked in her chair, moaning faintly.

"I did it for them," she stammered, and now her voice was full of anguish. "For my children."

33

Charles Godfrey stared truculently at his visitor this warm August day in 1922. Heat from the streets beat into the office but no breeze stirred the maroon velvet draperies. A great glare struck the opposite wall.

"We've been over this whole thing a score of times, Francis," said Charles. "You know the contents of Jerry's will. Ellen is to receive the interest and dividends from the whole estate, and even some of the capital if absolutely necessary, but only if absolutely necessary. We have a bad inflation now, as I don't need to tell you, but fortunately the Stock Market is booming and so, accordingly, is Ellen's income. We have been as conservative as possible, buying only blue-chip stocks and sound common, and good safe bonds. That was Jerry's way. He was never a gambler, when it came to money. He had too deep a respect for it, though it was not the greatest interest in his life."

"No. Women were," said Francis. Charles shrugged, dismissing the remark.

"We are not too optimistic about permanent prosperity," said Charles. "So we are being cautious. There has been no need to dip into the capital for Ellen and her children. The trust funds for Christian and Gabrielle remain intact; we are adding to them with any surplus income. No one can touch those funds, as you know. No one. Has Ellen suggested to you that she would like more income?"

"She knows nothing about money," said Francis with some bitterness. "But I am her husband, and I do have some rights, you know. I have the right to protest the amount of her income. When Jeremy's parents died two years ago they left their grandchildren a very handsome estate, though they left Ellen nothing at all. I think that most unfair. Considering that estate, I think Ellen's income should be increased."

Charles played with a pen and tapped it on his desk. "There is no way at all to do that," he said. "You're a lawyer, Francis. The children's estate, from their grandparents, is untouchable, according to their wills. They inherit the capital when they both reach twenty-one. In the meantime the estate is growing, though much of it is invested in what I consider dubious stock. Well."

He studied Francis keenly. Once Jeremy had mentioned Thoreau to the effect that reformers had a secret "ailment." He had said, to Charles, that it was very possible that Francis' "ailment" had been too strong and sensible a father, too dominant a father. Charles, watching the dangerous scarlet stain on Francis' thin cheekbones, suddenly doubted it; yet he did not know the answer either. It was impossible for him to guess that Francis did indeed have an "ailment," and that soul-illness arose from the fact that no one had ever really loved him in the way he had subconsciously craved, a love that asked nothing and understood everything, and gave with tenderness. Walter had loved his son, though not in the manner so desperately needed by that son, and so, in despair, Francis had come to hate his father and desire vengeance on him and all that he was and all that he represented. Francis never consciously suspected that he hated his father; that would have done violence to his rigid principles.

But something moved in Charles, in spite of his dislike of Francis and his exasperation. It was pity. Here was a very rich man who lusted after his wife's fortune, a man who spent very little on luxuries and was extremely penurious. He was living on Ellen's income almost entirely, though he had not as yet persuaded her to sell the house on Long Island, which Jeremy had purchased and loved. He saved all he could from his own law practice —he had not been re-elected the last time to Congress, a fact which he blamed on "the bourgeoisie who think of nothing but their purses." To many of Jeremy's old friends, Francis seemed detestable. Yet, Charles pitied him and did not know why.

He said, "I'm sorry, Francis, that Harvard did not accept Christian. But you listened to him when he insisted he couldn't stand Groton any longer, and you allowed him to enter a cheap, second-rate day school in New York. Your reasons are your own business. Still, had he been forced to continue at Groton he might have passed the entrance examinations to Harvard. Now I understand, from Ellen, that the best you can do for him is to get him accepted at City College, and even that will be a struggle. Too bad. He's a very intelligent young man, exceptionally intelligent, though lazy. He couldn't tolerate the discipline at Groton, either. It's very unfortunate. He seems to lack ambition, too, though I've heard he is very keen about money."

"He's not a brute. He's not grossly competitive! He's not materialistic like most young men of his age. I resent your implication that Christian is greedy, Charles. He has a sense of responsibility towards his fellow man; he wants to help. We have long talks about this, when we are alone. He is naturally humanitarian!"

Charles saw the indignant scarlet increasing on Francis' agitated face. Good God, he thought, Christian a humanitarian! So is a crocodile. Charles was amazed that even one such as Francis could be so naïve, so unperceptive. But men like Francis were adepts at deceiving themselves, if it served some hidden reason, some aching illness in themselves.

"Ellen understands," Francis continued, and his pince-nez glittered in the brilliant light of the day. "She is very happy that Christian has become so earnest concerning the necessary reforms we must have in our unjust society in America. She contributes lavishly to the many charities, and causes, I have been recommending to her. She is on many boards."

"Yes. I know," said Charles. He did not add: But it is her money, not yours, which you are using for your pet treasons against your country, the dangerous ideas, the malignant plots. And you aren't even aware of what they really are, you poor miserable wretch! Charles' light-gray eyes gleamed with quick temper.

He said, "Well, Gabrielle is doing very well at her finishing school in Connecticut, so we have no complaints there." But Francis obdurately came back to the initial subject.

"I have thought that perhaps it would be possible for Ellen to draw on the capital of Jeremy's estate for the purpose of contributing to worthwhile causes in this country. I think that would be possible under the terms of the estate—a necessary—shall we call it—expense?"

Charles was angry again. " 'Expense?' The will says 'if necessary.' That means," he added with an elaborately patient emphasis, "if she needs anything more for necessities for herself or her children. There is quite a difference between 'expense' and 'necessity,' as you doubtless know yourself."

"But, if it is her desire— If she gives from her present income, and then needs further income because her available funds have run short for necessities—"

"That," said Charles very calmly, "would be a little chicanery, wouldn't it, Francis?"

Francis sat up stiffly. "I do not see it in that light, Charles."

"Let me tell you something, Francis. Ellen's income is for her support. If she gives to 'charity,' let us call it with some kindness, it must come from her very adequate income, and not from the capital. Only in the case of a dire emergency, a prolonged illness or a period of wild inflation, could her funds be increased. I see none of these on the immediate horizon."

He deliberately glanced at his watch. Then he said, with some formality, "I haven't seen Ellen since you both returned from your tour of Europe. I hope you both enjoyed it. The last time Ellen had been there was with Jeremy, before the war broke out. How is she?"

"Somewhat disappointed that due to our breaking off relations with Russia we could not visit that fascinating country." Francis' pale eyes challenged Charles.

"Oh. You mean the Soviets. Well, I visited Russia before the war, when she was a comparatively free and civilized country, and well on the way to becoming a constitutional monarchy. I doubt Ellen would have been pleased to see the horror of that unfortunate country at the present time. She is entirely too sensitive to be happy in the company of assassins, murderers, slave masters, and bloody tyrants. I think that country would now turn the stomach of a stone alligator. Now, you really must excuse me, Francis, I must be in court in half an hour."

Francis had turned very white and had become still. He stood up. He looked down at Charles, who rudely did not rise. Francis said, "You don't know what you are talking about, Charles. You read too many of our excitable newspapers and vehement magazines and books, concerning Russia, and you listen to too many of our reactionary politicians, who have their own reasons for screeching lies."

"And what do you read?" said Charles, his eyes like the points of polished steel. "And how is it smuggled into America? And by whom?"

But Francis turned away and left the office and Charles sat there alone for several moments, his hands clenched on his desk.

He told his wife, Maude, that night, of this conversation with Francis Porter. She listened in silence, without comment. Then she said, "I am worried about Ellen. I haven't seen her since June, and neither have the majority of her friends, except for that execrable Kitty Wilder, who seems always to be in that house, according to rumor. But I have heard that she appears to be unusually subdued, even pathetic. Ellen never was assertive; I hear she is now too silent, too unsmiling, and rarely has a dinner party or goes to one. I have called a few times; she was 'not at home.' You know we have invited her and that man on several occasions to have dinner with us, or go to the opera with us, and she has invariably refused, with some dismal excuse. They have not invited us to their house for well over a year."

"I doubt that you'd enjoy the company of her new 'friends,' or rather, Francis' friends. Oh, they're impeccable socially and financially, but they are what we now call 'parlor pinks.' I've met a few of them. No, you wouldn't enjoy their company, nor would I."

"Is Ellen still on Long Island, alone?"

"Yes. Why?"

"I think," said Maude with quiet resolution, "that I will pay a visit to her tomorrow. Without calling first. I have some friends in the village, so if Ellen refuses to see me I can always call on them for an hour or two."

"I don't want you to be treated with discourtesy, Maude."

She widened her lovely dark eyes at him and smiled with tender amusement. "I never recognize discourtesy, Charles, for I am a lady. And Ellen has never been deliberately rude in her life. She, too, is a lady. I don't mind coldness and a lack of welcome, but Ellen is always polite even if she dislikes someone. As she dislikes us, for some reason still unknown. I am anxious about her, deeply anxious. Perhaps there is some way I can help her."

Ellen sat alone in the gardens behind the white house whose porches were filled with light and the sound of the sea. Here, in the gardens, it was more quiet; the strong hot wind agitated the dark pines, the maples, the birches, the elms, and the oaks, and blew their leaves against a brilliant sky. Ivy ran in green waves over the back of the house; the flower beds were almost hurtingly colorful in the radiance. Ellen sat in a wicker chair under an elm; she had been sewing some petit point for a purse. It lay idle on her knee now as she stared at the pines. She wore a pale-blue summer dress of lawn, embroidered, and with a wide lace collar, and blue slippers to match. She sat so still that she appeared not to breathe, or to be half asleep, for her lids drooped even as she gazed at the trees. She was past her mid-thirties now, yet she had retained a curious girlishness of figure. There were lines about her full mouth which had lost the bright color of her youth almost entirely, and her pale cheeks were almost flat, her eyes wreathed in fine wrinkles. Only her hair was alive, so wonderfully red and flaming, and the wind loosened tendrils of it over her smooth forehead and ears. Her daughter had often impatiently urged her to "bob" it, and be "modern," but Ellen could be unexpectedly firm at times. "Your father would not like it," she would say, faintly smiling.

She was not thinking in the full sense of the word as she sat under the tree, nor was she fully aware of where she was. In these past four years she had lived in a state of abeyance; she would acquiesce to almost anything suggested to her, not entirely out of her old anxiety to please but out of indifference. There was a look of chronic exhaustion about her, though she was never conscious of being tired or driven. She lived each day and went to bed each night with the thoughtless and mechanical motions of an animal, dressing, eating, bathing, visiting when politeness insisted, smiling when a smile was expected, speaking when spoken to in a subdued, gentle voice, but never offering an opinion of her own, never animated, never overtly interested, never stirred to quickness or dispute. She saw beauty but never felt it as once she did. It was as if she gazed at a painting, with appreciation for its loveliness but without passion or involvement. When she was with friends she felt as if she were watching a stranger, while she herself stood aside and listened, not very engaged in the conversation, and almost completely withdrawn.

She lived and had her physical being only on the surface. She would read books and never remember their contents. The world moved excitedly about her but she was apart from it. It had been three years since Francis had entered her bed or even her room. She had not denied him; it would never have occurred to her to do so. But Francis, intimidated by her lack of response, her distant gaze, her lifeless submission, her uninterest in him and what he did to her, had finally ceased his overtures, his demands. He became, as he had been before his marriage, totally impotent. He had not stopped loving his wife; he had loved her too long, too passionately, too despairingly, for that. But Ellen was now farther from him than she had been during her marriage to Jeremy. He would look at her yearningly, talk to her, and she would answer him pleasantly, and he would feel no desire for her body. It had been a year since he had even kissed her. After all, he would sometimes say to the loneliness and wordless longing in him, he was nearly fifty now and no longer young and desirous.

Still, often watching her in her silences, he would ask himself: Of what is she thinking? What does she want? He saw that she quickened when her children were present, but it was more a ripple than an actual animation. He knew that she loved her son and daughter; her voice would soften and her eyes brighten, if only slightly. Then she would relapse into a smiling distance as she listened to them. At these times Francis would tell himself that Ellen, too, was no longer young. She had reached the placidness of middle age, a good hostess, a good mother, an obedient wife, amiable and agreeable, ready to answer any need of her husband or her children. If she thought of the absence of her husband in her bed she showed no signs of it.

Of what is she thinking? Francis would ask himself. If he had asked her she would have looked at him with mild surprise and would have said, "Why, I'm thinking of nothing at all, really." This is what she believed. It was her only defense against life.

Sometimes she would tell Francis that she was grateful for his care for her children, and his concern for them. Christian was more mannerly and dignified than in earlier years, Gabrielle not so mischievous and quick with a cutting tongue. Yet sometimes her numb indifference was struck into uneasiness at a gesture from Christian, a fast sidelong look from Gabrielle, as they talked with their stepfather. The children, from the earliest childhood, had been extremely engaged with each other; they lived in an impenetrable world of their own from which they excluded all others, though they were excellent company to their friends, of whom they had many, and were very alive among guests. She often wondered at this aliveness, which fascinated outsiders, though it did not fascinate their mother. They seemed greedy for experience and adventure, for living. Everything interested them. They were indifferent to nothing.

Her own youth seemed infinitely remote to Ellen now,

as if it were a youth that had belonged to someone else. Only one thing lived in her, wild and glowing and pristine as the morning, and that was the memory of Jeremy. She existed only in that memory, timeless, deathless, immediate. She no longer cried in anguish at the thought of him, for she felt that she lived in the strong circle of his enduring life and he had never departed from her. She would smile in her sleep as she dreamt of him and talked with him, and laughed with him. For his sake, she endured. Everything else was shadowless, of two dimensions, painted, unreal, without emotion or passion, without actual being. She withheld herself from any participation in life, and only dimly did she know that such participation would awaken her into unbearable torment, would drive her mad. Her spirit knew, and so kept up a barrier between her and vivid awareness, and the instinct of her flesh joined in the conspiracy to keep her sentient, yet safe from reality.

Even old Cuthbert's death, two years ago, had not struck her with too much sorrow. She had attempted to feel grief; it was only another shadow, and for a time she reproached herself for being "unfeeling." One emotion did remain with her, however, and that was her old and chronic sensation of guilt when she was forced to refuse her children something or she did not always agree with Francis. Then she would attempt to placate, to pacify, and of this her children would take ruthless advantage. Francis would merely look hurt.

"I do my best to expand your horizons, Ellen," he would say in a stiff voice. "I do my best to educate you, you who have had little education and know so little of the world."

"I know, I know!" she would answer, sometimes touching his arm timidly. "I am a stupid woman, but I feel—"

"What do you feel, if anything, Ellen?"

She would smile uneasily. "Well, what you have just said—I just can't agree, Francis. I don't know why, but I can't agree. It is as if—Jeremy—doesn't agree, either."

The mention of that hated name would make Francis wince and Ellen would see that and feel guilt, a condition which Francis always tried to enhance. "I am your husband now, Ellen."

"Yes, of course." But she never believed it. Francis was still Mr. Francis to her, and she was always grateful to him though by now she had almost forgotten why, and sometimes she liked him as once she had liked him in her childhood. She never did anything without his permission, without consulting him. She often tried to please him, as one would try to please a solicitous friend, who had been inadvertently wounded. At these times she would remember her aunt, who lived painfully in the back of her consciousness and was always accusing and admonishing, reminding Ellen of her desertion. To appease that wraith Ellen would go to any extreme.

The acceptance, the forced tranquillity, of the years before she had married Francis, had left her. The marriage had destroyed, for her, any brave serenity in which she might have lived out her life. She had retreated to the time immediately following Jeremy's death. In many ways she had also retreated to the terrible years in the service of Mrs. Eccles, the motionless and hopeless years, the years without light or meaning. To all things she had become apathetic.

As Maude Godfrey approached Ellen over the garden grass she felt acutely the poignancy of Ellen's limp body in the wicker chair, the vacant blue stare Ellen fixed indifferently on her visitor. Maude made herself smile brightly.

"Good afternoon, Ellen," she said, her voice unnaturally vivacious. "I have been visiting the Freemans in the village and I thought I'd drop in to see you for a few minutes. How are you, Ellen?"

It actually took several moments before Ellen was completely aware of Maude. Then she smiled dimly, but her eyes became wary with the old mistrust and caution. She stood up with the movements of an old woman and extended her hand, which Maude took. The grasp was flaccid. "How nice," said Ellen. "Isn't it a lovely day? Have you had tea?"

"No, but it doesn't matter."

"Margie will bring it soon, Maude. Please sit down. How is Charles?"

"Busy, as usual. What a lovely place this is, to be sure. Charles promises to look at a house in East Hampton this summer—if he has time. We get away so seldom from the city. How are Christian and Gabrielle?"

"Christian is with friends in Boston, and Gabrielle is

with friends in Vermont. I see them very little these days, it seems." For a moment white distress appeared on Ellen's face.

"Well, young people, you know. They prefer the company of their peers, as it is called now. Very restless, but times have changed. Home is no longer the main attraction. Our own daughter is away for two weeks, too, at Plymouth, with her own friends."

But Ellen was thinking of something else. "Francis wants me to sell this house. He says it is a needless expense. Perhaps it is. I don't know."

"Jeremy," said Maude, "loved it." She watched Ellen carefully. Ellen looked down at her clasped hands. "Yes. I love it, too. But I feel guilty—spending money these days—"

"What is wrong with 'these days'?" asked Maude.

"So much is needed for social causes," said Ellen. Her voice was dead. "We can't be selfish any longer. We must have progress against injustice."

Maude studied her in silence, hearing the echo of Francis' pompous and reproving voice, he who would spend none of his own money on "social causes," but used Ellen's lavishly. Maude wondered if Ellen knew exactly what she was saying and decided not.

Maude reflected. She sat in a wicker chair, her figure as slight as a young girl's in its beige linen and silk lace. Her brown straw hat partly covered her sleek black hair, which she still wore in an old-fashioned cluster at her nape. Her smooth pale face with its delicate features had shown little ravishing from the years. Her old stillness and composure—which so disconcerted Ellen—had increased, so that, in spite of her fragile appearance, she appeared invulnerable. It was this very invulnerability which so intimidated the other woman.

Then Maude said, "I often think of what a great saint of the Church said, or wrote, in 1654—Baltasar Gracián, a Spanish Jesuit."

Ellen turned to her and for the first time there was a quickening on her empty face. Maude continued: " 'It is not the law of self-preservation that you must wish upon yourself lifelong regret in order to provide help to another. . . . *Never sin against your own happiness* in order to comfort another. . . . For in every situation which spells joy to another *and pain to you,* this is the proper rule: *It is better that your friend be downcast today than that you be tomorrow,* and helpless, to boot.'"

"That sounds very selfish to me," Ellen murmured, but there was an awakening in her eyes.

"I think Jeremy would agree with Baltasar Gracián— for he spoke common sense. If an action brings comfort and joy equally to the giver and the given, then it is good. But if it is only an exchange of misery, then it is bad. A man should care for himself first; that is a law of nature. He must always protect himself. If he does not, then he is a fool." Maude's calm voice rose a little.

"Then you don't believe in self-sacrifice, as Francis does?"

Maude gulped down a derisive sound. She said, "If self-sacrifice brings pain and suffering to the sacrificer, then it is stupid. Only if it brings pleasure should it be undertaken. Altruism is not only a sort of masochism but it frequently is a disguise for self-interest, or even something worse. Ellen, the ancient Jews had a law that a man must first serve his God and his country. Then he must provide for the present and the future of all his family of his household, which included his parents and other kin as well as his wife and children. Only when he had made full provision for the security of these was he obliged to give to others. This is a very sensible law. If a man does not care first for his own and protect them as fully as possible, in order to 'share' with others, then he has committed a crime against his community. He has opened up the probability that those he should guard first of all will become a burden on society, an unpardonable recklessness, an offense against his fellows, no matter how ostensibly 'noble' it seems. But really, Ellen, I didn't come to give you a lecture—" She saw that Ellen's face had become flushed.

"Jeremy provided well for his family," said Ellen in a voice which now had a little animation in it. "So there is money to spare—for others."

Maude shrugged. "I am not only speaking of money, Ellen. I am speaking of emotion, of inner integrity and soundness. Life is not truly, at all times, a place of suffering. I believe that God, according to what the Bible says itself, made this green garden of a world for our pleasure and enjoyment and it is filled with 'many good things' to give happiness to mankind. Happiness, of course, is not a perpetual thing, but it surely should be accepted when offered and not rejected in the name of something or other—sacrifice, for instance."

Ellen said, "When I'm in the city I work for many causes in which Francis is interested. It—it keeps me busy. I work for Hopewell House—"

That germinating ground for radicalism, thought Maude.

"It teaches young people, through many lecturers, to work for social justice and social consciousness, Maude. Eugene Debs is a frequent speaker there."

"I know," said Maude in a dispassionate tone. "Wasn't he once arrested for conspiracy to kill? Yes. Didn't he also violate the Espionage Act? Yes. He was also Socialist candidate for President many times, wasn't he? Do you know what Socialism is, Ellen?"

"Well, not exactly. I do think it has something to do with fair wages and equality—"

Maude smiled. "It has been said that Communism is only Socialism in a hurry. Do you know what is happening in Russia, Ellen, under a system they call Socialism? Don't you read the newspapers?"

Ellen looked uncomfortable. "Francis says that the newspapers lie. How can they possibly know anything about Russia seeing we have no diplomatic relations with her? So the newspapers use their imaginations—Francis said."

"They also use the reports of tens of thousands of refugees who were fortunate enough to escape the murderers."

"Aristocrats," said Ellen mechanically, and Maude again heard Francis' voice. "And the bourgeoisie."

Oh, God, thought Maude. How much of this world's anguish has been caused by envious spite!

A maid appeared with a tea tray and Ellen poured the tea. Her hands, now so frail, shook a little.

Maude said, cheered somewhat that she had aroused this apathetic woman if only to annoyance: "President Wilson said, after his first collapse, 'It would have been better if I had died.' What do you think he meant by that, Ellen?"

"I don't know. Do you, Maude?"

"I think so. He had brought America to disaster through

taking her into the war. He was long a Socialist, you know, or even something worse."

But Ellen's attention was now distracted. A look of exhaustion flowed over her face. "I'm sorry I can't serve you wine or sherry or brandy, Maude. Francis is a strict Prohibitionist, you know. He detests alcohol in any form. He worked for Prohibition—"

"I know," said Maude. "He also worked for the franchise for women, too."

"He says women will prevent future wars—"

"But wasn't he a fervent advocate of this one, Ellen? So it seems to me."

"This war was—different—from other wars. It was a war for freedom from tyranny, and the self-determination of small nations, and—democracy."

"No wars are different. They all bring calamity—and gain to the sinister, Ellen. They profit nobody, except a few. And war, as Benjamin Franklin said, never leaves a country where it found it. Well, never mind. When do you think you will return to the city, Ellen?"

"Before Labor Day." Ellen sighed. "I do wish Francis didn't dislike this house so much, and insist that I sell it. Even my children don't like it. They spend two weeks here in July with me, but I can see they are restless and bored. Only I—and Jeremy—love it." Maude noticed that Ellen used the present tense, and she felt a spasm of compassion.

"Then you must keep it, Ellen, if it gives you peace."

Then she was startled, for Ellen suddenly threw up her head and her face became taut and anguished, and she beat the wicker table with her fist.

"Nothing," she cried, "will ever give me peace! Nothing, nothing. I want my husband! I want Jeremy!"

To Maude's deep alarm Ellen flung back her chair, stumbled, then raced in a staggering swirl towards the house, her arms spread out to balance herself, her hair loosened and floating in the warm bright wind.

That night Maude said sadly to her husband, "Perhaps I shouldn't have aroused her. What I said reminded her of Jeremy."

"All the better, my darling. Jeremy's memory is a buffer between the poor soul and Francis Porter's suspect diatribes and schemes. By the way, it is rumored that he is a secret Communist."

"I don't doubt it at all," said Maude.

"Still, we mustn't get hysterical. Millions who have a vague liking for what they've heard of Communism are absolutely innocent of subversive intent, and don't know what Communism is. Many are just simple idealists, ignorant and naïve. We don't want wholesale witch-burning, do we? We just need to educate the American people."

"But Francis knows," said Maude. "Yes, he knows."

34

Christian Porter, though indolent and avaricious and not a brilliant scholar, understood more than did Francis himself what Francis was actually and dogmatically propounding. Christian had few if any neurotic impulses, but he did have a discerning and cynical intellect, and grasped at once the nuances of all that Francis taught him. He understood that Francis was driven by hatred and envy and that he subconsciously was aware of his intrinsic weaknesses and lack of ability. He knew that, like all weak men, Francis lusted for power in order to revenge himself on a world which comprehended his inferiority, and refused to pretend that he was superior to other men, and thus give him the rewards he believed he deserved. When Francis became vehement on the subject of the "oppressed common man" Christian was not deceived, and with inner hilarity he remarked to himself that if anyone truly detested the "common man" it was Francis Porter.

It was no laborious feat for Christian to guess that Francis was the archetype of the Socialist, the passionate reformer. It did not take Christian very long in his research to discover that Socialists rose not from the working class which they espoused so furiously, but from the upper middle class, and that the extremely rich exploiters used these men dexterously for their own advantage. Capitalism, Christian saw, had no quarrel with Communism; they practiced symbiosis to the perfect degree. It momentarily surprised Christian that Francis did not understand this himself. Francis truly believed that the extraordinarily rich capitalists who sympathized with Socialism, and "the workingman," were men of great heart and humanitarianism. Francis reverently extolled the enormous "foundations" set up by these men, and spoke of them with an almost religious awe, his voice fervent and deep with homage. Christian, at this, would raise his reddish eyebrows and laugh inwardly with contemptuous glee and malice.

Christian, rich in his own right, wanted even greater riches, though he had no intention of working for them. He was hedonistic, self-indulgent, and totally greedy. He considered politics, for he was very personable and handsome. But politics did require some effort and progress was often very slow and not immediately lucrative. Secure in his own self-esteem, he did not need adulation. But he did want wealth and power, and, unlike Francis, he knew why he wanted them. He did not want to impress; quite simply, he wanted to rule and in the ruling become very rich. He had thought of studying law, but this demanded application and tedious years of one's life. So he reflected for a time and finally arrived at an excellent solution: He would ask Francis to use his influence to get him a high position in one of the "charitable foundations." In that way he would become famous for his humanitarianism, a companion to the most powerful and ominous men in America, and could employ their political conspiracies to exalt himself. Christian, with unusual concentration and industry, read all he could of Lenin and Trotsky and Marx and Engels, and Fabianism and Populism, and similar subjects; he listened to Francis' friends with intense interest. Though now only twenty-three he had almost immediately attracted their attention; they had recognized, in him, one of their own.

So when Francis approached the head of one of the largest "charitable foundations" in New York he was received graciously. He did not mention that Christian had barely been graduated from City College, though they knew this only too well. They were not interested in intellectualism, except when they could employ it in such men as Francis Porter. They cared only for their own kind, and Christian was that kind, a completely conscienceless, cruel, exigent, intelligent, and pitiless man, absolutely aware, with no gauzy illusions such as Francis possessed, and no innocent hypocrisies. Christian would be a neophyte among them; later they would advance him. His beguiling appearance, his mental and physical strength, his compactness of character, his lack of self-deception, his forceful drive for power, his complete absence of any principles, his inherent willingness to commit any atrocity desired of him, were weighed and measured and pleasantly approved. They asked only one thing of him—dedication to their ambitions—and they knew immediately that they had an excellent recruit.

So Christian, in the autumn of 1926, became "corresponding secretary" of the David Rogers Foundation, based in New York but with interlocking and international affiliations, all of them secret and lethal, all of them controlled by some of the most astute and ruthless and sophisticated men in the world. The majority were financiers and bankers. But many of them were industrialists of giant fame and fortune, and shipowners and magnates. Despite the attitude of their own government in Washington towards Russia—and in contempt of it—they secretly assisted Communist Russia in commerce, industry, and technology, lending Russia vast sums at a low interest. It was of these men that Lenin wrote, "I, therefore, request all representatives in the Foreign Trade Department, the railroad administration, and all other representatives of the Soviet Government in Russia and abroad to render these gentlemen not only full consideration and complete attention, but every possible assistance, removing all formalities."

The David Rogers Foundation, ostensibly designed to assist various worthy charities of its own, and those of other organizations, was one of the largest and most influential and most highly regarded in the country. It also conducted a "graduate" school of its own in New York, another in San Francisco, one in Philadelphia, still others in Boston and in Chicago. The school was deftly called the "School of Democratic Studies." Here young men, and a few young women, were subtly indoctrinated in subversion, treason, crypto-Communism, and zeal for personal power and "public service," not to mention disgust for

truly democratic institutions and established government.
It set up scholarships for selected applicants, who were
sent abroad to "study." It built libraries for which books
were carefully selected. It bought publishing houses, which
produced only books written by radical writers. It bought
newspapers and magazines. It was very prudent in all
these things, moving quietly if relentlessly. It bought politicians, who were then praised for their "humanitarian
ideals" before election to a multitude of offices. It had no
particular party as its favorite, whether Republican or
Democratic. Its partiality was for men who would obey
orders.

It had two great enemies, the new President of the
United States, Calvin Coolidge, and Alfred Smith. But
though these enemies were formidable the David Rogers
Foundation, and its several brothers, had no doubt that
the gentlemen could be obliterated in one manner or another. The foundations began to plan even this early for
the elections of 1928. It was decided, after many national
and international conferences, that the currency of America—like that of Germany—must be debased to bring on
a terrible depression in the United States, and total chaos,
as in Germany. In this they were assisted ably by their
creature, the Federal Reserve System, which controlled
the banks. The best way to destroy American currency
was to eliminate the backing of gold and introduce fiat
money. The collapse of the American economy would be
arranged. The conspirators increased their activity. Once
the economy collapsed they would introduce many "reforms" which would lead to either overt or covert Communism in America. They looked about for a politician
who would serve them, in the years to come. They studied
Germany, and sought for "the man," through their German co-conspirators.

The fact that America was devoutly and strenuously
anti-Communist did not disturb them overmuch. Through
their various organizations they promoted disastrous strikes
and other public upheavals. For these they employed men
like Francis Porter—"Labor lawyers," fervid and dangerous innocents. They employed agents provocateur, cleverly
educated and directed. These agents were not innocents,
but were carefully trained: men of education and extraordinary deviousness and intelligence, men of eloquence
and stamina, men without nerves or scruples.

The David Rogers Foundation was the creation of the Rogers Brothers Steel Company, originally of Pittsburgh but now the owner of many subsidiary firms. It also owned various oil companies of smaller stature, and fabricators of steel and aluminum, and some coal mines and electric companies. It had been noted, in the past, that it had been scrutinized by Washington for obvious violations of the Antitrust Act, but had emerged with smug vindication. It had worked well and zealously in behalf of America's engagement in the Great War, and had been praised by politicians of considerable influence. It had recently bought a radio broadcasting company in New York, and one of its firms was manufacturing crystal sets preparatory to making more wieldy and sufficient instruments. It was also quietly buying whiskey futures in the sure conviction that Prohibition would be repealed. Its stock was one of the highest on Wall Street. The original David Rogers had been a confidence man before the War between the States, operating diligently, and profitably, in various northern cities. He had also owned a number of brothels in Pittsburgh. Frugal and canny, he had later bought a bankrupt small steel mill and had entered on real fortune. His portrait, piously improved so that he resembled a bishop, hung in the main office, in Pittsburgh.

In addition to introducing Christian to the David Rogers Foundation, Francis also introduced the young man to the Scardo Society and the Committee for Foreign Studies. They were noncommittal to Francis, whom they did not trust because he was a hysteric and believed his polemics, but they were deeply impressed by Christian, whom they recognized as one of themselves. They graciously permitted Francis to bring the young man to some of their peripheral meetings and discussions, none of which Francis fully understood. But the gentlemen saw, with gratification, that Christian understood immediately, though he was still a young man.

On the occasion of one discussion Francis vehemently complained that though the country was in a state of apparent roaring prosperity the average worker and the farmer were barely subsisting. He confessed his perplexity. Wall Street was doing a tremendous business; stockbrokers' loans reached $4,422 million. An air of wild euphoria filled the nation; shops teemed with customers; the streets were smoking with cars; the factories clamored day and night. Yet the real wages of workers remained extremely low and farms were going into bankruptcy. President Coolidge said, with great complacency, "Well, farmers never made much money at any time." It was hard for Francis to equate the obvious prosperity with the meanness of the lives of farmers and workers.

But Christian understood at once. The twin brothers, rampant capitalism and Communism, were working for one end only, and Christian knew that end. It amused him that Francis did not know. When Francis confided to him that he had joined the Communist Party, in low and despised esteem in America, in order, as Francis said, that "justice could be brought to the workers," Christian could hardly keep from laughing aloud. Francis urged the younger man to join also. Christian put on a serious expression. "It would be too dangerous for me," he said, "though I sympathize fully. I am with the Foundation, you know, and the Foundation is ostensibly anti-Communist."

"I see your point," admitted Francis, though he did not in the least. In the meantime stockbrokers' loans rose so steadily that they exceeded the amount of money in total circulation in America. The few Congressmen and Senators who expressed their alarm were jeered into silence. America had reached the plateau of permanent prosperity. When Alfred E. Smith, Governor of the state of New York, and called the "Happy Warrior," also expressed his alarm, his name was quietly removed from the consideration of the Committee for Foreign Studies. He had also annoyed the Committee by his authentic social reforms, improvements in education, and attempts to conserve natural resources. "But we are for these also," Francis said to his friends, who looked amusedly at each other.

But Christian understood that Mr. Smith's solid reforms were not what the Committee had in mind at all. It was not in their plans to improve society but to destroy it. Christian understood. He was growing more and more contemptuous of Francis, who now seemed unbearably naïve to the young man.

Crime, hedonism, irresponsibility, the increasing flouting of laws, were a phenomenon to Francis, a bewilderment. But not to Christian. Once a nation became morally degenerate it became weak and fragmented, unable to resist. The sinister men began to attack Alfred E. Smith, who constantly denounced this sudden reversal of American mores in the Twenties. Though he was quite outspoken in his desire for the Presidency, of which the Democratic Party approved, it was well understood in secret sessions that he had now destroyed his hopes. He would not be amenable to the enemies of his country. An innocuous man must be chosen, a man of obvious rectitude but a man who would follow discreet suggestions from "concerned gentlemen," without the slightest suspicion of the real motives of his supporters.

Gabrielle, home for the summer holidays, enlisted the support of Kitty Wilder against her mother. "I don't want to continue in college," Gabrielle told Kitty. "Here I am, twenty years old, and am treated like an infant. I want to do something exciting with my life."

"Such as what?" asked Kitty.

Gabrielle grinned. "Such as enjoying myself. I made my debut two years ago, yet I am supposed to be just a schoolgirl, by Mama. Christian has his own apartment, and I want mine. I've talked to Mama about this and she was horrified. Why, Christian was two years old when she was my age, and she'd been working since she was thirteen! I am certainly more mature than she ever was, in spite of the fact that she was earning her own living at an early time. Times have changed, Aunt Kitty. We're very sophisticated now, and understand life and living—as Mama never did. She still doesn't know. And she's forty, for heaven's sake! An old woman."

Kitty smiled affectionately though she winced inside and was resentful. She was well into her fifties now, and raddled and wizened, though the huge white flare of teeth had not diminished in her haggard face. As always, she was soignée and elegant, and the new styles of a flat breast and short skirts became her, as they certainly did not become Ellen with her full bosom. Her dyed hair was cropped and curled; she knew all the latest songs and international scandals and depravities. She could dance like the youngest "flapper." Her vivacity might be more feverish and more forced than it was in her youth, but it was still strong and lively. She looked at Gabrielle and envied her. Gabrielle was young and vibrant, her figure "boyish," her animation authentic, her piquant dark face shimmering and gleaming with vitality, her black eyes glowing, her black hair very short and tossed over her pretty head in a mass of springing and glossy curls. She wore a bright-red silk dress with a silver belt low over her narrow hips, and red slippers; the dress was very short and revealed rolled silk stockings, pretty bare knees, and delicate calves. Her lips were full and scarlet.

"Your mother is hardly ancient," said Kitty.

"Well, she looks and acts ancient. Look at her hair; down to her hips. Look at her skirts; they more than cover her knees, and as for her bosom—like a cow. She's got awful fat lately, too. That's because she is so lazy; she hardly moves from the house; she never goes anywhere, except to Europe once a year, and then to that awful house in the summer, on Long Island. She's practically a recluse. Sluggish. Not interested much in anything, except to interfere with me. And our terrible old brownstone, so shabby and in such a neighborhood! She doesn't realize how the neighborhood has decayed. I've tried to get her to buy a really beautiful house on upper Fifth Avenue. I even took her there; it belongs to the family of a friend of mine. Really exquisite, and only two hundred thousand dollars. Mama's become a miser, too. That's Uncle Charles' fault, always talking of 'conserving assets' and 'blue-chip stocks.' But then, he's old, too. It's time for the younger generation to take over. Mama's lived her life; I want to live mine."

"I agree with you," said Kitty with a sigh. "What does Francis say about all this?"

Gabrielle shrugged her thin shoulders. "Oh, Francis. So dreary. All he talks about is 'social consciousness.' And he's stingy, like Mama, too. He spends her money, but keeps his own. He does agree with me, though, that that old house on Long Island should be sold. In many ways, he's very sympathetic to Christian and me, and understands us. He often says, 'Youth must be served,' but I have the naughtiest conviction that he means youth in the factories, and dull clothes. Sometimes he tells me I'm too extravagant. Did I ever tell you that he wants me to be a volunteer for that dreadful pet charity of his, Hopewell House? All full of what he calls 'oppressed workers and immigrants.' "

They were sitting, this warm July day, in Kitty's cool and perfect living room, sipping illegal whiskey and ginger ale tinkling with ice. Fans whirred close by. Gabrielle

glanced about restlessly. "Your house is an old brownstone, too, Aunt Kitty, but in a better neighborhood. And
you are always redecorating. Mama won't touch a thing.
All that terrible damask silk on the walls, and gloom, and
silence. Mama never touches her piano any more, though
I should count that a blessing, considering her taste in
music. We rarely have visitors, or dinners. Mama seems
shut in on herself, hidden."

Kitty was surprised at the girl's perspicacity. "Well,
Ellen was always that way, even when she was married
to your father, whom she adored. I don't think she ever
got over his death, and her marriage to Francis seemed to
make her more—retiring."

"I think," said Gabrielle, watching Kitty closely, "that
Mama is mentally ill. I think she needs a psychiatrist.
Someone to take care of her."

Kitty understood immediately. She moistened her
painted lips and stared at Gabrielle with thoughtfulness.

"Have you mentioned this to Francis?"

Again Gabrielle shrugged. "In a way, he's as bad as
Mama. He sometimes fills the house with the most horrible
people, all jabbering excitedly, all socially impossible, all
dingy and smelling. I call them 'the dirty-underwear bri-
gade.' He wants me to join them occasionally—but no!
He says they are all 'concerned' people, concerned with
social progress and reforms. Me, I think they are a bunch
of Communists."

"Oh, hush," said Kitty, laughing. "That's libelous, you
know. They could sue you, Gaby."

Gabrielle laughed also. "I sometimes drop in on them,
in our musty parlors. I'm very serious with them, and nod
and agree. They don't seem to mind that I am dressed up
and perfumed and wear jewelry. They love inherited
wealth, but they hate people who make their own way in
life. I do, too. Nouveau riche. I agree with Francis that
the nouveau riche should be taxed heavily—but not those
with inherited wealth. Patricians. We must keep the upstarts down and force them to share the wealth with what
Francis calls the 'oppressed.' We don't want new chal-
lengers to our established positions, do we?"

"No, indeed," said Kitty.

"Francis is all in favor of taxing the middle class heavily
and forcing them to 'share,' as he calls it. He also calls it
equality. Of course, that wouldn't affect 'us.' I know some

girls at college whose fathers were what is called 'self-made men,' men who worked their way up and sacrificed and studied and did all those dreary things, and became rich. I agree that they should be taxed almost out of existence. Upstarts. The girls were so damned serious, too. One of them actually said to me, 'To work is to pray.' Bourgeoisie! What could be more stuffy and lightless?"

"Nothing," said Kitty.

"One of the girls' fathers was a Russian immigrant Jew who went into the clothing business in that horrible section—you know. He worked all the hours that God sent, and became rich. Then he sent for his relatives to rescue them, Esther said, from the Russian Communists. Esther is the dreariest girl. She talks politics, and other vulgar things. She wrote articles for the college newspaper—all very weighty, concerning God and duty and the Ten Commandments and the dangers of Socialism. We all laughed at her. Now, her illiterate father should really be crushingly taxed, and maybe Esther would be quiet for once. I agree with Francis when he quotes Karl Marx about taxing the middle class."

You are quite a little bitch, thought Kitty, smiling at her young visitor with deep affection. You forget who your mother is, and was. She looked at Gabrielle, with the restless licentious face, and speculated.

"Have you talked with Francis, about a psychiatrist for your mother?"

"Yes. I think he agrees. He and Mama rarely exchange a word, and he seems miserable. I heard about a psychiatrist, a Dr. Emil Lubish. His daughter goes to school with me. I've met him. A very wonderful man, though he does have a habit of pawing and calling me *Liebchen*. He's an Austrian, and was a student of Freud's. I once talked to him about Mama and he said, very gravely, that she needs 'help.' I told that to Francis, and I think he agrees with that, too, though Mama never quarrels with him, and does almost everything he suggests. Well, almost. She can be very obdurate and sullen, and Dr. Lubish calls that a 'syndrome.' Of what I don't know."

There was a little silence, while Kitty's mind hummed. Then she said, "Well, you wanted me to help you, dear, with something. What is it?"

"Frankly, I want you to help me to persuade Mama to

let me have my own apartment. Now. Oh, I can wait until next year, when I will be twenty-one. I'm rich, as you know, Aunt Kitty, but I can't touch my inheritance until next year, and even then Uncle Charles will be watching and scolding. So narrow. I also want a car of my own. A Cadillac. All the girls have their own cars. But I have to take taxis or the subway! Mortifying. And my allowance! Beggarly."

They refreshed their glasses. Kitty said, "Surely your mother, and Francis, know your position. No? Well, I'll talk to your mother if you wish. But you know how stubborn she can be. But I'm her dearest friend, and always was. Loyal. Devoted. Her only friend."

Francis Porter said to his wife with reproving distress: "You know it is illegal and unlawful, Ellen. Where do you get this—liquor? This bootleg poison?"

"I have to have it, Francis. It—soothes me. I have a very good bootlegger. This is genuine whiskey, imported."

"Why do you need 'soothing,' Ellen?"

Ellen was silent, frowning and considering. How could she explain to him the black horror of her life, her suffering, her memories? He had no point of reference through which he could understand her. She did not care whether he understood or not; she simply wanted to be relieved of reproaches. When he reproached her she almost groveled with guilt, though she did not understand her guilt, either. She only knew that she must have an anodyne. It was little enough, to shut out the recurring dreams of her terrible youth, the torment, the hunger, the hopelessness. It was little enough, to bring back the memories of Jeremy, to whom she talked and laughed in her sodden sleep. Without those memories of her husband she would surely die.

"I must live," she muttered. "I must live for my children."

Francis looked at her with genuine misery. Ellen had become fat and shapeless. Her face was bloated, her color gone forever. She sagged and sprawled. Only her brilliant hair was alive, disheveled though it was. She ate almost nothing—but still she was fat.

"I have done so much for Christian," Francis said, his lean body vibrating with anxiety. "You are not grateful, Ellen."

She sipped at her glass; the liquid was deep amber. "I am grateful, Francis. I can't tell you how much. But—I must have peace. You don't understand. I must—"

"Run away?"

Ellen was silent. Run away? Yes. Run away from a world that never cared for despair, but only exploited it. Run away from knowing, grinning faces which belonged to people who had no integrity, no decency, no honor, no love. What had Jeremy once said? "The sweet smell of money." It was a deadly effluvium. No. It was the stench of madness. The insidious reverie broke through her defenses and her mind shut it out.

"I only wanted to live," she said. "But that was denied me, until I knew Jeremy. Then he died. Now I cannot live."

"You are raving. You are drunk, Ellen."

"In vino veritas, Francis."

She looked at him blearily. "I remember something that Jeremy once said. 'Requiem for the innocent.' He meant that about America, Francis. But I often think that it means people like me, too."

Francis was exasperated. "Ellen! You never really loved or trusted anyone in your life! You deserted your aunt, and left her to die alone. You never really cared for your children. I am your husband, but you are not interested in me. My Aunt Hortense did everything for you, and look how you repaid her. The Porters—they were good to you, and you betrayed them, and alienated them from their son. You don't try to understand your children, and their needs and wants. You have left them to me alone. Ellen, you need a psychiatrist to enlighten you as to what a selfish woman you are. You were always selfish. That has been your curse."

Ellen drank deeply. Then she burst into tears and sobbed long and with anguish. Francis left her in disgust. She fell asleep in her chair in the library. Her last coherent thought was: What is it the world demands from people like me? And Jeremy? Corruption? Evil? Betrayal? No, they will never have it from us, even if we die.

I must call Dr. Lubish for her, thought Francis. Gabrielle is right. She is mentally ill. It is possible she always was.

That night Ellen dreamt of Mrs. Schwartz in the dry brown garden of the little cottage in Preston. The old woman was weeping. She stretched out her hand to Ellen and stammered, "Beautiful daughter of Toscar." Ellen reached for the rough hand extended to her but Mrs. Schwartz withdrew it, as if with terror and denial.

Part Three

REQUIEM FOR THE INNOCENT

35

Francis Porter sat in the suave office of Dr. Emil Lubish on a cold January day in 1928. Everything was brown, gold, umber, with pale-gold satin draperies. It was warm and luxurious here and very quiet, even though Fifth Avenue traffic raged outside. A dim snow was falling slowly, implacably.

"And how long would you say your wife has been an alcoholic, Congressman?" asked the doctor. He was a heavy man, heavy of body, heavy of face, heavy of eyes and brows and hair. Even the folds in his cheeks were heavy, and his chin and hands and thighs. Unlike other affected Viennese psychiatrists, he wore no beard, not even a mustache. His large ears drooped thickly. His clothing was European, though he had actually been in the United States for twenty years. He exuded an odor of peppermint, tobacco, and something curiously aromatic which Francis could not identify. He had very little accent.

Francis hesitated. The man intimidated him with his flickering eyes, strange eyes like round silver coins, intent, a little distended, and cold and probing.

"I should think about two years, though I am not sure. She always knew that I had an aversion for alcohol except for a little, a very little, sweet wine or sherry before dinner, and she knows the law now. After we were married, and that was before Prohibition, I never permitted strong spirits in the house, even for guests. She did not seem to care, for she did not drink herself, to my knowledge. I don't know where she gets the illegal whiskey, for she rarely leaves the house any longer, and I trust the servants, who do not particularly like my wife. She is too—vague. Too indifferent to notice them."

The doctor thought, humming like a dissonant bee, and

pursing up his heavy lips. He said, "From what you have told me lengthily, I see here the archetype of a deeply neurotic woman, not very intelligent or educated, engrossed with herself, selfish, withdrawn, sluggish, lethargic, self-indulgent, uncaring about her family, obstinate and hysterical, frigid, petty-minded, narrow of outlook, deliberately unaware of the world about her, dissociative, depressed, anxious, childish, sometimes hostile, with an infantile passivity. A classic case. You have told me she had no father she ever knew and that she came from the lower working class. No doubt she resents that unknown father though she has been searching for him. Her first husband apparently filled her need for a father image, and his death has left her the more lost. She has never outgrown, apparently, the oral, anal, or urethral phases of infantile development. Her addiction to the bottle also suggests that she was deprived of a mother's breast. Yes. Classic."

Francis had cringed at some of the mellifluent words, but he nodded solemnly.

"Her now total withdrawal from the world about her also suggests a portending psychotic condition. Have you considered institutionalizing her?"

"As I have told you, Dr. Lubish, she was institutionalized for two years following her first husband's death. I am afraid she has never fully recovered. During those years I visited her often, and she did not recognize me. For a year, I was told, she did not speak and seemed to move about in a trancelike condition. Only at night, I heard, did she show any emotion. She would cry for hours, even after sedation. On her return to her home, allegedly cured, she remained passive and indifferent even to her unfortunate children, who, I am glad to say, have become normal and healthy since I became their stepfather. She shows no gratitude for my guidance and my care for them, though they are deeply affectionate towards me and trust my judgment."

The doctor nodded. "They are indeed fortunate to have you, sir. Could you induce Mrs. Porter to visit me for therapy?"

"I doubt it. As I've said, she rarely leaves the house, though I take her each summer to Europe. But she has shown less and less interest in the museums of Europe, the art galleries, the opera, and other attractions. Yet I know that these used to interest her deeply before her husband's death. In fact, she was a patron of the Metropolitan Opera and the Metropolitan Museum and the ballet."

"And now she has regressed to the environment of the womb. Mindless. Protected. Nothing demanded of her. Warm sustenance. Self-engrossed. I fear a psychotic condition—"

"Could you visit her at our house, Doctor?"

The psychiatrist pursed up his lips again and the silvery orbs of his eyes studied Francis. "I should prefer her in a sheltered environment, such as the private psychiatric hospital to which I am attached, in Westchester. Intensive therapy, leading to an awakening to reality. Tell me, is she extravagant? Does she go out of the house on wild shopping expeditions, heedless of expense, then forgetful of her purchases? Is her shopping random, without direction or need?"

"Ellen is inclined to extravagance, yes, but less than she used to be. I have argued this hopelessly with the executors of her husband's estate. They insist she lives within her income, but I doubt it. We have four servants; two would be more than adequate. That is, they would be if Ellen aroused herself to an interest in her household and occupied herself with some of the domestic duties."

When Francis had called for an appointment the astute doctor had investigated his background and the background of his wife, and their financial condition, which he found very attractive and salutary. He had been discreetly informed of the great wealth of the pair, and the wealth of Ellen's children.

"I should like a consultation with the children of Mrs. Porter, also the executors of her husband's estate. Institutionalizing of a patient is often a very difficult thing, Congressman."

"You won't find Charles Godfrey and Jochan Wilder and the rest of the firm very sympathetic, Doctor. In fact, they all think I am an ogre, and dislike me intensely. They have done so from the beginning."

Again, the silvery eyes probed. Francis would have been astonished if he had known how thoroughly he had been investigated by this urbane man with the curious body odor.

"Lawyers are usually suspicious of a second husband if

the estate of the first is large," said Dr. Lubish. "You have no control of that estate? Sad. After all, lawyers want their huge administrative expenses, you know." He smiled. "However, if Mrs. Porter were institutionalized—after you received a court order to that effect—you could then move to be appointed her guardian, in control of her income. But you, as a lawyer, are aware of that."

The doctor was not surprised to see a sharp glow behind Francis' spectacles and a quick color on the emaciated cheekbones. Then Francis said, "You must understand, Doctor, that I deeply love my wife. I want the best for her. I—I have loved her since she was a child. It was very disastrous that her life took the course it did. She would have been happier in her natural environment as a servant."

"Displacement. Yes. Very traumatic to simple characters who by nature prefer an uncomplicated and directed life. Recently a patient of mine, a former bricklayer, an illiterate man without the slightest education, fortuitously came into a great inheritance from a distant relative, whom he had never seen." The doctor coughed. "Very sad for my patient. Thrust into a milieu alien to him, wealth, advantages, a rich house, cars, rich clothes, he went quite berserk. He spent like a madman; he drank copiously. He —wenched—is that the word? He flung his money about like that snow outside. Berserk. Fortunately friends came to his assistance, and lawyers. Just in time, as it happens, otherwise he would have been bankrupt. He is now in my little private hospital, where we hope he will eventually be cured. His son—er—was appointed his legal guardian. A very sensible young man who is prudent and concerned."

He thought. "I should like to see Mrs. Porter so I could form a definite opinion. Could you induce Miss Gabrielle and Mr. Christian to consult me first, before I visit your wife—as your friend?"

"They would be only too happy to consult with you, Doctor. In fact, Gabrielle, whom you know through your daughter, suggested I come to you. Christian agrees that his mother needs care. Christian is corresponding secretary of the David Rogers Foundation, and Gabrielle is studying dress designing—when she isn't traveling. They have separate establishments of their own. Very intelligent young people. Not yet married." Francis hesitated, then said with vexation, "Christian wishes to marry the daughter of

Charles Godfrey, and I am strenuously opposed to it. Most unsuitable, though the young lady is rich, I suppose. I know her mother, who is a very sly person and who was once a servant like my wife. A governess to Ellen's children until she—induced—Charles Godfrey to marry her, she a woman of no physical charms or family or money."

The doctor had noticed how often Francis had mentioned money during this consultation about his wife. The word seemed an obsession to him. As a shrewd man of radical politics, like Francis, he did not find this obsession disagreeable. He was a very sophisticated man, indeed, and knew many members of the David Rogers Foundation. In fact, the Foundation had helped to establish his private hospital, as one of their "charities." He was very rich himself. He sent considerable sums to Germany in behalf of an obscure but fiery man named Adolf Hitler, whom the Scardo Society and the Committee for Foreign Studies were studying with deep interest. One of the eminent doctor's friends was Colonel House, who had often said openly that he hoped to see America embracing Socialism—"Socialism as dreamed of by Karl Marx." Colonel House had completed an excellent piece of work in luring President Wilson into the Great War, which had accomplished the dream of Lenin and Trotsky and Marx and Engels. The world community, dominated by an established international elite, was well on its way.

Francis indeed would have been amazed by what the doctor knew, and in what he was secretly engaged.

He said, "I will ask Christian and Gabrielle to consult with you, Doctor, and then will give you a call."

Dr. Lubish said, "As Mrs. Porter is almost a recluse now, it is unfortunate that she has no friends or acquaintances who could support any conclusion to which we may come."

Francis said, "There is one. Mrs. Jochan Wilder, the divorced wife of one of Jeremy's executors. Kitty Wilder. She has often mentioned, with sorrow, the deterioration of my wife's personality over these last years. A very good friend."

Dr. Lubish knew Kitty very well, and he smiled. "I believe my wife knows her slightly. Good. I will await your call."

He did not think it necessary to inform Francis that Kitty Wilder was often a visitor to his wife, and that she had frequently spoken with jeering laughter of Ellen Porter and her husband. She was very vindictive, especially concerning Ellen, whom she designated as an ignorant fool, feeble of mind and intellect and entirely gross and unsophisticated.

Ellen drew aside the heavy draperies of her bedroom. It was three o'clock in the afternoon and she had just awakened from a sodden sleep. She saw the silent snow fluttering in a small wind. The street was almost empty except for the gloom of the late afternoon and the darkening of the sky. She leaned against the cold window and closed her smarting and swollen eyes and said to herself, "It is another day. When will the days end?" She thought of a line from Alexander Pope: "This long disease, my life."

She no longer had a personal maid. Francis had declared that "an undue extravagance," and she had permitted him to discharge the girl. It had not distressed her. She knew the house was becoming shabbier year by year, and she did not care. The house on Long Island had been sold last summer, and she had not protested. Even this house, which Jeremy had bought, no longer interested her. Her children were gone; she lived here alone with Francis, who had become a fretful shadow to her, and a fear.

It would have astounded him, but she knew all about Francis and his activities. She read his books and his literature, secretly, and she knew that this was what Jeremy had loathed the most. There were many times when she decided that she must appeal to Francis to leave her, to let her live out the years of her life in silence. Only in silence could she be herself, and think, and her thoughts were terrible. Some two years ago she had ceased to regress to her earlier years, and had become aware, but of this awareness she never spoke. When it became too acute she resorted to drink, for only alcohol could blunt her terror and her agony. Life was almost always unbearable; the anesthetic lay in her hidden stores. The houseman was able to secure her supplies from a "speakeasy." He was a crafty and slinking little man, whom Francis liked for no obvious reason except that he was obsequious to him. "He knows his place," he would say to Ellen, who would not reply. She detested Joey, but he was necessary to her. He robbed her when he bought the whiskey "right off the boat, ma'am." It was pure bootleg, at two dollars a pint; he charged Ellen six. It was Joey, who was very intelligent, who had guessed that she needed an anesthetic for her soul, and who had artfully urged her to drink. "Good for you, ma'am. Raise your spirits." She had refused at first, and then had succumbed. The liquor had kept her alive "for my children," and so she had no sense of guilt. She was even grateful to Joey at times.

She had tried to keep her children with her, but Francis had insisted that they needed to live a life of their own, though he had cringed at the thought of their spending "all that money on themselves." He had been deftly manipulated by Christian and Gabrielle. Gabrielle had been urging her mother to buy a house on upper Fifth Avenue, and to prevent this Francis had been able to persuade Ellen to agree that Gabrielle needed an establishment for herself. "After all, she is an adult, Ellen, and must live her own life." As for Christian, he was a man, and needed to live as a young bachelor, away from his mother.

Ellen had only one illusion left, and that was that her children loved her, if they no longer needed her. True, they had never shown her respect or deference or much overt affection, but she was convinced of their devotion in spite of sudden alarms in her mind and sudden overpowering doubts. She had given them everything they desired; Jeremy would wish that, she would say to herself, forgetting his discipline of his children. She had given them profound love, second only to the love she had given Jeremy. Why, then, should they not love her and be concerned for her? If she sometimes had felt a passionate urge to die the alcohol would soothe her, convince her again of her children's love. Did they not visit her once a week, expressing their affection and their anxiety about her? It was her only consolation. Her dresser, and the library, were full of photographs of her children and often she slept with one or two under her pillow.

Charles Godfrey had lost his influence over her, and sometimes she faintly berated him when he angrily told her that her children did not need the lavish gifts and money she gave them, for they had large incomes of their own. "But it gives me pleasure to give them happiness," she would protest. "Jeremy would want it this way." When he told her that Jeremy would not "want this," she would faintly smile and turn away, her eyes knowing. This drain on her resources, and Francis' spending of her money for his "causes," sometimes found her bereft of ready cash. But Charles would not let her touch the capital of the estate. When Francis took her to Europe they went second-class on the ships. "Ostentation is a crime," he would say. "There are others who need the money. We must not follow the example of the idle rich, Ellen. We have our charities to consider, our duty to the unfortunate."

She did not know exactly when she had become so fearful of Francis. It was a different fear than the one she had felt when she had first been married to him, and it was amorphous to her though always with her, like an omnipresent threat. But what the threat was she did not know. She only knew that when he was in the house she could not rest, and would keep glancing over her shoulder as if expecting some menace. She could barely bring herself to dine with him, and often left the table without eating at all, to go to her bedroom and drink, her hands trembling. When he slept in his bedroom, which was near hers, she would lie rigid, her hands clenched, her skin sweating. It was an animal fear, an animal dread. When he left the house for his office, or his endless "meetings," she would relax into exhaustion and sleep a little. She never mingled with his friends, nor did she sit at the table with them. The threat was with them also. He always told his friends that his wife was "unwell." She had seen them from a distance a number of times, and had shivered.

She would often ask herself what she feared in this solicitous man who genuinely loved her, who would look at her mournfully and try to talk with her. Sometimes she would desperately attempt to reply to him, but her tongue would become thick and she could only mumble and stammer, and then flee. Then, alone, she would be sickened by guilt and would weep, for was he not kind and was he not devoted to her children?

She did not connect her fear of him with the books and literature with which he strewed the house. Jeremy had hated these things, but she did not relate his hatred to her fear. She thought Francis obsessed with his "causes," and helped him, but she saw no reason to be frightened for herself or her children. Besides, were not the newspapers always avidly attacking the ideas which

Francis proclaimed? The editorials were full of derision and warnings. A few times she had called Francis' attention to them, and had shrank from the sudden silent rage on his face.

Francis seemed to her the least dangerous of men, yet she recoiled from him and her body and her mind pushed at him to go away from her forever. Old acquaintances did not visit her very often, nor did she visit them. There was something in the atmosphere which she could not name, but it affrighted her. Never in her life had she felt a deep alliance with the world except when Jeremy had been alive. Even then she had entered that world only because it contained him and it was not alien to him as it was to her, for earlier memory could not be obliterated. Still, memory could be dimmed when she had been with Jeremy, and she had enjoyed living, for she loved.

Her children made her feel dull and old and irrelevant. But, she would tell herself, were they not right? She rejoiced in their brilliance, their accomplishments, their popularity, their success as human beings. She would listen, rapt and humble, to their lively voices. When they visited her it was like a gift, for which she could not be grateful enough. That they wished for her death, so they could inherit, never entered her mind, for she was a mother. It was not possible for her to imagine any occasion when they would be her enemies, and injure her, or plot against her. Once Charles, desperate with anxiety for her, had said, "Ellen, you do not know your children. No parents do, and you least of all. Just be careful, please." She had shown her first arousal in years and had screamed at him, then had gone into hysterics. It was only when her children were in the house that she lost her fear of Francis, and could speak. In Christian's voice she heard Jeremy. In Gabrielle's dark appearance, she saw her husband.

Jeremy's portrait had been removed from the library. It hung on a wall in her bedroom. She would talk to it, in a drunken haze, and would smile and nod with a momentary warmth and a deep bliss.

There was but one person other than her children to whom she clung and that person was Kitty Wilder. She could talk to Kitty, and stammeringly speak of her vague but ever-present fears, and of her children and her pride in them. Kitty invariably listened with a great display of sympathy and affection, while inwardly she sneered and laughed at this fool, this ugly fool who had lost any of the looks she had once possessed. Lately, she had become more intent on Ellen's "ramblings," which she reported to Francis and Gabrielle. She would say to Francis, with false tears in her eyes, "I am afraid for Ellen. She doesn't seem—quite right. She was never one to make herself clear, but now she is positively incoherent. Yes, I am afraid for her. I think she needs—care."

"Good God," he would exclaim. "It's been fifteen, sixteen years since Jeremy's death! Yet you tell me she still talks of him incessantly. Why?"

Kitty would gloat over his obvious distress and sadness. She hated him, but now she hated Ellen more. It was she who had informed Francis, sorrowfully, that Ellen "was drinking heavily. Didn't you know, my dear?" Sometimes she would add, "You were never her husband, really."

"I know," he would say, and would look vulnerable and wretched and pathetic, and Kitty would rejoice. His open suffering delighted her. He had rejected her for that blowsy kitchen maid, and his misery was his own, the pleasure hers. She waited for her ultimate revenge.

Of none of these conversations was Ellen aware, nor did she even suspect them. She moved to her dressing table this cold and blustery winter day and stared at herself in the mirror. Her beautiful hair was rough and dimmed and hung in clots over her shoulders and down her back. Her face was bloated and the color of old lard, the fineness of bone and contour blurred, the chin dissolved in a roll of flesh. Her eyes no longer radiated blue fire; the whites were reddened, the lids swollen. Her enlarged body had lost its graceful lines and sagged unevenly. Her lips, once the color of a blooming apricot, were dry and colorless. Her crimson dressing gown was wrinkled and none too clean and had a tear on the shoulder.

She pushed back her hair and looked at herself dully. Her flesh ached, her bones ached and felt as heavy as stone. But she no longer cared, for Jeremy was not there to admire her and praise her and touch her with a gentle and passionate hand. How long had he been dead? Many years—but it was now as if only yesterday, only today. She leaned her cheek on her hand; she could smell her own rancid sweat. Nearby, on a table, the breakfast which had been indifferently left for her hours ago was cold, the eggs congealed, the pot of coffee chilled. She was as apathetic to food as she was to life. There was only a vague booming and echoing in the house and no other sound, except for the wind at the window, and it was the faintest and most mournful of cries. The temperature of the room was frigid, for no one had lit the fire for her and the furnace heat was now erratic and did not reach her apartment when it was needed. But she was insensible to the cold. She could only sit and wind a strand of her extinguished hair about her fingers.

She waited for the night when all was asleep and she could creep down to the library and read some of the books there, huddled together like a cowering animal. Then her thoughts were alive, teeming, despairing, deathly. In the most dreadful days of her youth she had not had to endure this hell which was in her soul and mind. She no longer prayed. Sometimes she would pass her piano and touch the keys so lightly that they made no tinkling, no answer. There were times when her feeble instinct for self-preservation awakened, and she would take a bath in tepid water, comb her hair, and dress and even speak to the servants, or take a slow walk down the street. But the desolation in her heart never lifted. She was in a world of strangers, a shadow among shadows.

It was necessary to one such as Ellen to love and trust. It was only when her children visited her, with more and more infrequency, that a light illuminated her darkness, and she could love and trust again. She never knew how she was betrayed, as all those who love and trust and are innocent are betrayed. She never suspected how evil the world of men was, and how frightful. This, and her children, saved her life.

However, she had begun to secrete the sleeping tablets her doctor had given her so that she could sleep. She was not fully aware of why she did this. She only knew that the cache was a comfort, a promise.

She stood up, heavy with exhaustion, and found her hidden bottle of harsh bootleg whiskey and drank deeply of it without a glass or water. It began to warm her. Perhaps her children, or at least one of them, would visit her tonight. The house, and herself, would awaken, and she could believe in life again and have some hope, and deceive herself that she was loved.

President Wilson had said, when he had worked so hard for the League of Nations: "I think of what Tennyson had written: 'The Parliament of man, the Federation of the world.' This League is conceived in love, in trust in the innate goodness of mankind, in the generosity and desire for peace in the human spirit. War is a madness, alien to the nature of men, an evil which makes men recoil. America must lead the way to the brotherhood of mankind, with love and trust. The League will accomplish all this. My prayer is that this will be ratified, for it is the dream of my life."

He had been as innocent as Ellen Porter, and like this woman he had never known he had dreamed a fantasy. For neither of them ever knew the boundless abysses of darkness in the human soul, the meanness and avarice, the treachery, the cruelty, the animal passion, the hatred and the lust. All these made the "dream of my life" incredible, and never to be realized.

36

Dr. Lubish had listened for long over an hour to Gabrielle's tearful pleas that he "help" her "poor mother." He had listened to Christian's deep voice speaking with solemnity and grave emphasis. He had listened to Francis. He was a very intelligent man, and it had not taken him long to realize that Francis was the only one present who loved the unfortunate woman. Her children were as lethal as serpents and as guileful, and wanted only their mother's money, and to have her removed from their lives. The silvery irises of his eyes flickered on the young people as he listened in silence.

He had no doubt that Ellen was not truly mentally ill; he also, being a cynical man, had no conviction that he could rescue her, nor had he the desire to do this. If she had withdrawn, then she had had reason to withdraw. He had asked a few astute questions and was convinced that though Ellen was probably somewhat neurotic—as who wasn't?—she was not psychotic. She was only a suffering woman. If she still mourned her dead husband, so did multitudes of other women. He had guessed, accurately, from what he had been told of Ellen's childhood and girl-hood, that the memories could not be erased, or resolved. Memory itself could be a terror, a haunter of the future, a pouncer on even the happiest moments. Women with more joyful memories, memories of loving parents and comfort and pleasant childhoods, and laughter and play, could cope with the direst calamities later in life. But women like Ellen could not, for they had been robbed of fortitude in their infancy.

Ellen, for a few years, had been sheltered by a strong and pragmatic man who had protected her from knowing the things which could kill her. She had lost that arm and that strength, and confronted now with reality she could not endure it, though it was evident that she did not know as yet that she was being confronted and only subconsciously recognized the fact. She could not accept her husband's death, for his life had been the only thing she had ever possessed.

No therapy could, like Hamlet attempting to exorcise the ghost of his murdered father, erase the memory of evil, or soothe the wounds of innocence. Yet the doctor felt no pity. The race was still to the swift, the battle to the strong, despite the pleas of the simpleminded. Life had no compassion for the innocent, the trusting, the kind, the generous, the tenderhearted, the self-sacrificing, the gentle, the loyal, the loving, the pure of heart. Why should it have? the doctor asked himself. These were the weak, the justifiably exploited, the eternal fools, and nature inevitably destroyed them through the offices of their fellow men. They were betrayed by their very virtues —if they were virtues, indeed, instead of lack of intelli-gence and acquaintance with reality, and absence of the instinct of self-preservation.

He saw before him now two exigent and pitiless young people, and a man who was as innocent, and foolish, as the woman he loved. The first would relegate their mother to a life-in-death, forgotten, obliterated from memory; they would deprive her of a significant existence, even if that existence was unbearable. They would reduce her to mere animalism in a comfortable prison—for her money, and to be rid of her inconvenient presence. (Why don't they simply strangle or poison her? the doctor reflected, and a faint smile lifted his heavy mouth. It would be more merciful, if illegal.) Francis was another matter. He sincerely, even passionately, wanted his wife "cured," to be made into another person entirely. He did not realize that this was impossible, nor did he realize that his very proximity in her house was making his wife's illness more emphatic.

The doctor himself was an extremely exigent man and he frankly acknowledged this with some complacence. He saw before him the probability of a rich patient, with a rich husband, and children who would be willing for Ellen Porter to be incarcerated for life, if it would "help" her. He understood that if Francis was given the guardianship of his wife he could easily be manipulated, not only by the son and daughter of Ellen but by himself. The patient was still comparatively young—forty-two—and with care and attention could live for years, physically if not mentally. Such an incarceration would destroy her for all time—but she would live on, profitably. In a way, it was good; through drugs she would be relieved of her misery and pain and live out her life as an imbecile, a happy if mindless existence. That was not too bad. Infancy had its consolations.

He said, "There are, of course, the attorneys of Mrs. Porter. Would they accede to any—suggestions—or would they reject them? Would they fight you in court, Congressman?"

Francis pondered. "Perhaps. But then you would have to persuade them that this was best for Ellen."

Christian said, "They wouldn't agree. I know them. After all, they are paid for administering my father's estate, and they wouldn't like that threatened."

Francis turned to him. "As a lawyer, I know we couldn't do anything about your father's estate, Francis, but only your mother's income for life, which is considerable. On her death, the whole estate, hers and your father's, would revert to you and Gabrielle. Of course, if she were declared incompetent, we would have control of her present income, and could, conceivably, dip into capital. Conceivably. For expenses, and such. I've told you this before." He cleared his throat. "Naturally, as her husband, I would have a right, on her death, to a legal share in her estate. But we should not be talking of her demise. We should be discussing what is best for her now."

Gabrielle and Christian concealed their huge mockery and contempt for him. "I am sure," he added, "that her expenses in Dr. Lubish's sanitarium wouldn't devour the whole of her income."

He did not know that Ellen's children ardently wished for her death, so he could not understand the intent gazes fixed on him. He went on, "Ellen herself, on the advice of her attorneys, has some very good investments of her own, and the value of them is increasing in the Stock Market. It has been only lately that she has not had enough money left for investments. She would never dip into what she has herself, for she has always been very fearful of poverty, which is natural, considering her early life. In the event of her confinement, those investments, by the order of the court, would be left to our own judiciousness."

The young people smiled like angels upon him, and the doctor was amused, as he was always amused at human nature. He was never horrified or revolted.

He said, "I think it best if I saw Mrs. Porter, and after some conversations come to a definite conclusion as to the state of her mind. Then, after that, I'd like to consult with her attorneys, and give them my opinion. You have spoken of Mrs. Wilder, Congressman. Would she be willing, as an old and valued and concerned friend, to testify in court as to Mrs. Porter's condition?"

"Yes," said Francis. "I've discussed all this with her. She agrees that my wife needs institutionalizing at once."

"It is possible," said the doctor, "that her attorneys will agree, too. They are reasonable men. I am sure they will want to do the best for their client." When the three had left he mused to himself: "Thank God I have no children." It was the nearest he came to compassion for Ellen.

Gabrielle had a quiet consultation with her brother,

and then the two went to Ellen, dolefully. Gabrielle had thought Francis' plan childish and ineffective: to bring Dr. Lubish into her mother's house, ostensibly as a "friend." Ellen would not see him under these false pretenses.

The housekeeper, Mrs. Akins, looked at the brother and sister with false regret when she admitted them to Ellen's chill and dingy house. "Madam," she said, significantly, and with a sigh, "isn't very well. I know it is three o'clock—but she is still asleep." Mrs. Akins was a tall and very thin woman, lanky of figure, sallow of face, long of feature, and with a nose that was perpetually damp. She had eyes the color of clams, and a thin tight mouth. Her lumpish brown hair was short and coarse. She was very religious. She hated Ellen, as did the other three servants, for Ellen, though vague and increasingly lost and dim of mood, had treated them all with the most timid but generous kindness, and never seemed aware of derelictions, petty thefts, dusty corners and cobwebs or badly cooked and served food. For this alone she deserved their contempt. They thought her a "booby," and stupid, for never did she raise her voice or speak to them with the severity they merited. They had, if possible, even less regard for Francis, whom they considered a poor and pompous thing, but at least he studied the bills and questioned them and talked to them, frequently, concerning the "rights of the workingman," and gave them Marxist tracts. He had solemnly informed them of his wife's background as a servant, which made them despise her the more, and resent her. Mrs. Akins had been with the Porters since the death of old Cuthbert, who had been a tyrant, the other servants told her.

Mrs. Akins and the other servants did not know that the unusually large wages they received were due to Ellen, over the protests of her husband, nor did they know that it was Ellen's money which supported the house, and to a great extent, Francis himself. Had they known, they would have jeered at her even more heartily, when speaking of her in their rooms or their kitchen.

Mrs. Akins was not overly fond of Gabrielle, with the delicately slashing tongue and the dark knowing eyes and the antic grin, but at least Miss Gabrielle was a lady born, unlike her mother. But the housekeeper was very fond of Christian, who always had a cheery and charming smile for her, and tipped her occasionally, and he was very handsome also and sometimes leered at her until she blushed. She was not afraid of him as she was of Gabrielle, who had sharp eyes and would pointedly remark on the dinner she was being served or stare meaningly at a dusty chandelier, or fastidiously wipe a dirty mirror with a lace handkerchief and call attention to it. So Mrs. Akins respected as well as feared Gabrielle.

Gabrielle said, with a sad and downcast face, "Well, this is very important, Mrs. Akins. Important for Mrs. Porter. Do, please, awaken her and ask her to come down to see us."

Mrs. Akins regarded her keenly. She thought to herself: Well, miss, anytime you feel anything for your ma, please tell me. I mean, really feel. She went upstairs to awaken Ellen. A radio was playing loudly in the upper regions, and Gabrielle began to throw out her pretty silken legs in the Charleston, and after a moment Christian joined her. They snapped their fingers and whirled and kicked; Gabrielle wore her stockings rolled and her round bare knees glimmered in the dusky light. She had flung her mink coat, with the huge shawled collar, onto a chair; her bright black curls danced a miniature and sprightly dance of their own over her small and elegant head. She was the prototype of the Harry Kemp "flapper" of the era, all tinkling with very long strings of clashing beads and bangles and long sparkling earrings and cigarettes in a jutting holder. Her olive cheeks were rosy, her lips painted a vivid purplish red. Christian loved and admired her deeply and wished that she was not his sister; he often had quite incestuous ideas about Gabrielle. As for Gabrielle, though she was twenty-three, she was not considering marriage in her immediate future. Her life was too exciting, and varied, and if she had any fears at all it was of becoming pregnant. Like her brother, she had no illusions, no conscience, and lived only for herself, and her appetites. It would have surprised Christian to know that she often reflected on him as he reflected on her, but her reflections were also amused and less tentative. She knew that he wanted to marry Genevieve, the pretty fair daughter of Charles and Maude Godfrey, and sometimes Gabrielle was sick with jealousy and derided the girl to her brother as a "vapid nothing with empty eyes and a little mouselike voice." Gabrielle was exercising her derision less and less lately, for she had seen that Christian resented her criticisms and once or twice had abruptly and angrily told her to "mind your own business."

They danced with vigor on the soiled Aubusson rug and so were not aware immediately that Ellen was standing, smiling with love and tenderness, on the threshold of the room. She was thinking how beautiful they were, her darlings, and how full of life and brimming with the wine of youth, and her heart so throbbed with devotion that it also was full of pain. They finally saw her, and stopped their wild dancing. She clapped a little and said, "How lovely. And what a wonderful surprise this is, to see you when I wasn't expecting you."

The room was not only dusky but had a smell of mold and dust, newly aroused from the unclean rug. Gabrielle ran to her mother and took her in her slender arms, which were covered with ruby velvet, and kissed her affectionately. Christian approached his mother also, and kissed her cheek, regarding her with very visible concern. "You don't look at all well, Mama. Does she, Gaby?"

"No, she doesn't," Gabrielle said, and studied Ellen with overly solicitous apprehension. She wrinkled her nose as the keen and acrid stench of bootleg whiskey assailed her nostrils. "You haven't looked well for a long time, Mama. And that's why we're here. To talk to you. How selfish of us that we didn't come to you like this sooner."

Ellen was a little bewildered. She smoothed down her drab brown wool bathrobe with trembling hands. Her hair clustered over her head in lusterless folds and loops. Her face was flabby and colorless, her lips burned and dry, her eyes swollen and reddened and without light. She was not yet old, but she appeared many years older than she was, shapeless and fallen of body, and bloated. She bemusedly let Gabrielle lead her to a chair and gently push her down into it. "I'm really very well," she said, and her once sonorously musical voice was faint and rusty. "You mustn't worry about me, dears." She paused. "You will stay for dinner?"

Gabrielle glanced at her brother, then shook a lovingly admonishing finger in Ellen's face. "Only if you will listen to us, and promise to take our advice."

Ellen was delighted. "I was so lonely," she said. After

a pause she added, "Francis is in Washington for a few days. At least, I think that is where he is." Her eyes became momentarily vacant. "What is your advice, my darlings?"

Gabrielle dropped to her knees before her mother, and took her hands firmly in her own. They were hot and feeble. "You know how we love you, Mama, don't you?"

"Of course," said Ellen, and her scorched eyes filled with tears and her lips shook. "You are all I live for." She looked up at Christian, for he had moved closer to her. "All I live for," she repeated. Only her children and her servants would have remained unmoved by her aspect, by her piteous attempts to smile.

"Well, then, live for us, and stop making us unhappy," said Gabrielle in a brisk tone.

"Unhappy?"

"Yes, you are making us very unhappy. We know you are sick and need a good doctor."

"But I have a good doctor, Gabrielle. I see him at least once a week." She began to be filled with a delicious warmth, and her extinguished face suddenly became pearly and translucent again with love.

"Oh, old Dr. Brighton! He's just a general practitioner! You need a special man, Mama, someone with far more medical knowledge, and younger, too. Someone who has studied in Europe as well as America. A specialist. You've heard me talk of Annabelle Lubish, haven't you? Well, Dr. Lubish is her father, and a brilliant—specialist. Please, Mama"—and Gabrielle's voice grew fervent, and she moved on her knees—"please see him—for us. Do something for us, just this one time, won't you? Think of us, just once, and not yourself."

For just an instant Ellen thought: But I've heard that before! I've heard that all my life! The warmth left her; guilt mixed with her grief, but she was confused again. In some way she had failed her children—as she had failed her aunt, and probably many others. She gazed at Gabrielle pleadingly.

"I—I'll have to talk to Francis about it—"

"But we've already talked to him, Mama, and he agrees with us. He is very worried about you. But we are the most important to you, aren't we, dearest?"

Never had Ellen heard her daughter speak so tenderly, so urgently, to her; Christian's hand was lovingly pressing her shoulder. All at once tears were sliding down her cheeks, and the warmth was returning in a flood of rapture. Still, she shrank a little at the thought of meeting a stranger, even if he was a doctor. She began to speak, then fell silent. Gabrielle kissed her; Christian bent and touched his lips to her hot forehead. God, that stink of bootleg! It would kill her in time, without any interference, but he had no time to lose. With distaste, he saw his mother blow her nose on a grimy handkerchief, she who was once so meticulous and wonderfully gowned. Didn't she ever give her servants orders?

Ellen said, her voice barely audible, "Yes. For you, my darlings. I'll do anything for you." She paused. "You may tell him to call on me. I'll see him any afternoon."

This was not in the plans. "Mama," said Gabrielle, "you must go to his office, where he has all the modern equipment. He couldn't examine you thoroughly here. Medicine is much more sophisticated and elaborate these days. I'll call for you tomorrow afternoon, at two. Mama? You will do this for us, won't you?"

The thought of leaving her house, which was now a cave to her, made Ellen shrink. But she looked into Gabrielle's brilliant eyes, so dilated, so insistent, and she nodded.

"I don't go out very much any more," she said. "But if it will relieve you and Christian, I will go with you tomorrow, Gabrielle."

Gabrielle pretended to be overcome. She wiped perfectly dry eyes. She kissed her mother. Christian kissed her also. Brother and sister exchanged triumphant and elated glances. Christian thought: Even one of those monstrous dinners she has now won't be too much to pay for this. What an old hag she's become. I'm convinced myself that she's mad.

Gabrielle and Christian waited in the luxurious sitting room adjoining Dr. Lubish's office and examining rooms. Gabrielle restlessly paced the room under the admiring eyes of the nurse-receptionist. Christian stood at a snow-streaked window, tense with expectation. Dr. Lubish had introduced brother and sister to "my associate, Dr. Enright. I'd like him present—for corroboration." Christian understood at once. Then Gabrielle had solicitously taken her mother's arm and had left her on the threshold of the office. "Be good, now, Mama dearest," she had murmured, and Ellen, stiff with fear, had nodded dumbly. "Tell the doctors everything, won't you?" Ellen had nodded again. The door had closed behind her.

Dr. Enright was a tall, youngish, and very fleshy man with huge spectacles, a round full face, and a relentless mouth. He was dark and nervous. He did not enter the examining room with Dr. Lubish and his new patient. He waited as tensely as Christian had waited. He knew the role he would have to play. He had played it a number of times.

Alone with Ellen, Dr. Lubish examined his new patient, for he was an expert and thorough physician as well as a psychiatrist. He wanted to make no errors on which he could be challenged by other and unfriendly, physicians. He made careful notes during the examination, which would be typed up later. "Not an alcoholic, but is becoming addicted. Release from mental stress. Patient dull, unresponsive, vague, confused. Apparently of only average intelligence, which has declined. Blood pressure 185/110. Bloated. Attrition of the large muscles, due to lack of exercise and poor diet. Heart palpitations. Some kidney dysfunction. Lungs—conspicuous rales. Forty-three, but physical condition is so deteriorated that she appears about sixty. Eyes without life; voice low, uncertain. Gives the impression that she is only existing and not living. Skin dry, face flaccid, hands hot though she has no fever. History . . ."

He continued to list physical symptoms. But he knew that these were only functional and not organic. It was his patient's mind that was sick, and this was reflected in her body. He felt his own elation. Still, he must be very careful. Ceremoniously, he suggested she dress and join him and Dr. Enright in his office. There he sat, murmuring in short sentences with the other doctor.

Ellen came timidly into the office and the two doctors rose, and she took the chair facing both of them. Her dark-blue suit was untidy and old; her black round hat sat wearily on her thick rough hair. Her face expressed apprehension. "I am not sick," she said with a stammer. "I—I am only tired."

Dr. Lubish regarded her mournfully. "We shall see," he said in an ominous but concerned voice. "Now, tell us something about yourself, Mrs. Porter. Your children have already told me about your marriages, the first to a gentleman of considerable fame, the second to Congressman Porter."

Ellen moistened her cracked lips. What had this to do with her need for good medical attention? Then she saw that Dr. Lubish was beaming at her as affectionately as a brother, and she was touched. Tears filled her eyes; she dabbed at them futilely. She said, "There is nothing to say. Nothing. But—but I will never forget Jeremy, my first husband. He was my life—" Her voice faded.

"He died a long time ago, didn't he, Mrs. Porter?"

Ellen was silent. She fixed her wet eyes on the lamp which was turned fully on her quivering face. Both doctors leaned alertly towards her. She said, "He never died, he never really died. I feel him closer to me every day. I feel him with me. He often tries to tell me—something —but I can't hear him—yet. He—he sounds afraid for me."

The doctors quickly made notes. "Hallucinations. Refuses to accept her first husband's death. Delusions that she sees and hears him. Suspect schizophrenic reactions. Progressive withdrawal from reality; avoids friends. Loss of adaptive power."

The gentle and insidious questions persisted. Ellen replied with faltering hesitations. But they were so kind to her, so anxious to help her. She began to relax. She became confiding. They questioned her about her childhood and girlhood, and they saw the raw pain on her exhausted face. They made more copious notes.

"Heavily preoccupied. Speaks in a dreamlike voice, as if repeating nightmares. Ideas of reference. Ruminations. Fantasizes. Introversion. Depersonalization. Flight of ideas. Stereotyped affectations; grimaces. Apathetic, even when speaking of painful past memories. From conversations with relatives, a close friend, and her husband, grave personality changes over the past ten years or so. Evidences of premature senility. Falls into short and stuporous states in the midst of answering questions. Speech incoherent. Emotional reactions shallow. Interest withdrawn. Poverty of ideas. Inaccessible. Blotchy skin. Inactivity. Repetition of words. Defense mechanisms against disavowed environment. Ambivalent attitude towards pres-

ent husband, sometimes hostile, sometimes with guilty
manifestations. Diminished response to social demands . . ."

The questioning went on and on, inexorably. The
snowy day darkened. Dr. Enright, moving soundlessly,
turned on more lamps. Ellen's exhaustion increased. She
knew she had been speaking as she never did these days,
but she kept forgetting what she had said. She craved
the solace of alcohol. At times she was extremely frightened by these men, and then admonished herself that they
were so very kind and only wanted to help her, and she
must assist them, if only to please her worried children.
Besides, she felt a far-off sense of alleviation, as if an
abscess had been opened. If only she didn't feel so tired!
Her legs ached with her tiredness, and spread.

Nearly two hours had passed. Then Dr. Lubish nodded
to his colleague and they both rose and went into the
waiting room. Ellen's son and daughter stood up, eagerly
searching the physicians' faces.

Dr. Lubish was very grave. "It is too early yet to reach
a definite prognosis, I am afraid. We will need an extended period of time—of treatment, for our conclusion.
We should like to see Mrs. Porter every week—"

Dr. Enright studied the two young people shrewdly
and knew them perfectly.

"We should also like to have a discussion with Mrs.
Porter's servants—"

Gabrielle's eyes were very vivid when she turned to her
brother, and she smiled, and Dr. Enright saw that smile
and knew its wickedness. He nodded to himself.

"In the meantime I have written a prescription for
Mrs. Porter. A light sedative. A quieting influence."

"Should we try to persuade her to give up drinking?"
asked Christian with bluntness.

Dr. Lubish appeared to hesitate. He delicately scratched
his chin. "No," he said at last. "She is not an alcoholic
—as yet. She drinks because she is mentally ill, I am
afraid. At least, that is what we suspect. We need more
time."

Time, time! thought Christian. He was disappointed.
"How much time?" he demanded.

Dr. Lubish shrugged. "That is something I cannot tell
you, Mr. Porter. It may be several months. But we must

be certain—there may be conflicting interests—we must be certain."

"Do you think you can help my mother, Doctor?" asked Gabrielle in a very sad and childish voice. He smiled at her broadly.

"Oh, I am sure we can help—everybody," he said. "But it will take time. We—er—must have a firm foundation. I am sure you understand that?"

There began, for Ellen, chaotic months of concentrated probing, of tears, of bewildered terrors, of distorted nightmares, of despair, of induced stupefaction, of drugged yet unrefreshing sleep. She knew nothing of the way of psychiatrists and did not even know that she was "being treated" by them. They always pretended to give her a physical examination three times a week, and they talked of blood pressure, kidney disorders, liver dysfunction, anemia, menopause. They suggested that she indulged in bizarre ideas and assumed unnatural attitudes, and when she protested they patted her arm or shoulder as if she were insane and needed humoring. They insisted on her confidences and listened critically, and sometimes brutally disputed with her and feigned anger at her replies. This frightened her more and more; she guiltily felt she ought to please them with "good" answers, but what those answers were she did not know. Sometimes she became hysterical when they chided her that she was not "helping them" to help her, and that her children were becoming extremely anxious. At this she would lapse into incoherences—which were duly recorded.

She expressed her instinctive fears to Kitty Wilder, and Kitty always listened with apparent sympathy—and Kitty always reported, with mendacious regret, to Dr. Lubish. "The poor girl is becoming more and more confused, I am afraid. Why, yesterday, she looked at me for a long time before recognizing me, her dearest and oldest friend! Then she could not remember my name at first! Later, she mumbled that she felt she was 'living in a dream,' and stared around her blankly. I don't think she is improving at all; I know it isn't your fault. She has been this way for a long time, though she is steadily getting much worse."

Dr. Lubish asked Kitty to bring Ellen's housekeeper with her the next time she had a secret conference with him. This Kitty did, in late November 1928. Dr. Lubish knew Mrs. Akins exactly for what she was—malevolent, envious, and hypocritically meek and "worried." This long and sallow woman with the damp nose would make an excellent witness, and Dr. Lubish called in his secretary to take down her remarks, concerning Ellen, verbatim.

"The poor Madam," she sniffled, wiping her blinking eyes, "she gets worse every day." The woman clutched her purse, in which was hidden a fifty-dollar gold bill, discreetly pushed into her hand by Kitty. ("There will be more, later.") She went on: "Only yesterday she said to Joey—he's the handyman—'Who are you?' And he's worked for her for years! When he reminded her that he was Joey, she asked about her 'kitten.' She never had a kitten. I keep having to remind her to take a bath or comb her hair or change her spotted dress. Really, the smell sometimes! And she prowls around the house at night and calling for her dead husband. It gives us all chills, and we lock our bedroom doors. Never can tell about people in her condition. If I didn't really love the poor thing I'd leave, bag and baggage, I'm that scared sometimes. She creeps up behind me, without a sound—"

There was much more, all lies and distortions. Joey was called in, and gave his own colorful interpretations, forgetting, of course, to mention that he pilfered regularly in Ellen's house and had taken some of her lesser pieces of jewelry. He, too, had been properly bribed. "Honest to God, sir, she puts her arms around me and even asked me to marry her, her with a husband! And she called me Jeremy, many times. Her eyes look queer all the time. I'm scared."

"Ah, but you mustn't leave the poor lady," said Dr. Lubish in a virtuous tone. "She needs every friend she has." Not that she has any, he added to himself with some bitter amusement. Well, she's a natural victim, and victims deserve to be victimized.

"She don't have any visitors any more," said Mrs. Akins. "Not that I blame them. She can't talk sensible to anybody, and she won't answer any phone calls and then only when her kids call, and then she cries and cries and begs them to come to her, and she forgets they come at least three, four times a week to see her."

"Sad, sad," said Dr. Lubish with satisfaction.

Only one was deeply concerned, and that was Francis

Porter, and he was beginning to despair. Sometimes, when he was alone at night, he would weep. Ellen was no wife to him, but he loved her, though she now would look at him startled and afraid, when she infrequently saw him. The doctors gave him little hope for the recovery of his wife, "unless she is institutionalized, and we must arrange that as soon as possible." When Francis was not counting the cost of the psychiatrists he was calculating the fees of Dr. Lubish's private sanitarium, and pacing his bedroom floor.

Ellen had been induced not to mention her "therapy" to Charles Godfrey. "You know how he is, Mama," Gabrielle would say. "He hates to part with a cent. And you've never liked his wife, either—that servant. She's sly, and a plotter. It wouldn't surprise me to find out that he has been robbing Papa's estate."

As Charles Godfrey always scrutinized Ellen's bills and expenditures, Dr. Lubish and his colleague discreetly sent her no bill. They were reimbursed by Christian and his sister.

The drugs which Ellen had been given made her more and more disoriented. She declined rapidly in health and in appearance, and her red hair was thickly streaked with gray. Her face was haunted, old, or blank, and heavily lined and dry.

37

In November 1928, Herbert Hoover was elected President of the United States, "by a landslide."

The conspirators had done well. Here was a gentleman of the most impeccable character and credentials. There was not a single stain on his reputation. Moreover, he was no Jacobin, no follower of Rousseau, who had always been erratic at the best and mad at the worst. In fact,

Mr. Hoover was the very antithesis of Rousseau. He admired excellence, unlike Rousseau, and did not believe that all men were born "equally endowed with intelligence and good character"; he also did not believe that if a man was poor he, per se, was sanctified. Mr. Hoover doubted that "the naked savage," so eulogized by Rousseau, was superior to civilized man. He was firmly convinced that a man should earn his "rights" as a man, in all areas of society. Property, in the main, except for that inherited, was the just reward of superiority.

Mr. Hoover had long been a student of the frightful French Revolution, and particularly of Maximilien Robespierre. He was becoming alarmed at a new and insidious tendency in the thoughts of Americans: Once classless in the true meaning of the word, with no established aristocracy and no authoritarian overlords and nobles, the American people had long known that it was the intrinsic worth of a man which was important, whatever his income. But now they were being deceived into believing that a class, amorphous, faceless, called "the Masses," existed and had sovereign rights above the rights of others. As no American felt that he himself was a part of that strange classification, it gave him a pleasant sensation of virtue to shout that "the Masses" must have something "done" in their behalf. However, he believed that they lived in another part of the country and not in his vicinity, no matter how poor his own resources. He had pride.

But the conspirators understood, and through their allies, the Communists and the vociferous Socialists, they began to invade the innocent American mind. In addition, they stealthily insinuated that America should no longer boast of her accomplishments, her freedoms, her form of government, her traditions and manliness. Like the France of Robespierre, Americans should, in all sincerity, become ashamed of their country's genius and drive. This perfidious idea was adopted, not by the workers of America, but by the self-designated "intelligentsia," and the upper classes. It became quite fashionable to hold this view, and it was earnestly argued in the best parlors, while the speakers sipped, delicately, the illegal wine. For the first time in American history the educated but mentally illiterate, and the effete, began to wonder, soberly, in conversations and periodicals, "if Washington should not intervene to bring about social justice." This alien thought spread assiduously in the colleges. The average American, however, still preferred that his central government remain far from him and his private concerns and hopeful ambitions, for instinctively he knew, as did the ancient Chinese, that "government is more to be feared than the audacious tiger."

He did not know, this sensible American, that his government was being invaded by Robespierres who were already in his banks and were active among the enormously wealthy. He did not know that he was about to become the victim of revolutions, planned economy, academic theorists, panics, and of "radical social change," as the assassin Robespierre had called it. He did not know that it was plotted that America commit suicide. He only knew that he was living in "an exciting time," as the newspapers proclaimed, though his own life was usually grim and dull. His entertainment and titillations came from moving pictures out of Hollywood, full of "glamour," and of reports of rich and murderous gangsters and bootleggers, and their "molls," and of the money to be acquired overnight in the Stock Market. He hardly believed any of it; inflation was devouring his poor wages; those he saw on screen or in photographs and police reports were part of a world beyond his comprehension, and it was his only source of color. If the "intelligentsia" were calling themselves "the lost generation," as they drank coffee in French cafés and mourned that they were expatriates from "American vulgarity, materialism, and exigency," the average American was unaware of their very existence. He did not know that they were part of the legions of death gathering together to assault the battlements of his very life, and overthrow all his dreams and sanctities.

Americans were hearing more and more about psychiatrists, and their hedonistic attacks on something they called "Puritanism and maladjustment." This was strange and foreign to Americans, but curiously interesting. It was not so interesting to American parents, however, that their children were already being corrupted in their schools by advocates of "sex freedom," and were craftily being induced to despise their parents for "suppressing" them or inhibiting them. They did not know that their children were subtly being taught that authority was evil, and that they should be "free souls." The seduction of children had begun.

Mr. Hoover heard all these things, but he thought them abstractions. He was more concerned with "keeping America prosperous—a car in every garage, two chickens in every pot." He had an uneasy and instinctive suspicion at times, but he was carefully insulated by his enemies. Moreover, he had faith in the sturdy American character. He thought the majority of men were as forthright and honorable as himself. That is why he had been chosen by the conspirators to be President of the United States. He was their ambush.

Mr. Alfred E. Smith, on the contrary, was a clear-eyed cynic with no delusions about the nature of mankind. He also knew a great deal concerning the enemies of his country. He was, in many ways, far more intelligent and realistic than Mr. Hoover, and far less innocent. Like Mr. Hoover, he had been a student of the French Revolution, and Robespierre. But unlike Mr. Hoover, he understood that something desperate and malign was moving against America from many quarters, and he saw the parallel between France of the Revolution and the United States.

He, therefore, was chosen to be defeated by Mr. Hoover. The enemy feared him. He was too pragmatic, too courageous; he could not be deluded or manipulated or "advised." He lacked trust and naïveté.

After the nominations of Mr. Hoover and Mr. Smith by their respective parties, a vicious whispering campaign was inaugurated against the latter. Those powerful Catholics who were part of the conspiracy—but did not believe in or practice their religion—began to "ask" if it were wise to invest a Catholic in the august robes of Chief Executive. "Should a President have a divided allegiance?" some bought editors anxiously inquired in the newspapers. As the average man hardly understood "divided allegiance," a cruder version was presented to him: "First a Catholic as President, with the Pope directing him, and then a Jew." Mr. Hoover, a just man, found this disgusting. But Mr. Smith understood without any doubts at all. On a few occasions he hinted at the identities of his enemies—and the enemies of his country—but he could do no more than hint. It would have been incredible to the trusting American, in his innocence, to believe that his death as a man was already designed, and the death of his country.

He did not know that the terrible ghost of Robespierre was looming over America. He was too busy, and too happy when he had a little money to spend, "making whoopee." He was too elated at the prospect of the Prince of Wales visiting his country to hear the approach of the universal glacier.

It was no surprise to the defeated Mr. Smith when, in 1929, the plotted collapse of the American economy arrived. Mr. Hoover did not, at first, believe it. When he finally did, he ascribed it "to the general depression in every nation as a result of the Great War." He did not know that the world depression had been well calculated decades before, and that behind his intrepid back and honor the plot was the better concealed—as it would never have been concealed had Mr. Smith been President.

"The poorhouse is vanishing from amongst us," said Mr. Hoover sincerely. "We shall soon, with the help of God, be in sight of the day when poverty will be banished from this nation."

He upheld Prohibition. But Mr. Smith made his fatal error when he pleaded for a return to States' Rights and the Constitution; this, the deadly quiet men could not endure. Mr. Smith also made another error: He warned that permanent prosperity was an illusion and that plans should now be made to prevent adversity, public despair, and depression. Such "plans," of course, were not on the enemies' agenda. It was necessary to destroy prosperity and evoke poverty, unemployment, and financial disaster. Hence, social change and revolution.

As the enemies were only human after all, they had made a serious mistake in financing Benito Mussolini and bringing him to power in Italy. Though a number of the plotters were Italians themselves, they forgot the fierce independence of the Italian spirit, its individualism, its intelligence, its diversity. Mussolini might, indeed, embody the Italian élan in operatic flamboyance and color and love of drama and extravagance. Mussolini might, indeed, be determined to alleviate the desperate financial misery of his people following the Great War. But he was first of all an Italian who passionately loved his country.

He could never be induced to betray it and enter into the Communist-financier conspiracy. He was no Stalinist.

Yet, astute and intelligent though he was, he failed to comprehend that Communism and Fascism were one and the same thing, and the invention of the malignant forces of the international conspirators. He was too intent on reviving the grandeur of ancient Rome in his country. His enemies took heart at this. They made grandiloquent promises—and he believed them.

Once Mussolini was well established—and beloved of his countrymen—the conspirators turned their attention to Adolf Hitler. The bankrupt and despairing German people were now beginning to believe that this creature of their murderous foes would rescue them from ultimate dissolution. He might still be in prison; he might still be anathema to the more understanding of their present leaders. But he gave them hope that their country could live again.

Their enemies edited his prison-written book, *Mein Kampf,* and gave him suggestions. His cruel hysteria, his naturally unstable temperament, combined with a shrewd insight though he was obsessed with an insane dream— which they encouraged—made him the perfect weapon for their purposes. Thoughtfully, they considered Sweden. Germany was now without arms and needed the best of steel, which Sweden produced. Swedish bankers were consulted, and a conference was arranged with them to meet with the followers of Hitler. American munitions makers were involved.

They had no trouble, these enemies, with Joseph Stalin. He understood them at once. Pragmatic, dogged, both patriotic and determined on world conquest under the euphemism of "dictatorship of the proletariat," he was, in all ways, their complete man. They had no need to indoctrinate him. He had known all about them from the very beginning, which was not true of either Mussolini or Hitler.

The final tragedy was somberly under rehearsal though the curtain as yet remained down.

Charles Godfrey, seriously alarmed, had a talk with his pretty young daughter, Genevieve. "Genny," he said, "I must ask you to see as little as possible of Christian Porter. You don't understand, in the least, about him—"

She looked at him with her own gray eyes, which were filled with gentle amusement. "But I do, Daddy," she said. "I know exactly what Christian is. He is great fun and intelligent and I like his company, for he is lively and interesting. But don't worry that I will consider him as a husband, though he has proposed several times. I know his character, and I wouldn't marry him for the world. In the meantime, I am only enjoying myself."

Then she frowned. "But as for his sister, Gabrielle— she is dangerous, Daddy, and I despise her. I think she is in love with him herself."

Charles was shocked. "Where, in God's name, did you ever learn about such things?"

Genevieve shrugged. "Daddy, everybody knows about these 'things.' Everybody always did. Did you think to keep me in a perpetual kindergarten? Oh, I am nice to Gaby; she is very amusing, too." The girl hesitated. "There is something going on in that family. I am trying to find out what it is."

38

In the meantime, the drugged Ellen Porter, the deliberately disoriented Ellen, submitted to the long "treatment" imposed on her by Dr. Lubish and his colleague. She became increasingly unaware of her surroundings; she never read a newspaper any longer, or a book or a magazine. Her house was a silent prison, with wardens always watching her. The solicitude of her children, the new pampering by her servants, warmed the confused woman, made her confide in them. Deprived of love, except for that of her dead aunt and her husband, Jeremy, she had no resources, no refuge. In her natural human hunger for affection she accepted the spurious brand offered her. She refused to see Charles Godfrey and Maude.

More and more was she convinced that Kitty Wilder was her dearest and only friend, and she clung to her with such strength that it might have moved anyone but Kitty Wilder. As for Francis, he grew dimmer in her consciousness and so she rarely thought of him. He was a shadow that came and went, and when he spoke to her she did not hear him. She only saw that his lips moved, like a shadow's lips, soundlessly. If he touched her hand, yearningly, she snatched it away, shuddering. She fled when she heard his footsteps, like one threatened.

Her dreams were her only reality and they became more vivid as time passed. She lived in them with Jeremy. Lately, however, to her distress, he seemed to be warning her urgently, but though she heard his beloved voice she could not comprehend his words. Once, in a dream, he grasped her arm and urgently led her to the door of their house and tried to propel her outside. She did catch one word: "Run!" Then again: "Ellen, my darling, run away!" She could not understand and looked at him pleadingly. She saw tears on his face, that face which grew younger all the time in her dreams.

"I think," said Dr. Lubish to Francis, Gabrielle, and Christian, "that we are now ready for the sad denouement. Mrs. Porter is not improving, I am sorry to say. In fact, she is steadily deteriorating and is a danger to herself. She must be institutionalized, for her own protection. We have good lawyers; we have all the evidence we need. We must have a consultation with Charles Godfrey at once." The time was the early week of August 1929.

Dr. Lubish said to Francis, "As Mrs. Porter's husband, ask Mr. Godfrey for a conference with him, without mentioning our names, though I think it wise if you suggest that Mrs. Porter's children be there also."

Francis nodded. He was very pale. He wanted only that Ellen be restored to health and sanity. "How long will she be in the institution?" he asked.

Dr. Lubish smiled at him fondly. "Only until she is recovered. It may be some time—but we have hope."

Charles sighed with exasperated boredom when Francis called him "for a consultation." He said, "Francis, let's not go over estate matters any longer. You know it is useless."

Francis said, "It's not exactly about the estates. It is something even more important."

Charles was alerted. "What?"

"Ellen. Please, Charles, let's not discuss it over the telephone. It's a very serious matter. Have you seen Ellen lately?"

"No. Not for nearly a year. What's wrong?"

But Francis repeated his request for an interview, and Charles, with a nameless apprehension, consented at once. That night he said to Maude, "I have the strangest feeling that Ellen is in some awful danger. Never mind, I am getting fanciful in my old age." He read the newspapers and forgot Ellen. The Stock Market was more exuberant than ever, and Mr. Hoover even more optimistic about "permanent prosperity." "I don't like it," Charles said to his wife. "Something's in the wind. I wish to God that Jeremy were alive. He knew more about these things than I do. I should have kept up——"

His apprehension about Ellen returned the next day, the day of the conference. He said to Jochan Wilder, "I'd like you to be present."

The August day was unusually hot, even for New York, and Charles was unaccountably very irritable. He could not concentrate on the papers on his desk. He could think only of Ellen, and her husband. He sweated; the fans did very little good in that sluggish humidity. Charles helped himself to a cold drink, clattering with ice. The whiskey was excellent, for he had a reliable bootlegger. But the whiskey did not calm him as usual. He said to Jochan, "Perhaps it's only the heat, but I am getting very jumpy, and I don't know why."

Jochan, the affable and smiling, said, "So am I. Jumpy. By the way, I'm selling a lot of my stocks. I hope you are, too, Charlie."

"Yes. Little by little. I don't like all the optimism in the country. I think it is being deliberately stimulated."

"Oh, come now. By whom?"

Charles frowned. "I wish Jeremy were alive. He'd know. He told me a lot about—this—before he was killed. Long ago."

"Crashes always follow booms," said Jochan. "That's why I am steadily selling."

"If everyone felt that way we really would have a bust," said Charles. "I just read that Professor Irving Fisher said, the other day, that the prices of stocks had reached 'what looks like a permanently high plateau.' That's what is worrying me. When economists are elated it's time for prudent investors to give the matter some thought. And when politicians are also elated it's time to head for the cyclone cellar."

His friend the Senator had died the year before, but earlier than that he had also warned Charles. "Get out of the Market as fast as possible, Charlie, or as much as you can. I am getting hints, though the picture is murkier than ever and more hidden. I think Mussolini and Hitler should be taken more seriously than they are, and Stalin also. Something's going on; I used to know considerable but I can't find out anything now. Those men are not the crackpots the newspapers declare they are. And some somebodies are supporting and financing all of them."

"What have they got to do with the Stock Market, Senator?"

"I don't know, exactly. But I think they are a part of the whole picture. I know it sounds fantastic, but fantasies are usually based on some secret reality."

At three o'clock, this hot August day, Francis and Christian and Gabrielle arrived, accompanied, to Charles' surprise, by three strangers. Francis, whose hands were tremulous, introduced them. Suddenly Charles recognized one of them: A Mr. William Wainwright, of one of New York's most prestigious law firms. Charles knew him slightly, and his vague alarm increased. The other two gentlemen, according to Francis, were a Dr. Emil Lubish and a Dr. Enright. Now Charles was deeply disturbed. "Medical doctors?" he asked when shaking hands. He studied Dr. Lubish, the heavy man, and the younger and fleshy Dr. Enright.

"Psychiatrists, sir," Dr. Lubish said, and looked properly solemn.

What the hell? thought Charles. He glanced at Gabrielle, in her blue linen dress and small blue cloche, and at Christian, and when he saw the sobriety of their faces he felt a hard tightening in himself, and a wariness.

"We can make this brief, I believe, Mr. Godfrey," said Mr. Wainright. "It's really a very simple matter. I represent Mr. Porter, Miss Porter, and Mr. Christian Porter. I have here a number of affidavits, by these physicians, and by Mr. Francis and Mr. Christian Porter, three domestics employed by Mrs. Francis Porter, and myself. I have consulted the others and have been present, in the background, when Mrs. Porter was being treated, psychiatrically, by Drs. Lubish and Enright—"

"Treated?" exclaimed Charles, and now he was sweating very visibly. He sat on the edge of his chair. "For what?"

Dr. Lubish said, "For a psychosis. Schizophrenia. Catatonic and paranoid types. She is definitely catatonic now."

Charles was so appalled and aghast that he could only sit in his chair, widely staring and dumfounded. Mr. Wainwright, whose reputation was not to be questioned even by Charles, ceremoniously laid a sheaf of papers before the other man. Jochan sat forward, silent, listening, his fair brows drawn together.

"There is here, also, an affidavit, very important, from Mrs. Jochan Wilder, Mrs. Porter's most devoted friend," said Mr. Wainwright.

"Ah," said Jochan, very softly, but only Charles heard him.

"Please read these affidavits," said Mr. Wainright, a gentleman of about fifty and conservatively dressed in dark-blue serge even on this hot day. He had a narrow and studious face with very bright blue and intelligent eyes. "It will explain everything. We lawyers know the value of time."

Still dumfounded, Charles began to read. His florid face became set and pallid. Silently, as he finished an affidavit, he passed it on to Jochan, who had begun to smile faintly, but not with amusement. The fans whirred in the thick hot silence. A dusky perfume wafted from Gabrielle. Christian smoked a cigarette. Francis sat tensely, his fingers laced together. The psychiatrists were relaxed and serene. Dr. Lubish smoked one of his large black cigars. The uproar of Fifth Avenue was unusually loud in the silence of the office, where only the crackle of turning papers could be heard. A fine golden dust danced in a stream of burning sunlight. Gabrielle kept dabbing her eyes with a scented handkerchief. Once she sobbed aloud and Jochan smiled sweetly at her, and she hated him.

When both Charles and Jochan had completed their swift reading Charles sat solidly back in his chair and regarded each of his visitors with cold and terrible eyes. But his face showed nothing.

"I see," he said. "It's Ellen's money, isn't it?" Now there was a violent hatred in his eyes. He fixed them on Francis. "So," he said.

Francis stammered, "I know you never liked me, Charles, and never understood my real solicitude for Ellen. I love her. You never believed it. I just want her restored to health."

Charles' mouth opened on an obscene expletive, and then he closed it. Amazed now, he believed Francis, and he felt a thrust of pity for him combined with his rage. "So, in a way, you are a victim too, aren't you, Frank?"

Francis looked bewildered and glanced mutely at Gabrielle and Christian. Charles stared at them. "Vampires," he said. But then he was never very original. "You'd institutionalize your poor mother and seize her money. Very simple."

He looked at the doctors. "You own a sanitarium, don't you? Mrs. Porter is scheduled to be confined there—until her death."

"Are you impugning our reputations as psychiatrists?" asked Dr. Enright, speaking for the first time in his hoarse voice. "I suggest you look up our medical credentials, and I warn you against slander and libel."

"I have my own opinion," said Charles, and his voice was ominous. "Yes, I see it all. I have the picture very complete in my mind. You are ready to take this case to court, have Mr. Porter assigned as Mrs. Porter's legal guardian, and lock her away for the rest of her life."

"Only until she is cured," said Francis in a piteous voice.

Charles regarded him. "Frank, she will never be cured. It was planned that way. Don't you understand, you damned innocent?"

"Slander!" exclaimed Dr. Lubish.

"I don't think so," said Mr. Wainwright. "This is a natural reaction from an old friend of Mrs. Porter's. Mr. Godfrey is also the administrator of the late Jeremy Porter's will."

"Oh, I understand," Charles interrupted. "I understand only too well." Again he looked at the children of Ellen. "I knew all about you both from the time you were born. And your father had his doubts about children, too. They are now justified."

"I object," said Mr. Wainwright, and his face flushed.

Charles smiled, and it was a ferocious smile. He quoted,
" 'Incompetent, irrelevant, and immaterial.' You haven't
sworn me, sir. I know you are a very reputable lawyer. I
am only sorry that you've been—hoodwinked."

"Hoodwinked?"

"Yes. Mrs. Porter is as sane as you are, sir."

"I've seen her, Mr. Godfrey. In my layman's opinion,
which isn't admissible, I know, she is insane."

"I wonder if it couldn't have been induced," said
Charles in a musing voice.

"By whom?" demanded Dr. Lubish, waving aside a
cloud of smoke.

"Oh, you won't get me there! I am just—wondering."

Mr. Wainright was beginning to look uncomfortable.
He had a Reputation. "Have you seen Mrs. Porter recently?"

"No, I haven't," said Charles with reluctance. "She's
become a recluse."

"She never recovered from her husband's murder," said
Dr. Lubish. "I have it there, in my own affidavit. A sad
case."

"I believe," said Mr. Wainwright, "that Dr. Lubish has
a recent photograph of Mrs. Porter, taken in his office."

"Ah, yes," said Dr. Lubish, moving heavily in his chair
and fumbling at a pocket. "Here it is." He presented the
cardboard to Charles. "I still have the negative," he
added.

Charles studied the snapshot. He was shocked. He
could not recognize Ellen in this old, haggard, and
devastated woman, with the graying hair, the vacant face,
the staring eyes, the dropped and open mouth, and the
disorder of her whole person. But he knew the aspects
of a drugged person, and his rage mounted.

"What have you been giving her?" he demanded.

"Mild sedatives, to allay her anxieties and apprehensions. By the way, do you know she is an alcoholic
also?"

"No, I didn't. And I don't believe it," said Charles.
There was something about that poor bloated face which
sickened him.

"I have but one concern—my unfortunate patient," said
Dr. Lubish. "She desperately needs institutionalization—if
she is to survive at all. If this is not accomplished very
soon, I fear for her very life. I am responsible—"

"I am sure you are," Charles interposed. Dr. Lubish's face darkened.

He looked at Gabrielle, and remembered what his daughter had told him. "You are quite a hussy, aren't you?" he asked. "You can't wait for your mother to die, can you?"

"Slander," said Christian. Charles turned to him. He almost lost control of himself.

"Do you know you have perjured yourself?" he demanded.

"Now," said Mr. Wainwright. "That is a very bad accusation."

"So is perjury," said Charles. He pushed back his chair. "Who has been paying her psychiatric bills?"

There was a little silence. Then Dr. Lubish said, "Her children. They are so distressed. They wanted to keep the matter confidential. Laymen, alas, still think there is something shameful about mental illness. I understand."

"So," said Charles, "that is why no bill has come to this office." He wanted to kill, preferably Gabrielle and Christian. But Francis' aspect, miserable and confused, and very open, assured Charles again that Francis was sincere. The only scoundrels were Ellen's children—and her psychiatrists. He knew all about psychiatrists and their dissident opinions in court. He knew one honest one, whom he frequently consulted in legal matters.

He said, in a very tight and threatening voice, "I am going to fight this, you know. Things are not going to be settled amiably. I demand that Mrs. Porter submit to an examination by a very reputable psychiatrist, whose word is respected in court. Dr. George Cosgrove."

For an instant dismay appeared on the faces of the two psychiatrists. Dr. Cosgrove had the most eminent credentials. Then Christian said, "I object."

Charles grinned at him. "You object? To another opinion? How do you think that would sound in court, laddie?"

"Mr. Godfrey is quite right," said Mr. Wainwright. "In fact, I suggested this myself, if you will remember, Mr. Porter."

Francis nodded. "I want that, too. I want Ellen to be well."

Charles almost liked him. "Then, it is settled. Before I agree to any court procedures we will consult Dr. Cosgrove. I will abide by his opinion." He looked at the two doctors. "Do you object?"

Dr. Lubish said, "Dr. Cosgrove has not treated Mrs. Porter for all these months. Over a year. I am sure our opinion, then, is better than his will be."

"We'll see," said Charles. He turned to Francis again. "Ellen must be examined by Dr. Cosgrove. If her children object—" He spread out his hands. "The case will be thrown out of court. I will take care of that."

He added, as if talking to himself, "I have just seen a play. *King Lady*. Perhaps Ellen is in the same situation. We'll see."

He touched the papers on his desk. "As for these affivadits, somebody—somebodies—are going to smoke very hotly over these. I will take care of that, after Dr. Cosgrove has been consulted." He smiled. "I believe judges don't care much for perjurers and liars."

The exit of the company was almost a rout. Only Mr. Wainwright remained for a moment. He said to Charles, "See here, Charles. I am very upset about all this. Do you actually believe there is some chicanery about the case?"

"Without doubt. And I intend to prove it in court—if it ever gets there. I want to spare poor Ellen that. Her personality is very fragile, and she is a loving and trusting woman. A court appearance, and the duplicity of her children—would probably kill her. She believes her children love her. It is all she has now. They anticipated that her personal appearance in court would not be expected, 'due to her condition.' I am beginning to believe that most children are a curse—that is, if money is involved. Jeremy was right. I give advice to parents whose children I suspect: Leave your money to schools and colleges and charities, and let your children know what you have done. You will be spared a lot of anguish and misery—and you may actually save your own life."

Mr. Wainwright thought, then he nodded and smiled sourly. "I've seen a lot of that myself. Do you suggest I withdraw from this case?"

Charles shook hands with him. "After we hear from Dr. Cosgrove. He will convince you. And then you must tell Ellen's children yourself why you have withdrawn."

After Mr. Wainwright had left, Charles turned to Jochan. "Well?" he said.

Jochan shook his head, smiling his sweet and amused

smile. "Dear Kitty," he said. "Dear, dear Kitty. She always hated Ellen. I heard she was after Francis Porter. This may be her revenge. But we'll manage that, won't we?"

"We will, indeed," said Charles. "By the way, have you any hold on Kitty, the love?"

"Well, I am paying her alimony, in addition to the divorce settlement. Of course, if she were convicted of perjury, or libel, or conspiracy—"

"I think," said Charles, "that you should have a talk with dear Kitty. After Dr. Cosgrove has examined Ellen. I don't think Kitty would enjoy the Tombs."

"And neither would poor Ellen's domestics. I think, Charlie, we should get very busy very soon."

That night Charles told Maude all about the interview, and she was tremendously agitated. "Now, calm yourself, sweetheart," said Charles. "It is quite a usual case— where money is involved. What did you say?"

"I think," said Maude, "that I will consult your Father Reynolds. Ellen needs comforting, at the very least. You are not going to tell her about her children, are you?"

Charles reflected. "No. It would kill her."

He called his daughter to him, and told her in confidence. "Do you know anything, Genny?"

His daughter was disconcerted. Then she said, "Daddy, Christian has told me, several times, that his mother is crazy. I didn't think anything of it, at first. But now I do. What a monster he is. And you thought I was in love with him! How could you have been so silly?"

He kissed her. He said, "All parents are silly—about their children." She did not see his dark expression. He added to himself: Where money is concerned no man is innocent. Especially children. He had left his daughter only a lifetime small income. He did not believe in inherited wealth.

39

Francis said to Gabrielle and Christian, "I don't think we need worry. Dr. Lubish will consult with Dr. Cosgrove—"

"Can he be reached?" asked Christian, who was much less wise than his sister. Gabrielle kicked him smartly in the ankle.

"Reached?" asked Francis.

"He means," said Gabrielle, "will Dr. Cosgrove be willing to examine our mother, and testify in court."

"Of course," said Francis with fervor.

They narrowed their eyes at him with cunning malice.

"We have no alternative," said Francis. "Charles Godfrey has given us the ultimatum: He will fight the case in court and bring in formidable psychiatrists—and psychiatrists often differ before the bar—or we have your mother privately examined by Dr. Cosgrove and abide by his opinion. He is a very eminent man. I have heard him in court myself."

Gabrielle's tongue daintily touched the side of her mouth.

"So we have to convince dear Mama to be examined by still another doctor," she said. She reflected. Drs. Lubish and Enright had assured her that "there would be no trouble at all" with Charles, or little, at the worst. Their reputations were manifestly good, and they were respected. Now this contretemps had arisen through that damned Charles Godfrey.

"What if Dr. Cosgrove disagrees with the other doctors, Francis?"

Francis was very earnest. "I doubt he will. Your poor mother is obviously mentally ill. Even a layman can see that; even her servants know it. Kitty Wilder, who has

495

known her since she was almost a child, sees the terrible change in her."

"Dear Aunt Kitty," said Christian with gloom. "I watched old Jochan when her name was mentioned. He almost chuckled aloud. I can see him as a witness against her, in spite of the fact that she divorced him. Everybody knows that our dear auntie frolics in bed with almost everyone."

Francis was shocked. "How can you say that of your mother's best friend?" But he was shaken.

"What if Cosgrove disagrees with our psychiatrists?" Gabrielle repeated. "It's a possibility, you know. We must be prepared for it."

"Then we must get still another."

They regarded him cynically. They knew what they knew, which Francis did not, that infernal innocent. "Well, we can only try," said Christian. He was very despondent, and full of anger and hatred and, above all, frustration. Even Gabrielle, the sprightly, was lugubrious.

They went to Ellen, and had difficulty in arousing her attention. They knew how heavily her doctors kept her under drugs, "to calm and soothe her." "Mama," said Gabrielle, catching the stench of liquor and wrinkling her nose, "your doctors aren't doing you much good. We've decided to consult another. You will help us, won't you?"

Ellen was dimly alarmed, then she smiled lovingly. "Certainly," she said. She frowned as if puzzled. "But I'm really feeling much better—some of the time. I sleep very well."

Gabrielle and Christian had had the thought of persuading Ellen to refuse to see Dr. Cosgrove, but had had second thoughts concerning it. Charles Godfrey, he had more than hinted himself, would petition the judge to demand other opinions, and the judge would naturally consent. After they had persuaded Ellen to see Dr. Cosgrove they approached him discreetly themselves. But he refused to see them.

"I want to form my own opinion," he told them on the telephone, in a deep quiet voice. "This is a serious matter, Miss Porter. I refuse to let you try to influence my conclusions. I assure you that if I believe your mother needs to be institutionalized I will so recommend it. No, I don't want to hear, just now, what Dr. Lubish and Dr. Enright have said. I do know, however, that their reputations are excellent." He did not add that he knew all about Dr. Lubish's private clinic.

"There is no need to tell all you know," he said to Charles, in the latter's office. "Yes, those men are authentic psychiatrists; they are no charlatans."

"What do you know about them privately, George?"

Dr. Cosgrove winked. He was a short, broad, and very jolly little man, with a rosy face and gay alert eyes. "Every man, it is said, has his price. Is that enough? I will talk to them myself, after I've seen Mrs. Porter." He became serious. "It is very possible that Mrs. Porter is indeed in need of institutionalization. If she is, Charles, I am going to agree with our noble friends."

Gabrielle expertly "dressed" her mother for the consultation with Dr. Cosgrove. "We must look our best," she chided Ellen. "You don't want us to be ashamed of you, do you? There, dear. You look wonderful." Gabrielle had applied a purplish layer of rouge on Ellen's ravished face and heavy lipstick on her sick dry mouth. She had frizzled Ellen's faded hair and had perched a very youthful new hat, a small one, on top of the shaking mound. She had bought Ellen a violently red tight dress, which stretched at the seams, and with a scandalously short skirt. Ellen feebly protested; even she could see the parody of an aging and raddled hag in her mirror. "But you look splendid!" cried her daughter, standing off and clapping her hands in mock delight. "Ten years younger, at least!" She became grave; she squatted on her heels before her mother. "Now, Mama, we are going to be very good— and honest—with Dr. Cosgrove, aren't we? We are going to tell him everything, so he can help you. We are going to tell him of our awful dreams, and forgetfulness, and our nightmares and our lack of appetite. We are going to tell him how you think Papa is with you all the time—"

"But he is, dear." Ellen's voice was small and smothered. Gabrielle nodded. "Good. Be sure and tell the doctor that, and how you hear Papa talking to you all the time. Promise?"

"Yes."

"And we are going to tell him about that nasty liquor, too, aren't we?"

Ellen colored under the streaks of gaudy rouge. But she said, "Yes," very humbly. "I do want to get well, dear."

As Dr. Cosgrove had told Francis that he was not to

bring the children of Ellen to his office, Francis brought her himself. He concealed his concern when he saw Ellen, for she had not spoken or taken his offered hand. But he said with brightness, "You really look very well, Mrs. Porter. That—er—dress, and that hat—they are very becoming. You are a good shopper."

Some of Ellen's fear of strangers left her. "I—I didn't buy them myself. My little daughter did—Gabrielle. She —she put this stuff on my face, too."

Dr. Cosgrove nodded. He had suspected such. Then Francis said, with stiffness, "I think it is all hideous, Doctor. Ellen doesn't usually wear paint and powder; I never saw them on her before, and her eyebrows aren't black and shaggy like that. And the dress and hat are horrible. They make her look like a clown."

Ellen stared at him, her dull eyes suddenly glinting. "My daughter knew best," she said. "Francis—go away— please." Her breath came hard and fast.

Dr. Cosgrove, prepared not to have much mercy on Francis, was now sympathetic. Charles had told him a great deal. "A real burning zealot, George. One of those ideological pure-in-hearts. But you've probably read much about him in the papers. I'll let you form your own opinion."

Francis retired to the waiting room, and Dr. Cosgrove saw Ellen's vague but poignant relief. He put her with kindness into a chair facing him. He saw her clenched hands, the rising fear in her poor face, her shrinking. She kept wetting her painted lips. Once, he thought, she was a beauty; it is in her bones, the hint of her former coloring. She has been destroyed, perhaps deliberately.

He smiled at her, a warm and generous smile. He sat in his chair and looked, Ellen thought distantly, like a Santa Claus without the beard. He rocked gently in his chair and continued to smile at her. But inwardly he was aghast. It was obvious that she was, indeed, very ill, physically at least. The white and shrunken neck; the mottled hands, beyond her actual years; the dried and sickly skin; the shapeless breast; the tremulousness about her mouth. Her constant blinking. She gazed at him fearfully. He said, "Haven't we had the hottest weather this summer? Do you mind it, Mrs. Porter?"

"No. Yes." She lapsed into dullness again. "I—I don't notice it. I don't go out very often. I don't remember when last I was out." In her voice he heard the echoes of once lovely cadences.

"Well, I don't blame you for not going out much," he said heartily. "Tell me. Did you bring the medication Dr. Lubish gave you?"

"No one told me to," said Ellen. But Dr. Cosgrove had specifically ordered Gabrielle, on the telephone, to have her mother bring her medication with her. His bright smile became set and mechanical. "I—I take a lot of pills," Ellen added, as if in apology. "Blue, pink, white, yellow—"

"With whiskey, too," the doctor said in a matter-of-fact tone. Again the unhealthy color flared out under the purplish rouge. But she saw he was not condemning her. "Yes," she faltered. "Dr. Lubish said it would be good for me. He even gave me prescriptions for it, so it would be— genuine—whiskey."

She looks at least sixty-five or seventy, thought Dr. Cosgrove, and his full red mouth thinned. Well, we'll see. He rang for his nurse and took Ellen, who was trembling again, into his examination room. She looked about her helplessly.

"What are you looking for, Mrs. Porter?" he said with compassion.

"Why, why—the dressing room—and the gown."

"Why?"

"The other doctors—they always examined me—every time."

Ah, thought Dr. Cosgrove. "We'll dispense with all that, Mrs. Porter. You've been examined enough. Except for your blood pressure and heart, and above all, your eyes. Your eyes." He had seen the dwindled pupils. "Then we'll have a little chat."

"Chat?" she repeated. Her voice trembled. "I've told the other doctors everything. They can tell you."

"No. Just tell me yourself. I will ask the questions." He saw her terror. He leaned towards her, over his paunch. "Mrs. Porter, don't be afraid of me, above anything else. I am your friend. Believe me, I am your friend. Nobody is going to hurt you, ever again. I promise you that."

He waited, compellingly. She began to relax. She even attempted a piteous smile. He nodded, reached out and touched her hand. His own was warm and firm, and all at once she trusted him, as never she had trusted Dr. Lubish.

He talked to her quietly and soothingly, and her eyes filled with tears. She began to sob, and he did not scold her as Dr. Lubish invariably did.

"I want my husband—Jeremy!" she cried, and wrung her hands.

"Certainly you do, Ellen, certainly you do. That is only natural. I'm a widower, and have been for twelve years. And I still want my wife. She is still my wife. And I believe, very surely, that someday we will be joined together again. Just as you will be joined to your husband."

"Well," said Charles Godfrey to Dr. Cosgrove as they sat in Charles' office two weeks later. "You've told me nothing, except that you have put Ellen in the hospital, with private nurses, and have forbidden any visitors. How you managed that I don't know. Congratulations, anyway."

"I had able help," said Dr. Cosgrove. "That burning zealot, her present husband. You were right. He honestly cares about her. I pity him. He is truly devastated; he wants her to be what he calls 'well.' He never questioned any of my orders. After all, thank God, as her husband he comes before her children, under the law at least. He even appears at night, until very late, to be sure that my orders are carried out, and Ellen's children refused admission. They've hounded him, of course. But he stands against them, just repeating what I've told him to say. And the nurses I ordered are grenadiers. Good women. I've told them a little, and they understand. They've seen such things before, unfortunately."

"What do you tell Ellen when she asks for her children?"

"I tell her that I've informed them that she must be quiet, and alone, for a while, and that they agree with me. God help her, with children like that. I'm glad I don't have any; no regrets. This is not an exceptional case. I've handled others just like that."

He took the drink the impatient Charles gave him, and pondered. He became somber. "She's been systematically drugged. She is suffering some withdrawal symptoms, which can't be helped. But she is not an alcoholic. I do permit her a drink or two a day, and it quiets her."

"Drugged!" Charles exclaimed. "I suspected that, but had no proof."

The doctor made a wry face. "There's another thing. I have no proof anyway, except her condition. I can't accuse those rascals of anything, in court. The law demands proof. At the very worst they can claim that they prescribed what they thought best for her—and who is to deny it? They can even swear they gave her only mild sedation, for her nerves and hysteria—and who is to prove differently? After all, into the bargain, they do have an excellent reputation, and the judges respect them. I asked Mr. Porter to bring me all of his wife's medicines, and he innocently brought a bottle of aspirin, Bromo-Seltzer, and a very mild sedative. There was nothing else in her rooms, he said, and I believe him. But who is to say who spirited it all away? Who is to accuse whom? We are on dangerous ground. My own accusations, and physical findings, and suspicions, would mean nothing without actual proof."

"George, you could have brought in another psychiatrist."

Dr. Cosgrove gave him another wry smile. "The medical fraternity sticks together. We don't want any scandals about our brethren. The American Medical Association doesn't like it at all. The public must have faith in its physicians. I see their point myself. After a friend of mine reminded me."

"Damn," said Charles.

Dr. Cosgrove comfortably filled the pipe. "Oh, I don't know. I've had a nice little visit with Lubish and Enright. We understood each other, without much argument. I named the drugs I suspected they had given her, and hinted that we found some forgotten bottles, secreted away. I recalled to them certain medical ethics— Well, to cut it all very short, they've discharged Ellen, and will not see her again."

"No!" cried Charles with delight. Then he was no longer delighted. "All right. Ellen is safe in the hospital, just now. But what will happen when she is discharged? Her children could get men like those other two, again, and it will start all over. She trusts her children implicitly, and, as you have said, God help her and other mothers like her."

But Dr. Cosgrove was not disturbed. "Let's not cross our bridges until we come to them." He was as unoriginal as Charles himself when it came to metaphors. "I've had a long talk with Francis Porter, too. He has written a formal letter—at my dictation—to Miss Gabrielle and Mr. Christian, and has warned them that as he is Ellen's husband he especially forbids them to visit her without his permission. They are also warned not to call any other physician for Ellen, without my express and written orders. By the way, your friend, Mr. Wainwright, has received a copy of that letter, and I have one here for you, too. Mr. Wainwright has withdrawn from the case."

Charles sat back, his face glowing with fresh delight. "You have been busy, haven't you? So Ellen is safe for a time. But you haven't told me all about her condition."

"She is extremely undernourished. We are forcing nutrition on her, telling her that she will cause her children much worry if she refuses. There has been an improvement, I am glad to say, in spite of the original, and continuing, withdrawal symptoms, which are subsiding. We hope to have her completely cleaned out in another week. The nurses take her on the garden roof, in the pavilion, every day for walks, in spite of her protests. But she is calmer. I repeat to her, over and over, that her late husband would be very angry if he knew that she was resisting all of us. I have told the nurses to encourage her to talk of him as much as possible." He sighed. "Such love as hers is frightening. I never encountered such devotion and passion before, in any woman. No one should love another like that. It is murderous, to the lover. But then, as you've told me, she never really had anyone else. Tragic. She will never get over it. But at least I hope that she will soon begin to accept it, as once she was so beginning, as you've told me, until she made this second marriage."

"Then you think you can cure her, George?"

The doctor hesitated. "In rare cases, such as hers, she cannot be completely cured of love. But I have discovered that she has a lot of courage, an unsuspected reservoir of fortitude. I doubt she will ever forget, but at least she will learn to endure. I wish she had some religion."

"She did. Until Jeremy was murdered."

"So? I wonder if there is any way of restoring it. It would be of magnificent help."

Charles mentioned Maude's suggestion, and the doctor nodded brightly. "Let the good Reverend try, at any rate. It won't do any harm. It may do some infinite good. If he is tactful."

"He is an old priest, and tactful, and old priests are very wise, George." Charles asked, "What of poor Francis?"

"Now, there is another sad case. I have advised him, as delicately as possible, not to try to see her for a long time, until she is discharged from the hospital."

"But I'm afraid her marriage to him precipitated her condition."

"Yes. We'll come to that, in time. She's not in the least psychotic, though she's neurotic, which is no wonder, considering her history. I had thought to ask him to leave his wife, but then remembered her children. So I told him that though it might be best, for a long period, for her not to be overtly aware of his presence, in her house, he must guard her. From her children. I had to do some subtle reasoning with him there. He believes her children to be devoted to their mother. He was considerably shocked, and incredulous. So I told him that they might, with the best of intentions, of course, bring other physicians to her in her house, or take her to their offices, and that would cause her to have a perhaps fatal relapse. He is really a very simple soul, in spite of his ideological madness. He is, himself, quite psychotic. Didn't you know that?"

"I suspected it. All his kind are, as Jeremy used to say."

"Yes. There is an old saying: 'Who will guard the city when madmen are the guards?' Well. There is a very thin line between sanity and insanity, as you know. They often overlap. We are all occasionally mad. But men like Francis Porter never are quite sane. We have one hold on him, fortunately. He loves his wife, and love is the best of guardians."

Charles was moved, thinking of his wife. Then he said, "Jochan Wilder, whom you know, has persuaded his former wife, Kitty, to leave the United States for a long, long world cruise, or something. She won't be bothering Ellen any longer, either."

Dr. Cosgrove was not certain of that. "At any rate, we'll come to some decision much later. By that time I hope to have Ellen restored, physically, and good health is, in itself, an excellent protection against knaves."

He sighed. "The more I see of my fellow men, the gloomier I become. We are all the sons of Cain. Murder is our familiar."

40

Charles called in Gabrielle and Christian Porter, "for a consultation."

He looked at the two with stern and bitter hatred, and condemnation.

"I don't need to beat about the bush. You have been warned by your own former attorney, Mr. Wainwright, that if you attempt, again, to injure your mother you will hear from him, and 'privileged communications' be damned. Above legal ethics there is the preservation, literally, of the innocent life of another, whose life is in danger from mortal enemies. You two are the mortal enemies of your mother. One more attempt out of either of you—and I will tell your mother everything. I will advise her, even force her, if necessary, to write a new will and leave you nothing. Nothing. That is the only thing you understand, isn't it? Money."

Christian did not pretend to be astounded or appalled. He smiled viciously at Charles. "A new will can be overthrown. She is insane."

"You'd like to believe that, wouldn't you? But she is not in the least insane. True, she has been driven to the edge of insanity—by her children. Her dear and beloved children. Damn you both! Push me too hard, drive me too hard again, and I'll bring legal action against you. Don't smile. To save themselves, Lubish and Enright will testify that your mother was never psychotic, and that you both, and others, lied to them about her and misled them. You've made affidavits, filled with perjuries. Do you know what the penalty for prejury is, in New York State? Fines, and imprisonment for five years."

He leaned back and grimly surveyed them. Their smiles were fixed and mechanical, and then they faded.

"I honestly wish you'd try something. I really do. Then I can see that you get what you deserve. By the way, Christian—and what a name was given you!—you are employed by the Rogers Foundation. I know all about them. They don't want any scandal about their employees. Very discreet, if sinister men. They don't want any nasty attention drawn to them; you do that, and you will no longer be corresponding secretary, as you call it. And I will follow you all the rest of my life. Believe me, I will."

He turned to the pert Gabrielle, who was gazing at him with raw hate. "You won't look so soignée, Gaby, after five years' imprisonment, for perjury. Believe me, I am not just threatening you. In fact, if it weren't for your poor mother I'd see both of you the hell in prison. For her sake, I am temporarily—refraining from doing what I'd love to do. And, by the way, there is always a grapevine among the medical fraternity. You'll get no more bought psychiatrists to 'treat' your mother and try to institutionalize her. That's another crime. I think the law thinks that more heinous than perjury itself. It doesn't look kindly at matricide—and that's what you attempted—matricide."

He stood up. "Now get your damned bodies out of my office, before I have you both kicked out. Just remember my warning."

They left without another word. He felt sick. He had to take a strong drink. He had won. But how long would the victory last? Murderers like Ellen's children could always find another way. The drink gagged him. "God damn them!" he said aloud.

Dr. Cosgrove entered Ellen's small hospital suite on this late warm and golden September day, and he was full of cheer. She was sitting in her sitting room, and was dressed in a becoming blue silk robe. She had lost most of her former puffiness of body and face, and her features were tranquil if sad. The blue shine of her eyes was slowly returning, and her hair, brushed and tended, was recovering its former brilliance. There was even some color in her lips, and her hands were once more smooth and white. Years had dropped from her appearance. When she saw Dr. Cosgrove she smiled timidly but trustfully.

"Well, we are beautiful today," he said. They were now such friends that she looked grateful when he kissed her

cheek. He pressed her hand. "Look what I've brought
you," he added. "A bottle of Dom Pérignon—champagne.
It's my birthday, and I thought you might like to celebrate
with me." He turned to the smiling nurse who sat nearby,
knitting contentedly. "Would you please get us a bucket
of ice?" He sat down in a nearby chair and regarded Ellen
with pride. She said, "When can my children visit me,
George?"

"Oh, in a short time, if you go on improving this way.
How's your appetite?"

"Miss Hendricks, my nurse, says it is quite good." The
sadness deepened on her face, and Dr. Cosgrove watched
her keenly.

"What's the matter, Ellen?"

She turned away her face. "I don't know why I am
living; I don't really want to live. No one needs me, not
even my children, for they are adults now. I'm useless.
What is there for me to live for any longer?"

"You've always lived for someone else, haven't you?
Don't you know, yet, that our first duty is to ourselves?
You, Ellen Porter, are unique and individual; God made
you that way. He had a reason for giving you life, and
that was not just to serve others. You say no one needs
you. God needs you. You can't live just through others,
Ellen dear. You can't take their reality as yours. You have
your own reality. Ellen, this is a beautiful world in spite
of the people in it. It is yours to know and enjoy."

She moved restlessly.

Dr. Cosgrove slapped his knee. "I have a friend just
outside the door waiting. A very good friend. I'd like you
to meet him, Ellen."

She was immediately alarmed, and shrank. "A stranger?
Oh, no! Please."

"You disappoint me, dear. I thought you had got over
your silly fears. He's here to help me, with you, celebrate
my birthday. Will you let him come in, for my sake?"

She was silent for a moment or two; her new color
faded. Then she said, "Yes, for you, George." But her
lips trembled and she looked at the closed door with
trepidation. The doctor went to the door, closed it briefly
behind him, then opened it again. Ellen looked at the
stranger, and was surprised. He was an old tall man,
almost bald, with a kind seamed face, and she recognized

him as a priest at once. She visibly relaxed. A clergyman would not threaten her.

"Father Reynolds, this is Mrs. Porter, my patient. She is going to help us celebrate my birthday. In fact, it's his, too," he added, much to the priest's amusement. He raised his white eyebrows and the doctor winked at him. The priest shook Ellen's hand and he was immediately compassionate, for her fingers were tremulous in his. But she smiled weakly at him, in silence. It had been decided that as Ellen mistrusted Charles Godfrey it would be best if Ellen were introduced to the priest by the doctor, who had her confidence.

The priest sat down and regarded Ellen with earnest if smiling attention. "It is very kind of you, Mrs. Porter, to let George and me—celebrate our—mutual—birthday, with you. There are not many occasions in life when we can truly celebrate. We should enjoy them fully when they occur, shouldn't we?"

"I—I don't know—Father. I don't seem to have much capacity to celebrate anything, any longer." Her voice, its old nuances almost restored, shook. She added, "No one to celebrate with."

He looked at her as if astonished. "Why, you have God, my dear! You also have the sun and the moon, the stars and the gardens, the trees and the clouds—all innocent things."

She smiled faintly. "I never thought of them being innocent. But they are, aren't they? Yet, they are insensate."

"And who told you that? They are part of God, just as we are. And as that part, and living, they are aware, with a different awareness than ours. No one need be alone, even if isolated from the human world; the world teems with friends of quite another world, and a beautiful one, unlike the human creation."

She looked at him with an interest which made Dr. Cosgrove rejoice. "I never thought of that," she said. She hesitated, while she thought. Her face changed. "I'm thinking of many people I've known. I'm beginning to realize that they weren't all nice, as I thought at first. I know you think that is uncharitable of me, and perhaps it is."

"An awareness of reality is not uncharitable, Ellen. May I call you Ellen? Thank you. Not to see things clearly and as they are, and that includes people, too, is to be deliberately and foolishly blind, not charitable. It's also dangerous. I am an old man now; I've been a priest for nearly sixty years. I've seen a multitude of people and have heard thousands of confessions. I know humanity, Ellen, I know its endless crimes and sins against God and man. I know there are very few really good people in the world, and they are very hard to find. As for the wicked, and their name is legion, we should not judge. We should have compassion, even while we recognize what they truly are. Compassion is not sentimentality or self-deception. We share the human predicament; we all have the capacity for evil. Evil is not strength; it is weakness, a violation against our immortal souls, and against God. Therefore, the strong, the good, should pity these malformed people —and pray for them."

Ellen pondered. "I always felt so guilty when I had uncharitable thoughts about others—"

"There is no guilt in recognizing the truth. The truth cannot only make you free—it can put you on guard and even save you. The recognition of truth does not mean you should condemn, though condemnation is often justified."

Her voice dropped. "There's another thing: When I do see people for what they are—I am thinking lately of some I have known—it depresses me and makes me feel— desperate—and frightened. I think that's what started my —illness." She made herself smile apologetically. "Truth, I think, can also kill you, can't it?"

He nodded. "Keats was quite wrong when he said that truth and beauty are the same. They are often mutually exclusive. But we should encourage strength in ourselves so that we can face even the worst of realities with fortitude. We can be brave. In fact"—and he smiled at her winningly—"I have presumed to add another Commandment to the Ten: 'Thou shalt be brave.' God knows, most of us are not brave at all. It is a virtue few possess, but it can be cultivated just as surely as the other virtues."

Ellen whispered, "I don't think I was ever very brave."

Priest and physician exchanged glances. The priest had already been fully informed of Ellen's life. The priest said, leaning towards her, his hands clasped between his black-clad and very thin legs, "I've never met you before, Ellen, but in some way I know, with absolute conviction, that you are one of the most courageous people I have ever known."

She looked at him in surprise. "I? Oh, you are wrong —Father! I have always been so afraid—"

"Fear and bravery are not—like truth and beauty— sometimes mutually exclusive. I think only those who have reason to fear can be greatly brave. Your soul, perhaps, recognized that reason even if you did not, consciously, yourself."

She shook her head slowly, and now there were tears in her eyes. "I was quite brave, when my husband was alive. Now I am not."

"I've heard about your husband, your first husband, Ellen. He was a brave man as well as courageous. Are you disappointing him?"

Her mouth trembled again at his use of the present tense. "I—I don't know if he—lives—any longer, though in my dreams—" She paused. "How can I be sure he is not—dead—his spirit dead, I mean?"

"You can be sure that he lives, for there is no death. That is a scientific fact, as well as a spiritual verity. Everything changes, but it never dies. The seas come and go, but they are never lost. Fiery stars collapse in on themselves, and are darkened. Then they explode into new fire and new life. Everything is always contemporary, Ellen. It is never the past. For present and past and future are all one and the same thing. You have surely read that love is deathless; it never dies, for it is an immortal force. So you can be absolutely certain that as your husband loved you, he still does. Can you imagine not loving *him*?"

Her color was returning; all at once she looked young and eager and alive. "No, I could never stop loving him! It is wonderful to think, perhaps, that he still loves me."

Without that surety, she suddenly thought, I would die. She said, "The very thought that perhaps he still loves me, as he once did, makes my life—worthwhile."

The priest gave her a beautiful smile. "He loves you, is waiting for you, and he knows, if you do not, that you as a human soul are 'worthwhile.' For your own sake. Not only he knows that, but God also."

She looked away. "I believed in God—and when Jeremy was killed, because he was a good and noble man, I lost faith."

"Sad," said the priest. "When we lose faith in the face of calamity our faith has not been so strong after all, has it?"

She smiled a little mischievously, and the doctor rejoiced. A dimple even appeared in her cheek. "You see how weak I am, Father. I told you I was not brave."

He replied with slow and somber emphasis, "Ellen, I am a priest. I was always a priest, even as a child, in my heart. Yet, there have been times when my faith was shaken. Once or twice it was totally lost. Then I was desolate, for I had alienated myself from God. Once knowing Him, then rejecting Him, is our present and future Hell, for we cannot live without Him, remembering the glory of our lost faith and our adopted sonhood with God. What, in this world, can replace the bliss of our former knowledge?"

Ellen thought of the sweet serenity which had pervaded her childhood, when she had had a child's utter faith, in spite of the circumstances of her life, and now the tears ran over her eyes in silence.

"How poor are they who have never known God," said the priest, taking her hand firmly. "Don't they deserve our utmost compassion, our prayers, our solicitude? For what is any man's life without the reality of God? It is a dream, a fantasy; it is barren and fruitless. When such men think they know life and its teeming, they are only seeing mirages in a desert. What gives everything reality is not there. The Godless are not alive; they are the truly dead. But then, they never lived, either."

Her tears, dropping heedlessly on her breast, spotted the silk darkly. But the priest knew they were healing tears. He raised his hand and blessed her, and she did not know what he was doing, though it strangely comforted her, as if a loving pact had been made between herself and a friend. When his hand dropped she took it like a child and held it, and smiled through her tears, and he knew that he did not need to promise her his prayers. She knew that he would pray for her.

Outside the suite, the priest said to Dr. Cosgrove, "She is a beautiful woman, in her soul as well as her flesh. She is also very fragile and delicate of personality. Yet, she also has an innate fortitude. That is not a paradox. We must teach her to endure, as she has the capacity for endurance, which she is no longer exercising. We must help her."

"I think she is already exercising her native bravery. She doesn't have the terrible nightmares she once had. So we have reason to hope."

Still, Dr. Cosgrove, natively cheerful and optimistic, felt a sudden terrible premonition. Without knowing exactly what he meant, he said, "God help her." He and the priest returned, smiling, to Ellen, for the champagne, and she laughed, as she had not laughed for years. Her face was young.

41

On October 24, 1929, Ellen was discharged from the hospital. Charles Godfrey had warned her children, "Pretend, as you always did, that you love her and want to help her. If you don't—then I promise you that I will do the very worst I can to you."

He said to Francis, "Don't intrude on Ellen at any time, Frank. I know you care about her. The best you can do for her is to see her as little as possible." He felt pity for the sorrowful man. "It isn't your fault that this is necessary. She'll never forget Jeremy. Yes, you may remain in her house. In fact, I recommend it. She needs protection from her children, and you must guard her. I know you don't believe how frightful they are, but I know."

"She looks so well now! When she saw me for the first time, a few days ago, she smiled at me, as once she used to smile, when she was young."

"Yes. Well. Be the 'Mr. Francis' to her, as you were in her childhood."

Maude, while Ellen was in the hospital, had rid Ellen's house of Mrs. Akins and Joey, and had replaced them with sound people. She had ordered the cleaning of the house and its redecoration, and it was as bright and as fresh as when Jeremy was alive, and filled with flowers. Ellen's old clothes had been thrown away, by Maude. She had bought gay new ones for the sick woman. Ellen did not know what her real friends had done for her, for she had never recognized them as friends.

So Ellen, returning to her house, felt its freshness and beauty, and it seemed alive to her with the presence of Jeremy. A surge of sweetness came to her, and comfort, and peace. She asked Gabrielle and Christian about Mrs. Akins and Joey, and Gabrielle, after a glance at her brother, said soothingly, "Oh, they were really no good, Mama. Very careless. We replaced them. I think they were stealing, too."

Gabrielle and her brother were simmering with hatred and frustration. They had passionately hoped that Ellen would die in the hospital, and so leave them free of her presence and, above all, give them access to her money, and the estate. They had always despised her and mocked her, from their earliest childhood. They hated her now for her renewed youth and health and the clarity of her eyes and her bright color. Her voice enraged them, because of its strength and cadences, the voice of her young womanhood. When she kissed and embraced them they wanted to strike her. They smiled at her lovingly. She had so far recovered that she could shake hands placidly with Francis, and the poor man was quite overcome. Perhaps, in spite of what the doctor had said, Ellen would forget Jeremy and look with kindness and affection at himself, as once she had done. That would be enough for him, and he asked nothing else.

Miss Hendricks, Ellen's nurse, was to remain with her in her house for a week or two. She was a cheerful and motherly woman, and she had come to love Ellen. She had her orders from Dr. Cosgrove, and she was wise. After the greetings to her children and her husband, Ellen was put firmly to bed by her nurse. "We must rest as much as possible. And every day we are going to have a nice walk, aren't we, and perhaps a nice drive. We will even go to the new talking pictures; it's really amazing to hear the actors' voices on the screen. Lifelike."

"I feel so alive," said Ellen, as she undressed and permitted herself to be put to bed. "Don't I have the most wonderful children? Imagine Gabrielle going to all that trouble to replace my wardrobe, and put all these flowers around, and have my house redecorated! And all those plants in the garden! I am blessed, in my children, aren't I, Miss Hendricks?"

"Yes," said Miss Hendricks, and her pleasant face became grim for a moment. She was grateful that she had never married and so had no children. Ellen, softly rapturous, smiled contentedly, and fell into a deep and quiet sleep. Gabrielle and Christian had gone to Wall Street. Something appalling was happening there, and they were concerned and apprehensive.

They had reason for this. The disquieting news had begun at ten o'clock that morning. It was a chill and cloudy day in New York, yet dusty. The gloom was not only on a frantic Wall Street, but in the natural air also. To the perceptive, it was as if the ground were rumbling in preparation for a devastating earthquake, and those tremors were reverberating all over the country, in every broker's office. By noon the rout was on. Charles E. Mitchell of the National City Bank in New York was reputed to have appeared suddenly on Wall Street, thrusting unheard-of millions into the Market. Standard Oil of New Jersey, the Aluminum Corporation of America, and the Bethlehem Steel Company, among many others, delivered even more millions of dollars for "call money." By one o'clock these loans had reached the incredible amount of over seven hundred and fifty millions. Now more than rumors were flying frenziedly about, and the rumors were proved true. Trading, selling, were frenzied. General Motors sold at 57½, twenty thousand shares; Kennecott Copper, twenty thousand shares, at 78. Brokers spoke wildly to their customers, and the selling mounted precipitously. U.S. Steel, which had sold, only a month ago, at 261, collapsed to 194.

Who was selling, and why? No one knew but the deadly quiet men, as Jeremy had called them. They were meeting today in the barred building of the Committee for Foreign Studies, and coded messages were constantly being delivered to them from all over the world. They smiled coldly together when news arrived that Thomas W. Lamont had met with the foremost bankers of New York, and had produced a two-hundred-and-fifty-million-dollar "fund" to stabilize the shaking Market. Richard Whitney, of J. P. Morgan and Company, bought twenty-five thousand shares of Big Steel at 205. In the meantime he also bought large blocks of the leading stocks at the last-quoted price. There was a sudden resurgence of hope among stockbrokers. But the tickers were over five hours late all over the country, and when they finally stopped their frantic clickings, some ominous facts were evident: A record had been established. Nearly fourteen million shares of stock had been sold, at a loss of nearly twelve billion dollars. Nothing like it had ever happened to the Market before.

"My God," said Charles Godfrey to Jochan Wilder, "so Jeremy was right, after all! It has begun—the planned economic collapse of America. Thanks to your own warnings, Jochan, I sold off much of my doubtful stock over the past three months." He paused, then smiled a tight small smile.

"Something's just given me a lot of pleasure. As Jerry's administrator and executor, I sold off a lot of somewhat doubtful stocks, and bought blue-chip and sound bonds, and so, so far, the estate is in a good position. But my real pleasure is in thinking about the estate left to Christian and Gaby Porter by their grandparents. Really all dubious stocks, and they've gone down almost to the vanishing point today. Those two were practically wiped out—in a few hours—and I could dance with joy. Of course, that doesn't affect what they will receive from Jerry's estate—" His smile vanished. "When Ellen dies."

Jochan said, his amiable smile wider, "They both shook off your advice, and bought the wilder stocks for themselves. You were too pessimistic, Christian said. He saw himself with about a two-million profit by the end of this year, and so did his sister. I wonder what they're thinking today."

Charles' pleasure returned, and he laughed. Then he was suddenly uneasy. Jeremy's estate, held in trust for Ellen during her lifetime, was in excellent order, though it, too, had rapidly declined to lower figures today. But the stocks and bonds were sound, if depreciated in value. The capital was intact, if not as large as only yesterday. Ellen could not take that stock and restore the fortunes of her children. Jeremy had planned well for her safety.

Only on her death would they inherit the capital—her children. Only on her death—

"Now what's wrong?" asked Jochan, seeing his friend's grim expression. So Charles told him. Jochan shook his head in smiling denial.

"Oh, come now. They might wish her dead, but they wouldn't dare do anything openly against Ellen. What they had tried wouldn't even be condemned by the most suspicious. They were just trying to 'help' their poor mother, and had engaged well-known and respected psychiatrists. They're no fools, Charlie. They aren't going to put themselves in jeopardy. Don't let your imagination stray. You've warned them enough, and they do love their precious selves. Do you actually fear they might poison or strangle or shoot Ellen?" Jochan laughed. "Covert and heartless bastard and bitch—but they'd never be grossly overt. Too dangerous."

Charles considered, and then he said sheepishly, "Of course, you're right. Smooth scoundrels. But—the coolest rascals, the most calculating and careful, can be driven mad—and do murder, when their fortunes are threatened. Never mind. I'm probably using my imagination, my Irish imagination, too vividly."

His uneasiness returned. If only Ellen trusted him; if only he could approach her as a realistic mother, with warnings. But Ellen did not trust him, and she loved her children with a passionate devotion, and she was not realistic and did not credit the full evil in the human heart, and its endless and bloody and very probable machinations, when it was forced to act, violently.

Charles began to think of the great financiers and bankers in New York who were buying up incredible amounts of stock. Why were they doing this? To stabilize the Market, to reassure the terrified country? To encourage more buying among the millions of smaller stockholders—to the latter's ultimate ruin? There I go again, thought Charles, using my imagination. But he now had another uneasiness, stronger than before.

"The sweet smell of money," Jeremy had once remarked to him. "Men lose their wits when it comes to money. They have no other allegiances."

When Ellen awoke from her afternoon rest she said to Miss Hendricks, "Are my children having dinner with me tonight?"

Miss Hendricks said, "I don't think so, dear. There was

a call for them, on Wall Street. Something to do with the Market."

Ellen was disappointed, but she said with firm brightness, "Yes. I read something about it last night, rumors, in the newspapers." Then she remembered something with vague alarm. What had Jeremy once told her? "The ultimate collapse of the American economy, planned for a long time, will soon arrive—then will come the tyrants and a planned economy and the slavery of the American people." She thought of her children's inheritance from their grandparents—surely that was safe? She did not think of her own income or the effect of a coming collapse on Jeremy's estate. Her anxiety grew, for Christian and Gabrielle. Ah, well, she had money, and so she could help them. At this thought there came to her a strange and disquieting stiffening in herself, a resistance, which alarmed her. Father Reynolds had visited her frequently in the hospital after his first visit. He had said to her, "He who does not protect himself, even from his family, has made himself contemptible and a victim. We have no right to tempt others. 'Thou shalt not tempt.' That is another of my amendments to the original Ten." He had smiled, but his eyes had remained grave.

Preoccupied, Ellen dressed herself for dinner. She did not understand the sharpness of her thoughts, and she waited for the familiar old softening and sense of guilt. They assaulted her, then, oddly enough, they faded away, and she felt a strength in herself, an alertness she had never known before. She smiled a little and thought: Ah, well, one must help one's family, mustn't one? To a certain extent—yes. But if I do not care for myself, why should they care for me? If I do not respect myself, how can I expect others to respect me?

As she dressed she looked at the portrait of Jeremy, and he seemed to be smiling at her, and she smiled in return. The crushing agony of before did not return to her; now she experienced peace and the conviction that Jeremy still loved and cared for her, and that his protection surrounded her as a wall. Above all, his love was her surety, her profound invincibility against all the evils of living.

She went down to the library for a glass of sherry. Francis was there, gloomily staring at the fire. He was biting his fingernails and restlessly moving in his chair. When he saw Ellen he stood up and looked at her with silent hope. She was surprised that she did not shrink and leave; she found herself even smiling. Francis saw that smile and he forgot all the terrifying things he had heard today, and the fact that suddenly he was not accessible to his "friends."

"Ellen?" he said tentatively. She smiled at him again. This was "Mr. Francis," the friend of her youth, and she felt sorrow that she had misjudged him and driven him away. He was, to her, not her husband, but the guardian of her childhood who had been kind to her and had helped her. She held out her hand to him, and her blue eyes shimmered with light.

"Will you have dinner with me, Francis?" she asked. "I would be happy if you would."

He held her hand. He was afraid to speak for a moment, for he felt a desire to cry. He kissed her hand and said, "Thank you, Ellen, thank you."

She sat down near him and accepted a glass of sherry. He could not look away from her; she was so renewed, so alert, so gracious, so the Ellen he had remembered through all the years. She said, "I have just been listening to the radio. It seems something very bad has been happening today, on Wall Street. What does it mean?"

Francis was beginning to know. He knew it was planned; he had heard it over many years, from his "friends," but they had been very guarded and noncommittal in his presence. "Changed economy," they had murmured, "leading to the freedom of the people from the oppression of capitalism, and their exploitation." He had accepted this as a necessary "social change." But he himself had been at the Stock Exchange that day, and had seen the terror and disorder of not mere "capitalists" but of "little" people who had invested in the Market in good faith, and under the songs of "permanent prosperity." He was confused. He had foreseen a "change" which did not beggar the "common people," or throw them into a desperate panic. He had reviewed his own portfolio. It was very vulnerable. Why had his "friends" not warned him a week ago? Why had these been so busy, in their guarded offices, that they could not spare the time to talk to him and reassure him and explain to him the events of the day? He was terribly frightened.

They were capitalists themselves, of enormous wealth. Were they feeling threatened as he was feeling threatened at the debacle of today? He had taken their advice over several years, buying what they recommended, and selling at their suggestion. Yet he had seen for himself, today, that his own portfolio had dwindled disastrously in value.

He said to Ellen, "I don't know what it means, Ellen. I know no more than does anyone else. I only know something calamitous has happened. But I've been hearing of all the huge purchases of stock in an effort to save the Market— It will probably be all right."

"I hope so," said Ellen. He looked at her glass of sherry and said, "Where did you get that, Ellen? You know it is illegal."

The old mischievous dimple, lost long ago, suddenly flashed in her cheek. "Oh, Father Reynolds gave it to me. It isn't sacramental wine; it was from his own cellar, he said." She sipped at the sherry and her eyes, so newly brilliant and intensely blue, flashed at Francis over the brim of her glass and he could not feel resentful. But he said, "I don't approve of—religion—Ellen, and particularly not of the Roman kind."

She removed the glass from her lips and said with gentleness, "Father Reynolds and Dr. Cosgrove brought me back to life, Francis. Whatever Father Reynolds does and says is truth to me. If I hadn't lost my faith I should not have been so ill, for so long. I—I lived in a wilderness. Now I see the earth and sky again. I am beginning to have hope."

He stared at her, and again his eyes moistened. Her voice had moved him more than her words. "Anything that helps you, Ellen, is wonderful for me, too. I can't tell you—I was in despair. To see you looking as you do now, to see the color in your lips and face—it is like—like seeing life returned to one who was thought dead."

In her turn she stared wonderingly at him, and knew for the first time that he loved her, and she was both abashed and filled with sadness, and regret.

"Thank you, Francis," she said, "thank you, so much. There isn't enough love and caring in this world, and they should be cherished." She added, after a moment, "You know, I never trusted Dr. Lubish and Dr. Enright. There was something—I don't know what it was, but I was afraid of them. I know you did your best, to engage them for me—"

He was perplexed, and thought. Then he said, "I didn't

know about them. It was Gabrielle, and Christian, who recommended those doctors to me, Ellen."

She looked at him intently. "My children?"

"Yes. Gabrielle knew his daughter—Dr. Lubish's daughter—and I went to see him at Gabrielle's suggestion. Frankly, I didn't like them much myself. They didn't help you in the least."

But she had paled. "Christian, and Gabrielle?"

"Yes." Ellen put down her glass and then gazed at it.

"They are very reputable men," said Francis. "I am sure they help many sick people. But they were not for you, it seems."

"No. Not for me," said Ellen slowly. She looked at him and her eyes seemed far away. "I am sure that my children thought they would help me, as you did."

"Of course, Ellen."

She was thinking of the last months she had been under "treatment," the increasing nightmares and lethargy, the mounting detachment from life, her suffering, her fear, the harsh accusations, the bewilderment and the anguish, the torment of her dimmed days, the grotesquerie of her daily hallucinations, the lost months of her existence, and, above all, her terrors.

"What is it, Ellen?" asked Francis.

"Nothing, really. I was just thinking of the difference between doctors. If I had continued with Dr. Lubish, I think I would have died. I might even have been dead now."

"You were very sick, my dear. I was almost out of my mind."

She heard the sincerity in his voice and she suddenly thought: Why, poor Mr. Francis! He is really very kind—and simple. It is strange that I never knew that before. How worn he looks, how old, how thin, and dejected. I must be kind to him, in return, and never forget what he once meant to me. She smiled suddenly at him, as at a neglected friend, and her face was translucent. She held out her hand to him and he took it. His own was cold and wet, and she felt a deep compassion for him.

"How really good you are," she said with impulsiveness, and she never feared him again, for she saw what he was, a deluded if pompous man, a fanatic, but a pitiable one. She had insights now that she had never possessed before, and was almost overwhelmed with her sadness.

"I am not very good," he murmured, and pressed his hand for a moment to his forehead. "Things seem very— peculiar—to me now. I'm shaken. I don't know what it is all about. I can't explain, Ellen. I can only say how happy I am that you are home now, and seem your old self."

They dined together, with the radio near at hand at Francis' request. Ellen listened with him. The voices were jubilant. The Market had "sustained a flurry today, but now all was well." The President had expressed his optimism. "A mere adjustment, temporarily," he had remarked. "We have reached a permanent prosperity for all Americans. Our country is sound and stable and rich and strong. There is no need for anxiety."

"That is good," said Ellen after the final broadcast was completed. But Francis, to her surprise, only glanced at her somberly. He had never had much appetite. He had barely stirred the food on his plate. They had not told him, he thought. He had not expected "this" to come so soon. He was both afraid and puzzled. But perhaps, after all, it was indeed just a "flurry." When the Market revived, as it surely must, tomorrow, he would begin to sell his stocks, at least a large part of them. If disaster threatened America, he wanted to be safe from the universal calamity. His friends had not warned him because there was no occasion for warning.

"I found a letter today, from dear Kitty," said Ellen. "At home. She had been so ill, you know, and her doctors had ordered her to take a long rest. All her community activities, and social affairs! But she is so lively she forgets that she's not young any longer. She expects to be back in New York in two days. I'll be so glad to see her again."

Francis turned his bemused face to her. "Kitty? Oh, yes, Kitty." He thought of her affidavit concerning Ellen. "She was much concerned about you, Ellen, and worried so much about you. But she had to go away, though I know she wanted to remain here and do what she could. It was all very sudden."

He was more bemused than ever, remembering the dark and crafty smile on Kitty's face whenever she mentioned Ellen. He said, and did not know why he said it, "Ellen, perhaps it would be better if you had other friends besides Kitty Wilder. She is too old for you; she is too 'worldly.' You aren't worldly in the least, my dear," added the man who was not worldly at all and never would be.

"But I don't have any other friends," said Ellen. "I—for years I avoided everybody and wouldn't see anybody. It isn't their fault; it is mine."

"Perhaps," he said. He remembered that Dr. Cosgrove warned him that Ellen must not be disturbed for a considerable period of time, so Francis smiled at his wife and she smiled in return.

"Before long, I must get in touch with my other friends," she said. "I must begin to live again." The deep peace of the last weeks came to her, and a sweetness and a hunger for living, and that odd strength. "All this must have been very hard on my children."

Gabrielle and Christian were sitting in the latter's apartment on East Forty-eighth street. They had been listening to the radio broadcasts in an almost complete silence. When the last broadcast had ended Gabrielle snapped off the radio and said very clamly, "It looks as if you and I are wiped out."

Christian said nothing. He was leaning forward in his chair, his clasped fists tight between his knees. His large red head was bright in the lamplight, but his face was tense and the muscles showed visibly.

"There's something—something going on I don't know about," he said. "My own office was in confusion today; no one worked. I couldn't find out anything, and that is what frightens me."

"But why should it?" He gave her an enigmatic look, then glanced away. "You don't know what is going on," he muttered. "I don't know much, either."

"What do you think is 'going on'?" she demanded, alert. But he could not tell her. His face became tighter, and she sensed he was in a cold rage. "They should have told me," he said at last.

"I don't know what you are talking about, Chris. The only thing I do know is that as of now we are practically beggars. That is, we will be if the Market collapses, in spite of all that tremendous buying."

Now they contemplated each other for a considerable space. Then Gabrielle said, in a gentle matter-of-fact voice, "If only she had died. If only she was dead."

"Yes," he replied. "The estate of my father is sound. If only she was dead. Why didn't she die?"

Gabrielle gave a short and ugly laugh. "Well, we tried

hard enough. If it hadn't been for that damned Charlie Godfrey— She'd have been dead now, and we wouldn't be here chewing our hearts out."

Her brother considered her. "We'll find a way, after all, Gaby. We'll find a way." He stood up and kissed her, and she clung to him. For the first time since she was a child she cried. "It's unfair, unfair!" she exclaimed.

42

It was not a surprise to Charles Godfrey when on the following Tuesday, October 29, the Market truly collapsed, and the bankers made no effort to save it.

The newspapers called the situation "a financial nightmare, comparable to nothing ever experienced before on Wall Street." Still, the next day America took some hope from the fact that John D. Rockefeller had just said, "Believing the fundamental conditions of the country are still sound, my son and I, for some days, have been buying sound common stocks." The calamity seemed halted for two days; prices did improve in a slight measure. Then the Stock Exchange governors declared a two-day holiday. For some reason this was regarded as "good" by the country, in spite of the past huge sales.

Francis Porter could not remain in his offices. He haunted Wall Street, among throngs of others. He still could not consult his "friends." They were all too busy. His only comfort now was that Ellen always greeted him with affection when he returned home, and that she was daily improving. They had contented hours together, while Ellen read a book and Francis studied the black headlines in the newspapers, and tried to hope. He would surely have known, wouldn't he, if "the day" had arrived? He would have been given warning months ago. He had even tried to discover if Christian "knew anything." Then he finally understood that Christian had no more information that he did himself. So—the day had not yet "arrived."

Gabrielle and Christian called once on their mother, hating her for her miraculously recovered health and appearance, her tender smiles, her solicitude for them. They gave her loving smiles in return, kissed her, and plotted. They were the first to visit Kitty Wilder on her return home. She looked wizened and fleshless, as tight and hard and gnarled as a wintry twig, but her huge white teeth glittered as ever on her dark face with the furrowed wrinkles.

"I had such a marvelous time in London and Paris and Rome, my dears! Such fun on the ships, too. And I've bought such clothes in Paris! Fantastic. We are out of style in America, Gaby, really provincial." She paused. "And how is your mother, my sweets?" Her face took on a sad expression.

"She looks," said Gabrielle, "twenty years younger. And healthy. And blooming. I'd like to know," she added with bitterness, "what that doctor is giving her. I could use it myself, these days."

Kitty's frenetic face expressed her disappointment. "Well, isn't that good news!" she said with enthusiasm. "I must really see her in a day or two, when all my trunks are unpacked, and I am settled." Her eyes narrowed on the two. "She isn't going to be institutionalized after all?"

"No. She's still under Cosgrove's care," said Christian. "And he and that priest—and that infernal Francis, too—guard her like lions."

"Ah," said Kitty thoughtfully. She said, "Well, we mustn't lose hope that she will recover, must we?"

They all exchanged significant looks, then the brother and sister smiled. "We are," said Christian, "relying on you, Aunt Kitty, to complete the—improvement."

They settled down to a discussion concerning the Stock Market. Kitty was optimistic, for in the last years she had bought only blue-chip stocks and sound bonds. "Never fear," she said, "that things are in a terrible state. They aren't. It is a passing thing; panics usually follow big booms, and then it all calms down and prices start to rise again."

As promised, she visited Ellen within two days, and Ellen greeted her with love and happiness. She led Kitty into the library for tea and chattered like a young girl.

Kitty sat down, and contemplated Ellen and made her face anxious and somber.

"Ellen, dear, I thought to find you much improved. But how thin you are! How pale, how haggard!" She stared at Ellen's fresh cheeks and shook her head. "Do you really feel quite well? You seem very nervous, and upset. Perhaps it would have been so much better for you to have been institutionalized than to have been in the gloomy hospital."

"Institutionalized?" asked Ellen. Now she lost her color. "What do you mean by that, Kitty? Whoever talked of such a thing? That's for mad people, isn't it?"

Kitty saw that she had made a serious blunder. But she was quick. "Well, dear, there was some talk of a sanitarium, where you could rest in cheerful surroundings, like a home, instead of a hospital."

"Who thought of that, Kitty?"

Kitty shrugged. "Dear me, I can't remember. It was quite a long time ago. And sanitariums aren't just for 'mad' people, dear. They are for people in distress, too, who need peace and quiet for some time. You are behind the times, Ellen."

Ellen silently poured tea. Kitty could not read "that stupid cowgirl face."

"How poor Francis and your poor children suffered, Ellen! It was tragic to see them. They became almost as sick as you were. Tragic."

Ellen's expression changed, became soft and tender again. "I know. Gabrielle just cried, and I thought Christian would cry, too. And Francis—he and I are good friends now. He is often a comfort to me, when I am feeling lonely." She smiled. "He is taking me to the theater next week, something lively, he says, to cheer me up. Ziegfeld Follies, I think. I have been away so long—"

"Francis? Ziegfeld Follies?" Kitty was momentarily diverted. "What a strange combination."

"Yes, isn't it? But he is determined to do all he can for me."

Kitty sipped her tea. She looked at Ellen's highly complimentary dark-blue dress with its bodice of silvery beads. It clung to her beautiful figure and heightened the color of her eyes and her brightening hair.

"Ellen, dear, who on earth bought that frock for you?

So out-of-date, and too young for you and too gaudy, for someone who has lost all her color—and youth. Really."

"Gabrielle chose it for me. She has excellent taste, Kitty," Ellen protested.

"Did she? I am surprised at Gaby. Really. Of course, the young never do seem to know what is appropriate for their elders."

Now Ellen widely smiled. For the first time in her life she spoke with something approximately like gentle malice. "I'm not that old, Kitty. I'm not quite forty-four yet; I won't be until January. And I am a lot younger than you, too."

Kitty felt a vicious spasm in herself. "Really? I thought you were near my age, dearest. What year were you born?"

"January 4, 1886."

Ellen was looking at her with a steadfast smile, and Kitty thought: I always thought you were sly and foxy, you housemaid, and now I am sure of it. First poor Jeremy, and now poor Francis, and from what I've heard they weren't the only ones, either. What the poor devils saw in you is beyond me. She said, with lightness, "Well, age is only numbers, isn't it? It is how you feel—"

"I feel eighteen again," said Ellen. She was astonished at herself. Poor Kitty was only trying to be kind, yet she, Ellen, felt no guilt at all, or very little, for her own repartee. Still, she said, placatingly, "Do have one of these hot biscuits, Kitty; they are filled with raspberry jam, your favorite. What gloomy weather we are having, aren't we? So chilly and dark and gray, and now all this financial fear and confusion. Of course, I have missed a lot that was going on the past year, and I am trying to catch up. If Jeremy were here he could explain it to me."

"Oh, I am sure he could." Kitty paused. "He would also be worried about his children. Gabrielle and Christian are sparing you, of course, but they are terribly worried. The stocks left to them by their grandparents are worth almost nothing now. I am distressed for them."

Ellen became serious. "I know nothing about these things, I am sorry to say. Surely, they are not in difficulties?"

"You must ask them yourself, when you are feeling better—much better than you are feeling now. After all, you must not be disturbed for a long time."

Ellen had felt new life springing in her before Kitty's visit, but now, all at once, she felt drained and tired and agitated. She bent her head and thought. She would have to ask her children; she would have to find a way to help them. However, she could not force herself to believe that they were in very great difficulties; they would surely have told her. But how thoughtful it was of them not to bother her just now.

She said, as if speaking to herself, "If Jeremy were here I would be afraid of nothing. Nothing. Neither for myself nor for my children. Still, I am not really afraid, for you see, Kitty, I feel he is here with me always; I feel he will never stop loving me, and loves me still. That is my— harbor," and she smiled a little. "My shelter. Knowing of Jeremy's love keeps me alive, keeps me hopeful, for his sake."

She wondered at the sudden intense silence which fell between her and Kitty, and wondered even more at Kitty's curious expression, almost of exultation. Then she saw fully, for the first time, that Kitty was very plain, even ugly, and that there was something malign glittering in her eyes and on her teeth.

Kitty said, and she lifted a cautioning finger like a dried stick, "Ellen, dear, you must be careful. I do hope you aren't having more hallucinations about poor Jeremy, poor dead Jeremy, being still 'alive.' What would your doctor think? He would pack you right back to the hospital."

But Ellen's face had regained its tranquillity. "No, he wouldn't. He was the one who assured me, with Father Reynolds, that Jeremy still lives and loves me."

"What absurdity, Ellen dear!"

Ellen shook her head. "No, it is the real verity, the one thing that is certain. Love does not die; it does not betray; it is immortal."

Again that intense silence suddenly filled the room like a malevolent presence. Kitty began to lick the corner of her lip. Her eyes, fixed on Ellen, were too vivid. She was elated. But she would have to think this over. The possibilities were tremendous, almost insanely exciting.

Francis came into the library, and he looked like a tall gray ghost in the twilight. He was startled to see Kitty, and greeted her with a new cold formality; then he studied Ellen with a touching earnestness. "How are you, my dear?" he asked, hesitated, then bent and kissed her cheek. She patted his hand lightly and said, "I am splendid, Francis. Will you have some tea?"

He glanced at Kitty and then he could not endure her presence. He said, seeing that she was watching him with a queer intentness, "I'm afraid not, my dear. I must go out again; I have an appointment. But I will be here for dinner. However, tomorrow, I am going to Washington. A client of mine is in some trouble."

When Kitty left, a few moments later, he said to Ellen, "Ellen, there's something about Kitty which I never knew before. I don't think she is good for you."

Ellen gazed at him uneasily, remembering her new responses to Kitty. She said, "I can't think what you mean, Francis. She's always been so kind to me, so thoughtful——"

He recalled Kitty's affidavit, and he knew now that Kitty had never had any affection for his wife but only envy and malice. She had always hated Ellen—Francis thought, with an insight alien to him. Still, he was a gentleman, and as such he could not speak meanly of a lady, especially one of Kitty's impressive background. So he said, "Perhaps you need younger friends, Ellen, those nearer your own age and own temperament. All the people you ever knew through Jeremy were much older than yourself, as was Jerry—and I."

He wondered why Ellen smiled so widely as she said, "Age is only numbers, isn't it?" But he rejoiced at the deep dimple coming in and out of her cheek, and he knew, as he had always known, that she was the only thing in his life that mattered, and the only thing he had ever deeply and tenderly loved.

Now he sat down and accepted a cup of tea from Ellen, after glancing briefly at his watch. He said, "I haven't seen that dress before, Ellen. I must admit that Maude Godfrey has good taste; it is so becoming."

"Maude? Maude Godfrey? Are you certain?" Ellen was disconcerted. "I thought it was Gabrielle—all my new clothes."

Francis frowned. "Did Gabrielle tell you that? No? You just jumped to conclusions, Ellen," and his voice took on a tinge of its old severity. "A bad habit of yours, I am sorry to say. I don't care much for Maude Godfrey, or her husband. But they were very considerate. Maude redecorated this house—and a pretty penny it cost, too—

and discharged your domestics, who were of doubtful character, I later discovered. I thought you knew."

"No, I didn't." Now real free guilt came to Ellen. "How kind of Maude. I haven't seen her since I came home, of course, but she never said a word in the notes she would write to me at the hospital, and neither did Charles. How I misunderstand people! I'm really sorry. I must call her tomorrow, and thank her."

"She and Charles also sent you all these plants, and a lot of flowers to the hospital. You honestly didn't know?"

"No." Ellen was close to tears. "Now, we mustn't be unjust to Gabrielle. She never even implied she bought my clothes and rearranged my house, and did all of the other considerate things. I just—jumped to conclusions. I am sure, though, that if Maude hadn't done all that, Gabrielle would have."

Would she? thought Francis. But he said, "Of course. Now, I must go for an hour or two. I will return in time for dinner. Rest in the meantime."

When Francis had left her she telephoned the Godfrey house, only to be told that Mr. Godfrey and his family were in Boston visiting his relatives, and would not be home for another two weeks. Ellen was both disappointed and relieved. She would write Maude and thank her, instead of speaking to her directly. She still could not like Maude, and now a faint resentment came to her that Maude had put her under obligation. And a fresh surge of guilt for feeling that resentment. But this was an entirely different guilt from that which she had known most of her life. It was a refreshing clean one, authentic, and so healthy and natural.

She went upstairs to her rooms. Miss Hendricks was rocking and knitting in her own bedroom. She stood up when Ellen appeared on the threshold. "Are we dressing for dinner, Mrs. Porter?" Then she saw Ellen's face. She said, "My, we look cross! Is there something the matter?"

"I'm annoyed with myself," said Ellen. Then, to her own astonishment, she laughed a little and she looked like a girl. "Did you ever feel like kicking yourself, Miss Hendricks?"

"Regularly," replied the nurse, delighted by the mischief on Ellen's mouth. "It's good for the soul—kicking yourself. That is, if you deserve it."

"Oh, this time I do," said Ellen. She listened to the

small radio; it was spurting with "good news." Ellen was deeply relieved. Nothing serious had happened to her children's fortune. They would have told her.

"I have the most wonderful idea, dears," said Kitty to Gabrielle and Christian the next day as they sat in her sitting room and drank cocktails. Her eyes were vivid with glee and spite. "It is so wonderful that I must think it all out clearly before I tell you about it."

"What is the idea?" asked Christian, with no hope. "Does it concern our money?"

"Yes. And something much more important, much more. But let me plan it all."

"If there was just some way to get rid of *her*," said Gabrielle. "Honestly, I can't stand visiting her, in that house. I hate that house; I hate everything about it. It is like a nightmare. But I force myself to visit dear Mama, much as I detest it."

"She does look well," said Kitty, always vindictive and happy to stir up the gall in her visitors. "I was quite surprised."

The next day Father Reynolds visited Ellen, for tea, and she took his hand as she would have taken the hand of a beloved father. "How well you look, Ellen," he said. "I hope you are following all the instructions of Dr. Cosgrove."

"I feel so well, Father," she said. "And so hopeful. I don't really know what I am hoping for—but it gives me joy. I am so expectant, too."

He sat down near the fire, and his long tired face was sweet with affection. He felt the new vibrancy in Ellen, the new awareness.

"To be expectant is to remain young," he said. "You are never old when you can feel that something joyous may be, will be, coming to you soon, even if you don't clearly know what it is."

He accepted a little cake, with pleasure. Then he was grave. "These are terrifying days for America. But Americans are resilient. They have passed through crises before, even when they thought it was the absolute end of their world. Still, I can't remember—and I am an old man—when I have seen such despair, such frantic despair. They say. this is the aftermath of the war; I think, though, it is something else."

"So did Jeremy, a long time ago," said Ellen. "I wish I had listened more to what he said then."

The priest shook his head. "I hate to be sententious," he said, "but it is a habit with me now, being a priest, I suppose. I always say, 'While there's life there's hope,' and often it is true. If a cliché. And sometimes it is stupid to say that. I feel calamity in the air—and it doesn't mean just this collapse of the Market. I feel, in some way, that this is the end of an era, for America, and—perhaps it is because I am old—I feel the new era will be terrible."

Ellen became grave also. "In what way, Father?"

He looked into his teacup, then put it aside. He clasped his hands together and stared at them. "I read the newspapers. Sometimes an item will seem obscure and not very interesting—and then it happens that it was the most vital news in the world, far more important than the current headlines."

Ellen waited. The old man sighed. "The end of an era —the beginning of a new and frightful one. I may be wrong; I pray I am wrong. I have been reading about an Austrian, Adolf Hitler. Have you been reading about him in the newspapers, Ellen?"

"I was ill for so long, Father. I didn't read anything or know anything. But lately, I have read something about him, in the hospital and here. He's just a revolutionist, or something, in poor Germany, isn't he?"

"I am afraid he is much more than that, Ellen. No one listens when I say so—but I feel it, know it. Poor Germany, broken by the Treaty of Versailles, and plunged into destitution and misery—she is looking for a savior. It is sad that when men and nations look for a savior they rarely look to God. They seek out malefactors, insane men, cruel and vicious and blasphemous men, criminals, mountebanks. And Satan obliges them, and gives them the most damnable." He paused. "Well, this Hitler, a man sentenced to prison for insurrection, has just formed what is called the Deutschvölkische Freiheitsbewegung, a radical Socialist party, and it is becoming very powerful in Germany."

"He's a Communist, then?"

"It is the same thing, Ellen—Socialism and Communism. The distinction is nil. Nazis and Communists—

they are one. American financiers and bankers and industrialists helped bring about the Russian Bolshevik Revolution, for their own purposes. I am wondering if they are not, now, supporting Hitler. If so—then the prospect for the whole world is appalling."

Ellen was acutely uneasy. "Francis—he is a Socialist. He told me that long ago, many years ago. I cannot believe he is cruel and a criminal—"

The priest tried to smile cheerfully at her. "Many good men, or innocent men—they are not always the same, Ellen—become deluded and fanatic, from some deep illness in themselves. I am sure your husband is not wicked. He could only be mistaken. Ah, well, you are looking despondent, and I am sorry. Let us change the subject."

He asked about her plans for the future and smiled affectionately at her when she spoke of taking her children abroad with her in the summer. Her face was alight, her eyes shining. Like a child herself, he thought. May God protect her.

That night he prayed, "Agnus Dei, Who taketh away the sins of the world—have mercy—"

Before sleeping that night Ellen stood on her bed and kissed the painted lips of Jeremy's portrait, and then the painted hand. "Never leave me, my love," she said. "Never leave me. You, my darling, are my hope and my joy. Don't forget me, don't stop loving me—keep me with you forever."

She smiled with passionate love at the portrait, sighed and lay down and slept.

43

Dr. Cosgrove refused to see Ellen in her house, for her own sake. He had suggested that she take a streetcar, or a bus or the subway, resorting to her car, driven by her new handyman, only during the worst of weather when transportation was almost impossible. He even was doubtful of a taxicab. He rejoiced contentedly when she came alone, and spoke of the crowds in the subway or her long wait for a Fifth Avenue bus. Daily her fears subsided more and more, and there was a freshness in her face and a sweet excitement as if she found the world not to be feared at every moment, but to be confronted with interest and participation.

She spoke to him with a childlike and trusting candor, and often she laughed, and daily her eyes brightened and her complexion regained a luster it had not had for many years. Once she proudly displayed a coat and hat she had purchased—alone—and was shyly delighted at his admiration. He began to suspect that not only was she now rejuvenated but she was exhibiting an attitude towards the world, and herself, she had not even known during her marriage to Jeremy Porter. There was an air of fortitude and endurance about her, which amazed even Dr. Cosgrove.

He said to her, "Remember always what I have told you before, Ellen: Your first duty is to yourself and your own welfare—as it is the duty of all men and all nations. Love for your fellow man is excellent and benign and Christian—but that love must always be the lesser compared with your own self-esteem and vital existence. You cannot help or love others honestly, and with kindness, unless you possess pride in yourself."

Ellen said, "So Maude Godfrey told me, long ago, quoting a Spanish Jesuit of the seventeenth century."

Dr. Cosgrove nodded. "To denigrate yourself, to believe yourself less worthy than those about you, is not noble, for you, too, are an immortal soul and as valuable in the sight of God as anyone else. In fact, not to remember this is to court the contempt of other people, and their exploitation of you, and that is a crime against them themselves. You have tempted them to degrade and dishonor you, a grave sin, and a sin against God."

He shook his head. "I have been told that in our schools and colleges, now, and even in our churches, they are teaching that the United States should have joined the League of Nations—to 'further peace and tranquillity among nations.' In short, America should abandon the memory of her glorious past and accomplishments and subvert herself to the service of other countries. That is not admirable humility, Ellen. It is gross stupidity. I am afraid America is becoming Europeanized, and that will mean the end of our strength, and our ultimate decay. America should take care of her own, protect her own, and never subject herself to any opinion or domination by those peoples who have lost their courage, their will to survive, their will to endure, nor should she make of herself an almshouse for the incompetents of alien cultures, who have proved themselves unworthy of survival. Do you understand, Ellen?"

"Yes."

"For a man to divest himself, or a nation herself, of what they have honestly and creatively earned, by their own efforts, is not charity or benevolence, Ellen. That only encourages mendicancy in others, and arrogance and ill will. It is very dangerous for all. Sharing indiscriminately impoverishes everyone and stimulates more poverty." He thought of Ellen's ruthless children, and the whining clamor in the League of Nations at the present time. "A proper care for one's own self, and one's country, inspires others."

Ellen moved uneasily for the first time. "This panic, Doctor: What if my children need my help?"

"Why should they demand help from their mother, if they have been too reckless or profligate to guard their own interests? If their greed inspires them to ruin, they have brought that fate on themselves." He was vaguely alarmed. "They are young, Ellen. They must find their own way, as you and your husband found your way. Struggle ennobles and strengthens a man; heedless 'help' from others dishonors and weakens him. God knows, we all need strength."

When Ellen was silent, he added, "If your children ask you for anything, ask yourself, 'Will this harm me and make me more vulnerable?' If the answer is 'yes,' then refuse. Will you promise me that?"

She hesitated, then said yes. Then she looked earnestly into his bright concerned eyes and said, "You don't know very much about my children, Doctor. They are most devoted and loving and thoughtful and considerate. They would never ask anything of me that would harm me or cause me distress."

She wondered at the sudden dark grimness of his face.

He was saying to himself: One of these days, when she is stronger, she must be told the truth about her children. He said, "Children are not the greatest blessing in the world to a parent, Ellen—that is, many of them. They can also be curses and can destroy their parents. It is cheap sentimentality—and dangerous—not to know that, or to deny it. What does the Bible say about children? 'The heart of a child is deceitful. . . . Man is wicked from his birth and evil from his youth.' Man is not born pure and noble and immaculate, as the psychiatrists are shouting just now. He is born human, with all humanity's innate cruelty and viciousness. Only strict discipline can make him a man."

Ellen thought of the children of her childhood. She thought of the crafty grins and the joy in her pain. Her face saddened. He said, very gently, "To know the truth, Ellen, is not always to gain happiness. It can bring sorrow. But it can bring strength, too."

When she was on the way home in the subway, Ellen thought, But he does not know Gabrielle and Christian! Her sadness lifted and she smiled. She had forgotten, long ago, all Jeremy's anxious warnings.

Gabrielle and Christian sat with Kitty Wilder in her living room. Their faces were drawn and pale, but she smiled at them. "Oh, don't worry so much, my dears! I am sure, from what I read now in the newspapers, that the panic is over, and the Market will stabilize itself. The President is very optimistic. I listened to him last night on the radio. Things were really very sound. Our national debt is only twenty billion dollars; we have all the gold in the world in the Treasury! Do cheer up."

"My stocks fell to a new low today, Aunt Kitty," said Christian, and Gabrielle said, "Mine also. We're not entirely wiped out, though Christian keeps getting demands for 'call money' from his brokers. Margin, you know. I didn't go so far out on margin as Christian did, but it's bad enough. I had to meet a demand for twelve thousand dollars today, and Christian got a demand for eighteen thousand. If it keeps up like this we'll truly be wiped out."

Kitty wanted to say with tartness, "Well, I never bought on margin, so I am in a sound position. I have only to wait until stocks start to rise again." But she smiled at the two with lovingkindness. "Cheer up. Things can't possibly get any worse. That is what the stockbrokers and bankers say."

"And if they do?" asked Christian.

"Then, we will put my idea into operation, darling. Let us wait and see. I am perfecting the idea. Very fast, indeed."

"Why won't you tell us about it, then, so we can be prepared?"

"Gaby, it may not be necessary." She paused. "In the meantime, I'd like you to talk over the whole situation with my own lawyers, about your father's will and your mother's income. The whole story, including her illness and how she was prevented from getting the institutionalization she still desperately needs. Why, she is as dreamy as ever, if not more so! She talks about your father as if he is still actually living, and inhabits her house, and always in the present tense! If that isn't mental illness I'd like to know what it is! Yesterday, I was quite frightened—the poor sick woman! She showed me some new clothes she had bought recently, and said she was sure Jeremy would like them, and she preened like a woman with a doting lover. Poor soul."

"Dear Francis encourages her," said Christian with a hating sneer. "I think he is as sick as she is, if not more so. Once he stood with us against her, and influenced her. Now the situation seems reversed. He actually hovers over her—and watches us—damn his soul."

"I really don't know what's come over Francis," said Kitty, sighing. "He seems to have lost his wits. But then, he lost them when he married your mother. To this day I can't think why he did that."

"Her money," said Gabrielle. "What else?"

"What else, indeed," said Kitty. "Now here are the names of my own lawyers. Be discreet, yet tell them everything that matters."

Christian took the card Kitty offered him. "Witcome and Spander. I've heard of them. They're very expensive, aren't they?"

"All lawyers are, my pet. But they can smell money quicker than can other lawyers. Do consult them as soon as possible. They are part of my idea. They'll ask for a retainer, or ask for a contingency basis. I've had them for years, and have never regretted it."

Gabrielle began to smile cunningly, as her brother

doubtfully fingered the card. "I am beginning to see," she said. She stood up and her piquant face became heavy with disgust. "Come along, Christian," she said to her brother. "We have to endure a visit, and a dinner, with dear Mama tonight. And listen to her insane babblings, all spoken with such a sickening air of brightness. Even gaiety, my God, at her age!"

Kitty did not love them so ardently for a moment or two. "I always thought your mother was older than she confesses. But then, it is possible she doesn't even know her actual age, does she?"

"She acts a hundred," said Christian, and Gabrielle, who had been watching Kitty closely, said, "She looks at least fifteen years older than you, Aunt Kitty. She never was vivacious and lively. Now she is completely washed out."

They went to visit their eagerly waiting mother, and the sight of her joy in them, her love and trust and tenderness, enraged them. She should have been incarcerated by this time, or decently dead, they thought. Again, she was an impediment in their lives, and time was running out. The newspapers were not so optimistic tonight. "I hate to open my mail in the morning," said Christian, "or to answer the telephone. Screams for more margin. I have exactly thirty thousand dollars in my checking account—and bundles of stock that are almost worthless, as of today."

"Cheer up," said Gabrielle as they entered Christian's fine new Packard, later. "I am beginning to see what darling Aunt Kitty has in mind. It's very clever, indeed. And our troubles will end."

On November 9, Charles Godfrey, in Boston, said to Maude, "I have a feeling, my love, that we should go back to New York tomorrow."

"You and your Irish 'feelings'!" said Maude, kissing him. "You are all fey, you Irish. I don't know why I listen to you so much, but I do. Very well. But tell me about your 'feelings.' "

"I don't know, frankly. But I am uneasy; I feel it is urgent that we go back. It's not the Market, thank God. I never bought on much margin, anyway. Perhaps it's the air of general foreboding—or something. I'm also thinking of Ellen Porter."

"But she is now so well, Dr. Cosgrove and Father Reynolds told us."

Charles nodded. "So they say. But I know Ellen. Perhaps better than they do. And there are those damned children of hers— I can never forget what they tried to do to her."

Maude knew that her husband still loved Ellen with the wistful and poetic love he had had for her from the beginning. But Maude was not jealous. Every man was entitled to his romantic devotion to the dream of fair women. Maude was contented to be his competent and sensible wife. A man without poetry in his soul was poor, indeed, even if that poetry concerned another woman. In fact, the more inaccessible the woman was, the more she was beautifully enhanced for him. It gave him an air of noble pathos, and chivalrous renunciation.

"Ellen's children wouldn't dare try to injure her again," said Maude. "They are too afraid of you."

"I hope you're right," said Charles. "But perfect greed casteth out fear, to paraphrase the Bible."

In the past days Ellen had actually taken the shy initiative with regard to the few friends she had had before she married Francis. They were astonished to hear from her; they had almost forgotten that she existed. But they were genuinely pleased to receive her calls, and to accept her invitation to tea on November 11. She felt quite elated at her own boldness, and sang softly to herself in her warm and comfortable house. She had let Miss Hendricks go a few days before, with regret. "Just you call me, Mrs. Porter, anytime you need me," Miss Hendricks said on the eve of her departure. "I'll come at once." She looked fondly at Ellen, with her sunny youthfulness and vivid complexion, and felt a personal triumph.

Ellen, just lately, had returned to her piano and admitted ruefully to herself that she needed a great many more lessons to restore her former skill. She called the teacher she had had at one time and was joyful that he would teach her again, if only once a week. He was also astounded to hear from her. "I have been ill," she said. "But now I want the happiness of music again. My husband would like that."

Her only regret was that her children did not appreciate the sort of music which entranced her. But then, they were young. They preferred "modern music," which, to Ellen, was only discord—all those blazing trumpets and those alleged singers they called "crooners," and the frantic beat. They were part of a world completely distasteful to Ellen, the world of stockbrokers and "company men," and gangsters and vulgar nightclubs, and Prohibition and avid and suspect women and "gang" murders, and shouting "movies" and very short skirts and shameless public scandal and activities. I must be getting old, she thought to herself with a smile. I suppose I should, like my children, find this all very exciting. I find it very shoddy and cheap and without substance or beauty. Tawdry and synthetic. Where in the world did all these strange people come from, to fill the air with their howlings and the streets with their sharp painted faces, and their rudeness? No longer was life rich and sedate and civilized. The Vandals had arrived. Would the true America ever be restored again, the America of principle and decency and decorum, the America of authentic values? The question itself was depressing. Ellen was determined never to be depressed again, and so she put aside the question. The world went on its merry way, for good and evil, and no one could halt it. One had to— adjust? As Dr. Cosgrove had called it.

But adjust to paltriness, to inanity, to the inferior and third-rate? Was it "progress" to accept the trashy and ugly and vile? Grace had vanished from the world; could it ever be restored? Ellen put this thought aside also. It was not the world she had made; this world had only contempt for the past and all its traditions.

The world of her youth, Ellen reflected, had not been a gentle world. It had been harsh and demanding. But it had also been strong. The competent and the able had been rewarded, justly. A man with bravery and courage and intelligence had always been able to succeed to the extent of his native capacity; he had always been able to deliver himself from adversity. If he suffered in the process it was an enabling suffering. People had had pride, even the humblest.

She was surprised, that afternoon, to receive a call from Maude Godfrey, and she became shy and abashed again. She stammered, "I do want to thank you, Maude, for your kindness to me. I just found out about it. You must have thought me very ungrateful."

"No," said Maude. "You could never be ungrateful, Ellen. It is not in your nature. I am glad you were pleased."

"And you will come to my tea at four o'clock on November 11?"

"Of course," said Maude with real pleasure. She paused. "Charles has been worried about you, that is why we returned earlier than we had expected."

"Oh, Charles is always worrying," said Ellen with a new lightness. "I am so splendid now, so happy. I can't be grateful enough to Charles for calling Dr. Cosgrove for me."

"You see," said Maude to Charles that night. "You were, thankfully enough, unduly worried about Ellen. I haven't heard her speak as she did today for many, many years."

Charles thought for a moment or two, and then he said, "I don't know why, but I am still uneasy about her. She is too vulnerable."

And I am so very competent, thought Maude, with amused annoyance.

When Charles spoke to George Cosgrove about Ellen, the latter said, "She is in a state of euphoria, such as one sees in a person who was almost moribund and then is restored to health. Life takes on a color never before seen. There is a light on everything, a surprised joy in existence, a discovery. When all this subsides somewhat in Ellen she will be completely mature, in a large way invincible, and will lead a reasonably happy life for many years, with contentment and balance. She will be able to resist almost any misfortune. And, I hope, she will have forgotten that nonsense of 'loving and trusting' anyone, save God."

"You sound as cynical as a lawyer, George."

"Well, I've heard enough in my professional career, God knows, to make me wonder, sometimes, why we aren't all swept from the face of the innocent earth. And, by the way, I am hoping to rid Ellen of her innocence, which has been her greatest enemy. I even hope to make her more sophisticated, tinged with a little skeptical humor. Too much to hope?"

"Well, as that German philosopher—Fichte?—said, we are born what we are and nothing can change it."

"We are also born with a measure of self-respect and

individualism, too, Charles, and a hearty and healthy
streak of selfishness. We ought to cultivate these in the
young, or we'll all end up, in America especially, slobber-
ing like infants and whimpering for our nice warm bottles
of milk—at someone else's expense."

Charles said, "To change Ellen, or to bring out good
latent qualities, will make her a different person, George.
I wonder—"

"I hope it does! She has been a victim of those she
loved and trusted too long." The doctor laughed. "When
she does a little gentle victimization herself, I will know
she is cured!"

44

Kitty, of course, did not know that the Godfreys had
returned to New York before they were expected. But she
did know that Francis would return this November night
of the tenth, from Washington. There should be no interference with her plans and the plans of Ellen's children.
She had enlightened them as to her "idea" a day or two
before. "Be sure it will succeed," she said to Christian,
who was somewhat doubtful. "Your enemies are out of
town, your mother is alone. We must act at once—that is,
if it is still your intention."

"We don't have any other choice," said Gabrielle. "It's
now or never. Tomorrow may be too late. Look what the
Market did today! Even my stockbrokers are gloomy,
and when a stockbroker is gloomy it is time to—what is
the old sea phrase?—trim your sails."

Gabrielle called her mother, speaking in a soft and
loving voice. "Mama, are you busy this afternoon? Christian and I, and Kitty, would like to have a drink—I mean
tea—with you at four o'clock. That is, if it is convenient."
She winked at her brother.

Ellen was overjoyed. "Do come! What a dismal day it has been, so dark and dull and windy, with some snow swirling. I was wondering what I would do with myself today, except reading. I am getting so restless, Gabrielle! It seems I want to go out to the theaters or museums or art galleries all the time! I have even been thinking of taking dancing lessons, so I can keep up with all you young people. Isn't that disgraceful of me?"

"Very." Gabrielle's voice was more than ironic. She hung up the telephone and turned to her brother. "Yes, we must act now. The old fool is even thinking of taking modern dancing lessons! What next? A divorce from Francis, and probably a new husband. It wouldn't surprise me. Childish, just about senile. Call your lawyers, Chris, and explain, and ask them to meet us outside of dear old Mom's house at four. Imperative."

"I am thinking of Charles Godfrey," said Christian.

"What can he do, when it's all settled? Signed, sealed, and delivered. The only way he can overthrow our plans or change them is to bring out the fact that Mama is incompetent and didn't know what she was doing. That would prove our case, don't you see?"

Elated at the thought of her beloved children's visit, Ellen dressed in a new frock, silvery blue velvet. She put on her sapphire necklace, earrings, ring, and bracelet—Jeremy's last gift to her. She considered her hair. The streaks of gray were softened now, and not so harsh; the red strands were glistening with life. She considered cutting her hair short, and wondered if Jeremy would like it. She rolled up the mass in a reasonable resemblance of a "bob." It was very becoming. She must ask Gabrielle, and Kitty, about it this afternoon. After all, she was not yet forty-four, and that was no great age any longer. Poor Aunt May, it was true, was an old woman then, worn thin by living and hunger and exhaustion. Ellen paused. She thought of May with sorrow and tenderness, but without the old destroying guilt. As Dr. Cosgrove had told her, she had done everything possible for a sick and suffering woman, and with love, and if that aunt had misunderstood, and had endlessly complained, one must remember that illness frequently had an evil effect on anyone's disposition. Ellen, he had said, must only keep in mind that her aunt had loved her and had worked for her, and in return she had given her aunt all of which she was capable. No one could be expected to do more.

"False guilt is a destroyer," he had told Ellen. "It is also a sort of masochism, a self-flagellation—a—a—" He had hesitated a moment, then had smiled widely at Ellen. "I will use a psychiatric term. It is often sexual in origin. A voluptuous self-indulgence. A kind of masturbation."

Ellen had blushed, then she had laughed, shaking her head.

"I have had cases," said the doctor, "where patients had even hired whippers to 'punish' them for sins they imagined they had committed. And then it was resolved in an orgasm, and the patients felt much better."

"Oh, Dr. Cosgrove!" But Ellen was laughing again. "Are you applying that to me?"

"Well, not exactly. But insistence on self-guilt is often only hidden sexual desire. Especially if there is no reason for guilt at all. It is a very strange thing, but the truly guilty never experience guilt. They are certain they are righteous, or were forced to do what they did, or were justified. That is why the wicked hate their victims; they must have a reason for their wickedness. A nice reason."

"I have certainly acquired a new way of looking at people," said Ellen. "I am not sure I like it, but at least it is real." Dr. Cosgrove was satisfied.

"Our Lord," said Dr. Cosgrove, "did not demand that we go unarmed in this dangerous world. In fact, St. Peter, and others, wore swords."

Thinking of all this, and smiling, and scented with jasmine, Ellen went singing down the stairs to the library to wait for her children and Kitty. She sat at her piano and played a little Debussy, the notes lifting and shining in the air like golden bubbles. She could see them dancing in the light of the fire, and tinkling like chimes. At four, her housekeeper, a competent and bustling woman, came to the door and announced Ellen's visitors, and she flew from the piano stool like a young girl full of anticipation. But she was surprised to see two strange men with her children, two small gray men with foxlike and intelligent faces and hard searching eyes.

Silently, she let them in. Kitty was there also, wrapped in sable. Ellen noticed, with sudden dismay, that her children looked very grave, even grim, and Gabrielle's eyes appeared to have been recently weeping. As for

Kitty, she spoke to Ellen in a subdued voice, asking her solicitously if she were "quite well." "You look so tired, dear, and so pale. Didn't you sleep last night?" She kissed Ellen's cheek as one kisses the cheek of an invalid.

Ellen stammered, "I feel very well." She looked at the strange men. "Mama," said Christian, "my lawyers, Mr. Witcome and Mr. Spander. Gentlemen, my mother, Mrs. Porter, who is just recovering—we hope—from a prolonged illness. We must make it brief. She is still in very precarious health."

The gentlemen bowed to Ellen with a lugubrious air and spoke softly and distinctly, like those who are careful not to disturb the fragility of a seriously ill person. Ellen became confused and distrait. "Please come into the library," she said. She led the way and glanced back over her shoulder at the strangers. "Lawyers, Christian? But why? Is something wrong?"

"Very wrong," said her son.

"Oh, Mama," said Gabrielle. "We are so sorry."

"Now, don't upset your mother too much," said Kitty in a shrill voice and insistent. "You know how ill she still is. We must be careful."

"Careful—of what?" asked Ellen. She remembered to be polite. "Please sit down. Tea will be here when I ring. Or would someone like sherry?"

Mr. Witcome and Mr. Spander looked like twin brothers, so uniformly dun and spectral were they, so sharp of feature yet so expressionless. They laid their briefcases on their knees and folded their hands on them. When the fire flickered on them it was as if it flickered on driftwood. Kitty had loosened her coat, but had not removed it. She looked aside; the fire jumped on her averted face, which appeared to be contorted by some grief or dire emotion. Ellen's bewilderment grew, yet a hard sick fear began to grow in her. She turned to her children. She had begun to tremble, as she had not trembled for a long time.

"Please," she said to Christian. "What is the trouble? Is it the Stock Market?"

Christian's large head bowed itself so that his chin almost rested on his chest. He wrung his hands. "No, Mama." His voice was subdued. "What does the Market matter when we are concerned only about you?"

"Mama, dear," said Gabrielle, and there were tears in her eyes. She put out her hand to Ellen in a pleading gesture. Ellen looked at that hand; she wanted to take it, but she could not, for some unknown reason, touch her daughter.

"Have I lost all my money?" she asked. She tried to smile. "Well, don't worry, dears. Charles has been very careful. I am sure that there will be at least something left over. If that is all that worries you—"

"Do you think that is why we are all here?" cried Kitty in a passionate loud voice. "You insult us, Ellen! We are here just to help you, just to save you."

"From what?" Now fright took Ellen. "Tell me what all this means. Why are you here, Christian, with your lawyers?"

"To save you," he echoed Kitty. "From thieves, and lying doctors. From people who would steal everything from you, and have you put away—"

"Put away!" exclaimed Ellen, and now her entire body felt cold, as if it had become stone. "Please stop all this mystery and tell me what you mean!"

"Be patient, dear Mama," said Gabrielle, crying. "You know how we love you, want to help you—"

Her mother was gazing at her with a peculiar intentness which the girl had never seen before. "Gabrielle," she said with a new directness which startled her daughter, "was it you who suggested that I be institutionalized, a long time ago?"

"Institutionalized?" Now Gabrielle was frightened and shaken. She looked at Kitty, and then her brother. They had both suddenly stiffened in their chairs.

"Yes," said Ellen. She turned to Kitty. "It was you who mentioned that, only recently. I asked you whose suggestion it was, and you were evasive. Now have you remembered?"

Kitty's dark and wizened face turned an ugly scarlet. She dared not look at Christian or Gabrielle. "I don't remember any such thing, Ellen! You are mistaken—or imagining things! Really! I am your best friend; would I lie to you? Have I ever lied to you?"

Kitty turned to the lawyers, who had become as alert as fox terriers. "Ellen herself will admit that for a long time, a very long time, she had been suffering from hallucinations and delusions, and hearing voices. She will admit it. She was in the hospital for weeks, too. Isn't that so, Ellen?"

Ellen was silent a moment, while they all awaited her answer. Then she said, "Yes, I was sick. I couldn't recover from my husband's death. I also had made a marriage which was—unsuitable. I wronged Francis. But all that is past and done with. I have completely recovered my health."

Mr. Witcome spoke in a low hoarse voice. "Who told you that, Mrs. Porter?"

"My doctor, Dr. Cosgrove."

The lawyer slowly took some papers from his briefcase. "I won't trouble you—in your present state—too long, Mrs. Porter. Believe me, I quite sympathize with you, and will spare you as much as possible. I have statements here, written long over a year ago, by Dr. Lubish and Dr. Enright, to the effect that you were seriously mentally ill, and needed to be institutionalized, if your life were to be saved. That was their informed opinion."

Ellen was completely white and rigid. "They are no longer my physicians. I have my own doctor, Dr. Cosgrove, who has cured me." She could hardly control her voice.

"Mama," said Gabrielle, leaning forward, "who persuaded you to go to Dr. Cosgrove?"

Ellen blinked. She said, "Why, you did, Gabrielle. But I found out that it was Charles' suggestion."

Gabrielle threw back her head and laughed bitterly. "He suggested that! What a liar he is! It was my idea, and Christian's, for you did not seem to improve very fast."

Ellen could not help it. Her old mistrust of Charles, and Maude, intruded itself like a sinuous finger into her heart, twisting. She clenched her hands on her knees.

"Do you believe a man like Charles Godfrey, who won't let you have enough income, and disbelieve your own children, who love you?" asked Gabrielle. "I assure you, he would have been only too glad to have had you institutionalized so he could seize your income, too, and dole it out at his own pleasure."

"You take his word before ours?" asked Christian, staring at her with her own large blue eyes. "Do you honestly want to think that, Mama?"

"How can you be so unjust, to your loving children?" Kitty asked.

Now the monstrous old guilt began to seep into Ellen, the old crippling guilt. She felt her chair tilting; she looked at her children and the pain of her love shattered her. They would not deceive her, her children. They wanted only the best for her. And then something moved against that guilt, like a strong repelling hand. She said, "What do you want of me, Gabrielle, Christian? What is all this leading to?"

They had never seen her like this, and had never heard her speak like this, before, and for a few moments they were hugely dismayed and helpless. Christian looked at his lawyers; they only looked back, impassively, at him, waiting.

"Mama," Christian said, and hated her more for her strength, inimical to him, which she was displaying. "I will put it very simply. You never did understand complicated things; it's not your fault. There is something—well, never mind. You see, someone is plotting to have you institutionalized, to claim you are insane, not in your right mind, since Papa died. We want to save you from that, and leave you in peace in your own house."

Her great blue eyes fixed themselves brilliantly on her son.

"Who is doing this, Christian?"

"Mama, you have such faith in people who are your enemies! You must take our word for it. There is no time to lose. Tomorrow may be too late. Our lawyers, here, have papers for you to sign. Kitty will be the witness, Aunt Kitty. You assign to me, and to Gabrielle, and to our lawyers, your entire present income and your money, and your future interest in Papa's estate, into our care and administration. We will then give you a proper income for your own use—in your own house, our father's house, which you love—and let you live in peace, and in safety. All your lifetime, which we hope will be long and healthy—after you have recovered."

Ellen continued to stare at him. Something enormously strange was happening to her, something like iron was expanding in her soul. It was as if she were looking at strangers. All Dr. Cosgrove's warnings, and the priest's warning, rushed in on her like a saving battalion, protecting her. But with it came a desolation she had never known before, even more terrible than that she had known on Jeremy's death. She felt herself suspended over an abyss; there was no foothold. She was alone as she had never been alone before.

But she said, "I must think about all this. I must talk to Charles, to Dr. Cosgrove—"

"Your enemies," said Gabrielle, and now her eyes were openly alive with her hatred for her mother. "You would consult with them, against us, your children? What will they do when you tell them? They will disgrace us; they could even have us arrested—and only because we love you and want to save you! Your enemies. They would destroy us, your children, who have come here tonight to help you. I can see now that you never loved us! You never loved anyone but yourself! It was always what you wanted—and the hell with anyone else! How could we have loved you so much, and so stupidly! You are no mother to us, after all. Or, tell me, Mama. Is Charlie Godfrey blackmailing you about something? Blackmail? That could be the only thing."

Ellen had listened, aghast. "Blackmail? You are out of your mind, Gabrielle. For what should anyone blackmail me? What have I done?"

Then Christian spoke, in a soft and ugly voice, "Your past, Mama, your past. Lawyers ferret out everything. Your past, in Preston, and in Wheatfield, Mama."

Ellen actually gaped at him, shaking her head as if to shake herself loose from a nightmare.

"My past?"

"Oh, Mama," he said wearily. "Our grandparents in Preston told us everything, long before they died, when we visited them. If Charles Godfrey carried out his threat, you couldn't live in New York any longer. You wouldn't have a single friend. Your disgrace would be complete. You deceived our father that you were a nice simple little girl when you married him—our grandparents told us. But you were only a—"

"Careful," said Mr. Witcome.

"Careful, hell," said Christian. "You can see the truth on her face now. Well, that's all past and gone. We didn't want to bring this up, but we had to. To warn her there there are—people—who are not only ready to blackmail her but to put her away for life. I'm sorry this all had to come out, but it was necessary." He looked at Ellen again. "Think what that would do to my poor father's reputation! He has enemies enough, even now. Why, the whole city would laugh at him! His reputation.

I suppose you haven't given a thought to that, Mama. Now, will you sign these papers?"

Ellen's mouth felt like thick clumsy soap, and she was sick as never she had been sick before, not even when she had been on the point of dying. "It is all money, isn't it?"

The lawyers were surprised. They had been led to believe that she was an illiterate former housemaid, unacquainted with reality and with money, a stupid, half-insane woman who needed institutionalizing, who was still mentally disturbed, and worse, and a former girl whose reputation had been infamous, and who had beguiled a susceptible man into marriage. Well, it was obvious that she had once been very beautiful, and men were men, and such women had made fools of men like her husband before, and always would. Now, the lawyers looked at each other doubtfully. They looked at Kitty, who was breathing fast and whose face was malign. They had many such cases before; they were careful men. They wanted to be very certain of their ground before acting.

"Things seem very confused," Mr. Spander said. "Perhaps we should consult further with you, Mr. Porter, and Miss Porter. There seems to be more here than the necessity to institutionalize your mother, or to persuade her—in her own interests—to sign these papers."

They turned to Ellen. But she was as rigid as the tragic marble she now resembled, and as unmoving. Only her eyes were animated; they gleamed with blue fire, and yet her features expressed such grief that it was almost beyond human flesh to endure. It was rare for them to feel pity. They felt pity for Ellen now. They were also uncomfortable. They stood up.

"We will meet with you, Mr. Porter, whenever you desire. In the meantime—"

But Christian was shouting at his mother, and his hatred was naked. "Think what it will do to Gabrielle and me—when it comes out about your past! When it comes out that you were treated for a long time by psychiatrists —because you are crazy! Crazy! Mad! Not only you will be driven out of New York, but we, too. Our futures ruined. A whole city, laughing, just when I am establishing myself! Do you think of that, dear Mama! Or, as always, are you just thinking of yourself, your own greed, your own stupid wishes?"

Ellen continued to look at him, then she turned slowly to Gabrielle. "Yes, I was wrong, all your lives. You hated me, even when you were children. I see it all; I tried to hide from the truth, the truth your father hinted. I always tried to hide from the truth."

Her voice was very calm. No one could know the hollow emptiness in her, the sorrow which was more than sorrow, the grief that was more than grief, the sickness that was mortal. Her face had become small and shriveled, but her eyes were huge and blazing.

"I always loved and trusted the wrong people—except your father. I mistrusted my true friends, and disliked them. I am not very bright, am I, to have believed the lies of my children, to have loved them? You have tried to make me feel guilty—for your own reasons, which are quite clear to me now. But I don't feel guilty, except for the guilt I feel concerning Maude and Charles Godfrey, because I did not believe they were my friends." She drew a deep and shuddering breath. "How can I live with this, knowing what you are, my children? Ah, but I will live with it; I will live it down. You are not going to destroy me, as you wish to do. God has given me strength to resist you, to put you out of my memory, to forget you forever."

But great tears rushed into her eyes and fell in a cascade over her quiet cheeks. "I have no children. You were never mine."

The lawyers unobtrusively withdrew and left the house, but no one heard them go. Ellen turned to Kitty.

"As for you—my friend, I was warned. By Jeremy, by Francis himself, by Charles and Dr. Cosgrove. It is all plain to me now, and I can look back over my life since I have known you, Kitty Wilder. You were my enemy from the start. I don't know why you have always hated me; I was devoted to you. But hate me you did. I don't know the answer; I don't care to know."

"But you must know!" Kitty grinned at her with savage glee. "I put up with you, as did your other friends, because of Jeremy, poor deceived Jeremy! I tried to civilize you, to make you a lady, for Jeremy's sake. It was all wasted, wasn't it? Your place is in the kitchen, my girl, and always will be. There! You have the truth at last!"

But Ellen was preternaturally calm and dignified. She stood up and faced the three of them, her children, her friend. She said, "Please leave my house, and never come here again. I do not know you. I will never know you."

The tears were faster now. "If only you had let me believe a lie! If only you had come to me and told me openly, and honestly, that you needed money! I, your mother, would have helped you as much as reasonable. But I am no longer your mother. The mother you knew is dead. This woman wants nothing of you any longer. Please leave my house."

The firelight danced over Ellen's expressionless face, that newly formidable face, and her children knew they were defeated and they were frenzied with despair. Their hatred was mad. Then Christian lost control of himself. He struck his mother fiercely across her composed face, and she staggered and she would have fallen but that she grasped the back of a chair in time. But she continued to look at her son, and there was no fear in her face, that still and quiet face.

"Damn you!" Christian screamed. "You bitch, you nothing, you thief! Why don't you die and make us all happy with your money, our father's money, which belongs to us and not you? Why don't you die!"

He would have struck her with his clenched fist, aiming at the breast which had nurtured him, but Gabrielle interposed. "Christian! Do you want to kill her? She isn't worth your going to prison or to the electric chair!" She seized the upraised arm of her brother, and clung to it when he would have thrown her off. "Christian!"

"You have already almost killed me, my children," said Ellen. "But I will live so you will have nothing, until what is left of me dies."

"Die!" shouted Christian. "Of what use are you, you miserable whimpering wretch?"

Gabrielle looked at her mother, the stillness of her, the deathly whiteness of her face, the distended eyes floating with tears, and for the first time in her life Gabrielle felt a hint of shame, a hint of remorse, and it almost unnerved her.

"You have always wanted me to die," said Ellen, looking only at her son. "It was there for me to see, all these years. You didn't dare kill me openly, as an honest man would do. You tried to kill me through your doctors, with drugs and threats and cruelty. You didn't succeed, for God was with me, and my friends." Something enormous broke in her, separated, bled, but she did not weaken.

She looked at Gabrielle. "My daughter," she said without emotion. "You, too."

Gabrielle's olive face was the color of saffron. She looked away. "Let's go, Christian," she said. "It's all over."

"No," said Kitty, "it isn't. I have something to say, too, to this woman who has denied that you are her children any longer, and wouldn't lift her hand, now, to save you from ruin. For you are ruined, you know."

She took a prancing step towards Ellen, almost daintily. Never had she looked so triumphantly evil. She cocked her head, pointed at Ellen with her fleshless finger, and grinned.

"Now it's my turn. You've always said that only the memory of Jeremy's love kept you alive. You still speak of him as if he still loves you, and lives.

"Now I will tell you the truth. He never loved you! He despised you! He ran from you, whenever he could—to other women. You bored the life out of him. He couldn't stand being with you—"

Ellen's voice was loud and clear. "You are a liar, Kitty. You were always a liar."

"Aha! Am I? Here I am a woman with a good reputation, which I could lose, am about to lose. I was his mistress for years, you fool! I slept with him in my bed; he held me in his arms; he kissed me and confided in me. Because you were sick, because he couldn't stand you any longer. He kissed my breasts; he lay on me, in my arms. You don't believe it?"

Ellen was silent. Her blue eyes seemed to fill all her face.

Kitty laughed aloud, her laughter shrill and wicked. She lifted her hand and swore, "Before God, I am telling you the truth! He was my lover, for years and years. There were times you enraged him, with your stupidity. I wasn't the only one. His other mistress was Emma Bedford—and there were others, too. Does a man take mistresses, and keep them, if he loves his wife? Even you, you imbecile, know better than that!"

She thrust out her hand on which a large opal flamed, surrounded by diamonds. "Look at this! He gave it to me for my birthday, two years before he died." She put it to her mouth and covered it with openly desperate kisses, and now her own tears ran down her face. "My darling, my Jeremy, my lover! I shall never forget you."

Ellen believed her. It came to her with gigantic force that Kitty had told the truth. She felt herself floating in darkness; she felt a frightful pain in her head and her heart; she felt herself dying. Jeremy had not loved her. He had betrayed her. It was not his fault, her husband. It was her own. She had had no right to marry him, to destroy his life, to make him wretched. Her aunt had been right in the beginning. His life had been a curse and a misery, because she had married him. All those years—he had endured her, for he had been an honorable man and had taken her in marriage. She remembered how somber he had often seemed, how abstracted. She had done this monstrous thing to him, and he had remained with her because he pitied her, and not out of love.

She closed her eyes, clinging to the chair. She did not feel the pain in her face where her son had struck her. Slowly, she did not feel any pain at all. When she finally opened her eyes it was to see that she was alone.

Alone. She had never had a husband; she had never had Jeremy. She had never had anyone at all. She felt no pity for herself. She felt only a guilt that was mortal, an anguish that no name could describe. And yet, there was no real pain in her. She was disembodied.

She had lived a lie, she had lied to herself all her existence. She had believed herself beloved by an unfortunate man who could, at the last, not endure the sight of her, but must take a woman like Kitty for consolation. Kitty Wilder! But it was all a dream.

Dreams must end. But so long as one lived, one would dream. Only death could end illusions. Only in death could agony subside. But first, one must do penance for crime against others. Then, peace and forgiveness.

"Forgive me, Jeremy," she whispered to the empty room, which was filled only by firelight. Then she turned and went upstairs, moving slowly but steadily.

The housekeeper appeared. "Shall I serve tea now, madam?" she asked. But Ellen did not hear her. She went upstairs and never once hesitated, never looked back.

45

Moving almost serenely, Ellen went to the beautiful German music box which Jeremy had given her many years ago. There was a china figure on the gilt top, which, when the music played, slowly and delicately and airily rotated, lifting fragile pale arms and gently bowing. Secreted within it lay a handful of yellow tablets, which she had begun to save years ago, small lethal sleeping tablets. She counted them and her fingers did not falter. There were twenty-five. She even smiled. She said, aloud, "I knew I would need them someday."

There was such a calm in her now, even a peace. She stood and looked at Jeremy's portrait. She climbed on the bed and humbly kissed, not the portrait's lips as usual, but the painted hand. "Do forgive me," she said. "Please forgive me, for the wrong I did you, my darling."

She undressed. She was conscious of no emotion in her at all, no agony, no terror, no grief, no despair, no betrayal. She was not even conscious of the house about her, and the servants within it. There was only a void, softly echoing with the music-box strains, and nothing else existed anywhere, not in the world, not even in herself. She put on her silk-and-lace nightgown, neatly hung up her dress. She brushed her hair. The image in her mirror was not Ellen Porter. It had no existence; it belonged to another woman. There was an abeyance in her, like a silent dream without substance. She filled a glass with water and, standing, slowly and methodically swallowed all the tablets, her eyes fixed and vacant and unseeing. Reality had left her. Yet, she felt she was living in the only true reality which she would ever know.

She had no thoughts. Thoughts were for the living, she said to herself, and she was already dead. She sighed. It was the sigh of a child who had given up all things, and was tired, and would soon sleep. In her sleep she would forget the nightmare of living. She repeated what Pope had said, "This long disease—my life." Now she was free of that disease, of that mortal illness.

She turned off her lamp and lay down on her bed and covered herself with the silken quilt and closed her eyes. Very slowly, a delicious warmth came to her, a softness, an enveloping night like a murmured tenderness, and she smiled, slept, and murmured once.

She was walking in the old garden she remembered, across long lawns on which the last sunlight fell, and there was a fragrant mist in the trees and the grass was alive and sweet under her feet. There was no end to the gardens. She wore a long pale dress sprigged with violets and a broad straw hat on her head, ringed with the same flowers. She carried a single white rose in her hand, its stem swinging in her fingers, its leaves like polished emeralds. Her step quickened; she began to run a little, breathless and smiling, to a rendezvous. The sun came more resplendently through the boughs of the trees and birds had begun to call and there was the distant sound of fountains.

A tall young man appeared across the lawns, emerging from the forest, and moving quickly towards her, holding out his arms and laughing.

"Jeremy!" she called. "Oh, Jeremy!"

He ran to her, as she ran to him, and he caught her and embraced her, and she felt the warmth of him, the strength of him, the surety, the joy, and the limitless peace and love. His lips were on hers; she raised her arms and put them about his neck.

"You found me. You never forgot me," she said, and her face was the face of a young girl of seventeen.

"I never lost you," he said. "I knew where you were all the time. And now, my love, we will go home, together, and never lose each other again."

"It was such a terrible dream, Jeremy," she said, holding his hand.

"Yes. But it was only a dream. Now you are home, with me."

It was an accident, they said. She had been very ill, they said. But "they" did not include Ellen Porter's murderers, and they did not speak to each other of it. However, from that time on Gabrielle was estranged from her brother. She, too, was cured of an old disease.

Francis Porter was broken. He had arrived home to hear from the housekeeper that Mrs. Porter had seemed tired and had gone right to bed. She had been called for dinner, but "she was sleeping so peacefully and I didn't want to wake her." Francis himself had gone to Ellen's bedroom at midnight, for he had become anxious. No one answered his knock; he looked within the room and by the dim light of the hall he saw his wife sleeping. He whispered, "Ellen? I'm home, from Washington." She did not answer. There was such a profound silence in the room that he did not want to disturb it. He had shut the door gently, and with love, and weary from his journey, had gone to bed. He had been able to see no one of consequence in Washington, which was in a state of black panic and fearful rumors.

"Why did she do it?" Maude asked her husband, weeping, but he had no answer. Nor did Dr. Cosgrove. "No one," he said to Charles, "has any answer to anything that happens in the world. At least, Ellen is done with all the weariness of living, and the disappointments and the betrayals. She has peace. It is all we can hope for." He paused. "No one can save anyone else. We can only save ourselves."

Ellen Porter was buried on November 13. On that day the Republic of the United States of America was buried also, never to live again. It was the end of an era.

Father Reynolds spoke of both in his prayers: "Requiescat in pace."

His tears were for the dead woman and his country, and in some way he felt that Ellen had epitomized America, and with both had died innocence, and both had been betrayed by trust.

ABOUT THE AUTHOR

One of America's most popular and prolific novelists, Taylor Caldwell has "always written"—since she learned to write at the age of four. She began writing novels at nine and by twelve her first novel was submitted to her grandfather, then on the staff of a major Philadelphia publishing house. He dismissed the book, refusing to believe a child could have written it, and advised her father, "Burn it; she'll cause you trouble." Undaunted by this early rejection, Miss Caldwell kept at her writing and went on to publish more than thirty books.

Born in a suburb of Manchester, England, of Scotch-Irish ancestry, Taylor Caldwell came with her family to the United States when she was six years old. She was graduated from the University of Buffalo (Miss Caldwell holds three doctorate degrees), and in 1938 she achieved instant literary fame with the publication of *Dynasty of Death*. Since that time she has written many bestsellers, including *The Sound of Thunder, Dear and Glorious Physician, A Pillar of Iron, Great Lion of God, Captains and the Kings,* and most recently, *Glory and the Lightning*.

Romantic Suspense

Here are the stories you love best. Tales about love, intrigue, wealth, power and of course romance. Books that will keep the reader turning pages deep into the night.

☐ CROCODILE ON THE SANDBANK—Peters	Q2752	1.50
☐ DARK INHERITANCE—Salisbury	23064-3	1.50
☐ THE DEVIL OF ASKE—P. Hill	23160-7	1.75
☐ THE HEATHERTON HERITAGE—P. Hill	23106-2	1.75
(Published in England as The Incumbent)		
☐ THE HOUSE BY EXMOOR—Stafford	23058-9	1.50
☐ IRONWOOD—Melville	22894-0	1.50
☐ LEGEND IN GREEN VELVET—Peters	23109-7	1.50
☐ THE LEGEND OF THE GREEN MAN—Hely	23029-5	1.50
☐ THE MALVIE INHERITANCE—P. Hill	23161-5	1.75
☐ MICHAEL'S WIFE—Millhiser	22903-3	1.50
☐ MONCRIEFF—Holland	23089-9	1.50
☐ THE NIGHT CHILD—DeBlasis	22941-6	1.50
☐ NUN'S CASTLE—Melville	P2412	1.25
☐ THE PEACOCK SPRING—Godden	23105-4	1.75
☐ THE PLACE OF SAPPHIRES—Randall	Q2853	1.50
☐ THE PRIDE OF THE TREVALLIONS—	P2751	1.25
Salisbury		
☐ THE SEVERING LINE—Cardiff	P2528	1.25
☐ STRANGER AT WILDINGS—Brent	23085-6	1.95
(Published in England as Kirkby's Changeling)		
☐ VELVET SHADOWS—Norton	23135-6	1.50
☐ THE WHITE JADE FOX—Norton	Q2865	1.50
☐ WHITTON'S FOLLY—Hill	X2863	1.75

Buy them at your local bookstores or use this handy coupon for ordering:

FAWCETT PUBLICATIONS, P.O. Box 1014, Greenwich Conn. 06830

Please send me the books I have checked above. Orders for less than 5 books must include 60c for the first book and 25c for each additional book to cover mailing and handling. Orders of 5 or more books postage is Free. I enclose $_____ in check or money order.

Mr/Mrs/Miss_____

Address_____

City_____ State/Zip_____

Please allow 4 to 5 weeks for delivery. This offer expires 6/78

A-18

BESTSELLERS

☐	BEGGAR ON HORSEBACK—Thorpe	23091-0	1.50
☐	THE TURQUOISE—Seton	23088-0	1.95
☐	STRANGER AT WILDINGS—Brent	23085-6	1.95
	(Pub. in England as Kirkby's Changeling)		
☐	MAKING ENDS MEET—Howar	23084-8	1.95
☐	THE LYNMARA LEGACY—Gaskin	23060-0	1.95
☐	THE TIME OF THE DRAGON—Eden	23059-7	1.95
☐	THE GOLDEN RENDEZVOUS—MacLean	23055-4	1.75
☐	TESTAMENT—Morrell	23033-3	1.95
☐	CAN YOU WAIT TIL FRIDAY?—	23022-8	1.75
	Olson, M.D.		
☐	HARRY'S GAME—Seymour	23019-8	1.95
☐	TRADING UP—Lea	23014-7	1.95
☐	CAPTAINS AND THE KINGS—Caldwell	23069-4	2.25
☐	"I AIN'T WELL—BUT I SURE AM	23007-4	1.75
	BETTER"—Lair		
☐	THE GOLDEN PANTHER—Thorpe	23006-6	1.50
☐	IN THE BEGINNING—Potok	22980-7	1.95
☐	DRUM—Onstott	22920-3	1.95
☐	LORD OF THE FAR ISLAND—Holt	22874-6	1.95
☐	DEVIL WATER—Seton	22888-6	1.95
☐	CSARDAS—Pearson	22885-1	1.95
☐	CIRCUS—MacLean	22875-4	1.95
☐	WINNING THROUGH INTIMIDATION—	22836-3	1.95
	Ringer		
☐	THE POWER OF POSITIVE THINKING—	22819-3	1.75
	Peale		
☐	VOYAGE OF THE DAMNED—	22449-X	1.75
	Thomas & Witts		
☐	THINK AND GROW RICH—Hill	X2812	1.75
☐	EDEN—Ellis	X2772	1.75

Buy them at your local bookstores or use this handy coupon for ordering:

FAWCETT PUBLICATIONS, P.O. Box 1014, Greenwich Conn. 06830

Please send me the books I have checked above. Orders for less than 5 books must include 60c for the first book and 25c for each additional book to cover mailing and handling. Orders of 5 or more books postage is Free. I enclose $_____ in check or money order.

Mr/Mrs/Miss_____

Address_____

City_____ State/Zip_____

Please allow 4 to 5 weeks for delivery. This offer expires 6/78.   A-14